F
AKS

Aksenov, Vasilii
Pavlovich,
1932-

Generations of
winter.

$25.00

DATE			

GENERATIONS OF WINTER

GENERATIONS
OF WINTER

——— ☆ ———

Vassily Aksyonov

*Translated from the Russian by John Glad
and Christopher Morris*

RANDOM HOUSE

NEW YORK

Grateful acknowledgment is made to Harvard University Press for permission
to reprint one poem from *The King of Time: Poems, Fictions, Visions of the
Future* by Vladimir Khlebnikov, translated by Paul Schmidt, edited by
Charlotte Douglass. Cambridge, Mass.: Harvard University Press. Copyright ©
1985 by the Dia Art Foundation. Reprinted by permission.

Library of Congress Cataloging-in-Publication Data
Aksyonov, Vassily Pavlovich
    Generations of winter / Vassily Aksyonov ; translated from the
  Russian by John Glad and Christopher Morris
      p. cm.
      ISBN 0-394-56961-X
    1. Soviet Union—History—1925–1953—Fiction. I. Title.
  PG3478.K7G4 1994
  891.73′44—dc20   93-30655

Book design by Tanya M. Pérez

Manufactured in the United States of America

98765432

First Edition

IN MEMORY OF MY PARENTS,

Pavel Aksyonov and Eugenia Ginzburg

CONTENTS

VOLUME II

WAR AND JAIL

VOLUME I

———— ☆ ————

Generations of Winter

LELI-LELI—the snow of locust flowers shielding a rifle

CHEÉCHECHÁCHA—the shine of sabers

NEE-EH-ÉNZAI—the scarlet of banners

ZEE-EH-ÉGZOI—the words of an oath

BÓBO-BE'EBA—the stripe of scarlet

MEEPEEÓPEE—the glitter of the gray-eyed troops

CHÚCHU BE'EZA—the glitter of swear words

MEE-VEH-ÁH-A—the heavens

MEEPEEÓPEE—the glitter of eyes

VE-E-ÁH-VA—the green of the troops!

MEEMOMÁYA—the dark blue of hussars

ZEEZOZÉYA—the sun's handwriting, a rye field of sun-eyed sabers

LELI-LÍLI—the snow of locust flowers

SOSESÁO—mountains of buildings

—Vladimir Khlebnikov*

*Translated by Paul Schmidt, *The King of Time*, Harvard University Press.

CHAPTER ONE

Scythian Helmets

★

Just think—in 1925, the eighth year of the Revolution, a traffic jam in Moscow! All Nikolskaya Street, which runs from the Lubyanka prison through the heart of Kitai-gorod down to Red Square, is filled with streetcars, wagons, and automobiles. Next to the open-air market, they're unloading crates of fresh fish from heavy carts. Beneath the arch on Tretyakovsky Street one can hear the neighing of horses, the tooting of truck drivers' horns, and the swearing of a cart driver. The police will hurry to the scene, blowing their whistles ingenuously, as if not yet entirely convinced of the reality of their exclusively local, nonpolitical—that is, perfectly normal—role. Everything has the appearance of an amateur production, even the people's fury seems put on. The most important thing, though, is that everyone's happy to play along. The traffic jam on Nikolskaya Street is, in fact, a cause for rejoicing, like a glass of hot milk for someone who has been shivering with fever: life is coming back, along with dreams of prosperity.

"Just think, only four years ago there were famines and epidemics here, crippled men were wandering about from place to place, people were lining up hopelessly for a handout of a few sprouted potatoes, and the only vehicles on Nikolskaya Street were the Black Marias of the Cheka," says Professor Ustryalov. "There, Mr. Reston, you see the 'Change of Landmarks' theory in its practical application."

Two gentlemen of approximately the same age—around thirty-five or forty, one would say—are sitting in the backseat of a Packard stuck on Nikolskaya Street. Both are dressed in Western European style, in well-cut three-piece suits from the finest stores, but a few apparently insignificant, yet unmistakable signs make it easy to tell that one of them is a Russian while the other is a foreigner—the genuine article—and an American at that.

On his first trip to the Russia of the Reds, Townsend Reston, Paris correspondent of the *Chicago Tribune*, was struggling with fits of annoyance. As a matter of fact, one couldn't even say he was having fits—his irritation never left him for a moment. It was just that at times it affected him like a nagging toothache, while at others it felt like the symptoms of food poisoning.

In fact, maybe it had all started with the food, on the day of his arrival, when his Soviet "colleagues"—that unbearable Koltsov, that showoff Bukharin—had treated him to their delicacies. This caviar—why was everyone in Paris so crazy about the stuff? he wondered. Apparently they considered it a powerful aphrodisiac. Why, it's nothing but fish eggs, mesdames et messieurs! It's nothing but a prehistoric fish covered with a cartilagelike shell. . . .

Yet the biggest problem was the never-ending histrionics, the faintly nauseating exultation and elevated language, the boastfulness . . . and at the same time the uncertainty, the eyes peering at him with unspoken questions. They had already taken the measure of Europe, but they were baffled by America. And Reston was baffled by things here. At one time, he had thought he understood the ins and outs of revolutions. His reports from Mexico had been considered first-class journalism in their day, and he had interviewed members of the rebel juntas of numerous Latin American countries. Damn it, now he could see that those "gorillas" were closer to him than these "controllers of history" with their confounded fish eggs. Really, did these Bolsheviks seriously think they made the world turn? Everything would be so much easier if it were a simple question of seizing and holding on to power, of changing the ruling elite. However . . .

In preparation for the trip, Reston had read translations of the newspaper articles and speeches by the Soviet leaders. At the end of August, the Bolshevik Party had been shaken by a tragic story involving the United States. Two prominent Bolsheviks—Isaac Khurgin, chairman of the Commission on Trade with America, and Ephraim Skliansky, Trotsky's closest aide throughout the Civil War, had drowned while boating on a lake somewhere in Maine. At the funeral in Moscow, the omnipotent "leader of the world proletariat" managed to force a few words that seemed to express a strange, almost metaphysical, confusion: "Our comrade Ephraim Markovich Skliansky . . . having passed through the worst storms of the October Revolution . . . perished in some insignificant little lake. . . ."

This business of contempt for the lake, of being bewildered by "extrahistorical" death. Really, they think they're the gods of Valhalla, or at least mythological titans! Good Lord, hardly anyone in America would understand that these people are more obsessed by the class struggle than by the aura of power. They call this a revolution? How much more decadent is it possible to get?

In front of them, a streetcar filled with black overcoats and soldiers' great-coats shuddered and moved ten yards or so. With a groan the chauffeur of the Commissariat for Foreign Affairs' Packard turned the wheel to line up behind the trolley's tail. Reston, sucking at his now-extinguished pipe, looked out the side windows. Extremely beautiful women, looking almost Parisian, flashed by from time to time in the awkward-looking crowds. Two young Red officers stood at the entrance to an imposing building containing a drugstore. Trim and ruddy complexioned, wearing tightly drawn belts, they were chatting with each other, taking no notice of anyone else. Their uniforms were distinguished by the same decadent savagery as the entire Revolution, as all the authorities here: the strangest sharp-cornered hats with a red star sewn on the front, very long overcoats with red stripes across the chest, no epaulettes but rather mysterious geometrical figures on the sleeves and collar—an army of chaos, Gog and Magog . . .

"Professor, let me ask you one—as we say in America—provocative question: after eight years of this regime, what do you consider to be the greatest achievement of the Revolution?"

To emphasize the seriousness of the question, Reston drew out his Mont Blanc and prepared to note the answer in the margin of a page in his Baedeker.

Professor Ustryalov burst out laughing. He was someone who simply adored all this caviar and salmon.

"My dear Reston, don't think I'm laughing at you, but the greatest achievement of the Revolution is the fact that the Central Committee has become eight years older."

To tell the truth, even this companion for a day, with his fumbling English combined with the self-assured modulations of his voice, annoyed Reston. Just where did the Russians get this habit of automatically assuming they were superior to Westerners? An unfathomable figure, this man—a former minister in the Siberian government of the Whites during the Civil War, an émigré who had settled in Harbin, a leader of the Change of Landmarks movement, he was a frequent visitor to the Moscow of the Reds. His latest book, *Under the Sign of Revolution*, had been the subject of a great deal of talk in Europe, and even here not a single political article appeared that did not mention his name.

Zinoviev had called Ustryalov a "class enemy," all the more dangerous because of his acceptance (publicly, at least) of Lenin's ideas, his talk about the benefits of "transforming the center," about "putting on the brakes," about the "normalization" of Bolshevik power and hope for the bourgeois New Economic Policy and the "strong peasant."

Zinoviev made fun of Ustryalov in typically Bolshevik fashion, quipping that "the chicken has dreams of chicken feed." "Mr. Ustryalov won't see kulakization any more than he will ever see his own ears." Bukharin called him a "worshiper of Caesarism." Curious, that last one—of what and whom was it hinting?

In his conversation with Ustryalov, Reston was playing the fool, the superficial American newspaperman, in order not to betray his preparation.

"Everything comes full circle in the end," continued Ustryalov. "The angel of revolution is quietly deserting the country."

Reston understood that he was quoting his own words.

"Revolutionary ardor is already a thing of the past. . . . It is not Marxism that will triumph, but electrical engineering. . . . Just look, sir, upon these striking changes. Only yesterday they demanded instant communism, today there flourishes private property. Yesterday they called for world revolution, today they seek only trade agreements with the Western bourgeoisie. Yesterday it was militant atheism, today it's 'compromise with the Church'; yesterday it was unrestrained internationalism, today it's 'considering patriotic attitudes'; yesterday they proclaimed unconditional antimilitarism and anti-imperialism, wanted to give the land to all the peoples of Russia, today it's 'the Red Army, pride of the Revolution,' and, in fact, they're gathering the Russian lands together. The country is finding its age-old 'Eurasian' mission."

As the unloading of the carts at the open-air market continued, the traffic on Nikolskaya Street began to edge forward again. Animated scenes of a crowd that really seemed rather optimistic drifted by.

The street vendors were invigorated by the slight October nip in the air. A woman selling meat pies had rosy cheeks that made her look like the merchant's wife from a painting by Kustodiev. A cheerful invalid with a wooden leg was stretching the bellows of an accordion. Next to him someone was selling toy figures in glass jars. The passing American had no idea that this novelty was called "American underwater dweller."

"I say, the Sytin bookstall is open!" exclaimed Ustryalov, before he realized the name meant nothing to his companion. "In the domain of literature and art, everything is in full bloom now, sir. Cooperative and private publishing houses are open. Even the newspapers, though they have remained in Bolshevik hands, are being used much less now for high-flown propaganda and more for giving the news directly. In a word, the sickness is behind us. Russia is quickly coming back to health!"

From the side wall of a house, which here as in Germany is called a *Brandmauer*, a cinema poster looked down, depicting a man in a top hat who looked like Douglas Fairbanks and a blonde in curls who might well have been Mary Pickford. On the same wall there was another poster with some badly done drawings in the cubist style and large Cyrillic letters. Had Reston been able to speak Russian, he would have understood that next to the poster for the Hollywood film the Department of Public Health hung the appeal "There is no room for lice in socialism!"

"Yes, and what about the people in the Party, the army, and the Cheka?" Reston asked Ustryalov—he pronounced it "Astrelow"—"Do you think they're undergoing the same sort of transformation?"

With the liveliness characteristic of the soft Slavic features, the professor's expression quickly changed from exaltation to a serious, almost pained thoughtfulness.

"You've touched on the most important question, Reston. You see, just yesterday I was calling the Bolsheviks 'iron monsters with cast-iron hearts and machines for souls.' Maybe metallurgy is not entirely inappropriate here, if you will recall the pseudonyms of various Party men—Molotov, Stalin— Molotov, meaning sledgehammer, Stalin, meaning steel."

"Stalin, it seems, is one of—" interrupted the journalist.

"General secretary of the Politburo," Ustryalov explained. "The founding leaders apparently do not trust him much, but it looks as though this Georgian represents the growing moderate forces." Ustryalov went on, "Only such monsters with their reflecting mirrors and concentrated energy could tear down the great Russian fortress in which so much evil had accumulated before the Revolution. Right now, however . . . we begin to see the effects of the eros of power, which is very highly developed with these people. Mechanical theories are being replaced by human flesh."

"Interesting," muttered Reston, scribbling nonstop in the margins of his Baedeker. Ustryalov smirked. Interesting? How could it be otherwise?

"It seems to me this process is happening in all domains, in the Party and particularly in the army. You looked interested by those two young officers outside the drugstore. Such bearing, such posture! They weren't ragtag Chapaev guerrillas but real professional soldiers, though they were in uniforms that must seem strange to Western eyes. About their uniforms, by the way—many think they were sewn almost by Army Commander Budyonny himself, but in fact they were made in 1916, according to the designs of the artist Vasnetsov. So here we see a kind of direct passing on of tradition . . . Scythian motifs, my friend, memory of our ancestors!"

Ustryalov broke off and looked at the American in surprise. Why is he writing all the time, as though he understands everything I'm saying to him? Who among them could understand this, these murmurings from middle earth mixed with fifteen centuries of a people's history? Again and again, he had to stop himself on a note of exaltation. How many times did he have to repeat to himself—follow the British rules? Understatement, there was the keystone of their stability. He coughed and said: "As far as the OGPU or, as you would have it, the secret police, are concerned, do you suppose that four years ago an émigré historian could have driven around Moscow with a foreign journalist in a government automobile?"

"So you're not afraid?" asked Reston with the directness of a quarterback shotgunning the ball across midfield into his opponent's territory.

Meanwhile, the car had come to the end of Nikolskaya Street at what must have been a prearranged stopping point, next to the ornate façade of the shopping area. Here Professor Ustryalov and Reston left the vehicle and continued on foot in the direction of Red Square. Straining to hear, the chauffeur could still make out the high voice of the adherent of the Change of Landmarks movement: ". . . it goes without saying that I understand how ambiguous my position is—in émigré circles they all but call me an agent of the Cheka, while in Moscow, just the other day, Bukharin said that—" Then their words were drowned out by the roar of the bustling city.

No sooner were the two figures in English overcoats out of sight than a man in a lambskin cap came up to the Packard. Before the Revolution private detectives had dressed in those same green overcoats, and they had not changed an iota since then.

"Well, driver, what were the foreign spies talking about?" he asked the chauffeur.

The driver rubbed his eyes tiredly with his palms and only then looked at his interlocutor, giving him such a look that the policeman realized the man before him wasn't a chauffeur at all.

"My friend, you don't really think I'm going to translate from English for you?" Suddenly, snowflakes began to fly over the jammed streets of old Kitai-gorod; it was the first, invigorating snowfall of the autumn of 1925.

Meanwhile, the young officers whose appearance had given rise to such a serious conversation between the two gentlemen of our prologue were still chatting at the entrance of Ferrein's Pharmacy. Brigade Commander Nikita Gradov and Regimental Commander Vadim Vuinovich were both twenty-five years old, and so, by the standards of the time, they were already mature men.

Gradov was on the headquarters staff of Tukhachevsky, the commander of the Western Military District, while Vuinovich was special affairs officer for the Revolutionary Military Council, a post that made him one of the most important aides to High Commissar Mikhail Vasilevich Frunze, the army-navy commander. The two friends had not seen each other for several months. A native Muscovite, Gradov had been posted to the backwater of Minsk, while Vuinovich, from the Urals, had turned into a real city dweller after his assignment to the Revolutionary Military Council. This twist of fate amused him greatly and gave him a means of poking fun at Nikita.

Strolling about Moscow with his friend, he would notice theater bills and in an offhand way would begin a conversation about premieres: "How do you like that? Meyerhold is doing a job on Gogol again." He pretended to remember suddenly: "Oh, but you people in Minsk probably haven't heard about that yet, out there in the provinces . . . ," and so on in that vein, that is, with good-natured humor.

Then again, these young men in peaked caps didn't talk much about the theater: their conversation always seemed to move on to weightier themes. They were serious young men who had attained ranks that no one in the army of the old regime could have reached before the age of forty.

Nikita had come to Moscow with his commander to take part in a conference on military reform. The conference was to take place in the Kremlin, and in secret, since almost the entire Politburo was going to sit in. Even then, everyone was obsessed by secrecy. A joke of the leading Bolshevik wit, Karl Radek, was making the rounds of Moscow: "The Party can't seem to get out of the habit of working underground." Matters were complicated by the fact that Vuinovich's chief, Frunze, had been in the hospital for two weeks now with a severe duodenal ulcer. Out of brotherly concern for the health of the working classes' most beloved servant, legendary army commander, and destroyer of Kolchak and Wrangel, the Central Committee had proposed that the conference take place in his absence and that his top aide be provided with a report. Frunze, however, insisted categorically on participating, and also that his illness was not that serious at all. This was the very matter the two young officers were discussing in front of Ferrein's Pharmacy while waiting for Veronika, Gradov's wife, to arrive.

"The commander goes crazy whenever they talk to him about this damned ulcer," said Vuinovich, a broad-shouldered man with south Slavic features, bushy eyebrows and mustache, and bright eyes. Though he had grown up in an industrial town in the Urals, he had realized where his real homeland lay when his unit saw action on the south coast of the Crimea—there, among the rocks, foaming waves, cypresses, and vineyards.

If we were to succumb to the temptation to romanticize our story, we would have to make Nikita Gradov the polar opposite of his friend—that is, a native of the wide-open spaces of the North, a representative of some sort of Russian Gothic (if such a thing exists)—and lend a Varangian tint to our Scythian-Macedonian color scheme. However, for the sake of the truth, we have to overcome this temptation and not fail to mention that Nikita, too, belonged to the Mediterranean "cradle of civilization," even if only partly: his mother, Mary Vakhtangovna, was descended from a Georgian family named Gudiashvili. Then again, there was nothing of the Georgian in his features, unless you count a certain redness of hair and prominence of nose that could just have easily been put down as Slavic or Varangian or even, with no less chance of being right, as Irish—a people who as yet had played no part in the world revolution.

"Listen, Vadya, what do the doctors say?" Nikita asked.

Vuinovich smiled. "The doctors say less about it than the members of the Politburo. At their last consultation at the hospital, they came to the conclusion that it could be treated with medicines and a special diet, but the higher-ups are still insisting that he have an operation. You know Mikhail Vasilevich, he never blinked under machine-gun fire, but a surgeon's knife sends him into a blue funk."

Nikita pulled back his overcoat flap and drew from his light blue trousers a gold pocket watch, a gift from his commanding officer after the completion of the Kronstadt operation in 1921. Veronika had disappeared into the labyrinthine pharmacy forty minutes ago.

"You know," he said, still looking at the expensive, heavy, magnificent object he held in his hand, "it sometimes seems to me that a lot of the Party leaders don't like army commanders to have too much energy."

Vuinovich drew out a long, hollow-tipped Herzegovina Fleur cigarette but then flung it away.

"Stalin is working particularly hard at it," he said sharply. "The Party, don't you see, can't allow Frunze to be ill. Maybe Lenin was wrong, eh, Nikita? Maybe 'Stalin the cook' isn't going to 'prepare food that's too spicy'? Or maybe it's the other way around, and that's why he's against the diet and for the knife!"

Gradov put a hand on the shoulder of his friend, who had worked himself up into a state of agitation. "Calm down, calm down," he said, glancing around meaningfully.

Just then Veronika, an attractive woman in a sealskin coat, darted out of the pharmacy, her blue eyes sparkling like signal lights on the yacht of an overthrown monarch. She said jokingly and with terrible timing, "Comrades, why so serious? Are you planning a military coup?"

Vuinovich took a rather heavy bag from her hands—what could you possibly get in a pharmacy that would weigh so much? he thought—and then they walked off in the direction of the Hotel Metropole, down Teatralny Lane, past the monument to Fyodorov, Russia's first printer of books.

Every time he saw his friend's wife, he made an effort to shake off certain sensual impulses, which were at once fleeting and strong. As soon as she appeared, everything would turn to sham, make-believe. The only honest relationship he could have with this woman would be in bed, and even then . . . Turning cold out of shame and sadness, he realized he was ready to do to Veronika what he had once done to a noblewoman in a train captured from the Whites—turn her back to him, give her a push, bend her over, pull her skirts up . . . Moreover, this was the image that flashed before his eyes every time he saw Veronika. Boorish impulses, he thought, flagellating himself—a hateful legacy of the Civil War and a disgrace for a commander of the regular Red Army. Nikita is my friend and Veronika is my friend, and I, their good friend, am a hypocrite.

In front of the Metropole they went their separate ways. Vuinovich had a bachelor apartment in the hotel, directly beneath Vrubel's mosaic of the Princess of Dreams. The Gradovs hurried to their streetcar to begin their long journey, including three transfers, out to the suburb of Silver Forest.

While they were rattling along Tverskaya Street in the jam-packed trolley with its repellent odors and glances from other passengers, Nikita didn't say a word.

"Well, what's wrong now?" whispered Veronika.

"You're flirting with Vadim," muttered the brigade commander. "I can feel it. You may not even be aware of it yourself, but you're flirting with him."

Veronika burst into laughter. Someone glanced at her with a smile—a beautiful woman laughing on a streetcar, a sign of life returning to normal. A severe-looking woman bit her lip in indignation.

"You silly goose," Veronika whispered gently.

A sparse white down was falling from the clear pinkish-green skies, and a light frost seemed to promise the joys of ice-skating. They went past the crumbling ruins of Khoroshovo, on the outskirts of Moscow, and then the half-empty streetcar arrived at the Silver Forest station, the end of the line. The age-old pine trees of the parks, Lake Bezdonka, frozen over and covered with a thin film of the season's first snow, and behind fences dachas in which lights were already turned on and stoves lit—it was unexpectedly idyllic after the hustle and bustle and—as always, at least in part—the madness of Moscow.

From the station, they still had to walk several hundred yards to Nikita's parents' house.

"What's in your bag that's so heavy?" asked Nikita.

"A month's supply of bromides," Veronika replied cheerfully with a sidelong glance at her husband.

Suffering always made his freckled face look comical. He stared down at the ground. "To hell with your bromides," he muttered.

"Oh, stop it, Nikita," she said angrily. "You haven't slept for two weeks since you came back from your trip. This Kronstadt business has exhausted you!"

. . .

The mission to Kronstadt in October had seemed like an ordinary trip for an upper-echelon commander—a special train to Leningrad, from there a launch to the moorage at Ust'-Rogatki. Calm and order reigned everywhere: in the harbor, on the shore, in the city. All the seaborne services were back to their natural, measured rhythm. Platoons of sailors marched to and from the bathhouses with a crisp step. Some of them sang "Lizaveta" in chorus. On the battleships they were perfecting the signal equipment. The latest hydroplanes were flying about over the bay like pelicans. For everyone there, the passage of time was marked by clearly sounded bells. It was a clean-scrubbed, nautical world, one might almost say English—in any case, considerably removed from the Russian everyday.

There was nothing there, and no one left, to remind Nikita of what had happened there four years before. Only once, as he was walking toward the top of Fort Totleben, he had heard a quiet voice behind him say: "I see, Comrade Brigade Commander, that you already know the way quite well."

He turned around sharply and looked into the gaze of an old artilleryman. "You . . . you were here? Then? Is it possible?" Later, Nikita had felt quite awkward after he realized that under the surface of his confusion, there lay another implicit question: "Why weren't you shot?"

"I was on leave," said the artilleryman simply, without betraying the slightest emotion.

"Well, I stormed your fort! That's how I know the way!" Nikita said with a note of defiance in his voice, even though he knew the challenge was directed at the wrong person. After all, if the artilleryman hadn't been shot, he must have been considered trustworthy. Otherwise, he would have shared the fate of all those who had had to answer before the people and the Revolution for the violent anti-Bolshevik explosion of March 1921.

Then again, maybe the challenge was not entirely misdirected, considering the way the artilleryman averted his eyes and, indicating a ladder, made a silent gesture of invitation that seemed to say, "Go ahead, be my guest."

Nikita spent the entire day inspecting the installation of new Obukhov guns on forts Totleben, Pyotr, and Rif. He delved into the plans, as well as the oral reports from the gunners, with representatives from the munitions factory and the commanders of the Baltic Fleet. It was only toward evening that he begged off because of fatigue, found himself alone, and headed back to the city on foot. He felt drawn toward Anchor Square, which had been in the middle of the events of 1921.

From a road running alongside the water he surveyed a roadstead and saw the silhouettes of two giants, the very same ones, it seemed to him. No matter how hard you try, he thought, you'll never expel the fury of these battleships, with their cannons and smokestacks, from your memory.

Freshness and a feeling of things washed clean wafted through the air of the October evening, from the lush waters all around, from the small craft furrowing the waters of the roadstead, from the winking signal lights of the gigantic ships.

But back in those days the entire expanse had been white, seemingly frozen forever, and hostile. Battleships had ridden side by side at the harbor wall, covered with ice to the tops of their superstructures and with snow scattered over their decks. Nikita caught himself thinking that even he, a spy, had had feelings of hostility toward the frozen "Marquis' puddle," as the sailors and marines called the Gulf of Finland. Endless chains of punitive troops in white uniforms had marched along that ice to the fortress.

Four and a half years later, Red Army Commander Nikita Gradov, standing at the foot of a bronze Peter the Great, caught himself thinking something else: if the mutiny had occurred a month later, there would have been no coping with it. Having freed themselves from the trap of the ice, the battleships would have had clear sailing to Oranienbaum and with point-blank fire would have put an end to any attempt by the government forces to consolidate. Two other dreadnoughts, the *Gangut* and the *Poltava*, which in March had still been frozen in the mouth of the Neva, would undoubtedly have joined them, and other ships in the Baltic Fleet would have followed. It would have been difficult to count on even the legendary cruiser *Aurora*—after all, just a week before the Kronstadt base rebelled, it had been considered the proud bastion of the Revolution.

The invincibility of the mutinous Baltic Fleet would almost certainly have lit a fuse, setting off a series of explosions throughout the country. The peasant revolt in Tambov Province was already in full swing. No wonder, then, that Lenin had said that the Kronstadt uprising was more dangerous than the armies of Denikin, Kolchak, and Wrangel combined. Clear sailing for the Baltic Fleet would have put an end to the Bolshevik Republic.

The ice saved us, he thought. Historically determined events and the ungovernable forces of nature depend on each other in a strange—no, make that disgraceful—way. Ice turned out to be our best ally in both the storming of the Crimea and the suppression of Kronstadt. So shouldn't we erect a monument to ice? What, base the laws of class struggle on ice, on the slowing down of some pitiful molecules? What rubbish!

However, these paradoxes were not Brigade Commander Gradov's chief source of worry. The fact was that at certain moments of his life he suddenly began to see himself as a traitor, if not someone who had stifled freedom. It was as if a heroic mission had been assigned to a fiery twenty-year-old revolutionary ready to sacrifice his life at any time for the Red Republic and that he had heroically carried the mission out—and yet . . .

He walked slowly along the yellow-and-white columns of the Naval Officers' Club building, raising his hand in a salute to the soldiers and sailors who passed him and even returning women's glances with a smile—Kronstadt had always been famous for the wives of its men—and remembered how in that March blizzard, in the twilight, having left his white smock made of two sheets sewn together on the ice, he had climbed up onto a pier, run across the street, then made his way along this very building, wearing a bogus sailor's uniform that made him fit right in—there was even a new tattoo on his chest that said "Armored Train Red Partisan."

A scouting party of a dozen men had been chosen personally by Tukhachevsky from among the most selfless of the outfit. They were supposed to put the forts' guns out of action and open the gates by the time the final assault was launched, and they would be working alone. Every hour was precious; the first damp western winds were beginning to blow over the bay.

That night he reached the flat that served as their hideout without being challenged, but the next morning . . . the next morning his torments began.

He awoke to the sounds of a military band. Along the street bathed in sunlight marched a column of sailors with broad grins on their faces. A hastily made banner fluttered in the still partly cloudy skies, clearly announcing the shattering slogan of that March:

DOWN WITH THE COMMISSARS!

Signs of rebellion were everywhere. The first thing Nikita saw when he came out into the street, carrying a package containing two Mausers, four hand grenades, and forged papers from the Sevastopol Sailors' Committee, were leaflets bearing the headline "News of the Kronstadt Council" posted on a wall. They contained proclamations of their Revolutionary Committee, news about an attack that had been repulsed and the distribution of provisions, as well as mocking jingles directed at the Bolshevik leaders.

> *When old Kalinin does arrive,*
> *His tongue is soft, and oh so live.*
> *Like a robin he does sing,*
> *But no one here would call him king.*
> *So this chicken commissar*
> *Rides off in his fleeing car!*
> *But then arrives the ultimatum:*
> *Trotsky says he woulda ate'm—*

Alive or served up piping hot,
Like garnished quails in a pot,
Or—better yet—just have them shot.
But these lads ain't sweet old biddies,
They've picked their troikas and committees
Crossed one leg over the other
And shot away—all in a bother.

The men of Kronstadt continued to throng Yakornaya Square, arriving singly, in small detachments, and even in large groups, forming a huge crowd of peakless caps and blue collars in front of the Naval Congress Building and around the monument to Admiral Makarov. The few soldiers and civilians who were sprinkled throughout the crowd stood out sharply in the mass of naval personnel in their army and sheepskin overcoats. Small boys were scampering about here and there, and occasionally one even saw women's excited faces. These people made up the "Kronstadt crew."

Several bands were playing. Together, they drowned out the noise of the constantly increasing rumble of artillery from the bay. As for the Bolsheviks' airplanes, their engines could not be heard at all above the din of the guns and the brass bands, and they could have seemed like attractions at a fair if not for the death-dealing explosive packages that fell from them from time to time, along with leaflets full of threats from "Red Field Marshal Trotsky."

The mood of the crowd was festive. Nikita could not believe his eyes— instead of hardened sinister conspirators led by White Guards, he saw people on a huge outing—many thousands of them, caught up by the excitement.

It was a strange place. A Byzantine hulk of a cathedral and a monument to a man in an ordinary coat. A military orchestra was playing the waltz "Waves of the Amur" to the accompaniment of explosions. The machines in the sky seemed like toys, surrounded by white cottony clouds of exploding antiaircraft shells. Was it all just some fatalistic game, or a new communion, the religion of mutiny?

Snatches of the speeches of the orators on the platform could be heard:

"Comrades, we have appealed to the whole world by radio!"

"The Bolsheviks are lying about the French gold!"

"Councils without monsters!"

Almost every sentence was greeted by a roar from the "crew."

"Comrade Petrichenko, representative from the Revolutionary Committee, has the floor!"

A man in a tight-fitting striped jersey stepped forward from the black coats on the platform. "He's not afraid of catching cold," Nikita said to himself.

"You won't hit him from here with a Mauser. Maybe one of our lads has him in his sights right now?"

"Comrades, I would like to put the battleships' second resolution to a vote! Reject Trotsky's ultimatum, and fight on to victory!"

A shaken Nikita looked around him at the throats roaring "Victory! Victory!" with a single voice. Then he suddenly remembered himself and began to wave his hat in the air and shout "Victory!" Someone slapped him on the back. An old marine with a mustache was looking into his young face with a pleased expression.

"We'll get Russia on her feet, eh, sonny?"

"Hurrah!" Nikita bellowed even louder, and suddenly he felt a chill come over him. He felt as though he meant what he was shouting, as though he was being sucked into the funnel of the crowd's enthusiasm, as though here, for the first time, he was finding what he had been looking for vaguely all these years since the storming of the Metropole in 1917, when as a seventeen-year-old kid he had joined Frunze's outfit.

All the same, these traitors and scoundrels had put the very Revolution in danger by their sailors' arrogance, by acting like spoiled children, by their anarchism and devil-may-care attitude. How could anyone feel any emotion or sentiment where this rabble was concerned?

The doors of the cathedral opened, and a priest with a large cross came out onto the porch. They began to bring out the coffins bearing the bodies of those who had died repulsing the last Bolshevik assault. The bands struck up "The Marseillaise." Sailors removed their hats, and Gradov the spy did the same. At this moment of collective sorrow, his skin was cold as ice, his muscles trembled. . . . This was it, the orgy could not go on any longer, four years of evil actions in the name of the fight against evil. His eyes filled with tears—why, this is the medieval Novgorod *veche* all around you, free Russia, and you're going to stab them in the back!

When it was all over, Nikita and two others of the detachment who had survived the operation were each awarded a gold Swiss watch. Then he was taken to the hospital. For several days he alternated between delirium and unconsciousness, coming around only long enough to notice the ice-laden branches and bullfinches outside his window.

No one ever told him exactly what kind of a fever he had or any details about his illness. He simply got better and then returned to the ranks. Military and Party circles avoided talking about the Kronstadt affair, but there were vague rumors going about that it had brought Lenin to a state of "downright hysteria." It was said he had been laughing and shrieking, "We shot workers, comrades! Workers and peasants!"

No one in these circles, naturally, talked about the fact that it was indeed Kronstadt that had led the country out of the plague of war communism, turned her in the direction of the New Economic Policy (NEP), and started warming her up again. If this row hadn't arisen, the higher-ups would not have renounced their theories "in earnest and for a long time to come."

Veronika, the daughter of a prominent Moscow lawyer, had been married to Nikita for three years and naturally knew quite a bit about her husband's secret wound, though she understood that she didn't know everything about it. In the two weeks since he had come back from his assignment, she had begun to worry seriously about the state of his nerves. He had almost stopped sleeping, paced the floors at night, smoked constantly, and, when he did fall into something approximating a doze, he began talking in his sleep. From his muttering emerged, like phantoms, sentences, cries, and lines from the newspapers of the Kronstadt free troops: "From Zavgorodin—two days of bread rations and a bag of homegrown tobacco; from Ivanov, stoker on the *Sevastopol*—an overcoat; from Member of the Revolutionary Committee Tsimmerman—cigarettes; from Putilin, chemical laboratory worker—one pair of boots . . ."

". . . complete confidence in Comrade Battery Commander Gribanov!"

"Kupolov, goddammit, Kupolov the doctor—have you seen him, boys?"

". . . the crew has been thinking a lot, and they need some literature to exchange with the officer trainees . . ."

> . . . *Arise, people and peasants*
> *Arise to the rising of the dawn.*
> *We'll throw off Trotsky's fetters*
> *And the Lenin tsar will be cast down . . .*

". . . to all the working people of Russia, to all the working people of Russia . . ."

One day, screwing up her courage, she asked if it wouldn't be better for him to leave the army and follow in his father's footsteps by studying medicine at the university. After all, he was only twenty-five, he would be a qualified doctor by the age of thirty . . . Strangely enough, he didn't shout at her but only nodded his head thoughtfully—"It's late, Vika, too late" . . . but it seemed he wasn't thinking about age.

Finally, they came up to the gate in the fence around the dacha bearing a shiny brass plaque that read "Dr. B. N. Gradov," just like in the old days, only in the new orthography. Inside the gate, a brick path wound its way in the shape of an *S* up to the porch, to the well-appointed doors covered with oilcloth, to the large two-story house with a garret, a terrace, and an added wing.

Anyone crossing the threshold of this house would think: here is an oasis of common sense and order, a real stronghold of the enlightened Russian intelligentsia. The older Gradov, Boris Nikitovich, was a professor at the First Medical Institute and a senior staff member at the Soldatyonkovskaya Hospital, and was considered one of the best surgeons in Moscow. Even "makers of history" had to reckon with specialists of his caliber. The Party knew that even though its leaders were relatively young, their health in many cases had been undermined by years of working in the underground, arrest, exile, and wounds. As a result, particular respect was always accorded to the high priests of medicine. Even during the years of war communism, when many of the dachas of Silver Forest had been partially dismantled for firewood, the Gradov house had always had a fire in the hearth and lights in the windows, and now, during the prosperity of NEP, everything seemed to have come full circle, to "prehistoric times," as Leonid Valentinovich Pulkovo, a friend of the family, put it. For example, the piano was constantly heard. The lady of the house, Mary Vakhtangovna, had graduated from a conservatory, where she had studied the piano. Though she joked, "Alas, my greatest concerts turned out to be my children," she never missed an opportunity to immerse herself in music. The professor joked, "Mary keeps the evil spirits away with Chopin."

A large, good-natured German shepherd trotted about on the carpets. The sound of men's voices usually drifted from the library in one of those eternal Slavic debates. A nanny, who had played no small part in Mary Vakhtangovna's three "greatest concerts," puttered about from room to room with piles of clean bed linen or stood in the vestibule paying for the latest delivery of milk and sour cream.

Nikita hung his coat and Veronika's on the deer's antlers that served as a hook—his coat weighed probably about five times as much as his wife's sealskin. He tried to be quiet as he followed his wife up to their room in the garret, so as not to disrupt Chopin, but his mother heard him and called out in her unusually youthful voice, "Nikita, my boy, be nice—there's a meeting of everyone tonight after supper!"

In the garret, from whose windows one could see a bend in the Moscow River and the cupolas of the Khoroshovo and Sokol churches, he began to undress his wife. As he kissed her shoulders, tenderness and a sensuous attraction seemed to crowd out the gloom of Kronstadt. How marvelous it is, he thought, that women can buy silk underwear again. Well, maybe Vuinovich was right when he said we had to crush our brothers in order for the Russian state to be reborn?

CHAPTER TWO

The Kremlin and Its Neighborhood

☆

Rumors and whispers have always hovered around the Kremlin in no fewer numbers than swallows around its towers on fine summer days. What else can one expect from the present day, when the leaders of the world proletariat have been occupying the fortress for eight years? Paradoxes everywhere you turn! Take, for example, one of those Kremlin towers, the Spasskaya, or Savior's Tower. Even though it still bears the name of the Savior, it has come to symbolize something quite different. It is still topped by a two-headed eagle, but now the midday chimes sound the "Internationale" and at midnight they play a popular tune from the Civil War.

Rumor in the city has it that they're building an entire network of hiding places and secret tunnels beneath the Kremlin, for reasons no one knows. The most fantastic stories are going around about the lives of the Kamenev and Stalin households, and about the Bolsheviks' court poet, Demyan Bedny, who has taken up residence right next door to the leaders in what used to be the Arsenal building. The literary circles of the capital have taken to calling him "Demyan-the-Flunky Pridvorov," a pun on the fact that his real name—Pridvorov—came from the Russian word for "courtier."

The stories only increased when, after the death of the Kremlin's most important inhabitant, they embalmed him, carried him out of the fortress, and put him on display in a crystal coffin. What strange twists of reasoning. How does one square them with materialist philosophy, or with the example of Engels, who left instructions for his ashes to be scattered over the ocean?

The great churches of the Kremlin are closed, but their cross-bearing cupolas are still shining. As soon as the sun breaks through the central Russian haze, they glisten alongside the red spurts of the new flags bearing the spidery symbol of the crossed instruments of labor.

This proud Italian fortress, set on the peak of Borovitsky Hill, was burned down three times at two-hundred-year intervals—by the Crimean Tatar Khan Tokhtamysh in the fifteenth century, by Hetman Honsevsky in the seventeenth century, and by Napoleon—and raised its turrets and its swallowtail walls again. What else awaits you in this unpredictable world?

Three Rolls-Royces belonging to the Commissariat for Defense cut across Red Square. It looked as though they were heading in the direction of the gates of Spasskaya Tower, but unexpectedly they raced past them, drove down toward the Moscow River, went around the south and west sides of the fortress, then rolled inside through the potbellied Kutafia Tower at the foot of the bridge. This sudden change of route had been worked out in order to thwart any terrorist actions. The plan, it must be said, was not very complicated, being based on the age-old bit of wisdom that "God watches over the protected." Even so, if someone were to have prepared an ambush anywhere around the Spasskaya Tower gates (and there was, after all, no shortage of combat-ready anti-Soviets, either at home or abroad), the Worker-Peasant Red Army would have been decapitated with one blow. The first car was carrying Commissar for Defense Frunze, the second Tukhachevsky, commander in chief of the Western Military District, and the third Vasily Blücher, Knight of the Order of the Red Banner and commander in chief of the Far East Military District.

Frunze was in a somber mood. He was on his way to the conference despite the decision of the Politburo. This circumstance weighed more heavily on him than his illness. In just the last few days his cursed ulcer had been hurting less. The consulting physicians were hopeful—the tests did not rule out the possibility that a scar was forming, that is, that the ulcer was healing itself. And yet there was this burdensome and ever-growing concern on the part of the Party men. Of course, it was understandable in many cases—the tragedy of the previous year, Lenin's death, had shaken the Party terribly. Still, weren't they showing excessive caution? And maybe, if one wanted to call a spade a spade, they were playing some sort of strange double-dealing game?

Frunze did not like to raise his voice. The thing he feared more than anything else was changing from a Red Army commander, a conscious revolutionary, into a despot and a martinet of the old regime. So he had learned quite well how to impart to his voice a tone that immediately made it clear to those around him that it would be useless to argue. It was in just these tones that he had given orders that morning to have his full dress uniform brought to his billet. After dressing, he went straight to his office and from there to the Kremlin.

In the car, he did not talk to anyone. He even tried to avoid looking at the faithful Vuinovich. Strange, the customs that develop among leaders, he thought. Consider a few people separately; the further away they get from the feverish days of the Civil War, that is, the more they advance into maturity, if not into old age, the more they begin to display unattractive qualities—

Zinoviev and his absurdities, Stalin and his sinister inscrutability, Bukharin and his I-don't-give-a-damn attitude, the litigious Unshlikht, and Klim Voroshilov, who quite simply was good for nothing. You know the individual worth of each one of them, and yet, taken together, they become the "will of the Party." The problem is that we can't get along without that idea, Frunze thought. Lenin understood that without this mystique, everything would crumble.

The thought that today he would be transgressing the "higher ideal"—even if it were for the good of the cause, for the good of the republic itself, it was still an act of willfulness and indiscipline—bothered Frunze. He had an uneasy feeling, and when the Rolls-Royce began bumping over the paving stones of Red Square, it even seemed to him that he could feel this motion in his stomach. He wiped his brow with his glove.

The cadets on duty in the government offices were standing at attention. One could read the admiration in their faces, even though in principle they were supposed to remain impassive. Three legendary army commanders with their aides—adjutants, they used to be called—right on their heels mounting the steps of the Kremlin palace and walking down its corridors . . . Wasn't this the sort of event a man remembers for the rest of his life? Their steps were firm, and to the cadets they represented an ideal of masculinity and youthful maturity. Indeed, they were right: Frunze, the oldest of them, was forty, Blücher thirty-five, Tukhachevsky thirty-two. Had there ever been an army in the history of the world whose command at once was so young and had so much battlefield experience?

The last pair of cadets, standing guard at the "holy of holies," opened the doors. The army commanders entered the conference hall: it had large windows, moldings on the ceiling, a crystal chandelier, and a huge oval table. Some of the participants of the conference were still ambling about on the spongy Bukhara rug and trading jokes, while others were already seated at the table and were absorbed in reading documents. All these men were, as they say, in the prime of life—if any of them was over fifty, then it was not by much—and they were all in a good humor. Things in the country had never been better. They were dressed either in well-cut business suits or in the paramilitary uniform of the Party: a service jacket with large pockets, riding breeches, and boots. They addressed each other with the slightly coarse yet friendly and gently ironic comradeship that had long been the custom in the Party.

An attentive outside observer like Professor Ustryalov, who made a fleeting appearance in our prologue, might have noticed the beginnings of a certain stratification, of what would later be called "Party etiquette," according to which one person might be allowed to address someone else as "Nikolai" or "Grigory," while another might be obliged to emphasize how far removed he was from the omnipotent boss by calling a man by his patronymic, or even the official "Comrade So-and-So." For the time being, however, we cannot help emphasizing the fact that these were all members of the same crowd.

The partisans of the Change of Landmarks movement, like all Russian intellectuals, loved to fasten facts onto preconceived theories. They would obviously have looked for signs of their beloved "aura of power" in this group, and they would probably have found them easily in such trivial details as, say, the fact that the men had put on some weight, that they were better dressed and showed a certain nonchalance in their movements, or that they bore the marks of statesmanship in their wrinkles. For our part, we can just as easily attribute these traits to other causes, and as for their lined faces, we can weigh the following question, though not without a shudder: might they not be the signs of their violence and cruelty—which not long ago had been boundless—that were now overtaking them like a sort of leprosy?

When the military men came into the hall, everyone turned toward them. "Why, Mikhail, it's you! Isn't this a surprise!" Voroshilov exclaimed in a display of cheap theatrics, even though everyone had known for some time that Frunze had left the hospital and was headed for the Kremlin. Several men exchanged glances—it was as though Klim's sham exclamation had underlined the strange, and to some degree insoluble, sense of ambiguity that had grown up around the commissar of the army and navy. Rykov, the chairman of the Council of People's Commissars, invited all to take their seats. Sitting down, both the members of the Politburo and their guests continued to trade rejoinders, looked through their papers, did anything to make it clear that their attention was not riveted on Frunze, neither on him as a person nor as a sick man.

Those who had shaken his hand when he entered the room tried not to attach any significance to their observation that though his hand was as firm as always, it was extremely damp, and those whose gaze met the army commander's as though by chance suppressed the thought that they were looking for signs of blood circulation deficiencies.

Meanwhile, Frunze, beneath the weight of so many stares, was feeling that something was wrong. Fearing he might create a scene, he ducked behind the cover of a pile of dossiers to take his prescribed tablets out of his pocket and swallow one but then decided against the idea. Turning to Shkiryatov, he asked, "So where's Stalin?"

Shkiryatov moved his entire body forward, closer to Frunze. It seemed as though his eyes were trying to penetrate more deeply into the army commander, and the expression on his face was one of pure hypocrisy, which accentuated his natural lack of symmetry.

"Comrade Stalin asked to be excused. He is just now concluding a meeting with a Cantonese delegation."

Frunze felt a pain that reminded him of the attack he had suffered in the Crimea in September. The pain was not very severe, but the fear that another, stronger pain would follow it, that he would make a spectacle of himself in front of the Politburo, and moreover—and here the image began to take shape in his mind for the first time—that he would let himself be taken away to go under the knife seemed to knock the floor out from under him. The geometrical order of the world was quickly becoming blurred before his eyes.

"That's odd. I thought Unshlikht had already discussed everything with Generalissimo Ku Khan-min—"

"What's wrong with you, Mikhail Vasilevich?"

Frunze had not even noticed Rykov's signal to the other participants in the conference that seemed to say "Leave him alone." He vaguely realized that according to the predetermined agenda Tukhachevsky would be the first to speak.

On the agenda was Frunze's "baby"—military reform—which he was more proud of than the taking of Perekop during the Crimean campaign. In accordance with this measure, the Worker-Peasant Red Army would be reduced by 560,000 men, which would, however, make it twice as strong and three times more professional. A mixed personnel and territorial administrative system was being introduced, a law of compulsory military service was being passed, as well as the long-awaited establishment of unified command—that is, the removal of the political commissars, those constant sources of demagoguery and chaos. The military reform would get rid of the guerrilla amateurs once and for all and lay the foundations of an indestructible armed force.

Frunze's head fell onto the table with a strange, inanimate sound that made the very fibers of the mighty council shudder. He immediately stood up and made as if to leave. Halfway to the door, though, he felt sick to his stomach and raised his handkerchief to his mouth. The handkerchief turned red with blood, and the army commander sank to the floor.

The cadets on guard, clearly not yet trained in how to act in such circumstances, began scurrying around in confusion. Some rushed over to the fallen man, some to the windows, some to the telephone. At this point—that is, almost immediately—several medical orderlies appeared with a stretcher. It was difficult to tell whether this stretcher was part of the normal inventory of the medical service that was always on call at Politburo sessions, or if it had been ordered especially for that day.

In the panic, even our impartial observer might have been distracted and failed to notice the more than somewhat peculiar glances exchanged by several of the conference's participants. Then again, he would soon have been brought back to reality by Voroshilov's tragic cry: "The Crimea didn't help Mikhail!"

Then, in the movement that had arisen around the prone form, movement that would have looked right at home on the stage—any court, particularly during a period of interregnum, resembles a theater, and the Kremlin was no exception—our observer would have heard Zinoviev's venomous whisper: "On the other hand, it did help Iosif . . ."

It's hard to say whether or not everyone present heard this utterance, but it is certain that it reached Stalin's ears. He had slipped in unnoticed through a small door flush with the wall and had crossed the hall soundlessly in his soft Caucasian boots. Walking around the table and going around Zinoviev with particular care—the latter suddenly had the feeling that a wildcat was passing by—Stalin approached the stretcher.

At that moment they were giving Frunze an injection of camphor. He had come out of his fainting spell and was quietly moaning, "It's my nerves, my nerves . . ." The stretcher bearers lifted him up. Stalin put his hand to the army commander's shoulder as a parting gesture.

"We must bring in the best doctors," announced Stalin. "Burdenko, Rozanov, Gradov . . . the Party cannot allow such a son to be lost."

Trotsky was right, thought Zinoviev. This man will say whatever raises him higher than anyone else, even if only an inch.

Stalin walked over to the table and sat down. His seat, though one of many, suddenly appeared to be the center of the oval. Perhaps, in accordance with the rules of drama, attention was fixed on him because he had appeared at a decisive moment, or perhaps it was something else; whatever the reason, it was indeed Stalin whom the dazed members of the Politburo and the government were looking at. It was obvious that, all the different interpretations of the meaning of Frunze's illness notwithstanding, a motif of fate and gloom had been introduced beneath the arches of the Kremlin, as though a flight of Valkyries had winged past.

Stalin looked out the window for a minute or two at the indifferent clouds passing in the October sky, then intoned: ". . . but eternally green is the tree of life . . ."

The Party men, who had long experience in emigration behind them, remembered that the great man himself, Lenin, had loved to repeat this line from *Faust*.

"Let's continue." With a benign gesture, Stalin proposed that they return to the order of business.

. . .

Toward evening of that same day, guests began to gather at Professor Gradov's dacha in Silver Forest. A Russian-Georgian feast was being prepared in honor of the forty-fifth birthday of the lady of the house, Mary Vakhtangovna.

Galaktion Vakhtangovich Gudiashvili, the older brother of the cause of the festivities, had come from Tiflis along with two nephews, their sisters' sons Otari and Nugzar.

No one doubted, of course, that Galaktion would be the *tamada** of the evening. The powerfully built epicurean from the Transcaucasus considered feasting much more essential to life than his work as a respectable pharmacist on Mount King David. The storms of revolution, the collapse of the Georgians' short-lived independent state, even last year's uprising, which had been savagely put down by the agents of Blümkin's Cheka—none of these things was reflected in either the outward aspect or the worldview of this "Mediterranean man," whose very appearance seemed as promising as the beginning of an Italian opera, or at least a vial of love potion.

It goes without saying that Uncle Galaktion had not come to Silver Forest empty-handed. He had brought along his two nephews, "those good-for-nothings," as he called them, to help him transport three barrels of wine from Klarety's private cellars, a half-dozen smoked piglets, three quarter-sections of fresh and fragrant chachi—"like the kiss of a child," as Lermontov had put it—a sack of mixed nuts and another of figs, two baskets of tangerines from the Ajara region, a basket of ripe pears that resembled the breasts of young Greek girls—how could I visit my sister without bringing her these pears?—a pot of satsivi the size of an ancient amphora, two buckets of Georgian-style beans, and a few other condiments—ajika, tkemali, shashmika, shmekali.

Immediately on arrival, Uncle Galaktion went to inspect the preparations for the feast and was greatly impressed by his host's stores: here were vodka and cognac, every possible kind of jellied hors d'oeuvres, as well as delicacies that had almost been forgotten but had reappeared now that NEP was in full swing. There were anchovies and herring, an absolute landslide of mushrooms, cucumbers, and tomatoes that made the heart glad, several different varieties of cheese, from those of the chaste outpost of Holland to the decadent Roquefort. There was even sturgeon, the food of aristocrats. A saddle of mutton was languishing in the oven, much to everyone's satisfaction.

"Mary, my dear, happy birthday! So this is NEP, kind ladies and gentlemen?

*"Toastmaster."

The best new economic policy is the old economic policy, and the best policy is 'To hell with all politics!' " exclaimed this Georgian Falstaff.

Most of the guests who had already arrived burst into laughter, but the young poet Kalistratov, the one who was always interested in the whereabouts of the Gradovs' younger daughter, Nina, recited some lines from Mayakovsky:

> *They asked me once:*
> *"Do you like NEP?"*
> *"I like it," I replied,*
> *"When it's not inept."*

Not everyone, you see, was in a tranquil frame of mind that evening. The Gradovs' middle child, their son Kirill, who only that spring had graduated from the university with a degree in history and Marxism, angrily shrugged his shoulders at his uncle's politically tactless joke.

"I can't stand all these smirks and bits of doggerel that are going around about NEP," he said to Kalistratov. "It always seems to them that it's the end of us, when in fact it's not going to go on forever, even though it will take some time!"

"I've seen enough for my lifetime," sighed the unprincipled Kalistratov, who, not wasting any time, made a beeline for the buffet.

Kirill, standing erect, pale and serious, wearing a peasant shirt with the collar fastened at the side, resembled one of the old-time fanatics of the underground and stood out distinctly from the well-dressed guests. Had he not been afraid of offending his mother, he would have left the party long ago to go to his room to read. Damn NEP! All the has-beens of history were crowing about it, the White emigration was following it with bated breath and, breathing a sigh of relief, deciding that in fact one could turn back the clock. Well, all right, he thought, you can't expect very much from Uncle Galaktion; Father generally acts as though politics didn't exist, a perfectly typical specialist; Mama is always occupied with her Chopin pieces, prays on the sly, and still worships the Symbolist poets and their "The wind brought from afar the hint of a spring song." Our generation, though, has been affected by something noxious—even my brother the Red Army brigade commander, not to mention Veronika . . .

The indignation of this young Puritan was easily understandable if one looked at his parents. They no more conformed to the revolutionary aesthetic than their Muscovite hospitality would have compared with the inventory of any Soviet mass dining hall. Mary was a striking woman in a low-cut silk dress, a string of pearls around her neck and her luxuriant hair tied up in an old-fashioned bun. She was well matched by the professor, fifty-year-old Boris Nikitovich Gradov, a still-fit man in a well-tailored suit. His neatly trimmed beard, even though it did not go perfectly with his modern necktie, was indispensable to the enlargement of the gallery of great Russian doctors. On this festive evening they both looked at least ten years or so younger than their age, and it was clear to everyone that they were filled with tenderness for and devotion to each other in the best tradition of the not yet totally vanquished Russian intelligentsia.

Most of the Gradovs' guests belonged to that tribe that had now been declared in Marxist terms a "stratum," or a "layer," as if it were part of a layer cake. At the beginning of the evening, with obvious pleasure, they had all crowded around the physicist Leonid Valentinovich Pulkovo, who had just returned from an official visit to England. "Why, look at him," everyone said. "He looks just like an Englishman, a regular Sherlock Holmes!"

But no, the real Englishman of the evening turned out to be another guest, the writer Mikhail Afanasievich Bulgakov. He even sported a monocle! On the other hand, Veronika, who was helping her mother-in-law to greet the guests at the door, caught the celebrated man of letters glancing at her in a not very English—that is, a not very restrained—manner.

"Listen to me, Verochka," Mary Vakhtangovna said to her. Her use of this name alone was enough to indicate the presence of that old platitude of family relations, friction between a woman and her daughter-in-law. The latter had been asking everyone to call her "Vika" while the former seemed to keep forgetting, calling her "Vera" instead. "Tell me, darling," Mary said, and Veronika immediately thought, Darling? From what Tiflis salon did you come to visit? "Where is your husband, my dear?" Veronika shrugged her shoulders in such a way that Bulgakov could only say "Oh!" after which he moved away.

"I don't know, Maman." It seemed to her that by calling her mother-in-law "Maman" she was parrying her "Vera darling," but Mary Vakhtangovna did not seem to notice anything unusual about this form of address. "This morning he was accompanying his commander in chief to the Kremlin, but he should have been back three hours ago."

It's a good thing he hasn't come back, thought Bulgakov as he passed by with a glass of wine.

"To the health of dearest Mary, in her room I'd surely tarry!" some loudmouth shouted.

People began to propose spontaneous toasts. Uncle Galaktion protested vociferously, saying that it wasn't yet time for the toasts and that proposing toasts was part of a refined culture. Russians, with their barbaric manners, would do better to learn from more ancient civilizations, which had already been making fine wines in the days when the Scythians were only just learning to chew on wild hemp.

A general chaotic merriment was starting, just the sort that later allows one to say "The evening was a success," when suddenly fireworks began going off outside. Someone was beating a drum and youthful voices were heard chanting some ridiculous verses—"Seven years since Revolution, / Away with bourgeois evolution, / Down with family collusion!" The "Blue Shirts," a pro-Bolshevik theater troupe, were the latest enthusiasm of the youngest Gradov, eighteen-year-old Nina.

The guests poured out onto the porch and the terrace to watch the show a group of six players was putting on. "We are beginning a spectacle-bouffe entitled *Family Revolution!*" announced the leader, who then turned a cartwheel. The leader was Nina herself, who had inherited her mother's thick dark locks, which at the moment were mercilessly cropped in the proletarian fashion. She had her father's bright eyes, filled with a lively positivism, and she had absorbed from the rest of the universe, which so delighted her entire young being, such a healthy dose of enthusiasm that at times she seemed to be not a separate entity but rather a part of the enchanted world among the stars sparkling high over the pine trees, the verses of Pasternak, and the towers of the Third International. This dazzling creature has such an important role to play in our story that we can surely derive no real pleasure from being told that the acrobatic movement with which she made her entry onto these pages turned out badly, with a fall and even a somewhat absurd landing on her buttocks, which fortunately turned out to be fairly resilient.

On the whole, the entire "bouffe" turned out to be an absurd bit of hackwork, not to mention the fact that it was tactless.

A tall, robust young man, a proletarian friend of Nina named Semyon Stroilo, threw a ridiculous purple cloak over his shoulders, stuck a top hat that was too small for him on his head, and began to declaim in a wooden voice,

> *I'm a retrograde professor,*
> *And I sure like my rubles, yessir!*
> *When my wife asks me for money,*
> *I kick her ass and think it's funny.*

The remaining members of the troupe built a rather rickety pyramid behind him and began to shout,

> *Like Kollontai create an Eden,*
> *Bestow upon your wife her freedom!*

Barricades mean revolution,
Not a lot of noise pollution!
Down with capital's oppression,
Mary needs a useful session,
Trade unions teach us all a lesson!

Every exclamation point, it seemed, produced new, ever more frightful swayings of the pyramid, and the guests were following not the idiotic words but the fragile equilibrium. In the end the pyramid collapsed. Fortunately, no one was hurt, but there was a terrible feeling of awkwardness in the air, and not even because of the clumsiness of the performance but rather because everyone secretly sensed that the feelings behind its "spirit of rebellion" were false: no matter how one looked at it, the Blue Shirts were on the side of the ruling ideology, and the liberal "bourgeois" who had come together at the Gradovs' that evening always pictured themselves as the opposition.

"Dinner is served, ladies and gentlemen! Dinner is served, comrades!" yelled Uncle Galaktion.

Emboldened by this summons, Otari and Nugzar broke into a song in their native language and then began to whirl around Nina in a Georgian dance. The failure of the sketch *Family Revolution* affected Nina just as deeply as the failure of Treplev's play in Chekhov's *The Seagull* had affected her namesake. She was not, however, as embittered by the vicissitudes of life as that other Nina, and so, quickly forgetting about proletarian aesthetics, she delved into her ancient roots, tiptoeing past her cousins like a Georgian peahen.

"It seems as though she is your best work," Boris Nikitovich was told by his best friend, the physicist Pulkovo.

Everyone was scrambling to find a seat around the gigantic table, and in the confusion the two old friends moved over to the window. Outside, the moonlit sky of Moscow was shining through the pines.

"So what do you think of all of this after England?" asked Boris Nikitovich.

Leonid Valentinovich shrugged. "I've been back for a week now, Bo, and Oxford already seems like a strange place to me. How do they manage without all of our—er—well, in a word, without all the excitement we have here?"

"Tell me, Leonid, didn't you feel like staying there? After all, you're a bachelor. You have no anchor here, so to speak, and the possibilities for research there are incomparably better."

Pulkovo grinned and slapped Gradov on the shoulder. "That's what it means to be a surgeon—he goes right to the sore spot! You know, Bo, Rutherford offered me a position in his laboratory, but—well—in fact I really do have an anchor here . . ."

Engrossed in their conversation, they did not notice that something unforeseen was happening in the living room, that a dissonant note had sounded amid the festive babble of voices. Two army officers in full uniform had come into the house and were looking around the room without taking off their overcoats—Nikita and Vadim.

"Well!" exclaimed Pulkovo finally. "What do you know about that? Nikita, a brigade commander? Unbelievable! So all your offspring have joined the cause now, Bo—are you satisfied with your children?"

"Well, how can I put it—" Boris Nikitovich already realized that something important had happened and was now following his son with his eyes. "We have good children, but . . . well, you know, they're rather too caught up in—er—the fact is . . . no one is carrying on the family tradition . . ."

Nikita had finally seen his father and was coming across the room toward him, freeing himself as delicately as he could from his sister, who was hanging on his left shoulder, gently pushing away Veronika, who was peppering him with questions on his right, politely but steadily forcing his way through the crowd of guests. Vadim Vuinovich followed on his heels, serious, with a stern expression and without a glance at Veronika. Even though their manners were impeccable, a feeling of something not quite right emanated from these two figures clad in the uniform of the triumphant Worker-Peasant Red Army. Perhaps this was caused by a special air that seemed to waft behind them into the unconcern of the party—an odor of spaces too vast, a mixture of the dampness of fall, gasoline, vast living quarters, riding schools, and barracks, perhaps even hospitals.

"Delighted to see you, Leonid Valentinovich, welcome, welcome back, but I have urgent business with my father." With these words Nikita took Boris Nikitovich by the arm and with assurance, as though he were the elder, led him into his study.

Vuinovich, continuing to follow Nikita, stopped for a moment to unfasten the hook at the collar of his overcoat. That moment would remain in his memory for the rest of his life as the most intense moment of his youth. Veronika whispered to him, "What's wrong with the two of you, Vadim?"

"Some very important events have occurred, Father. Commander Frunze's ulcer has become exacerbated. He was taken ill during a conference at the Kremlin. The Politburo is insisting that he have an operation, but the doctors are divided in their opinions. They are asking you to come and participate in a consultation. Stalin himself mentioned your name. Your opinion could be decisive. I'm sorry that things turned out like this, but I know Mama will understand. Regimental Commander Vuinovich will take you to the hospital and bring you back as well."

Nikita was speaking in short bursts, as though he were reading a telegraph ticker. Already making ready to go, the professor suddenly thought about how many things the events of the past few years had robbed them of, both his son and himself: his firstborn son's youth, with all the delightful pranks and horseplay a family looks forward to, had ended before it had ever really started. It is normally later in life that one discusses important world events with seriousness, but his son had stepped from adolescence straight into those damned events, and from that moment on it had been impossible to speak to him any other way except with great seriousness.

"You, I hope, will stay here with your mother?"

"Yes, yes."

None of those at the party, least of all the cause of the festivities, was surprised by the unexpected departure of their host in the company of the handsome young officer. A successful surgeon was often called away at the most inconvenient moments. A few whispers went around about goings on "at the top," but they were soon crowded out by the strong aroma of spiced saddle of mutton.

"On the X rays, gentlemen—rather, comra—in a word, respected colleagues—we can clearly see an example of the 'niche effect' on the walls of the duodenum. However, there is reason to believe that what we are dealing with here is an intensive process of scar formation, if not an actually healed ulcer. As for this latest hemorrhage, it seems to me that it was caused by a superficial ulceration of the walls of the stomach, the result of a chronic inflammation. That was, in fact, the impression that I had when I examined the patient, and I trust my own fingers, gen—pardon me, colleagues—more than I do X rays." The elderly Professor Lunts coughed and stopped but then finished his sentence by saying in irritation, "gentlemen and comrades!"

The large study in the administrative building of the Soldatyonkovskaya Hospital was filled to capacity. The chairman of the meeting, or the man who in any case was sitting in the center of the room by the X-ray projector, was Dr. Mandryka, chief of staff. He was considered to be the man who knew the V.I.P. patient better than anyone else, since he had been supervising his cure during the past few months and had also accompanied him on his recent trip to the Crimea. It was going to be difficult for even Mandryka to play the leading role in this gathering, though: no less than a dozen leading lights of Soviet medicine were on hand—Grekov, Martianov, Pletnyov, Rozanov, Obrasov, Abrikosov, Lunts, Gradov, who had just arrived, the celebrated Professor Vishnevsky, who was expected from Kazan . . .

Also present at the consultation were several individuals who clearly had no direct relation to the medical profession, even though they were dressed in white hospital gowns. To a man they were serious and attentive, sitting in a corner and taking in every word, and though they said nothing themselves, they made it clear by their mere presence that the matter at hand was one of the highest importance to the state.

Lunts is right, thought Professor Gradov as he took a folder containing the consulting physicians' notes and the test reports from Mandryka's hand—some here are "gentlemen," others are "comrades."

"So, what is your diagnosis, Vsevolod Karlovich?" Mandryka asked him. "Do we need to resort to an operation?"

Lunts was perspiring profusely, and his face was covered with blemishes produced by nervous tension. He was constantly taking out a large handkerchief that was already soaked around the edges. "In my clinic, friends, I treat such things with special diets and mineral water. Ordinarily, the patients—"

"But can we take the risk?" Mandryka cut in. "After all, this is no ordinary patient!"

"Don't interrupt me!" said Lunts, slamming his hand down on a table in anger. "To me, all patients are ordinary!"

"May I examine the army commander?" Boris Nikitovich asked Dr. Ochkin in a whisper.

As they were walking along the corridor, Regimental Commander Vuinovich followed. Two soldiers were posted by the doors leading to a stairwell. In the antechamber of Frunze's room, Professor Gradov noticed the overcoat of the army-navy commissar hanging from a hanger—four rectangular shapes in the buttonholes and a large star on the sleeve.

Meanwhile, one of the many paradoxical events of the Revolution was taking place at the dacha in Silver Forest: it turned out that the Charleston, the *dernier cri* of the season, delighted the "old fogeys" of the bourgeoisie but outraged the "progressive" young people.

"What the hell do we want with that kind of decadence?" asked, for example, Nina's friend Semyon Stroilo. "It's just some shaking-about invented by the capitalists as a distraction, bread and circuses for the masses. It's of no use to the proletariat."

"Yes, but the proletariat abroad does dance the Charleston," said Pulkovo, who had recently traveled halfway across Europe after his studies at Oxford. "Young men and girls from the lower classes, and just about anyone who has the energy."

"A Western whim," said Stroilo with a dismissive wave of his hand that had a touch of class arrogance about it.

"And I suppose that you, my friend, propose to introduce country folk dances into everyday proletarian life?" Mikhail Afanasievich Bulgakov, his monocle flashing, addressed the question mockingly to the young people who were arguing.

"No, no, nothing of the kind!" said Nina heatedly, coming to the defense of her friend. "The Revolution is creating a whole new aesthetic, and that includes new dances!"

"Will they be like the old marches?" asked Savva Kitaigorodsky, a graduate student in the department of Nina's father and the embodiment of intellectualism and good manners.

"Don't play the provocateur," said Stroilo. He did not address these words to the future doctor directly but clearly intended him to understand that he mustn't go too far, he shouldn't be too hard on Nina; the "broad" belonged to him, Stroilo, as a trophy of the class struggle.

"Comrades! Comrades!" exclaimed Nina, who wanted so much for everyone to be set afire by the same flame instead of just smoldering in their own way. "Think about it, really—what foolishness, the Charleston! What is it to us at the heights we've attained? We can afford to be indulgent! Why, we can even dance it ourselves, as a sort of parody!"

She turned around with a jerk—all movements had to be precipitous, awkward, part of the New Left Front of Art (LEF) aesthetic—cranked up the phonograph, put on a record called "Mama, Buy Me a Yellow Bonnet," grabbed Styopa Kalistratov, and pulled him forward. "Let's do a parody!"

"Parody, parody," the poet cackled like a rooster, and with great eagerness he began to throw his legs out to the side at the knees, showing that he was quite well informed about how it was done, and throwing open his stylish jacket that he had bought secondhand especially for the evening.

Well, Nina wasn't doing so badly herself, taking great pleasure at parodying the decadent dance that had washed up beneath the gloomy Russian skies from Georgia and South Carolina, coming from people who never used words like "decadence."

Soon everyone was dancing, "parodying," including Uncle Galaktion, despite the two hundred and fifty pounds of his hedonism, as well as his two nephews, the agile young knights from the Caucasus. Even the birthday lady joined in, though not without a great deal of charming timidity, raising her heavy silk skirts up to her bony knees. The dacha floor was shaking violently, the maid looked in from the kitchen in alarm, and the dog was barking frightfully . . . The old world may be doomed, but it's the dacha that's going to collapse first! she thought. Even Nikita the brigade commander, the "kombrig," was drawn in by his seductive wife, who seemed to be radiating a strawberry warmth, and did no less than a dozen or so ironic steps; even

Stroilo, filled with contempt, was banging on the floor, not keeping time but all the same in a healthy frenzy . . . Only Kirill Gradov, a doctrinaire Marxist, remained true to his principles, standing in the loft and glaring fiercely down at the tremulous revelry.

His elder brother came up to the loft with a bottle in his right hand and two shot glasses in his left and told him, "Stop making such a fuss, Kir—let's drink to Mama's health!"

"I've already had enough to drink," growled Kirill. "And it looks as though you've had more than enough, Comrade Kombrig."

Nikita, who had come only halfway up the staircase, began to go back down, assuming a comical expression of hurt. Funny guy, that Kirill, he thought, standing up there like a member of a military tribunal.

The kombrig had indeed had quite a bit to drink, no less than six shot glasses of vodka and another two or three glasses of Georgian wine. It was only after taking all this in that the tension of the day had begun to leave him. At the beginning of the evening he had felt like a sort of ghost, like a gendarme messenger in Gogol's *Inspector General*, the only difference being that no one fainted at the sight of him—on the contrary, everyone skirted around his frozen form with unusual agility. He had made several telephone calls to headquarters and to the commissariat, and only after he learned that Frunze had regained consciousness and "felt fine" did he join the party.

He continued for some time to look at everyone with a strange smile, feeling as though he were the only real person among the guests and relatives, representing the only world that was real, the world of the army. Then the alcohol, good food, the joyful noise, that silly Charleston, the beautiful young woman radiating success and warmth who belonged to him and him only, all these things had their effect on Nikita, and he forgot about the chevrons on his sleeve and suddenly became an ordinary young man of twenty-five, strolling from room to room with a glass in his hand, mixing in conversations, laughing at jokes louder than anyone else, twirling his nimble sister about. . . . He had a go at the "bourgeois parody," tried to get his surly younger brother to show some life . . . until he suddenly saw his splendid wife surrounded by men and laughing. A vile thought occurred to him: they're standing around Veronika like dogs who want to mate. He suddenly realized he was very drunk.

Just then a loathsome voice cut through the noise from a crowd standing next to him. It belonged to a haggard-looking young man with purple rings beneath his eyes. "It was Youth that led us in the cavalry campaigns, young men who threw us onto the ice at Kronstadt . . ."

Nikita knew his type very well: one of those staff officers with bohemian ways who use cocaine, always have a swollen nose and lips, and are forever irritated about something. They reminded him of suckers on a plant. It was just these sorts who were always muddling heads with their versifying and their white powder . . . muddling the heads of whom? Why, our young women, of course, pulling them into back rooms of headquarters buildings . . . these "romantics," defiling our young women in storerooms, in wardrobes, even in latrines; they drag our girls around all over the place, using them on sofas, behind sofas, on grand pianos, on pool tables, underneath pianos, underneath tables, in cellars, on rooftops, in moldering smashed greenhouses . . . and then they palm them off on commissars, agents of the Cheka, any swine that comes along . . . our Smolyanka and Bestuzhev girls, with a chorus of staff officer riffraff in the background . . . and their ridiculous guitars and putting paper flowers in their curls . . . youth, revolution . . .

He still understood that what was running through his head was some idiotic, and what was more, White Guard rubbish, that he really hadn't met that many defiled women who were, as he put it, "our girls" in the headquarters units. Nevertheless, fury had already raised him up to the crest of its wave, and, almost incapable of resisting it any longer, he strode over to the romantic of the Revolution.

"Pardon my asking, but were you at Kronstadt yourself?"

"What do you suppose, Kombrig? Of course I was there!" the "youth" snarled at him, apparently eager to accept the challenge. With his clear eyes and twitching cheeks, the "youth" was in fact no younger than the brigade commander. "I took part in the final assault!"

"Aha!" said Nikita and seized him tightly by the shoulder, moving close to him. "So that means you saw the executions? You saw how they shot sailors by the dozens, by the hundreds?"

"They executed ours, too!" said the "youth," struggling to free himself from the grip of the brigade commander. "The Whites ruled by terror in the fortress!"

"That's a lie!" cried Nikita so threateningly that a hush fell over everything around them, except for the meowing voice of a Negro singer coming from the phonograph. "They didn't shoot anyone from our side! The Kronstadt sailors didn't execute Bolsheviks!" The circle of faces that had formed around Nikita suddenly took on the appearance of a strange film, having no depth, only flat surfaces, and he released the soft shoulder. "The boots were confiscated from all the men who were arrested, that's true," he muttered. "They distributed them to the men of the command who had no shoes. The Communists received bark sandals in return." Suddenly he flared up again: "Sandals, comrades! There were no executions! Even me, a spy, they didn't shoot! We did it to them later . . . like butchers . . . like beasts!"

The guests, taken aback, were silent. All of a sudden, Kirill came racing down the steps from the loft and flew at his brother in a rage. "Nikita, how dare you! Don't repeat slander!"

Veronika was already hanging on to her husband's shoulder, pulling him away into the depths of the house. Mama Mary followed them with a tray of small pharmacist's vials. Uncle Galaktion brought up the rear, making reassuring gestures to the guests. Nothing to worry about, everything is all right. From the threshold, Nikita once again yelled, "Murderers! A bloodbath! You know what you can do with your romanticism!"

The army-navy commissar did in fact feel much better. He smiled at Professor Gradov as the latter's fingers—each of which seemed to be a separate earnest researcher—probed his abdomen and diaphragm.

"They say that your son, Professor, is one of Tukhachevsky's staff officers, isn't that so? I know Nikita, a brave soldier and a real revolutionary."

Boris Nikitovich was sitting on the edge of the bed, his hip leaning against the army commander's. The famous medical man had examined thousands of patients, yet never before, not even in his student days, had he found anything strange in the fact that a man in his care turned from a social concept into one of diseased physiology. From this body, even in its outstretched position beneath the doctor's fingers, emanated the magic of power. A foolish thought occurred to him: maybe everything is different with this one? Maybe his stomach flows into the Perekop isthmus, where he won his famous battle?

Examining the triangular area over the duodenum and probing more deeply into a sizable layer of fat, the doctor discovered several points that were rather sensitive. Perhaps exudation was taking place, as well as a slight irritation of the peritoneum. His liver seems to be in perfect order, he thought, now let's auscultate his heart.

As he bent over his chest, that is, over the receptacle of the heroic legend, Frunze momentarily pushed his stethoscope aside and whispered directly into his ear, "Professor, I don't need an operation! Do you understand? In no case do I need an operation . . ."

Their eyes met. The whites of Frunze's eyes were faintly jaundiced. He closed one eyelid for a second to signal to Professor Gradov that he had his full and confidential trust.

Something is not quite right here, thought Boris Nikitovich as he was leaving the commander's room. The unusual zeal of Mandryka, the patient's whisper . . . guards and strange people everywhere . . . the hospital seemed to be occupied by the army and the secret police . . .

He had not taken ten steps down the corridor when someone tugged at his sleeve, saying to him in a tone of utmost seriousness, "If you please, Professor, come this way. They're waiting for you."

In the same tone, the man said to his escort, Vuinovich, "As for you, Comrade Regimental Commander, they are not waiting for you."

When he entered the office of the ward director, two pairs of eyes seized him. The white gowns over their cloth uniforms did not conceal their real affiliation in the slightest. Then again, they were not trying to conceal it.

"We have orders from the government to learn your diagnosis after your examination of Comrade Frunze."

"I'm going to give a report at the consilium in a moment." In trying to conceal his bewilderment, he had spoken almost rudely.

"To us first," said one of the agents. I wouldn't think twice about shooting you, you son of a bitch, his eyes seemed to say.

The second man was—oh, yes—decidedly more gentle.

"You understand, of course, Professor, the significance that is attached to the recovery of Comrade Frunze."

Boris Nikitovich sank into the chair that was offered to him and, trying to conceal his annoyance (what else could his excessive perspiration have been caused by except annoyance?), said he was inclined to agree with Dr. Lunts—the illness was serious, but there was no need for an operation.

"Your opinion differs from that of the Politburo." The words were pronounced slowly, with every word emphasized, by the one whom Boris Nikitovich almost subconsciously recognized as an expert in torture, an executioner.

"To my knowledge, there are no doctors in the Politburo," he replied in as pleasant a tone as he could manage. "Isn't that why they called me in to the consultation?"

The "executioner" fixed his gaze upon him. It was almost unbearable.

"By taking that position, Gradov, you are increasing the distrust that has accumulated in your case."

"The distrust that has accumulated . . ." Now he was covered in sweat, could feel the moisture trickling from his armpits, and realized that it was caused not by annoyance, but by a staggering fear.

The secret police agent drew a thick folder from his briefcase—without any doubt one of the well-known dossiers . . . the personal OGPU file of Professor B. N. Gradov.

"Let us be precise, Gradov. Why did you never indicate in any of your documents that your uncle was a deputy of the commissar of finance in the provisional government of Samara? You didn't think it was important? Or did you forget? And you didn't know his Paris address—88, rue Vaugirard? And here, didn't your friend Pulkovo visit your uncle? Tell us, now—didn't you yourself meet with Professor Ustryalov? What instructions did he bring from the leaders of the emigration?"

These seven questions felt like seven mighty blows of a *knout*, and only after the seventh was there a pause. He felt as though he were suffocating.

"What are you saying, comrade? Why, how can you talk that way, comrade?"

The lovingly ironed handkerchief he pressed to his forehead instantly became an abject rag. The "executioner" pounded the table in a rage. "You'll find no comrades here! The wolf in the forest is your comrade."

Boris Nikitovich pulled his expensive necktie to one side. Later, in analyzing his state and his humiliating actions, he always justified it by saying that they had been caused by the surprise of it all. Unexpected it obviously was: how could he have supposed that in the clinical surroundings so familiar to him he would be subjected to an interrogation?

The second agent, the more "liberal" of the two, turned to his coworker indignantly. "Get ahold of yourself, Benedikt!" He moved closer to Gradov and laid a hand on his shoulder. "Pardon us, Professor. Benedikt's nerves are in an awful state. You know, a consequence of the Civil War . . . he went through the hell of the White torture chambers. The class struggle, Boris Nikitovich, sometimes takes on cruel forms. What can we do? Sometimes we become the victims of history, and that is why we wish to avoid any possible mistakes and to dispel this suspicion that has grown up around you, and, as a consequence—alas, almost automatically—around your children. The enormous respect that we have for your medical skills notwithstanding, it is particularly important that a scientist of your reputation occupy a post that is worthy of him and that he should demonstrate that he is not indifferent to the fate of the republic, that he is with us in his heart—in his heart and not because of the cold calculations of a bourgeois 'expert.' And so, in a case as important as the saving of our hero Army Commander Frunze, it would be desirable to see that you are not a man to take cover behind false objectivity. Do not remain aloof."

Boris Nikitovich bowed his head, then took an irrevocable step into cowardice. "All things considered," he muttered, "I never said an operation was out of the question."

The comforting hand on his shoulder tightened almost imperceptibly; a sort of intimacy was established between the shoulder and the hand.

"To a certain extent, radical measures are always more effective than therapy."

The hand moved away. Without raising his head, the professor sensed that the secret policemen were exchanging looks of satisfaction.

. . .

Vadim Vuinovich, holding down the map case that was slapping against his hip, rushed headlong down the stairs toward Army Commander Bazilevich, who had just arrived from the Moscow Military District headquarters with two of his aides. "Request permission to report, Comrade Bazilevich. The commissar decided to have the operation. The Politburo proposal was backed by the doctors after consultation."

The Moscow District commander slowly unbuttoned his overcoat, as though by this action he wished to make the breathless, nervous young officer slow down. He surveyed the vestibule, the staircase, and the windows, in which black tree trunks covered with white bands of the first snow stood out in relief against the autumnal grayness.

"Reinforce the state security guards with our people," he said quietly to one of his aides.

"Yes, sir," came the brief reply.

Vadim could not hide a sigh of relief. The arrival of Bazilevich made it seem that things might turn out all right, that the potent logic of the Red Army would have its say in the matter, that the strange, ominous uncertainty that had established itself under the roof of the Soldatyonkovskaya Hospital would turn out to be only a figment of his imagination.

By midnight a good half of the guests—that is, the respectable people—had already left the Gradov dacha, which inspired the indefatigable toastmaster, Galaktion Gudiashvili, once again to reflect gloomily on the nature of his "big brothers," the Russians. "It makes me sad to look at the Muscovites. Some of them, you understand, have become too European, just like the Germans—they don't know how to have a good time," he said, having forgotten about his recent sallies about the "Scythian barbarians." Nevertheless, he continued to hold court around the melancholy table, trying to get those who remained at least to drink themselves senseless.

Even more than the respectable people, Uncle Galaktion was distressed by the young people. They didn't get into the spirit of things and paid hardly any attention to the sumptuous supply of drink. Having apparently forgotten that one is young only once—just once, dear Mary, you know it as well as I do—the young people had congregated in the kitchen, making a racket like a *kinto*—a street vendor in an outdoor market—arguing the questions of the world revolution, a subject the peoples of the Mediterranean basin were already sick and tired of.

These arguments had broken out spontaneously, it seemed, yet no one had doubted they would. It would have been odd if, when all was said and done, trivialities had not been forgotten, the wine, flirting, jokes, poetry, theater gossip, and odd if it had not happened in the kitchen—where else but in the kitchen, among the dirty dishes? It was quite characteristic of the disputes of the youth of the intellectual class, as well as those of the Party and its surrounding circles when the topic got around to politics. It goes without saying that the passionate revolutionaries were a crushing majority in this case, though there were as many different plans for the road to human happiness as there were people present. This group of young was not yet particularly afraid of the "organs," as they supposed that the Cheka-OGPU was an appendage of their own power and that therefore they were permitted to tax their vocal cords, wave their arms, and not conceal their sympathies for one or another of the various factions: the Trotskyites with their "permanent Revolution," a certain "Kotov-Usachenko platform," which no one had heard of before that evening, the supposedly antibureaucratic "new opposition," even the "rock-hard" Stalinists, who, cheerless and dismal as they might be, still had the right to express themselves, after all. You can't stifle anyone, lads—why, the very sense of Party democracy resides in that principle!

From the general hubbub, we will pick out for the time being only a few phrases and ask the reader to imagine what a resounding echo they were producing in the student assemblies of the time.

"It's time to finish with the NEP, or else we're going to choke on satiety."

"Socialism will perish without Europe's support!"

"Your Europe is dancing the Charleston!"

"LEF—they're bogus revolutionaries! Snobs and aesthetes!"

"Bukharin dances to the tune of the kulaks!"

"Have you heard, brothers, that in Munich they've formed a 'National Bolshevik Party'? There's really no end to petit bourgeois rot!"

"Why are they keeping Lenin's testament from the people? Stalin is usurping power!"

"You're just imitating the Trotskyites!"

"Better to be in a lion's tail than in a shoemaker's backside like Stalin!"

"In the old days you would have had your face smashed for that!"

Since times were still "new," they managed to get along without any face-smashing, though Nina's "proletarian friend" Semyon Nikiforovich Stroilo was seen longingly weighing an unopened jar of saffron milkcap mushrooms in his hand more than once.

Mechanically scrubbing his hands and forearms, Professor Gradov was trying not to look at his colleagues. For that matter, all the other doctors of the operating team—Grekov, Rozanov, Martianov, and Mandryka—were scrubbing silently, absorbed in their own thoughts. It didn't occur to anyone that night to show off any of the much-loved "professor stuff"—telling jokes or perhaps bellowing an operatic aria, sniggering and snorting, all the eccentricities these Moscow luminaries were so fond of and that were so revered by the surgical assistants, especially the women. Never before within these walls had five of the country's greatest surgeons scrubbed up at once, and never before had there been so much tension in the air.

Ochkin and Neiman emerged from the operating room to say that the anesthesia was proceeding normally. The patient was asleep. Gradov, who was supposed to begin, that is, to open the abdominal cavity, gave orders that the patient's pulse and blood pressure should be checked every minute without fail. Were the cardiovascular resuscitation machines ready? This was the most important aspect of the operation.

He had already put on rubber gloves when Mandryka, who had also finished his preparations, took him aside and asked to have a word with him.

"What's wrong with you, Boris Nikitovich?"

"Everything's fine," muttered Gradov.

"I don't like the look of you today, my friend. Your facial muscles are twitching, and your hands seem to be trembling."

"No, no, everything is fine. I beg you not to touch me—you understand, before an operation . . . it's odd . . . not very ethical somehow . . ."

"Yes, yes," said Mandryka, who seemed to be studying Gradov's face line by line. "Perhaps, dear friend, you shouldn't participate directly. Just stand by in case anything unforeseen occurs, and we'll begin, praying . . ."

Good Lord, thought Gradov, he didn't have to take part in this. He didn't understand what it was all about, he had been deceived and his mind wasn't on his work—and now, taken off *this*, liberated, he shrugged, trying not to betray his emotions.

"Well, you're the boss. Do you want me to get out of here?"

"Absolutely not, old man!" Mandryka said abruptly. "There are no bosses here. All of us, and you too, are equal participants in this operation. Be prepared!"

Gradov sat down on a couch in the corner of the preoperating room, threw his head back, and closed his eyes. He did not see the four surgeons, their gloved hands "prepared," as they passed through the frosted-glass door like the priests of some ancient pagan cult.

Toward the end of the night, no less than a dozen of the young people went down to the banks of the Moscow River. The ice of small frozen puddles crunched beneath their feet. The stars were still shining through the pines in the clear night air, and there was "a moon young and golden, knowing neither days nor years," in the words of Mandelstam, quoted by Styopa Kalistratov. "I heard him read those lines recently at the House of Architects."

"And do you remember this, at the same reading?" cried Nina. "I'll never forget that voice . . . 'I will rush through the gypsy band of a dark street, beyond the crumbling cherry tree in a black spring carriage, beyond the bonnet of snow, beyond the noise of the mill . . .' Semyon . . . are you listening, Syoma?"

She seemed to be drawing her loutish suitor, Stroilo, by the hand, dragging him, constantly tugging at him, and he in turn seemed to be condescending to her, simply allowing himself to be drawn, though at times Nina's gusts of enthusiasm broke his stride and pulled him into a trot unworthy of the proletariat. Now there was a puddle beneath his feet, then a hummock, and they were making their way to the river, now some roots, the poetry of this Mandelstam, the quirks of the professor's children . . .

"What's all this about gypsy bands and bonnets? It's all some kind of puzzle," he said in a deep voice.

"Why, Syomka!" whimpered Nina in an offended tone. "It's genius, simply genius."

"Semyon may be right," said Savva Kitaigorodsky. He was wearing a long black coat, and his starched shirt shone in the moonlight. "A cherry blossom and snow somehow don't go together."

How magnanimous he is to a rival, thought Nina slyly and joyfully. She shouted to Kalistratov, who was walking ahead, "And what do you think, Styopa?"

"I have no wish to enter into a polemic with jackasses!" he replied without turning around.

The intensity of the moment nearly caused Nina's throat to seize up. All three of them were in love with her, this was all a game around her, it was all . . . she let go of Semyon's hand, ran ahead, and reached the precipice first.

Below, the bend of the river was shining like silver, and faintly golden in spots. Beyond, the sparse lights of Khoroshovo and Sokol could be distinguished in the predawn light. It was still long before dawn, yet the distant rooftops and bell towers of Moscow formed a distinct outline, which meant that the first day of November 1925 would be bathed by the tremendous light of Russia's infrequent guest, the star called the sun.

Nina turned to the approaching group, her suitors and friends: Syomka, Styopa, Savva, Lyubka Fogelman, Misha Kantorovich, her brother Kirill, her cousins Otari and Nugzar, Olechka Lazeikina, Celia Rosenbloom, Miriam Mek-Nazar. Their faces were clearly visible, illuminated perhaps by the moon, perhaps by the approaching dawn, perhaps simply by their youth and the Revolution. How happy we are, Nina Gradov wanted to shout, how happy I am right now!

.   .   .

Morning found them near the park of the Temiriazev Academy of Agriculture, at the Invalids' Market. They were laughing and drinking kvas when suddenly a radio loudspeaker mounted on a column came hoarsely to life. Through the static they could make out "Citizens of the Soviet Union . . ." Then they heard some cacophonous sounds that gradually took shape as a mournful tune from Wagner's *Götterdämmerung*. Finally the announcer began to read:

"An appeal by the Central Committee of the Bolshevik Party to all members of the Party, to all workers and peasants . . . More than once did Comrade Frunze escape from mortal danger. More than once did death stand with his scythe poised above him. He escaped unscathed from the heroic battles of the Civil War and gave all his seething energy, all his creative might to the construction of our triumphant Red Army. Now he, an aging warrior, has left us forever. A great Communist and revolutionary is dead. Our glorious comrade in arms is dead."

"Kirill!" yelled Nina to her brother. "Hurry! There's a trolley! Let's go home! We have to go home!"

As always, the first thing the Gradovs tried to do when any turning point of history or fate occurred was to race home and gather together. It was only later, in the thirties, that the house began to seem no longer a fortress but a trap.

Boris Nikitovich was standing on the steps of the surgical building, waiting for his driver. He was trembling as though he had a terrible hangover, and he was afraid to look at the unexpectedly golden morning. Coming down the stairs, he had been pursued by a group of people, some wearing hospital gowns and some not, shoving one form after another at him for his signature. He signed everything without reading, thinking only just one thing—getting home as soon as possible.

A car pulled up, and a soldier jumped out. Regimental Commander Vuinovich crossed over to him. Gradov was seemingly carried along by a wave of hostility from his powerful body. He heard a voice: "Fokin, take this shit home!"

FIRST INTERMISSION
THE NEWSPAPERS

"Loss of consciousness occurred forty minutes before death. The cause of death was postoperative coronary paralysis . . ."

"A funeral commission has been formed of the following members: comrades Yenukidze, Unshlikht, Bubnov, Lyubimov, Mikhailov . . ."

"In the person of the deceased a most prominent member of the government was laid in the grave . . ."

"A session of the Revolutionary Military Council took place, Unshlikht, Comrade Frunze's aide, presiding. Present were Members of the RMC Voroshilov, Kamenev, Bubnov, Budyonny, Ordzhonikidze, Lashevich, Baranov, Zof, Yegorov, Zatonsky, Eliva, Khadyr-Aliev . . ."

"To fire a salute from both ship and shore batteries at Kronstadt and Sevastopol: in the first, fifty guns, in the second, twenty-five . . ."

"To take part in the funeral ceremonies: a detachment of political commissars, an overflight of aircraft, and the First Combined Company of the Baltic Fleet. The senior officer will be Comrade Fabritsius, commander of the XVII Corps . . ."

"There is no place for dejection! Close ranks!"

From the autopsy:
In the abdominal cavity, some 200 cm³ of a bloody viscous substance containing pus . . . bacteriological examination revealed streptococcus. . . . Anatomical diagnosis: healed round duodenal ulcer. Severe infectious inflammation of the peritoneum. . . . Abnormally large thymus. . . . The surgery caused the intensification of a process of inflammation that had existed since 1916 as the result of an appendectomy, and this in combination with an anesthesia-induced weakening of the system occasioned a sharp decrease in cardiovascular activity and fatal consequences.

Recent hemorrhaging was a consequence of superficial ulceration.

Autopsy conducted by Professor A. I. Abrikosov . . .

Telegram from Comrade Trotsky to the Central Committee: "Shaken! What a terrible breach in the first rank! What a terrible blow on the eighth anniversary of the October Revolution!"

"After embalming, the body was moved to the conference hall. Among those in the honor guard were members of the general staff, as well as his close comrades Rykov, Kamenev, Stalin, Zinoviev, Molotov. . . . Cadets of the All-Union Academy stood guard."

.   .   .

"Condolences: from the Japanese embassy, from the Turkish military attaché, Mr. Bedy-Bey, from the Estonian military attaché, Mr. Kursk . . ."

N. Bukharin: "Though the embodiment of gentleness, Frunze was a devastating military leader . . ."

C. Zorin: "The shining path . . ."

M. Koltsov: "The core of the Bolshevik guard bears the indelible imprint of czarist persecution. . . . The Central Committee must pay serious attention to its thinning ranks . . ."

"In view of the interest of the public and in connection with the discussions about the operation, we are printing excerpts from the case history.

"The doctors were in ceaseless consultation from 8 October onwards. Drs. Semashko, Burdenko, Gradov, Martianov, Rozanov, Lunts, Kapel, Kramer, Levin, Pletnyov, Obrasov, Mandryka, and others participated. . . . The patient's tendency to hemorrhage required surgical intervention."

"The automobiles pull up. The Chinese Generalissimo Ku Khan-min has arrived . . . delegations from factories . . . a gold side arm on the lid of the casket. . . . In the Hall of Columns, the entire Politburo . . . *Götterdämmerung* is replaced by the 'International' . . . on the fifth of November . . . snow . . . Stalin's speech:

" 'Comrades, this year was a curse for us. It snatched a whole series of distinguished comrades from our midst. Perhaps it is just and necessary that our old comrades should go to their graves quietly and simply. Unfortunately, it is neither easy nor simple for our young comrades to replace the old ones. We believe, we hope, that the Party and the working class will take all possible measures to make easier the forging of new comrades to replace the old . . .'

"Tukhachevsky: 'Dear, beloved friend! We met when the eastern front was in a state of collapse. Calm and certainty shone through in the entire glorious figure of Comrade Frunze. Farewell!'

"The Central Committee of the USSR has decreed the appointment of Comrade Voroshilov as people's commissar of the army and navy; first deputy assistant, M. M. Lashevich; second assistant, I. S. Unshlikht . . ."

SECOND INTERMISSION
THE FLIGHT OF THE OWL

Four-hundred-year-old Tokhtamysh rarely left his long-established nest beneath the top of Vodovzvodnaya Tower. The old bird seemed to have had only one task—to sit through all these centuries in a drowsy state of deep thought. What all this sitting was for, I'm afraid not even he, she, or it knew. And only when something happened in the fortress to disrupt the order of the days did Tokhtamysh tumble out through an aperture he alone knew about into a current of Moscow air and circumnavigate the tower, as if he wanted to make sure—will they be able to hold out? So it was that on that night, having sensed in one of his diaphragms—one that had escaped the notice of ornithologists—the agitation of the new princes, known as commissars, Tokhtamysh set off in his soundless, not particularly graceful flight that was nonetheless filled with ontological certainty.

He rose about three hundred feet into the air and saw nothing but a pair of ravens who had taken up permanent residence in the tower. There was an odor of smoke and outhouses in the air, but as usual, he did not smell the gunpowder, and he described a wide circle above his perch before he flew down past the Borovitskaya Tower, flew if not floated over the State Armory and the Poteshny Palace, then approached the Arsenal.

Everything was quiet, sticky, and damp, the guards were in their places, doors were bolted, and outwardly nothing betrayed the inquietude of the commissars that Tokhtamysh had detected. It was only in the Arsenal courtyard that anything was stirring.

Tokhtamysh landed on the rain gutter, squeamishly turning aside at the sight of a sparrow's carcass floating in it—it had been some 150 years since he had eaten offal—and stared at the thing that was making the disturbance, at Demyan, the local court poet, who called himself "The Poor," even though he was richer than most.

The owl had already glimpsed the man once before, had immediately disliked him and remembered him. Demyan concealed his mouselike restlessness with revolutionary romanticism and his lack of talent by writing topical doggerel.

Why, then, is he bustling about like a badger gobbling down berries in a wood? Ah, yes, inspiration! In the days of the devastating raid, Tokhtamysh had been known for his keen hearing. Now he tried to get it back and catch the man's mutterings.

"Friend, dear friend," muttered Demyan, bending his arms and raising his fleshy face toward the heavens, perhaps looking for the moon or perhaps taking the owl's two shining eyes for the stars of a favorable constellation.

"Was it long ago? So clearly I recall . . . hmm . . . all, what rhymes with that? . . . To write some verses I had sped . . . —ed, —ed . . . Aloud to you from the wall . . . —all, —all . . . one of Wrangel's leaflets I read . . . —ed, —ed . . . *Ich fange an,* . . . How we mocked the enemy together! . . . —ether, —ether . . . what was it like? —ike, —ike, —ike . . . You were all aglow, our fighters keen for the endeavor . . . —ever, —ever . . . In a week or two to strike . . . —ike, —ike . . . what next? . . . We looked at the sea through a telescope . . . —ope, —ope . . . In our Soviet annals with an iron hand you have written 'Red Perekop' . . . —op, —op . . . Where's the pity, then? . . .

"What now . . . right now inspiration's the thing, I'll worry about the rhymes later. . . . Now then . . . There occurred an unexpected twist of fate . . . I can't understand . . . —and, —and . . . I bend down to your dead face . . . —ace . . . and I see before me a face . . . hmm, what kind? Living? . . . —ing, —ing . . . A modest and wise hero . . . a swarm of sorrowful thoughts . . . —oughts, —oughts . . . Not bad at all, it's almost like Pushkin! . . . I haven't the strength to express a farewell in words . . . must call *Pravda* immediately . . . —ly, —ly . . ."

Tokhtamysh could not bear any further outrages against the art of nocturnal versifying, so he dived down and blew a current of air over the poet with his fearful wing, that his dirty maw might shut.

CHAPTER THREE

The Chopin Cure

☆

The year ended with the rustle of the always ambiguous newspapers, with the rumble of Moscow's ever-growing streetcar network, with the whirling of blackbirds, those seemingly charred inhabitants of the Moscow skyline, and the spreading syncopated rhythms of the Charleston issuing a challenge to the proletarian trumpets, which advanced, though at times as slowly as spilled heating oil, with a triumphal howl.

The snows came and the snows went, and the gardens had already been covered and come back to life again by the time our story resumes in October 1926, entering the Gradovs' dacha in the tracks of the milkmaid Petrovna.

The doors to all the downstairs rooms were open. Everything was vacant, clean, and well lit. Chopin could be heard from the library. Mary Vakhtan-govna was playing stormily, as always, with inspiration, imparting a certain Caucasian staccato to measures imported from the Central European plain. From time to time, however, she shot quick, attentive glances at her husband, who sat in a deep armchair, covering his eyes with his hand.

Pythagoras was sitting next to his master in the classic pose of the young, attentive dog. His long ears were also taking in the stream of not disagreeable sounds. Agasha, the maid, occasionally passed noiselessly from one room to another in woolen socks, arranging clean sheets and towels on the shelves, glancing at her master and wiping the corners of her eyes with her handker-chief as she did so.

Boris Nikitovich was contemplating the regal profile of his wife through the cracks between his fingers. Strange, he thought, her profile never struck me as erotic before. Yet when she turned toward me with her high peasant cheekbones and her full lips . . . But why am I thinking about her in the past tense? We're still young, after all, and our libido is still . . .

Petrovna banged in through the door with her heavy milk cans, basket, and pail and saw the matinal idyll. What do you know, she thought with tender gratification, the bourgeois life is alive and well.

"Good Lord, Petrovna, do be quieter!" said Agasha, hastening up to her. "Come along, let's go to the kitchen!"

In the kitchen, unloading her cargo of sour cream and cottage cheese, Petrovna asked: "What's going on, ma'am?"

"The professor is taking a music cure."

"Do you mean he's caught a cold?"

"Oh, Petrovna, Petrovna," said the cultivated Agasha, shaking her head.

"The only treatment my old man recognizes is booze. If one glass doesn't help, then he just has another—then everything is fine."

"Get along with you now, Petrovna."

Having paid her, Agasha showed the woman, who was the picture of health and cleanliness, to the door, then stopped by the lintel to listen.

Mary concluded the concert with a dazzling glissando and then stood up. Boris Nikitovich also rose from his chair. "Thank you, Mary! You know, I always find that prelude helpful."

He walked over to his wife and took her by the shoulders, trying in the most delicate way to turn her face toward his. Mary Vakhtangovna avoided his gaze and pointed toward the window. "Look, Pulkovo is already here!"

Along the walk from the gate to the house, through the flying yellow leaves, came Leonid Valentinovich Pulkovo at an unhurried pace in his English Sherlock Holmes overcoat.

"Lyonka may be slovenly, but he's always punctual," said the professor with a smile.

"Well, why don't you both go for a walk? Pythagoras, you go with Daddy, too."

The dog joyfully ran in circles around them, occasionally kicking up his hind legs like a hare.

Agasha was already standing in the doorway with the professor's hat and coat. "Permit me to remind you, Boris, Mary, Nikita, and Veronika are coming for dinner directly from the train station."

"Oh yes, Bo, you haven't forgotten? We're all getting together in two hours." Mary Vakhtangovna pronounced the words severely, trying to restrain her joy at the fullness of her life.

The dog could not control an obviously similar feeling and jumped up to lick his master on the chin.

"Yes, yes, Pyth, you haven't forgotten!" she said delightedly. "I see, I see! Just make sure to remind your daddy, in case he decides to go to the racetrack instead of taking a nice healthy walk."

For the whole past year, Boris Nikitovich, despite fits of depression, had worked like a madman. Even before, as a matter of course, he had had no equal at the operating table: mere mastery had long ago yielded its place to work of the highest caliber, to virtuosity. The lancet and clamps in his hands felt at once like the baton of a conductor and the violin of a soloist. In moments of inspiration—oh, yes, at times he did feel true surgical inspiration!—it seemed to him that the entire sphere of life was under his rule: the assistants, the nurses, the instruments, the outstretched patient; all life at that moment seized the meaning not only of his words, snorts, coughs, and smallest gestures, but also his thoughts. His lectures always drew large audiences. Doctors from Moscow clinics and the provinces fought for seats with students. It was said that even liberal arts students came to hear him, supposedly to reassure themselves of the viability and the ideological wholeness of one part of the Russian intelligentsia that had survived.

He had attained still greater successes in the theoretical domain and in the creation of a school of thought. Articles intended for the development of his original ideas about surgical intervention gave rise to lively discussions at the meetings of the medical society and in the press, both at home, and even, yes, abroad. The young doctors who followed in his footsteps, foremost among them the prodigiously talented Savva Kitaigorodsky, proudly called themselves "Gradovites." In a word . . . how to put it . . . be that as it may . . . oh, to hell with it . . .

Who of these "Gradovites," except for maybe Savva, would ever have guessed that from time to time their idol, moaning and grinding his teeth, would collapse onto a sofa, on his side, then, slipping down along the leather incline to the carpet, would kneel, watching one corner of the room while glowering wildly and raising his beard toward the ceiling in an attitude of prayer as though he were looking for an icon—which, of course, as a hereditary positivist and a man of his century, he did not keep in the house. Over and over again he asked himself—just what happened at Soldatyonkovskaya Hospital? Nothing; I was simply put out of the way and not consulted, he would say to himself at first with audacious pride—think of me as you will, Your Honor the Supreme Judge, he would say to himself, but I consider myself neither a liar nor a coward.

After some brief sobs and trembling, however—provided Mary did not come into the room and rush to the piano—he would begin to yield a bit. Well, maybe I was a coward, and, well, yes, I was afraid of the Cheka, but who isn't afraid of those monsters? . . . Well, that's all there is to it, O merciful one! And it was only in the third phase—again, if Mary did not manage to intervene—that Boris Nikitovich would begin to permit himself to do some violence to his clothing, sometimes ripping his shirt like a Kronstadt sailor and sometimes tearing his vest and crying out loudly, "Collaborator! Collaborator!"

Yes, at such moments he considered himself a direct participant in the murder of Army Commander Frunze, and just then Mary would appear with a stiff bromide, her warm bosom, and the Chopin that was his salvation.

Of course, it wasn't because the commissar, a hero, a mighty man of the state had been killed that Boris Nikitovich punished himself so—that man had been no better than the rest of them, just another fiend who had executed prisoners—but because he had been a patient, a body sacred in the conscience of a doctor.

Fortunately, these accesses of injustice to himself—for injustice is just what it was—were becoming rarer and rarer. On quiet days, even when Professor Gradov remembered that October night of the previous year, he thought only about the question of how exactly Rozanov and Mandryka had dispatched the commissar to the "unreal reality." Even now, despite the ill-concealed cynicism of these people, which he had seen for himself, he would not let himself think that any of his colleagues could be capable of, say, simply severing an artery. After all, we're not Budyonny's cavalry, we're doctors, don't you see, doctors!

Streetcar bells clanged in the distance. Happy children rode by on bicycles. The less fortunate, but deliriously happy for all that, were racing homemade scooters. A flock of rooks flew away noisily, momentarily stirring up a whirlwind of falling leaves.

Two men who had been friends since their high school days, Professors

Boris Nikitovich Gradov and Leonid Valentinovich Pulkovo, walked in the classic style of the Moscow intelligentsia: hats tilted back slightly, overcoats unbuttoned, hands behind the back, faces illuminated by thought and mutual sympathy. As they strolled along, they walked sometimes beside long fences and sometimes moved away into a grove of trees, then emerged again next to the trolley tracks. Then Pythagoras beckoned to them with his sly, open muzzle, and one of them took hold of his leash for a moment.

"Yes, Bo," said Pulkovo, pausing for an instant, "the other day I came across a report about you in the evening paper. Why aren't you bragging about it? You've been named chief surgeon of the Red Army! Don't you think it's tremendous?"

Gradov frowned slightly, then adopted the tone that had been prescribed at the high schools of the old regime: "Yes, sir, we're now a general officer, too good for the likes of you. You shall address me as 'Your Excellency'! You, a poor physicist, won't be able to afford a bicycle, while I'll have a private car with a Red Army chauffeur!"

Pulkovo took off his hat and bowed deeply like a true sycophant. "We understand the matter well, Your Excellency, even very well, and respect most respectfully . . ."

Gradov came to a sudden stop and angrily poked the trunk of the nearest pine with his walking stick. "I know what you're getting at, Leo! My sudden advancement during the past year! Only yesterday without any honors at all, but now assistant chairman of a department at the university, chief consultant to the Commissariat for Health, and now the Red Army." He was becoming more and more agitated and seemed as though he were no longer addressing his bosom friend Leo but instead hurling a challenge at a large audience. "You know, I hope, that I don't give a damn about all these titles? I'm only a doctor, just a Russian doctor, like my father and my grandfather and his father before him! I've done nothing wrong, certainly nothing heroic—I'm just a doctor, not a . . . not a . . ."

Pulkovo took his friend by the arm and led him further down the empty tree-lined walk. Pythagoras came from their left, circling around and peering at them.

"What are you getting so upset about, Bo? No one is expecting heroics of you, only kindness and help."

Gradov looked gratefully at Pulkovo—he always knew just the right thing to say. "That's just it," he said more gently. "That's the only reason I'm taking these posts, for the benefit of the sick. For the sake of medicine, you understand, Leo, especially for the sake of the advancement of my system of local anesthesia for abdominal operations. Do you understand how important it is?"

"Please explain," said Pulkovo seriously, one scientist to another.

Gradov was immediately enthusiastic and in the best tradition took his friend by the buttonhole and led him to the side of the path.

"You see, general anesthesia, at least in the form in which it is normally used here, is an extremely dangerous business. The slightest overdose, and the consequences can be—" He broke off, as though astonished by this speculation. "The slightest overdose, and—" He leaned his shoulder against the trunk of a pine tree and breathed heavily.

How is it I didn't think of this before? he thought. Ether mixed with chloroform. They pumped an extra bottle of that damned mixture into the army commander, and the deed was done. Yes, yes, now I remember—even then it occurred to me that the smell of ether was stronger than usual. And yet—

Now Pulkovo was pulling him along again. "Well, let's go, Bo, let's go! Let's get some air, have a stroll, stretch our old bones!"

For a quarter of an hour they walked rapidly along a cleared path through the forest without saying a word. Then they turned in to a sparse birch forest and walked along separate paths among the high white trunks. Pythagoras continued on between them as if he were maintaining their communication. Soon, their intercourse reestablished itself on a new, verbal level. Leonid Valentinovich started it, obviously trying to remind Boris Nikitovich of the days when as high school students they had taken walks in the woods the same way, from time to time launching into operatic duets.

"Give me your hand, O maiden fair!" demanded Pulkovo in a booming bass.

"No, the maiden fair will not give it you," replied Gradov in a tenor, a regular Caruso.

The forest soon came to an end. They came out onto a precipice above the Moscow River and walked along it in the direction of home. Pulkovo, with the feeling that he had done his duty—now he's got his bearings again, he thought, he's caught his breath—lit his pipe.

"And how are things with you, Leo?" asked Gradov.

"Strange things are happening to me," said Pulkovo with a grin. "For some time now, I've been followed."

"Followed by women, as always?" asked Gradov with a broad smile. In their circle the physicist, a confirmed bachelor, had a well-established reputation as a ladies' man, even though no one could remember any particular instance when he had acted like one.

Pulkovo grinned again. "If only it were women. For the time being, it's men with the Lubyanka prison written all over their faces. Then again, I suppose they have women to do this sort of work as well."

"Them! Them again!" exclaimed Gradov. "What the hell do they want from you, Leo?"

The physicist shrugged. "I don't have any idea. Could it be my trip to England, my correspondence with Rutherford? It's absurd. Who in the OGPU could possibly be interested in theoretical nuclear physics?"

Boris Nikitovich gave his friend, always so self-assured and ironic, a side-long glance, and the thought suddenly occurred to him that he was closer to Leonid than anyone else in the world.

"Listen, Leo, do you want me to talk to someone there, in the upper echelons, to see what I can find out?"

"No, no, Bo, there's no need. I was talking about nothing in particular, really. But then, maybe just in case."

"Why don't you move in with us for a while, say, for six months? Let them see that you're not alone, that you have a big family."

Leonid Valentinovich, deeply touched, put his hand on his friend's shoulder. "Thank you, Bo, but that's not necessary. War communism is finished, after all."

That evening in the dacha there took place one of those dinners that were milestones of a sort in the life of the family: the entire clan was reunited. These meetings were usually called when Brigade Commander Nikita and Veronika arrived from Minsk. Everyone knew, though, that seeing one another again was only a superficial reason for these gatherings and that their principal value was that they allowed all of them to check the solidity of the foundations and the degree of animation of that feeling of fullness that sometimes took Mama Mary's breath away.

Thus everyone, or almost everyone, was assembled around the table. Only Nina was absent, but she was always late.

"Where is that dratted Nina?" pouted Veronika.

The attractive woman had ballooned up in the course of the year and now barely fit into her wide, specially tailored dress, of the sort they wear in the Polesye region. Her lips and nose had swollen, and she was always on the verge of tears.

I'm just a few years older than Nina, she thought, and I'm sitting here like a fat fool from the country while Nina is probably at a Pasternak reading or hanging around at Meyerhold's. . . . And Nikita, this is just like him, the disgusting egoist . . .

A radiant Boris Nikitovich turned to the young woman, kissed her on the cheek, then raised his glass and spoke to her enormous stomach.

"Respected sir, Boris the Fourth! I hope that you can hear me and are ready to affirm that you, as opposed to the present generation of revolutionaries, are prepared to reestablish and continue the Gradov medical dynasty!"

Veronika contorted her mouth. Her father-in-law's joke seemed even more nauseating to her than all the sumptuous dishes spread out on the table. Nikita turned to her in alarm, but she managed to overcome her disgust and, surprising even herself, answered with a passably good joke.

"He asks what medical school do you want him to go to, Moscow or Leningrad?"

"What a question!" thundered Boris III, that is, Professor Gradov. "To my institute, of course, under his grandfather's wing!"

Everyone began eating and clinking glasses and silverware, while Veronika —once again to her own amazement—had a sudden craving for pickled tomatoes and pulled the entire bowl over to herself.

The front doors banged then, quick steps sounded, and Nina burst into the dining room. Her dark chestnut hair was disheveled, her bright blue eyes were shining, the collar of her overcoat was turned up, and she was carrying a briefcase under her arm, as well as a knapsack full of books.

"Hello, family!" she yelped. She rushed over to Veronika, kissed her on the lips and once on the stomach, then flopped down for a moment onto Nikita's lap, shook the hand of Kirill the Party worker, and said with tragic serious-ness, "All that we have is yours, comrades tough as stone!" Like an English lady, she extended her hand to be kissed by Leonid Valentinovich Pulkovo and then bestowed a kiss upon everyone else. The most tender kiss of all, of course, went to Pythagoras.

"You could at least be on time when your brother comes to visit," grum-bled Mary Vakhtangovna.

Nina, who was still breathless from her run, or maybe from her antics, or maybe even from the "excitement of history," drew a new copy of *Novy Mir* out of her rucksack and threw it down on the table so hard that the meat pies jumped.

"Well, what do you think about that? You wouldn't believe the scandal in the city—the Stalinists are snarling with rage! Imagine, guys, the entire edition of *Novy Mir* with 'The Tale of the Unextinguished Moon' has been confiscated!"

Everyone around the table smiled. Even Mama Mary knitted her brows in mock seriousness, trying hard to conceal her adoration. Only Kirill frowned in earnest. He tapped his fingers severely on the table top and looked at his sister with narrowed eyes, almost like an OGPU investigator.

Nina suddenly realized in amazement that no one in the room was *au courant*. The storm that was raging at her university, for that matter all over "young Moscow," here in Silver Forest was only a far-off noise, like a streetcar rumbling by in the distance.

"Would you be so good as to inform us, miss, what exactly is this 'Unextin-guished Moon' that has created such a stir?" asked Pulkovo.

"A story by Pilnyak—do you mean you haven't heard of it?"

"And what is this story about, child?" asked her father.

"You folks are really something!" chortled Nina. "Don't you remember, last fall? The death of Army Commander Frunze in the Soldatyonkovskaya Hospital? Well, I haven't read it yet, but the story is about precisely that, and Pilnyak hints at certain suspicious circumstances—"

She stopped short, having noticed the frozen expressions on the faces around the table. "What's wrong with you all?"

An awkward silence reigned. Nina's glance moved around the table from one person to another. Her father sat motionless, his eyes closed. Her mother was looking at him with consternation and in a trembling voice was muttering something of which only a few snatches could be heard: "Really, what unseemly . . . strange . . . such rubbish . . . stupid gossip . . ." Pulkovo was frozen holding a glass of vodka halfway to his mouth. Pythagoras began to whimper quietly. Agasha, her lips in a firm line, was wiping a perfectly clean dish with a towel. Kirill was absorbed in gazing into the bowl of vinaigrette. An expression of almost unconcealed pain was written on Nikita's face. The eyes of Veronika, the pregnant beauty, quickly became moist.

The tension was broken by the doorbell. Agasha went with mincing steps to open the door, and when she came back, a robust man with a ruddy complexion in a military uniform was with her. He clicked his heels in prerevolutionary fashion, saluted, and bellowed, "Junior Commander Slabopetukhovsky reporting! As you ordered, Comrade Professor, a car is here from the Soldatyonkovskaya Hospital for you!"

Boris Nikitovich glanced at his watch and sighed weakly, "Oh, it's already seven-thirty." Then he stood up and kissed Mary Vakhtangovna. "I'll come back right after the operation."

Junior Commander Slabopetukhovsky headed for the door, twirling his comical mustache as he went, and whispered something to the blushing old maid Agasha. The professor went out behind him.

Mary Vakhtangovna had raised her quivering chin proudly and was deliberately trying not to look in her daughter's direction. "What cruelty!" she said. "What conceit! How could anyone be so unmindful of things? Father sacrifices everything for the sake of his patients, even professional advancement! He doesn't know the meaning of day or night."

"What in the world is going on, anyway?" asked Nina excitedly. "This is all like a scene at the Moscow Art Theater!"

Nikita laid his weighty, chevroned arm around his sister's shoulder. "Easy, Nina." He turned to their mother and said softly, "Mama, maybe we ought to explain things to Nina?"

Mary Vakhtangovna rose sharply from the table. "I don't see any reason to! There is nothing here that requires an explanation!" Clasping her hands dramatically to her breast, she moved briskly from the room. Nikita, after whispering, "We'll talk about it tomorrow" to his sister, followed his mother. The meal, which had begun so joyfully, now lay in smoking ruins.

Kirill pushed the issue of *Novy Mir* away from him with his fingertips almost squeamishly and scowled at Nina. "If this slanderous issue of the journal was suppressed, where did you get it—if you don't mind my asking?"

Nina snatched the journal and blurted directly into her brother's face, "None of your business, you Stalinist toady!"

Kirill, in his best Party manner, banged his fist down on the table. "Do you think you're some sort of high-minded Trotskyite? You silly fool! Just stick to writing your little poems and don't join the opposition!"

After pushing back their chairs, the two young Gradov offspring flew from the dining room in opposite directions.

Agasha let out a shriek that was not at all in the style of the Moscow Art Theater, but in her own natural rural way—the style of the Maly Theater—and took refuge in the kitchen. Pythagoras was running about in bewilderment on the parquet floors.

At the table, so densely populated a short time before, only Pulkovo and Veronika remained. She dabbed at her eyes with a handkerchief, trying not to burst into tears, but then blew her nose and suddenly burst out laughing.

"Our Kirill has gone batty over the Party line," she said.

Pulkovo poured himself another glass and took hold of a small bowl of pickled mushrooms. "Yes, madam, and everywhere are fateful passions," he pronounced, uttering the words just as a gentleman bachelor ought to after witnessing a family quarrel.

Veronika smiled at him, showing that she remembered how they had almost flirted with each other in the house a year ago.

"Just a year ago, Leonid Valentinovich, if you remember, it was Mary's birthday, and I was dancing and flirting, but now—" She pointed to her stomach with her palms outstretched as though they were wings. "You can see how ugly I've become."

"Your beauty, Veronika Yevgenievna, will come back right after you give birth."

"Do you think so?" she asked like a child and then pouted. "Oh, I'm such a fool!"

Pulkovo looked at his watch, stood up to say good-bye, and took Veronika's hand in both of his. "By the way, I often play billiards now with an interesting soldier, Regimental Commander Vadim Georgievich Vuinovich. He frequently talks about you and Nikita—you in particular."

"Don't tell him we're here!" she cried out.

A moment later they both shuddered at the sound of the stormy, dramatic passages of piano music that began to come from the study. Pythagoras rushed to the doors and struck at them with his front paws. Agasha jumped out of the kitchen and seized him by the collar.

"Hush, Pythy, hush! Mama is treating herself now!"

Mary Vakhtangovna spent the rest of the evening at her music. Nina, in her room upstairs, sometimes had the impression the piano was speaking directly to her, sometimes demanding and other times cajoling her to come downstairs to talk things over. These imagined invitations angered her: first they hide things from me, she thought, then they make a scene. They accuse me of indifference, but they couldn't care less about their daughter's life! When has Mama or Papa, let alone my brothers, ever asked about how things were going in my theater troupe, or my literature club, or with my friends, or with Semyon—even once? They always speak to me in a mischievous tone that was decided upon once and for all a long time ago, as though I'm not growing up and aren't troubled by the problems of the Revolution. What's the Revolution to them anyway? They're quite happy it's being pushed into the background of daily life, that their old comfortable everyday routine is coming back so quickly. What's the basic difference between my parents and the NEP men, someone like the director of the Moscow Eastern Society of Mutual Credit, which Mikhail Koltsov recently wrote an article about? That man rejoices in his bank guarded by doormen in green uniforms, and here, aristocratic suffering is played out on the piano, people put on evening dress to go to the opera. . . . A real "return to normalcy"—what luck!

Nina flopped down on her bed without undressing and tried to read Pilnyak's "Tale of the Unextinguished Moon," but she couldn't concentrate on reading. The lines on the page slipped away, and annoying thoughts ran through her mind one after another: I'm not living the way I should, I'm doing everything wrong, why do I let Semyon act the way he does toward me, why am I ashamed of being a romantic, of the poetry I like, why aren't I honest with myself and admit that I'm bored in the Party cell, why don't I—

She fell asleep with her copy of *Novy Mir* on her stomach and was awakened only by the sound of an automobile approaching the house. The front gate banged. Nina looked out of the window and saw her beloved father. He was skipping up the path to the house in the moonlight with his coat unbuttoned—the operation must have been a success. The sound of the front door opening and closing was followed by the tapping of heels—her mother hurrying to greet her husband. She heard their cheerful voices.

Nina put out her lamp but remained sitting up with her forehead pressed against the windowpane. In the clear sky the moon soared over the pines of Silver Forest. Junior Commander Slabopetukhovsky was walking along the path to the house with his military shoulders held as though he were on parade. She heard his voice, which sounded like a steam engine: "I see your kitchen stove puts out a bit of smoke, Agafia Yermolaevna!"

Agasha, whose voice was shrill, she was so happy, replied, "Oh, don't remind me, Comrade Slabopetukhovsky. It's not a stove, it's a regular hippopotamus. It eats a pile of wood ten feet high in a week!"

Nina took out her thin volume of Pasternak, opened to a page at random, and read:

> *Imagine a house*
> *Where silence like a spotless cheetah*
> *Lies in a far room beneath a billiard table,*
> *Its paws curled around a fallen sphere.*

The silence in the end did actually settle down. Through her drowsiness, Nina thought she could hear the sounds of lovemaking next door in her parents' room. Impossible, thought Nina with a smile, and she fell asleep.

CHAPTER FOUR

The General Line

☆

The next morning, the faltering Indian summer turned into a cold, driving rain devoid of any poetic content whatsoever. Kirill Gradov, wearing a short coat and worker's cap, protecting his books by clutching them to his chest, was walking down a village street to the streetcar stop. He was halfway there when a small car pulled alongside him. His brother, in full dress uniform, was sitting next to the driver. The car came to a stop, and Nikita opened the door and called to Kirill.

"Listen, I'm on my way to headquarters. Get in, I'll drop you off!"

Without slowing down, Kirill waved him off. "No, thanks, I'm going by streetcar!"

At a sign from Nikita, the chauffeur slowed the car to the pace of the young man walking. The Red Army officer looked at the sulking Party activist with a smile.

"Don't be stupid, Kir—you'll get soaked!"

"Makes no difference," muttered Kirill. Then he added angrily, "Drive on, drive on, Your Excellency! We're not good enough for the general's car!"

Nikita then got a bit hot under the collar himself. "My goodness, what high-minded Marxists we have these days! You're getting pretty high in the ranks of the city administration yourself—it's no joke to be the second secretary of the Krasnaya Presnya District Committee!"

Without answering, Kirill sharply turned the corner. The chauffeur looked to the officer for instructions—straight ahead or to the right? Nikita motioned to him: follow him! The car turned and drove in Kirill's direction and accidentally drove through a puddle, splashing the walking man with murky water. Nikita opened the door, climbed halfway out of the car, and stood with one leg on the running board.

"Listen, Kir, I've been meaning to ask you for a long time: why do you cultivate this pseudo-proletarian style? I mean, where did you dig up that coat? There are at least three good woolen overcoats hanging in a closet at home not doing anything, and you go out wearing that rag! Your trousers are so worn at the seat that you can practically see your reflection in them! What exactly are you trying to prove, and to whom?"

"Exactly nothing to no one at all!" his younger brother roared. "Leave me alone, all of you! I receive a stipend of a hundred and twenty-three rubles a month, and I have to feed and clothe myself on that. There's still some revolutionary thinking left in the Party. We don't follow those who want to instill the spirit of the czarist officer corps in the Worker-Peasant Red Army!"

Nikita laughed defiantly. He even forgot about the presence of his chauffeur with the red triangular insignia of rank on his uniform. "Ha-ha, so you think the leaders so dear to your heart are as ascetic as you are?"

Kirill wrathfully pointed his index finger at his brother. "You're repeating petit bourgeois slander, Brigade Commander!"

At that moment, the trolley appeared at the end of the street. An advertisement by the well-known LEF artist Alexander Rodchenko was fixed to it: "Don't be sad and don't be lonely, just gulp down your macaroni." Without another glance at his brother, Kirill dashed headlong for his stop. Nikita angrily slammed the car door shut. Driving by the station, he saw people rushing to get on the car, determined to get a seat. He had to admit he had forgotten what it was like.

On a streetcar in dry weather, despite the crush of people, passengers always rustle their newspapers, contrive to open them over their heads or between their legs. Today the wet newspapers were not rustling and did not unfurl easily, but there were still many people reading. Progressive-minded foreigners always notice that the USSR has the largest reading public in the world. Not long ago, Kirill had been discussing the question of freedom of the press with Savva Kitaigorodsky. Strictly speaking, it hadn't been a discussion—after all, what can you discuss with a typical bourgeois liberal? He was only checking Savva's views against the correct Party position.

Naturally, Monsieur Kitaigorodsky was dissatisfied. What good are the relaxations of NEP if the press still remains in the hands of the ruling Party, if not a single newspaper from before the Revolution has been reopened?

So that's what they want: not only privately owned shops but an untrammeled press as well. That means we're pursuing the right course in the matter. No indulgence for the press—in that respect Trotsky was right, it's the Party's sharpest sword!

Kirill stood in a corner of the rocking car, pressed on three sides by three wet, gloomy passengers who looked as proletarian as he did. Newspaper headlines loomed before his eyes. The Party press is always full of news, and it's a good thing events are reported with a Party slant—that way a man isn't left on his own, at the mercy of the facts. On the contrary, a man learns to use facts, to evaluate them from a position of class consciousness.

Embezzlement is punishable by execution; kulaks, Church leaders, and former czarist officials are deprived of the right to vote; timber exports are increasing; anyone caught buying an apartment will be evicted; a play *Roar, China!;* a combined soccer team of workers from a sugar refinery and the Commissariat for Trade beats "Proletarian Smithy"; new airplanes at the Trotsky aerodrome: the *Narkomvoenmor,* the *L. B. Krasin,* and the *Comrade Nette,* and the flight of a hot-air balloon piloted by Comrade Fyodorov, a cadet at the Air Force Academy. There are many, many such facts; the Red republic is seething with life . . . here's another—rebuke to Marshal Pilsudski; and there's advertising for you—paints, henna, triple eau de cologne, Vegetal . . . all for the petit bourgeois.

Turning back to the window, Kirill got out his own reading matter, a thick book. He pretended not to notice two rather attractive young women of about twenty, secretaries or typists from the look of them, who had been traveling in the car with him for some time, looking at him and giggling.

"All the same, he's not bad looking, don't you think?" said one of them.

"Very serious, though," said the other. "What's he reading?" Without any dissimulation she looked beneath Kirill's elbows to see. "Well, well—*The Hindi Language!*"

Kirill said nothing and gritted his teeth as the Hindi words flickered meaninglessly before his eyes, as though they served only to add more nonsense to the general sum of rubbish that surrounded his well-developed personality:

the quarrels with Nina and Nikita, his wet, odious clothing, the idiocy of the newspaper ads, his agitation and cowardice in the proximity of these two girls.

The trolley was approaching a major transfer point. The passengers were readying themselves for another assault.

The reason Brigade Commander Gradov had been summoned to Moscow this time was, from his point of view, a bit far-fetched. Kliment Yefremovich Voroshilov, the new army-navy commissar, was going to read an important paper on modern military strategy. Well, all right, good luck! But why drag so many field commanders away from pressing practical matters, in particular from working on the coordination of cavalry and light tanks in offensive operations on wooded steppe? Furthermore, the trip could not have come at a worse time for him personally. Veronika was in the last month of her pregnancy, and Nikita had hoped that this time she would stay in Minsk under the watchful eye of the experienced doctors at the local hospital. The doctors were accustomed to them, and in addition, they knew all her quirks, but she would not hear of it. Let slip the opportunity of a trip to her native Moscow, the capital simmering with activity, a chance to get away from stagnant Minsk if only for a week? Unthinkable!

The fact that they were vegetating in a provincial city and spending the best years of their lives uselessly were constant themes of their conversations at home. On good days he joked with her, calling her "Chekhov's fourth sister," since she was forever echoing their cranelike call "To Moscow, to Moscow!" On bad days, when she was brooding darkly, Nikita sometimes just stormed out of the house and went off to headquarters for no reason at all. Once there, he would often sit in his darkened office trying to drive away his own gloomy thoughts about Kronstadt.

And now here he was sitting in the commissariat's large conference hall, looking at the glistening features of the man delivering the paper but thinking only about his wife. God forbid she should go into labor in some trolley car or in one of the fashionable shops that she'd probably visit near the Lubyanka!

Voroshilov, it seemed, relished his role of commander in chief, military philosopher, and strategist. Stocky, robust, with a small, neatly trimmed mustache, even in a well-fitting uniform that was clearly custom tailored he looked like a prosperous merchant from Kuznetsky Most. Upon closer observation of his face with its shrewd eyes, one could catch occasional flashes of pure stupidity. From time to time, as though reminding himself of just who he was, Kliment Yefremovich would pause for a moment and fix his attention on his monumentality.

After the lecture Nikita was hailed in the corridor by three dashing young officers. He immediately recognized one of them—Okhotnikov! They embraced. Okhotnikov looked at his chevrons and said, "Aha, so you're already a brigade commander, Nikita!"

"I certainly wasn't expecting to see you here, Yakov," said Nikita. "Have you been back from the Transcaucasus for long?"

"At the moment I'm taking courses at the academy, getting wisdom," said Okhotnikov with a laugh. "I'd like you to meet a couple of my classmates—Arkady Geller and Volodya Petenko."

Nikita could tell by their handshakes that they were solid, regular army men.

"Delighted. Pardon me, Arkady, but don't you have the feeling that we've already met somewhere?"

"Of course," said Geller. "On the Polish front in October of 1920. On the armored train *October Thunderstorm*."

"That's right!" exclaimed Nikita.

At that moment, Voroshilov came out of the conference accompanied by several other high-ranking officers. Beneath his arm he carried a folder containing the speech he had just delivered. His round face turned toward those smoking in the corridor, obviously expecting them to greet him with delighted expressions. Okhotnikov rather casually tossed his head in the direction of the army commander. "Well, what did you think of the speech by the new boss?"

Nikita shrugged diplomatically.

"What, he's not the new Clausewitz?" whispered Geller gleefully.

"A gre-ea-t theoretician," laughed Petenko.

Nikita laughed too. "I can see, my friends, that Moscow is having its seditious effect on you, too."

"And why not? The opposition, of course, is too loudmouthed, but they're right about quite a few things. The army understands the grip of the bureaucrats better than anyone."

Remembering this brief conversation later, Nikita came to the conclusion that it had made him aware of several topics that were aggravating the city. "Bureaucrats" here meant Stalinists, that is, the majority of the present Politburo. The students of the Frunze Military Academy were close to the upper echelons of command. The thoughts expressed by Geller and Petenko clearly showed that irritation was growing in these circles at the "bureaucratic" style of leadership being forced on the Red Army. Even if these circles did not openly ally themselves with the opposition, they at least sympathized with them, if for no other reason than that they were against those who had promoted a mediocrity like Voroshilov to the highest post in the army after the fall of two brilliant men, Trotsky and Frunze. The sympathies of the army, after all, are an important matter.

As a matter of fact, the conversation was interrupted just when it was really getting interesting, thought Nikita with regret. He had seen Regimental Commander Vuinovich passing by in the corridor. Their eyes met, but Vuinovich immediately looked away without showing the slightest desire to stop.

"Vadim!" shouted Nikita.

Vuinovich continued down the corridor without turning around and went around a corner.

"Vadim, what the hell is wrong with you?"

Leaving the "academics," Nikita raced down the corridor, turned the corner, and stopped. They were now in an empty wing of the building. Vuinovich's feet tapped smartly on the floor as he walked away.

It's so silly, thought Nikita, to fall out with your best friend just because of an awkward situation my father got into. Even if he was mixed up in that dirty business, what's that got to do with me? In any case, he's not mixed up in it at all, it's just that—just that—oh, how stupid it all is!

"Don't be a fool, Vadim! Let's talk about it!"

Without turning around, Vuinovich opened a door onto a staircase and disappeared.

The secretaries, office workers, and guards of the Moscow Party Committee were not particularly happy, to put it mildly, about the invasion of the working masses in leather jackets and military shirts, caps and red kerchiefs. Proper order had been established at their institution for quite some time— the parquet floors had been scrubbed and carpeted paths laid out, barmaids in white aprons ran from office to office bearing tea and sandwiches, conversations were held in muffled tones, the ashtrays were emptied constantly, the busts of the great Lenin were polished in the most careful way, perhaps even better than the marble nymphs that had preceded him when the building had belonged to the Chamber of Commerce, and suddenly the proletariat—what else could you call them?—had appeared, calling loudly to one another, stamping their feet, blowing their noses, shaking dirt from the soles of their shoes, spreading an odor of uncleanliness and cheap tobacco, as though war communism had returned.

The conference hall on the third floor was filled with functionaries of the City and District Committees as well as Party activists of the largest business concerns. Kirill Gradov, in his eternal jacket over a peasant shirt, looked more like a working-class type than a city slicker, and he was quite happy about it. Moreover, his superiors in the Party esteemed his "theoretical grounding" highly and were indulgent toward his pseudo-democratic eccentricities—this young man, they said, has plenty of time to learn the unwritten rules of Party etiquette. The secretary of the Moscow Committee was speaking, looking like an absolutely typical representative of the growing Party masses of the mid-twenties, wearing a service jacket like the ones favored by Stalin, a small beard like Rykov's, and an omniscient smirk like Bukharin's.

"Comrades," he said, "the opposition is making desperate efforts to appeal to the workers over the head of the Party. A group of their leaders showed up at the cell meeting of an aircraft factory and made a bald-faced attempt to undermine Party decrees. Another group organized a meeting of a cell of Ryazan railroad workers, who were forced to accept the chairmanship of such dubious comrades as Tkachov and Sopronov. Politburo Member Trotsky made a speech, and Reingold appeared at a meeting of the cell of the Commissariat for Finance.

"The opposition has been sending these road shows to any number of factories. To our sorrow, we must point out that the State Planning Agency and the Red Institute of Professors have become outposts of opposition, and their people are constantly traveling to various manufacturing institutions to agitate among the workers.

"The same thing is happening in Leningrad, but for now that is not our concern. The principal task of the Communists of Moscow is to sever all contacts between the leaders of the opposition and the workers. Frankly, the best way to resolve the question would be to bring in the OGPU, but for now we cannot go that far—there would be an uproar. Today we must send out groups of our activists to all the enterprises where, according to our information—"

The secretary smiled faintly. An eloquent smirk, thought Kirill, peculiar to the secret police—an omnipotent, impudent, ominous smirk. He felt a sudden hatred for the man but immediately squashed this traitorous "liberal" feeling. Why, he thought, should I see him as a repulsive person, or as an individual at all? He is a representative of the Party, and right now we have only one task—to prevent a schism!

"—where, according to our information," continued the secretary, "new attempts to undermine Party decrees will be undertaken this evening. Comrade Samokha, proceed immediately to the division of our comrades into groups."

Having finished his speech, the secretary stepped down into the crowd and answered a few questions, for the most part referring those who asked them to Comrade Samokha. Then, with obvious relief, he withdrew from the scene to the private offices further inside the building.

Comrade Samokha, a wiry secret police operative in the leather jacket traditional to the service—though his had clearly seen better days—was distributing passes to the factories. Handing Kirill a document with the stamp of the All-Union Council of Trade Unions, he said, "Gradov, you and your group will go to the Ryazan Railway Yard, to the unified meeting of locomotive engineers, track workers, and electrical technicians. Our comrades in the local administration will meet you. The situation is tense. The highest leadership of the opposition might appear. There is ferment among the workers down there, and everyone knows what a hypnotic effect Lev Davidovich can have on a crowd. You've got to get their resolutions rejected, by any means possible! Stay in constant touch with the OGPU! Have as many personal discussions with the workers as you can. Remember anyone who might be wavering. Is everything clear?"

So this is where my war begins, thought Kirill—flanking maneuvers, diversionary actions, smokescreens. "Everything is clear, Comrade Samokha!"

After the passes had been handed out, the Party activists were invited to lunch in the building's dining hall. They did not go unwillingly—things like smoked salmon, stewed duck, and pork chops in aspic promised to be on the menu. Kirill, however, remained true to his principles. The comrades might laugh at my egalitarian attitude, he thought, but a man of my privileged bourgeois background needs to stick to his guns.

He left the City Committee building and went to the local greasy spoon, where cabbage soup with meat, navy-style macaroni, and a fruit dessert cost him less than a ruble—more precisely, 87 kopecks. Sitting by the window with his food, he looked at the people eating beneath the arched-ceilinged hall and out the window at the Muscovites, whose entire life seemed to revolve around streetcars: jumping on and off them, looking at their watches while they waited for them, running from one stop to another. For some reason an incredible hurried feeling had arisen in Moscow over the past few years—everybody ran, leapt on, leapt off, shouted, "Bye now!" or "So long"; and no one would even guess that events were about to take place today that might determine the future of the country for the rest of the period of reconstruction.

Early in the evening of the same day, Veronika Gradov, young military wife, was sitting in a square on the corner of Kuznetsky and Petrovka streets. All day she had been making the rounds of the stores, pricing things, but you couldn't try anything on except hats anymore. In the end she had bought herself something she had wanted for as long as she could remember, a smuggled Polish jacket. Not long ago, she had read Mayakovsky's satirical verses in *Izvestia:* "On Petrovka, broads in jackets walk in a band, they bring those Polish jackets to us as contraband," and the feeling had been aroused in her in Minsk—I have to, just have to go to Petrovka Street and get one of those jackets. I won't always be lumbering around with a big belly, she'd thought, soon I'll put on the wasp-waisted jacket and join the "band of broads" on Petrovka. The satirist, without meaning to, had out of a negative image created a sort of clan of dedicated and daring Moscow women in "Polish jackets."

She suddenly realized that what hurt her more than anything else was the absence, or complete indifference, of men's glances. Before, the eyes of every man who saw her had appeared slightly dazed, and none of them, not a single one, had failed to turn and look at the beautiful woman after she passed. Now no one looks at me, she thought, everything is lost. Being pregnant means getting old before your time.

She looked nervously at her watch: Nikita was late. Boris IV kicked a couple of times. Why was everyone so sure it would be a boy? The infamous Gradov patriarchism . . . I'll go and give birth to a girl, then leave my soldier husband, go to Paris, and stay with my uncle. I'll raise my daughter as a French girl, she'll become a movie star, the next Greta Garbo . . . I'll follow her to Hollywood, and some day my face—her face—will come back to this lousy Moscow, like the Mary Pickford posters they put up on the kiosks.

She began to feel nauseated, she put her hand to her stomach beneath her ample coat and had trouble getting her breath—oh, God, don't let it begin here, behind a kiosk bearing the names of Pickford, Fairbanks, and Jackie Coogan, as well as the Larionov Gymnastic Troupe. Suddenly a coachman stopped his cab on the street in front of her, and a soldier got out. She did not realize right away that it was Nikita.

"Well, it's about time!" she cried out as he and all his chevrons and stripes approached her.

Nikita smiled and kissed her. "A woman in your condition, my lady, ought to be at home in bed, not making dates with officers!"

Veronika was becoming fretful, biting her lip and trying to keep back tears. "Don't you understand that I can't live without Moscow? Even just to walk along Stoleshnikov Lane is true bliss! What's it to me to come to Moscow once in a blue moon and then sit out in Silver Forest like a breeding machine growing the Gradovs' male heir? It's all just a mockery!"

Nikita began kissing her on her cheeks and swollen nose. "Take it easy, darling. It'll all be over soon!"

Veronika turned away. "You're only worried about your kid—you don't give a damn about me!"

"Why, Vika, what a thing to say!"

She wiped her face, then asked in a calmer voice, "So what's going on at your silly Commissariat? Have they finally transferred you to Moscow?"

"On the contrary, I've been appointed aide to the commander of headquarters of the Western Military District."

"That means back to stinking Minsk," Veronika said, drawing out her words dejectedly. "If at least Warsaw were ours . . ."

Nikita shuddered. This frivolous woman had unknowingly gone right to the heart of the secret conferences on strategy, as if she were sticking a pin in a map. "Warsaw! Shut up, Vika."

"Well, why not? Anywhere you please, but at least it's a capital city, it's European." She realized she had touched on a very sensitive area, so she craftily played the fool, taking the same pleasure in it as she formerly had. "We should just take Warsaw, live there awhile, then move away. Propose it to the War Department."

Nikita was already holding his sides with laughter. "Oh, sweetheart, stop clowning around. Look at the surprise I have for you—tickets to the Meyerhold play!"

Veronika was stunned. "Tickets to Meyerhold? You mean for *The Mandate?* Why, Nikita, you've outdone yourself!" He had not seen her so radiant for a long time. "When is it? This evening?" Her face clouded momentarily. "But I won't be able to dress properly!"

"Oh, Vika, listen to me, my dear. Why would you have to dress up specially? You're already dressed for—" It suddenly occurred to him that he was about to say something tactless, and he corrected himself: "—for the revolutionary theater, anyway. We'll still have time to have dinner at the National, and you'll see, this dress of yours with the Byelorussian embroidery will take everyone's breath away."

Veronika grumbled with unexpected good humor, "In other words, I'm already dressed for someone with a belly this size. You know, Nikita, of all the rotten husbands around, you're not the worst by far. Lord, how I've dreamed of seeing the Meyerhold performance!"

The unified meeting of the cells of the Ryazan railway workers took place in a huge locomotive repair depot. The depot was so big that one corner of it was large enough to accommodate the meeting, for which a temporary platform had been erected, with a portrait of the immortal Lenin suspended from a bridge crane. Meanwhile, at the back of the huge crowd loomed the silent locomotives, imparting a Middle Eastern coloring to the event, like elephants trained for battle sealing off the exits from some Babylonian square. The majority of the listeners were dressed in coveralls, not having had time to change after their shift. Most of the heads were covered by caps and kerchiefs. The deputies who had received their orders from the Moscow Party Committee earlier in the day were sitting in small groups with "leather jackets" sprinkled among them and looking around with attentive eyes. From time to time they saw individuals in everyday coats and ties. These they viewed with suspicion, particularly if the outfit was topped off with a hat and even more so if the man wore glasses.

The air was damp and foul, and many in the crowd were sweating like pigs. The shop workers did not sit idly by; the non-Party workers opened the gigantic, one might even say Cyclopean, gates and the inclement late October winds came howling in.

Why didn't I just study linguistics, Kirill Gradov thought sadly. After all, I love languages! Right now I'd be sitting in a library . . . Then again, who would fight for genuine socialism if the intellectuals all just went their separate ways, hiding out in linguistics or microbiology?

On the tribune beneath the portrait of Lenin were seated both members of the opposition and proponents of the Party line. Karl Radek, an individual whom the Russian proletariat considered an outsider, and maybe even suspicious, was making a speech. Not a week went by without Radek's jokes about "Soviet bureaucrats who make heads roll" making the rounds in Moscow, jokes that were insulting not only to the Stalinists but in a certain measure to the masses as well, since they seemed to hint at the supposed eternal narrow-mindedness of the Russian people. Radek spoke grammatically correct Russian, but with a heavy accent and an intonation that made it difficult to follow him.

Just the way that he mangled the word "tovarishch" was enough to make the workers begin exchanging glances and smiles. Of course, as conscientious Party members and internationalists, they were not heard to express any opinion about the speaker's nationality, but one could almost guarantee that everyone was thinking something along the lines of "This character they sent overdoes the Jewish bit" or "How much more Jewish can you get?" and in extreme cases "This Jewish comrade isn't one of us." Meanwhile the orator continued to develop his logically murderous theses:

"The idea of the present Central Committee concerning the development of socialism in one country reeks of the mustiness of centuries past. Really, comrades . . ." His way of saying "really" made it sound like an expression of pain rather than exhortation. "This thesis by its absurdity cannot help but remind one of those old Russian provincial dimwits in the writings of the nineteenth-century satirist Saltykov-Shchedrin. Comrades, the Stalinist Central Committee is regaling the workers with doses of cheap patriotism as gigantic as Gulliver in Lilliput, while at the same time the soviets are losing their core of workingmen, industrialization is hampered by private capital, and in the international arenas we're spinning our wheels, we're losing our authority in the eyes of the revolutionary masses! Comrades, the leader of the world proletariat, Comrade Trotsky, together with others who were close to our great leader Lenin, calls on you—let us breathe new life into our revolution!"

Radek left the speakers' platform with a feeling of disenchantment—it seemed as though the railroad workers were a different audience from a week ago. At the beginning of his speech, smatterings of applause and approving shouts of "Right!" "Hurrah!" and "Down with the centrists!" could be heard, but now this clapping and yelling was replaced by hissing, whistling, and angry cries of "Down with the Trotskyites!" "Pull him off the platform, brothers!" "No compromises with the opposition!" "Shut your mouth!" and "Get out of the Party!" After a time individual sounds could no longer be distinguished, there was simply a storm of indignation. He realized his opponents had done their job well, that it had been a mistake to think he could just sail into this depot and make a speech of this sort, with all these allusions to Saltykov-Shchedrin and Gulliver . . . and had it not perhaps been a mistake to join the anti-Stalinist wing of the Party at all, to stick his neck so far out?

Kirill Gradov, going along with the majority, had raged against the speaker, jumped out of his seat, and brandished his fist in the air while shouting something rather incoherent. He was seized by a blissful, inspiring feeling of unity. This is what class feeling is all about, he said to himself, it's finally come.

At the rear of the crowd stood a group of OGPU operatives led by Samokha. It would clearly be incorrect to say that a feeling of class consciousness had come over them at that moment, simply because it had never left them. They were surveying the crowd of railroad workers and Party members with a businesslike air, whispering to one another from time to time. So far, everything was going as planned.

Kirill Gradov shouted to the platform from his seat in the third row, "I request the floor!" The chairman of the meeting raised his hand and rang a small bell. Both the gesture and the sound looked ridiculous in the face of a shouting crowd in a railroad depot. Finally, though, the chairman's voice could be heard through the tumult: "Attention, comrades! The debate shall continue! According to our list of those who have signed up to take part, it is now the turn of Comrade Preobrazhensky!"

Preobrazhensky, an opposition leader, stood up decisively from his seat on the presidium and, tucking the sturdy cloth of his paramilitary shirt under his belt, moved toward the speaker's place.

"I demand the floor on a point of order!" shouted Kirill.

Suddenly, two lads in peaked caps jumped up onto the platform, looking more like hoodlums from the Marina Roshcha area than workers. Spreading their arms and flashing a crooked grin, they barred the way of the opposition speaker. The powerfully built Preobrazhensky continued to try to get through to speak, but the two lads hung on to him. They were unable to knock him off his feet, but they prevented him from advancing.

"This is an outrage! Get off, you lowlifes!"

In reply, horselaughs resounded from all over the hall.

At that moment Kirill leapt onto the platform from the opposite end and took the floor. "Comrades, I ask your attention for a moment!" he shouted as loudly as he could. The crowd quieted down slightly, though whistling and boos could still be heard here and there.

"Comrades, I am a young Communist," Kirill went on. "Party unity is more important to us than the air we breathe! I move that we condemn the schismatic, arrogant, and autocratic actions of comrades Trotsky, Zinoviev, and Pyatakov! I move that we adopt a resolution for a halt to all discussions with the opposition!"

A wave of emotion surged through the crowd. The vast majority, caps in hands, was now yelling, "Right you are! Enough undermining the Party! We won't allow any more splits! Down with discussion!"

Preobrazhensky finally freed himself from his pursuers, walked up to the lectern, and banged his fist on it. "What's going on here? An organized provocation? I demand the right to speak!"

Kirill shouted into the hall without looking at the man standing next to him, whose chest was heaving with emotion while streams of sweat trickled down his face. "I move that Comrade Preobrazhensky be denied the right to speak!"

A new wave of antiopposition feeling answered him. "Down with them! Down with them! Down with them!"

Preobrazhensky waved his hand in disgust and returned to his seat.

Nevertheless, the meeting went on for another two hours and finished at nightfall. The opposition had been smashed.

Going their separate ways in the darkness, stumbling now and then on the rails, the different factions continued to exchange insults. Preobrazhensky was walking silently with a group of friends. Somehow this passage across railroad territory reminded him of a scene out of the prerevolutionary days of emigration. We're being pushed out, he thought. We're becoming foreigners here, and we may have to emigrate all over again. Looking behind him, he saw the young man who had deprived him of his turn to speak. Letting his comrades walk on ahead, he waited for him.

"Gradov, can I talk to you for a minute?"

Traces of unfeigned enthusiasm still seemed to be trembling on the young man's features, unless, of course, they were traces of shame, which was unlikely.

Kirill stopped. "What do you want, Comrade Preobrazhensky?"

Preobrazhensky offered him a cigarette, then lit one himself. "Tell me, do you seriously mean to say you don't understand the meaning of what happened here tonight? Don't you understand that the opposition is simply an attempt to stop Stalin?"

"Stalin is fighting for the unity of the Party, and that's enough about that!" Kirill riposted.

Preobrazhensky looked at his face attentively. "Is your father Gradov the surgeon?"

"Yes. What does that have to do with anything?" he asked, lurching forward.

Preobrazhensky tossed his cigarette aside and walked away. "Good night, Comrade Gradov," he said without looking back, almost flinging the words at him.

CHAPTER FIVE

The Theatrical Avant-Garde

★

That evening, when Veronika and Nikita Gradov were on their way to a performance of *The Mandate*, there was a meeting in the rehearsal hall of the Meyerhold Theater of the performing company and the theater's active fans. The actors who were to perform that evening were already in their costumes and makeup, and the rest were wearing the latest fashions in suits and sweaters and, of course, scarves—long, multicolored, thrown over the shoulders, worn as a shawl or wrapped around the neck. An impressive range of Moscow's bohemian underground was represented there.

As for the fans, jamming the back rows of seats, standing along the walls, even sitting in the aisles, they were mostly young students.

The meeting, it was understood, was a meeting in name only. In fact it was a rare visitation of his people by the Master.

Meyerhold and Zinaida Reich had only just returned from a trip to Europe. The "First Lady" was dazzling and in a wonderful, generous mood. Her fashions, from the most elegant Parisian couturiers, were so cosmically inaccessible that they did not even inspire envy among the women in the company, only delight. In the hall one could make out the desirous stares of men who would clearly have liked to introduce some disorder into her impeccable outfit.

Meyerhold, wearing a broad gray herringbone suit that was also obviously from abroad, appeared rather glum. He had already learned that the recent premiere of his *Inspector General* had been hooted down by the press. Casually tossing out sentences with his long right hand, the Honorary Red Soldier was recounting his impressions of his voyage.

Everything in the European theater was at a standstill. No one abroad was getting any further than the Austrian playwright Max Reinhardt. The direction was on the level of the Maly Theater, the sets were primitively realistic. There was a complete absence of style and innovation. Even in Italy things were in decline. Luigi Pirandello's company was barely eking out a living on government subsidies.

In spite of everything, though, there had been some interesting things. Magnificent church services, for example—now, that was theater! Or the Negro Dixieland jazz bands that were such a hit in Germany. We ought to organize a touring company with some of our Gypsies—in the meantime, I'm trying to get some of those Negro musicians to play with us. Take it easy, nothing is certain yet, negotiations are still going on. The French didn't want to give us entry visas, they're afraid of the "Red virus," while at the same time in Paris itself, and in London too, there is a tremendous interest in our theater in left-wing artistic circles.

Moscow is becoming a theatrical Mecca for such people. Our school has been proclaimed the only current movement with any life, which is why the bad reviews of *The Inspector General* that appeared in the press here look like an inept conspiracy on the part of the stinking bourgeoisie. What is the value, for example, of that rot they printed in *Izvestia*?

He picked up a newspaper from the small table in front of him, held it by the edges, and shook it with revulsion, then opened it and read aloud, "The murderer. A review in epigrams of Meyerhold's production of *The Inspector General*."

> *Who is as bold as Meyerhold*
> *and apes the ass that killed the laugh?*
> *Gogol cries, the director lies.*

The hackneyed, rather arrogant meter failed completely and produced one of the countless small moments of joy at Meyerhold's rehearsals. The lame epigrams had been read in such a way that everyone burst into laughter, as if they could see with their own eyes the Soviet hack who had created them. Meyerhold smiled in satisfaction. He was glad to be back in Moscow, with his own people.

Nina Gradov was standing at the back of the theater in the crowd of supporters, her cheeks glowing with delight, her eyes and teeth sparkling with constant movement, her hair tousled. Meyerhold was like a god to her. To see and hear him was not just a pleasure, it was a moment of Olympian enlightenment. She had already forgotten that this evening was more than just an ordinary trip to the theater, that among those assembled was Albov himself, the leader of the underground Trotskyite cell, and that an "action" was being prepared.

From the very beginning, Nikolai Erdman's play *The Mandate* had revealed itself to be, as it were, a bottle of kerosene that would set off Moscow's Party-Komsomol and intellectual-artistic circles, already red hot. It was said that literally every line was a double entendre, that every scene contained not only satire and buffoonery but a direct attack on the Central Committee, the secret police, the centrists, in short, all of the evil forces which, by making the bureaucracy all powerful, were gradually but stubbornly rooting all romanticism out of the Revolution.

It had indeed seemed that at the play's premiere at the Meyerhold Theater the year before, every line had sprayed kerosene into the glowing coals. Half the audience had roared with laughter and applauded, enraptured, while the other half had whistled and hissed in indignation, left the theater with cries of "Shame!" and "It's an insult!," stamped their feet and shaken their "Party fists," which Mayakovsky had recently described in an impressive phrase that sent shivers down one's spine: "The Party is a hand with a million fingers, clenched into one crushing fist!"

Perhaps at that time it was only in Moscow that an avant-garde performance could become the arena of a struggle between two political forces, the opposition and the official Party line.

The Mandate was on again that evening for the *n*th time, and nothing extraordinary was expected to happen, though the audience, as always, responded immediately to the audacious cues coming from the stage. For example, when the drunken organ-grinder hobbled unsteadily to the front of the stage and announced from the side of his mouth, "Little Pavel, when he was just a tiny little thing, used to come and sit on my knee, and he kept saying, 'I love the proletariat, Uncle! Oh, how I love them!' " the audience guffawed and applauded, excited by the atmosphere of light-hearted conspiracy. Veronika laughed happily, forgetting all about her belly, and her husband, Nikita Gradov, brigade commander of the Worker-Peasant Red Army, clapped his "hands of steel."

Suddenly, a piercing, girlish voice from the balcony cut through the carnivallike atmosphere: "Shame to the Stalinist hypocrites!"

Immediately, several tightly bunched groups of young people rose from their seats and as if under the direction of a conductor's baton began to chant in unison,

> *Down with stupidity and rage,*
> *Stick Wily Koba in a cage!*

Nikita looked back up at the balcony and whispered to his wife, "I'd swear that one of those is our Nina!"

"Oh, my God!" said Veronika in horror.

Absolute chaos took over. Many of the theatergoers were fuming and could be heard saying, "It's an outrage! What hooligans! Have your meetings at school, don't bring them to the theater! They're ruining the show! Someone should call the police!" A second faction supported the oppositionists: "They're right! Down with the Stalinist protégés! We're fed up with them!" Another part of the audience was simply laughing: it's all merry and cheeky, what do you want to bet Meyerhold himself thought it up? A fourth group was consumed by curiosity: what will happen next? A fifth faction was prudently trying to leave the hall altogether. An old usher holding his head in his hand started up the aisle toward the balcony. Styopa Kalistratov and his gang of poets, loudly laughing and obviously not entirely sober, met him as they came down toward the stage.

Stepan yelled to a friend of his who was acting in the play, "Congratulations, Goshka! It's even better today than at the premiere! That's the way it ought to be! That's where the meaning of modern theater lies—in scandal! Theater means scandal!"

After pronouncing this exclusive, innovative phrase that even Griboyedov had known about, Styopa looked back over his shoulder to his sidekick Fomka Frukht and said, "Make a note of that!"

"It's done! Noted!" replied Frukht.

The commotion was increasing. Nikita, looking at the seething crowd around him, forgot about his wife for a moment. When he looked at her again, he went cold and began yelling more like a high school student than a brigade commander.

"What are we going to do? What are we going to do?"

Veronika's contractions were beginning, and she was gripped by panic. She gritted her teeth and gasped for air. Sweat streamed down her face. Her dress was already soaking wet. Cursing himself for losing his head like an idiot, Nikita caught Veronika under the arms and began to help her toward the exit.

"Let us through, citizens! Let us through! My wife is about to give birth! Call an ambulance, please!"

In the melee in front of them, a youth burst into laughter and pointed a finger at them. "Look, look, only in our theater! A brigade commander dragging his wife out! Meyerhold's the daddy!"

The furious Nikita kicked the youth squarely in the backside. "Let us through, you scum!" In a rage, he drew his revolver out of its holster. "Get out of the way or I'll shoot!"

That kind of threat was still fresh in the minds of the theatergoers, and they immediately cleared a path. He once again took Veronika, who was screaming in pain, by the arm and started in the direction of the exit.

Styopka Kalistratov caught Nina running headlong down the stairs from the balcony. "Hello there, citizen! Listen, the Armenians are here—the poets—there's going to be a blast. Champagne! Free!"

Nina, in his arms, laughed. Isn't that happiness, to hold a laughing nymph in your arms, the thought flashed through Styopka's noggin.

Alas, Nina had already slipped out of his grasp and was moving away. "You, Stepan, are an incorrigible bohemian decadent!"

What the hell, he thought, you can't hold a girl like that, laughing and full of blessed fire, in your arms forever. And for that moment, thank you, Providence.

Semyon Stroilo the proletarian came thumping down the stairs.

"So you're still with this Stoilo?" said the poet with a grin. "The word means 'farm'—'animal stall.' "

"It's not Stoilo, but Stroilo, from the verb 'stroit,' 'to build,' if you don't mind!" Nina replied heatedly. She attached herself to her chosen suitor and went down the steps with him, almost hanging from his shoulder, which allowed her to look back once again at the dejected Stepan.

Thank you anyway, Providence, thought the poet.

The members of Nina's band swept by. Among them was a man who must have been more than thirty with hair like a lion's mane and professorial glasses—Albov. The "action," he concluded, was a success.

Toward morning, the doctor on call at the Grauerman Maternity Hospital came out to see Nikita Gradov, who was agonizing in the waiting room, and announced to him that he had a son. The doctor already knew that his patient was the wife of a brigade commander, Professor Gradov's son. He told him it was a healthy, bouncing baby of normal weight. "Go on home, Comrade Kombrig, get some sleep, come back in the afternoon, and we'll show you your firstborn."

Nikita went out onto the street in a half-conscious state, his overcoat unbuttoned, and set off in no particular direction, for some reason walking faster and faster, turning corners sharply and holding on to drainpipes. One of them was so rusty it bent in his hand. The backstreets of the Arbat were deserted and dark, but in the distance he saw the vista of a weakly illuminated shop window containing a large globe. The globe had a sort of stimulating effect on the brigade commander, and he suddenly shook the cobwebs out of his head and realized what had happened that night.

"It's a boy!" he yelled and ran in the direction of the globe. In the window he saw his approaching reflection, the billowing flaps of his overcoat and his shiny high boots. He ran out onto the main street of the Arbat. Above the rooftops he saw the cross of a small church that had escaped damage. "A son, a son . . . my son is born!" He crossed himself once, then twice, then took the three fingers that he used for the gesture away from his forehead, away from the red star on his cap. Then he drew out his revolver and fired a shot into the air. "Hurrah!"

"Stop shooting!" said a voice nearby. Nikita looked and saw the figure of an old man with a nightstick standing beneath the entrance to a building. Must be a watchman, he thought.

"There's nothing to be afraid of, everything is all right—it's just that I've just had a son, Boris Gradov the Fourth, Russian doctor!"

"All the same, that's no cause for shooting," said the old man, coming out of the doorway and walking by Nikita, who could see then that he wasn't an old man at all but rather middle-aged, in an old-fashioned but expensive coat. His steeply sloping forehead and bald pate were shining. An ephemeral golden-silver flora, translucent, flickering effect wound about these lofty heights, the highest on his body. Was it the poet and novelist Andrei Bely?

CHAPTER SIX

$$\sqrt{RCP(b)}*$$

★

Toward evening on a beautiful fall day—the height of Indian summer—Instructor Semyon Stroilo of SOSUAF—the Society for the Support of the Armed Forces—was waiting for Nina Gradov in the Office of Visual Aids, which was located on the second floor of the Krasnaya Presnya District House of Culture.

*Russian Communist Party (Bolsheviks).

A ray of sunlight coming in through the narrow window lit up the thick dust covering the books and training materials, grenades, gas masks, and parachutists' knapsacks, hinting at a certain lazy streak on the part of the respected Comrade Instructor.

Semyon couldn't stand all of the laziness and understood absolutely nothing about it. He had gotten this job as a reward for having a spotless record, but he wasn't planning to stay in it for very long: he had a long road in front of him. For the time being he was content—it was a "let sleeping dogs lie" kind of job, and most important of all, he had the keys to three of the offices, which were very handy places to meet girls.

A Maxim heavy machine gun, cut in half lengthwise in order to show its iron innards, was on display in the middle of the room. On the walls hung propaganda posters, which Semyon managed to dust from time to time. One of them showed a gigantic proletarian fist smashing an English battleship that looked like a pathetic lizard: "Our answer to Lord Curzon!" Another showed a flight of airships in the sky beneath a radiant hammer and sickle: "We will build a fleet of dirigibles in the name of Lenin!"

The room was hot. Semyon was sitting on a couch wearing a T-shirt that bore the emblem of the *Stormy Petrel.* He was smoking, sipping from a bottle of cheap wine, and reading a rather soiled copy of a sensational romantic novel.

Now she'll come, the stupid cow, he thought, and she'll see me lying around in just my undershirt, drinking, reading this trash, and she'll go into raptures—oh, how simple and free you are! What a bitch . . .

On the one hand, Semyon Stroilo was delighted with his romance with Nina Gradov, the spoiled professor's daughter, and on the other, it irritated him tremendously: it was as though he constantly had to play the role forced on him by the imagination of this kid who had always gotten her own way. She saw in him her ideal of the "simple and free" proletarian holding the world in his hands. As a consequence, he always had to show simplicity, act the man of the urban masses, show confidence and even move with a relaxed awkwardness, and have the rock-hard muscles of a weightlifter. In fact, Semyon Stroilo was by nature restless, convoluted in his thinking, and not even physically very strong; he hated muscles. In short, Nina looked on him more as a proletarian toy than a genuine proletarian, which, the purity of his background notwithstanding, he had never been. Descended from Marina Roshcha warehouse workers, neither his father nor his grandfather had done anything of great value. All things considered, there was no reason to get offended about what was going on: a sweet girl whom he got a lot of use out of, but still . . .

He heard steps running from the staircase into the corridor—she's coming, damn her, right on time!

Nina ran across the vestibule at the end of the corridor, and anyone who had met her in that huge building would have been dumbfounded—what makes that girl so radiant? Where does she get so much optimism, ten years after the Revolution?

The cleaning lady smiled knowingly after her and pointed her out to the watchman with a gnarled index finger. "See that? She's running to her date with the instructor!"

The watchman smacked his lips and wiped his brow with his sleeve. "She's a real cutie. I could—"

Nina flew down the corridor, nearly tore the hinges off the door marked "Visual Aids," and burst into the room waving a brand-new copy of the journal *Red Virgin Soil.* "Semyon, you loafer, get up! Look, one of my poems is in *Red Virgin Soil!*"

She opened the review, propped her elbows on the half of a machine gun, and read aloud forcefully:

> *Could I in my moments of striving*
> *Not recall, O Odysseus, your eyes, your lips?*
> *The jasmine bloom of your flotilla at midnight,*
> *Shadows of the fortress,*
> *The ring of distant trumpets?*

Semyon gave a measured yawn, thinking, my proletarian maw is showing. "What's it about?"

Nina did not answer, looking at some invisible point.

"What's it about, this poem?" repeated Semyon.

"About night," she said.

Semyon tossed his book under the couch, stood up, and stretched. "Want some grub, Nina?" He gestured toward an open tin of canned meat and a loaf of Moscow bread.

Nina shook her head.

"You don't want this first-rate stuff?" he said in surprise. "How about some wine? Come on, sister, you're not going to turn down this vintage, are you?" A sweet feeling of attraction ran through his body, and he began to undo the belt of his trousers. "All right now, Miss Fine-and-Pretty Fiddle-dee-dee, come over here!"

Nina took a step backward, almost in annoyance, though she herself hungered for only one thing, to perform the act with him. "What's the matter with you, Syomka? I'm trying to talk about poetry and right away you—"

He pulled her toward him, and in a commanding way raised her skirt. "Come on, come on . . . enough of this pussyfooting around! How many times do you have to be told, 'Be simpler, Nina!' "

Closing her eyes, she was yielding to him more and more, muttering, "Yes, yes, you're right, my love . . . be simpler . . ." though in fact, she was imagining herself, as always, as a victim of proletarian rape, a trophy brought back by the triumphant class.

The cleaning woman, mopping the corridor, went up to the door in order to listen to the loud, extended squeaking of the couch springs. The watchman shuffled over as well.

In the gathering dusk, Nina went on kissing his cheeks and neck for a long time and smoothed the damp hair of her exhausted conqueror.

"You're my Czar SOSUAF," she whispered.

Semyon, now satisfied, said resoundingly: "Cut out the childish mush!" He took another drink from the bottle and lit a cigarette. "Listen, Nina, there's something I want to point out to you. You're a great kid, of course, but you need to get a bit more involved, know what I mean? When the moment comes, you need to do like this—" He demonstrated with his hand how to do it, indicating a splashing wave. "You, dear lady, don't do it!"

She laughed, taking no offense. "Oh, Syomka, Syomka . . . you're such a blockhead!"

He got up from the couch, pulled on his pants and his undershirt, and sat down on a chair. "And here's another observation for you, my dear, and not a personal one from anybody in our group, but from Albov himself. He told me to tell you that he's not happy with you. Not enough time with the collective, too much time spent on—" He shook the copy of *Red Virgin Soil* disdainfully. "—'the jasmine bloom of your flotilla at midnight' and what have you. You're in the Komsomol, after all, you shouldn't be going around with fellow travelers like Styopka Kalistratov!"

Nina exploded with laughter. "Why, you're jealous, Mr. SOSUAF!"

Semyon slammed his fist down on the table in front of him. Though his fist wasn't what you could call massive, at times like these it seemed like a sledgehammer even to him. "What? I'm talking seriously, and you're still playing the flirt? You just can't shake off your high-class upbringing, can you?"

Nina sat up on the couch. "Albov himself really said that?"

Semyon nodded. "It's a fact. 'We're working in the underground, as it were,' he said, 'while Gradov flits around at LEF poetry readings.'"

Nina looked at her watch and jumped to her feet. In the musty air of the classroom, she threw on one article of clothing after another—skirt, blouse, sweater, scarf. In a flash she was dressed, and it was as though her submission to her sinful desires at the feet of the pagan idol of a disassembled Red Army machine gun just a short time before had never happened. "Syomka, we're going to be late to the university!"

Comrade Stroilo was already pulling a thick bag of printed matter from beneath the table.

They made it to Manège Square in half an hour. They were forced to take a horse-drawn cab at their cell's expense, otherwise the whole expedition would have been ruined for no reason that they could explain.

It was rush hour, activity was at its peak. Overcrowded streetcars crawled past the university building, clanging and throwing showers of sparks from their wires. Vendors selling meat pies containing giblets, or, to use the modern term, "production leftovers," were crying out joyfully like students. Now and again a student flashed by with one of the meat pies stuck halfway out of his mouth and his eyes dazed from the culinary assault.

An announcement had been hung from a lamppost by the university gates: "Communist Auditorium. This evening at 8 P.M. LEF! 'Algebra of the Revolution,' read by the poet Sergei Tretyakov. Also appearing: the poet Stepan Kalistratov with 'Untitled'; the designer Vladimir Tatlin with a story about a device called 'Letatlin.' "

Stroilo and Nina, glancing at the poster, quickly passed through the gates, cut across the square past the statue of Lomonosov, and dashed up the grand staircase.

The hall was still nearly empty when Nina and Semyon entered, though in preparation for the evening a huge futuristic flying machine in the form of a pterodactyl had been suspended over the lecturer's seat.

"We made it. Thank the God of Labor there's no one here," whispered Nina.

"Let's get to work," commanded Semyon.

They ran up the aisles, distributing packages of flyers along the rows. Their work was finished quickly, and then they settled in close to the stage in the first row, opening their textbooks and giving the impression that they were reading diligently while waiting for a concert to begin. From time to time they looked at each other and giggled. In addition to everything else, thought Nina, Syomka and I are comrades-in-arms. Oh me, Semyon thought about her, what eyes!

A few minutes later the auditorium began to fill quickly with students. Someone had already found one of the leaflets and read out, "The salvation of the Revolution is in your hands! Down with Stalin!"

From another row, another variation was heard: "We shall stop this attempt to repeat Thermidor! Shame to the Stalinist Central Committee!"

Subversive Trotskyite and opposition leaflets were nothing new to the students. They found them in their dormitories and dining halls, sometimes pasted to a wall, other times in packs with a notice attached urging the students to distribute them among their comrades. Many sympathized with the leaflets, others couldn't have cared less. Sometimes political meetings flared up, other times a student could be seen racing to the bathroom with one of the leaflets in his hand. On this occasion the students seemed to be ignited right away and began to cry out, "Down with . . ." and "Shame!" but then there were the local wits in attendance, and how can anyone avoid clowning around for the girls when he's out for the evening? "Down with binary!" "Shame to ternary!" "Down with squared!" The laughter grew. "There's the 'algebra of the Revolution' for you!" The mood that evening was plainly not going to be very political.

Meanwhile, the Communist Auditorium had gotten so full that latecomers were being turned away. People were standing in the aisles and in the doorways. Among those who arrived late was Professor Gradov's assistant, the young doctor Savva Kitaigorodsky. He was hemmed in at the entrance, and he managed to drift over into a corner, where he could rest his shoulder lightly against the wall. The poet Sergei Tretyakov was already on stage, but Savva was not looking in his direction. His eyes were searching for the desired face in the hall. Finally, he found the face that he was looking for: Nina Gradov! Even if she was with that numbskull of hers, at least she was here! He thought of some lines from Blok: "I enter into the darkened temples / I perform my poor rite . . ." The young doctor had a liking for poetry, but his tastes had not gone much beyond the Symbolists, and he had no desire for them to.

The crowd roared and burst into applause. Then a hush fell. The popular Sergei Tretyakov, a friend of Mayakovsky's, had come to the edge of the stage to read. He was very tall, no shorter than "Mayak" himself, yet he did not have the appearance of an orator but seemed rather to have more in common with people like Savva Kitaigorodsky, that is, with intellectuals: he wore spectacles and a three-piece suit. Mayakovsky wore a monster suit, which made Tretyakov's seem puny by comparison. Because of this, the LEF militancy in his reading style—the snarling and waving of his clenched fist—seemed a little out of place. He read:

> *The square root of the RCP(b)*
> *Multiplied by*
> *Forward! Look Ahead!*
> *Plus!*
> *Electricity! Linkage! Training!*
> *Plus*
> *We want the world!*
> *We praise Lenin!*
> *Minus*

Lie!
Minus
Filth!
Minus
Boredom!
That is
      October's
        Path!

The final cry of the percussive verses favorably emphasized the weak rhyme of "filth" and "path," which the poet was proud of, apparently unaware of the unfortunate connotations that could be attached to the juxtaposition of the two words. The students of the philological faculty roared their approval:

"Bravo, Sergei! Bravo, LEF!"

Next to Savva stood a "literary girl"—her hair in long, angular bangs and the back of her head shaved—who turned to him and asked, "Did you like it?"

Savva shrugged his shoulders. The girl laughed. "I didn't care for it much either. What kind of 'algebra' was he talking about? Basic fourth-grade arithmetic!"

The crowd began to rock back and forth. The girl's stomach was pressed against Savva's. A great deal of wholly inappropriate pushing and shoving began. The "literary girl" grinned in mock embarrassment. "Pardon me." Savva squirmed, trying to make a space between the extremities of their different sexes. "It's so crowded . . ."

In their row, Nina was tugging at Semyon's sleeve. "Don't you find that kind of poetry closer to you? Come on, tell me, Syomka! It's very important to me!"

Stroilo rumbled in his best offhand proletarian style, "It's crap . . . I feel like my bladder's about to bust, I'm going to the john."

He began to make his way toward the exit over the legs of their neighbors. Nina whispered to him from behind, "My simple darling!" He turned around and barked, "Cut it out!" Then he said to the displeased students, "You say I'm stepping on your feet? What do you want me to do, walk on top of your heads?"

Stroilo went into the old university's spacious washroom with its high ceiling and glazed tile floor and saw at the window a young man in a paramilitary uniform who seemed to be waiting for him. He went about his business. The young man approached him.

"A salute to you, Stroilo!"

"A physical culture greeting to you!" replied Stroilo, shaking himself off.

"Shall we hop on up to the Party Committee hall?" the young man asked in a tone that demonstrated how inclined he was toward positive thinking.

The Party Committee hall was of nearly the same dimensions as the washroom. At that hour, there was no one in the room except for a middle-aged man sitting at the far end next to a table lamp leafing through some papers. A large, elaborately framed portrait of Vladimir Iliich Ulyanov/Lenin dominated the hall.

At the sight of the two youths entering the room, the little man rose and walked toward them.

"Greetings, Comrade Stroilo! Let's get right down to business—how many attended the last meeting of the circle?"

"Twelve, Comrade Commissar," Stroilo replied crisply. He unbuttoned one of his pockets and drew out a piece of paper. "Here's the list."

The commissar took the list and read the first several names aloud: "Albov, Brekhno, Gradov, Galat—" Then he thrust the piece of paper into his pocket and firmly shook Stroilo's hand. "Thank you, Semyon. This is a very big, very important job that you're doing for us."

Stroilo beamed and as a result looked somewhat like an oversized statue. He drew himself up and said, "I serve the Soviet Union!"

Meanwhile, in the auditorium, Sergei Tretyakov had been replaced by Stepan Kalistratov, who wore a crumpled velvet shirt, had thrown a scarf over his shoulders, and displayed a disheveled hairdo known as "the Esenin look." As usual, it was hard to tell how drunk Stepan was at the moment—tipsy, barely able to walk, or simply "smashed." Somehow or other, he managed to read with an inspired feeling of gloom:

> *On a flat and empty earth*
> *Factories near and far hoot eerily,*
> *Then fall so silent during the watch*
> *That even the angels' voices can't be heard . . .*
> *Our consolation comes*
> *From tavern revelations*
> *And "Arzamasian anguish."*

Nina Gradov was watching him, spellbound. Maybe even more than Tretyakov, Stepan was a favorite with the public, particularly women. Every one of his poems was received with rapturous applause.

Perhaps the only person in the auditorium who was paying almost no attention to the poet was Savva Kitaigorodsky. He could not take his eyes off Nina's thoughtful face, which seemed illuminated from within. When she doesn't have some "proletarian" sitting next to her, he thought, she immediately changes, she lights up in just this way, and therein, kind ladies and gentlemen, lies her essence!

A whisper from the "literary girl" just in front of him distracted Savva from these thoughts.

"You know, Kalistratov is on the point of a break with LEF!"

Savva shuddered. "Why, what are you saying? What about the Revolution?"

She looked back at him over her shoulder and smiled. "Some people are already fed up with it."

Someone in the audience threw Stepan a bouquet of flowers. With a dexterity that was surprising for an eternally drunk bohemian he caught it before it hit the floor, clutched it to his chest, then reached down into the first row of seats and handed it to Nina Gradov.

The students all craned their necks to see who had received this greeting from the poet. Nina's bright red cheeks could be seen through the carnations.

The "literary girl" whispered directly into Savva's ear: "Do you know that person? The young poetess Nina Gradov. They say that—"

"Excuse me," said Savva hastily, interrupting her, and began to make his way to the door.

Meanwhile, Semyon Stroilo, again paying no attention whatsoever to the feet of the people sitting in the same row, was returning to his place next to Nina. Flopping into his seat without saying a word, he snatched the bouquet out of her hands and tossed it behind her seat, one row higher up in the amphitheater.

In the meantime Stepan was delivering his most celebrated poem, "The Dance of the Sailors," puffing up his lungs more and more with each line.

The young Pythagoras, powerful but of a gentle disposition, tried not to make too much noise as his clawed paws struck the floor, moving from room to empty room illuminated only by strips of moonlight filtered through the shutters. Sometimes he would go to the kitchen and, standing on his hind legs, look through the open window. Finally, he saw what he had been waiting for so zealously, raced to the front door, and sat down next to it, whimpering softly.

A key turned in the lock, and Nina came in. Immediately she began to remove her shoes, so as to glide along the floors as lightly as possible, not waking family members but rather wafting sweet dreams their way. The dog rushed up to his favorite sister to give her a kiss. She hugged him in return. "Thanks for waiting up, Pythy, and for not barking."

Accompanied by Pythagoras, she crossed the dining room and the living room, then suddenly noticed a small lamp on in her father's study. She peeked in and saw her father. He was sitting on the couch in his dressing gown and slippers reading the copy of *Novy Mir* containing "The Tale of the Unextinguished Moon."

Nina was very touched—dear, sweet Papa, she thought, and was about to cross over to the staircase, when he suddenly raised his head and saw two favorite faces: one with big eyes, the other with big ears. He put down the journal.

"Nina, come sit with me awhile."

She sat down on the rug, at his feet. He tousled her short hair.

"This short story you brought into the house . . . it happened to end up here in my study. . . . It's rather an abstract work . . . though if one wanted to . . ." He mumbled on in this way for a short while but then said with sudden firmness, "You have to know that I wasn't there. I was pushed aside at the last minute. And of course, if I had been there, then . . . do you understand what I mean?"

Nina took his hand and pressed her cheek against it. "I understand, Papa. I understand everything now. I don't believe you were there at all."

He sighed. "Alas, that's not entirely true. I'll tell you about it all later, but . . . They, of course, think I'm not one of them. They kick me upstairs as though they were trying to tie everything up in one neat package, they reward me, but all the time they understand perfectly well that I'm not one of them. My whole school and I, we're just Russian doctors, even kids like Savva Kitaigorodsky."

"How's he doing, that Savva?" asked Nina in a tone that showed that she was not entirely indifferent to him.

How wonderfully she asked about him, thought her father. I would certainly want to know if any girl were asking about me that way.

"Oh," he said, "Savva is a rising star, believe me. We're doing good work together on local anesthesia. He has a rather hard time of it, you know—he supports his sister's family, and you know that young doctors are paid very poorly. He moonlights in the emergency room."

"And why is it that he's stopped . . . visiting us?" asked Nina, again to the delight of her father, this time because of an exquisite cunning in her voice.

He chuckled.

"You know perfectly well why, you little fox. Because you've joined the other side."

She caressed his hand like a kitten and said: "What nonsense!"

Pythagoras, lying next to her, began eagerly licking her leg.

Upstairs, Mary Vakhtangovna came out of the bedroom and quietly descended the stairs. She stopped in the doorway of the study, looking at her husband and daughter, who had not noticed her.

"Oh, if only we had all been born fifty years earlier!" sighed the professor.

Nina's temper ignited, and she dropped her father's hand. "Oh, no! Believe it or not, just as you please, but I'm happy that I'm living right at this moment! Happy that I'm young right at this moment, in the twenties of the twentieth century! All other times pale beside ours!"

Her father looked at her. "Please don't shout, Nina, but I think you need to leave Moscow for a while."

Nina, of course, immediately began to shout: "Have you lost your mind, Papa? Where would I go?"

At that moment, her mother sat down beside her and took her by the shoulders. "Maybe to Tiflis, to stay with Uncle Galaktion," she said in a gentle murmur. "Sweetie, you've gone too far with your passion for politics. Your papa's chauffeur, Junior Commander Slabopetukhovsky, said just the other day to Agasha that the OGPU is taking an interest in you."

Nina, even though her heart skipped a beat, squeezed out a laugh. "Oh, that's rubbish! You believe Slabopetukhovsky, of all people! Of course the OGPU is full of nitwits, but still, this isn't the Mussolini regime!"

She suddenly jumped up and took her mother by the hand. "Wouldn't it be better if you played for us, Mama!"

Mary Vakhtangovna smiled.

"We're not allowed to play at night anymore. There's a baby in the house. We might wake little Boris."

Nina insisted and tugged at her mother's hand. "Please, please, very quietly! Play that Chopin nocturne, you know the one." She had almost gotten her way, and her mother pulled herself up from the carpet.

Laughing, she sat down at the piano. "Why, this is just old palace romanticism, you should renounce it—after all, you love jazz, the avant-garde."

She began to play, so softly she could barely be heard. Her husband and her daughter listened reverently, exchanging affectionate glances. Pythagoras began to listen as well, sitting up in the ideal pose of the obedient dog and twitching his ears. Agasha appeared and stood in the doorway. Nikita and Veronika came down from their bedroom upstairs. Now that she had given birth, Veronika had returned to her usual business—that is, looking beautiful. Kirill, it turned out, had already been sitting on the stairs for a long time, listening with his eyes closed. When both of the wide doors to the study were opened, it was as though one could see the entire extent of the sturdy old house. Nina looked around at the expanse of the family nest. My God, she thought, how I love them all, even that silly Kirill! I just don't have the right to love them all so much.

In the bedroom the awakened child began to cry. Mary Vakhtangovna stopped playing. "Well, there you have it, Boris the Fourth is displeased!"

The first snow fell at the end of October. Physicist Leonid Valentinovich Pulkovo was traveling in a streetcar in the Chistye Prudy quarter when the almost weightless crystals began gliding across the milky white streaks of the light blue sky. Automatically registering that Indian summer was over, he prepared to get off at his stop. He was in no mood to take much notice of nature—in the last few days, the men shadowing him had become more than merely annoying; now it was as if they were making a show of it. Take, for example, that character in the derby waiting on the observation platform— obviously a spook. Not only is he not trying to hide, it's as though he wants to be seen. He is showing, as though he were acting in a film, that it is precisely that gentleman in the English raglan and round astrakhan who is the object of concern. Even the Muscovites, who were never surprised by anything, turned and looked.

The streetcar braked at the stop, and the police operative, again demonstratively drawing attention to himself, leaned out of the car and pointed at Pulkovo—here he is, said the gesture, everything is in order!

Two men were waiting for Pulkovo. They were not hiding either. They made a sign of reply to the gesticulations of the man on the streetcar and grinned slyly at the professor getting off.

Pulkovo tipped his hat ironically as he passed them. The two men went into fits of giggles and looked at each other, then set off after the "noneradicated bourgeois," keeping the accepted distance—that is, following very closely.

Over the last few days Pulkovo had begun to regret that he had not accepted Bo's invitation to move to Silver Forest. He could no longer be sure someone wouldn't break into his bachelor apartment while he was out. He could not even be sure there wouldn't be a burglary during the night as he slept.

He ran into spooks everywhere he went—on the stairs or entrance of his building, in trolleys, in bookstores, inside and outside the Institute, even at concerts at the Conservatory, to which he had been a ticket subscriber for years. What was to be done? To appeal to the regular police would be ridiculous; to write a letter of complaint to the OGPU would be humiliating.

He turned into the street where he lived and saw a large black automobile parked immediately beneath the frosted-glass art nouveau marquee. A man in a Red Army uniform was sitting behind the wheel. That's what I like to see, he thought, and he began to feel better: at last everything would be cleared up. Two men, one in a civilian overcoat, the other in the uniform of the OGPU, got out of the car and came toward him.

"Professor Pulkovo, Leonid Valentinovich?" asked the first agent. "Hello, we are from the OGPU. Please familiarize yourself with this document. It's an order to search your apartment."

After holding the order, correct in all its particulars, in his strangely steady hand for a second—where did this self-control come from? he thought— Pulkovo returned the document to the man who had handed it to him.

"What are you looking for, then?" he asked with a smile. The second agent immediately fired back in a somber, mechanical voice: "We'll ask the questions here!"

The Red Army soldier, his hand resting on the handle of a large-caliber pistol suspended from his belt, had already taken up a position behind the professor. With a courtly gesture, Pulkovo invited them all to come inside.

The search was almost finished. The first police operative, having rooted through the professor's desk, closed all the drawers and joined his partner, who had gone over all of the upper bookshelves. Pulkovo, as was proper, was sitting in his deep armchair smoking a pipe, his cat nestled in his lap.

From the cat's point of view, nothing out of the ordinary was happening in the cozy bachelor apartment, where, unfortunately, the odor of tobacco usually prevailed over those of his feline charms. Just two book lovers who had come to see Papa. Not even the fact that there was a soldier standing stock still in the doorway seemed unusual to the cat. "Well, that's it," said the first agent, the man in expensive civilian clothes. "We're confiscating nothing except for this." He pointed to a map of England on the wall, with little flags marking the places the professor had visited.

"What do you want with that?" said the professor in some amazement.

"Everything will be explained to you later. Right now, though, Professor, you'll have to come with us."

"Am I to understand that I'm under arrest?" Pulkovo quickly uttered the words he had been turning over in his mind while the secret policemen went through his papers and books.

The agent smiled. "Let's call it an extremely important meeting."

Pulkovo shrugged. "Then I can decline to go, if it's not a formal arrest."

"That is impossible, Professor. You will go." He bent down and took Pulkovo's luxuriant Persian cat from his knees.

The cat did not like it at all. No one except Papa had the right to pick him up by the stomach. He hissed and scratched the hand of the "bibliophile."

The second secret policeman, the one whose insignia indicated his junior rank, took the map of England down from the wall and began to roll it up. It was only then, at the sight of this seemingly perfectly normal action, that Pulkovo gave a sort of inadequate, almost convulsive, shudder.

"Do you have any iodine?" asked the first agent, holding his clawed hand.

Dusk was just beginning to fall when the car carrying Pulkovo emerged onto Lubyanka Square, teeming with horse-drawn carts and trucks. The massive, regrettably well known prison building in the fin-de-siècle style was coming closer through the ever-increasing snow. At present, at the height of NEP, the building, which had at one time been the offices of a peaceful insurance company, did not inspire the same sort of trepidation that it had in the days of the Red terror and war communism, though even now people as a general rule preferred not to mention it, and if the subject came up, it was touched on obliquely, with an ambiguous smile, a momentary awkward change of gesture or gait, all of which was indisputable proof of people's ingrained fear of the place. In the bars, when the weather was cold, the men of Moscow would sometimes have conversations about "the cellars of the Lubyanka," where, even now, supposedly, dirty work was still going on. Rumors were going around the city about the three most ruthless Lubyanka executioners, who were nicknamed as though after characters in a gothic tale by Nikolai Gogol—Fish, Maga, and Gel.

The intellectual circles were saying all kinds of things about Vyacheslav Rudolfovich Menzhinsky, the new chairman of the OGPU, a secret police veteran who had once again made his way to the top of the heap. It was known that he had come from St. Petersburg, from the family of a high government official of Polish nobility, which meant that like his predecessor, Dzerzhinsky, he was a Catholic who had apostatized at the time of the Revolution. In the days before the catastrophes of war and civil war, he had hardly been what one might call a Leninist stalwart, on occasion even publishing insulting pamphlets directed at the leader of the laboring masses. Lenin, however, precisely because of Menzhinsky's exceptional intellect, had named him to the post of people's commissar for finance and later, because of certain other exceptional capabilities, had made him chairman of the Cheka, a position he had occupied during the years 1919 to 1923. The talk about his personal conduct contained rumors that directly contradicted one another— according to some, he was a shameless profligate, a womanizer, and an adulterer, while others held that he was a complete ascetic, a sort of a sectarian fanatic like his predecessor, Felix Edmundovich.

The car rolled by the huge heavy portals that led into the Lubyanka's interior courtyard and stopped before an impressive entrance. Slightly encouraged that they had not driven into the closed interior yard, Leonid Valentinovich climbed out at a sign from one of the men in the car, and, looking at the façade before him, said with a nervous laugh: "Aha, here we are at the 'Salamander'!"

The agent behind him coldly cut off this ill-timed joke. "This is the State Political Directorate."

"Everyone but the birds in the trees knows that," said Pulkovo, still trying to make light of the affair. "But we Moscow old-timers still remember your predecessors, the Salamander Insurance Company."

"Follow me, Citizen Pulkovo!" said the agent.

Leonid Valentinovich felt cold all over and then almost immediately broke out in streams of warm perspiration. He suddenly realized that not once so far had they called him "comrade," the term of respect, but only "professor," and now even this cold, alienated title had turned into the ominous "citizen," the form of address used with people under arrest, prisoners and enemies. Holding on nonetheless to the gallows humor in which he found his saving grace, he murmured, "Aha, now I understand. . . . The equation is reaching its solution. . . ."

They're probably going to send me to Solovki, he thought, as he walked along the corridors of the "Luba" in the company of the two agents. They say you can survive there, that there are lots of intelligent people. After all, they're not going to kill me—it's not as though they're going to send me to the cellars.

Meanwhile, there seemed to be nothing sinister about his surroundings. He was led first into a huge entrance hall with a portrait of Lenin, where several guards, laughing among themselves, took no notice of him. Then they went up one flight of an ornate staircase, which had been designed to make an impression of solidity on Salamander clientele, and went into an elevator.

Then, however, instead of the expected ascent, the elevator went down. Leonid Valentinovich's heart sank like a stone into the ocean depths. So we're going to the cellars after all? The elevator came to a stop. But instead of gloomy arches and instruments of torture, Pulkovo saw before him a brightly lit corridor lined by numerous doors. The soothing clatter of typewriters could be heard from behind several of the doors. Suddenly a long, fierce howl could be heard from somewhere: must be a man being tortured, he thought. They led the professor into another elevator, and this time they went up. Finally, pale and bewildered, he was led up to two carved stained-oak doors.

The office of the Salamander director (the firm's name had been attractive to its clients—we won't burn in a fire, it seemed to say) was now, quite logically, the office of V. R. Menzhinsky, chairman of the OGPU. Pulkovo looked around at the mahogany furniture, the large Persian rug, the desk with a green fabric top, and the portraits of Lenin and Dzerzhinsky.

Behind the desk sat a man of intelligent appearance with a part in his hair. He rose as though he had been pleasantly surprised and, hand outstretched, strode toward Pulkovo, who had just come in, or rather just been led in.

"Very pleased to meet you, Comrade Pulkovo. Thank you for coming. I'm Menzhinsky."

Pulkovo shook his hand and, making no attempt to hide his relief, took out a handkerchief and began to mop his face and brow energetically. "A pleasure for me too, Comrade Menzhinsky." He tried to remember another bit of primordial gallows humor but came out with only a weak attempt. "I must confess that it was quite a journey from his 'citizen,' " he said, indicating one of the agents with his eyes, "to your 'comrade.' "

Menzhinsky laughed good-naturedly. "Our comrades do go a bit over the top sometimes." He took the professor by the arm, led him further into the office, and said in a confiding tone, "They're men with a heroic past, but their nerves aren't always the steadiest."

He then conducted Pulkovo over to a corner of the office where there were two chairs and a small table. He turned to the agents.

"Comrades, why didn't you simply explain to Comrade Pulkovo that I wanted to talk to him? What's all this secrecy, then? Very well, you can go."

There would be no point in bringing up the search, thought Pulkovo.

Menzhinsky turned back to him. "Have a seat, Leonid Valentinovich. Would you like some cognac?"

"Thank you, I won't say no."

Menzhinsky poured the cognac and showed the professor the label. "It used to be called Shustov cognac, now it's just Armenian. Five stars! In my opinion, it beats Martel. Here's to your health!" He took a large swallow, then moved his chair forward and smilingly watched for a few seconds as his guest's face flushed and returned to life. Then he proceeded to the matter at hand.

"Leonid Valentinovich, I've heard a great deal about your voyage to England last year. The government finds that it was beneficial for Soviet science. In principle, that's just what I wished to speak with you about—some of the perspectives of modern science. However, before we begin I should like to clarify our information about some of the meetings you had there with certain people . . ."

Once again, everything seemed to crumble inside the motionless Pulkovo, who was rapidly becoming petrified. Could it be they've gotten wind of it? What's wrong with it, in the final analysis? After all, it's strictly personal, a private matter . . . do they mean to say even *this* is criminal now?

"First of all, your meeting with Mr. Krasin," continued Menzhinsky without taking his cold, inquiring, and frankly not particularly gentlemanly eyes off the professor.

The sigh of relief that escaped from Pulkovo did not go unnoticed. It seemed as though even the slightest twitch of his facial muscles was recorded by that stare.

"Excuse me, Vyacheslav Rudolfovich, but are you talking about Comrade Krasin, our ambassador? The one who died several months ago?"

The unblinking eyes came closer. "He died at a very convenient time, this Mr. Krasin. Do you take my meaning?"

"Forgive me, but no, I understand nothing whatsoever. After all, Krasin was our ambassador to France at the time that I visited that country. It was in Paris, on the return trip from England, that I was introduced—"

"We know that," Menzhinsky cut in. "But what about England? During your stay there, Krasin went to England twice. Didn't he introduce you to some members of the British government?"

"How could he introduce me to anyone if I never saw him?" muttered Pulkovo.

Menzhinsky forced a laugh. "A sound answer, Comrade Pulkovo."

A thought that was neither here nor there suddenly came to Pulkovo—had it not been for the Revolution, Menzhinsky would never have become head of the secret police. He would have been some sort of left-wing journalist, or maybe a stockbroker. Maybe the Revolution can make a police agent out of anyone?

"It is your good fortune, Leonid Valentinovich—" continued Menzhinsky in a light, amicable tone, "—your good fortune that you did not meet Krasin in England, my friend . . . neither in the hotel where you stayed on your way to Cambridge from London, nor in the Athenaeum Club. . . . It's a good thing you met him nowhere else besides Paris. . . . Where was the meeting? I can't remember offhand—in the reception room of the political representative's office, I believe. . . . I'll open the shades a bit if you like. You see, Krasin has already been canonized, as it were, and the truth about his ties to the British will never come out, though things will go badly for the people who had the misfortune to be involved with him in this connection.

"I appreciate your worth as a scientist, Leonid Valentinovich. I have something of an amateur interest in modern physics, you know. This branch of science is the wave of the future. It would be very distressing if our most talented minds were to become mixed up in unsavory political matters. People such as Krasin and his friends in British intelligence are no fit company for you, Professor. You would do better to stick to your own kind, my dear man. For example, be as friendly as you please with Ernest Rutherford . . . by the way, do tell me about him!"

In saying all of this, the chief of the mighty department had poured himself two more glasses of cognac without offering so much as a sip to his guest. It even seemed to Pulkovo that those all-penetrating eyes were beginning to cloud over slightly. He began to talk to Menzhinsky about Rutherford's work. What is there to say about a scientific genius if one doesn't talk about his work?

"After inducing an artificial nuclear reaction for the first time, Rutherford has confined his work to this domain. He has predicted the existence of neutrinos and hopes to isolate one of these particles in the course of laboratory experiments. Yes, we are good friends—Ernest is very interested in my research in the area of cryogenics and in the idea of high-quality electrical discharges in solid gases . . ."

Menzhinsky listened attentively, nodding, then suddenly slapped Pulkovo on the knee and laughed drunkenly. "Well, what do you think of Meyerhold, Leonid? He made fools out of all of us with his Gogol! You know, I went to see *The Inspector General*—incognito, of course—to relax, have a laugh . . . but instead of relaxation . . . well, up on the stage they were babbling all kinds of nonsense, the scenery was a horror, everything smelled of sulfur. . . . I ask you, that isn't the sort of thing our workers and peasants need, is it?"

Without waiting for a reply, Menzhinsky rose and went over to his desk. He changed his mind en route and instead headed toward a small door in a far corner of the office. His walk was now decidedly unsteady. Reaching the door, he turned to the physicist. "We're living on the edge of some sort of mysticism," he said. "I read recently that your friend Rutherford has proposed a theory of the planetary construction of the atom. Does that mean our solar system could turn out to be a mere atom and the earth one of its electrons?"

"One cannot exclude the possibility," said Pulkovo.

"Ha, ha!" cried Menzhinsky. "Very impressive!" Still laughing, he opened the door and went into an adjacent room.

For several minutes Pulkovo sat by himself, trying to gather his thoughts, which seemed as elusive as neutrinos, trying to understand what all of this meant and why the secret police had suddenly taken such an interest in nuclear physics.

When Menzhinsky came back, he was perfectly sober—it was impossible to tell whether he had really been drunk just a minute before or if he had only been acting—and sat down next to Pulkovo. For a few seconds he regarded him silently and then asked severely, "Leonid Valentinovich, is it true that atomic research could lead to the creation of a weapon of mass destruction?"

By nightfall the snow was quickly melting in the sudden thaw that had arrived in the Moscow region. While the strong southerly wind tore umbrellas from the hands of their owners and sent them flapping along the ground, two friends, Leo and Bo, were leaning on each other as they walked down an empty dacha-lined street in Silver Forest.

"How did you answer the question about an atomic weapon?" asked Gradov.

Pulkovo shrugged. "I said it would take at least another hundred years."

Gradov smiled. "They're strange people, these Bolsheviks. In spite of all their materialism, their actions seem to be dictated by some kind of mysticism. How do you explain, for example, embalming Lenin and then putting his remains on display to be worshiped? As far as time is concerned, it seems to me that they want to unceremoniously divide it by four. Maybe the atomic weapon has saved you, Leo—they want to have it within a quarter of a century . . ."

A big figure of a drunk man in a police uniform rose up from behind a fence and roared gleefully, "That's right, Professor! You'll give them that weapon within a quarter of a century!"

"Slabopetukhovsky!" shouted Professor Gradov. "What are you doing here? Eavesdropping again? And why are you in the uniform of the regular police?"

Slabopetukhovsky, very pleased with the effect that he had produced, reported gaily, "I've been discharged from the heroic Worker-Peasant Red Army, and I've joined our heroic police force, Comrade Professor. Agafia Yermolaevna won't let me get away with anything; I've been your district constable for three days now. Let me ask a personal question—you wouldn't happen to have three rubles in your pocket that aren't doing anything, would you?"

At the end of the month Nikita, Veronika, and Boris IV went back to Minsk. Strictly speaking, only the parents were returning—the child, a haughty native Muscovite, was making his first journey.

The Gradov family gathered, with much shoving and commotion, at the Byelorussia Station, on the platform next to the so-called "international" sleeping car. Mary came from the house, bringing her favorite grandson; Boris Nikitovich arrived shortly after her; and then Kirill approached with an intent stride.

Nikita held Boris IV in his arms—the hefty little tot breathed on his cheek in faint snorts, filling the entire being of the division commander with an unheard-of tenderness. Agasha, former Junior Officer and now Local Constable Slabopetukhovsky, and an unknown Red Army officer sent from the Commissariat for Defense were finishing loading the baggage.

"Why are there so many military people on the platform?" Kirill asked his older brother. The fact that he had the right to ask such a question, and that he expected an answer, was clearly written on his youthful face.

"Important maneuvers at the Polish frontier."

"Here now," said Mary, "let me hold the very best child in the world." Boris IV made the trip to her arms and now began to sniffle on her cheek as well.

"Where's Veronika, then?" asked Boris Nikitovich.

"She stopped off on the way to buy newspapers," said Nikita and mounted the first step into the car in order to try to see his wife above the crowd. "There she is! That's her favorite trick—forgetting about everything in the world!"

Veronika was slowly advancing with a rustle of newspapers through the crowds of the arriving and the departing, civilians and soldiers, peasants and government workers. Engrossed in one of her papers, she noticed nothing around her, not even a suspicious band of street urchins.

Suddenly someone from the crowd approached her and spoke to her softly: "Veronika Yevgenievna!"

She looked up and recognized Regimental Commander Vadim Vuinovich. Swarthy, broad at the shoulders, and slim at the waist, looking even more like someone from the Caucasus than the half-Georgian Nikita, he looked at her with undisguised delight, or rather with delight that he could not have hidden anyway. It seemed as though at any second he would throw himself upon her in a fit of amorous dizziness.

Veronika laughed. "Vadim! You scared me! Whispering like a spy, 'Veronika Yevgenievna!' " She had long understood the sort of feeling the man had for her and instinctively always tried to lower the tone, to transform any passionate theatrics into light, ambiguous repartee.

"Pardon me, I didn't want to speak to you, but—but—" mumbled Vadim.

"Are you going to Minsk too?" she asked. "Come along to our compartment. You can meet his Highness, Boris the Fourth."

From the step of the car Nikita saw Veronika and Vadim walking alongside each other. He knew his former friend had no business here except shadowing his wife. A certain gloom descended upon him, and then he noticed a small detachment of sailors, perhaps half a platoon, marching energetically down the platform in their black uniforms with shiny buttons, ribbons fluttering from their visorless caps, led by a broad-chested seaman with a boatswain's whistle. Nikita had a sudden feeling that at any moment they would take aim at him, thereby avenging themselves for Kronstadt—instantaneously and without ceremony.

"No, I'm not going to come to your compartment," Vadim said to Veronika quietly. "I only wanted to wish you happiness."

Veronika laughed even more brightly and took him by the hand. "What a strange fellow! To wish me happiness!'' She waved to her husband with the pile of newspapers she had just bought. ''Nikita, look who I've found!''

Vadim let go of her hand, walked away, and disappeared into the crowd.

The detachment of sailors stopped and executed a left face beside the "international" sleeper, which was carrying not only Division Commander Gradov but Tukhachevsky, commander in chief of the Western Military District, as well. It turned out that they were nothing more than musicians. A moment later they struck up "The Red Partisans."

At the last minute before the train pulled out, Nina came rushing down the platform like a speedboat. She had just enough time to hug her brother, give her sister-in-law a kiss, and to bounce her haughty nephew in the air.

The train began to move off slowly. Nikita and Veronika were standing in the door of the car with their arms around each other, laughing and blowing kisses. Everything was going just as planned to the strains of a bravura performance of a song that had been sung by both sides in the Civil War. Those who had brought them to the station were waving their hands, handkerchiefs, and hats. Mary Vakhtangovna, who could not bear to see the departure of her beloved grandson, buried her face in her husband's scarf. Police Officer Slabopetukhovsky kept reaching into his boot to draw out a small flask of vodka. He clearly seemed to be traveling back in time in his mind, shouting, "The division has moved forward! On to Warsaw!" after the train.

"Stop it, Slabopetukhovsky!" Kirill Gradov said to him severely. "Don't you understand what nonsense you're talking?"

The policeman extended his prized flask toward the young Party member and was very surprised when his generous hand was soundly repulsed.

CHAPTER SEVEN

Trotsky's on the Wall, Glasses on His Nose!

*

In November 1927, Townsend Reston once again left his headquarters in Paris in order to take a trip to the "Red East." The purpose for this visit, unlike the one of two years before, was quite clearly defined—to shed some light on the grandiose celebrations in preparation for the tenth anniversary of the October Revolution.

It had been a decade of undreamed-of power, next to which even the black-shirted witches' Sabbath of Mussolini and his speeches seemed like commedia dell'arte. The Soviet government stood unshakable, with no intention of changing, that is, of losing any of its inconceivability, of returning to something more like normalcy, as predicted by Mr. "Astrelow," as Reston called his interlocutor of two years ago, the theoretician of the Change of Landmarks movement.

In contrast to the émigré professor, Reston did not feel any sort of holy fear of the "historical mission of Russia," assuming that he had ever supposed that such a mission existed and that the civilized world would have to reckon with it. He saw only the utter absurdity and brazen impudence of the government that had arisen from the ashes of the old empire and did not doubt for a minute that they would crush this NEP of theirs as soon as it had ceased to be useful to them.

Reston's first series of articles on Russia, which he had in fact written in the form of discussions with "a historian whose counsel he had sought," had been a success. Afterward, Reston kept his eyes forever riveted on the East. He knew about the struggle that was going on within the Party, and didn't believe either side for a second. Ustryalov, of course, would have seized on the fact that the official party line was wearing down the opposition with its ultrarevolutionary slogans as proof that the idea of stable government was taking hold. Stalin is a pragmatist, he would say, he needs a strong central authority, not a worldwide conflagration, he needs NEP, financial solvency, a reliable system of supply, and a satisfied, adequately fed people. "Bullshit," muttered Reston in reply to this imagined thesis. Communism, he thought, is getting stronger and more sinister in this country every year, and it is the Party line that's doing it, not those windbags in the opposition. The opposition, all of its demoniac energy notwithstanding, is still just a vestige of liberalism. Genuine communism will begin with Stalin.

On the morning of the seventh of November Reston left the National Hotel and headed on foot for Red Square, which he had obtained written permission to enter through the efforts of the All-Union Society for Cultural Ties with Foreign Countries. He was accompanied by a translator supplied by the society—Galina, a young blond creature with the mannerisms of a poorly trained racehorse. She was constantly making jerky movements to one side or the other and trying to look in every direction at once.

Maybe I should sleep with her after all, thought Reston. It probably wouldn't be a very pleasurable experience, but at least he could boast to Hemingway, next time they were at the Closerie des Lilas, that he had slept with an agent of the Russian secret police.

He put his hand on her just below her waist. Galina's rump immediately slipped away from beneath his hand the way a drifting block of ice might slip out from under a boot when stepped on. Her heavy boots broke into a nervous trot.

"Please translate these slogans for me," Reston asked.

The entire length of Manège Square was filled with groups of parade participants, who were standing at ease, marching in place, or beginning to move off in the direction of the Kremlin. The grayness of the day was warmed by monochromatic red banners blazing everywhere. Portraits of Lenin, Stalin, Bukharin, and other members of the Politburo looked down from the walls of the Historical Museum, the Grand Hotel, and the former Duma building. Actually, thought Reston, all of these pictures are of only one face, they just change the beards and mustaches around.

In a triumphant voice, Galina translated the exhortations on the gigantic banner on the façade of the Historical Museum.

"Red banners, higher! Workers of the world! Toilers of the soil! Prepare yourselves, organize the victory of the worldwide revolution!"

So that's how it is, thought Reston with an ironic smile. Where, then, are your differences of principle, Mr. Ustryalov?

The Red Army units passing by were trying out something new—an egg-shaped steel helmet. A women's medical unit passed by with their heads covered by blue kerchiefs. A civil defense regiment marched in place. Next to them stood a regiment of the Red frontline fighters of Germany, some of whom, despite the damp Moscow cold, were wearing *Lederhosen.* Their thighs were a healthy milk-white color. The frontline fighters were a source of amazement to the Moscow crowd. A tipsy fellow in a proletarian forage cap shouted to them in a voice on the verge of tears, "Machine guns, brothers, machine guns are what you need! Then you'd show Hindenburg a thing or two!"

"Sieg heil!" roared the Germans, who had been well fed during their stay in Moscow.

The speech which Bukharin was delivering from the tribune above the Lenin Mausoleum began to crackle over the loudspeakers installed at various places around the square. The parade began, and Reston and his translator picked up their pace.

"Workers!" Bukharin called out theatrically. "Laboring peasants! Fighting men of the army and navy! For five years we struggled, rifle in hand, against forces of the enemy incalculable in number! We smashed them to pieces! We broke the back of the landowner! We overthrew the capitalist rabble! For five years we fought against poverty and ruin, against the parasites of private capital! We raised the country up out of the abyss, and we are now advancing! We are closing in on the capitalist, surrounding the kulak! Who are we? The masses! Millions! Laborers, workers, and peasants! Long live the Great October Revolution!"

And after speeches like that people still hope for something, thought Reston.

Meanwhile, as he walked along and, without slowing down, made notes on a small stenographic pad with his gold-tipped Mont Blanc, Galina was watching him, "a difficult guest, even dangerous," as she had been warned. Besides, why shouldn't he give me his fountain pen as a present? Oh, I'd go crazy over a pen like that!

"Tell me, Galina, is it true that the opposition is preparing to come out today?" asked Reston. "They say there's going to be some sort of counter-demonstration—or haven't you heard?"

She began to tremble all over. They were right to warn me, she thought—a dangerous man!

"How can you ask things like that on such a day, Mr. Reston? A national holiday, Mr. Reston! Do you mean you are not sympathetic toward our country?"

"No, I'm not," growled Reston under his breath.

At ten o'clock, a fiery Roman numeral X was lit on the Kremlin wall. Commissar Voroshilov emerged from the gates of Spasskaya Tower riding a white horse. He was a competent horseman and looked comfortable in the saddle. He plainly relished the day's assignment—to be watched by thousands as the "first Red officer"!

After the ceremony of the delivery of reports was finished, Budyonny's cavalry went past the Mausoleum. The horsemen were wearing their characteristic helmets, which terminated in a sharp point, and carrying staffs with different colored flags.

A strange uniform, scribbled Reston, repeating his notes of 1925. An army of chaos, Gog and Magog.

As if to strengthen this impression on the part of the "dangerous guest," a regiment drawn from one of the Caucasian nationalities thundered across the square at full gallop, their black felt cloaks and blue hoods flying.

In the stands that had been set up for foreign guests, chiefly delegations of the Communist parties of various countries, everyone was delighted. Looking around, Reston saw numerous people with shining eyes and fists raised in a proletarian greeting.

Someone, apparently the Spaniards, broke into the "International." Immediately the entire tribune erupted into song as well, each group singing it in its own language. Someone put his hand on Reston's shoulder, thinking that he was with them. You bastards, thought the journalist, smiling and showing all thirty-two of his American teeth.

. . .

The lounge behind the tribune contained a buffet well stocked with wine, zakuski, and a huge samovar. There was a constant traffic of party leaders in and out of the room, among them the all-too-familiar faces of Molotov, Kalinin, Tomsky, Yenukidze, Klara Zetkin, Galakher, Weyan, Couturier. . . . The music and noise of the parade could be heard through the open doors.

Stalin and Bukharin were sitting in a corner sipping tea. Nikolai Ivanovich was rattling his glass in its holder in his hand, which had nothing of the working class about it. Iosif Vissarionovich, the embodiment of steady nerves, was eating one piece of caviar-smeared bread after another. Like all Georgians, he was a great eater. Bukharin, a true descendant of the talentless class of positivist intellectuals, was gulping his food down without much relish. He whispered, "Iosif, we have precise information that the opposition is going to come out, at least in Moscow and Leningrad."

Stalin smiled, which in his case meant only that behind the mustache his mouth lost some of its hardness. "Don't worry, Nikolai. The working class will not permit a handful of scoundrels to get away with their outrages."

"Has Menzhinsky been informed?" asked Bukharin nervously.

Stalin cracked another enigmatic smile. "Don't worry, dear friend."

Meanwhile, the character of the noise outside had changed. The measured tread of marching feet died away. Several different military bands were playing at once, and the soles of thousands more shoes came shuffling along, mixed with a chaotic babble of voices and ardent shouts of love and support for the government. The demonstration of the workers of the capital had begun.

Reston asked his translator to explain whom the wildly caricatured effigies the crowd was carrying were supposed to represent. At first Galina sighed. Then she rolled her eyes in resignation—well, why not? It's just political satire. But then, biting her lip, almost maliciously, in a tone that seemed to say "You and your damned curiosity!" she replied, "MacDonald and Chamberlain, the leaders of British imperialism."

Aha, it's clear now, thought Reston. Even he was beginning to make sense out of things. Next came a huge plywood figure of a worker with a sledgehammer, and before him several imperialists in top hats, smoking cigars, their teeth bared in an evil grin. The moving sledgehammer would deliver a just punishment to the imperialists, then it would rise and the top hats would spring back into place. "Funny how he can't deliver a crushing blow once and for all, or else there wouldn't be any more show," wrote Reston with malicious glee in his notebook.

After that came a huge column of Chinese, carrying imperialist scarecrows on poles, and then that was all for the satirical symbolism. Next were columns of Moscow workers bearing posters and cheerful diagrams with moving parts that testified to their achievements. Here and there portraits of Stalin, Kalinin, and Rykov bobbed by. The representatives of the various enterprises were yelling through galvanized tin megaphones: "Long live Stalin!"

"Long live Kalinin, our great Elder of the Union!" "Long live the Soviet government of our motherland!"

The workers of the Iliich factory unfurled a wide banner that read FOR LENINISM, AGAINST TROTSKYISM!

Tverskaya Street, Moscow's main thoroughfare, lined with hotels, restaurants, and shops, was jammed with demonstrators slowly making their way toward Red Square. On the whole the weather favored an outpouring of emotion, not to mention of invigorating spirits. The bands were cheering people up, too, and all was going well.

Above the crowd, six of the leading organizers of the parade were standing on the balcony of the Hotel Paris. They greeted the columns of marchers, shouted revolutionary slogans through megaphones, and scattered leaflets celebrating the holiday. The Mikhelson factory workers passing beneath the balcony responded with loud hurrahs and applause.

"Who are you applauding, comrades?" Kirill Gradov yelled at the top of his lungs. "They belong to the opposition! They're Trotskyites! Schismatics!"

He was standing on the back of a truck with the sidings pushed down. Several other agitators from the Krasnaya Presnya Committee were shouting in all directions along with him.

At first the Mikhelson factory workers only applauded, but then it began to dawn on them that what these comrades were shouting wasn't quite suited to the day's festivities. Then they took a closer look through more class-conscious eyes at the Hotel Paris—there were portraits of Trotsky and Zinoviev in the windows, and what the people up on the balcony were yelling was, if they heard rightly, "Down with Stalinist bureaucracy!" There's another leaflet falling, grab it, Petro, let's read it! Not much here, just a cartoon about our party, comrades. Here, take a look—"The Bolshevik Party behind bars."

"Things are getting sticky now, brothers!" said someone with a laugh. Someone else was waving his fist, roaring: "You've swindled us, you sons of bitches, you've ruined the celebration!" A group of red-cheeked thugs emerged from a side street and began pelting the balcony with apples, shouting, "Beat the scum!"

A dense crowd of at least two hundred opposition supporters was standing in front of the hotel entrance. Most of them looked like students and intellectuals, but there were quite a few workers in their ranks as well. A few opposition slogans were tossed about: "Long live the opposition!" "Long live Comrades Trotsky and Zinoviev, the leaders of the world proletariat!"

More and more young toughs came out of the side streets, disrupting the columns, pulling marchers from the ranks and punching them or throwing them to the ground. More and more rotten apples and galoshes came hurtling in the direction of the speakers on the balcony. The opposition supporters, seeing that serious trouble was brewing, tried to link arms while shouting, "Down with Stalin! Down with Stalinism!" in unison, but their attempts to defend themselves were unskilled and ineffective. It looked more like a gathering of Tolstoyan Christians than one of militant Communists.

Police paddy wagons were now arriving on the scene, along with an ever-increasing number of organized Party loyalists. Together with still other marchers from passing columns, they began to turn the pressure on the opposition forces into a full-scale rout. The oppositionists were throwing away their picket signs, trying to escape from the crowd and hide in entranceways. They were immediately seized by the police and thrown into the wagons.

Kirill could not help trembling as from the back of the Party truck he watched the scene develop. As a member of the Gradov household, he was naturally well versed in literary allusions, and they compelled him to compare what was going on to an incident from the "shameful past," history repeating itself, a case of déjà vu: the Butchers' raid on the Social Democrats' meeting.

Comrade Samokha, beside himself with joy, stood next to him rubbing his hands gleefully. Fighting back his disgust, Kirill buttonholed the secret police agent.

"What's going on, Samokha? Were you the one who unleashed those thugs from Marina Roshcha?"

Samokha, a tall, well-built man, did not even turn back to face the youth. "It's nothing, don't worry about it," he said. "They'll do just fine. Don't be an intellectual sissy, Gradov! History doesn't like to joke around!"

Maybe he's right, thought Kirill. In fact, he's certainly right, it's time to take the white gloves off once and for all, just as Lenin taught. What makes me better than Samokha, anyway? Didn't I happily look on when those two thugs in short-brimmed caps blocked him from coming to the podium?

All of a sudden, not far away, he saw two men—of the same kind he had just been thinking of, wearing those same hats with the visor cut off— dragging away a woman carrying a large picture of Trotsky. One of them tore the picture out of her hands, the other seized her by the hair. Forgetting himself, Kirill leaped from the truck and rushed to her rescue.

Trotsky and the broken stick on which he had been mounted flew sharply out of her hands and was seen one last time for a fraction of a second fixed at an oblique angle over the seething crowd. Then it was trampled in the dirt underfoot, and the ridged sole of a boot stepped on the legendary face. How recently they had sung to the accompaniment of an accordion:

Trotsky's on the wall,
Glasses on his nose,
Just have a look and see
All you dirty bourgeoisie!

Throwing the woman aside, the two lads turned their attention to Kirill. They seized him by the shirt and shoved him up against a door. Their animal snouts were beaming with happiness—ah, life is a carnival!

Kirill resisted, which only made them happier. Now one of them took him by the neck and forced his head down to the ground, while the other twisted his arm behind his back. "Let me go!" Kirill howled in desperation. "I'm not—I'm not a Trotskyite! I'm for—the general line!" The two young toughs brayed in return: "You're for the generals' line, but we're for the soldiers'!"

Samokha, the "knight of the Revolution," clad in his leather armor, approached the struggling threesome at a pace that made it clear that he was in no particular hurry to prevent harm from coming to the "sissy" Gradov. Then he flashed his OGPU identification, a small red booklet, to the two thugs, and they released the Marxist.

Meanwhile, in another part of the capital, on the corner of Mokhovaya and Vozdvizhenka streets, in full view of the Kremlin's stout Kutafia Tower, events were unfolding somewhat differently. Here the opposition had managed to organize itself better. The meeting was better attended and more peaceful. There were no attempts to disrupt the slogans of the "schismatics" or to harm their posters and picket signs. The façade of the Fourth House of Unions Building was decorated with a large picture of Trotsky. The real one appeared from time to time in a window not far away, waving a bundle of theses, just like in his days on the southern front of the Civil War in 1920, and addressed the throng: "The question is very simple, comrades: either the Revolution or Thermidor!"

Thunderous applause and shouts of greeting came up from the street below. Trotsky struck a pose, then turned away from the window and swallowed an aspirin. He had a splitting headache. We should have acted three years ago, he reproached himself. It was the machine gunners we should have appealed to, not students.

Columns of marchers in the official parade were passing along the periphery of the crowd as they moved toward Red Square. They eyed the meeting but expressed no feelings about the slogans they saw on the banners. When Trotsky appeared in the window, though, everyone oohed and ahed. The great leader winced, sure that this was a reaction of curiosity on their part, not of solidarity. They would say "Ah!" the same way, and maybe even more loudly, if Shalyapin were to appear.

One of the dense columns moving by was made up of young people. An observer who looked at this group closely might have thought that they belonged to the opposition rather than to the obedient majority. Nonetheless they advanced quietly, one would have almost said apathetically, trying to pay no attention to the inflammatory appeals coming from the Fourth House of Unions. Semyon Stroilo was carrying a picket reading "Glory to October!" Nina Gradov bore a portrait of the "All-Union Wise Man." The lascivious Kalinin with his beard like a billy goat's and even Albov, the leader of the underground circle, had unashamedly taken up a picture of the despised "Koba." The only thing that mattered to them was reaching Red Square without incident.

The procession of columns again came to a standstill, and Albov's group found itself just opposite the Fourth House of Unions along with the hundreds of young Trotskyites. The small group now couldn't help staring at the people on their side from afar, at the picture of their beloved leader, and at the open window in which the man himself periodically appeared. Albov looked in alarm at his comrades, who were trembling with excitement: Whatever happens, don't break!

Nina Gradov, surveying the scene, whispered to Semyon, "I guarantee this place is crawling with Stalin's agents! Look at those jackals scurrying around, Syomka!"

"It's a fact. Where else would they be?" said Semyon in a deep, strained voice. He put his arm around her shoulders, as if he wished to impart to her the composure of their class, sure of its own rightness. He was scarcely able to keep up the sweeping and measured movement that was the most important element in his masquerade. Everything inside him was quivering and urging him on to the exact opposite—to fidget, look over his shoulder, hide his face. Soon everything will come out. It's sure that she'll understand, finally, who I am, and then they'll see: do you love me or not, professor's daughter? That's when the sincerity of your feelings will be put to the test— which is more important to you, your shitty Trotskyism or your beloved man? After all, I would proudly walk by your side into a new life!

The pretty face of Olechka Lazeikina emerged from behind the signs as though from behind one of Meyerhold's set decorations, and her impassioned whisper could be heard: "There he is, look! It's Lev Davidovich!"

Trotsky had indeed popped up in the window again. He remained motionless for a moment, his hand upraised, and then began to hurl appeals down to the crowd:

"We are for immediate industrialization! We are for Party democracy! Comrades, the flame of the Revolution is about to catch on in Europe and India! China is already growling! The bureaucrats are fetters on the legs of the world revolution!"

The throng beneath the windows once again erupted in applause and shouts of approval, hats were thrown into the air. The workers in the official columns continued to look at the proceedings as though it were a theatrical spectacle. The slow movement toward the Kremlin resumed. Albov whispered to his people, "Easy, lads! We're going to go on quietly. Our objective is Red Square."

Suddenly everyone on Vozdvizhenka Street came to a stop. Someone was letting down a hook from the roof of the Fourth House of Unions. Two pairs of hands reaching from a dormer window were manipulating the rope, trying to maneuver the hook under the edge of the portrait of Trotsky. The opposition supporters were shouting indignantly. A piercing cry of enthusiasm came up from somewhere in the columns: "Look, they're trying to pull down the portrait!"

Trotsky went on for some time shouting his call to arms, oblivious to what was happening, and then froze in another historical posture. The window next to him opened, and his closest ally, Muralov, appeared with a long floor brush in his hands. Climbing halfway out of the window, he scraped the brush along the wall, trying to intercept the sinister OGPU device.

"Hurrah!" roared the delighted marchers, shifting from foot to foot. The battle of the broom and the hook had captivated everyone's attention. Trotsky stepped back from the window and said to those around him, "We've lost. The masses are inert." The state of affairs, however, was quite the opposite: the broom had pushed away the hook, which was retreating in disgrace. The crowd applauded enthusiastically. The leader of the Permanent Revolution was prevented from taking advantage of his only chance by his lack of a sense of humor.

The parade was going to go on all day. The servants in the lounge behind the Mausoleum had already restocked the buffet for the tenth time. From time to time the door to the tribune opened to reveal the stocky figures of the leaders greeting the masses of parade participants. The columns continued to march noisily by, the bands blared, and the ardent shouts of support of the regime's partisans could still be heard.

Stalin's personal Caucasian guard was standing watch inside the Mausoleum. Armed with pistols and daggers, two chevaliers were standing at the doors of the underground tunnel leading from inside the Kremlin grounds into the Mausoleum. Suddenly one of them heard a suspicious noise. Opening the door and peering into the tunnel, he saw three Red Army officers approaching rapidly. "Who let you in here?" yelped the guard. "Stop or I'll shoot!"

Two more members of the guard came running up, their hands on the hilts of their daggers. The three officers came right up to them, trying to push their way through and waving passes in the air. One of them said in a booming voice, "What the hell is this? The head of the academy himself, Robert Petrovich Edelman, sent us on a matter of government security. Here are our passes—Regimental Commander Okhotnikov and Battalion Commanders Geller and Petenko! Get out of the way!"

The leader of the guards took their passes and began to look them over. The Red Army officers, strangely, were bouncing up and down on the balls of their feet, scanning the room where the buffet was being served as though they were looking for someone amid the comings and goings of the Party bosses. The Ossetian guard flung the piercing glance of a wildcat at Okhotnikov, the man with the booming voice. Rising intently on his toes as he did so, the guard leaned forward like a greyhound at the gate.

"There's an improper seal on your pass. Why?"

The guard was still hesitating as to whether or not to presume the worst, but his instinct told him: if you don't act immediately, in another second it may be too late.

Petenko ripped the pass out of his hands. "Even without the seal, can't you see who we are? You can't see our medals, you savage?"

The guard blew his whistle. The lounge immediately filled with reinforcements and workers of the Party Secretariat. A voice rang out: "Lay down your arms!" The door leading to the tribune opened, and Stalin, Rykov, and Yenukidze entered. Someone said in surprise, "What's going on here, comrades?"

At the sight of Stalin, Okhotnikov, Geller, and Petenko rushed forward. The Caucasians hung on, trying to stop them. Everything looked quite absurd: tables were overturned, bottles and plates were smashed to bits, the samovar fell over with a crash in the corner and began to spew forth steam as the frightened Party leaders looked on and the tussle between the Caucasian guard and the officers, by now beside themselves with indignation, continued. Holding sway over everything was the odor of the cognac that had been spilled, so strong as to be nauseating.

All of this went on for several seconds, and during that time Stalin realized that something extremely unpleasant was happening, maybe even the stuff of those excruciatingly detailed nightmares that kept him awake at night. It was happening in broad daylight, over the Revolution's most sacred body. I must get away immediately, he thought, I haven't the right to risk myself.

A moment later Okhotnikov succeeded in throwing off two of the guards. He leapt at Stalin and with all his strength threw a punch that struck the first secretary in the head. Stalin's boots shot outward in different directions from the puddle of cognac in which he was standing, then he collapsed in a corner. "It's the end of the Revolution" flashed through his mind before he lost consciousness. The Ossetian came up behind Okhotnikov and plunged his dagger into his shoulder. Blood spurted.

"Take them alive!" bellowed Yenukidze. Stalin was lying in a corner in a ridiculous pose, with zakuski that had fallen from the table scattered all around him. Okhotnikov was holding his wound with his right hand, the whole left side of his back was soaked with blood, and he now held his revolver in his left. He was unable to get a clear shot at Stalin in the confusion, and for some reason this Red Army hero and cutthroat could not bring himself to shoot an innocent bystander.

In another few seconds the Red Army officers, pistols in hand, had managed to reach the tunnel and take off running. Two motorcycles were waiting for them outside the Kremlin walls.

"They got away, the bastards! Iosif, how are you?" asked Rykov, bending over Stalin solicitously.

Stalin sat wincing, looking as though he had gulped down some vinegar by mistake. He unbuttoned his overcoat in order to straighten out the folds that had gathered up onto his stomach. "They won't get far," he muttered.

Meanwhile, the demonstration was still going on. "We are the Red Cavalry, and great epics will be written about us," sang, or rather wailed, a group of girls in pigtails. The column into which Albov's group was squeezed was approaching Red Square, carrying all the appropriate paraphernalia: a huge coffin bearing the words "Russian capitalism," a "hydra of counterrevolution" with a Chamberlain head, and a model of the future Dnepr hydroelectric dam. The column passed by the façade of the GUM department store and flowed around the monument to Minin and Pozharsky.

That was the spot where Albov dashed from the ranks and, drawing his arm well back, flung the picture of Stalin as far away onto the cobblestones as he could. The portrait, bewhiskered face upward, slid along the slimy pavement in the direction of a group of soldiers standing in formation before the Mausoleum. "It's time, comrades!" Albov shouted to his followers.

The Trotskyites had already thrown away their official posters and unfurled over their heads a banner that they had managed to keep concealed until then—"Down with the Thermidorians!" Another huge banner bearing the same slogan was unrolled from the windows of GUM in full view of the members of the government on the tribune atop the Mausoleum and their invited guests: "Down with the Thermidorians!"

"Down with them! Down with them!" chanted the young people. Nina held on to Semyon's shoulder when she wasn't waving her arms in the air. "Down with them! Down with them!" Icy waves of joy washed over her, exciting her. At moments like these, one would be willing to charge machine guns, to perish and disappear! "Down with them!"

The authorities lost no time in taking action. An entire infantry company carrying rifles with fixed bayonets came charging across the square. Their orders were to thrash the demonstrators with their gun butts, to show no mercy. A squadron of cavalry cut through the rear of the column. Honest laborers scattered to make way for them, pointing the way for the horsemen: "It's not us you want, brothers, it's those Yids over there!" They waved their fists wrathfully after them, shouting, "Beat the scum!"

The task of the riders was not to beat anyone, though, but rather to push the group off the square toward the rear of GUM. Policemen came running up from all sides in an uncoordinated attack, blowing their whistles and creating a wild panic. "Catch the traitors!"

Albov's group linked arms and defended its banner until it was forced by the might of the horses and flying rifle butts beneath the somber arc of the connecting passage. "Our job is done! Everyone scatter!" the leader was heard to say.

Unfortunately, there was nowhere for them to disperse to. In a few minutes they found themselves in the narrow Bumazhny Passage, separated from Red Square by the massive covered mall. This was where the real beatings began. Policemen and soldiers charged, armed with nightsticks, rifle butts, and sheathed sabers. Bloodied, disfigured faces could be seen here and there. "Fascists! Murderers!" the Trotskyites cried. They were knocked off their feet and dragged into waiting paddy wagons. Some tried to escape by mingling with the crowds of onlookers. They were recognized, dragged out, and given another beating. Bedlam reigned.

Two soldiers, cackling, were dragging Nina Gradov away. One held her from behind while the other ripped the buttons from her coat. "Now we're going to plug you, you bitch! Come on, Kolya, let's get her over behind the barrels! We'll give it to her there!"

Shrieking "Semyon! Semyon!" so loudly she thought she might burst, Nina tried to free herself from the stinking mongrels. A wave of people and horse-men howling in anger arrived on the scene and broke the grip the two men had on Nina. She was thrown against the doors of a notions store. The door opened, and a greasy face poked out of the darkness. "Come in here, miss, save yourself!" She stepped back in horror and began to cry "Semyon! Semyon!" again. Then she saw him.

In the midst of all this dismal brawling, the civil defense instructor was cheerful, even radiant. He was standing on one of the high porches of the trade stalls with a group of OGPU agents, showing them whom to take from the crowd. Unable to believe her eyes, she began to make her away along a low wall toward the porch. Once more she screamed, "Semyon!" and this time he heard her and extended a hand to her with a smile. Through the commotion she heard him say, "The game's over, Nina Borisovna! Climb on up here!" She watched as one of the OGPU men nudged Semyon and gestured inquiringly at someone in the churning crowd—"What about that one?"— and Semyon nodded—"Yes, that one."

"An informer?" shrieked Nina hysterically. "Semyon, you're an informer?"

The crowd once again swirled up around her and carried her away. Looking back, she noticed that Semyon was pointing her out to the OGPU agents as well: that one too, he was saying. A moment later, a horseman dealt her a blow on the head with the staff of his parade lance. Nina lost consciousness and fell beneath the feet of the crowd.

The struggle was over. The police were shoving the beaten Trotskyites into the paddy wagons. A fat-faced cop with a large backside dragged the unconscious Nina to a corner of Nikolskaya Street. Suddenly the guardian of order was surrounded by a mob of beggars and street vendors.

"Look, people, look! The monsters have killed a girl! Those bandits, those blood-sucking fiends have done in a pretty schoolgirl!"

The cop looked around in bewilderment. "Why, what are you talking about? She's alive! She's under arrest as a Trotskyite!"

A woman threw a stale meat pie at him, and then the other merchants let fly with their unsold wares. Women and beggars yelled, "You're the Trotskyite, you are! A heathen! You and your shameful snout will find yourselves in the dock!"

The cop spat, let go of Nina, and escaped from the crowd, that classless element. Several women picked up Nina and looked at her—it was true, she was alive—and they wiped her bruised and cut face with their handkerchiefs. Screening her from the police, they led her further down Nikolskaya, where several ambulances were standing at the ready. Suddenly, a lanky blond doctor leaped out of one of the cars, gave a cry of dismay, and staggered. "My God, Nina!" he shouted. "Nina!" He was close to collapse himself.

Everything had come together. An act of banditry in Kitai-gorod, and the beaten princess was in the hands of Savva Kitaigorodsky.

Inside the wagon, Savva laid Nina on a stretcher, gave her an injection of morphine, wiped her face with some gauze, painted iodine on her cuts as well as the places where her skin had been roughed up, and wrapped a bandage around her badly injured hand. On the way to Sheremetiev Hospital she drifted in and out of consciousness, moaning quietly, even though she felt no pain because of the morphine. She wanted Savva to bring his face closer to hers.

And what a face! she thought. A face of such fineness and purity, without a hair or a wart, simply an unblemished human face. I've never seen such a face in my life! She didn't understand what was happening to her or where she was being taken, but she could feel the warmth, the calm, and the fact that she, a little whimperer, was the object of concern. "Savva, Savva, it's you! Don't go away, please . . ."

Savva, who felt himself on the point of expiring from happiness and tenderness, nestled up to her on the floor of the trembling conveyance and held her hand, muttering, "Ninochka, try to hold on a little longer, everything will be all right now . . ."

Suddenly, remembering the hateful faces of the Red Army soldiers who had rained blows from their rifle butts down upon her, she gave a terrible scream and sat up, leaning on one elbow.

"Ohh . . . what did they do to us? Scoundrels! Fascists! Savva, Savva, the Revolution is destroyed!"

To hell with it, your tyrant of a Revolution, thought Savva. The only good thing it has ever done has been to bring you here to me!

"Calm down, Ninochka," he pleaded. "After all, you're still alive, aren't you? Your youth, you know, and your poetry are still alive!"

She threw herself back on the stretcher, and then a narcotic-induced smile again came over her face. "What a face you have, Savva," she whispered. "Compare the two faces, yours and mine. Well, mine is a mug and yours is exquisite. Could you and your face kiss my ugly mug? Kiss me there, where it isn't smashed."

He carefully looked for and found an undamaged spot on her face just above the point of her chin and touched it with his lips.

There was considerable confusion in the stands that had been erected for foreign guests by the Mausoleum. Many of them had noticed that something peculiar was going on among the members of the government—Stalin and Rykov had disappeared somewhere, and all the while Bukharin was glancing about nervously. After a while Stalin resumed his place in the middle atop the Mausoleum, but he plainly was not himself, and his face seemed dark. Then there was a commotion at the other end of the square, and a detachment of cavalry galloped in that direction. A banner with a short inscription had been hung askew on the massive building opposite the tribune, and an obvious battle was taking place around it—some people were trying to pull it down, others were defending it.

Reston was greatly annoyed that his translator had managed to vanish just at the most crucial moment—or maybe she had disappeared on purpose, so as not to have to translate the threatening inscription. He tried to make some sense out of the indecipherable Cyrillic letters, and all of a sudden, however strange it may seem, he managed to understand something, he figured out that the second word came from the French "Thermidor," which meant that it had to do with Trotsky's challenge to the ruling wing of the Party. That meant that the opposition had come out. And here I am, he thought, hanging around in these silly bleachers in the middle of a crowd of Communist nitwits missing important moments of history.

He walked up along an aisle trying to find one of his colleagues, a "journalist of the imperialist press." A few of the international revolutionaries were singing "Bandera Rossa" or "Die Fahne Hoch" almost mournfully. Their enthusiasm was crowded out by the oppressive ambiguity of the situation. Suddenly, he found himself face to face with a familiar gentleman in a fine tweed raglan. "Well, Professor Ustryalov! What a coincidence! Do you remember me?"

Ustryalov stopped, though obviously unwillingly. Of course he recognized him immediately, but he made a show of trying to remember . . . wait, give me a second . . . a quick glance backward over his shoulder, mm, yes . . . "Ah, yes, you are . . . pardon me—oh, yes, Reston! You're from Chicago, are you not?"

Reston took him under the arm in a gesture intended to show that they were equals, and to say "stop playing the fool."

"What's going on here, Ustryalov? Is it true what they say, that some other demonstration is going on?"

"I hardly know any more than you do," said Ustryalov, trying to free himself.

"Can you give me a brief interview? Five minutes outside the Mausoleum after two years—not bad, eh?" Reston continued to squeeze.

Ustryalov yanked his arm away, and his eyes were constantly looking off in other directions, as if he hardly noticed the American with whom he had

had such an informative discussion two years before. "I'm sorry, but right now that is out of the question. . . . Once again I ask you to pardon me, but I am in a hurry . . ."

He ran down the wooden steps and even looked at his watch again to emphasize—I'm in a hurry. Reston, a true jackal of the pen, nevertheless shouted a provocative question at his back: "Does this mean your theory has collapsed, Ustryalov?"

The professor stumbled slightly, hurried on for several more steps, but then turned around anyway and shouted so loudly that it startled the delegation of the Dutch Communist Party: "Not at all! It is the Russian state growing still stronger!"

Reston tiredly put his pen and pad back in his pocket. Galina showed up holding two silly balloons with a red Roman numeral X painted on each of them. Reston had the impression at that moment of supreme irritation that these two Xs represented some kind of diabolical threat: "X—X." That's enough, he thought, I'm getting out of here. There are lots of other stories to write. I'll go to Spain—at least there I won't have to depend on an interpreter.

"Where's the exit?" he asked Galina. "I'm tired."

"Comrade Reston!" exclaimed the girl in an offended tone.

"I'm not your damned comrade," he growled.

The Trotskyite slogan had long since been taken down from the façade of GUM. The endless procession of workers continued to spill onto Red Square. Reston looked at the portraits of Stalin bobbing into view from behind the Historical Museum one after another. Then he took out his pad and wrote four words: "The overture is finished." That cheered him up a bit—it would make a good headline.

THIRD INTERMISSION
THE PRESS

Anyone caught purchasing an apartment is subject to expulsion from Moscow: laboring elements within one month, nonlaboring elements within one week.

Religious believers are subject to examination by a special commission set up to handle evasion of service.

At the Meyerhold State Theater: *Roar, China!* a play by S. Tretyakov.

At the Nic-Diavolo Circus: Loop the Loop on a Bicycle.

Stars of the screen at the movies: Gloria Swanson, Jackie Coogan, Xenia Desny, Charlie Chaplin.

The following groups are deprived of the right to vote: kulaks, clergy, former czarist functionaries, suspicious individuals of free professions.

Burglars have broken into the store of Mikhailov & Lane at 20 Pokrovka Street.

T. Semashko has discovered the reason for increasing hooliganism among our young people: they grew up in the era of autocracy.

Nikolai Sergeyevich Lorentz, twenty-nine years old, has disappeared.

Archdeacon and Professor of Theology N. I. Bogolyubsky has quietly passed away.

Member of the Academy of the Commissariat for Foreign Affairs Comrade Rothstein has returned from sabbatical.

World-famous Chlorodont toothpaste! Basma henna! Triple eau de cologne for the bedroom!

Department of Divisional Supply. Deals. Cabbage and potatoes by the sack.

Forty-nine Latvian spies unmasked and neutralized.

The International Workers' Committee "Rus" has produced its own film of Gorky's novel *The Mother*. The leading roles are played by V. Baranovskaya and N. Batalov. Director V. Pudovkin, cameraman I. Golovnya.

Sun Chuan-fan defeated again.

Editorialist beaten up in Odessa.

Cartoon of "dry America": a stream of moonshine liquor flowing from a lawbook.

Nail. Corks. Saws. Underclothes.

The theses of Comrade A. I. Rykov presented at the XIV Party Congress: "On the Agricultural Situation in the Country and the Tasks of the Party."

Fiftieth anniversary of the death of Mikhail Bakunin. Main hall of Moscow State University packed. Speakers: University Rector A. I. Vyshinsky, Commissar for Public Enlightenment A. V. Lunacharsky . . . "We do not disown our predecessors!"

Academician P. P. Lazarev: "The brilliant research of Lobachevsky demonstrated the existence of new forms of space, distinct by their properties from the spaces in which we live . . ."

A long poem by L. Ovalov: *The Steel Propagandist*, dedicated to Alexei Ivanovich Rykov.

Mikhail Koltsov. Art or the Party? This Moscow student with the seat of his trousers worn as shiny as a mirror has many questions. This is what he lives on: a stipend of twenty-three rubles, pork chops with buckwheat kasha, faith in the worldwide revolution, hot water in his dormitory, three pounds of fatback from his stepfather, and occasional tickets to a show.

Here are his liabilities: his workload—studying, Party and professional tasks, civil defense volunteer work, painfully blinding shop windows, unpaid Party dues, frostbite through his opportunistic boots.

Comrade N. Pomorsky on New York: ". . . to our surprise, the Statue of Liberty turned out to be hollow inside. . . . One cannot smell anything in the city center except the stench of gasoline. . . . New York with its highest skyscrapers—up to fifty-eight stories—arouses a feeling of malice in the soul. . . . The workers' revolution will have to liquidate this monstrous city."

"The union of workers and scientists, rising up as one, will crush all obstacles on the road to progress in its iron embrace!"—Ferdinand Lassalle.

"The spirit of Lenin is hovering over the dry columns of figures!"—L. Trotsky.

Mikhail Koltsov. It is absolutely out of the question that we should return our commerce to the worn-out rails of capitalism. . . . The State cannot permit the anarchy of a market economy, of the "free play of prices." . . . There is nothing shameful about the competent organs calling someone to order . . .

FOURTH INTERMISSION
DANCE OF THE DOG

Young Prince Andrei, mistakenly named Pythagoras by his present owners, was running through the pines in his usual ecstatic mood, barking at ravens and chasing squirrels. From a distance he was fearful to look at: he had a wide chest, a long back covered with black fur, powerful light-gray paws, large ears standing sharply erect, and a muzzle filled with awesome, shining weapons. Squirrels should have been scared to death of this approaching storm, run away, scattering in all directions, racing up the trunks of the pine trees to the highest branches, and though they did run away and climb the trees, they did not appear afraid. One must confess that they didn't climb to the highest branches, either, but rather perched on the lowest ones and watched Prince Andrei from there. Sometimes it seemed to him that they were simply playing with him, that's what it was.

What would I do if I caught one of them? he sometimes thought. I couldn't pick it up in my teeth, I might hurt an innocent creature's fur. What can I do? he would sigh. I run too fast for them—basically, it's just not worth it for me to catch them.

One day, however, he didn't even need to catch up. A squirrel rushing away before him suddenly stopped and glanced back at him with the same look as that Chukhonets woman he had met in a field near Derpt during the First Livonian Campaign. And just as he had sat astride his horse then, he now sat down on his back paws. A wave of amorous thirst, joyful timidity, and youthful exultation washed over him. The squirrel regarded him without fear just as that girl in the linen dress had looked at the gleaming Russian warrior of long ago. Then its animal instinct was aroused, and it immediately shot up to the unattainable top of a tree.

Prince Andrei Kurbsky was as sure that it had been that girl as he was that he, Pythagoras Gradov, three-year-old German shepherd, had already been on earth once before in the body of a Russian prince. There she is now, jumping from branch to branch with her companions, coupling with the male of her species, furtively glancing at him from time to time with the eyes of an animal. It is quite unlikely that she fully understands who she is at that moment, but on the other hand, he does not fully grasp the meaning of the ideas of "Prince," "Russia," or "Czar Ivan" either. Prince Andrei, of course, did not know his own name, perhaps because he was still too young. He loved it when older people called him Pythagoras by mistake, or even better, Pythy, which more than made up for the error.

He loved his entire family: Mother Mary, Father Bo, Uncle Leo, his second mother, Agafia, his second uncle, Slabopetukhovsky (every time anyone mentioned that name, he wanted to repeat it with a laugh), his older brothers, Nikita and Kirill, his sister Veronika, who not long ago had brought into the house a puppy named Boris IV who wasn't bad at all, and, most of all, of course, his little sister, Nina, who unfortunately didn't play with him much anymore.

Everything that he remembered about the past now appeared to him like bright flashes of happiness: the broad horizons before the final advance on Kazan or the sparkling expanses of water when he and his retinue had broken through to the Baltic for the first time, moments of appeasing his hunger or quenching his thirst, encounters with women, the gesture of drawing the flaps of a tent closed, the glance of a friend who had not yet become a fiend . . .

At this point, when he was taking in the glance of this seeming friend, Prince Andrei gave a low growl and shook his ears to drive away the thought of what came next and set off again at a trot around the pines, or around the furniture if he was indoors, once again in the cheerful rays of light of the present and the past.

One morning, Savva, who wanted to gain entrance to the family of Prince Andrei, brought Nina in a motorcar and carried her from the car in his arms, saying that she could not stay in a hospital. Her mother cried in fright, "What happened?" They carried Nina upstairs to her room. Prince Andrei managed to slip in ahead of them and lie beneath the bed. He flatly refused to come out and even snarled faintly when his second mother was about to seize him by the collar. Then Father said: "Leave him there."

A gloomy, burnt-out area now appeared before his eyes, a smoking battlefield after the fight, the shadows of marauders; the absence of life assumed the tangible form of black flakes swirling about like crows over the unbearable stench of the outrages below. He felt as though these flakes were descending more and more densely upon his beloved sister, and consequently upon him as well . . . and now out of the past a host of horrors began to advance on him: horizons were closed, the world narrowed to a cage in a dungeon, to the well from which they dragged him not in order to save him but to inflict upon him the most terrible torture yet, to face the hardened features of the beast who had once been his friend, Czar Ivan.

How much time had passed Prince Andrei did not know, and he did not even ask himself the question. He tried not to whimper, even though whimpering was the only thing that could help him now. Suddenly Nina's arm fell from the bed and dangled in front of his nose. He touched her with his perpetually cold and wet nose, which even so seemed cold to her. He began to lick her arm warmly with his tongue, long and always hot like a stream of lava. Suddenly her hand sprang up and took him by the ears. "Pythy, darling," whispered his sister's voice.

The flakes of nonlife were dispersed as though frightened by a winged horseman. The dog danced beneath the moon, and the cells of the dungeon burst open as if the walls had been flattened by a mighty wind. His youth was calling him back, his days of running came full circle to the green Lithuanian hills.

CHAPTER EIGHT

The Village of Gorelovo and the Luch Collective Farm

☆

Toward evening one day in the early autumn of 1930, passengers began boarding the Moscow-Tambov train at the Kazan Station right on schedule, or almost on time—in any case, to the delight of everyone who was waiting.

Whenever Soviet people boarded a train in those days, they were inevitably seized by a feeling of nervousness bordering on panic. The transportation system was operating like clockwork, but it still seemed like a miracle, all the more so since hard times had once again come to the country and many items that had been available in any shop during NEP were in such short supply that one had to go to Moscow to get them. These peasants from Tambov Province, bags and sacks of all kinds draped over their best plush jackets, were already preparing themselves to do battle for seat and shelf space in the train as they entered beneath the giant arches of the station, which was supposed to evoke the sixteenth century but in fact reminded one only of more recent twentieth-century modernism. Old women raced along the platform at a remarkable speed and still were able to shout to their companions, "Come on, come on! Don't fall behind, Masha! Whose child is this? Has anyone lost a child?" At their backs, the people of Moscow, represented at the station by no class any higher than porters, addressed splendid parting words to them. The prerevolutionary gentility of the station had not yet been reestablished, and obviously never would be. Swarms of huddled Tatars and Chuvashes covered the tiled floors. People did their washing as best they could in the rest rooms. The air was filled with the unforgettable odor of the Kazan Station: a mixture of disinfectant, urine, dried fruit that had gotten wet, and all kinds of spilled food.

The Gradov brothers were in no hurry. They walked slowly along a platform with the certainty of young men who occupy respectable positions in society, paying no attention to anyone except each other. Nikita had arrived from Minsk with his family only that morning, and when he had learned that his younger brother was leaving for Tambov, he had volunteered to see him off at the station. Kirill had not objected.

During the previous two years Kirill's hard-line positions had softened somewhat, and he had not even objected when his brother had called a car for them from the commissariat. Even his facial features seemed to have softened, and now it was difficult not to recognize him, despite the fact that he was dressed like a shop foreman, as a young man "from a good family." Then again, perhaps he owed this effect to a new article of his apparel, wire-rimmed glasses. They immediately lent him the appearance of someone not of the working class.

As always, Nikita was in the full uniform of a ranking officer in the Worker-Peasant Red Army, everything properly adjusted right down to the smallest crease. It was this precision, as well as a better cut of cloth, that distinguished the uniforms of the officers of the upper echelons from those in the middle or at the bottom. On the surface, it seemed to be the same uniform—the shirt, the straps, the riding breeches, the boots—and yet a senior officer could always be spotted even from a distance without looking at his insignia of rank.

In recent years the two brothers had seldom seen each other and even less often socialized together, except at the dinner table in Silver Forest. The quarrels that had arisen between them seemingly out of nowhere had nonetheless blazed up with a violent flame—over Kronstadt, over the privileges of the officer class—and had distanced them from each other. This send-off at the Kazan Station, then, was an attempt to overcome this alienation, and in the glances Nikita and Kirill exchanged one could clearly read one look that said "Come on, Kir, stop sulking" and another in reply that said "What made you think I was sulking?" In other words, things were returning to the way they had always been: loving condescension on the part of Nikita and loving defensiveness on the part of Kirill.

The younger of the two brothers had idolized the other ever since "Nika," their mother's favorite, had abruptly and irrevocably gone over to the Reds, fought heroically on all the fronts of the Civil War, and then made a career in the military, advancing so rapidly that it made one's head spin. Kirill would never admit even to himself, though, that it was precisely this choice of his brother's which had pushed him into the arms of "the most progressive teachings of our times." That had nothing to do with it, he would say to himself—the fact is that he had been intelligent enough to realize which direction the ship of history was sailing in. After all, didn't Nikita's strange development—even now, he seemed to be nursing an absence of ideological fervor—prove that Kirill was entirely his own man?

The boarding of the train for Tambov was beginning to resemble the storming of the Winter Palace. Escaping the sacks and suitcases that went flying past, Nikita and Kirill stopped at a light pole to smoke a cigarette. Just then the lights all over the station went on. At the end of the platform on the wall of the terminal, a large picture of Stalin, with the words "Long Live the Stalin Five-Year Plan!" below, was illuminated. Nikita drew out a pack of expensive Kazbek cigarettes and looked at the familiar black silhouette of a horseman galloping along on a background of snow white mountains and a bright blue sky. Kirill declined, however, preferring his downscale Nords.

"Anyway, what are you going to do in Tambov Province?" asked Nikita.

Kirill did not answer for a moment, seemingly absorbed in trying to light his densely packed cigarette, then muttered, "They're setting up an ideological enlightenment network there."

"Just what farmers need most of all, right?" said Nikita with a grin.

Kirill did not respond to the irony: he didn't want the conversation to slip away into serious, if not dismal, topics, and to lead to another clash between the high-mindedness of a Party ideologue and the intentional cynicism of a military professional.

"And where exactly in Tambov are you going?" continued Nikita in a cautious voice.

"To Gorelovo and to several new collective farms in the surrounding area," said Kirill. He would have preferred to steer the conversation toward family matters, but Nikita smiled again.

"New collective farms in the Gorelovo district!" He clapped his hand on his brother's shoulder. "Better watch out for yourself down there, Kir."

"What do you mean?"

"In 1921, all the Gorelovo peasants joined Antonov's army. We had to take the place by storm twice in one month."

"There you go again!" Kirill exclaimed in considerable annoyance.

Nikita was clearly embarrassed, and this time his smile was apparently directed at himself. "Yes, little brother, I'm still thinking about these nightmares. How is it that we, the army of the rebellious, so quickly turned into the army of executioners?"

Kirill was ready again to flare up: the affection he felt for his brother was struggling with resentment at this insult to the Party. "Oh, Nikita, it's been almost ten years, collectivization is in full swing, and you're still thinking about the Kronstadt anarchists and Antonov's bandits!"

"Strange naiveté," his older brother intoned gloomily. "It seems to me that right now is the very time to recall such things. Do you really think that the people are overjoyed that NEP has been wiped out lock, stock, and barrel, that they've seized the lands and started collectivization? Damn it all, isn't it Trotskyism of the highest order?"

"Naiveté, Commander? Have you ever read even one book by Marx in your life?"

"That again!" Nikita shouted in reply, in the same ardently polemical tone. "Of course I haven't, and I'm not going to! And I hope my eyes never need a bicycle like that!" He put his index finger on the bridge of Kirill's traitorous glasses.

At first Kirill was dumbfounded. Then he burst out laughing. He was grateful to his brother for so unexpectedly cracking a joke.

Nikita smiled contentedly. "What do you hear about Nina?" he asked a minute or so later.

Kirill shrugged his shoulders. "The latest news is that *Red Virgin Soil* has published a long poem by her. It's modernist rubbish. She defended her thesis down in Tiflis two months ago, but for some reason she's in no hurry to return. Mother doesn't understand what's wrong, but I'm sure that it's just her latest silly love affair."

Nikita smiled. "And what about you?"

"What about me?" inquired the bewildered Kirill.

"Haven't fallen in love yet?"

"Me? In love? What kind of nonsense is that?"

Nikita chuckled and embraced his brother. "Only after collectivization is done with, right? After industrialization? After the fulfillment of the Five-Year Plan, Kir?"

Almost at the same instant, the train whistle sounded and the bell rang, followed by the blood-curdling yelp of the conductor: "Citizens who are departing, citizens who are seeing travelers off, the train is leaving!" Upon hearing the announcement, citizens began rushing in different directions, some getting on the train, some getting off, and there was one last series of collisions. Kirill began working his way through the crowd.

Some ten minutes after this mad rush, the train had still not yet moved. Kirill was standing, pressed against a murky window, hemmed in on three sides by peasant sacks, plywood suitcases with padlocks dangling from them, baskets filled with groceries bought in the city—aromatic blocks of strong household soap, three-liter bottles of vegetable oil, "heads" of sugar protruding from blue wrapping paper, a combination of colors that, let it be said in passing, recalled in its boundless simplicity the recently mentioned pack of Kazbek cigarettes.

Finding it impossible to move his arms, Kirill tried to approximate what he wanted to signal to his brother by means of facial expressions and gestures with his chin—"Go on, what are you standing around for?"—but his brother did not go away. He remained standing there smiling, easily distinguished from the wretched crowd of Five-Year Plan workers by his graceful figure and proud bearing, not to mention by his uniform.

He has no ideological grounding, he's just someone appropriated by the military circles—and what a cynic, too! thought Kirill. He's exactly the same sort of officer here that he would be in France, or England, or . . . well, naturally, in the czarist army, or in the White army. How is it that I never saw it before? In spite of all his regalia, Nikita is just a simple, old-regime Russian officer . . .

The train finally moved off, Nikita drifted away, and the platform and the station with its picture of Stalin, its slogan, and its spire on the roof dissolved into darkness.

After traveling for at least sixteen hours, perhaps closer to twenty, the train stopped at a way station where there was nothing but a booth for the switchman and a wretched shack a hundred yards away that was his home. Kirill, exhausted from the journey, jumped, or rather tumbled, off the suitcase he was perched on, and then off the train. Blissfully inhaling the cold autumn air of the empty Russian steppes, he took off his hat and set his face to the wind. The train chugged off again, heading for the city of Tambov, the provincial capital, which had once been famous for the balls that were given in the Assembly House of the local nobility. A peasant lad no older than twenty, wearing a service cap bearing a red star, was outlined against the steppe and the background of gently sloping hills laced with dark coppices. "Comrade Gradov? Hello there! I'm Pyotr Nikanorych Ptakhin, secretary of the Gorelovo Komsomol cell. I've been instructed to trans—er, transport you."

Like all of the workers who had recently been promoted to positions of responsibility, Petya Ptakhin loved new foreign words. It was not surprising, since the Russian ideological language was now stuffed with these garlicky foreign borrowings. The proletariat is "expropriating the expropriators," thought Petya Ptakhin, even though he had difficulty pronouncing the foreign words.

Their "transport" was halfway between the small station and the switchman's shack, tethered to the frame of a well—an old nag harnessed to a cart. A generous amount of straw had been spread in the bottom of the wagon to make the journey more comfortable.

"Is it a long way to Gorelovo?" asked Kirill. A strange feeling seized him. Looking at Ptakhin's humble uniform, his wagon, and the bare fields where some sort of black bird appeared for an instant and then was gone, he suddenly experienced a feeling of deep attachment to this countryside, as though he had his roots there himself . . . but an oppressive, languishing feeling swept over him as well, one that was like an endless reproach, shame at the impossibility of ever overcoming this country, if only because it was the place of some unthinkable and distant love that would have been unimaginable anywhere else.

Petya Ptakhin cheerfully untied the horse. "Getting there, there's nothing to it, Comrade Gradov, about three hours in this rig. So, I'll gladly—er, submit a report about our collectivization. We've achieved great things, Comrade Gradov!"

Dusk was gathering as they drove along, and by the time they entered the village it was completely dark. Even so, the peasant shacks along the edges of the bumpy road were still visible. Oil lamps and candles were smoldering here and there, and then all of a sudden, in the midst of these pathetic sources of light, another one appeared, hot and powerful—the remains of a burning building, radiating a heat so intense that the air around it was absolutely clear and giving off rose-colored smoke. Living tongues of flame danced along the fallen rafters. A woeful feeling of alarm took possession of Kirill. "So this is Gorelovo," he muttered. "Gorelovo the Hungry, No-Harvest Gorelovo . . ."

Petya Ptakhin watched the blaze with great interest and explained excitedly, "That happened just this afternoon, Comrade Gradov—Fedka Sapunov, that kulak scoundrel, torched his whole farm, a real big place, just so that he wouldn't have to join the collective. Slaughtered his whole family and all his cattle and then took off himself to meet his God—but he's only going to end up roasting in Hell, the damned Antonovite!"

The fire at the Sapunov place was obviously the biggest thing happening in the village. Several figures loomed up, silhouetted against the glow, and the sounds of women wailing could be heard. Ptakhin drew up the horse not far away and watched the smoldering logs and the little serpentine flames darting here and there, muttering in a trancelike voice, "A big place, yes sir, a big place . . ."

By the way that Ptakhin's lips were trembling and that he wiped his forehead with his cap, Kirill understood that the ruin of the Sapunovs also marked the end of the past life of the frail young Komsomol leader.

CHAPTER NINE

Bags of Oxygen

★

From the crumbling culture of the grain growers of the Russian center we now take a leap into the Mediterranean civilization of olives, plums, and grapes, one that was still stubbornly resisting the implacably advancing time of rationing.

Take, for example, the humpbacked streets of old Tiflis. Here it would never occur to you that the First Five-Year Plan was going on in the world outside. Like a hundred years earlier, or even two hundred years, the steady clop-clop of the shoes of horses pulling carts resounded in these streets. Housewives called to one another from shady balconies and verandas. To say that they called to each other in guttural voices would be to give the stereotype of the Georgian its due, but it is in fact true that the sound of a Georgian's speech originates in his larynx, not in the remote recesses of his belly, and from there it beats its way frantically upward as though it were gushing from a fountain and nearly always encounters a silver pea in its flight, an obstacle the characteristic gesturing of his hands helps him to overcome. That early autumn, as in days of old, the fences were overhung by dense foliage weighed down with peaches and pears. And just as they had always done before, before the "Catastrophe," by which was meant the happy annexation of Georgia to Bolshevik Russia—to use the expression of a few pharmacists who lacked political consciousness—two frosted globes ornamented the entrance to a pharmacy on a small square, and on the other side of the large window of the establishment was, as always, Uncle Galaktion, decked out in a starched white smock and intent on his discussions with his clients, for the most part Georgian women wearing dark capes. While it was true that the sign reading

"Gudiashvili Pharmacy" above the entrance was rather carelessly daubed—what else would you expect from this new government, if not crudity and carelessness?—it was easily distinguished. In any case, it attracted the attention of the public far more readily than the thin wooden plaque hung at a cockeyed angle by the entrance reading "Pharmacy No. 18."

"Make a stop at the Gudiashvili Pharmacy, dear friend!"

"Yes sir, boss!"

The gently clattering horseshoes of the animal drawing the cab obediently came to a halt. The passenger, Lado Kakhabidze by name, looked about with delight. He was a typical man of the region—stout, in his fifties, wearing a shirt gathered together with a studded leather belt. He had spent several years up north carrying out an important assignment for the Party, had just returned, and now was very pleased with what he saw around him. Not much has changed in Tiflis, he said to himself and immediately suppressed his next thought, which would have been something along the lines of "We haven't gone to ruin here yet."

With a spryness surprising for a man of his age, Kakhabidze jumped out of the carriage and went into the pharmacy. The driver—like all Tiflis cabbies, he was not wanting in curiosity—noticed how the arrival of the important government passenger astonished and delighted Uncle Galaktion. Throwing up a bar that formed part of the counter so suddenly that some of the customers gave a start, he ran toward the man entering the store with his arms outstretched. The customers looked on, beaming.

The arrival of Kakhabidze, by the way, had been watched with interest from the second floor of the pharmacy building. There, in the pharmacist's private apartment, more exactly in a large shuttered room with mirrors and filled with ancestral portraits—that is, in the living room, or, as they say in the Caucasus, the "salon"—stood Galaktion's nephew Nugzar, who had once made such an impression on the guests at the Gradov party with his fiery dancing of the lezginka. Peeping through a small crack in the shutters, he watched the arrival of the great Party leader and then, opening the door to the stairs slightly, listened to the joyous exclamations of greeting below. The sound of tapping heels on a parquet floor came from somewhere else in the apartment, and Nina Gradov came into the salon. Her face showed no sign of the bruises and cuts with which we left her three years ago. The enormously important historical events that had occurred in that span of time notwithstanding, she was now only twenty-three years old. On the other hand, the flourishing beauty that she was now bore only a vague resemblance to the "Blue Shirt" wind-up toy she was in our early chapters. Without noticing Nugzar, Nina went to a mirror and straightened her hair and the straps of her décolleté dress. Nugzar coughed by way of announcing himself.

She barely accorded a glance to the young man, whose presence was not only habitual but even importunate.

"Hi, Nina!" he said. "Listen, I give you my word as a man of the Caucasus, you look simply irresistible in that dress. Where are you going today, mademoiselle? Oh, pardon, pardon, madame!"

"Paolo is celebrating the publication of his new book," replied Nina. "All the poets are getting together at the funicular."

Nugzar made a clucking sound with his tongue. "Paolo Yashvili! So that's the kind of people you associate with, young lady! Downright literary celebrities!"

He approached her from the rear and stopped just behind her back, so that his reflection appeared in the mirror. "You and I don't look bad together, eh, Nina?"

She turned around to face him with some exasperation. "I'm a poet myself, or have you forgotten?"

"To me you're only a woman for whom I would wither away and die," replied Nugzar in a somewhat downcast voice.

Nina chortled merrily. "What an oddball! You're just an incurable womanizer, Nugzar!"

There was always a certain lack of definition in their relationship, as if nothing was taken seriously—how else could Nina react to his constant advances, especially when it seemed as though she had humiliated him by rebuffing them? No need to make a scene! He's just fooling around, a handsome lad spoiled by women.

"Me, a womanizer?" he retorted in apparent indignation. "Just look at me. I'm suffering because you won't put out."

"You punk!" cried Nina. "It seems you've forgotten that we're close relatives!"

Now indignation was growing on both sides—perhaps it was genuine, or perhaps only put on.

"Ha, ha!" Nugzar guffawed sarcastically. "And this coming from one of the most free-thinking women of the twentieth century? What happened to the theory that sex is no different from drinking a glass of water? Or your idol Alexandra Kollontai and her 'love between the worker bees'? Why is it that Paolo gets his glass of water but Nugzar doesn't? Why is there honey for Titzian and none for Nugzar? Relatives? Tell me you're married, too!"

"Yes, I'm married, you swindling nincompoop. Who blabbed to you about Paolo and Titzian?"

"Your husband is useless, he's not even a man!" shouted Nugzar. All of a sudden everything turned serious. He threw himself on her and began kissing her neck and shoulders. Enraged, Nina freed herself from his grasp and picked up a large candelabra. Nugzar, breathing heavily, retreated to a corner on the opposite side of the room, then whirled sharply as if he were brandishing a sword.

"I know the real reason you came to the University of Tiflis! Your parents insisted on it when your strange doings with the Trotskyite opposition came to light!"

"You trash!" shrieked Nina in reply. "Where do you hear these dirty rumors?"

Nugzar suddenly realized he had said too much. He smiled, and the "sword" in his hand turned out to be nothing more than a sweet pear.

"I was only joking, Nina, pay no attention to me. I'm sorry, it was just a stupid joke. You know how it is, a beautiful woman is always surrounded by chatter and jokes. . . . Why, I'm just your page, your Highness. 'The queen was playing Chopin in the castle tower, and, catching the sound of the music, her page fell in love with her . . .' You see, even Georgian lads know something about Russian poetry."

Nina was already heading for the door, but he ran in front of her and continued to play the page, dancing in circles and barring the way out.

"Stop clowning and let me by!"

Nugzar, dancing on his tiptoe, pretended he was fanning her. "And might I drive you to Paolo's feast, your Highness? Imagine yourself arriving on Mount King David in a real American Packard with three silver claxons! A friend of mine has one, and he will lend it for your use."

Again she was unable to keep a serious expression on her face. Finally she laughed. "Go on down to the stable, page, and tell them you're to be whipped!" Then she ducked around the cavorting Nugzar and ran out of the room.

She popped down to the store to say good-bye to Galaktion, and she saw him embracing a man who was at least as massive as he was.

"Nina, you won't believe your eyes!" called out Galaktion. "Look who has come back! It's him all right, the valiant Kakhabidze! As a relative, you have the right to call him Uncle Lado!"

Nina suddenly felt another opera coming on—"The Meeting of the Valiant Kakhabidze." Life in Tiflis seemed to her to be a constant round of operatic stories.

"Uncle Lado! Welcome, my dear! Welcome back, *genatsvale**!" she sang out in reply. Then she swung through the door out onto the street.

Nugzar leaped nimbly into the store right after her. He began to embrace the visitor as soon as he crossed the threshold, without waiting for an intro-

*A Georgian form of address.

duction. "I can't believe my eyes! Uncle Lado in the flesh! The legendary commissar! How did I know, you ask? Why, I read about you in the newspapers, saw your picture in hundreds of houses!"

Nina, standing on the corner, hailed a horse-drawn taxi. Nugzar left the store and headed for the center of town with its large French-style hotels.

Meanwhile, in the shop, Galaktion and Vladimir could not seem to get enough of looking at each other, slapping each other on the back and laughing.

"Galaktion, wake me up, I must be dreaming! Is it really you?"

"Lado, are you really here, in my old pharmacy? Please don't wake me—if it's a dream, let it go on!"

Kakhabidze walked around the store, taking everything in. He touched the revolving cabinets with their rows of drawers, each one bearing a drawing of an herb. He had known the shop since he was a child and could remember the time when Galaktion's father, Vakhtang, had run it. He ran his hand over the National cash register and the glass-covered cases. All solid items, of old-fashioned Russo-German manufacture . . .

"Everything here is just as it was," he pronounced with pleasure. Then he sighed. "Except that you are no longer the boss, dear Galaktion, now you're a simple Soviet 'director.' "

Gudiashvili wagged a finger at him. "You're mistaken, dear Lado, I'm not the director but the deputy director. Our director is Party Comrade Bulbenko. He was transferred here from the railroad depot—he was director there, too. A lot of our leaders have experience directing deputies."

Kakhabidze laughed. He was clearly enjoying the conversation and appreciated the wit of his school friend and relation. "Lucky man, this Bulbenko. My goodness, if only I'd had just one deputy like you in the Urals, Galaktion! On the whole, though, business is doing well, isn't it?"

Galaktion sighed. "So-so. You know, Lado, I never thought my store would run short of belladonna, ipecacuanha, calcium chlorate. . . . Now sometimes I just throw up my hands: suspended deliveries, suspended deliveries . . ."

Lado Kakhabidze's face took on an expression of feigned concern. "A shortage of belladonna? They haven't delivered enough ipecacuanha? Why, this is a disgrace to our Soviet pharmacology! I promise you, I'll take care of this right away! You'll see, my dear Don Basilio, by the end of the Five-Year Plan, the laboring masses will enjoy a bumper crop of belladonna, an abundance of ipecacuanha!"

Galaktion laughed so hard he had to hold his stomach. "Do you want to know the truth, Lado? You're the only Communist bigwig I've ever liked. This evening we'll organize a feast in your honor!"

They were about to leave to start preparing for the feast properly when an elderly woman burst into the shop. She was out of breath, wringing her hands, sobbing and crying, "Save us, good people, good Galaktion, save us!"

"What's happened, dear Manan?" said the pharmacist, rushing up to her.

A great man, thought Kakhabidze. I don't know anyone else who is so quick to go to someone's aid. There's no one like that in the Party, in any case.

"Oh my, my, my . . ." wailed Manan. "My husband, my faithful husband, Avessalom, is dying. He may even have died while I was running to get you, noble Galaktion, our only hope in these difficult times—God bless you and all your ancestors and all your descendants and all your relatives forever and ever!"

Galaktion hastened behind the counter to a small pantry with an energy that was surprising for a man of his size, drew out two oxygen bags, then dashed to the exit. Lado Kakhabidze was right behind him, and Manan, having realized what was going on, followed.

All of the hunchbacked little street, which they ascended at a run, together with all of its adjoining side streets, was taking part in the event. People were leaning out of their windows and over their balconies to see the two portly men rushing past. The two puffy oxygen bags gave them the appearance of thieves making a getaway, but everyone understood what was happening, all the more since Manan was there to clarify matters, continuing even on the run to offer up praise "to the whole Gudiashvili line, and to all pharmacists and artists" and to lament her "unforgettable Avessalom."

Galaktion explained to his friend trotting alongside, "No one in town has any oxygenators except Gudiashvili! Right now, everyone is constantly having problems with camphorous monobromide except me!"

Cries of "God save our noble druggist! God save his oxygen bags!" carried down to them from the windows and balconies.

Not even Lenin could have dreamed of something like this, thought Lado Kakhabidze, gasping for breath.

When they came to their destination, they saw the rotund Avessalom in front of the house. He was sitting beneath the branches of a fig tree playing a quiet game of nardy with a neighbor. When he saw the two breathless men and the wailing Manan with them, he jumped, sprang to his feet, and began to beat his chest.

"Sorry I'm not dead!" he shouted. "Please find it in your hearts to forgive me! My dear Galaktion, the very thought of you and the oxygen bags saved me! My God, who is that I see in the company of our miracle worker? I swear by the prophets, I've never had such famous guests in my house! *Gagemard-zhos, Lado-batono.** We're all delighted that you've come back! Manan, we

---

*"Greetings, my esteemed Mr. Vladimir" in Georgian.

won't let these gentlemen go until they've broken bread with us. Come and eat, come and eat, gentlemen!"

Manan did not have to be asked twice. She immediately hastened to the large table that had been standing beneath the plane tree in the yard for a hundred years, followed, after an amazingly short time, by her neighbors carrying dishes of all sorts of food. The table rapidly filled with heaps of fruits and vegetables, cups of lobio beans, plates of smoked chicken, cheese, and various condiments, along with earthen jugs of local wine. People from all over the neighborhood arrived—bakers, barbers, postmen . . . This is a good sign, thought Kakhabidze: my first evening back in Tiflis, and I'm with the people—it looks as though they're going to make me toastmaster!

And indeed he was selected as honorary toastmaster. He stood up with a wine-filled ram's horn in his hand.

"Dear friends, I gave several years of my life to the building of socialism in the Urals. I used to dream of my generous homeland during the cold, blizzard-swept nights. And now the Party has sent me back to an important post in my native Republic. I drink to Georgia, to our republic, in which there shall be no more thievery or corruption, where a Leninist, truly Leninist, style of working will flourish!"

Now there's style for you, the bakers and postmen nodded gravely. Style? The barber raised his eyebrows in surprise. How did a man like my Lado get stuck with them? Galaktion sighed. "Let Georgia become a true showcase of socialism in our great USSR!" said Kakhabidze, concluding his speech.

With shouts of affirmation, the bakers, barbers, and postmen raised their horns and drained them. Galaktion drained his too, though not without a sarcastic grimace.

"I drink to bumper crops of belladonna, to an abundance of ipecacuanha!"

"To your oxygen bags, dear friend!" said Avessalom in a whisper.

There are several intersections in Tiflis where you'd swear that you were in Paris. On one side of us we see, let's say, the façades of fin-de-siècle or art nouveau houses and on the other, an intricate cast-iron grating, a park fence.

It is night and the streets are deserted. A large black automobile, with three silver horns mounted on one side that make it seem all the more like a mirage, is waiting by the park fence, seemingly taking its own presence there for granted. Then again, the passenger, whom one might be able to catch a glimpse of through a lowered window, didn't look much a typical laborer of the Five-Year Plan: prematurely balding, extremely well groomed, with a strange look in his eyes sparkling behind the pince-nez on his fleshy nose. Looks like some capitalist, a pedestrian who happened to be passing might think, and then he would exclaim to himself quietly: "Why, it's Lavrenty Beria, the number one man in the OGPU!" Then the Parisian mirage would vanish.

Nugzar emerged from a side street with a purposeful stride and went straight to the Packard. Beria extended a hand to him through the window, palm upward. Nugzar slapped it with his palm as he approached. He bent down and whispered right under the nose of his old friend, "He's here, Lavrenty! I saw him myself in my uncle's house and embraced him."

"Get in, we're going," said Beria.

Nugzar dived into the backseat. The driver revved the Packard's engine, and the car roared off. A beggar standing on the corner crossed himself fearfully.

On a slope of Mount King David facing the city stood a large white house. The neighbors had already forgotten that it had belonged to a tea and coffee merchant before the Revolution and knew only that they were forbidden to go near it. It was there the Packard was heading.

Officially, the mansion was one of the "guest houses" administered by the government, but in fact the OGPU had absolute power over the place.

When they drove up, several black cars were already parked next to the porch. Plainclothes agents were standing guard beneath the windows and along the walls around the grounds. Their swarthy faces provided an Italian touch, like a meeting of the Mafia, or maybe a gathering of Blackshirts in the early days of Fascism.

Nugzar could not pretend to be Beria's equal here, so he walked to the porch deferentially, not like a friend but like an assistant.

The chief of the security guards drew himself to attention before Beria, who saluted. "Good evening, comrades! Is everything going well?"

"Yes, Comrade Beria!"

Inside the house, the similarity to the Sicilian Mafia was even more pronounced. About a dozen corpulent men, some in heavy three-piece suits and others in paramilitary uniforms, were sitting around a large table. Several of them wore badges on the lapels of their jackets that identified them as members of the Central Executive Committee, that is, of the Party elite, and that did nothing to weaken the Italian motif.

Taciturn guards brought in wine and zakuski, arranged them on the table, then left again. The participants in the meeting raised their glasses. "To our friendship!" Restrained smiles of the type usually described in Soviet literature as "sparing" appeared on the faces around the room. Beria was the first to speak. "We have gathered together here, comrades, to talk about Lado Kakhabidze, who has just returned to Georgia to assume the post of chairman of the Party Control Commission. Who is he—is he a genuinely good man, or is he just pretending? Nestor, Sergo, Archil, you've known Lado since 1905— are you sure that he's our friend, that he's a good comrade? Vakhtang, Givi, Vano, Murman, Rezo, Boris, Zakhar—you too, Nugzar, don't be shy, my boy—let's talk this over like Party men!"

Despite the encouragement of his friend, Nugzar tried to behave himself as he thought befitted him as the youngest—modestly and hanging on every word—and every participant in the conference, or let us rather say "assemblage," could read this modesty and diligence on his face.

Silence reigned at the table for several minutes. The Party men looked at one another. Finally Nestor, who was the same age as Kakhabidze, the man they were discussing, said, "I never liked him, this Lado."

Sergo, another veteran, spoke up. "Comrade Kakhabidze thinks a great deal of himself. He is, though, you understand, a pure Leninist. Everything else about him is fishy."

With a frown on his face, Archil was drumming his fingers on the table. All present were sure they already knew what he was about to say, and they turned out to be right.

"Before the Revolution, he was our party's representative in the interparty counterintelligence service, whose chief, Burtsev the Socialist Revolutionary, fled abroad. Now Lado walks around looking as though he has something on everyone concerning security matters."

Beria, his pince-nez sitting far down his nose, looked as though he were going to dive forward and take Archil by the arm. "Including?"

"Including whom, I'm afraid to say," replied Archil meeting his gaze. "He suspects everyone of 'betraying Leninist ideals.' He has no respect for the Party leaders. They say he's now fighting corruption in Georgia as though there were still capitalists here."

Another minute or two of gloomy silence passed while everyone digested this devastating bit of information. Then the young Vano turned to Beria. "Is it true he calls Comrade Stalin 'Koba'?"

Beria smiled benevolently. "Many of the old comrades call Comrade Stalin 'Koba.' It was his Party nickname in the underground days, there's nothing that can be done about it." Then he added severely, "Nevertheless, it is unseemly to call the leader of the peoples of the USSR 'Koba'!"

"Listen, Lavrenty, why did they appoint him chairman of the commission? I think that—" Vakhtang said hotly, but Beria interrupted him with a gentle wave of his hand.

"Just a minute, Vakhtang. Do you think it is appropriate, comrades, for Lado always to start chattering, after only one drink, about the fact that

Comrade Stalin has six toes on one foot, that he has seen it with his own eyes?"

Once again silence reigned, only this time it was not deadening or temporizing but rather a sort of animated silence, during which a glimmer of thought appeared in the eyes of some while others smiled faintly or said "Ooh . . ." ironically, as if to say "So that's what they're so scared about." Finally someone chuckled mischievously.

"Why make such a fuss about it?" said Sergo. "If you've got only five instead of six, no one bothers about it . . ."

Nestor stroked his mustache briefly, then threw up his hands. "Really, what difference does it make, five or six?"

"That's not the point!" said Vano sharply.

"Quite right, Vano, that's not the point!" said Beria enthusiastically.

Rezo moved his chair closer to the table and cut to the heart of the matter. "Comrade Stalin simply doesn't know Lado Kakhabidze is mocking him, making indecent hints about the past, speaking in overly familiar terms about his body, otherwise Moscow would never have appointed him to such an important post in our Party!"

"Bravo, Comrades!" exclaimed Beria. He put his hand on Rezo's shoulder, as if to emphasize that good friends can interrupt each other sometimes, and with his other hand squeezed Nugzar's wrist. Again he seemed to be almost sailing forward, his eyes flashing. The key moment of the "friendly discussion" was approaching.

"And maybe Comrade Stalin is already perfectly well aware of Lado's views?" he asked in a voice that was almost a whisper. "And that is just the reason for his appointment? Maybe Comrade Stalin has confidence in his faithful comrades in our republic and knows we won't let him down?"

Again there followed a silence. Each man at the table looked at everyone else, and everyone else looked at him. Then everyone broke into a smile at the same time. A toast was proposed: "To loyalty!"

While the loyal members of the Party were conferring on the slopes of Mount King David, the feast of poets was going on at its summit. At the end of a cable bridge stood the terrace of a restaurant, seemingly suspended in the night sky. Below it lay God's creation, the Kura valley. A full moon illuminated the huddled rooftops of Tiflis, the Metekhis Castle, the bends of the river flowing through the city. Just go ahead and try to imagine a more poetic landscape! thought an old organ grinder, standing with his contraption in a corner of the terrace, right above the beautiful scene. "You can walk, walk through the whole ancient world, live more years than you know what to do with, turn into the wandering Jew, but you'll still be delighted by the simple moon." He turned the crank of the instrument, wringing from it an almost indecipherable Caucasian music. Two parrots perched on his shoulders flew off among the tables with pink slips of paper predicting the fortunes of the guests written on them: "For happiness and good luck."

The poets, who numbered no less than thirty, were sitting around a large table. Apparently Paolo Yashvili was squandering the entire royalties from his book that very evening. Nina's place was between the cause of the festivities and the toastmaster, another celebrated poet named Titzian Tabidze. Toasts were proposed ceaselessly, each one more flowery than the last.

". . . and also this evening, which has given the *Argo* wind in its sails and right now is turning the pages of your book, dear Paolo! *Alaverdi,** Titzian *batono*†!"

Titzian Tabidze had already been on his feet with a glass for some time. As toastmaster, he was expected to show himself to be an excessively verbose speaker and not to wait for the wine to take effect. "I propose a toast to the wind!" he said. "And Paolo, of course, will drink with me to that eternal wind that brought to us a certain being! That individual who has been the inspiration of Georgian poetry for the last two years. Brother poets, let us raise our glasses to the Beautiful Lady of Tiflis! To our girl! The title will always remain hers, no matter how many years go by and no matter where she lives, be it in Moscow, in Paris, or on Mars! To Nina Gradov!"

Paolo jumped to his feet and raised his drinking horn over his head. Just then, one of the parrots alighted on the shoulder of the beaming and somewhat embarrassed Nina. In its beak was one of the rose-colored slips of paper. She unrolled it and read aloud:

> *The person whom you love the most*
> *Will come to help you at your post.*

The entire table exploded with laughter, and everyone, of course, began yelling that the man had already come and that naturally he would help such a girl. Nina laughed along with the rest. She was happy that the parrot had managed so successfully to lower the tone of the mealtime bombast of which the Georgians knew no limits or bounds. The poets, on the other hand, even though they were laughing—no one present was entirely devoid of a sense of humor—were still a bit annoyed that the flow of eloquence had been interrupted. Paolo Yashvili lost no time in getting to his feet, brandishing his horn, as soon as the laughter had quieted a bit.

*"I pass my toast to you" in Georgian.
†"Esteemed" in Georgian.

"Snatching up the *alaverdi* of my brother Titzian, my friends, I would like to profit from the freedom given to us by our Eternal Motherland to give Our Girl—"

Just then the ritual was interrupted again. At the far end of the table, a drunken and disheveled lad stood up, if "stood up" are the right words to describe someone who looked as if he barely had the energy to do so. It was Nina's lawful husband, a former member of LEF, a former Imagist poet who had moved like a nomad through every imaginable poetic movement of the twenties: Styopa Kalistratov. Then, despite his drooping appearance, he yelled in the mighty, resonant voice with which he had once spoken from stages: "I beg your pardon, but could we try it without the *alaverdi*. . . . Is Your Girl's husband not allowed to say a few words? Hey, you, poets! You puff yourselves up with wine, gobble down shashlik, drag yourselves along after my lousy charmer of a wife, as though everything were fine, as though the carnival were going to go on forever. . . . But no, it's curtains! Disgrace and misery, that's our future! Seryozhka Esenin is dead, and Volodya Mayakovsky too! The star charts are not favorable to us, brothers! And your humble servant Styopa Kalistratov is barely alive himself!"

After delivering this speech, which had visibly exhausted all his energy, Stepan collapsed into his chair and into the embrace of his friend Otari, Uncle Galaktion's other nephew, a surprisingly languid and silent creature who reminded one of a deer.

The poets, disregarding the fact that they were Georgians, were not angry with Stepan for disrupting the mealtime ritual. Someone, if the truth be told, muttered, "There you have it, the typical Russian scandal in a noble family," while someone else objected, "Oh, drop it—this is just a vestige of Futurism, after all," but the majority were simply filled with pity: "Stepan is a suffering soul! He's a genius! Let's drink to him!"

Suddenly one of the restaurant's bouncers crossed the terrace running and whispered into the ear of Yashvili, whose eyes grew wide. Everyone turned toward the door in expectation of a new arrival. A small man of about forty came out, or rather flew out, onto the terrace like a little sparrow. He extended his arms toward the poets' table and in a high voice on the point of breaking from pride and delight began to recite:

> Let me tell it to you straight:
> Life is candy, cherry brandy,
> Ain't that dandy, sweetie pie?

The others all jumped to their feet, and in the din someone cried, "Osip! Why it's Osip himself in the flesh! Glory to Mandelstam!"

Nina was shaken. Like all of literary Tiflis, she knew that the poet Mandelstam was somewhere in the Caucasus, that he had spent several days in the city at Zdanevich's flat and was then going on to Armenia, or maybe it was Azerbaijan, but could she ever have imagined that her idol would suddenly appear from nowhere here above the city and beneath the moon, in a bacchic haze, that very night when she, bare-shouldered, was so irresistible (she knew it perfectly well)—or that he, with a high, noble forehead, would look at her wild-eyed while he was embracing Paolo and Titzian, as though he recognized in her one of those "beauties of the year 1913," maybe even the celebrated Solominka herself, also a Georgian? Perhaps that night she was Salomeia Andronikov* herself?

"Where have you come from, Osip?" inquired Paolo loudly, playing a scene of two members of the worldwide brotherhood of writers before the understanding audience.

"From Armenia!" shouted Mandelstam in return. "Barely managed to drag myself away from the place! Listen, here are a few lines I've just written!" He began to recite, clearly addressing the lines to Nina. "There in Nagorno-Karabakh, in the predatory city of Shusha, I experienced the fears that are related to my soul . . ." He stopped reciting and asked in a stage whisper, "For God's sake, Paolo, who is she?"

Paolo introduced her proudly: "Nina Gradov, a young poetess to whom we have just given the title 'Our Girl'!"

Mandelstam extended his cold hand and snatched at Nina's palm. "Nina, you . . . I'm simply staggered. . . . You look as though you've come straight from the Stray Dog Café!"

" 'I shall teach you the blessed words—Lenore, Solominka, Ligea, Serafita,' " said Nina in a trancelike voice.

"Oh, you remember!" whispered Mandelstam.

The organ grinder approached them, cranking out music for all he was worth. The parrots flew from his shoulders again with a stormy flutter. Mandelstam began rummaging through his pockets. "As usual, I don't have a single ruble."

"It's not necessary," said the old man.

Even Georgian feasts sometimes finish, and at the end of the night Mandelstam and Nina were by themselves in the center of town. The moon was still in the sky, illuminating numerous portraits of Stalin and signs bearing slogans of the First Five-Year Plan. They were walking along a row of wretched shop windows that had once belonged to luxury stores.

---

*"Solominka" is a poem by Osip Mandelstam, dedicated to Salomeia Andronikov.

"This Tiflis . . ." muttered Mandelstam. "Even in spite of the cat's face everywhere . . ." Without any circumspection, he indicated a portrait of the bewhiskered leader with his finger. "Here it seems that the house has not yet been completely ransacked, that at least NEP is still alive. Look over there, at the end of that little street—not a single portrait or slogan, just a fountain, and water streaming from it . . . streaming, Nina, just like before the Catastrophe . . . and on the tables, my God, what delicacies! . . . and around the tables, such lively faces free of suffering . . . and you, Nina . . . why has fate bestowed such a gift upon me?"

"Let's be precise, Osip Emilievich," said Nina. "Who or what is a gift of fate, I or Tiflis?"

"For me, you will always be inseparable," said Mandelstam.

"As for me, I'm afraid I'm already coming apart," she smiled. "I'm going back to the real world. You see, I'm a Muscovite."

Nina was trying to impart a sense of irony to their nighttime stroll, in order to avoid taking up his tone and soaring into exultation. Mandelstam, who obviously did not want to adopt such a tone, looked at her in confusion.

"I heard about you in Moscow, Nina," said Mandelstam. "And I read your long poem in *Red Virgin Soil.* Believe it or not, I saw your face through its lines." He discreetly took her by the arm just above the elbow.

"Listen to me, Osip Emilievich," she said, distancing herself from him slightly. She was a bit taller than he was. But that's probably because of my shoes, she thought. If I took them off, we would be the same height.

Somewhere behind their backs, down an empty street, they heard a noise that increased in volume. They had scarcely managed to turn around when a large black automobile with three silver horns on the side drove past. Nina shuddered. She had been telling her fellow writers about Nugzar's joke just before the start of the feast, and one of them had told her, sotto voce, who it was who drove around Tiflis in that car.

Her fright did not escape Mandelstam's notice. His hand moved slightly higher on her arm, suggestively.

"Those black automobiles . . ." he said. Suddenly the look in his eyes became a glassy stare, and he forgot about the proposed embrace. "When I see them, something large and black rises up from the depths of my soul. I'm pursued by a vision of something horrible, something that will inevitably crush us all . . ."

"I know that feeling," she said.

Mandelstam, noticeably stretching up, looked directly into her face. "You're still young for that."

"I went through a bitter disappointment," she pronounced with gravity.

"In love?" he asked, thinking: now she's going to tell me about her unhappy love affair.

"With the Revolution," she said.

Suddenly he trembled all over and thought: she's bewitching!

They stopped beside the softly gurgling fountain—the tall young beauty and the pitiful, aging sparrow. He now took her by both arms without any hesitation. Now, it seemed, deceptions were scattered to the winds and utter sincerity was called for.

"Nowadays, after everything that has been and before everything that will be, I see every moment of peace or beauty as an unheard-of gift I don't deserve. Nina!" He tried to get closer to her, and at that moment someone nearby guffawed loudly and then could be heard saying "Ha, ha" in a hoarse voice.

Jumping back from one another, Nina and Mandelstam peered into the darkness and made out Styopa Kalistratov. The poet was lying on the rim of the fountain, with his long hair dangling in the water. Next to him sat Otari like a sculpted figure of a mourner.

"Go on, kiss him, my mangy wife!" said Styopa in encouragement. "Don't lose your nerve. Your biographers will write that you slept with Mandelstam. I give you my permission."

He stopped speaking and turned away, almost faded away into the darkness, and the only thing that could be heard was a splashing sound—not quite a splash, but something like the lapping of waves—and Otari's cigarette flickered like an entreaty in the night.

Nina looked at the spot where Stepan was lying, and she recalled the New Year's Eve three years before when the two of them had arrived in Silver Forest in a horse-drawn cab and burst into the house red-faced and tipsy, and how she had announced to all those present, "Well, everybody, you've talked me into it, I'm going away to Tiflis—not alone, but with Styopka, my legal husband!" And she remembered how Savva Kitaigorodsky had quickly crossed the living room with his head down, ignoring all the rules of decorum he had been brought up with, snatched up his coat out of a pile, and disappeared. A pang of pity pierced her now. Pity for whom? For Savva, for Stepan in his degradation, for herself, or for the fact that those years were irretrievable? She rushed over to Stepan as though spurred on and then turned back to Mandelstam.

"Forgive me, Osip Emilievich, this is my husband. My poor, dissolute 'fellow traveler.' "

Seizing Stepan by the shoulders, she began to shake him. "Stand up, stand up, you dunce! Let's go home!"

Somehow Stepan managed to get to his feet. Nina supported him. Otari trudged along behind them. His cigarette had gone out. Mandelstam stood motionless. Even here, in this peaceful corner reminiscent of the time before the Catastrophe, a picture of Stalin was watching him through the branches.

CHAPTER TEN

Keen Eyes, Doves, and Little Stars

☆

Is there anything on earth more desolate than a street in a Russian village? Quite apart from the poverty of its material condition, is there anything more hopelessly remote from the carnival of life, from the enchanting spectacle of the Revolution? These thoughts, in the spirit of Gogol, were those of Party propagandist Kirill Gradov as he passed clusters of ramshackle huts in the streets of Gorelovo early one evening. He wondered why the suffering faces of peasant women were looking at him from behind every wattle fence.

The women, though, were peering at an approaching cloud of dust. They emerged from behind the fences and stopped at their gates, frozen, with their hands folded on their chests. They were obviously incapable of recognizing that what was happening to them was contrary to common sense and to the Russian countryside itself. Mooing that sounded like distant thunder was approaching along with the dust cloud. A herd of underfed collectivized cattle was being led into the village by bewildered Komsomol shepherds.

Kirill stopped to let the cows pass by. The closer the herd came, the more the composure of the women began to dissolve—they could no longer control themselves and began loudly wailing and crying out to their former "children" and providers with the same melancholic tenderness that had always characterized the relations between Russian women and their cows. "Keen Eyes, my little mother! Why have they taken you away from me?" "My dove, my own little girl! Look at your mama just once, at least out of the corner of your eye!" "Little Star, my provider, why, no one has washed or brushed you! These collective farm heathens have ruined you!"

On seeing the farms of their birth, the memory of which had not yet grown cold, and hearing the still familiar voices, first one, then another cow began to stray from the herd and, as in former recent times, to head for home to be cared for and caressed. Some of the women ran toward them in sorrowful desperation. The confused Komsomolists cracked their whips down onto the backs of the cows and the heads of the women indiscriminately. A woman recognized one of the herders as her own son, dragged him away by the hair, and gave him a kick in the backside.

Something's not right here, thought Kirill, as he watched the scene, something's not quite right. Nothing else entered his mind. Paralyzed by the senseless, piercing quality of what he had seen as well as by the defensive dullness of his own mind, he stood stone-faced by the wattle fence. The sunset glared in his eyes. Suddenly a thought distinctly appeared and swam before his eyes like a ticker coming from a telegraph: "Is there anything in the world dearer to me than these cows and these women?"

Party Cell Secretary Petya Ptakhin walked up, red-faced and clearly perturbed, and muttered, "I hope you'll pay no mind to these women, Comrade Gradov. Their class consciousness is zero, they just have the in—instinct, or in-stick, or whatever—of private property. Inspinkters, that's what they are, all right . . ."

The herd passed. The street grew quiet. The dust settled. Kirill and Ptakhin continued on their way to the village club. It hardly needs saying that the club was located in the church, so that there, as everywhere else, "enlightenment" would get the upper hand over "prejudice." The building was half falling down, the cupolas were full of holes, and the cross was twisted out of shape— perhaps all of this was the consequence of a battle, perhaps the result of peaceful profanation. Two posters hung next to each other over the entrance. One read "Collectivization and the Wiping Out of Boundaries Between City and Countryside. Lecturer: Comrade Gradov." The second announced "The Machinations of British Imperialism in the Far East. Lecturer: Comrade Rosenbloom."

Both lectures were scheduled for exactly the same day and time. Above the two banners in the middle, as if mediating a compromise between them, hung a portrait of Stalin with a banner attached to it like a red beard: "For 100% Collectivization!"

A crowd of morose peasants in front of the church were smoking cigarettes from homegrown tobacco. "Hello, comrades!" said Kirill. No one answered, nor did anyone even look in his direction. Many, however, eyed the Komsomol secretary in an unfriendly fashion.

"What's this, Ptakhin—you've scheduled two lectures at exactly the same time?" asked Kirill. "Why the competition?"

Ptakhin, after flashing a sign to the peasants that said "Keep quiet, no fooling around" answered officiously, "Please don't worry, Comrade Gradov. Our people, from Gorelovo, have been called to come and hear you, while the members of the collective farm Precepts of Lenin are coming to hear Comrade Rosenbloom. There's more than enough room for everyone."

. . .

Kirill failed to captivate his audience either with a historical excursion to the utopian communes of Saint-Simon or by talking about the bright prospects for the future. The Gorelovo peasants sat expressionless, and whenever a face did begin to show some animation, one had the impression that it was because the man wanted to draw a bead on the lecturer from Moscow. Meanwhile, from the hall next door where the mysterious Rosenbloom was giving what for to British imperialism, there were constant outbursts of friendly laughter and applause. Kirill decided on a change in strategy and, skipping several paragraphs, proceeded directly to his powerful conclusion.

"The Party program, comrades, envisages the creation of enormous agricultural complexes in which the most modern conditions will be created for the labor and everyday life of the collective farmers. The boundary between city and countryside, as the great Lenin taught, will be wiped out as rapidly as possible, and then the 'idiocy of village life,' which Marx noted even in his day, will be forgotten!"

The lecture was evidently over, but the peasants were still sitting there just as they were before, without stirring. So maybe I won't take a bow, thought Kirill. Ptakhin finally stirred and began clapping. The peasants then clapped too. Kirill, who was red in the face from embarrassment, began to gather his papers.

"Questions, people, ask questions!" shouted Ptakhin. "Comrade Gradov will answer any questions!"

An old man with a beard who looked like a wood sprite got to his feet. "And where are you going to treat the people, Citizen Explainer? In the hospital?"

"To treat them? Treat them for what?" asked the baffled Kirill.

"Where will they go to get cured from the village idiocy?"

Kirill mopped his brow in bewilderment. Was the old man having him on or had he really not understood anything?

Petya Ptakhin, however, knew how to conduct the Party line. "You, Uncle Rodion, think your idiocy is in your backside, but in your case it's in your head. Understand?"

The peasants snorted rather listlessly, as if only for the sake of appearances. The old man said gloomily, "And so it is."

"The lecture is over, comrades," said Kirill. Then he realized that none of these people cared to have him as a comrade.

Everyone went out into the corridor. From the neighboring hall, or rather the church entrance hall, one could still hear laughter and awkward carrying on. Kirill broke his cigarette in half in annoyance. "This Rosenbloom really knows how to find a common language with the farmers. Don't you hear it, Ptakhin? What a lively reaction!"

"Well, the only reason for that is they brought in a few jugs of moonshine—that's how they got that reaction."

The doors opened, seemingly under an onslaught of stormy applause. The peasants from the neighboring village of Neelov came out, red-faced, aroused, and laughing. Some of them couldn't walk a straight line. And the lecturer, that source of knowledge of the peasant soul, turned out to Kirill's amazement to be none other than Cecilia Rosenbloom, one of Nina's Blue Shirt friends, with whom he had closed ranks more than once during heated discussions in Silver Forest on the basis of their mutual nearness to the Party line. She was a young redhead, not at all unattractive despite her profuse crop of freckles. Her outfit was a most peculiar ensemble and even created a new style—a hat that would have been fashionable twenty years earlier, a military shirt belted with an officer's strap, a long skirt suitable for a lecturer or a poet at a recitation, and high riding boots.

"Yes, comrades, that's right," Cecilia was saying to the peasants walking with her. "The British lion is now the principal foe of the world proletariat."

The peasants reacted with respect.

"The lion is, of course, a serious beast—supple and well provided for. He needs something to gobble down, too!" One man sniggered, another burst out laughing. The lecture had clearly been a success—painless in more ways than one.

Kirill looked at Cecilia in astonishment. Her appearance in this godforsaken place, where everything was so unlike the theoretical model—where, to be honest, he was on the point of throwing up his hands, where his strongest convictions were evaporating—gladdened and inspired him: here is one of our girls, a Muscovite, a Marxist, and a Bolshevik, daringly working here in this hotbed of former Antonovites. That must mean that our people are everywhere, by the thousands—we'll clear the eyes of these country folk. Cecilia noticed him standing against a wall on which the rubbed-away traces of holy images were still visible, laughed, and came up to him with her hand outstretched.

"Gradov, hello in the name of fitness! Let me shake your revolutionary hand!"

Shaking her hand firmly, Kirill exclaimed, "Rosenbloom! I never thought this Rosenbloom giving the lecture was you! How long will you be here?"

"About five days," said Cecilia.

"Me, too! That means we'll be traveling together!"

They both smiled. A banner reading "We will cut off the claws of the kulaks!" extended over them on the pockmarked wall.

"Let's go get some chow!" offered Cecilia.

"All right, let's go chow down!" Kirill agreed delightedly, even though at one time, he had found this sort of Moscow Communist slang repulsive.

A happy expression flickered over the face of Petya Ptakhin, also on the scene. Obviously, he was thinking of the Party's educational system.

. . .

On one of the five days that followed, on one of the most gloomy afternoons of vile weather, to be exact, Kirill and Cecilia were making their way through almost impassable streams of muck. Rain was inundating Gorelovo. The harvest was rotting in the fields, and the collective farm era was dawning as gloomily as a piglet contemplating its future. The young people were continuing their argument about Marxist theory.

Cecilia, marking the rhythm of her words with her hand, announced, "The countryside is now developing in strict accordance with our theory, and Stalin, as a great Marxist, understands perfectly that we cannot deviate from it. It's a scientific law, Gradov, understand? An elementary dialectic of the Revolution!"

Kirill, nodding pensively, followed the progress of her ideas from her mouth down to the dreary mud. "I agree with you, Rosenbloom. In theory we have no disagreement, but in practice it seems to me we sometimes bend the stick a bit too far . . ."

They rounded the corner of the only two-story building in the village, a stone house where the council and administration of the collective farm sat, and the debate was interrupted. Something unusual was happening at the edge of the village by the main gate. A column of a half dozen or so army trucks with their sides let down were parked in the road. Soldiers carrying rifles with fixed bayonets were running into peasant huts on both sides of the road, driving out sobbing and crying women, children shrieking in terror, and dazed old men and dumping their meager possessions in the mud. Village activists whirling about the scene were "collectivizing" what remained of the domestic cattle, as well as the ducks and chickens, and driving away with kicks and stones the useless members of the household such as dogs and cats. The cats, true to their nature, immediately took off, some disappearing, others taking refuge on inaccessible branches of trees in order to watch the proceedings in the same way their species had been observing history since the time of the Pyramids. The dogs, incapable of overcoming their loyalty to their homes, were the only ones who resisted, barking and hurling themselves at the bandits. Kirill and Cecilia heard people shouting on all sides: "What are you doing, you monsters?" "Godless heathens!" "A curse on you, you torturers! Bloodsuckers!"

The commander of the detachment showed up and with a piercing yell drew his revolver from its holster. "Shut up, you kulak scum, or I'll shoot!" He fired into the air anyway.

Shaken by the display of "practice" they had witnessed, Kirill and Cecilia forgot about theory. They walked slowly along the column, unable to say a word. They happened on their Gorelovo counterpart, the Komsomol leader

Ptakhin, by one of the trucks. He was noting something down on a pad with a businesslike air. "What in hell is going on here, Ptakhin?" asked Kirill.

"De-por-ta-tion of the alien class elements, Comrade Gradov," Ptakhin began in what he had hoped would be a severe tone, but then giggled nervously. "For their own good, we are sending the families of the kulaks to the wide-open spaces of the brotherly Republic of Kazakhstan. Not on foot, Comrade Gradov—you can see that automobiles have been sent for them, what care is being taken for them."

"These people here are kulaks, you say?" asked Kirill, barely able to keep himself from trembling. Cecilia took his hand to be ready for anything. "Unfortunately, practice sometimes differs from theory, I'm sorry to say—there are unavoidable costs. Just the same, Pyotr, are you sure they're all kulaks?"

Kirill had always seen something of a prerevolutionary overseer in Ptakhin's efficiency—then again, how could a bureaucrat come out of a roach-ville like this?

"Please don't worry, Comrade Gradov, or you, Comrade Rosenbloom," said Ptakhin hastily. "Everything has been checked and rechecked. I have them all on my list as kulaks or middle-class peasants, and the list was compiled up there!" In a deeply meaningful gesture, he pointed toward the sky with his index finger, and a dirty-looking storm cloud now moving over the village seemed to leave no doubt about his statement.

Kirill and Cecilia left Ptakhin and increased their pace in order to leave the distressing scene behind as quickly as possible. Meanwhile, the pogrom continued. The soldiers snatched from the women any possessions that they considered unnecessary and threw them into the mud—blankets, pillows, grandfather clocks, frying pans, pots. From time to time rifle butts were used for purposes of clarification and warning shots were fired.

As soon as Kirill and Cecilia left the village behind, all of this seemed to recede quickly, like a nightmare of a civilization that might have been poor and miserable but was a civilization all the same. Nature and this age-old land, not even possessing the name of "Rus," brought peace and even in the gloom promised open spaces and a broad horizon.

They turned onto a side road where it was drier, and Cecilia sighed, "What can you do? It's the class struggle."

Kirill remained silent for a moment. Then he picked up a stick, broke it over his knee, and stopped. "No, this is just too much, Rosenbloom! You saw those kulaks . . . poor, wretched people. I'd heard talk about these things and I didn't want to believe it, but—they sent some unheard-of requisition orders down here, maybe to pay them back for the Antonov uprising. . . . These kinds of extremes are no good to anyone! We're destroying the very essence of Russian agriculture! I don't know about you, but I'm going to go to the Central Committee and report on what I saw!"

His face was red with excitement, and she was looking at him in a new way.

"Listen, Gradov, haven't you ever heard the expression 'You can't make an omelette without breaking eggs'? Stalin knows about all of this and understands the situation and its excesses perfectly well. Enough!" Suddenly she put her hands onto Kirill's shoulders and looked deeply into his eyes. "Listen, Gradov, what would you say to a small sexual adventure?"

Kirill recoiled, flabbergasted. "What do you have in mind, Rosenbloom?"

A vague smile, thin as a dragonfly's shadow, appeared briefly on her freckled face. "Well, just a bit of physiological satisfaction. Don't you think we've earned it after a week of political enlightenment? Come on, Gradov, don't be a bourgeois mama's boy! Look over there, there's a barn on the hill—it's the perfect spot for this business!"

There had been a rusty lock on the door, but they had managed to separate the boards of the wall and go inside without any effort. The abandoned barn hardly seemed suitable for "this business." Gaping holes yawned in the roof, and there were puddles on the decaying floor and in the barrels stored in the shed.

Cecilia looked around in a matter-of-fact way. She quickly found a more or less dry corner and threw an armful of more or less dry hay into it. She spread her overcoat there, took off Kirill's coat, and then with the same air of efficiency took off her skirt, revealing somewhat repulsive lilac knickers that extended to her knees. She unbuttoned her blouse and turned to Kirill. "Well, come on, Gradov!"

Kirill couldn't "come on"—he was completely confused and didn't know what to do. She threw out her chest, and Kirill was staggered by the sight of her breasts, which seemed to him as large as two white geese. Where did such things come from? he wondered. Continuing to smile, she took matters in hand.

When the "small sexual adventure" was completed, they lay next to each other and looked at the holes in the roof, and at the sky, which was growing still murkier and darker. Kirill, overwhelmed by a flood of emotions that were new to him, whispered, "You're—you're amazing, Rosenbloom . . . you're simply a wonder . . ."

Cecilia sat up and coughed like the inveterate smoker she was. Her white geese rippled up and down unbecomingly as though they had been caught out on the water by a sudden gust of wind. She exhaled the smoke from her cigarette and asked derisively, "How is it, Gradov, that you managed to keep your virginity until you were twenty-eight years old?" She leaned forward and began kissing Kirill with unexpected tenderness. "Well, welcome to the world of adults, professor's little boy!"

Suddenly she noticed that Kirill's attention was distracted from the amorous game and that he was looking over her shoulder with alarm. She looked around and saw a pair of eyes watching them from behind a pile of rubbish in a corner. They both jumped up.

"Who's hiding back there? Come out!" yelled Kirill.

The eyes disappeared. Kirill raced to the corner, threw aside the disintegrating barrels and abandoned harnesses, and dragged out a young boy of about seven or eight, smelly and utterly exhausted. The boy tried to wriggle free, to defend himself by waving his arms, but he had strength left only to clench his fists. He even tried to bite Kirill, but his teeth left only faint impressions on Kirill's arm. A feeling of pity so keen as to be almost unbearable stabbed at Kirill as he watched the lad's pathetic attempts to protect himself.

"You little louse, why were you watching us?" he yelled. But he soon calmed down, stopped yanking the boy about, and held him up instead. "What are you doing here, boy? What's your name? Who are your parents?"

The boy opened his mouth wide as though he were going to shout, but his cry sounded like a whisper. "Let me go! Bloodsuckers, godless torturers! At least let me die! I don't want to go to Kazakhstan!"

Finally he passed out in Kirill's arms.

By the time Kirill, carrying the boy in his arms with Cecilia following after, appeared on the main street of the village, the operation of loading the "socially alien elements" into the trucks was almost complete. The soldiers, like harvest hands at the end of a good day's work, were relaxing by the wattle fence, trading wisecracks and sharing their tobacco. Petya Ptakhin was satisfied: he had checked all his lists, and everything tallied—more or less. Only the women, with their lack of political consciousness, were acting incorrectly. Makarevna, for example, was brandishing her fist at him from the back of one of the trucks, calling him the "Antichrist."

"Stop chattering, Makarevna!" Ptakhin called out to her good-naturedly. "Since there was no Christ, that means that there's no Antichrist, either."

"Do you hear that, Gradov?" laughed Cecilia, who had overheard the exchange. "Ptakhin knows his Dostoevsky!"

The Komsomol leader turned around, saw Kirill with the lad in his arms, and emitted a happy cry. "Ah, what luck! Where did you catch him, Comrade Gradov?"

"Who is he?" asked Kirill.

"Why, none other than Mitka Sapunov, a member of the kulak family! Throw him right into the truck, Comrade Gradov. It's loaded to bursting, but I think we can squeeze in one more all the same. A little tight, but no offense, I hope, girls?"

"Where are his parents?" asked Kirill.

"Why, they burned everything! You saw the ashes yourself, Comrade Gradov. Mitka's father, Fyodor, said a long time ago that before he'd go into the collective, he'd put the torch to everything he had, and to himself and his family too. He did his wrecking just as the comrades were about to come to his place with the order. Come on, now, Comrade Gradov, I'll help you stick Mitya in."

"No, hands off!" said Kirill with a ferocity that surprised even him. "Forget about this kid, Ptakhin. He's going to Moscow with me and Comrade Rosenbloom."

The Komsomol leader went pale at this turn of events, bustled about absurdly for a moment, and then drew a folder from beneath his belt.

"How can that be, Comrade Gradov? These are the new instructions, after all, and according to them, all kulak elements must be removed from here, regardless of age! They're to be sent to Kazakhstan to take up a more useful way of life! You're acting against instructions, Comrade Gradov. I can't allow someone to do just as he likes! There has to be proper no-ti-fi-cation!"

He looked around for the commander of the detachment, but he was nowhere in sight, and Ptakhin was afraid to run after him for fear that Gradov would make off with the kulak offspring. Kirill was also seized with a certain amount of panic. For some reason he could not even imagine how he could bring himself to part with the small body that was whimpering and moaning faintly in semiconsciousness in his arms. And yet, if the commander of the detachment appeared in the next few seconds, the game would be up.

Cecilia now went into action, taking the Komsomolist by the arm and leading him to one side, applying pressure to his elbow and wrist, transferring feminine warmth to them.

"Did it ever cross your mind, Comrade Ptakhin, that your interpretation of the Party's class policy might not always be the right one? Have you really never suffered from a lack of education? I can loan you a few works by some of our greatest theoreticians." She took several pamphlets from the bulging bag over her shoulder and began thrusting them under Ptakhin's belt. "Here you are, Ptakhin, you have Zinoviev, Kalinin, Bukharin, Iosif Vissarionovich Stalin. . . . Take them, Comrade Ptakhin, and study them. Study, study, and study, as Vladimir Iliich taught!"

Ptakhin put his hands on his waist, a dazed, reverent expression on his face. Cecilia finally released him from her comradely semiembrace and gave him an affectionate push that seemed to say, "Go on, study!" Kirill, meanwhile, walked away with Mitka in his arms. Cecilia followed after him with a good Party stride.

Some ten minutes later the column of army trucks roared past them, swaying as they ran over potholes and splashed through puddles. From the trucks came a sobbing and wailing that sounded remarkably like the mooing of cows.

CHAPTER ELEVEN

Tennis, Surgery, and Defensive Measures

☆

The autumn of 1930 was taking its time. Sometimes in the morning the smell of snow was clearly in the air and it seemed as though the first scarcely noticeable white flake would come fluttering down from the sky at any moment, but then, all of a sudden, as though it were made to order for our story, Indian summer would return, and Silver Forest in all its doubtful azure glory presented itself as the brightest and most luxurious palace of nature imaginable.

It was on such a morning that Nikita came out of the gate to the Gradovs' yard, as always in full uniform and carrying the briefcase he was never without whenever he went to the Commissariat for Defense. He was accompanied by Veronika, who wore a tennis dress and carried her racquet under her arm. Their son, Boris IV, in a sailor outfit and at the age of four already carrying a toy saber slung over his shoulder, was with them as well.

"Please remember, Nikita!" Veronika was speaking in a capricious yet severe tone, which meant she was quite serious. "Under no circumstances am I going back to Byelorussia. I've had enough! I'm a native of Moscow, after all! I haven't the slightest desire to waste my best years stuck in the provinces! You have to tell the commissariat straight out that you want a transfer to Moscow! Your articles are published in the journals, you're considered a theoretician! Pluck up your courage for once!"

Nikita was becoming jumpy, and glanced at his watch. "All right, all right, please calm down. I'm sure we'll stay in Moscow. Uborevich said unmistakably that he sees me as a member of the General Staff. I'm just almost sure that . . ."

A Defense Commissariat car came around a corner. Boris IV was in the clutches of two contradictory impulses—should he run toward the car or stay next to his mother? Chivalry won out.

"Mama's right," he said to his father. "It's better here. I want to live with Pythagoras too."

"Do you think I don't understand?" said the division commander in a hesitating, guilty tone. "You can believe me when I say I want it myself . . ."

Finally Veronika smiled.

"I'm absolutely sure," said the division commander more confidently. "Almost absolutely sure of an imminent transfer to headquarters!"

He kissed his wife and son and got into the car.

"Why aren't you playing tennis, Papa?" asked Boris IV sternly.

Life is filled with secrets, thought Nikita. It was only yesterday that the little one couldn't do anything but smack his lips and sniffle, and now he's asking existential questions about life.

The car started off.

Veronika was already on the court with her doubles partner, a handsome, elderly man, as well as their opponents, two other athletes who were no longer young, waiting to begin. All three were representatives of the "famous lawyer" type, a class that had survived the Revolution, returned fully to life, and now would take any case except one involving the defense of an accused man. The match started off smoothly, and within a few minutes Veronika was running all over the court, determined and flushed from exertion, fully aware that she looked simply enchanting and—well—irresistible!

"We're beating the daylights out of you, boys!" she shouted to her opponents, who beamed at being called "boys" and seemed to be rejuvenated by the strokes of the Red general's wife.

"Oh, Veronika, you're a tennis goddess!"

Boris IV was doing his part, too, running around the court and catching the balls that went out. Among the handful of spectators in the stands made of planks sat a military man with his hat pulled down over his eyes. Veronika had already noticed that it was none other than Regimental Commander Vuinovich.

Meanwhile, in one of the large rooms at the Commissariat for Defense, a group of upper-echelon Red Army officers was in a conference. A map showing the USSR and its neighboring countries was spread out over one wall. One of the best senior officers in the service, Commander of the Special Far East

Army Vasily Blücher, was walking up and down in front of the map with a pointer in his hands, representing the epitome of controlled might. Nikita Gradov was no less captivated by this report on the strategic situation than his wife was by tennis.

"The center of the military-political activity directed against our country is now shifting to the Far East," said Blücher. "Japan's plan to create a puppet Manchurian state on our border is of particular significance. I ask you once again to pay attention to the map, comrades. The blue arrows represent the recent movements of Japanese land and sea forces."

The blue arrows representing the Japanese forces poked like nettles into the udder and tail of the gigantic cow that was the Soviet Union. Blücher adjusted them slightly with his pointer. The commanders were absorbed in making notes on their pads.

"In the months to come we must be prepared for a serious confrontation," continued Blücher, "perhaps even for head-on clashes with a very powerful foe. The Japanese know how to fight—" He smiled and added, "—and like to." The army commander's smile clearly meant "Just as we like to," and all those present understood it that way as well.

Blücher crossed the room and stopped beside Nikita Gradov, putting his shiny boot on the rung of his chair. "It is precisely on our front, in the Far East, Nikita Borisovich, that you will find an application for your talents as a strategist. I'm offering you the chance to become my chief of staff in Khabarovsk."

A stunned Nikita found himself staring at the army commander's boottop rather than the man's face. Everyone present turned in his direction, smiling. The offer was of the sort a young officer can only dream about! What was it but a trampoline to a brilliant ascension?

"This is very unexpected, Vasily Konstantinovich," muttered Nikita. "Me, chief of staff in Khabarovsk?"

Blücher offered him his hand. "Well, do you agree?"

"How could I refuse such an offer?" Nikita stood up briskly, straightened the creases around the strap running diagonally across his chest, and shook the proffered hand. A thought suddenly occurred to him: Blücher has something in common with the late Frunze. Everyone in the room was now applauding: the Red martial spirit, the brotherhood of battle!

After he had finished his report, Blücher walked out into the corridor, accompanied by Nikita and a group of his subordinates from Khabarovsk. As he walked, he gave practical orders for the transfer.

"Nikita Borisovich, meet Regimental Commander Strelnikov, who will be your second in command. Battalion Commander Setanykh will be your senior adjutant. The remaining members of your staff you will select yourself. That's all for now. Everyone is free until 1435 hours."

Everyone then went off in different directions. Nikita slowly walked down the corridor and then stopped by yet another map of the USSR—the commissariat was well supplied with them. The green of the valleys and the brown hump of the Urals, followed by the expansive plains of western Siberia, the Altai Mountains rising in the south, and so on . . . Khabarovsk—five thousand miles from Moscow . . . Veronika will leave me. . . . Someone behind him clapped him hard on the shoulder. He shuddered. This sort of overly familiar greeting had been out of fashion for a long time now, and as for Nikita, he had learned to dislike it as long ago as the Civil War and certainly wanted no part of it now. Particularly if the someone who slaps you on the back with all his strength then stands there beaming right into your face wearing the uniform of a major in the NKVD. Nikita did not immediately recognize Semyon Stroilo. Since Nina's departure for Tiflis, not only had he not seen him, he had forgotten about him altogether.

Stroilo trumpeted, "Congratulations, Division Commander! What luck, eh? That means we'll be working together. I was just appointed to the Special Department of your staff!"

"Forgive me, but I don't believe I've had the honor," said Nikita with venom. Stroilo caught the intonation right away and began to play along. "Why, what's all this, Nikita, putting on airs like an old-style guard officer! I almost became related to you before Nina fled her Trotskyite friends and went to Tiflis . . ."

Nikita abruptly pushed him aside, surprised that Stroilo wasn't as strong a man as he appeared, and walked away with rapid strides. Stroilo, a crooked smile on his lips, watched him go. His invented and long-forgotten proletarian instincts were now aroused and deeply wounded.

Nikita went directly to Blücher's temporary office. The commander was sitting beneath a picture of Stalin, writing. Nikita approached his desk decisively. "Forgive me for coming in without an invitation, Vasily Konstantinovich, but I will have to refuse the position of chief of staff of the Special Far East Army."

Blücher finished the sentence he was writing and then looked up with a frown. Like all people who have armies of thousands of soldiers under their command, he immediately changed his behavior toward anyone who crossed him.

"Your reason?"

"A man has been appointed to the Special Department of my headquarters whom I completely and utterly distrust," said Nikita, who thought that at that moment he was making for himself a mighty and implacable enemy.

However, the unpleasantness on the commander's face vanished as instantaneously as it had appeared. He could understand Nikita's position. His subordinates chose their own subordinates—it was understandable, the military way, and without hypocrisy. He took out the list of the new appointments. He stopped his gold-tipped German fountain pen next to Stroilo's name.

"This one?"

Nikita nodded coolly. "Yes. NKVD Major Semyon Stroilo."

The golden pen point drew a sharp line through the undesirable name. Blücher looked carefully at Division Commander Gradov to see whether or not he appreciated this act of trust and saw that he did.

Perhaps it was at that very moment that Veronika decided that she'd had enough of dancing about the tennis court and interrupted the game. It was then that she acknowledged Vuinovich.

"Vadim, what brings you here? I imagine I must look a fright now! Where have you been all this time? It's as if you simply evaporated!"

Vuinovich, absolutely mortified, was cursing himself for not having left five minutes earlier—what could he do, though? He had been unable to take his eyes off of those graceful leaps, and now he twisted in his hands the hat that had not concealed him while muttering things he could not believe he heard himself saying:

"... blind fate ... a remarkable coincidence ... I was walking by and heard the sound of the racquets hitting the balls ... lawn tennis ... I've never seen it before ... I came in and then ... you, in person ... you were the last person I expected to see ..."

She gazed at him with a smile, as if she wanted to let him know that she had no objection to his passion for her so long as it remained in its present sweetly romantic proportions. He stopped talking, and then she came out again in the same tone, which seemed to her perfectly chosen: "Oh, really? So you never think about me? A good friend you turned out to be! Well, all right, all right—you're under arrest, Regimental Commander! Come to the dacha, everyone will be delighted to see you!"

Vadim's facial muscles began to tremble noticeably. The professor would be particularly delighted, he thought. He put on his hat and put his fingers to the visor in a courteous gesture.

"Forgive me, Veronika Yevgenievna, but I can't. I'm in a hurry to get to the train station. Today, in fact, I'm going to Tadzhikistan."

"For a long time?" she exclaimed in vexation, thinking: it's just like something that happens in books.

"Perhaps forever," said Vadim and hurried toward the exit.

What a strong, handsome figure he has, she thought, following him with her gaze. It's easy to imagine how he would take me. . . . Just then Boris IV, a bit off his head from running in circles for two hours, came running up.

.   .   .

Taking advantage of the unexpected blessings of Indian summer, the Gradovs had brought the samovar out onto the veranda. They were having a typical summer tea, with different sorts of homemade cookies along with rolls from a state store. At the table that evening were Boris Nikitovich, his assistant Savva Kitaigorodsky, Mary Vakhtangovna, their servant, or, as she would now be called, "domestic worker," Agasha, "tennis goddess" Veronika, her son, Boris IV, filled with dignity, and the new member of the family, the "kulak offspring" Mitya Sapunov.

A little more than two weeks had passed since the little boy had been brought only half alive to Moscow and installed in the dacha in Silver Forest, much to the consternation of the entire family. Now he was nearly unrecognizable: fed, washed, given a haircut, and wearing a good sweater. Only his eyes still looked scared; it would have been easy to say it was the look of a hunted wolf, if not for the fact that at times one could see in it something incomprehensible and terrible. But the look appeared less and less often now, and sometimes Mitya even smiled when Mama Mary looked him over and then gave him a bit of ham and cheese. And his smile became quite loving when Pythagoras, the friend of the entire house, breathed on him warmly and laid his muzzle in the crook of his arm.

Meanwhile, Boris Nikitovich and Savva continued to discuss professional matters.

"Our colleagues in the commissariat have approved our proposal. So get ready, Savva," said Gradov.

"Did they really?" asked Savva with joyful nervousness. "That means we can put the idea into practice? The introduction of the Gradov method of anesthesia is not far off?"

The professor smiled. "Not only is it not far off, but to be more precise, we're operating the day after tomorrow."

At that very moment, our young Marxist couple began to mount the steps from the garden to the veranda. They were holding hands and gazing at each other through their spectacles. Everyone was watching them, but they were paying no attention to anyone else. Agasha fetched them some tea, and they sat down together next to the samovar. Its red-hot side seemed to make Cecilia's freckles even more vivid than usual. Neither the tea nor the cookies held any interest for Kirill, who had eyes only for those freckles.

"Kirill, what's wrong with you?" asked Mary Vakhtangovna severely. One could scarcely say she was ecstatic about her youngest son's choice.

"Rosenbloom and I just registered our marriage."

Agasha clapped her hands. "Good gracious! And without a proper wedding?"

Veronika snorted derisively. "What I'd like to know is, do you call each other by your last names even in bed?"

"Veronika!" exclaimed her mother-in-law.

Kirill only giggled at Veronika, nodded to no one in particular, and squeezed Cecilia's hand beneath the table. The sullen dogmatist had disappeared, yielding to the love-struck schoolboy. He was even making jokes!

"Once we acquired an eight-year-old son, we had to get married!"

Mary Vakhtangovna was troubled again. "You don't think it would be better for Mitya if Bo and I adopted him?"

The romantic gleam disappeared from Cecilia's eyes, and she spoke decisively. "I beg your pardon, Mary Vakhtangovna, but the child must remain with his parents, that is, with us!"

"Well, here I am a grandfather again!" announced Boris Nikitovich happily. "I could have become a father four times, but instead twice became a grandfather!"

"And what do you think about it yourself, Mitya?" Mary asked the little boy.

With his mouth full he shuddered, then opened his eyes and muttered, "I'm drinking tea."

"An answer worthy of Socrates!" sang out the professor. Everyone applauded.

Mary remained serious, her voice quavering slightly. "I insist—I demand, even—that Mitya stay with us at least until you find a decent apartment." Assuming an expression of wounded dignity, she left the veranda with her chin held high. Almost immediately afterward the agitated rumble of the piano was heard from the house.

"Do you hear that?" Boris Nikitovich asked Kirill in an intimidating tone, after which he turned to his assistant and disassociated himself from the tangled affairs of the family.

"Tomorrow just take it easy, Savva, don't do anything. Relax, have a rest. The operation has to go off without a hitch, brilliantly, my boy."

Savva prepared to go home, though he did not want to leave. Every time he came to Silver Forest, it seemed to him he would see Nina. Agasha, who understood the sorrows of the young specialist perfectly, brought him some of her famous meat pies wrapped up in paper. From the threshold to the kitchen she announced in a sweet, singsong voice, "And here's Nikita, just now returning from the Commissariat for Defense. He looks very happy, yes sir."

Veronika saw him walking up the path from the front gate, and lit a cigarette. "Somehow he looks too happy," she murmured.

. . .

A day later, the long-awaited operation using the new anesthetic technique took place in the surgical clinic of the First Moscow Medical Institute. There were no empty seats in the amphitheater around the operating table, even though the observers had been limited to doctors and advanced students. The lower-course students crowded behind the glass window of the balcony.

Everything went surprisingly smoothly. The anesthetics they had developed over the previous months acted perfectly on the nerve extensors and endings. The patient was calm, joking with the nurses. "How do you feel, Iosif Alexandrovich?" Gradov asked him every five minutes. Every time, the esteemed piano tuner replied with unchanging good cheer, "Just fine, Boris Nikitovich." Now Savva Kitaigorodsky was sewing the final stitches. Soon the patient would be wheeled out. The surgeons stepped back from the table and removed their masks. The amphitheater burst into applause.

"And so, comrades, one may consider that as of today, the Gradov-Kitaigorodsky method of anesthesia has attained the status of standard practice!" declared the professor loudly.

Savva looked at his boss with a stunned expression, and everyone in the hall was surprised as well: there were very few professors who would so easily share the glory with their young assistants.

When they were alone together in Gradov's study, a nurse brought them two measuring glasses of diluted grain alcohol. Savva and Boris Nikitovich clinked their glasses together.

"Phew!" said Savva, running his hands over his face. "What's all this, then, Boris Nikitovich? The 'Gradov-Kitaigorodsky method'? My goodness, I don't deserve it!"

"Yes, you do, and very much so," countered the professor. "You were with me from the very beginning, Savva, working like an ox in the laboratory and in the clinic, and contributing so many brilliant ideas! And in any case—" He almost added, "you're like a son to me." Instead, he put his hand on the young man's shoulder. "Tell me, Savva, how is it that you didn't marry Nina back in '27?"

Savva was greatly embarrassed. A feeling of bittersweet sadness, so out of place within the walls of the surgical clinic, welled up quickly in his throat. "Well . . . to tell the truth, I don't know. At first there was Semyon, then Stepan . . . her disenchantment with Semyon, her attraction to Stepan . . . after all, Nina and Styopa are both poets, aren't they? And me? Just a modest small-time doctor. . . . My God, I love your daughter more than anyone else in the world! She's all I think about when . . . when I'm not operating, Boris Nikitovich . . ."

"She's coming back soon, my friend," said Gradov. He felt a sharp pang of pity and compassion for his assistant. When he had been courting Mary at the end of the last century, a medical diploma had been considered the height of prestige. Under the present regime, the old sources of prestige were subject to all kinds of humiliations.

"Nina's coming back!" Savva shouted, though he immediately cut himself short and turned away to the window. Outside, a sparrow was swaying back and forth on the branch of a birch tree. A tiny drop fell away from beneath his tail. Ruffling its feathers triumphantly, it soared off toward a destination unknown.

CHAPTER TWELVE

The Charlatan Organ Grinder

☆

In clear weather, the mountain range to the north of the Georgian capital was visible. The mountain peaks that shone forth from the plywood sign standing just beyond the entrance to the city zoo were even more impressive. In front of that mountain range there was drawn a picture of a well-built, wasp-waisted Caucasian mountaineer in his native costume with a cartridge belt across his chest and a dagger on his belt. There was an oval-shaped hole where the face should have been. The round Russian visage of dissolute fellow traveler Styopa Kalistratov now appeared in it. Voilà—he was a romantic mountaineer partisan. The photographer, who wore a mustache à la Kaiser Wilhelm—or like that of Semyon Budyonny, commander of the First Cavalry—raised the magnesium flash and dived beneath the curtain.

"Say 'kishmish,'* my good man!"

"Kishmish," Stepan called out. The magnesium went off. The photographer reemerged.

"Bravo! You're my best model so far this year! Where would you like to have the photograph sent? Moscow, Paris, Monte Carlo?"

"To Solovki, my beloved barbed-wire island, Monsieur! All decent people take their holidays now on the Solovki Islands, so it looks like that will be my address in the near future," the poet replied. He was clearly trying to put on a show, but when he looked around he was disappointed to see no one but

*"Cheese" in Georgian.

the faithful Otari, the knight of the sorrowful image. The audience he was trying to play to, the group of laughing young people that included his wife, Nina, was not far away, but was paying no attention to Styopa.

The whole group—Nina, her cousin Nugzar, the young poet Mimino, the dancer Shaliko, and the artist Sandro Pevzner—was cavorting in front of a cage from which a huge brown bear, risen onto his hind legs, was glaring at them. It was difficult to tell who was the audience and who was the performer. All of them, including, it seemed, even the bear, were filled with the sort of counterfeit irony and cheap theatricality that sometimes prevails in groups of young people after a long night of feasting and then more drinking the morning after.

Nina was trying particularly hard, extending her arms and calling out to the bear, "My dear Russian bear! My countryman and compatriot! My life's companion! Poor dear, what did you feel when you woke up after a pleasant nap to find yourself in this vile cage? My child! You are my Lermontov, abandoned in the Caucasus! How I want to kiss you!" She seemed oblivious to everyone around her, but out of the corner of her eye she saw her husband and his faithful Otari, and through the unrestrained haze of alcohol a sudden anger rose up inside her. Without realizing what she was doing, she jumped over the fence, ran up to the cage, and tore at the door. The lock, which turned out to be open, flew off, and the door swung wide. The bear, like Sobakevich in a theatrical version of Gogol's great epic poem, turned toward her slowly. Without even thinking, Nina tiptoed up to him and planted a magnificent kiss right on his snout. Again looking from the corner of her eye, Nina saw Stepan running as fast as he could in the direction of the action, Otari hurrying along behind him wringing his hands. She heard her husband shouting, "Nina, have you lost your mind?"

Nugzar seized him near the cage, covered his mouth, and commanded in a harsh tone, "Stop howling!"

Meanwhile, the bear had put his front paws onto Nina's shoulders and was shuffling in a circle around her, again like Sobakevich in the living room, as though he were afraid of stepping on her foot. His maw was partly opened, giving off a terrible odor. Everyone had stopped laughing long ago. Who could predict what the bear might do once he was bored? Only Nina pretended not to be afraid, trying not to spoil the scene. "My poor bear! My Lermontov! Child of mine!"

In fact, she was afraid to stir beneath the bear's paws. The thought even came into her mind: what an unthinkable end! The bear obviously was not going to let this once-in-a-lifetime opportunity to have fun get away.

Stepan pushed Nugzar away, and screamed hysterically, "Call the guard! Bring a fire hose!"

Sandro Pevzner, pale, overcoming his muddled head, was on the point of climbing over the fence without knowing why. What could he do? He might frighten the beast into maiming the Beloved, Our Girl, the star of Tiflis. Nugzar pulled him back with an iron hand and then, demonstrating absolute sang-froid, followed in Nina's footsteps. The bear's backside was facing him at that moment. He opened the door, went in, and gave the bear a forceful kick. The surprised animal returned to all fours. In a flash, Nugzar dragged Nina out of the cage, banging the door behind them. The bear howled wildly in disappointment. Several of the zoo's employees were now arriving on the scene. "It's an outrage!" roared the man in charge. "Hooliganism! You're all under arrest!" He seized Sandro by the lapels of his coat. "Who are you, you parasite?"

"I'm Sandro Pevzner, artist." A haze of hangover and shame fell over the young avant-garde painter, who had recently been advised by certain comrades in no uncertain terms to change to the path of realist proletarian art.

"So he's the ringleader!" roared the keeper. "Pevzner is the ringleader!" Once again, Nugzar came to the rescue. With a vivid air of authority he took the zookeeper aside, flashed his red NKVD identification discreetly enough so that no one else saw, and said weightily, "Take it easy, take it easy, dear comrade. No one was hurt, and the animal in your charge is alive and well. The girl was making a joke, taking a small poetic liberty. And *you* ought to keep the cages locked, sir, so that hostile elements cannot get in . . ."

The keeper held his tongue and forgot about pressing charges. The band of bohemians headed for the exit. The alcoholic haze had evaporated. All except Nugzar felt loathsome for the lack of courage they had shown. Nina was cursing herself for having done something so foolhardy and affected.

Nugzar glanced at his watch. "Sorry, everybody, but I have to run. I'll see you tonight at Papa Niko's."

He gave Nina a kiss on the cheek like a relative and then walked away with his usual purposeful stride, disappearing around the next corner. Soon afterward the rest of the group dispersed.

Early in the evening that same day, Nina and Stepan were walking along a humpbacked side street in the historic part of the city toward a small restaurant marked with an old sign reading "Papa Niko's Restaurant." Above the sign was another daubed with red and white letters in what was apparently supposed to be a primitive cubist style, reading "Dining Hall No. 7, City Food Administration." From time to time Stepan dropped several steps behind his wife. At one point she turned around and saw him inhaling a white powder into his nose. She shrugged contemptuously.

"Stop it, Stepan! You can't take a step anymore without that stuff! Tell me, did you pack your things? Or did you forget we're leaving for Moscow tomorrow?"

Stepan shot her a strange glance and muttered, "Wait awhile, Nina, we have to talk. Let's go into Papa Niko's first."

Despite Stalin's Five-Year Plan, the atmosphere peculiar to Tiflis still prevailed inside the restaurant, which had always been a favorite gathering place for coachmen and the artistic bohemia of the city. Bright primitivist paintings in the style of Pirosmani hung on the walls. Only Papa Niko himself, "King of the restaurateurs," as he was known in town, was unhappy. Instead of meeting guests at the door and wrapping them in an embrace as he usually did, he was sitting at the bar with an artist friend complaining that he was no longer the boss but the "assistant director."

"They collected everything, nationalized every pot and pan, everything except your paintings. I'm nobody now. They sent a Party man to take my place. It's the end of an era, my friend!"

The artist was comforting the restaurateur with the frivolity common to members of his profession. "Niko, just wait, old boy. Time will pass, and you'll get millions for my pictures."

Nina and Stepan sat down at a corner table and ordered a bottle of wine. "A large one," Stepan called after the waiter. "In fact, you can bring two," added Nina. "What's going on, Styopka?" she asked, putting her hand bearing two rings given to her by Paolo and Titzian on his trembling fist.

Stepan felt his head begin to swim, assumed an expression as though he had a toothache to show her—look how I'm suffering!—and then shook himself, pushed his hair back with both hands, and said, "I'm not going to Moscow."

Noise and commotion reigned in the city center at that hour. Overcrowded streetcars approached from every direction. Automobiles honked their horns. Cart drivers yelled at one another. Nugzar was cutting through the crowd like a torpedo boat. He approached a lemonade stand. The vendor handed him a small, heavy package along with his glass. Nugzar put the package into his pocket and emptied the glass with satisfaction. Then he disappeared beneath the arch of a passageway.

Nina and Stepan were drinking without looking at each other.

"Something in our relationship has burst, Nina," said Stepan sadly.

"A good word, 'burst,' " said Nina even more sadly. "Just like a balloon . . ."

"You're successful now, and I'm going down," said Stepan.

"What are you talking about, what success?" she said in exasperation.

Stepan suddenly flared up. "It's that damned bear—everything became clear to me after that! It was a sort of test that fate put me to, and I turned out to be absolute shit!"

"That's rubbish," she replied with a mixture of dejection and annoyance.

At the same time, Lado Kakhabidze, chairman of the Party Control Commission, was sitting in his spacious office beneath a picture of his beloved leader reading *Pravda*. A portrait of Stalin was conspicuous, if not glaring, by its absence. Anyone entering received an invitation to put himself in a serious mood in which he would be mindful of Party purity, for what could be more serious in all the world than Lenin reading *Pravda*? After a full day of conferences and meetings, Lado Kakhabidze was sitting by himself reading papers and making notes.

Somewhere far away in the building a door creaked, followed by swift, light steps. They were coming closer. The door of the office opened. Kakhabidze looked up. The visitor aimed a pistol at him. Before he could open his mouth, Kakhabidze was dead on the spot.

Meanwhile, at Papa Niko's, the organ grinder with parrots had wandered in. The threesome and the old musical contraption were in good form, cranking out an easily recognizable old melody as the organ grinder hummed along and the parrots fluttered from table to table. The people of Tiflis often argued about why the parrots didn't fly away from the organ grinder—some claimed he had tied invisible threads to their claws, though it was only the occasional drunk who figured out that the old man represented a sort of motherland for the birds.

Stepan was speaking heatedly to his wife. "I love you as much as ever, Nina, but I can't go with you. I've come to be afraid of the North. The North will devour me the same way that mammoths used to devour goats."

"Mammoths were herbivorous, you ignoramus," countered the irritated Nina. "What are you going to do here all alone, Stepan? You won't even be able to make enough to feed yourself."

The heat with which Stepan had been speaking was enough for only one sentence. He suddenly went limp again and murmured listlessly, "I'll think of something . . . the wine is cheap here . . . there's cheese . . . and vegetables . . . and don't forget that Otari is always with me."

That was what she was always forgetting—how could you remember the shadow of another man? And that youth did in fact follow her husband everywhere, just like a shadow. Otari, languid as a swan, was sitting at a small table by himself, clearly waiting for their conversation to end. Suddenly Nina was struck by an idea—she had finally guessed the reason for the magnetic inseparability of the two men. "Ah, so that's what it's all about! And I never guessed, fool that I am!" She began to laugh uproariously and kept on laughing until she had to put her head in her hands.

Just then a husky man wearing a military belt, the newly appointed director of the City Food Administration Dining Hall, emerged from the doors leading into the restaurant's kitchen. He made his way decisively past the tables of customers and began to push the organ grinder toward the door with both hands. "Get out, you miserable bandit! No private trade allowed!"

The two parrots landed on the old man's shoulders, bearing pink slips of paper in their beaks. The director instinctively made a grab for his belt, where not long ago a revolver had hung. Papa Niko sighed bitterly: the era is dead, long live the era! And it will end, sighed the exhausted philosopher, by a private undertaking on the part of God.

That night, confusion and disorder reigned at the house of the pharmacist Galaktion Gudiashvili. Women ran in and out crying, "Oh grief! Oh horror!" The master of the house lay on a couch in a semiconscious state, repeating only, "No, no, I don't believe it, my Lado must be alive . . ." His favorite nephew, Nugzar, his face hardened by the tragedy, sat on one of the bolsters of the couch holding his uncle's dangling arm by the wrist.

Suddenly Nina burst into the house and rushed to her uncle's side. "What happened, Uncle Galaktion?"

Her uncle covered his eyes with his palm and said, "Nugzar came running with terrible news, that Lado was shot at point-blank range in his own office. . . . The neighbors all came over, they say that the whole city is already . . . no, no, I don't believe it, my Lado must be alive . . ."

Nina clutched at her head, then raised her hands in the same imploring gesture as all the Georgian women in the house. Nugzar came up and led her off to the side of the room. "Nina, be brave."

"Who could have done this?" she asked, for some reason in a whisper.

"I heard the Trotskyites had some old scores to settle with him."

"That's rubbish, the Trotskyites don't resort to personal terrorism!" she replied with a dismissive wave of her hand.

He looked at her full in the face, quite sincerely, it seemed to her. "How do you know that, Nina?"

Nina struck her palm with her other fist, snatched up an open pack of cigarettes from a table, then threw it away. "It's as though Pandora's box has opened!" she exclaimed.

"What else has happened?" asked Nugzar briskly.

"Nothing has happened," she said, pacing around fitfully, "but I have a train tomorrow . . . do you understand? In the morning I'm leaving for Moscow . . . my things aren't packed . . . everything has collapsed . . . this news . . ."

"Your things are no problem," said Nugzar with assurance. "Let's go, I'll help you get ready. Trust your cousin."

Struck by the last phrase, Nina came to a stop with her back to him, then looked slowly over her shoulder. A wave of feral joy passed through Nugzar's body. Today is my day, he thought. Without saying a word, she went upstairs. He followed after her.

Everything in her room was in disorder, empty suitcases lay open everywhere. Coming in, Nina began to throw everything that came to hand—undergarments, shoes, books—into her cases. Nugzar came in behind her, took her by the shoulders, and pulled her to him. Today she was unable to resist him. On the contrary, she felt herself drawn to some unknown goal by some unknown person—finally to get to the end of things, to some end that was unknown to her, that is, finally to be open about things. He sensed this and said in a breaking voice, "You're the kind of girl I like, no bear is going to scare you off."

"I'm not afraid of beasts that are even scarier," she whispered with a dark smirk and began to unbutton his shirt. He removed her jacket from her shoulders. Their movements were deliberate, as if they were taking pains that not one second of this melancholy tryst should pass unnoticed.

When that train of moments had finally passed, Nina found it impossible to remain still. She kissed the shoulders and neck of her man with her eyes closed. Suddenly an infinitely odious voice reached her ears. "I see you liked the *abrek.**"

Everything came to an end. She opened her eyes. "You, an *abrek*?"

Nugzar burst out laughing. "Of course I'm a bandit, a bold *abrek*!"

Nina moved away from him. Their nudity suddenly seemed shameful to her. "*Abreks* didn't blackmail women," she said, though she understood perfectly well what was happening—after a stormy series of confessions and admissions, she was beginning to resort to guile, to imagine herself as a

*Georgian for "bandit."

frightened victim. Understanding swept over her, and she sat up in bed. "Of course! Now I understand everything! It was you who killed Uncle Lado Kakhabidze!"

Nugzar threw himself at her and fell on her heavily, seizing one of her breasts with one hand, covering her mouth with the palm of the other, and whispering hotly into her ear, "Never repeat that nonsense again, you fool! Otherwise we'll all get killed—you, me, and anyone who hears it! Understand?"

Then everything began all over again. Turning her head away, Nina looked at one of the darkened windows with eyes full of fear.

CHAPTER THIRTEEN

Life-Giving Bacilli

☆

Another family morning idyll began at the Gradov dacha in Silver Forest. The whole family was gathered for breakfast: the professor and his wife; their eldest son, the division commander; his lovely wife and their haughty son, Boris IV; their younger son the Marxist with his equally Marxist wife and their son, Mitya; Agafia bustling about and managing everything; and of course, the chief ideologist of such moments of harmony, Pythagoras.

"Everyone should have one glass of yogurt every morning," Boris Nikitovich was insisting. "The great Metchnikoff discovered life-giving bacilli in it, the secret of a long life. Everybody will drink yogurt, without exception. Nikita, that means you too!"

The chief of staff of the Special Far East Army shuddered. "How's that—'me too'?" He hurriedly emptied his glass. Mary gave him a look that said "Good boy."

"What the hell good is long life to us?" said the tennis player defiantly. "So that we can rot in the swamps of the Far East?"

Nikita lowered his eyes. Mary returned the serve. "Veronika, what kind of a way is that to talk? There are children here!"

Mitya, who had become the favorite of the family, went off into gales of laughter. "What the hell, what the hell good is long life to us?"

Boris IV, declining in importance, jumped up on his chair. "What the hell! What the hell!"

Despite the difference in their ages, the two boys had become friends, and the "kulak offspring" had changed to the point of being unrecognizable. Agasha even parted his hair at a slant so that he would look like a child "from a good family." It was only at night that he sometimes tossed and turned in his sleep, running off somewhere in his dreams and making a sound that sounded like mooing, but it happened less and less often.

Boris Nikitovich wagged his finger at Veronika, and the whole tribe surveyed the scene with mock seriousness. Satisfied with his performance, he looked at the clock and rose from the table. Something was preventing him from feeling true matinal comfort. Then it came to him—the opera! The fearful, righteous lord of justice immediately vanished, and the professor reappeared. "Marichka, can I speak to you for a moment?"

Sensing that something was wrong, Mary followed him into his study. "What's happened, Bo?"

"Marichka, we're going to have to put off our excursion to the opera."

"Oh, I just knew it! We'll never get to the opera!"

He muttered hastily, "Don't you understand, Mary, the Chief Medical Directorate of the Commissariat for Defense is asking for a report at the earliest possible moment on our new method of local anesthesia. That means I have to summon our entire research group. We simply won't be finished by the time the performance begins."

Mary was deeply disappointed. The "excursion," as he put it, to the Bolshoi to see the new production of *Carmen* was a big event for her—this morning she had woken up with joyful anticipation—while for him it was only an annoying reason to hurry, an obstacle on the road to new successes. Somehow everything looked different when I was young! she thought. Yes, of course there is work, life and its struggles, but all that exists alongside music and pure inspiration, otherwise we are deprived of spiritual freedom!

"I see, Boris, that you've lost the ability to say no to the leadership! You've won all your awards and high positions, but you've lost your spiritual freedom!"

Gradov made a gesture of entreaty. "You're wrong, my dear!"

At that moment someone was ringing the front doorbell over and over again. Agasha rustled to the door to answer it. On the threshold stood the imposing figure of a former junior officer in the Worker-Peasant Red Army, now District Constable Slabopetukhovsky. He whispered something into Agasha's ear. She clapped her hands and grabbed his sleeve, then led him into the professor's study by a roundabout path so that those in the dining room would not see them. Now she was kicking at him, waving her fists, hissing at him in a loud whisper, and gesturing to her masters.

"Boryushka, Maryushka, you won't believe it—Slabopetukhovsky has come for Mitya! May my eyes never see such a thing! Get out, you shameless creature!"

The constable's face broke out in spots from indignation, his mustache drooped, and his cheekbones protruded like a Scythian burial mound. "And what does Slabopetukhovsky have to do with it, Agafia Yermolaevna? Slabopetukhovsky was summoned by the proper authorities, told to stand at attention, and then given an order. We received a report from Tambov Province. A kulak element under legal age was unlawfully taken away and housed with the family of Professor Gradov. According to the orders that were drawn up, the underage child must be removed from the family immediately and placed in an orphanage. Why do you treat me this way, Agafia Yermolaevna, calling me a shameless creature? You can eat those words!"

Greatly offended, he turned away and through a series of doorways saw the kitchen cupboard containing cut-glass cups and glasses, among which, as he knew better than anyone else, there was always a decanter full of some strong drink.

"They've really gone off their heads this time, the scoundrels!" shrieked Mary. Her Georgian temperament had never needed much provocation.

"This is simply beyond good and evil," said Gradov, his temper boiling. "Making off with an underage child, the idea!" He could barely restrain himself from taking up his wife's cry: Scoundrels! Scoundrels corrupted by their impunity, devils incarnate!

"I trust you won't allow this, Bo?" Mary said to him in the same angry tone.

Gradov suddenly began barking orders as though he himself were the local representative of the Bolshevik bureaucracy. "Mary, stay here! Slabopetukhovsky and Agafia, you can go! Wait! Not a word to anyone!"

In the kitchen, the constable put one arm around Agasha and with the other reached for the decanter, as was his habit. Agasha weakened in his half embrace. "Slabopetukhovsky, how could you? What about your oath, Slabopetukhovsky? Why, they're all just like family to me, and Mitenka is closest of all to me, the poor orphan." Suddenly she shook off his large hand and said in a commanding tone, "Well, just go to your superiors now and tell them that Mitya isn't here. Tell them his mama, Cecilia, has taken him to a Party sanitorium!"

Slabopetukhovsky was delighted at the resourcefulness of his friend and looked much happier. "Right away, Agafia Yermolaevna, though permit me to use the cavalry method of plucking up courage and ask you for a kiss and a good glass of strong drink."

Meanwhile, in the study, Boris Nikitovich resolutely walked over to the telephone, but before he could put his hand on the receiver, the telephone rang. Mary folded her hands on her chest in a tragic gesture.

"Savva?" said Gradov into the phone. "It's good you've called. Please tell everyone concerned that I am canceling today's operation and all my appointments. . . . What? You're happy? How should I take that? . . . Oh, so that's it! Well, all right, I'll see you this evening." He put the receiver down and turned to his wife. "Imagine, Nina and Stepan are coming back today. She sent Savva a telegram, and he's in ecstasy."

Even this news had no effect on Mary. "Please, Bo, Nina comes later! Right now Mitya, Mitya, only Mitya! We must save that little boy!"

Sitting at his desk, the professor opened a morocco-bound notebook in which he found the number of the Kremlin operator. Lord, how he wished he didn't have to call there! Every moment he could delay seemed to him a gain. "Mary, please bring my suit—you know, the one with all those idiotic medals on it." As soon as she had gone out of the room, he picked up the receiver. "Miss, please connect me with Chairman of the Central Executive Committee Comrade Kalinin!"

Mary was already flying back to the study, carrying the dark suit with the two Orders of the Red Banner on one of the lapels. These days, someone came to give him an award on the occasion of almost every holiday, and all these medals, good-sized badges, had to be worn on his "on parade" suit. Without putting the telephone down, he began to change. Just as he was taking off his jacket, the connection with Kalinin's office was completed, and the jaunty voice of some newly promoted peasant crackled over the line. Gradov said firmly, "Hello, this is the surgeon Boris Nikitovich Gradov, professor and laureate, speaking. It is urgent that I speak with Comrade Kalinin. . . . I'm sorry, the matter cannot be put off. . . . Yes, yes. . . . You'll do what, comrade? Ventilate the situation? Please, ventilate by all means. . . . Yes, I'll wait."

He had removed his shoes and trousers and had already taken his official suit from his wife when he heard the rapid speech of a provincial small businessman on the line—Kalinin.

Why didn't I ever notice that dark blue vein on Bo's right calf before? thought Mary, as she looked at her trouserless husband. It must be because of so many hours of standing during operations.

Gradov was speaking to Kalinin with assurance and the requisite amount of respect—in other words, just as one was supposed to address the "Wise Man of all the Russias" with his beard like a billy goat's, who, while not considered a villain in Moscow, generally passed for a malingerer and a coward. "I must speak with you, Mikhail Ivanovich. I urgently request that you receive me today. I won't take up more than fifteen minutes of your time." Cocking his head to one side to hold the receiver between his ear and shoulder, Gradov knotted his tie with a few deft movements. "Yes? I'm extremely grateful. They'll come for me right away?"

Hanging up the receiver, he stood before his wife in full regalia. Mary kissed him, then stepped back to admire him. Even those barbaric medals suited him.

"I was wrong, Bo. You haven't lost your freedom of spirit!"

By that evening everything had been resolved, definitively and with the happiest outcome imaginable. The password of the Kremlin leaders—"You can work in peace, Comrade Gradov"—had been uttered. A joyous atmosphere prevailed at the dacha. Mitya was chasing Boris IV all over the house, not even suspecting that he had been so recently marked for "removal," feeling only the festive excitement that always seized the house on days of "all hands present." The phonograph was playing in the dining room, bottles were opened. It goes without saying that the happiest of them all was Pythagoras, who knew everything. Besides—and this was maybe even more important—Nina, his favorite sister, Nina, had come! Mary, quite flushed, was constantly bestowing kisses upon that bearer of unshakable spiritual freedom, her husband.

"Our papa is a hero today! Our papa is a hero today!"

Boris Nikitovich recounted his audience with Kalinin in deeply meaningful tones, though not without restrained humor. "That is what it means to be a Russian doctor, my friends! A member of the government . . . yes, sir . . . hmm . . . and of such a government as this one, at that . . . speaks to you as an equal!"

He looked intently at Nina. His daughter was pale, as though she had just come from foggy Petersburg, rather than from the South. Suddenly he realized that she was alone. "Well, then, where is Stepan?"

Nina did not answer, but Savva Kitaigorodsky stepped forward instead, almost beside himself with excitement, if not actually radiant with happiness. "Imagine, ladies and gentlemen, the train pulls in, Nina jumps down from the car, and I see that she—she's alone, ladies and gentlemen! I look around: alas, Stepan's not there, occupies no space. I even went into the car to look for him, but he wasn't there. He was simply and dramatically absent, ladies and gentlemen!"

He glanced at Nina, and she smiled at him—smiled at him personally, a teaching assistant in the Department of General Surgery. It was a slightly distracted smile, but she clearly had a recipient in mind. It was not just directed to the air.

The professor also smiled, understandingly, and said to Savva, "And you were terribly depressed by his absence, weren't you? It's a bit awkward when one is expecting to meet two people but only one shows up." It was perhaps the first time since the days of the Frunze affair that Boris Nikitovich had been as animated as he was today. He caught his grandson Boris IV on the run and sat him on his knee.

"I hope that at least this one of my offspring, Boris the Fourth, will follow in the footsteps of his grandfather and become a great Russian doctor."

"I'll follow, I'll follow, Grandpa! Where are your footsteps?" Boris IV cried out.

From the kitchen, Slabopetukhovsky raised his glass to all present. Agasha was going back and forth with dishes of meat pies and aspic. Nikita, Veronika, Cecilia, Kirill, Nina, and Savva—that is, all the young people of a grown-up age in the Gradov house at this point in the story, 1930, the year of the "great breaking point," a year when they continued, against all odds, to grow stronger—went out onto the veranda to smoke.

"Just think," said Nikita, lighting a cigarette, "without saying a word to anyone, the old man arranged everything himself. After all, I could have done something through Blücher—he's a member of the Central Committee . . ."

"Quiet, comrades, Mitya doesn't know anything about it," warned Cecilia. "And he doesn't need to know anything about his past, either. Let him grow up as a full-fledged Soviet man."

Nina flung a furious, purely Georgian gaze at her but said nothing. Nikita snickered. "All the same, Cel and Kir, this case doesn't fit in very well with your historic classifications, does it?"

"Exceptions don't invalidate the whole process as such," countered Kirill in a gentle academic tone that was unusual for him.

Veronika laughed shortly. "I'd still rather be treated as an exception than as part of the process!"

The "happy ending" of the second part of our story was approaching. Agasha called everyone to the dinner table. A feeling of generalized joyous affection was spreading throughout the house, in spite of all the ups and downs in the life of the family—and perhaps even because of them—and the ideological disputes. "Why, oh why can't we all live together always?" exclaimed Mama Mary.

Only Nina smiled, a forced, unnatural smile. She still had not really arrived. Slowly, like a train going through a switching station, the events of the past few days passed through her mind: her discussion with Stepan, the murder of Lado Kakhabidze and the night she had spent with his killer, and finally a brief incident that had occurred on the trip north, the railroad impression of a modern-day Anna Karenina.

The train had been passing slowly through a switching station at Rostov-Nakhichevan. Nina was standing in the corridor of her "international" car, smoking. She could not take her eyes away from the window. By the nauseating station light, she watched a seemingly endless procession of boxcars drifting by, carrying kulak families from the Ukraine and the Kuban to the East for permanent resettlement. Each car could carry either forty human beings or eight horses.

In the tiny windows beneath the boxcar roofs appeared a jumble of eyes, lips, and faces uniformly pale to the point of being jaundiced. Here and there the doors had been opened a crack to allow air to circulate, clearly against regulations. The sound of curses, cries, and children howling carried across the tracks. Suddenly a harmonica began to wail. It was impossible to tell how many "horses" were in the cars, but they were undoubtedly filled past capacity. Red Army soldiers from Kirghizia were posted along the tracks with rifles. From time to time, members of the NKVD special forces passed by, leading guard dogs on leashes.

Nina could not take her eyes off these wagons of death. And then someone answered her glance. The terrible and swollen face of a person of an indeterminate sex was looking at the beautiful young woman in the "international" car—it was in fact a collective face with an uncountable number of eyes, looking at her with hatred and contempt.

FIFTH INTERMISSION
THE PRESS

The XVI Congress of the Communist Party is proceeding, taking as its slogan "It is time to put an end to the rightist opposition!" The Party has tried its best and is trying patiently to correct the line of the comrades who have strayed from the Leninist path. However, the leaders of the rightist opposition have not yet indicated that they are ready to make amends for the mistakes that they have made, refusing to abandon the smallest opening for rightist opportunistic hesitation. The article by Comrade Bukharin not only mentions none of the errors he has committed but might well lead one to believe that he still holds to his rightist opportunistic position. What the rightist leaders Comrades Uglanov, Tomsky, and Rykov said at the congress will force the Party to be on its guard. The Party is fully justified in expecting Comrade Rykov to provide more direct and clearer responses. Propagandistic activities for and the defense of rightist views are incompatible with membership in the Communist Party. Former adherents of such theories must show real proof that they are now struggling against the rightists. The Party is not Noah's Ark but a fighting union of ideological allies. Only unity will afford us the possibility of vanquishing all the foes of communism.

An early mass subscription to the state bond "The Five-Year Plan in Four Years" has been noted in the factories and plants of Leningrad. A mass wave of initiatives has swept the Urals.

According to an announcement by the Moscow authorities, meat ration coupons for the third ten-day period in June, the thirteenth, fourteenth, and fifteenth inclusive, will be valid until July 3, inclusive. The validity period of children's and workers' coupons for manufactured goods has been extended to the third quarter.

In honor of the twenty-fifth anniversary of the 1905 uprising: a showing of the world-famous film *The Battleship Potyomkin.*

Bring in the full harvest from the fields of the collective farms! Lead individuals by setting a Bolshevik example!

The All-Union auto-bike-motorcycle relay race is coming to Moscow. Reports will be broadcast from Dynamo Stadium.

Turn in wastepaper before the end of the month!

Japanese crab fishing boats are poaching in Soviet waters.

From the closing address of Comrade Stalin, July 3, 1930:
"The rightist leaders must break once and for all with their past, rearm themselves, and merge united with the Central Committee of our Party in its struggle for a Bolshevik rate of development, in its struggle with rightist deviation. There are no other means. If the former leaders of the rightist opposition manage to do this, well and good. If not, they will have only themselves to blame . . ." Prolonged applause throughout the hall. Everyone stands and sings the "International."

.   .   .

To all workers on the construction of the airship *Pravda,* to all cooperative groups of newspaper editors: You are requested to announce the amount of the funds that you have collected and to transfer the collected funds to the current account of the airship *Pravda,* No. 564.

Textile worker Ivanov has contributed twenty-five rubles in gold: "I am sending you twenty-five gold rubles to be placed in the proletarian treasury. I have been saving them for some time, I wanted to make gold teeth from them for myself, but I can see that this is not the time for that. I propose that a collection drive for gold items be opened. Everybody is holding on to something. With comradely greetings, Ivanov."

Journalists vacationing in the Sochi rest home and typesetters, instead of laying a wreath on the grave of Taras Kostrov, have contributed 420 rubles.

By September twenty-seventh the account had received 193,452 rubles and 97 kopecks, 3,000 Italian lire, 150 rupees, 7 German marks, 4 gold rings, and various items of value. *Pravda* will soar over the Soviet earth!

Make up for the September shortfall with plenteous columns of bread!

Step up the attack on the kulak and the rightist opportunists putting the brakes on collectivization!

We must rely more strongly and broadly on the initiative of the masses in the struggle for the new millions of collective farmers!

We, individual farm owners of the village of Zarient in the Margelan region, are convinced of the advantages of being collective farmers and rejoice in joining the Stalin Collective Farm!

Construction of Airship Excites Enormous Interest!

From the audience. Under a mask of anonymity. The debates at the Platonov Institute about the results of the Party Congress supposedly showed agreement with the Party line . . . and yet the fact that a significant number of anonymous notes were handed to the speakers from the audience testifies to the presence among the participants of comrades who are either in disagreement with the resolutions of the congress or those who doubt their correctness. Some of the authors of these anonymous notes mockingly claim that collectivization is a failure.

. . . In discussing the resolutions of the XVI Party Congress, the cell of the Platonov Institute of Agriculture in Moscow must pay greater attention to conciliatory tendencies manifested by some of the Party members and rebuff their advances soundly.

Harvest and store with a fighting spirit!

Call to strict accountability persons guilty of ruining vegetable production! There are suspects, why haven't they been put on trial?!

Mobilize thirty writers within the next two weeks and include them in the shock worker brigades! Put an end to literature's lagging behind the needs of socialist construction!

News of the day. In Anapa the trial of the wreckers of cooperatives has begun. First reported closures of distribution centers in Leningrad. Sizable deposits of lead have been discovered. In Stalinabad, the trial of automobile assembly line worker Kubitsky, accused of the murder of a Tadzhik taxi driver, has begun. Society indignantly condemns this case of obvious Great Russian chauvinism.

In the decisive phase of liquidation of the kulaks:

"For the time being, the question of 'who will triumph over whom' has not been decided, and the class struggle in our country continues to intensify. Small manufacturing every day, every hour gives rise to capitalism. . . . With full collectivization as a starting point, we shall strike a powerful blow against the kulak, particularly in the grain-growing regions. He is straining with his last desperate efforts beneath the wheels of the chariot of socialism triumphant, trying to drag the middle-class and poor peasant down with him, along with isolated strata of the urban proletariat. The task of the liquidation of the kulaks as a class is our principal task."

Two new groups of "former people" have been liquidated by the organs of the Moscow OGPU. One of them was headed by the typical kulak ideologist Professor Kondratiev. Alongside it existed a fully formed group of intellectuals continuing to propagate Menshevik ideology—Groman, Bazarov, Sukhanov, and others.

News from abroad. Suspicious overflights by Polish aircraft. Indigenous uprising in Indochina. An increase in White Guard activity in Harbin. The leader of the German Fascists, Hitler, is negotiating with the industrial magnates of the Ruhr.

The OGPU has uncovered a network of spies and wreckers in the public food supply system, an organization having as its aim the creation of famine in the countryside and dissatisfaction among the working masses, thereby contributing to the overthrow of the dictatorship of the proletariat. The following food industries have been infiltrated by the wreckers: meat, fish, canned goods, citrus fruits, and other corresponding links in the People's Commissariat for Trade.

From the testimony of Professor Ryazantsev, former landowner and general in the Quartermaster Corps: "I always believed that the fundamental class, the bearer of culture, is the bourgeoisie."

Professor Korotygin, former editor of a Kadet newspaper: "Disbelief that agriculture can be restored in this country by Soviet rule, the rejection of collectivization, reliance upon private farming, the preservation of private property relations, are all characteristic of us. . . . For my wrecking in the refrigerator affair I received a total of 2,500 rubles from Ryazantsev . . ."

Levandovsky, manager of the department of sales and distribution of the state meat company: "We want the state to get out of the meat business, to hand the market over to private capital . . ."

Responses in the countryside to the unmasking of the group of wreckers: "Crush the saboteur snakes mercilessly! A salute to the OGPU, the guardian of the revolution! Greater vigilance!"

The workers are responding to sabotage in the food production industry by rallying in ever greater numbers around the Bolshevik Party, by pledging on their honor to fulfill the third and decisive year of the Five-Year Plan. The working class will produce hundreds and thousands of organizers of socialist construction to take the places of the isolated wreckers.

The metalworkers in the electrical components factory demand a ruthless sentence. The Amo Factory workers send greetings to the OGPU, the sword of the dictatorship of the proletariat. We demand that the supreme punishment be applied to the wreckers—death by firing squad!

Proletarian poet Demyan Bedny:

And so the wreckers lost the war,
But we have captured every whore.
This Kondratievna-German snot,
This egghead counterrevolution's not
About to get its canned goods hot.

Put them against a wall! We demand retribution against the agents of the international bourgeoisie!

> After carrying out the assignment of the Central Executive Committee of Soviets of Workers, Peasants, and Soldiers to examine the case of the counterrevolutionary organization in the domain of food supply, colleagues of the OGPU reached the following conclusion:
>
> Ryazantsev, Korotygin, Karpenko, Estrin, Dardyk, Levandovsky, Voiloshchikov, Kupchin, Ginzburg, Bykovsky, Sokolov—in all, forty-eight men—as active participants in the wrecking organization and implacable foes of Soviet rule—WERE CONDEMNED TO BE SHOT.

> Sentence has been carried out.

> Chairman of the OGPU Menzhinsky

"The struggle for quality in production is the struggle for socialism!" From the address of Comrade Kuibyshev at the production quality conference.

> To the editor of the newspaper *Pravda*. Respected Comrade Editor! I ask you to publish my declaration.
>
> In *Pravda* No. 9 my article "Toward the XVI Party Congress" was included on the discussion page. I have now come to the conclusion that I was entirely wrong, and that the comrades who spoke out against me were right. My views on collectivization did not correspond to those of the Party, but to the right-opportunist line. I recognize my address as harmful and fallacious, and I fully share the Party's views on questions concerning collectivization. I will make a genuine effort to rectify the mistakes that I have made.

> With Communist greetings,

> Mamaev

SIXTH INTERMISSION
THE OAK RUSTLES

Among the numerous trees of Neskuchny Garden, above the Moscow River, stood an eighty-year-old oak tree on a gently sloping hill, almost by itself. Its uppermost branches made a noise that sounded like "Butashevich, Butashevich!," the branches in the middle of the tree and lower down chimed in with "Petrashevsky!," while the crossbills perching in the oak whistled, "Dost! Dost!"

Unlike the other trees in the park, this one had originally been planted far away, many miles away in the semidarkness of the North, in the damp mouth of a short but voluminous river. After that discussion circle had been broken up, it was reincarnated into a young oak, almost without any form at all at that point, and continued to live for a long time above the mouth of the river and its channels, in which were reflected palaces and bridges, spires and clouds, and even the utterly invisible, almost nonexistent future oak, embodying the idea of the disbanded liberal Petrashevsky discussion group. One day, however, a storm came up, and the oak, which, just being born, or rather the idea of an oak, was uprooted by the turbulent southerly wind and flew along with other ideas, particles, disputes, and tiny frogs yanked from their swamps until it ended up on a gently sloping hill in the Neskuchny Garden in the old capital.

One warm and stuffy night, when winds from the north and south were struggling against each other in the sky, everything was suddenly lit up by a flash, illuminating the columns of a pavilion in which a daring couple was making love, the trunks of trees, ripples on a pond, and the rough surface of the river. The nascent oak dug itself into its now-native soil, recently turned over by someone who lived in the area, strong smelling, black after a downpour, a loose, sticky substance, and thought forlornly: Will I really take root? It did. And eighty years later, in 1930, it stood, swaggering in the wind, occupied like all those around it with the usual business of trees. According to the recent discoveries of science, photosynthesis was all it was supposed to do, but in its branches, or rather among its branches, still lived the memory of the group, or more accurately the group's indistinct ideas, the booming sound of leather galoshes being thrown off in the entrance hall, the exchange of literature and viewpoints, Belinsky's letter to Gogol—Fyodor, my dear, do read aloud!—the baffling interrogations, the steady beating of the drums at the mock execution.

One day toward evening, a couple appeared in the pavilion—a man of around forty and a young woman. Like his White opponent Kolchak, Red Army Commander Blücher was in love with one of his female adjutants. Her head lay on his broad, leathery shoulder, her nose, touching in its smallness, next to his marshal's star, and he looked at the branches of the oak and thought: something has to be done, maybe at this very moment, maybe later will be too late—time to take a chance and then to go down in history as the savior of the Revolution. Not a bad idea, thought the oak, waving its branches and sending him a reassuring breeze. Go on thinking . . . Technically, it wouldn't be hard to manage, Vasily continued his thought. On the next trip from Khabarovsk, a full guard detachment could enter the Kremlin and arrest the bastards, particularly the one at the top, that red-headed cockroach . . . then go on the radio and ask everyone to stay in place, to put an end to collectivization, to bring back NEP and head off the coming famine.

A traitorous dampness was advancing from the direction of the river. A dense, low-flying cloud of fear was slowly moving away from the city center like steam from the turbines of an electrical power station. The oak was trying to distract the army commander's attention from these bothersome details by singing its refrain: Butashe-e-e-vich, Petra-a-a-shevsky, while the crossbills chirped, "Dost! Dost!" Tiny streams of dejection, though, trickled in beneath the leather harness, disturbing both the star and the touchingly small nose. Such a plan had very little chance of succeeding, very little chance indeed. To undertake such an operation without allies at the top would be unthinkable, but to seek out such allies would mean failure—Menzhinsky's spies are everywhere. The fact that he would be killed was unimportant—the important thing was that he would go down in history not as the savior of the Revolution but as its betrayer.

Meanwhile, yet another savior of the Revolution was approaching the pavilion in the shade of the oak on the deserted path in the Neskuchny Garden, the butcher of Kronstadt and Tambov, the chief of staff of the Red Army, Mikhail Tukhachevsky. There was a military maiden on his shoulder as well, a hairdresser from the commissariat. The trend was clear: the iron men of the regime were seeking comfort in romance.

The oak was aroused in every fiber of its being. Come closer together, lads, Vasya and Mitya, it exhorted, become friends—after all, you're both thinking the same thing.

But once they noticed each other, the two army commanders hurriedly dismounted from their poses as future equestrian statues, their hearts beating faster in fear. Tukhachevsky turned his companion sharply in another direction and vanished into the twilight shadows of the spruce trees. At the same time, Blücher, taking hold of his lady with the small nose, dashed down the steps of the summerhouse, then disappeared down a path, his boots tapping noisily on the asphalt surface. Among other things, neither army commander could be sure that his companion was not working for Menzhinsky.

Fainthearted men, rustled the oak in its crown, and then it devoted its attention wholeheartedly to the sunset over the Moscow River.

CHAPTER FOURTEEN

Count Olsufiev's Mansion

☆

By day Moscow looked like its usual self—a seething anthill crisscrossed by streetcar lines. Any form of public transport—streetcars, buses, or the newer trolleys—was covered with swarms of these creatures. Horse-drawn cabs had almost disappeared, replaced by the motorized taxis, and there were now so few of them that they belonged more to the realm of legend than of public transport. In 1935, with much attendant pomp and circumstance, the first passengers had been admitted into the metro with its marble-floored stations, ceiling mosaics, and escalators. Two years had already passed, and the propaganda orchestra and its accompanying fountains had not ceased for so much as a day. There was even less practical sense in the single line running from Sokolniki Park to the Park of Culture on the Moscow River than there had been in the project that had been drawn up before the First World War that proposed to construct a tunnel from the Zamoskvorechie district to the Tver gates, that is, to unite the two halves of the city. The propaganda value of the Moscow metro, however, overshadowed all practical considerations. The best in the world! Underground palaces! The triumphs of the Komsomolists and the construction workers! The hearts of the laboring masses are filled with pride! It is the concern of the Party and the government, and of Comrade Stalin personally!

The advertisements of the NEP era had been replaced by "agitation and propaganda by visual aids," which sometimes appeared in the most unexpected places: slogans, portraits of Stalin as well as the other members of the leadership who remained after the waves of executions, pieces of sculpture and diagrams. The Muscovite who, in looking around, no longer even took in the meaning of these devices, but only realized inwardly that they were there and would always be there, all around him, had already received the message that was coming from behind the crenelated walls of the Kremlin: sit still, don't complain!

Otherwise, everything seemed to be going along normally, organized streams of people going to and from work, languishing in queues, on Sundays going to the Spartak-Dynamo match, or else to the cinema to see the buoyant comedies of Grigory Alexandrov, The Circus, and The Happy Boys. The show trials of yesterday's leaders were on—Rykov, Bukharin, Zinoviev, Kamenev—but these trials had no other effect on the daily whirl of Moscow life than to cause some occasional pushing and shoving of men at the newsstands. For the most part, they read the speeches of the prosecutor, Vyshinsky, in silence, and only rarely would someone come out with "Now there's an orator!" Immediately after a brief exchange of opinions, they would scatter for the various modes of transport. Meeting the heroic pilots who had flown to the North Pole, however, was another matter! That brought them out onto the streets by the thousands. Smiles, shouts, bands, confetti . . . So, on the whole, Moscow passed the days in an ordinary way.

It was only at night that fear began to creep along the streets; scores of Black Marias emerged from the iron gates of the Lubyanka and drove to different buildings throughout the city. All in Moscow averted their eyes at the sight of these vans, the same way any man drives the thought of the inevitability of death from his mind. Please, God, don't let them come for me, or any of our family—ah, thank the Lord, they've passed by! The Black Marias stopped where the orders said they were supposed to, and the agents of the secret police entered homes unhurriedly. The sound of footfalls on the stairs or the noise of an elevator rising in the middle of the night became the habitual background of Moscow's nocturnal terror. People pressed close to the doors of their communal apartments and trembled in their rooms. "They aren't coming to our floor, are they?" "No, they're going higher." "Oh, of course, they've come for the Kolebanskys—you had to expect it sooner or later." "I just knew it." "Really, you too?" "Oh yes, yes—they never make mistakes . . ." Sometimes in the home of the arrestee there would be sobbing—muffled, suppressed, of course, at first, but turning into hysteria that was unseemly in Soviet society but still very much alive, which was then cut off by the shouts of the "knights of the Revolution": Moscow does not believe in tears! Then the sobs would cease altogether, with shame and accompanying whispers: forgive us, it's just nerves. More often, though, everything went off like clockwork, with high marks for discipline. Come on, come on, *they'll* straighten everything out!

The literature of socialist realism was in full flower. Formalism had already been completely rooted out. Soviet poets, playwrights, and novelists had been gathered up in a single union and were vigorously turning out the works the people needed.

They did not avoid public life, either. For example, the first letters of workers demanding the execution of the accused in the "enemies of the people" trial had been published yesterday in *Pravda* and the other central newspapers, and already today the writers were gathering in their well-appointed mansion on Vorovsky Street, once known as Povarskaya Street. They were composing an appeal to the humane Soviet government. There are times one must suspend humane behavior, dear Comrade Government, when enemies must be punished without mercy!

The meeting was taking place in the large hall that was the restaurant, from which the tables had been removed and replaced by extra chairs and platforms for the speakers. "Where the feast table stood now lies a coffin," thought many, though of course they kept such thoughts to themselves. Shoot them, shoot them! The fighting words of the Party thundered forth beneath the lofty ceiling, wrapped around the large chandeliers, were daubed on the panes of the high lancet windows and weightily squeaked along the parquet floors, where only twenty years before, the children of Count Olsufiev, the former owner, had played with their governesses. The poet Vitya Gusev decided to add some poetry to the general feeling of irreconcilability. He leaped up onto the speakers' platform and threw his hair back with a brusque movement of his head. "I am a poet, comrades! I express my feelings in verse!":

> *The people's rage roils in a single word,*
> *From my lip it trips—Execute!*
> *Execute the traitors of the Fatherland,*
> *Remember all things living, think of our human band,*
> *Dream the dream of happiness—Shoot!*

The young fellow received a round of applause from the meeting. The representatives from the cultural division of the Central Committee smiled paternally: a poet of exceptional talent, the son of a simple laborer; we'll be all right, comrades, we can get along without the decadents!

Nina Gradov was sitting in the mezzanine behind a spiral wooden column. Her eyes were closed. Shame and sadness showed plainly on her face. Her neighbor, a repented critic from the Formalist school who was trying to woo her, glanced up at the ceiling and, without stopping his "tempestuous applause," whispered, "Cut it out, Nina! They're watching you—clap, just clap!"

She opened her eyes and did in fact see several stares directed at her. Her brother writers, timid as rabbits, could clearly read the challenge in the taut muscles of her face and her motionless hands. Most of these stares immediately turned away when she made eye contact with them, but two or three remained on her for a moment, as though to remind her of where she was.

Then two piercing, attentive, observant glances cut through the crowd from two directions, gauging the levels of enthusiasm. Bowing her head and blushing like the young Countess Masha Olsufieva at her first ball, Nina joined the applause.

Someone in the Presidium was saying: "Draft resolution: to request the Soviet government to inflict the supreme punishment upon the band of Trotskyite hirelings: to shoot them like mad dogs. Let us proceed to a vote: who is in favor of the resolution, comrades? Who is against? Who wishes to abstain? . . . The resolution is passed unanimously!"

Again a storm of applause followed, accompanied by a few shouts, and again Nina was clapping, clapping with everyone, only this time she had suddenly had the terrible feeling that she was clapping even more energetically than the rest of the crowd. The writers, along with the entire people—miners, metallurgists, milkmaids, swineherds, garment workers, tractor drivers, border guards, railroad engineers, and weavers, as well as doctors, teachers, artists of all sorts, volcanologists, paleontologists, not to mention shepherds, fishermen, ornithologists, watchmakers, weighers, lexicographers, diamond cutters, pharmacists, sailors, and fliers—were demanding that the government put the members of the double-dealing group to death.

The meeting broke up in a cheerful mood, with everyone feeling reinvigorated by a sense of common purpose, all conflicts between groups, personal enmities, and rivalries forgotten for a time. Many stopped at the buffet, asked for "a good shot of cognac," sampled the excellent sturgeon sandwiches, hailed one another, asked their colleagues how their novel or play was coming along, when they were planning to take their seaside holiday, and so on.

The onetime Formalist critic was enthusiastically recounting to Nina some idiotic review that had appeared in the *Literary Gazette* and seemed to be asking her to put out of her mind everything that had just happened—it was a formality, something purely superficial that required no soul-searching, as necessary as, well, an umbrella in bad weather, just some laughable foolishness that required no moral commitments. They were slowly walking down Vorovsky Street past a row of foreign embassies in the direction of the Arbat. A marble-faced diplomat from Afghanistan looked down at them from his country's embassy; from the Swedish embassy, an indeterminate Swede; and at the Norwegian embassy, a young damsel with a milky complexion and bewildered glance flashed past the window.

"Well, what do you think, Kazimir—we applauded, didn't we?" said Nina suddenly, interrupting her elegant companion. "We certainly clapped up a storm, don't you think? Clap-clap-clap with our hands and stamp-stamp-stamp with our feet, eh? Russian writers demand the death penalty, marvelous!"

The critic continued on for a few steps in silence, then waved his hand in a gesture of resignation and turned and walked in the opposite direction.

Nina crossed Arbat Square and then went down Gogol Boulevard in the direction of the Palace of Soviets metro station, that is, to the place where the ruins of the demolished Church of Christ the Savior were still visible behind a dirty fence. The peaceful life of the boulevard, seemingly unspoiled by Stalinism, and the warm breeze of the late summer evening not only did not serve to calm her but plunged her into an even greater state of confusion. With wild eyes she met the admiring glances of passing men. Are there any men left in this city? she asked herself. And what makes the women any better? Are there any women left, either? Who are we all? The great devil leads us all in dancing and singing, and we just follow along behind him like lesser demons.

Savva was waiting for her by the entrance to the station, everything about the way he looked refuting her gloom and pessimism. Tall, clear-eyed, dressed in a gray suit and dark blue necktie, leaning one shoulder against a lamppost, he was calmly reading a small, elegant book with a soft leather cover whose gilt edging was discolored by time. He's interested in the secondhand book business, looks for rare editions in his spare time, reads foreign novels, philosophy, is perfecting his French . . . why, for his appearance alone right now he could be arrested! Nina rushed up to her husband, buried her nose in the gray fabric of his suit, and put her arms around his shoulders.

"Savva, dear, imagine—everyone voted to have them shot, demanded their execution . . . that appalling Vitka Gusev had written a poem about it, and everyone applauded it, even I joined in! I applauded it, Savva, and that means that I was calling for the execution as well! I didn't get up and walk out, I just stayed and cheered with the rest, like a contemptible little mass-produced doll!"

He kissed her, took out his handkerchief, and applied it to her nose and forehead, taking care to blot around her eyes so as not to smudge her makeup.

"To walk out would have been suicide," he muttered. What else could he say?

"Russian writers!" she went on. "They don't vote for mercy or clemency— no, they demand death by firing squad!"

They were walking along the boulevard in the direction from which Nina had come. On their way home—they now lived in Savva's apartment not far from Gorky Street—they had to stop by the nursery and pick up their daughter, Lena.

"We had a similar meeting today at the hospital," he said. "They're going on everywhere now. Everywhere, you see, without exception."

"And you voted for the execution as well?" she said with horror.

He shrugged guiltily. "Fortunately, I happened to be in surgery at the time . . ."

They went two stops in a streetcar and then got off right next to his street. The nursery was on the other side of the boulevard. Savva directed Nina's attention to the entrance of their building.

"Do you see that? Rogalsky just came out, finally emerged from hiding. The other day he was expelled from the Party and in a unanimous vote—unanimous, understand?—dismissed from the Academy of Sciences, stripped of all his awards. Do you see how the neighbors are getting out of his way? Look there—Anna Stepanovna has crossed over to the other side of the street just so she won't have to say hello to him!"

The man who yesterday had been a professor of history, invariably jaunty and at pains to emphasize his lack of involvement with the daily lives of his small-minded fellow citizens, was walking toward the corner of the street slowly, as though he were severely handicapped. The stigma surrounding him weighed him down, and his very presence on the street seemed inappropriate. They saw that he was carrying, for the first time since they had known him, a string bag with two empty milk bottles in it.

"Hello, Yakov Mironovich," said Savva.

"Good evening, Yakov Mironovich," said Nina in a deliberately loud voice of which she was immediately ashamed: shallow, stupid, as if I were casting a challenge, I'm saying hello to this man as though I wanted to make up for my own cowardice and loathsome conduct.

"Hello," Rogalsky replied indifferently. He did not even look up to see where the greeting had come from.

Savva watched him walk away. "He's not even with us anymore. His life is over, he's waiting for his arrest. They say he's already packed his things in a bundle and he's just waiting."

Nina dropped her hands in despair. "Well, why is he just waiting, Savva? Why doesn't he try to get away? Fleeing danger is instinctive! Why doesn't he just leave, go to the South, at least he could enjoy the South one last time! Why are they all paralyzed by these conclusions and procedures?"

"Excuse me, dear Nina, but why did you applaud 'that appalling Gusev' today?" asked Savva, taking her by the shoulders.

"I was afraid, that's all," she whispered.

"No, it wasn't just fear," he objected. "There's something here more powerful than fear . . ."

"Some sort of mass hypnosis, you mean?" she murmured.

"Exactly," he nodded. "And it was all of us who created this hypnosis!"

"And you?" She shot him a quick glance. She felt the muscles in his arm tighten.

His voice grew harder. "I never took part in this dirty masquerade."

"What do you mean by that?" She brought her face up to his. From a distance they looked like two lovers whispering endearments to each other. "You mean everything as a whole? The Revolution, right?"

"Yes," he said.

"Shut up!" she whispered hurriedly and closed her husband's mouth with her hand. He kissed her palm.

CHAPTER FIFTEEN

Indestructible and Legendary

☆

In those years the genre of mighty Soviet singing was born. Singers and choruses learned to swell with greatness and enthusiasm until they were at the point of bursting. The creation of a national radio network carried these voices from the black dishes of the transmitters to the most remote regions of the country.

> *From Moscow to the highlands,*
> *From southern hills to northern seas,*
> *Man is master of his homeland,*
> *Of tiny ants and giant trees.*
>
> *Full as life the Volga courses,*
> *Open, wide-eyed, ripe with thunder!*
> *Where our youths urge on the horses*
> *And the old folks bask in honor.*
>
> *A raging source of fearsome power,*
> *Never tamed at any hour,*
> *This is the country of my dreams,*
> *Bound firmly by life's loving seams.*

As it went out through all eleven time zones, so it rang out in the Far East, from a speaker on a column next to a railroad crossing barrier at a small station in Priamur.

The weather was vile—a steady, endless rain was falling, and bubbles that augured nothing good for the future were swimming in the puddles. " 'Everyone today will put on a coat / And a drop will get caught on a thicket / And none of them will notice / That I'm drunk on bad weather again,' " muttered Nikita, quoting his favorite semiforbidden poet . . . and only out beyond the river, that is, in Chinese territory, did there appear a few hints in the mass of clouds that summer might still get the upper hand.

The staff car of Corps Commander Gradov stopped directly in front of the lowered barrier. A red light was blinking. Along the branch of the Trans-Siberian Railroad that intersected the village road at this point, a train of boxcars was passing as slowly and endlessly as the rain. Nikita stared fixedly at the gloomy procession clacking along the rails. He and everyone else in the area knew what sort of load these boxcars were carrying: human cargo, prisoners being taken to Vladivostok and Vanino for transfer to the camps in Kolyma. It obviously was no secret to the driver of the car, Sergeant Vaskov, either. He kept on sighing as he watched the train, clearly wanting to say something.

"Well, what's wrong, Vaskov? Can't catch your breath?" asked Nikita glumly.

"It just never occurred to me before, Comrade Corps Commander, that there were so many enemies of the people hidden away in our country," muttered the driver without looking at his superior. His simple face reflected a native cunning.

"Drop the subject, Vaskov," said Nikita. "Just keep your thoughts to yourself. Understand?"

The sergeant scratched his nose and uttered a muffled "Yes, sir." In their endless travels around the military district, he had become accustomed to having a somewhat overly familiar rapport with the army commander's operations officer, and it had just been sharply broken off—though he didn't see how one could avoid speaking during a long stop at a railroad crossing.

Suddenly, the bumpers of the cars all along the line clashed together and the train came to a stop. Some people were running toward the front of the train, here and there some of the car doors opened slightly, guards stuck their heads out, shouts were heard in the distance. Something was going on.

Meanwhile, a fairly large number of collective farm wagons had drawn up behind Gradov's car, along with many military vehicles returning from the armored forces training zones. "There, he's going himself," said Vaskov gloomily, pointing at one of the wing mirrors. Nikita looked over and saw the camouflaged armored car that was known to the entire sector, the one belonging to Blücher, the local commander in chief.

Nikita got out of the staff car. The marshal was already approaching him with his usual more than self-assured stride that made him seem as though he were on the attack. They shook hands.

"What's happening here, Nikita Borisovich?"

"There's a special train going by, Vasily Konstantinovich."

Blücher smiled darkly: "A special train . . ." He pushed aside the flap of his leather overcoat, reached into his pocket for a cigarette case, and offered Gradov a smoke. In all their years together, exchanging cigarettes had been the only sign of informality between them. They still used the formal form of address, called each other by name and patronymic, and kept the distance between them that was prescribed by army rules of conduct—rules both written and unwritten. In the past few months, their mutual alienation had become even greater. Nikita had not shared his irritation where Blücher was concerned with anyone, not even with Veronika, and he did not even admit entirely to himself that he no longer trusted his commanding officer. In May, in full view of the headquarters staff, the NKVD had brazenly hauled away one of the most respected commanders in the Special Red Banner Far East Army, Corps Commander of Aviation Albert Lapin, and Blücher had not lifted a finger to save him. Men were being arrested all along the chain of command, and then the affair of the "military-fascist conspiracy" that had shaken the entire Red Army had erupted, immediately and irrevocably spattering many icons of the Revolution with mud—Tukhachevsky, Uborevich, Yakir, Gamarnik, Eideman . . . Even more of a disturbance had been caused by the fact that Blücher, Belov, and Kashirin, among others, had been members of the court that condemned them to death. That would be just like me pronouncing sentence on Kirill and Nina, thought Nikita. When he thought of these things, his body felt as though it were filling with lead, and he imagined he saw the blood-spattered wall of the fort at Kronstadt . . .

Something out of the ordinary was happening on the special train. Blücher and Gradov were standing some twenty yards from one of the halted cars. They could hear the sounds of some sort of confusion and a muffled babble of voices. Suddenly a howl that sent shivers down the spine cut through the commotion:

"Comrades! Red commanders! Don't believe the false accusations! We are not enemies! We are Communists! We are faithful to the cause of Lenin and Stalin!" The yell was immediately drowned out by an incomprehensible chorus of bellowing male voices. Soon, the soldiers and peasants gathered at the crossing were able to distinguish the frenzied performance as the Party anthem, the "International." One of the boards in the upper part of the boxcar's siding fell away, and a hand flung out a package of letters folded in a triangular shape in the direction of the barrier. "For God's sake, mail these letters!" said one voice that cut through the "International." The atheist hymn was at once a roar and a supplication. The triangles flew in different directions, some of the letters falling directly on the roadbed, some being carried by an air current to the hillocks next to the tracks. One landed right next to Corps Commander Gradov's shiny boots. Nikita picked it up and thrust it into his pocket. Blücher glanced at him with a frown and pretended he had not seen anything. He knew how his staff felt about him. Every officer, of course, was thinking: am I going to be the next one sent off, Comrade Marshal? If only they knew . . .

Several armed guards ran up to the mutinous car, pistols in hand, and then, pulling the door aside and helping one another up, climbed inside into the darkness where the faces of the singers were visible. "Shut up, you motherfuckers! We'll teach you to sing, you sons of bitches!" Meanwhile, a handcar rolled up to the crossing on a parallel track, and some important officials of the railroad jumped off. Two scared-looking men ran up to Blücher, obviously wanting to explain to him what was happening on the tracks. The marshal was not about to listen. Without taking his hands from the pockets of his leather coat, he barked, "Clear this crossing immediately! Take the train apart if you have to! I'm giving you ten minutes and not a second more!"

Turning sharply on his heel, he went back to his armored car. Nikita stood silent, his eyes on the ground. The singing in the boxcar stopped. Once again—he could no longer count how many times—the ice of Kronstadt and the wall of the fort, three Red Army envoys standing before it, loomed up in his mind. One of the three men was shouting into a megaphone: "Sailors, we have brought an ultimatum from Trotsky, the commander in chief. If you want to save your lives, give up!"

The sailors on the parapets burst into laughter. Nikita the spy was up there with them himself. It was just then that he had left for Anchor Square.

The corps commander shook his head to drive away these painful memories and succeeded, unless one counts an ephemeral moment when the fort flashed before his eyes again, this time as the scene of the execution of his brothers. And there he was, the young Nikita, in the ranks of the victors . . .

For Veronika, the corps commander's wife, life in Khabarovsk had turned out to be not so bad. They lived in a spacious apartment in a building in the constructivist style on the city's main street. They had three rooms, a large kitchen, and a bathroom with a water heater. They had managed to find some quite charming furniture. Nikita thought the flat looked ridiculous, but what did he know? There was a music theater in the city and a tennis group at the Army club. She had found some fairly good partners—Berg, a doctor, and First Lieutenant Veresaev from Air Corps headquarters, who frankly had the eyes of a madman. It was amusing to watch the rivalry of these two with—well, with others. One had to maintain a hospitable home. Nikita was often away but with equal frequency burst into the flat with a crowd of his fellow officers, whom Veronika had to entertain and feed. She managed to keep herself in perfect trim for sports and to get out to premieres, such as the recent jazz concert of Leonid Utyosov and his orchestra. They sounded a bit like a sideshow at an Odessa carnival, but then again he had played a few original blues numbers. At the age of thirty-five, Veronika was simply a knockout! The only sad thing was that the years were passing so quickly, just flashing by.

They went fairly often to Vladivostok, or "Vladik," as the locals called it. Here, on the shores of the Golden Horn, beneath the excited glances of sailors, Veronika was seized by a mood that was something like a return to her youth. She remembered some lines from Alexander Blok:

> *By chance, on a pocket knife,*
> *You shall find the dust of far-off lands*
> *And strange, vague colors will wrap your life.*

She was looking at the ships in the bay and was lost in a daydream. Let's imagine, then, that the Soviet armed forces have been smashed once and for all. Poor Nikita has been captured, but in the end, of course, he'll come back alive and unharmed. For the time being we're standing on a hill looking at the horizon, waiting. Once again, as in Blok's poem, we're waiting for the ships. Puffs of smoke have already been sighted, the victors' squadron is on its way. Who are they? The Japanese? No, that would be too much—do it with a Japanese? But they say they're all so persnickety anyway. No, no, they'll be Americans, white-toothed cowboys, that's it, and among them some Californian built like a knight . . . the soft strains of the blues . . . something to remember all your life . . . oh, rubbish!

She had little time to read, but she managed a bit anyway, for the most part the journal *International Literature*. Modern Soviet literature had become unbearable, nothing but a "social order." They had been to Moscow three times during their years here, and every time they went there, events simply flowed along one right after another. Riding around in some magnificent official automobile, dashing out of it and then back into it with her purchases, while all around people were stunned by her blazing blue eyes, as a poet would have said. Sometimes you think it's better to pop into Moscow for a visit rather than to live in its routine. Well, there you go, that's all that's happened, strictly speaking. Oh, yes, a daughter had been born during that time, as well. That means, then, that they had an eleven-year-old son and a three-year-old daughter, and we will stop there—that's enough, the problem of the perpetuation of the species has been entirely taken care of.

One evening an unbelievable event occurred. Their old friend Regimental Commander Vadim Vuinovich came for a visit after a twelve-year absence, not counting their "accidental" meetings at the train station and the tennis court. It was just as though he had fallen from the sky! From his Kiplingesque Turkestan he had come to the Far East! Had he made the trip specially?

She served tea in the living room—from a tea service a connoisseur would have immediately recognized as having been made by la maison Kuznetzov. She had found it in a Moscow commission shop, but Vadim was clearly no connoisseur of tea services and paid it no attention, seemingly not even noticing what he was drinking—and now she was sitting across from the officer, the blazing of her eyes held in check and smiling a faint, sweet smile.

"I can't believe my eyes! Vadim, is it really you? Just look at you—graying at the temples, mustache à l'anglais . . . do you know what? You've become even more attractive, or in any case more stylish, with the years. So, tell me about your life, my dear Evgeny Onegin. Are you married?"

Every time they met, it seemed to her that in the next moment some sort of erotic storm would break but that the moment had yet to arrive—even though twelve years had elapsed.

He spoke in a quiet, melancholy voice, though it was perfectly clear that he . . . well, what could he do? Of course that was what came first of all, flowing out of him, he couldn't forget about her for so much as a second . . .

"Yes, I'm married. I'm thirty-seven and still only a regimental commander. We live in a godforsaken hole near the Afghan border. My wife is a wild animal. We have three children. I love 'em. That's about all, really . . ."

He smiled again. His happiness in looking at her was clearly overwhelming him. She understood. She suddenly had a strange feeling—it seemed to her that without this admirer she would lose her beauty, even though she was thousands of miles distant from him.

"I see you're still a romantic! Admit it, Vadim!"

The electrical field between them was becoming too excited, and they had to wait a moment, at least, to allow a part of those swollen arrow-bearing electrons to disperse. After an awkward pause, he said, "Was I ever really a romantic? Then again . . . You know, Veronika, you don't remember, of course, but I can't forget one fleeting moment twelve years ago. . . . It really was just a moment, no more than a second. . . . Of course, you don't remember anything about it, but . . . it was light and heat, noise and breathing . . . the very essence of our youth . . . and you gave it to me, and I remember it as if it were yesterday.''

Staggered by this confession and by a stream of hazy emotions, she looked at him. It suddenly seemed to her that she might remember what he was talking about—another second, just one more . . . but everything slipped away from her, and in the next moment there was a noise at the door, and then the faithful Corps Commander Gradov appeared. "Vadya!" "Nika! What a surprise! Where on earth did you come from?" They slapped one another hard on the back and boxed playfully, their long-standing feud seemingly forgotten. "Come, come on and tell us everything over dinner! It's great that I have the day off tomorrow!"

They sat talking until long after midnight—in the kitchen, naturally, the way it's always done when Russian friends get together. Veronika's table arrangement had long since become mixed up. The head of the house even tried to fish a few sprats directly from a can. They had gone through three bottles of Moskovskaya vodka and had just opened a fourth—for the road. Conversations about the good old days kept on turning into discussions of the current military and political situation. In the end Veronika found it more than she could bear. "Well, you lads can just go to blazes! Go on talking about your 'serious questions' without me. I'm going to bed!"

She stood and walked out of the kitchen, enchantingly unsteady on her feet. Vadim followed her with his eyes, took out another cigarette, then crumpled it and threw it away, shaking his head as if ordering himself to sober up. He put a hand on the shoulder of his friend, who was sitting next to him with his collar bearing the insignia of a general's rank undone. A strange sort of subordination had always existed between these two men. Nikita had always seen Vadim, a man of his own age, as his senior, and now, despite the great difference in their rank, he felt this sensation more strongly than ever.

"Nikita, be straight with me," suggested Vadim. "You know, of course, the reasons why I stopped seeing the two of you twelve years ago?"

"I know one reason," said Nikita.

"You know the second one, too!" replied Vadim with a slap on his friend's shoulder.

Nikita smiled. "I'm not sure, though, which is the first and which is the second."

Vadim rocked back in his chair, which creaked beneath his weight. "Well, okay, that's not important. The important thing is that I have two reasons for coming back."

Nikita moved from the table to the windowsill. The only visible light in the gloom outside was the star shining atop the House of the Red Army.

"Tell me the first one," he said, rocking back and forth. He took a deep breath, then added, "The second I already know."

A strained silence followed. Now what, was he going to choose this moment to unburden himself, to pour forth his lyricism, to open up to the husband of his ideal? A provincial garrison officer is likely to say anything when he's been drinking! When Nikita looked at Vadim, though, he realized immediately that any sort of condescension was inappropriate. By the expression on Vadim's face, Nikita could tell that Vadim was again about to put himself in an exposed position.

"I came to see you, Nikita, in order to find out what you think about what is going on right now in the country, and in the armed forces."

"Meaning what?" Nikita started to say. Then he realized there was no need to ask questions. What else could they talk about at such a time and in such a place when all the barriers between the two friends had come down and all misunderstandings had been forgiven? Why, about the very subject no one discussed with anyone, not with friends, not with husbands or wives—the purges.

"Do you know the extent of the arrests?" Vadim asked.

"I can guess. It's hellish."

"And what do you make of the confessions of the commanders of the army, their confessions to taking part in a fascist conspiracy?"

"There's only one possible answer."

"What, you mean torture? After all, it's not boys they were dealing with, but heroes! Just imagine them—when you yourself fell into the hands of Wrangel's counterintelligence . . ."

"Things would have been easier there."

"Maybe you're right. It's more painful coming from your own side. When it's your own people that are doing it, it must be unbearable . . ."

"That may be true, but maybe our people are simply crueler, more nightmarish . . ."

"But why? What for? What more do they want? He's already a god, an unimpeachable idol. Maybe he's still afraid of the army? Fascist plot—nonsense! He's playing right into Hitler's hands. The army is being decapitated right on the eve of an unavoidable war! Tukhachevsky—"

"Keep your voice down, will you?"

"What's the matter? The walls in your place are thick enough, Corps Commander. Two years ago Tukhachevsky was already predicting an unavoidable clash with Germany, but now the general staff is talking about a possible alliance with the Nazis against the Entente powers. They're mad!"

Dawn was breaking, and they were finishing their sixth pack of cigarettes. Nikita thought with dull anger that his morning had been ruined—waking up with Veronika, half an hour of weight lifting followed by a cold shower, drying himself with a shaggy Turkish towel, followed by a healthy "Metchnikoff" yogurt breakfast. Vadim's lips were trembling, and from time to time his body was shaken by a shudder. In the course of the conversation he had pulled out all the stops.

"Listen, Nikita, they say that not only was Blücher an official member of the court but that he gave some of the most damaging evidence against Tukhachevsky. Is that right?"

"The other marshals convinced him he should help out in the investigation," Nikita murmured.

Vadim laughed bitterly. "Well, I guess now it'll be his turn to go to the Lubyanka! They probably already have a cell prepared for our hero."

Nikita said nothing. The entire conversation seemed to him like a prolonged nightmare. Here it was, the repayment for the delightful days when he was still a young man. "Youth led us on a saber campaign . . ."

"Then again, he could prevent it," said Vadim quietly, looking at the outlined trees beginning to appear in the fog. Nothing was yet visible beyond the park, but the presence of the Amur River could be felt.

"How?" asked Nikita, instinctively lowering his voice. The thought occurred to him that Vadim was once again directing the conversation.

"You ought to know how," said the regimental commander through clenched teeth. "A military man is supposed to know how to deter enemy action."

Nikita's head began to spin, and he grabbed at the railing of the balcony. Below, he saw Khariton the doorman pulling himself out of the cellar dragging a broom.

"Well, you know, Vadim," muttered Nikita. "How can you even think of such a thing? To put the Revolution in danger?"

"What Revolution is there still?" Vadim had opened his mouth so wide that he shrieked the question almost soundlessly. "There hasn't been any Revolution for a long time. What's wrong with you? Don't you understand?"

He fell silent and looked at Nikita expectantly. The corps commander glowered back at the colonel like a small boy. He could not say a word. Of course he understood that there had not been any Revolution for a long time, but he only understood it; he had never put the thought into words, neither inwardly nor aloud, and no one he knew had ever dared say it. Now, for the first time, it had been uttered by his comrade in arms.

Stunned by this realization and the summons to action it implied, he was speechless. Realizing he was not going to get an answer, Vadim hammered the railing with his fist. "Everything is falling apart. It's a fucking mess! We're all doomed! Well, if that's the way things are, so be it! Do you want me to tell you the other reason I came here, old man?"

Nikita shrugged. "Don't get mad, Vadya. After all, I already told you I know the second reason."

"But I want to tell you about it all the same," insisted Vadim. "About what you know perfectly well. I suppose you'll know it even better then. I'm in love with your wife. I think about her every minute of every day, and I dream of her at night. I've been dreaming about her for four thousand three hundred and eighty days . . ."

Nikita embraced him and then shook him lightly by the shoulders, as if to say, all right, all right, go easy. We're grown men and soldiers, we've seen it all. Come on, now, you've said your piece, that's enough. You've told me about it, friend, I heard you. Everything else will just fly away as life goes by. Then he remembered something important that, fortunately, had nothing to do with either the first or the second reason. He drew from his pocket the letter folded into a triangle that he had intended to post that very day but had forgotten.

"Listen, Vadya, you're going to Moscow from here, aren't you? This letter has a Moscow address . . ."

"I'll deliver it," growled Vadim. "I know what kind of a letter it is— prisoners in the gulag fold them this way. I'll deliver it as soon as I get there." He smiled. "That much at least I can do . . ."

The daily business of the Special Far East Army headquarters usually dispelled Nikita's gloomy premonitions and feelings of depression. Everything went along precisely, even energetically: young adjutants ran in and out, guards clicked their heels when they came to attention, secretaries' typewriters clacked away, commanders of large units and carefree fellows from the frontier reconnaissance units arrived, phones rang, and radio contact with all the units scattered throughout the Far East from Alaska to Korea was maintained.

The situation in the southern part of the region was getting hotter with each passing month. The Japanese were obviously probing the Red Army, trying to determine its fighting strength. It was not difficult to guess their long-range plans: in case of a war in the West, they would attack and occupy the coastal area that included Vladivostok and Khabarovsk, and they might go even further, to Lake Baikal.

Corps Commander Gradov, chief of operations, was in a private conference with the commanders of several large units. Marshal Blücher, the commander in chief, was nearly always present at these meetings. "Their plans are clear to us in their broad outlines, comrades," said Nikita, "though it is sometimes difficult for us to pinpoint their day-to-day strategy in spite of, I will say without any false modesty, the fact that our intelligence service doesn't function at all badly."

Bending over to the southeast corner of the huge map in the room, he began pointing out troop movements in General Toguchi's army as well as a concentration of strength in the area of Lake Hasan, the meaning of which was not clear. The pointer's movement resembled that of a wood-carving tool. Along with the other commanders, Blücher was watching the lithe figure of his best lieutenant in the Far East force, a figure that always seemed to be in the right place, inspiring certainty in the expediency of a job that at times seemed to the marshal to be a senseless game played by treacherous idiots. I hope that at least I won't be—he said to himself, breaking off his thought. After the arrest of Lapin, and particularly after the harsh punishment of Tukhachevsky, this thought, applied to all of his closest collaborators, almost plagued . . . no, there was no almost about it, tortured and exhausted him, perhaps more than anything by the fact that it remained incomplete, that he was always too cowardly to follow the thought to its conclusion. He finished the thought only at night, in his dreams, when it took the form of a bitchy ticker tape from an old telegraph, appearing in Morse code: "I—hope—that—at—least—I—the—coward—who—betrayed—his—friend—Misha—won't—be—arrested," and then the mighty marshal jumped out of his bed like a ten-year-old boy.

The conference was interrupted by the appearance of the head of radio communications. He was bringing a coded message from Voroshilov. The commander of the Special Far East Army was being urgently summoned to Moscow. Blücher, the coded message in his hand, allowed his thoughts momentarily to drift away from the problems of the Far East: perhaps this is the completion of my incomplete thought, and . . . ? A moment later he rose to his feet sharply and, as usual, adjusted his shirt, said, "Carry on, comrades," then left the operations room. Having understood immediately that the message contained something serious, the senior officers concentrated on their notes. In an earlier time they would have exchanged silent glances, but now any glance could be read as a manifestation of treason.

After the conference, Nikita went to Blücher's office, as he usually did. The commander briefed him on the contents of the coded message. There was an unusual smell in the office. Tobacco, Nikita guessed, and then he saw the ashes and three cigarettes that had been lit, then snuffed out. But Blücher had recently quit. Blücher started to discuss the secret transfer of two mechanized brigades. "This movement must be started even before I come back from Moscow," he said.

A silence ensued, and then Nikita raised his glance from his notepad and looked the marshal directly in the eye. "Vasily Konstantinovich, do you really intend to go to Moscow right now?"

The marshal's eyes were filled with gloom; it was impossible to say whether it was fear or a threatening look.

"What a strange question, Nikita Borisovich," he answered slowly. "How can I not go, if the commissariat summons me? I'm going, and right away, too, as soon as my plane is ready."

Nikita did not take his eyes off the marshal's. "Yes, yes, I understand, but —Vasily Konstantinovich, are you really going to go to Moscow alone, without a detachment of bodyguards?"

The gloom in the marshal's eyes began to take on a leaden shine. "One more question like that, Nikita Borisovich, and I'll have you arrested."

Another second passed before their eyes could look off in different directions. That's exactly what's devouring us all right now, thought Nikita, fear and helplessness. Then they took their leave of each other.

Nothing special is happening. The only thing that's happening is a silent conspiracy of millions upon millions of people who have reached a tacit agreement that nothing is happening. Anything unusual that is going on is happening to the guilty, but *we're* all right, everything is normal. "We will sing and laugh like children amid the usual struggles and labor . . ." And yet it is not only the arrest victims who are being tortured, but all of us.

These were the thoughts of Corps Commander Nikita Gradov as he leafed through the pages of foreign military journals in the quiet and comfort of his apartment, which had been "Veronikized," as they always joked. The doorbell rang, followed by a thunderous knocking. Well, that's it! Straight off, his wife began to sob. No cry of surprise, just an immediate flood of tears. So she had been expecting it.

The room filled with agents of the NKVD. There were no less than seven of them, three of them holding pistols. After all, they were arresting a military man, and he might try something stupid. Nikita did not try anything stupid. The agent in charge approached him with an unpleasant smile. "You'll have to come with us, Gradov. Here is the arrest order." Nikita recognized the young major. He had caught his gaze as the man stared at him and his wife during one of the concerts given at the army club. At the Leonid Utyosov jazz concert, it seemed to him. It might have been an unremarkable incident—men were always looking at Veronika—but there was something about his face, his blond-haired, blue-eyed features, like someone in a film melodrama, that had made an impression. Nikita held the loathsome little paper containing the order in his hand. The idea for a childish ploy emerged from his memory. Unfold the piece of paper. Want to see a trick? Yes, yes, I do! Crumple up this paper. Good, you've crumpled it! Thanks, now hand it here! The treacherous jokester ran off to the bathroom with the crumpled paper.

"What is the reason for my arrest, Major?" asked Nikita.

The officer raised his eyebrows in surprise: his rank insignia was not visible beneath his civilian coat. Then he smirked. "Can't you guess, Gradov? We'll soon help you."

Where had they learned these grinning thieves' mannerisms? They acted like a gang ransacking the flat. The agents were opening the cupboards and taking books down from the shelves. If only he could keep from looking at the sobbing Veronika, could keep from bursting into tears himself. They're making a point of addressing me not as "comrade" nor by my rank, he thought. It might not be anything personal, they only want to make clear what is happening; everything is finished—you're not a corps commander anymore, neither are you a comrade . . .

"I demand—"

"Forget that word, Gradov!"

So I'm not "General Gradov" anymore, thought Nikita.

"You would do better, Gradov, to think about your association with former Marshal Blücher, an enemy of the people and the Party."

They began beating him in the Black Maria. One of them punched him on the jaw, another in the eye, a third in the ear. The major ripped off Gradov's shirt and tore it to shreds. After a minute or so the stunned Nikita stopped trying to avoid the blows. Then again, they didn't even feel like blows to him. It seemed like some sort of glittering battle taking place on a red-hot surface. Flashes and shellbursts all over the sky. We're resisting. A superior force is crushing us. The end.

CHAPTER SIXTEEN

Come on, Girls, Lend a Hand, Beauties!

☆

Two weeks after her husband's arrest, Veronika reached Moscow with her children. Her last days in Khabarovsk had been the most humiliating of her life. Literally the morning after the catastrophe, representatives had come from the city housing authority and told her she would have to vacate the premises as soon as possible. The neighbors shunned her like a leper. The youngsters who the day before had been the playmates of her children now taunted them with shouts of "Trotskyite Fascists!" Boris IV had gotten into a fight with his friend, the son of the regional prosecutor, and came home with a bloody nose. The prosecutor, however, was soon hauled away himself, and before the Gradovs' departure the two boys made up. When she went to the NKVD offices to inquire about her husband, she was treated rudely or, even worse, with indifference. Fat, odious sergeants with the soapy faces of castrati were sitting behind the front desk. Sexless women with fat behinds, in military uniform, passed by, their boots squeaking. We have no information about Citizen Gradov, she was told. What do you mean, you don't have any information? Why, he was only arrested a couple of days ago! Then they said: for the time being, we have none—come back in a few days, in two days, in a day, tomorrow. She sat in that antechamber of villains, beneath the portrait of the omniscient Lenin, across from a portrait of Dzerzhinsky wearing the usual bright, sadistic smile, and wept helplessly. Finally, a blue-eyed villain descended the villainous staircase from the villainous upper floors and said that Gradov had been sent to Moscow for investigation. Then, looking her over attentively with his somehow not entirely masculine eyes, he advised her that she would do better to think less about a traitor to the Motherland and more about her own life.

She rushed to the train station and bought a ticket, then to her son's school to get his school record. Then she began packing and dragging things to a commission store to sell. Furniture appraisers came to the pulled-apart flat and offered her prices that were a joke but that she accepted. She stood in the midst of absolute emptiness, as though she had not lived in this city for seven years, as though she had never even been there, like the former queen of the ball who would not now be chosen by anyone. Not by Berg the military doctor, nor by First Lieutenant Veresaev from Air Corps headquarters, not to mention the other tennis players of a lesser caliber. Who knows, maybe they, too, will soon find themselves far from the courts. Apparently, a full-scale pogrom was under way in the upper echelons of the Far East Army. Only Sergeant Vaskov, the former corps commander's driver, had come to help with the preparations for the trip. He walked through the rooms, glancing about briskly—either he was a spy, or he was looking for something to steal. Then again, perhaps he felt genuinely sorry for the children. Let him walk around, at least there's another living soul in the place.

Just before boarding the train, Veronika sent a telegram to Silver Forest. "Coming back with children. Nikita apparently in Moscow. Kisses. Tears. Veronika." They would surely understand what had happened, if they didn't already know. On the other hand, how could they not know? Blücher's arrest had been reported in the newspapers, and it was quite likely that Nikita had been mentioned in connection with him: "Yet another group of Fascist conspirators has been uncovered and neutralized . . ." The Siberian days seemed to go on forever. The railroad car was stuffy and the windows could not be opened, a stench of rotting food hung in the air, everyone was scratching lice, the children were becoming uncontrollable from inactivity, and everywhere were the sounds of people snoring and breaking wind, but most of all chewing; after the stop at Lake Baikal, people chewed the famous local salmon, and before coming into Omsk, they started on some sort of smoked lard that was supposed to be quite well known, and everywhere was the sound of hard-cooked eggs, the only food that would keep on such a long journey, being broken open. The conductors would come in from time to time and sprinkle disinfectant powder about so that the passengers would not pass germs to one another. After a few drinks, some of the know-it-alls moping here and there launched into endless discussions. This was the first time Veronika had ever traveled third class. Her only comfort was a small book of Pushkin's poetry. Curling up in a corner, she endlessly repeated, sometimes aloud in a whisper and at other times to herself, "Farewell, love letter! Farewell—she has commanded . . . Enough then, the time has come. Burn, love letter . . . It is done! The darkened pages have curled. Kind ashes, a poor delight in my cheerless fate, remain on my sorrowful breast forever . . ." The bitter lines comforted her. We are not the only ones, she thought, who have had everything smashed and destroyed, Pushkin once saw everything go to pieces, too; even in the sadness of human destinies there is a certain rhythm—like the rocking of a cradle . . . it may be all we have left, but it's something.

Finally, the "Nikita-ites," as their part of the family was known in Silver Forest, exhausted, worn out from scratching themselves, and dazed, stumbled out of the train at the Yaroslav Station directly into the arms of Boris Nikitovich and Mary Vakhtangovna. The women, including little Vera, huddled together sobbing. The two Borises stood by silently. The professor noticed on the face of his favorite grandson a scowl just like the one Mitya had been wearing when he had first been brought from Gorelovo.

The "Nikita-ites" spent the rest of the day washing and scrubbing themselves, then drying off. Then they crawled between immaculate sheets under the old, seemingly ancient, Gradov quilts. The children immediately fell asleep. Veronika curled up in a ball on the bed so familiar to her, in which, in all probability, Boris IV had been conceived. She lay there, listening to the sounds of the old house: to the squeaking of the parquet floor below, to the comforting wail of the wind through the attic, to the voice of Agasha as she bustled about, to the steps, cries, and sudden, inquiring barks of Pythagoras. For some reason, she was not thinking about Nikita. She was not really thinking about anything, only feeling the tranquil joy of being in a safe haven. In one of these blissful moments, she heard someone downstairs announce that a telegram had come from her parents, who were on holiday at a writers' colony in the Crimea, and that from the writers' colony they sent warm embraces to their daughter and their charming grandchildren. She did not stir from beneath the quilt, in order not to disrupt the joy of her haven.

In the evening all the Gradovs gathered for dinner. Around the table sat Boris Nikitovich and Mary; Kirill, his wife, Cecilia, and fourteen-year-old Mitya, who, even though he was an adopted son, considered Silver Forest his home; Nina, Savva, and their two-and-a-half-year-old daughter, Elena; the family friend and eternal bachelor Pulkovo; Pythagoras, who despite his solid appearance of a mature dog still considered himself a puppy; Agasha, if one could properly say that she was sitting, since she was constantly running back and forth between the table and the kitchen. Also at the table was Slabopetukhovsky, her almost legal "life's companion," and a very popular man in that part of suburban Moscow, who in addition to his duties as a constable was now moonlighting as an inspector in the District Financial Agency and had managed to get himself assigned to the adjacent forest district, though he usually spent most of his time when at the house in the kitchen near the liquor cabinet and only rarely came to the table to liven up the evening with the latest stories of what Mussolini was up to in Abyssinia. And, of course, there were the guests of honor, Veronika, Vera, and Boris IV. The only one lacking was everyone's favorite, Nikita, their "Red general," who here at home at the dinner table always behaved informally, almost like a small boy, more the confidant of Nina or even Pythagoras than of his severe younger brother, and because he was not there, the triumphal atmosphere of earlier years was absent as well; silence reigned, accompanied by sighs and sheepish glances. The feeling was almost that of a wake.

Mary looked at Veronika, who was sitting next to her, then kissed her on the cheek and shoulder. For the first time, a genuine closeness had formed between the wife and her mother-in-law. Boris Nikitovich tousled his grandson's hair with one hand and with the other raised a glass of brandy.

"Let's drink to our Nikita! I'm sure he'll come out of the terrible experience with honor! I hope, Mary and Veronika, I sincerely hope that all this will soon be behind us. An extremely important person whispered to me yesterday: 'Be patient, Professor, mistakes can happen . . .' That's just what he said— 'mistakes' . . ."

Everyone, of course, remembered the time seven years before, when Boris Nikitovich had so convincingly demonstrated the strength of his connections with the Kremlin, and so this whisper from one of the higher-ups was taken seriously, everyone's spirits rose hopefully, and the members of the family nodded calmly.

Kirill said with assurance, "I'm sure Nikita will be found innocent. It might take a month or two—the Blücher case is very complicated for a number of reasons, very contradictory, and some innocent people have clearly been sucked into the whirlpool—but I'm sure that as soon as they clear up everything, Nikita will be freed."

"If he's innocent, that is," Cecilia interjected quickly. Everyone looked at her in amazement and suddenly perceived her as an alien quantity, as someone who had spoken out of turn, and in whose stiff posture they could read a declaration of membership in a more serious circle of society than the Gradovs'.

Nina flushed and glared fiercely at Cecilia. "You said 'if,' Cecilia? What does that mean? What do you mean by 'innocent'? Have you gone off your head?"

Cecilia turned her head only slightly in the direction of her erstwhile comrade in the Blue Shirts who was now a relation, her sister-in-law. With a pronounced, though not excessive, hauteur and an air of ideological superiority, she explained her position: "In principle, the organs of the dictatorship of the proletariat cannot act wrongly or unjustly. Of course, in the conditions of the escalation of the class struggle there can be errors, but they are extremely rare. You see, comrades . . ." Clearly, she felt as though she were giving a lecture; forgetting about Nina's attack, she drew up her large bosom, and her freckles shone forth more brightly as the enlightenment of the masses proceeded. "You understand, comrades, the very fact of the arrest already shows that there was something improper in the political or ideological conduct of the arrested person. In these difficult times, when a new, gigantic geopolitical conspiracy has been organized against the Soviet Union, creating as-yet-unused agencies all over the country, no one can vouch even for himself, much less friends or relatives. The organs know the situation better than any of us, they're putting things in their proper places, they're taking care of everything. Boundless confidence in the competent authorities is an indispensable element of true Party-spiritedness!"

Kirill sat with his eyes lowered. On his face shone a sort of cubist spot formed by the light of the rays of the setting sun refracted through the blue-and-red rhomboid shapes in the window. If one departed from the class ideology, then what his wife was saying now was simply monstrous, but from a class-conscious standpoint, from the Party point of view, she was perfectly right. Anyway, hadn't he always noticed a certain, say, insufficiency of ideological conviction on the part of his brother?

"What is she saying?" exclaimed Nina. "Listen to the rubbish she's talking!"

Only Cecilia spoke, replying caustically to Nina. "What does the member of the Union of Soviet Writers find strange about my words?"

"According to your logic, Celia, you would approve of the arrest of your own father, would you? You place the organs above your father, is that right?" Nina hissed.

"Yes!" Cecilia yelled into her face.

Kirill reacted to this cry as though he had been struck on the ear with a club. "Rosenbloom!" he shouted.

"Gradov!" Cecilia slammed her fist down on the table. "I love my father, but as a Communist, I love the Party and its authorities even more!"

Mary Vakhtangovna said only "Nina!" and laid a hand on her daughter's trembling arm. An uncomfortable silence followed. It was suddenly clear that even here around the family dinner table one could not speak forthrightly. Veronika cried quietly into her handkerchief. "Oh, Mary," she whispered, "if you could only have seen their faces, those monstrous, animallike snouts . . ."

Mary rose and tugged at Veronika's arm. "Come into the study, my darling, I'll play some Chopin for you . . ."

Pulkovo stood up as well. "May I come with you?"

"I'm coming, too," joined in Boris Nikitovich.

The music lovers took their places in the study as if according to stage directions: Mary at the keyboard; Leo leaning with his elbows on the instrument; Gradov in his favorite armchair, the very one in which he had once taken his "music cure"; Veronika sitting on the carpet at his feet with a hand on one of his knees; her young daughter, Vera, with her cheek nestled against her. Tiny Elena Kitaigorodsky came stamping into the room on her little feet and joined them on the carpet, gazing up at "Grandma."

Mary embarked upon a bravura rendition of a polonaise, drowning out the row in the dining room and rebutting the NKVD from the very first measures. Suddenly, the pianist stopped playing, jumped up from the stool in alarm, and dashed to the door shouting: "Where are the boys? Has anyone seen Mitya and Boris?" The entire house was thrown into a panic: they had indeed forgotten all about the boys. They turned up in the garden. In the gathering dusk, Boris IV, lively and quick, was playing football with Mitya, awkward and adolescent, with an almost invisible ball. The tops of the pine trees were illuminated by a rose-colored light, and above the dense verdure, the star of the Gradov house was already visible. It seemed to be weeping softly for them.

Back then life was never slow to provide those ironic twists of fate that are its peculiar property. Several days after the "all hands on deck" gathering in Silver Forest, Cecilia Rosenbloom was working as usual in the library at the Institute of the International Workers' Movement. She found it a very pleasant place to enrich her theoretical baggage, and there was no shortage of current information, since the library subscribed to a good dozen foreign newspapers, the combat publications of the Comintern.

One could only imagine the longing and hope with which the proletariat of England, France, and the United States of America looked to the East, to Moscow, when they marched in picket lines and blockaded the gates of factories to keep strikebreakers from getting through. Quite remarkable, Cecilia thought, the cynicism of Hitler and his followers, calling themselves a socialist workers' party as well. And all the while they send ultramodern aircraft to bomb the republican forces in Spain! Cecilia's table was jammed with piles of classical Marxist-Leninist tomes forming a mighty bulwark against the savagery of everyday life. Inside this preserve she rustled her Communist newspapers. Here was harmony, only here—in spite of the contradictions in the International Workers' Movement, it existed here; we create harmony for ourselves, she thought.

A colleague came down the aisle to ask her to come to the telephone. "They said Gradov wants to talk to you about something," he said with a smile. The romance of the "stern youth"—which Kirill had remained to that day, his thirty-five years notwithstanding—and the slovenly, absent-minded, and rather absurd "Rosenbloomer" was a constant source of humorous conversations in the "theoretical circles" of Moscow.

The telephone was on the wall near the circulation desk. A small table and a Viennese-style chair stood beneath it. The receiver was dangling upside down. Cecilia felt a sharp inward pang at the sight of it for some reason. Some secret instinct, an atavistic twinge, stirred within her. The beloved voice of Comrade Gradov soon stopped this small leak in her materialist's outlook.

"Hello, Rosenbloom, this is Gradov!"

Cecilia sighed happily. "Hello, Gradov! Why are you calling? Are you coming home late?"

"No," replied Kirill. His voice, or rather his presence on the line, seemed to drift off somewhere and then come back again. "It's not about that. Just—just don't wait up for me."

"What do you mean, 'Don't wait up for me'? Are you going out of town? Where? For how long?" She had developed a habit, from her constant teaching in seminars, of speaking in simple phrases and stressing every word.

"Listen, Cecilia," said Kirill, calling her by her given name for the first time in all the years that they had known one another. "I'm calling from the office of an NKVD investigator. I was summoned here. At first I thought it had something to do with Nikita, but I was wrong. It had to do with me. They have an order for my arrest."

"Kirill!" shrieked Cecilia so that the entire hall heard her. She heard a click in the receiver, and the line went dead. She let out a low, animal wail that seemed to originate in the innermost depths of her body, then tumbled from the chair onto the floor. The fallen receiver bobbed up and down in the air for a few seconds and then was still. Her colleagues seated at the small tables around the hall went on diligently studying what they were reading without raising their heads. No one dared come to the aid of her crumpled form— everyone understood perfectly well what had happened. The jokes about their comical love affair were over, the source of humor had dried up.

When she came to, she jumped to her feet and ran out of the Institute of the International Workers' Movement. The scene was like something from a futuristic movie: shots of trees with rooks perched in their branches, the gates of the institute, the large-pored face of a watchman, the raised hood of a bus, steam rising from its overheated engine, swooped down on one another in dizzying succession, taking one another's places, flashed before the running woman who had gained weight in the previous few years. Putting theory into practice and vice versa, and vice versa again, and practice, like a steamroller, flattened the delicate surface of theory. . . . So it was that in the third year of the First Five-Year plan, two staunch Bolsheviks had passed over into a more intimate manner of addressing each other.

Several days later, a general Party meeting took place at the institute. Cecilia was given a place in the first row of seats: everyone knew she would be expected to make a speech disassociating herself from the enemy of the people K. B. Gradov. Despite their swinish work, most of the Party activists were not swine at all, and they felt sorry for poor Cecilia: it is difficult, after all, to renounce one's husband, even in the name of a great general cause. All of them unconsciously, or perhaps even consciously, imagined themselves in her place: maybe tomorrow will be my turn, the machinery of the purges is picking up more and more steam. One could ascribe the unavoidable excitement and anticipation that gripped the hall to residual humanist feelings.

From the wall above the presidium four overlapping profiles looked down with lofty indifference on the birds hopping about outside the window—Fritz Engels, stuck between Marx and Lenin, could only wink, while Iosif Vissarionovich Stalin, who was closest to the auditorium, displayed the full expanse of his cheek, showing that he was entirely independent and unattached. The chairman of the meeting, Party Committee Secretary Repa—a Latvian veteran of the Civil War—began to speak.

"We have gathered here today, comrades, in order to express our approval of the arrest by the organs of the NKVD of Gradov, a former member of our Educational Council, and to condemn the pernicious activities of this man, who, on assignment from an undermining anti-Soviet center of activity, crept into our—" At that point the speaker hesitated. He wanted to say "into our healthy collective," but held his tongue: what kind of "healthy collective" was it when seven of its members had been taken away in the past two months? If you say "healthy collective," he thought, then later on it will be remembered as an attempt to shield other conspirators. He coughed severely and finished the sentence by saying, "—into our collective." The interruption did not go unnoticed, but no one dared exchange a look. These days, one did not exchange glances in the presence of such mysteries; rather, one lowered one's eyes.

Meetings of this sort in Party institutions had become something on the order of a ritual in recent years, like retirements, though they were organized by proxy—without the presence of the arrested person. Orators spoke with a heat that was fired up to the point of hatred. The public was accustomed to the procedure: a man who minds his own business, a senior or a junior research fellow who gathers union dues or posts wall newspapers, worries about getting his children off to Young Pioneers camp, one day stops showing up at work—that means that either he has gone on sick leave or he's been hauled off; the latter was the more likely. That meant that a meeting of condemnation and disassociation would have to be organized. His coworkers, mistresses, and relatives would have to disown him. If a crazy thought like "My turn could be next" came into one's mind, then it would immediately be pushed out with a resounding "Really, though, I haven't done anything."

Well, what if Providence suddenly asked you a horrifying, numbing question like "And what did Gradov do, you bastard?" Why, then, with a quick turn of the head you avoided the questions of Providence.

That day everything was going according to the usual plan. Several of Kirill's coworkers got up to speak. They said that even in Gradov's early writings certain painstakingly concealed premises tending to support the Right-Trotskyite bloc could be detected. They spoke of his possible ties to the opposition in the twenties, of his sympathy for the kulaks. They spoke of the need to be done once and for all with all concealed forms of counterrevolution. They were waiting to hear the speech of Doctor of Historical Sciences Cecilia Rosenbloom, who was still the lawful spouse of the exposed enemy. Some of the women in the hall, particularly library workers, secret admirers of Akhmatova's verse, inwardly reproached Cecilia: she had not absolutely had to come, she could have fallen ill, collapsed beneath the weight of prostration . . . Comrade Repa yielded the floor to Comrade Rosenbloom. As she made her way to the speakers' platform, the image of her father appeared before her eyes, that same abstract father about whom a heated argument had broken out not long ago at the Gradovs' dacha. Her real, concrete father, a quite timid, modest accountant named Naum, had himself said, "Don't go to the meeting, Celia—keep your humanity." She was trembling all over and could not seem to get control of herself. The podium, which was actually quite steady, began to shake at the first contact with her body, decanters and glasses clinked together.

"Comrades," she began. "This is the most terrible moment of my life. It would be a thousand times easier for me to die for the Party and for socialism. I always knew Gradov as an uncompromising supporter of the Party line, as a faithful Leninist and an unshakable Stalinist. He always opposed the slightest deviation from the course set by the Stalinist Politburo. Comrades, even though I have the greatest respect for the glorious organs of our dictatorship of the proletariat, I have to say that in this case they have made a mistake. I urge the leadership of the NKVD to reconsider its decision with regard to the arrest of Kirill Gradov, and if such a reconsideration does not bring the results that I wish, well—" She threw back her head and looked as though she were choking, at the same time seizing her throat with both hands as though she were trying to stifle a howl. "—then let them take me! Please, arrest me, too! He and I are one! Gradov and Rosenbloom are one and the same! I can't live without him, comrades!"

The stunned auditorium was silent: no one had anticipated such a spectacle. Cecilia spun away from the podium and, clearing empty chairs out of her path, made her way to the wall, stepped down into the hall, then crashed back down into her seat in a semiconscious state. A librarian, one of the secret admirers of Akhmatova, ran to fetch some water. Comrade Repa, with a fear that was intensified by anger, banged his fist down on the table on the presidium and thundered: "What sort of outrageous speech was that? Rosenbloom has no respect for her comrades, for the organization of her Party! Instead of admitting her insufficient vigilance with regard to this carefully concealed enemy, she has weakened our defensive obstacles and allowed sex to rear its ugly head, as they say! This is unworthy of a Party member! It's a disgrace! I propose that Cecilia Rosenbloom be severely reprimanded and the matter be referred to the District Party Committee!"

Meanwhile, a march tune was ringing out from speakers on public squares and in apartments throughout the country:

> *Ah my lasses, ah my beauties,*
> *Let the country sing our glory,*
> *Tell a tale of wondrous duties,*
> *Tell of heroes such a story.*

Millions of people throughout the country, including the secret police and those who would by tomorrow be their victims, remembered with pleasure the scene from the film of the splendid, full-breasted girls marching across the screen; forward march, happy friends, the country will give shelter to every heart, thoughtful hands are needed everywhere, and laughing, buoyant broads!

The cult of the Soviet blonde had come into being. Built on Lenin Hills, or Sparrow Hills, as they had once been called, the huge film studio Mosfilm, the Soviet Hollywood, created the mirage of the happy years of the Five-Year Plan. Girls with white teeth, golden curls, and even rather long legs like Lyubov Orlov, Marina Ladynina, and Lidia Smirnova marched along in the columns of enthusiasts, tenderly seeing off heroic lads on their journeys—fliers, tank crews, polar explorers, NKVD agents. Every film concluded with a luxuriant apotheosis—superficially resembling a Hollywood production, but in actual fact filled with deep socialist content—of distinctive fountains of red banners and triumphal staircases either for the ascent into the glorious future or for coming down to the exultant masses. The happy ending went hand in hand with light comedies, with lyricism; crêpe-de-chine dresses fluttered, white shoes and apache shirts flashed by; but even here, in love stories, there flourished fundamentally new relations between the builders of the new society, replete with high-minded humanism, as opposed to the immorality and lack of ideological grounding of bourgeois culture. It was the first time in history that optimism had so mightily flourished in the vast space of the earth, or more exactly on one sixth of it, on the part of its dry surface turned toward the North Star.

In the textbooks of Soviet history schoolchildren, under the supervision of their teachers, smeared ink thickly over the names and pictures of the old heroes, now become enemies. The next year, the textbooks were handed down to younger students, and no one remembered the names that had vanished into the inky night. No shortage of heroes was felt, though. Life went on giving birth to a new hero almost every week. Stalin's glorious young eagles have saved the winter camp of the *Cheliuskin* icebreaker crew! Here you are, the first Heroes of the Soviet Union, the pilots Liapidievsky and Vodopyanov, here's the glorious bearded hero Otto Iulevich Schmidt! Papanin's mobile exploration camp has reached the North Pole! The icebreaker *Leonid Krasin* is coming to give them a hand! The miner Alexander Stakhanov has set a record for the mining of coal! Chkalov, Baidukov, and Belyakov have flown nonstop over the North Pole to America! The people thronged the streets by the thousands to greet these magnificent sons of the Motherland! They rode in open cars down the center of the recently widened Gorky Street, their white-toothed smiles flashing in the whirl of confetti and paper streamers. Students of the Komsomol! Soldiers of the Party! Soviet composers were writing more and more remarkable songs. "I know of no other country where a man can breathe so freely!" crackled from the speakers. Children ran with armfuls of flowers toward the Lenin Mausoleum. The fathers of the nation, those of Stalin's bandits who were still alive at the moment, stretched their noble, honorable arms toward them. An Uzbek girl named Mamlakat, who had set a record for picking cotton, pressed the peach down of her young cheek against the pocked moonscape of the Leader's visage. And the loudspeaker blared: "The sun shines more brightly. And the blood quickens. And Stalin looks on with a smile, a simple Soviet man."

Oh, how attractive Moscow is becoming! The police have been issued white helmets and knitted gloves! Entire blocks have been raised from their foundations and moved in order to widen streets. Our own Soviet automobiles roll past on them! Republican Spain, beating back the Fascist offensive with our help, sends us oranges, each one delicately wrapped in beautiful paper. Sporting life is in full swing! Our football teams can compete with the best in Europe! The incomparable discus thrower Nina Dumbadze, a countrywoman of our Leader, masterfully leads a column of legs, while the incomparable Nikolai Ozolin stuns all with his feats in the pole vault. And so many lyric poems all around! "Sasha, do you remember our meetings in the seaside park, on the coast? Sasha, do you remember that evening, that spring evening, when the chestnut tree was in bloom?" In the enchanted twilight of the imagination, marble staircases, vases, sculptures seem to float by, and all belong to the people, and the government holiday sanitoriums are splashed with girlish laughter, playfulness tender and pure, pursuit with only the most honorable intentions, only in order to say, "Vera, I'm flying out tomorrow, but I can't say where, do you understand?" "Yes, I understand! Come back as soon as you can!" That means she loves him!

> *Farewell, my dear, our young fighter!*
> *Guard your native shores!*
> *When you return, she'll dance with you,*
> *This proud love of yours!*

Meanwhile, the Black Marias continued to roll along the streets at night, not interfering with anyone's routine of living, loving, and working. Lovers took no notice of them. When all was said and done, people were simply minding their own business. Muscovites still shuddered when they heard an elevator going up in the night and strained to hear for a few minutes, then relaxed—the moment had passed, seemed even to have subsided entirely. You watch for a moment, then the cup passes from you, and tomorrow is a day off, for a soccer match, or the movies, or the circus, or a show by the comedian Smirnov-Sokolsky!

At Tushino Airport, the trumpets of the latest holiday were sounding. An excited crowd packed the stands and overflowed onto the field. Everyone's attention was riveted on the silver trimotor that was parked a short distance away and would have reminded one of a gigantic stuffed bird if not for the letters "USSR" painted on its side. Bands were playing, banners were fluttering, and groups of the Soviet answer to the Boy Scouts—the Pioneers—were playing bugles and drums as they marched past in review. A rally to celebrate the forthcoming nonstop flight by a female crew made up of Valentina Grizodubova, Polina Osipenko, and Marina Raskova was in progress. A huge picture of Stalin in a stone-hard Bolshevik service cap was fixed on the curved façade of the Central Aviation Club building. Smaller pictures, in some of which he wore the same hat, dotted the field. Here and there there flashed into view a two-headed portrait that had recently come into use—the catlike Stalin embracing Mamlakat, a happy little mouse with wide cheekbones.

The crowd was kept away from the airplane, and all the activity was concentrated on the wooden platform on which the three flyers, powerfully built women in flight suits and leather helmets, were standing. From the tribune shouted slogans were greeted with bursts of enthusiasm by the crowd. Flashbulbs were popping everywhere, photographers were working their cameras.

Nina Gradov had missed the beginning of the ceremonies and was now energetically making her way through the crowd. The stuffed bird of a plane, Stalin's hat, the two-headed picture . . . She dismissed the anti-Soviet thoughts that were creeping into her mind and then showed her red booklet identifying her as a correspondent of the newspaper *Working Woman* to the right and to the left. She finally reached the tribune itself and shouted to Grizodubov, "Hello, Valentina! I'm from *Working Woman.* As the commander of this flight, which is unprecedented in world history, could you please say a few words to our readers?"

Grizodubov noticed her, then extended a hand and helped her up onto the platform. She had a callused, masculine paw. Nina drew from her jacket pocket a notepad and a stylish Mont Blanc fountain pen, a gift from the writer Ilya Ehrenburg, who had just come back from a trip abroad. Grizodubov, trying to be heard above the noise, shouted directly into her ear—like a motor running at full throttle.

"Women! Girls! We live in a fabulous time! Who could have predicted that Russian women would cast off the fetters of age-old slavery and come to pilot airplanes, command ships, and drive tractors and tanks? No one could ever have predicted it, just as the modern enslaved woman in the bourgeois West cannot even imagine it! We are dedicating our flight to the great Stalin constitution, the most democratic constitution in the world, and to its creator, the sun of our Fatherland, Iosif Vissarionovich Stalin!"

Having said all this, Grizodubov took out a pack of cigarettes and offered one to Nina. "Do you smoke, friend?" They lit up and then smiled at one another not unsympathetically. A treacherous, cloying feeling of being a part of the whole spectacle suddenly came over Nina. She jumped down from the platform and began pushing her way through the crowd to the exit.

If I have to work somewhere, then why not at *Working Woman?* There's nowhere to hide from propaganda and lies, and here at least, in the essay department, I feel at home, surrounded by people who understand everything, see things rather ironically, modern women who, in addition, like my poetry. Such were the thoughts of Nina every time she approached the paper's offices on Pushkin Square, by force of habit searching with her glance for signs of life in the city that had nothing to do with "them": the statue of the poet, the iron lampposts, the swarms of blackbirds, the domes of a church that had survived, the Birth of the Virgin Mary in Putinka. . . . So here I am, a Blue Shirt, a Futurist, longing for the old days, searching my memory for fragments of childhood, of a world where such madness does not exist . . .

In the editorial offices she quickly banged out her article about the Tushino rally and gave it to Irina, the head of the department, with whom she had become close friends despite a ten-year difference in their ages. "Bacheloress Irina" often accompanied Nina and Savva to concerts at the conservatory or to performances at the Moscow Art Theater. There was nowhere else to go in Moscow anymore; the exhibitions were nothing but hog farms, the avant-garde artists had all gone underground, becoming court jesters doing doodlings of a constructive, inspiring nature. Miracles, though, still happened. Out of nowhere, *International Literature* had printed some staggering prose by someone named Joyce, and a two-volume set of Proust had come out. Luckily, Ernest Hemingway, the writer of the Lost Generation, had aligned himself with the "forces of progress," taking up a sharply anti-Fascist stance in Spain, which meant that he could be published. And the same journal had published several stories that included the surprising "The Cat in the Rain"; it was in an entirely new style—so much could be read between the lines of the simple dialogue. In a word, there was still something left to discuss, and they talked about Western literature in the kitchen, or while strolling along the boulevards, for hours at a time. As for their own former colleagues, some of them from quite recent times, it was better not to talk about them, it would lead to nothing good. There were many whom it was wiser not to mention at all, as though they had never existed.

A teakettle was whistling in the corner of the editorial office. "Teatime, girls!" The staff unwrapped sandwiches, someone produced a basket filled with homemade cookies, and a happy atmosphere of relaxation prevailed. Everyone knew that both of Nina's brothers had been arrested, but no one ever asked her about them. Talking about arrest victims in public places was simply not done. Nina surprised herself in thinking that not only was talking about her sorrows in public places unseemly, even thinking about them was as well, as though arrests and Soviet offices belonged to different worlds that had no contact with each other. Perhaps it was fear that imposed this rule, or perhaps it was the secret hope that one fine day the nightmare must end and therefore it was better to keep quiet about it. Then again, maybe it would be better to shout about it, to wail and shriek, Nina sometimes thought, though she immediately reproached herself: you won't yell for long, and nobody will be able to hear you.

In any case, everyone laughed while they drank their tea. Nina was recounting the story of her recent trip to the Crimea to interview an important man, Comrade Ibragimov, the chairman of the local Central Committee. In atrocious Russian he had described the status of the modern Tartar woman in the following terms: "Before, Tartar woman slave, like horse, but now she public woman—like seagull!" They laughed until tears ran down their cheeks.

After the tea break, Irina took Nina into her office to discuss her article. Nina looked over her shoulder—the page was streaked with red!

"Nina, forgive me, but I took the liberty of cleaning it up a bit," said the department head. "It's a wonderful article, but your habitual irony . . ."

Nina laughed. "You found that it contained my habitual irony?"

Irina laughed in reply. "Traces of your habitual irony, let's put it that way."

"Irina!"

"Nina!"

They looked each other in the eye. Irina had a peculiar nose, not quite a pug nose, but with the nostrils flaring outward, which in combination with her closely cropped hair and editor's glasses gave her a rather fierce appearance. In fact, though, she was a gentle, lonely soul. She extended her hand across the desk and laid it on top of Nina's. "The time for irony is over, Nina. It is our fate to live in heroic times."

Nina shrugged. "Without irony, Irka, it's simply impossible to get through these heroic times."

"And with it, it's difficult not to disappear," said Irina.

"Now there's a bit of sophistry!"

They both laughed sadly.

CHAPTER SEVENTEEN

Above the Eternal Rest

☆

Like all the prisons in the country, the terrible Lefortovo was also overcrowded, but fights for a place in the cell bunks rarely broke out, since the cells were occupied for the most part by political prisoners, a better class than ordinary criminals, people who were for the most part intelligent and inclined even to display a solidarity characteristic of the days before the Revolution. In many cells they had even worked out a rotation system for using the bunks. One hour at a time in a horizontal position, sleep if you can, dream about a woman, then yield your place to one of your comrades in the historical process. The prisoners who were waiting to "go horizontal" either stood against the wall or sat huddled together on the slippery floor. In this position, many began to have the sensation of traveling somewhere in a monstrous streetcar. There were, of course, exceptions to the rules, particularly with regard to anyone returning from interrogation. Any man who was carried back from the interrogation cells was given a bunk without waiting. But if he came back walking he had to wait his turn like everyone else. There was a queue system for the latrine bucket; someone was always sitting on it, releasing various gases into the overpacked crowd of people. However, there were not only depressing minuses but a few encouraging pluses as well. Just look, two Moscow University professors, a philologist and a biologist who wound up in a cell together, whispered to one another: even with all the physical deprivation, such as the stuffy air, the stench, the absence of a place to lie down, there were still some psychological advantages. First of all, when they push you into a cell like this, you can't help thinking: look at all these people, I'm not alone! And that—have you noticed?—cheers a man up. And then, take the queue system for the bunks and the latrine bucket, isn't that a demonstration of humanity? There's an old Russian saying to the effect that, with people around, even death is beautiful, but even in this state of approximation, people encourage you, won't let you surrender entirely. There's always some joker to boost your spirits. See how Mishanin questions the new arrivals. No, the classic Marxist authors knew the power of the collective. And they knew how to bank on it, the scoundrels. Who were the scoundrels? That's right, the classics!

Mishanin, a lively little man who had been a driver on the outside, kept himself entertained and entertained others as well. He would sidle up to a new arrival and ask him with a businesslike air, like someone he had met at a train station, "So, comrade, what are you in for?"

The new arrival, looking at the businesslike features of his questioner, suddenly understood that his case was not the end of civilization as we know it. He shrugged and answered, "Connections with Polish intelligence services. Don't know why with the Poles and not with someone a bit more substantial. Maybe it's because my last name ends in -sky? In short, I'm an 'S.E.'— suspicion of espionage."

Mishanin nodded in understanding, gave the man's hand an encouraging squeeze, then moved on to the next newcomer. "And you, friend, what are you in for?"

"Sabotage," he replied eagerly. "I worked as a cook, you understand, at the ball bearing factory, and of course we conspired to poison the workers—that's about the size of it."

Mishanin nodded respectfully to the cook as well and said with a knowing grin, "Where there's food, there's a sentence not far behind." Then he made his way over to a man whose peasant garb made him stand out among his urban mates. "And you, strawfoot, what are you here for?"

The peasant, observing Tolstoy's version of the folk tradition, looked at him good-naturedly. "For Marx, dear friend. In the club on the collective farm there was a lecture with the title 'Is There Life on Marx?' so I asked, 'Are you recruiting people to go to this planet Marx?' and that very day they arrested me, told me I was undermining the structure of the collective, showing signs of Bukharinist Trotskyism."

Mishanin roared with laughter, slapped the peasant on the back, poked his nose into the man's rucksack: how are you fixed for bacon, Marxist? Quite a group we've got here this time, comrades: a Polish spy, a saboteur-poisoner, and a Trotskyite-Bukharinite-Marxist!

The bars clanked, the door opened, and two guards came into the cell while a third barked from the corridor, "Gradov, to interrogation!"

Nikita freed himself from the wall. He was barely alive: they were interrogating him daily, sometimes twice a day. "Stand tall, Corps Commander," Mishanin whispered behind him, though he himself didn't stand tall at the interrogations at all, cheerfully signing any nonsense that the investigating officer put before him. "Stand tall, Corps Commander" had a nice ring to it, though, a sense of the poetry of an NKVD jail, and so every time the shadow was dragged off to be beaten at an interrogation, he would mutter this incantation to him.

Suddenly a heartrending cry flew up from the bottom of the stairwell like a tongue of fire: "Nikita!" The corps commander, who was being dragged along by two guards, stumbled slightly. The shout from the bottom floor, made louder by the resonance of the stairwell, seemed to reach his ears through the firmly packed, mute, and senseless cotton wadding of years past and illuminated for an instant a scene from his childhood: he and his friend Kholmsky were rowing in a skiff toward a bend in the Moscow River, and little Kirill was standing on shore shouting in desperation—they had forgotten him!

Kirill, also led by two thugs, rushed to the railing, forgetting everything else. Right there on the landing, two flights up, one of the people dearest to him in the world, his older brother, flashed by. Then he could no longer see anyone, but he kept on waving one hand and shouting, "Nikita! I saw you! Nikita, brother!"

The guards, who had become flustered for an instant, yanked him back from the bannister. He looked at them with an expression of joy and amazement, as though he had just seen his brother on the deck of a boat on a pleasure cruise. "Comrades, I just saw my brother up there!" One of the warders gave him a blow between the shoulder blades with the butt of his pistol, while the other drove a knee into his groin. They began kicking the fallen man methodically with their crude artificial leather boots. They cackled, "The wolf is your comrade! The pig is your brother!" Then they began dragging the prisoner who had violated regulations along the floor toward an open latrine. "Stick him snout first in the bucket! Let this Trotskyite eat shit!"

An hour later, they threw the half-alive Nikita back into his cell. His face, neck, and chest were covered with blood, his eyes were swollen puffs, and there was a dark stain between his legs—whether it was blood or urine, no one could tell.

One of the lower bunks was immediately cleared for him. They laid him on his back, wiped away the blood with a rag, and gave him something to drink. The corps commander did not groan, and it was not even clear whether or not he felt any pain. A few minutes later, he began to mutter. Mishanin bent over him, and caught a few words that made no sense to him: "From Zavgorodin—two days of bread rations and a bag of homegrown tobacco . . . from Ivanov the stoker—an overcoat . . . from Tsimmerman—cigarettes . . . from Putilin—one pair of boots . . ." Mishanin scratched his head—not the sort of thing you'd expect from a delirious corps commander, he thought.

The philologist whispered to the biologist, "Just look at that—you know, this is beyond me. I never thought our people would resort to such torture."

The biologist looked at him and smiled. He's lived to be forty, has landed in Lefortovo, and he's still surprised by "our people"! "Why, it's not even torture at all, my friend, it's the 'twenty-two methods of active investigation,' as the agent in charge of my case explained it to me. 'Yezhov mittens,' he laughed. Right now, they're trying them out on the stubbornest ones, and then they'll make them available for mass consumption, for the common sinners."

The philologist shuddered. "I don't know about you, but I wouldn't be able to stand it for a minute. I'd sign anything they put in front of me, even if it meant being shot!"

The biologist looked sadly at his colleague from the Moscow University faculty. "There are worse things than one's own execution, my friend." The philologist answered with a barely audible moan, as if his jaw were racked by a terrible pain in the roots of his teeth. No, no, just shooting—I hope they'll just put me up against the wall, nothing more . . .

A laugh came from the far corner of the cell. The omnipresent Mishanin was telling the story of how he had landed in jail. "Pure laziness, comrades, I'm a victim of my own laziness. No one's guilty except for my own worthless ass, dear comrades. You want to know how it happened, strawfoot? You're a stranger, of course, to such a thing as laziness? All right, I'll tell you a story as simple as one by Shakespeare. I've got this friend named Vaska Leshchinsky . . . move over; I want to lie down. One day, me and him picked up a dozen Zhiguli beers, and we were sitting around real late in the garage with three quarter-liters of Moscow Osobaya vodka, plus a couple one-ounce bottles. We were shooting the breeze about something—girls, or the Spartak-Dynamo soccer match, I don't remember what. Anyway, all of sudden we started arguing about who's the best-looking of the Party bigwigs. I was all for Voroshilov, and he was for Kaganovich, the Iron Commissar. We started fighting something terrible, grabbing each other, and trying to remember Stalin and all was no good. That night in the cot at home, I thought, 'I ought to inform on Vasenka Leshchinsky.' But I didn't want to get out from under the covers: it was warm, I'd had one too many, the wife was next to me. In the morning, I thought, 'Before my shift I'll hop over to see the authorities.' Well, that very next morning they came for me. Vasenka Leshchinsky, him, he didn't turn out to be so lazy . . ."

No one was interested whether or not Meshanin had really been turned in by this friend on whom he himself had wanted to inform. The important thing was that this outgoing fellow presented the whole secret police nightmare in an everyday, even comical light. The tension was decreasing, it was beginning to seem as though the authorities were taking their time, like a drunken apartment block manager, but it didn't matter—someone, most likely Stalin himself, would take care of these dawdlers and restore order.

After another spell of fainting and delirium, Nikita had emerged into the invigorating reality around him in time to hear the end of Meshanin's cheerful little tale. Then he regained consciousness entirely. Maybe Vadim Vuinovich back then, in Khabarovsk, had been just as energetic? This thought, as a matter of fact, had been tormenting him ever since the first moment following his arrest. Had it been Vadim? Had he really lost his nerve and informed to the police about a conversation that he himself had initiated? Maybe he had even been sent as some kind of provocation? No, that's impossible . . . Vadim and his chivalrous code of honor—an agent provocateur and stool pigeon? Better to suspect yourself of anything you want, but leave a man like that alone. On the other hand . . .

Vuinovich's name had not been so much as mentioned in the interrogations. The investigators, beside themselves with their own cruelty, came out with all sorts of nonsense, making up one scenario of treason and espionage after another, each more idiotic than the one before, when in fact the only really critical moment that would have been grounds for criminal proceedings and a firing squad had been that conversation on the balcony in the wee hours of the morning that had essentially been about plotting an uprising. The inspectors knew nothing about it—or did they? Were they only biding their time, intending to break him with Vadim's denunciation and thereby crush his resistance?

Today's interrogation had begun with all of them hurling themselves on him right away, tearing him to shreds. One of them took off his belt and lashed at Nikita's face, shoulders, and chest with the buckle. Then they proceeded to "methods of active investigation," their favorite of which involved squeezing the victim's genitals in a wooden vise. The pain was so far beyond being merely unbearable that it seemed almost nonexistent. The corps commander laughed and sobbed in a childish voice, quite unaware of himself. Suddenly, through a narrow crack in his hellish surroundings, he imagined Veronika at a moment when she had been running her fingers along his now swollen and crushed member. Then a doctor, their doctor, took his pulse and announced that it was permissible to continue. They turned him upside down, stuck him into a narrow box, head down, and went away. Everything disappeared, all sense of spatial orientation disappeared, he was starting on the final journey, but then they suddenly came back and he heard the doctor's voice saying, "That's enough for today."

Here it is, Nikita thought, my retribution has finally come, for Kronstadt, for Tambov . . . retribution for my cowardice, for my damned fear of thinking things through to the end, for the hypnosis of the Revolution. We were all daredevils as long as we were together, caught up in the herd instinct of the war, the romanticism of the herd, but when we were alone with our thoughts, we were cowards. That was the source of the present Stalinist hypnosis. Vadim turned out to have more courage than I did, he had overcome it. By pushing away Vadim, I knew I had given up any chance of doing it myself, but I did value my own skin, after all . . . Perhaps this would all pass by me? It would be disgraceful to perish at the hands of these secret police scum. It would have been better to have caught a sailor's bullet at Kronstadt.

Strange as it seemed, Vadim's idea had a chance of succeeding. There were several tactical schemes which were feasible. One of them involved dispatching a battalion of scouts to Moscow by train. Army transport by rail was a confused business, no one would figure out what unit they were and where they were headed. The battalion would arrive in Moscow just before a session of the Supreme Soviet, storm the Kremlin, and arrest Stalin. Another plan called for a strike force to land in Moscow in three airplanes. Even if both these plans failed, it would still be possible to flee and mount an uprising on a broad scale, to liberate the prisoners in Kolyma and the Northwest, to try to establish an independent republic in the Far East. They would offer the presidency to Blücher, and if he refused, then I could risk it myself or nominate Vadim. All great triumphs start from nothing. In short, one has to take risks, not just sit and wait to be slaughtered . . .

In the reprieves between interrogations, Corps Commander Gradov sometimes thought about these things, and any number of times he reached a point in his heroic daydreams where he found a traitorous thought galloping through his mind: what if Vadim had been sent by the NKVD? Then everything was ruined.

"Nikita Borisovich, are you asleep?" asked a delicate voice in his ear. Nikita turned his head with difficulty and saw Kolbasiev. The erstwhile signalman in the Baltic Fleet was still in communications—even in a Lefortovo cell. His place between the heating pipes was inviolable. He was on duty around the clock, receiving and transmitting messages tapped out from the deepest bowels of the dungeons on the pipes of the prison grapevine. Even on the outside Nikita had heard about Kolbasiev, an intellectual and jazz aficionado from Leningrad. A man like that, of course, could not avoid being swept up by the broom of the Cheka. On the one hand, it was a horrifying thought that the police were purging the country of its best people, but on the other, it was the basis for a certain pride—you were sharing the fate of good men, not those from the gutter.

"There's a telegram addressed to you, Nikita Borisovich."

There were visible bruises on Kolbasiev's face, traces of interrogations, but they were overshadowed by his bright, ever-curious technician's eyes. "In all probability, it came from the third floor through the Disinfection Unit. Listen, here it is." He lowered his voice as much as he could and whispered directly into Nikita's ear: "To Nikita Gradov from his brother, Kirill. I saw you on the stairs. I'm on the third floor. Our family is all right. Veronika has brought the children. The investigation of my case is over. I confessed. Don't put yourself through torture. Sign any documents. I love you."

Nikita burst into uncontrollable sobbing. So Kir had been arrested. Maybe even Nina, too. It was hard to imagine that she would get off after being linked to the opposition, to participation in a pro-Trotsky demonstration. They might even arrest his father.

The thought that they might do to his loved ones what they were doing to him now was absolutely unbearable. It's the end, he thought, our world is crumbling. Everything will be wiped out, it's obvious. Suddenly, a line from the blasphemer Mayakovsky emerged from somewhere in his mind: "God, if You are there, if it was You who wove the carpet of the stars . . ."

A hush came over the cell, whose inhabitants were hearing for the first time a sound the investigators delighted in at every interrogation, the unrestrained, infantile sobbing of the iron corps commander. Kolbasiev squeezed his hand. Nikita muttered, "Thank you, Sergei Nikolaevich" in reply to the handshake. Finally he managed to control his sobs and even sat up a bit, leaning one shoulder against the wall.

"Do you want me to sing you something by Sidney Bechet?" asked the signalman. In a whisper, he began to sing a spicy, syncopated melody punctuated by beats of his palms on his knees. It was surprisingly familiar.

"What is that tune, Sergei Nikolaevich?"

" 'The Yellow Bonnet,' " replied Kolbasiev and went on humming. Yes, it was the very same song that had been blaring from the phonograph all night long, thirteen, I think, years ago—yes, that was it, in 1925 . . . of course, on Mama's birthday, in Silver Forest, that evening when Vadim had driven his father to the Soldatyonkovskaya Hospital, the night of the death of Commissar Frunze. "Mama, buy me a yellow bonnet," Kolbasiev sang softly and then clicked out the breaks with his tongue and his hands. With these melodies in his head, the charming sailor disappeared forever and without a trace into the slime of the Russian penal system, into the incinerating frost of the ruins.

Quite recently, Semyon Nikiforovich Stroilo had received a considerable promotion, becoming a senior investigator and colonel in the NKVD, and had moved into an office in the "holy of holies"—the Lubyanka itself, whose very name struck fear into the hearts of the enemies of the Revolution throughout the world and all the vipers inside the country.

The office boasted a high, sculpted ceiling with a magnificent palatial chandelier, two large windows with a view of the wide expanse of Moscow—from the square with its new subway station up to the Kremlin spires emerging from the crowded rooftops of Kitai-gorod—and walls covered with irreproachable claret-colored wallpaper and paintings that would brook no objections—portraits of Lenin, Dzerzhinsky, and Stalin. The heavy desk was covered with a green fabric, with copper corners that had been through it all. On the wall, Levitan's landscape *Above the Eternal Rest* presented a grandiose allegory of the greatness of the spirit of the people. Here, in these surroundings, would be the place to receive visitors, to hear petitions, to delve into details. . . . Alas, the intensification of the class struggle and the approaching triumph of socialism occasioned some dirty work, in particular checking the effectiveness of the new investigative methods.

Colonel Stroilo was approaching forty and had become a strapping, self-assured man. All of his Komsomol prankishness, much less the whispering and giggling inherited from his parents, had disappeared. Now he was standing at the window with three junior officers. They were enjoying an extended break from their work, smoking, telling Jewish jokes, and laughing.

"Someone comes running up to Abraham. 'Abraham, Abraham, your wife is cheating on you with our bookkeeper.' 'With what bookkeeper?' Abraham shouts in a rage and picks up a heavy object. 'Well, you know, the tall, dark one with glasses.' Abraham waves him off with relief: 'Oh, he's not *our* bookkeeper . . .' "

Meanwhile, an enemy of the people sat slumped in a chair in the middle of the office, the rags of his military uniform hanging from his chest and shoulders. A young lieutenant was still working him over. Grabbing the prisoner by the chin, he moved the man's head back and up at such an angle that it was possible to recognize Regimental Commander Vuinovich in his smashed and swollen features. The lieutenant bent down next to his ear and whispered in an anguished voice, "Enough of this foolish stubbornness, Vuinovich! Confess and make it easy on yourself. Don't you understand that they'll skin you like a cat in here?"

"Go fuck yourself, you creep," said Vuinovich, moving his tongue and lips only with great effort.

The lieutenant immediately flew into a rage that swept away any signs of compassion. He delivered a chop to the captive's neck. Stroilo turned at the sound of the blow and looked at his watch. "Smoke break's over, boys. Time to go back to work." He sat down in his chair, which fit in well with the decor—the kind of chair in which a man might sit with a girl on his knee—and plunged into some documents. In overseeing ongoing inquests, he also had to familiarize himself with a large quantity of cases that were already closed—to see if all the regulations had been followed, all the proper documents had been signed: socialist justice had to be on a proper level. The remaining officers (a word which, once considered a shameful appendage of the Whites, was now used more and more often) slowly approached Vuinovich. Four strapping young lads surrounded one enemy of the people on his last legs. Why so many for just one man? Because of a black mark in his file that had followed him all the way from the Turkestan Military District: "inclined to insubordination."

The major brought his lit cigarette to a point immediately in front of the prisoner's eyes and lazily drawled, "Well, let's go on, Vuinovich. Come on, now, don't look so surly, let's have a chat. Tell us about your meetings with the French military attaché. Who took you there, where it was, how long it took them to recruit you . . . ah, forgotten everything, have we? Your memory fails you again? Ah, that's too bad—we'll just have to jog it a bit . . ."

They had come for Vadim at his post right after his return from the Far East, and as a result he had not been able to read the announcement in the newspapers that a group of enemies who had managed to infiltrate the High Command of the Special Far East Army had been unmasked and arrested: Marshal Blücher, Corps Commander Gradov, and others. The remains of his naiveté prompted him to think that perhaps this was why he had been arrested: after all, he had met his old comrades in arms on several occasions in the past few months and sometimes engaged them in open discussion about the possibility of the army rising up against the NKVD. One could not exclude the possibility that he had been informed upon: men who had been the bravest fighters in the past now jumped at the slightest squeak. He had compromised Nikita: the corps commander's silence that morning in response to his unambiguous summons had been painful. All that aside, Nikita had reason enough to dislike his former friend, who had insulted his father and mooned over his wife for so long. Of course, Nikita was a man of unimpeachable honor and pride, and in earlier times such a vile thought would never have crossed Vadim's mind, but times had changed, and now everyone lived according to the principle of "you today, me tomorrow." What sort of insurrection could there possibly be when a pathetic rabble of Cheka agents could come onto a military post in broad daylight and arrest a well-liked commanding officer in front of his entire staff?

It became clear right away in the investigation that the NKVD knew nothing about his recent travels and attempts to sound out the mood of the armed forces. They had their own clumsily concocted scenario of his criminal activities. Some absurd meetings with foreign military attachés, negotiations with tribal chieftains from the other side of the Afghan frontier, having as their goal detaching Turkestan from the fraternal family of peoples and creating a White Guard emirate on its territory. Even to offer resistance to these lunatic ravings seemed to Vadim a senseless, awkward, and humiliating business, but he could not help putting up a fight. Thank God they're on the wrong track, the idea of conducting a real investigation never came into the minds of these nitwits! Still, it would be better to be tortured for something I had done!

In Tashkent they had worked him over the old-fashioned way. They surrounded him in threes or fours, began by asking threatening questions in a mocking tone, then roared at him. Then one of them, as though unable to bear the treachery and impudence of his enemy, kicked or punched him in the side of the head, joined by another, then another, and then they were all on him at once. He was familiar with these methods of interrogation, had seen them used in the Civil War, and, he might as well admit it, had taken part in them once or twice himself, when, as the commander of detachment of cavalry scouts, he had brought some White prisoners in to headquarters. Now you know, Vadim, on your own skin what it must have been like for those men.

Then again, the "22 methods of active investigation" had not yet been thought of at the time of the Civil War, and Vadim began making their acquaintance once he was shipped from Tashkent to the Lubyanka for questioning. The regimental commander had continued to hold out here, too. Today, however, a decisive moment had arrived. It was no accident that they were conducting this interrogation not in the usual cell but in this commander's office, where a man in a Cheka uniform with a vaguely familiar face was sitting behind a desk. From all appearances he gathered that today they had determined to get what they wanted from him by their favorite, most bestial methods, and if he didn't break today, sign the confession, they would simply send him off to the cellars. Vuinovich had heard from his cellmates that those who stubbornly held out were eventually put up against the wall, after which the Cheka would arrange the paperwork to suit themselves.

Any movement, however slight, now brought agony. He lifted his head and surveyed the four investigators. Two of them, a major and a captain, he already knew from previous interrogations, and they had come to feel a sort of sadistic affection for him, as though he were one of their in-laws or even a blood relative. The other two, both lieutenants, he had seen for the first time today. As for the one behind the desk, he didn't seem to be taking part directly, absorbed as he was in more serious matters . . . but no, he would look up from time to time with a weighty glance, and as soon as Vadim met that gaze, he knew: it's all over.

The first part of the interrogation went as usual: they repeated their idiotic question about Frenchmen and Afghan tribesmen, now and again striking him addling blows to the head and stomach. Then the torturers decided to have a smoke, and they entered into the second, serious part of the "conversation." The major snapped his fingers, and one of the lieutenants rolled over a small metal table that looked like it might belong in an operating room, though it obviously was not sterile. The "investigative instruments" were lying on it. One glance at the table sent a shudder through Vadim. Two or three methods had been tried already, but the worst was yet to come! I won't give up, I won't! I'll go down fighting, the dogs! Maybe one of them won't be able to stand it and will just want to shoot me, then I might be able to grab the gun, get to the windows, and rip out the bars. . . . All of this roared through his mind like a whirlwind, and in the next second, the regimental commander jumped to his feet, overturned the "surgical" table with a kick, raised his chair over his head, and began to swing it, uttering the savage, senseless howl of a hunted beast finally run to ground.

Colonel Stroilo watched the scene with a grimace. Just to be on the safe side, he unbuttoned his revolver holster. Well, it's a beast we've got on our hands, simply an animal! I've seen this one somewhere before—he glanced at his papers—Vuinovich. I'll be damned, wasn't it at the Gradovs' dacha in the twenties? One of Nikita's buddies . . . well, that makes it all clear: the White Guard poison was flowing out of all of them even then.

From behind, one of the lieutenants jumped onto the shoulders of the enraged regimental commander, who managed to crash the chair down onto the major's head. In the end, four Cheka agents mastered one half-dead insurgent. Their fury knew no bounds. They went at him with all their extremities, even their heads.

"Go easy, comrades!" warned Stroilo. He understood and sympathized with his colleagues. You couldn't help but become a beast in this line of work. What can you do? From time to time certain paradoxical emotions are awakened in our people as a result of their contact with human filth. An incident which, viewed objectively, was rather unpleasant had recently happened even to him. In his presence, another brigade using the same methods had been interrogating a woman from the so-called "old Bolsheviks," though in fact she was just a Jew viper who had long ago sold out to the Italian Fascists. Everything was going as it should have until the feeble old scum flew into a rage. She began by shouting, "The czarist police interrogated me, but never—they never laid a hand on a woman! The Whites never treated me the way you have! No one, ever!" Then a thought seemed to strike her: "Only the Gestapo behaves the way you do! You're just agents of the Gestapo! The Gestapo, I say!" Something suddenly snapped in Colonel Stroilo, who could not keep a cool head, as Felix Edmundovich had always taught—his ardent heart was acting up, and his hands at that point were relatively unstained. He rushed forward, pushed aside his comrades surrounding the criminal, threw the old woman onto the couch, yanked her skirt off, bared the bitch's rear end, took off his solid, heavy belt with a star on the buckle, and went to work with it on her flaccid, decrepit buttocks. He kept at it until the bitch stopped howling and until he went into convulsions, convulsions of fountain-like ejaculations, as had sometimes happened in the days of his youth, many years before, with the professor's daughter; he felt very awkward then in front of his comrades. On top of that, an unbearable stench was spreading through the office, both from the old woman and from the colonel. No, that won't do, friends, one has to learn restraint, though we understand that these things can happen to any of us: when you work with the dregs of the human race, excesses are unavoidable.

The agents snapped handcuffs onto Vuinovich's wrists and bound his legs. Head thrown back, the regimental commander was lying on the parquet floor, while the upside-down expanse of Levitan's painting *Above the Eternal Rest* soared over him. He suddenly realized, in the sharpest and most penetrating way imaginable, what the artist had been trying to say with his colors and had failed to get across, something that no paints, no words, not even any music could express. Shaken by this understanding, he forgot about his own sufferings and about the agents, forgot everything that he lived for, forgot

Veronika, about whom he had in fact not forgotten even at the moment when he thought that he had. The only thing he passionately desired was to hold on to that moment of enlightenment, but almost immediately it slipped away from him. The agents unbuttoned his trousers, pulled out his "equipment," and prepared the vice. Only three of them were at work. The fourth, a young lieutenant, was throwing up in a sink in the corner. Stroilo gathered his documents together and locked them away. On the desk remained only Vuinovich's file, opened to a typewritten page with one line standing alone at the bottom: "I recognize the conclusions reached by the investigators as correct." All that was needed was the merest trifle, the signature of the man under investigation, and it was because of this trifle that all of this circus was being played out, with its yells and struggles and the foul odor of the lieutenant's undigested food.

On his way out, Stroilo said to the officers, "Carry on, comrades, don't stop until the son of a bitch signs." The major just gave him a dirty look.

The colonel had one more important matter to take care of that day—inspection of the new equipment in the cell block where the supreme measure of termination of criminal activities was to be carried out. Descending to one of the subterranean levels of the Lubyanka, he walked along a network of corridors to a row of unremarkable portals, those very doors behind which were located the execution cellars. Those who were condemned to death, naturally, arrived by a different route. This door was for the use of personnel. On the prisoners' side of the door, everything sparkled with fresh paint and cleanliness. Two sergeants were playing checkers in the recreation room. A radio was softly crooning the operetta *Mademoiselle Netouche*. Another twenty yards down the corridor, and the colonel found himself in what could properly be called the industrial section. Here everything was done with peak efficiency. Here was the spacious waiting room for the condemned. From here they would be led one by one to the execution cell, where they would be put face to the wall, the backs of their heads facing a marksman in a special booth. The process was almost reminiscent of a medical procedure, like, say, taking an X ray. An assistant sitting behind a glass window would turn a key to start up an automobile engine that had been installed to drown out gunshots and other undesirable sounds, particularly shouted propaganda slogans, which some of the enemies continued yelling right up to the last moment. The results of the work—that is, the corpse—would be transferred from the execution chamber to the refrigerated transport room, to be piled up with the other bodies until the arrival of the special transport. The truck would back up to a window in an inner courtyard. Then the bodies would slide down an inclined chute directly into the back of the truck, in which they would be transported to the competent authorities. Having examined the premises and the devices contained therein, Colonel Stroilo was satisfied: even in this business, after all, one has to maintain modern humane standards.

He had already left the remodeled execution block when its first party of clients, a dozen men taken from various Moscow jails, was brought in. Among them was Meshanin, the joker. Right up to the end he did not understand the seriousness of what was happening to him. "A pretty nice bathhouse, boys!" he announced cheerfully in the waiting room. "Do we take our clothes off, or what?"

"Just sit there, don't move!" a guard barked at him. The duty officer arrived. The sergeants abandoned their game of checkers and went off to do their job.

CHAPTER EIGHTEEN

I Recommend That You Not Cry!

★

Silver Forest was enjoying an exultant Indian summer, with deep blue skies over the gold, crimson, and ocher leaves and the seemingly rejuvenated pines. A gentle breeze was blowing through the groves as if in reassurance: everything was as it should have been, everything was marvelous, a few leaves had fallen, but only for aesthetic effect, only to bring an added touch of harmony to the overall picture by their flight. Spiderwebs stirred faintly as butterflies newly emerged from their abandoned chrysalides flitted between them with no other aim than, again, to add to the harmony. They had the beauty that comes with unreliability.

". . . then again, perhaps the other way around," Leonid Valentinovich Pulkovo thought aloud.

"What are you talking about, Leo?" asked Boris Nikitovich Gradov.

"About beauty," said the physicist. "Can beauty be relied upon?"

"You'd do better to address that question to our poetess," said Gradov with a smile that immediately turned into a frown as he remembered that of his three children, two were in jail and only his daughter remained free, only little Nina, to whom he advised his friend to refer his question about beauty.

The two old friends—and they were old not only in the sense of the length of time they had been friends but also because they were both past sixty—were standing on a high bank of the Moscow River. A small tugboat was towing a barrel-laden barge along the river. High above the water, eerily, two broad-winged gliders floated sightlessly.

"Just think, to soar like that without any engine," said Pulkovo, shielding his eyes with his palm as he watched the gliders. "Have you noticed, Bo, that young people nowadays have a positive mania for flying? All these gliders, aerostats, parachutes . . . where on earth does such bravery come from?"

"Bravery has relocated to the skies," noted Gradov sarcastically. "There's no trace of it on earth."

"Maybe the old sort of bravery is dead and a new one has been born in its place, a sort that's unknown to us?"

"If that's true, then cowardice has undergone some kind of radical metamorphosis," replied the surgeon.

They laughed grimly.

"Just listen to us philosophizing today," said Gradov, turning his back to the river. "Let's keep going."

The edge of the grove above the river had long been a favorite spot for picnickers. Here and there traces of Sunday comings and goings were visible: empty wine, vodka, and beer bottles, canning jars, eggshells, candy bar wrappers, even the peels of Spanish oranges: food shortages in the country were suddenly a thing of the past, and with each passing year the stores were filling up with a greater assortment of what were still called "vittles" out of habit formed in the years of hunger. Scraps of newspapers showed up in the grass and in shrubs, the scattered letters only occasionally joining together to form a more or less comprehensible, and more often than not frightful, message: "Shame to the Trait . . . ," "Get Your Filthy Paws off . . . ," "Severe sentence pas . . ."

"The pollution of nature," said Pulkovo. "One day it's going to become a colossal problem."

"Where we live, in Silver Forest, it's already a colossal problem," growled Gradov.

They were walking at a brisk pace along a path leading past some dachas. As in the old days, they were taking a fitness walk before lunch, moving energetically, to the point of exhaustion. "Then again, there are problems that are even somewhat more colossal." Gradov looked back over his shoulder—no one was there—and with his cane he indicated one of the dachas, whose peaceful windows reflected the blue skies and the pines, and also flashes of the squirrels that densely populated the area.

"Do you see that dacha, Leo? Do you remember a Volkov, from the Commissariat for Heavy Industry? He was taken away a week ago, and the dacha was sealed off. They're planning to confiscate it. And this one here on the other side, the third in the row, the Yarchenkos lived here. If you recall, he was a prominent functionary in the Commissariat for Finance. Even though he was more or less promoted from the ranks, he was a highly valued specialist, and they visited us often. They evicted his family the very same day he was arrested and boarded up the house. Over there, a bit further into the woods by the pond—the same story. Trifonov, an important man in the Party, his son Yury often played tennis and soccer with our Mitya. . . . They comb Silver Forest every night. It looks as though my turn is coming. What else can I expect after the arrests of the two boys?''

The last two sentences were pronounced with a certain lightness of tone that left no doubt that his upcoming arrest was the only thing Boris Nikitovich now thought about. Who doesn't think about it these days, except for me, Pulkovo asked himself. Only—something strange is happening to me. I don't think about it as having anything to do with myself—as though they couldn't just take me any day, all the more considering the baggage I bring from the twenties, the search, being taken to the "Luba" . . . You couldn't call it fatalism, though—fatalists think only about *fatum,* but my only thoughts are about my way of life, my experiments, my scientific papers, my ideas for trips, my most important plans, as though there were no obstacles standing in their way and could be none. It was a strange game he was playing with himself, perhaps even one unworthy of him . . .

Small dry twigs crunching beneath their feet yielded now and again to a springy carpet of pine needles. Again and again squirrels darted across the path. A large male was perched on a branch above the fence of the finance expert Yarchenko's dacha. "Mr. Squirrel," Pulkovo thought to himself in English. He turned back to look at it again as he passed. The squirrel was sitting in the classic pose with a pine cone and reminded Pulkovo of Lenin absorbed in reading *Pravda.* Leonid Valentinovich noticed that Boris Nikitovich was looking at the squirrel as well. "What do you know about that?" he muttered. They looked at each other and laughed.

"Listen, Bo, try not to think about being arrested," said Pulkovo. "God only knows what they're up to—sometimes I have the impression that they're simply picking people up at random, unsystematically. It's impossible to predict anything, they're like a swarm of stray bullets. It doesn't necessarily follow that one of them will hit you. Try to think about other things—you certainly have enough of them. If you insist on dwelling on the arrests, then think about the boys and how to help them, about your neighbors, about anyone except yourself. Do you understand? For some reason that works for me.''

While his friend was saying this, Gradov looked at the ground pensively and then said calmly, without any emotion, "Do you think, perhaps, that I'm playing the coward again? As I did back in 1925? No, there's none of that now . . ."

Pulkovo looked back over his shoulder. There was no one behind them except the big squirrel, occupied with his own business. "Well, everything else aside, Bo, the higher-ups are getting older, they need doctors, and they see you for exactly what you are: a leading surgeon and a healer, a miracle worker, at that. They need you!"

Gradov shrugged. "That's no guarantee. They considered Professor Pletnyov a miracle worker and healer, too, but they accused him of poisoning Gorky. My position in the Kremlin medical system has yet to be of any help to my boys. You know, Leo, something monstrous is going on in the Party leadership right now, some kind of pernicious leukemia. . . . Just the other day, Alexander Nikolaevich—you know whom I'm talking about—told me an ominous story. As a matter of fact, he would never have told it to me if it hadn't been for the decanter of Agasha's brandy that happened to be right at hand. He suddenly burst into tears and began to unburden himself. You remember Ordzhonikidze's sudden death? Alexander Nikolaevich was summoned to sign the death certificate. He examined the body along with six other great, prominent figures, who are indeed remarkable doctors, whatever one might think about them as individuals, and all of them saw a bullet wound in his temple with their own eyes, and then all of them signed the certificate stating that the death had been the result of a heart attack. In other words, they did what was demanded of them without a word of protest. No further questions were asked, and then they were all taken to their homes after being warned that they were dealing with a state secret of the highest importance. Permit me to ask you, Leo—is that a state secret, or—" He stopped his friend and whispered directly into his ear: "—or the work of a criminal gang?"

Chills ran up and down Pulkovo's spine. "How did you manage to avoid it, Bo? I must admit, I was surprised not to find your name in the 'synod.' "

Gradov, bowing his head and crossing his hands behind his back, continued walking. "I know what you're talking about," he said. "The way things turned out, I couldn't get out of it in 1925, but this time I did. To tell the truth, it was Mary who saved me. She pulled down the shades, locked the office, and told all callers and visitors that Boris Nikitovich wasn't there, that he was in Leningrad or Murmansk, at the moment she couldn't say exactly. Of course, if I had been at the concilium, I would have signed, too, there's no doubt about it, but . . . that's not what I'm getting at, Leo, I'm not talking about us weak and sinful people. . . ."

They walked on for a while in silence. A chill wind suddenly broke through the transparent Indian summer veil. It blew the bits of refuse on the forest path about in a whirl, along with the thin tufts of hair on the two friends' heads. "Ah, Bo, my dear Bo!" said Pulkovo unexpectedly, and Gradov stumbled slightly from surprise: this kind of epithet had hardly been accepted usage in their restrained friendship of a half century. Leonid Valentinovich, of course, understood straightaway that he had committed a faux pas, that he had awkwardly put things onto a different footing, had spoken with almost childish heedlessness. It did not sound very natural, either, but he nevertheless began to extricate himself little by little from his sentimental slip of the tongue.

"You know, I always envied you because you're a doctor, because you do such a ripping good job"—he even used the outmoded expression from their high school days—"such a ripping good job in your field, which is, after all, a genuinely useful and practical one, while I'm bogged down in endless abstract experiments—"

"But now you no longer envy me?" Boris Nikitovich asked with an ironic grin.

"Now I wish that you were a physicist, and that you were working with me in the same institute."

"Why is that, then?" asked Gradov in amazement.

"Because it's begun to seem to me at times that in the midst of the present madness, my science offers some kind of strange guarantee. Small and limited it may be, but nevertheless it's a guarantee. Do you remember that decade-old conversation of mine with Menzhinsky? Well, just now the question of a superweapon is worrying them a hundred times more. No matter what anyone says, their intelligence service is first class."

"What do you mean, 'their' intelligence service?" asked Gradov.

"Sorry, I mean 'our,' " Pulkovo corrected himself and went on. "And the intelligence services are bringing in more and more information about nuclear research in Great Britain, Germany, and the North American states. They're simply terrified of falling behind the West. From my point of view, for the time being there's nothing to fear, since it's necessary to produce a chain fission reaction to produce an atomic weapon, and to do that one has to amass a colossal quantity of the constituent elements—a fantastic thing like heavy water, for example . . . well, all things considered, we could talk about this for hours, but . . . but if there is a breakthrough, one cannot exclude the possibility, because there are physics geniuses working over there—Einstein himself, Bohr, too, and even that young American lad Bob Oppenheimer—that the USSR could end up defenseless and would be forced to capitulate!"

"That's terrible!" cried Gradov. "What are you talking about, Leo? What a horror!"

Pulkovo looked rather strangely at this man horrified by the possibility of the USSR's capitulation, then smiled and shrugged. "Well, this is all in the realm of theory, Bo, you must understand. Who will capitulate to whom. . . . The Devil himself would get confused in the current political situation. The principal thing that I wanted to say is this: we physicists are now surrounded by the colossal 'paternal concern' of the Party. They have given us a fivefold raise, they shower us with privileges. They come from the Central Committee, from the NKVD, they stroll around the laboratories, saying, 'Work in peace, comrades.' They do everything but scratch your ear. 'If you have any requests, if there's anything you want, just let us know immediately.' Can you imagine, they've even given me permission to go to Cambridge on official business for two months."

At that moment, Gradov really stumbled, because his head was spinning. "To Cambridge, Leo? You mean you're going abroad, to England?"

Pulkovo took him firmly by the arm. "Yes, Bo, I'm leaving in two days, and this is the most important thing I wanted to say to you today. I can't even imagine it, Bo, I'm ashamed to be leaving in these terrible days, but after all, I haven't even dared to dream of it for all these years! To see both of them!"

" 'Both of them,' Leo?" The flabbergasted Gradov could hardly go another step. "Who's this 'both of them'?"

They sat on a pile of sawed-up logs that were ready for transporting, and Leo revealed his closely guarded secret to Bo. In 1925 in Cambridge a romance had been kindled between himself and a young German girl named Claudia, one of Rutherford's assistants. "Claudia, or as we Russians would say, Klava . . . a remarkable girl, with a scientific potential like Marie Curie's, and Mary Pickford had nothing on her for looks. She was twenty-five then, and the old man leading her into sin, like you, my upright contemporary and paterfamilias, was already half a century old.

"Nothing more beautiful than that romance has ever happened in my life, Bo. The age difference gave it a kind of spin that we were both mad about. We went to Paris and stayed in a cheap hotel in the Latin Quarter. We had a wonderful time there, drinking and dancing. We spoke a mixture of languages, a 'lexical desecration,' as she put it, but it worked marvelously. Then we went to Brighton in the fall, spent hours wandering the deserted beaches, writing equations on the sand. . . . What more can I say!

"I left and began sadly to forget about her, supposing that she too was sadly forgetting me. It turned out, though, that I had left her with a weighty souvenir that was getting heavier all the time. In 1926 she gave birth to a son! I found out about this by accident from one of our mutual friends, who, as a matter of fact, knew nothing about our affair. I wrote to Claudia—you remember those days, when it was permitted to correspond with people abroad?—and asked—obliquely, of course—if I should not consider myself the father of the child. She replied that I was indeed the father, but that it did not place me under any obligation, that I did not have to worry, Alexander— she had intentionally chosen such an international name—would be brought up by her and her parents. A woman of surprising tact and dignity!

"In 1927 we exchanged a few letters and I began to think about submitting an application for a second research trip, but by that time my investigation was under way. More than anything, I feared that the OGPU might bring up the subject of my beloved and son. Ties to a foreign woman were still not enough to incriminate you at that time, NEP was still on, after all, but the very mention of their names in that institution filled me with horror. As it turned out, the secret police knew nothing about it all, otherwise Menzhinsky would not have let slip the possibility of blackmailing me a little. Even now, naturally, they know nothing about it. Would they really give me approval to make the trip if they knew I had a family in England? In fact, no one else in the world knew about this until this moment. Now you know, Bo. As long ago as that same year of 1927 I wrote her a letter and gave her to understand that our correspondence would have to end. Knowing her, I imagined that she was following the situation in Russia and understood where things in our country were leading. Now all these years have gone by. From time to time our mutual friend shows up—he enjoys the reputation here of a 'progressive foreigner,' and when we go to visit him in his hotel, he passes on greetings from her, not to us, but to the entire USSR. It was from him that I learned that her parents emigrated from Germany—they have some Jews in their family tree—and now they live together just outside London, which means that Sasha is spending his childhood in a family of loving people. Last year, this friend brought me a journal from her containing her address at a seminar on elementary particles, but the most important thing was contained not in her talk, but in . . . here, Bo, look . . ." In great agitation, Pulkovo drew from his raincoat pocket a copy of a scientific journal folded in half. There, in the midst of the fine print of texts, equations, and diagrams, was a small photograph. "Group photo of the participants in the Grace Fountain Villa Seminar" read the caption. Ten or so scientists were sitting in wicker chairs on a typical English lawn. There was one woman among them. Boris Nikitovich saw no resemblance between her and Mary Pickford but, paradoxically, saw in her something of his own Mary in her youth. The most unnerving thing was that in the background, next to the terrace, one could see a little boy of about ten and could even tell that he had a football under his foot. "That's him," whispered Leonid Valentinovich, scarcely breathing. "I'm sure that's Sasha. He's the same age as Boris the Fourth. Of course that's why she sent the journal, so that I would see my son. Just look, Bo, do you see? A boy like that, a part in his hair, a little round nose, his whole appearance. . . . Well, what do you think?"

"Really, he does look like you," pronounced Gradov, saying the words Pulkovo so passionately desired to hear. The old physicist's face lit up for a moment. Even in their romantic student years, Gradov had never seen his friend in such a maelstrom of emotion. He himself was in a state of unheard-of agitation. This Pulkovo, you always expect the unexpected from him, but something like this! To start a family for yourself in England . . . well, what do you know about that!

"You know, I have a first-rate magnifying glass in my study," he said. "We'll go have a look at your Sasha right now."

They stood up. For some time they walked silently. The rooftops and garret windows of the Gradov dacha were already in sight. Boris Nikitovich came to a sudden stop and said without looking at Pulkovo, "As I understand it, we'll never see each other again . . . in this life, in any case. Right now I want to tell you one thing, Leonid, perhaps the most serious thing I've ever said in my life. You and I have never spoken forthrightly about the events of 1925, about the operation on Commissar Frunze. Despite everything, I have remained, and shall remain always, an honest doctor. Do you understand? The same Russian doctor my father and grandfather were . . ."

At these words, the flawless, self-contained dandy, the professor of physics, abruptly hugged Boris Nikitovich and dissolved into sobs, muttering, "Bo, my dear man . . . my only friend . . ."

By its great predilection for the little word "we," the Soviet intelligentsia has often put its foot in its mouth. After all, you don't say "We are carrying out purges" if you yourself are to be purged, or "We are struggling with enemies of the people" if you yourself suddenly turn out to be just such an enemy. In the past few days, Boris Nikitovich had for some reason become stuck on the subject of the "they-we" difference. Considering himself quite legitimately a man of the old regime, he usually used "they" with regard to the rulers, but suddenly in his conversation with Pulkovo, he had been cut to the quick when the latter had remarked, "No matter what anyone says, their intelligence service . . ." A purely logical confusion—what had he meant by "their," the West's or ours, in the USSR? Aha, it's not just a matter of logic, you're already identifying yourself with this state. Its staggering totality has already begun to leave its mark on you. You growl, even fly into a rage, talking about "us" instead of "them." In saying "we," you're referring not to the regime, not even to the state, but to society, Russia, finally. Think back, though—did you ever speak that way in the days of the old regime, in the reign of the "rotten liberal" Nikolai Romanov? You always set "them" apart—the czar, the secret police, the Okhrana, the government clerks. Here, however, admit that when you say "we," you are subconsciously including everything, maybe first of all Stalin himself, the Politburo, the Cheka, even if you can't stand them . . .

In desperation he thought, well, how can I say "we" and include in that concept those who arrested my boys? In horror, he imagined his sons in the secret police prison. Muted rumors were going around the city that terrible tortures were used there. No, that's just too much, that can't happen in our country, in "our" . . .

He had been prepared for some time. Unknown to Mary, he had packed a small suitcase should he be taken—a change of underclothes, a sweater, toiletries—and hidden it in his lower desk drawer in the study. At Moscow's Lenin Medical Institute, where he headed a department, there had already been a series of arrests. Until now they had been confined to the lower echelons. The same thing was happening at the Academy of Military Medicine. The professors who held the leading chairs had not yet suffered, but they all expected their turn to come soon. "Are you waiting, my good fellow?" old man Lunts had asked him the other day. "As for me, I'm only guessing where I'll go first—to the Lubyanka, or to those happy Elysian Fields where no one can reach me."

The most painful thing of all was to look at Mary. In a few months she had aged ten years. Forgotten were all her proud poses, her stormy exits, the staccato of her emotions, and she had not touched the piano for a long time. It was clear that she spent every hour, every minute thinking about Nikita, Kirill, her grandsons, and their ruined hearth, of which she had always been so proud. A wave of determination passed over her face now and again, giving way to the expression of helplessness and simplicity Boris Nikitovich so adored.

The house sank into a stupor. Even Pythagoras, elderly but still fully possessed of his powers, trailed the boys in the garden less often, preferring to sit next to Mary, or at least near Agasha in the kitchen. The latter no longer made the dough for her stupendous meat pies, which everyone loved so much, and even prepared her jars of boiled and pickled preserves for winter without her former enthusiasm. Slabopetukhovsky, who during this time had managed to marry the daughter of the chief of the police directorate and even to father children, had not broken off his friendship with Agafia and her cut-glass decanter. Nowadays he often showed up with a morose expression, sat in the kitchen, and told Agasha that in "certain circles" they were saying things about the Gradov dacha that boded ill, that it seemed as though they were reckoning that they would have to deal with it in the near future.

"What do you advise us to do, Slabopetukhovsky, what do you advise us to do?" questioned Agasha desperately.

"In this case, there's no advice to give," answered Slabopetukhovsky in a downcast voice. "My information has no influence on them. Go to a church and light a candle, that's all the advice I can give."

After several weeks in a semiprostrate state, Veronika was gradually beginning to come around. Every two days she went to the Lubyanka to make inquiries about her husband. Again and again she received the same reply: "Investigation continuing, messages and visits not permitted." The lines before the little windows behind which the NKVD human robots sat were unbearable. Wide-faced, with skin the color of soap, the robots were of an indeterminate sex. One could never tell whether these eunuchs really knew something or whether they were automatically telling lies. Smiles had no effect on them.

As for the wider strata of the male population of Moscow, they continued to be not indifferent to Veronika's appearance, regardless of what was going on. Some of their representatives simply gave a start at the sight of her, as though the fulfillment of some lifelong dream were approaching. Despite the tragedy of her position, Veronika had not forgotten how to enjoy being adored by the capital. To travel on the Kuznetsky and Petrovsky lines, "to make an impression," had always counted for something and still did even now. Nikita had always understood this perfectly and had never let pass an opportunity to take his beloved with him when he went to Moscow on official business. After all, he knew she was no cheap woman and that even if she sometimes permitted herself to flirt with the men who surrounded her, she never got up to any whore's tricks. Even now, she could unfailingly guess which men in a Moscow crowd would be suitable for her entourage and even allowed a few of them to approach her. Alas, as soon as they found out she was the wife of Corps Commander Gradov, it was as if the wind blew them away. It even happened one day that the celebrated and fearless pilot Valery Chkalov offered her a ride in his car out to Silver Forest, yet as soon as he found out who she was he began to fidget disgracefully, said that he was in a hurry to get somewhere, and let her off at a streetcar stop. The same thing happened at the tennis court. No sooner would she arrive than her former partners would begin hurrying off.

The men in this country are degenerating, she thought, there'll be no one left to wage war.

Perhaps it would in fact be dangerous to play a set or two with her on a Silver Forest court? Take, for example, Morkoviev, a member of the Foreign

Law Department. He plucked up his courage, elegantly lost the match, then disappeared the next day. Then again, a number of her partners had disappeared without being compromised by her, and quite some time ago.

Well, if they put everyone who is brave and honorable into jail, who is going to fight against imperialism? she wondered.

Veronika began to spend more time with the children, particularly with Verochka, one of God's gentlest creations, who spent her time gathering plants for her herbarium and was a tireless artist. With Boris it was difficult to spend more time, because he did not give her any of his time. He was forever staying at school after his lessons were over for some aviation club, or else going to the stadium together with Mitya.

To begin with, they had had some unpleasantness at school. One day, a math teacher began to upbraid Boris in front of everyone for his poorly done homework assignments, for copying an answer from his desk neighbor, and suddenly cried out, directing an accusatory finger at the twelve-year-old boy, "Now we see it all: like father, like son! The apple never falls far from the tree!"

Boris IV came home choking back tears of rage, and Veronika tore into the school to withdraw him. The director, however, convinced her not to do so: Borya is liked by everyone, he's a brilliant soccer player, let's forget about this regrettable episode, our colleague got a bit carried away—after all, Stalin himself has emphasized that "the son is not responsible for the father." Let's just transfer Boris to another class. For the first time, Veronika read almost unconcealed sympathy in the eyes of an outsider, and it was difficult for her to hold back tears herself.

In a word, Boris continued to go to the fourth grade in the same school on the Khoroshovo highway, where his closest friend and adoptive cousin, Mitya, the former Sapunov, who had nearly forgotten his original family name in the Gradov clan, was in the seventh grade. Despite the difference in their ages, the two lads were almost inseparable, assembling their model airplanes together, going on bicycle rides together, waiting together on the tennis court for dusk, when the adult players dispersed, in order to be able to hit an almost invisible ball back and forth a few times. Yury Trifonov, another of their friends and a former neighbor, ironically called them "the twilight school players," including himself in that number.

One day Mitya looked at Boris over their chessboard. "See here, Borya, we'll grow up, and then we'll show them, the snakes," he said, interrupting his playing of the Capablanca gambit. Boris IV was a bit upset: he thought he was really winning, but it turned out that Mitya had his mind on something else entirely. "Who?" he asked. "The Communists and the Cheka," Mitya said with hardness. "The ones who ruined our fathers. Oh, I hate them so much!" "What about Stalin?" asked Boris IV quietly. "Stalin's not to blame. He doesn't know what they're up to," Mitya pronounced assuredly. "He's a great leader, the leader of the world, understand? He can't know about everything. They're deceiving him!"

Their school was taking part in the November seventh parade celebrating the October Revolution, and they marched together in the ranks of their aviation club, holding their model airplanes over their heads. As they approached Red Square, both boys were seized by an ever greater, almost staggering excitement, and when the Mausoleum came into view and Stalin appeared as a clear gray dot in an overcoat, a feeling of unimaginable triumph and jubilation took hold of them and merged with that of the exultant crowd of many thousands. He's there, he's in his place, at the country's most important spot, and that means everything will work out, our fathers will come back, justice will be reestablished. If he were to order me to die on the spot, thought Boris IV, without hesitation I'd charge into machine guns or barbed wire, blow up a Fascist battleship with a torpedo! Mitya, the former kulak offspring, was experiencing the very same emotions. "Wait, Borya, just you wait," he whispered. "When we grow up we'll let Stalin know who his friends and enemies really are!"

Mitya had long ago come to consider himself an integral part of the Gradov family and in the depths of his soul considered Mary Vakhtangovna his mother, not the erratic, slovenly Cecilia. After Kirill's arrest, Cecilia had rapidly let herself go, had stopped combing her hair and doing her laundry. Now she often gave off a sharp, repugnant smell, the odor of ill fortune, insurmountable grief, and dissolution. For Mitya it was sheer torture to be at "home" in their small room, a communal burrow on the fifth floor of Merchants' Court on Solyanka Square, where the woman would sit in front of books for hours on end without saying a word and then would suddenly begin to sniffle and whimper, looking with unseeing eyes at her beloved bust of Karl Marx, which stood against the wall beneath a map of the world, his curly hair seemingly supporting the icy pillow of Antarctica. Suddenly she would jump to her feet—"Why, why do you always want to go there? You're my son, you should be with me! Are you hungry? Do you want me to fix you some soup?" She would rush to the communal kitchen, turn on the stove, break several matches, and senselessly try to pump in more kerosene, but nothing worked, she only burned her hands. The neighbors made crude jokes about the antics of "the Jewess." Mitya pleaded with her, "Aunt Cecilia, I don't want any soup. It would be better if you gave me some money for a roll and some liver sausage." Cecilia's soups were an opus of the absurd. Grandfather Matvey said with a shrug of his shoulders, "Our Cecilia has a grown child? It's the paradox of the century." Finally Mary would arrive, either alone or with Grandfather Bo, and Mitya would go off to his native country, where by night the pines rocked and whistled over the big, warm house, where his loving friend Pythagoras roamed, where there was a joyful smell of fresh pancakes in the morning, and where, finally, there was Boris IV, who had come into the world, as everyone said, in order to carry on the dynasty.

It was Mitya himself, it seems, who was the first to see the Model T–like sedan with blinds drawn tightly over the side windows pull up to their gate. He didn't even know what had awakened him in the middle of the night. A strong wind was blowing, the pines were rustling, and the light car's engine was barely distinguishable through the din. He looked out of the window and saw the car's stubby body enter into the swaying dot illuminated by the headlights and stop just opposite their gate.

On the other hand, it might not have been Mitya who was the first to see the Cheka car arrive but rather Grandfather Bo himself, who had already suffered through several sleepless nights in a row. "There they are, they've come," he whispered, with relief as it later seemed to him, and began to get into his dressing gown so as to open the door to their nighttime visitors. Mary was already standing right behind him, as though she had not been sleeping either, but waiting.

The nocturnal team got out of the car unhurriedly: a man in a military service cap and uniform but a civilian overcoat, a woman in a leather coat and man's cap, though it was cocked at a feminine angle, and a young soldier leading a German shepherd on a leash. "Good Lord, what do they want with a dog? What is there to sniff out here?" muttered Gradov.

The young officer thrust his hand through the fence with a knowing gesture, pulled back the bolt of the gate, then let the dog through and came in behind it. The man and the woman followed.

Taking their time, they came closer, like figures in a nightmare. The dog was not distracted by the smells of the forest, which would have set the head of any normal dog in a whirl.

Boris Nikitovich embraced his wife. "Well, there you see it, they've come even for me now."

Mrs. Gradov, née Gudiashvili, flared up and trembled all over in one last access of Georgian rage. "I won't let them into my house! Go, call Kalinin, Stalin, call the bald devil himself if it will help!"

Boris Nikitovich kissed her on the cheek and stroked her shoulder. "Stop it, Mary, my dear! You can't deceive fate. All things considered, they need doctors there, too. Who knows, we might survive after all. If they don't confiscate everything, try to sell the dacha and go to stay with Galaktion in Tiflis. And now . . . in my study, behind the medical encyclopedia . . . a small bag . . . I was prepared for this eventuality . . ."

The trembling left Mary. Hunching over, she turned away from her husband and whispered, "I've known about this bag for a long time. I even packed wool socks in it for you . . ."

Downstairs they were already ringing the doorbell, once, twice, three times, followed by the sharp, insolent banging of fists and boots and shouts of "Open up! Open the door immediately!" The Gradov household was awakening in a panic. Pythagoras began to howl, Agasha set to bustling about, the boys could be heard rumbling downstairs. Boris Nikitovich walked to the door decisively, still in his dressing gown but already wearing his trousers and shoes. "Who is it, then, Borya, at this hour?" whispered Agasha. "Someone to drag you out for an operation?"

He opened the door and was struck by the expressiveness of the faces he saw before him. There was anything but indifference in them. It seemed that they were so enraptured with life that they could barely keep themselves from shouting. They were not only specialists at this night work but obviously enthusiastic about their total, ruthless power. The only impassive professional among them was the bitch of the same breed as Pythagoras, and, having only glanced at her, the old dog broke into a melancholy whimper and began backing up until he reached the kitchen and hid beneath a couch.

"We're from the NKVD," said the senior officer in the overcoat. "We have an order for the arrest of—"

"Come in," Gradov said quickly. "I'm ready." Having already rehearsed the scene in his mind many times, he had determined that he would show no emotion, as if he had nothing to do with these people. They would not even see contempt from him. It was as though grave-digging automatons, not living creatures, had appeared.

The senior officer smirked. Obviously, he had already come across these stoic types. He was clearly no robot. He liked to watch the squirming of helpless people suspected of carrying the dirtiest kind of syphilis—state treason.

The group came inside. The senior officer quickly looked over those present. He turned to Boris Nikitovich and smirked again with outrageous contempt.

"Don't worry, Professor Gradov. It isn't for you that we've come. Our order is for the arrest of Citizen Gradov, Veronika Yevgenievna, your daughter-in-law."

"Mama! Mama!" Boris IV cried out, just like a child. Veronika, who had only just come down the stairs and was fastening the front of her dressing gown, sat down on a step and lowered her head into her hands.

"*Vai!*" exclaimed Mary in Georgian and hurried to Veronika.

Little Vera, awakened in her mother's room, started to cry. Agasha began to moan sorrowfully. Veronika's shoulders were trembling. She began to sob with strange low sounds that one would have thought her incapable of producing.

The female agent in the leather coat stepped forward and with the voice of someone who had experience in orchestrating such proceedings announced, "All those resident in the present living quarters are required to gather downstairs in the dining room. I recommend that you not cry! Moscow doesn't believe in tears. Right now, the witnesses will come along and we will begin the search."

The agent with the dog smiled crookedly at Agasha. "You live here bourgeois style, I see!" He glanced beneath the sofa at the cringing Pythagoras. "Tie your animal somewhere in the pantry, otherwise something unpleasant might happen," he said, pointedly clapping his hand to his holstered pistol.

Boris Nikitovich was flabbergasted and unnerved. From the fact that they had come not for him but for someone else, leaving him in freedom, he derived not the slightest joy, not even subconsciously—as opposed to Mary, it must be admitted, who would later punish herself endlessly for allowing an involuntary note of joy to be heard in her first *"Vai!"*—the cup had passed, after all, from the man closest to her, while he, by contrast, was simply devastated by the turn of events. The blow that he had so long expected and was prepared to absorb, as a man, as a scientific figure—the hard traveling of a Russian doctor along the path of martyrdom—this blow had suddenly been redirected at a gentle, defenseless creature, an entirely guiltless—as though he were guilty of anything himself—woman! By now there was no longer a question of any sort of restraint where these loathsome robots were concerned; he was seething with rage. "On what grounds are you taking not me but a defenseless woman?" he suddenly shouted at the senior officer.

The officer sat down at the dining room table, spread some documents before him, and gave the old man an evil look. "You would do better not to raise your voice with us, Professor. Your daughter-in-law is wanted as an accessory in the case of your son Gradov, Nikita Borisovich. Let's turn to the matter at hand. For how long has Citizen Gradov, Veronika, lived with you?"

The witnesses came in, accompanied by a regular policeman. They turned out to be the lady from the newspaper kiosk at the streetcar stop, and . . . none other than Comrade Slabopetukhovsky. All the vicissitudes of the latter's life were reflected on his face. During the entire search he sat in a corner as silently as an Easter Island statue.

The arrest procedure took two or three hours to complete. Inasmuch as Citizen Gradov, V. Y., had apparently lived not in a separate room but all over the house, the whole house was subject to search, yet the idiotic search was carried out only for the sake of appearances. For some reason or other the sergeant with the dog went through all the rooms. The dog obviously did not understand what it was that was wanted of her and became nervous, getting down on all fours, coming to a halt for no reason, then pointlessly striving to go somewhere else. The woman agent went through the motions of searching the library and again found nothing that related to the case except for some photo albums containing a few snapshots that showed Nikita in the company of other officers of the Worker-Peasant Red Army.

"Don't you dare touch that!" cried Mary Vakhtangovna. "Those are ours! They're not hers and they're not his. Ours! Mine, and my husband's, a distinguished doctor of the Russian Republic, three times decorated. Take your hands off!"

Grimacing almost squeamishly, the agent tossed the album back to her and then got down to the real business at hand: compiling a list of Veronika's personal property, that is, her wardrobe, which had seen no small travels along the roads of the twentieth century, from Paris shops to Moscow commission stores, from there to the distant frontiers of Soviet reign and then back to Moscow, ready to hang on the hooks of the secondhand stores once again. Here there were things that sent the NKVD woman into a rage: garments of chiffon, crêpe de chine, a fur coat, tennis racquets, vials of French perfume. If it had been up to her, she would have had this little lady put against the wall for these items alone—after having let her pass through the hands of the "guys and gals" first, of course, in keeping with the rules. In addition to the clothes, there were also Veronika's personal photo albums, bundles of letters—what the hell was she keeping these old letters for, and with dried flowers from the Crimea thrown in?—and the most important things: her bankbook and letters of credit for a tidy sum.

The senior officer carefully noted down all these goods. "The question of personal property will be decided later. For the time being, we will put everything in the detainee's room and seal it." At the word "seal" Boris IV's eyes widened. He caught himself in the realization that the procedure of melting wax and smacking a lead stamp into it excited a burning curiosity in him.

On the whole, it must be said that all of the recent events, the arrests of his father and uncle and now of his mother—in other words, the catastrophic collapse of the family—had not been the cause of only grief and dejection in the boy's heart, but also a strange sort of excitement, keen sense of the newness of his life. Sometimes he imagined himself as an incorrigible vagabond, an old hand, like Jack London's heroes who joined up with oyster pirates and made a living with them in the San Francisco Bay.

Suddenly he shuddered at hearing his name spoken in an improbable fashion by the commander of the group himself, the keeper of the seal.

"Gradov, Boris Nikitovich, twelve years old, and his sister, Vera Nikitina, six years old, pending special orders, will temporarily remain in the care of their grandparents. Sign right here, Professor."

"What do you mean, 'temporarily'?" Mary shrieked like a wounded mother eagle. "They will always stay with us! To the end of our days!"

"The question will be reviewed," said the senior officer. "We do not exclude the possibility that the state will take them into its care."

"Over my dead body!" wailed Mary.

"Hmm . . ." said the senior officer and looked at her attentively, as if to let her know that if she continued to have these attacks of nerves, then that eventuality might well come to pass.

"Mary, dear, calm down!" The professor put his arms around his wife. "In no case will we hand over the children. Tomorrow we'll submit an application to adopt Boba and Verulya."

"Well, that's all," said the commander. "Say good-bye to your family, Veronika Yevgenievna." As he stood up, he caught the glance of the adolescent Dmitry Kirillovich Gradov, né Sapunov, born 1923, upon him—a look of total, final hatred, irreconcilable under any circumstances. It's ones like him that ought to be hauled away, he thought. They're the ones who will kill us if anyone does. They ought to be finished off, right down to the lowest classes.

Mary and Veronika converged in an embrace, both of them spilling floods of tears. Had there ever really existed a rivalry between these two women? "Veronika, my darling, my little dove . . ."

"All right, enough of this sniffling," said the woman agent. "You didn't sniffle about your dirty tricks, and now you're boo-hooing all over the place!"

Veronika wiped away the tears and suddenly stood before everyone in an entirely unexpected, severe and composed posture. "Good-bye, children, don't be afraid of anything. You're not surrounded only by beasts, there are people, too. Boba, look after Verulya. Mitya, I'm begging you, take care of my children. Children, heed your grandparents and watch out for them. Good-bye, my dear Marichka. Good-bye, dear Bo. Kiss Ninka, Savva, and Lenochka for me. Prepare my parents for the news. Good-bye, Agashenka, I'll always remember you. All the best to you too, Slabopetukhovsky!"

"All the best to you, my dearest Veronika Yevgenievna!" Slabopetukhovsky said with sudden firmness. His face contorted like a stone cracking.

CHAPTER NINETEEN

"I Dream of Hunchbacked Tiflis"

★

Numbness and confusion still prevailed at Silver Forest after that terrible night, when a raucous alarm clock went off directly beneath the ear of the head of the house in the apartment of a happy Moscow family. Out of habit the head, the newly qualified Professor and Doctor of Science, Savva Kitaigorodsky, extended a muscular arm to turn it off so as not to wake his wife and daughter early. It was only then that he noticed that he was lying in bed alone and saw Nina through the half-open door puttering around the kitchen in a Spartak soccer jersey and a billowing pair of flannel pants. With a cracking of joints, he stretched happily. I'll lie here for another ten minutes, he thought, and if I'm half an hour late today, nothing will happen—a professor can permit himself certain things. In all probability Nina was fussing with her jingles intended for posters, writing so-called *khokhmas. Khokhma,* which meant "joke," was a word that was all the rage in Moscow now, having recently sailed into the capital beneath the banner of Leonid Utyosov and the southern school of writers. All one heard now was *khokhma.* "Are there any new *khokhmas?*" "Now there's a *khokhma!*" "Stop your *khokhmas!*"

The Kitaigorodskys belonged to that number of Moscow fortunates who had their own flat instead of a room in a communal apartment. In gratitude for a successful operation, one of Savva's patients, a functionary of the Moscow City Executive Committee, had sent Savva's application through the right channels, and as a result the Kitaigorodskys had been given a one-room apartment in a ten-story building in the "Russian modern" style on Bolshoi Gnezdnikovsky Street. The building was unique. Built not long before World War I, it resembled a hotel more than a block of flats. The singular thing was that it had been built for bachelors, young Muscovite intellectual professionals: lawyers, dentists, bank clerks, and so on. Every apartment, or "studio," as they had been called then, consisted of a single rather large room with a picture window, a kitchen, and a bathroom. Nowadays, of course . . . well, never mind about bachelors, all the flats were jammed with entire households, sometimes made up of people from different branches of one family. Nonetheless, no more than a single family was housed in each one, and for this reason all the residents were content and took pride in the fact that they all lived in their own apartments! The elevators had functioned reliably until now, and the building had a handsome, wide, tiled roof, designed with a view to strolling young bachelors absorbed in thinking about their professions, Symbolist poetry, stock dividends, and most of all, girls. Naturally, children now played on the roof. A high steel cage that had protected the prerevolutionary bachelors from any superfluous symbolism now protected the children from any excessive imitations of airplanes.

There were no telephones in the apartments, but on the other hand, by a happy irony of fate, the entire reconstructed tenth floor was occupied by the infamous Soviet Writer publishing house, and Nina could dash up to some friend's office at any time and "give someone a jingle" from there.

Even to the offices of *Working Woman* it was literally two minutes' walk—turn right onto Gorky Street, cross, turn right again, and Pushkin Square is right around the corner, that's all there is to it. Nina continued to work for *Working Woman* despite the fact that her friend the department head had disappeared several months before. She disappeared, and that was it—end of story. So where's Irina? We have a new department head now, Ninochka—I'd like you to meet Angelika Dormidontovna, a pace-setting worker from Gzhatsk. Pleased to meet you, but where's Irina? She no longer works for us. And where is she working now? Nina, really, don't ask naive questions. Oh, that's how it is—it's the same all over, all from the same opera, there was a person, now she's gone, and don't ask naive questions! There's a *khokhma* for you!

In other Moscow intellectual circles, the endless circular terror of the NKVD no longer inspired horror but a feeling of black comedy, of gallows humor. In her kitchen, Nina, for example, had hung a sign, an appeal to her faithful partner: "If they take you away first and in my absence, make sure you've turned off the gas to the stove and any electrical appliances!" It made life just a bit easier in spite of everything. The vanished Irina had been wrong, vestiges of humor did help, and in any case, running away would do nothing to save you. In all other respects—if one could even refer to what was left as "other respects"—Nina and Savva's life could almost be called happy. Elenka was going on three, and both her parents doted on her. In the romantic sense, Nina had, as they say, settled down. Above all, she had suddenly discovered that the man who had sighed over her for so long, the comical intellectual Savva, was an exceptionally handsome man. Earlier, she had for some reason never paid any attention to his features, and it was only when she shared a bed with him that she discovered that he had broad, muscular shoulders, a supple waist, and long, narrow thighs. When he bent over her and his fair hair fell down, he seemed to her a genuine knight of the North, the essence of the "blond beast." A sweet, strong lover, a faithful husband, a real gentleman, a wonderful friend—what else could a woman ask for, even if she did consider herself a "contradictory poetess"?

As far as Savva was concerned, not only did he not try to analyze his domestic harmony, he simply could not imagine himself with another woman. Of course, he suffered sometimes—I can't give Nina everything she needs for her work, he thought. She's a poet, she needs a few sharp turns now and again, rises and falls, some kind of roller coaster of emotions, otherwise the Muses will fly away from her, and I can give her only my love, an even, everyday motion. Well, why not . . .

It sometimes even seemed to Nina that he had written her a sort of free pass to go into spirals of short duration. Thus she was almost certain that her several meetings with Ehrenburg, just returned from Europe, had not slipped by him. The celebrated "Muscovite Parisian," the poet and world-famous journalist . . . she had seen him at the National Hotel sitting alone by a window, with a pipe between his teeth and a glass of cognac. She had even stumbled like a horse whose bridle had been pulled. "There's Ehrenburg over there, just back from Spain, via Paris, of course. Want to meet him?" someone asked. Everything was clear from the very first moment. They met several times at the apartment of his friend. He sat on a windowsill, looking off to one side as usual, reading to her from a small notebook:

"Forgive me for living in that forest, for having gone through it all and survived, for the fact that I will take the immense twilights of Paris to my grave . . ."

As she had once done with other poets, and sometimes with contemptible men, she unbuttoned his shirt. It seemed that the old intoxicating fog was returning, that she was eagerly devouring some quintessence of existence. Someone had let her know that the secret police literally followed on his heels, which meant they had already taken note of her, but she was scarcely in a state to listen, and of course the police were what she thought about least of all—and then, all of a sudden, to her sorrow, she discovered that everything had vanished, that there was no need to meet him anymore. This secret eventually flowed out into a cycle of poems, about which the parties concerned spoke in secret with ambiguous smiles, and the poetess, after sighing deeply before the face of the cool and stormy sea, went back to her masculine ideal, Professor Kitaigorodsky.

Well, I knew whom I was marrying, thought Savva. I've known her for so long, I know her a thousand times better than she knows me. When all is said and done, my happiness lies precisely in the way she is!

He stretched his arms and legs one more time, then jumped briskly out from under the covers. He did exercises that stretched his left extremities, then the right. Ten squats, followed by a handstand, and then he went to get little Elena out of bed. "Up you get, little fritter, time to go to work," he said. The little girl had been calling her day nursery "work" for a long time now.

With his daughter in his arms, he walked over to the kitchen and saw that Nina was pinning to the wall a new rhyme-covered poster, on which he himself was depicted in a caricature that still managed to be flattering.

> *Savva is a young professor,*
> *And in surgery no lesser*
> *Than the curse of spleen and sadness,*
> *Bringing ladies joy and gladness.*
> *When he bought a record player,*
> *Adding value to his cargo,*
> *Cables foreign crowned him mayor:*
> *"Yes, I love you, darling!—Garbo."*

Everyone roared with laughter, Elenka loudest of all. She had not yet learned to read and insisted on having the verses repeated to her so that she could memorize them and recite them at "work."

"Just don't repeat the part about Greta Garbo, Elenka," said Nina. "Otherwise you'll reveal our foreign connections. Instead of 'I love you, darling—Greta Garbo,' say 'I approve, signed—Doctor Karpov.' "

"All right," said Elenka, "that's even better."

"Who's this Doctor Karpov?" asked Savva indignantly. "Your mother is an incorrigible Blue Shirt, Elenka. Only cares about the concerns of the moment. I'm ready to risk my hide for the sake of Greta Garbo."

He took his daughter off to wash and had a shower himself. A private bathroom—is that not luxury, isn't it bliss? Then he made some kasha for the little girl's breakfast while Nina was cooking the scrambled eggs. Everyone finally sat down to the table.

"As far as your hide is concerned, Professor, yours is like an elephant's," said Nina. "The elevator went up and down again three times during the night, and you couldn't have cared less, you just went right on snoring."

"And why shouldn't I sleep, if it's not my turn yet?" asked Savva. "They're coming for someone else, and I'm supposed to jump out of bed, is that it?"

"Now that's logic!" exulted Nina.

"And who got taken away in the night?" he asked overcasually, with a certain worldly satiety.

In reply, Nina perfectly assumed the pose of a bored *grande dame*. "The doorman told me when I went down for the paper that three were arrested. No particular surprises. Let's see, Golenpolsky was taken, Margarita Nazarovna Yakovleva, and Shapiro . . . his wife was taken as well."

"That makes four, not three," said Savva.

"What?" asked Nina, searching for the day's radio listings in the newspaper.

"If Shapiro was taken with his wife, that means that four were arrested last night," said Savva.

"Well, of course," nodded Nina. "Golenpolsky was arrested alone, Margarita Nazarovna, too, but Shapiro and his wife went together. That means four were taken."

Little Elena was already gagging slightly on her kasha in anticipation of an explosion of laughter. Savva nodded his head with evident approval. "A good catch."

Nina could not hold it in and guffawed. Elenka burst into gleeful laughter. At that moment the doorbell sounded.

"There it is, they've come for a fifth!" Savva sang out joyfully.

"And maybe for a sixth as well?" offered the poetess craftily.

Savva went to open the door. It was nonsense, of course—the secret police don't operate during the day, he thought. There was no record of them ever showing up anywhere at such an early hour, when people were getting ready to go to work—this must be the hour when they themselves change shifts. Maybe it's just a telegram from Greta Garbo? It should be pointed out that the passion of the young Moscow doctor Savva Kitaigorodsky for the distant Hollywood beauty had for some time been the subject of discussion in their family and among their friends.

Then again, Savva thought suddenly, perhaps we've brought on calamity by our own *khokhmas.* He opened the door. Indeed, on the other side of the door stood Calamity in the form of an old woman of Middle Eastern appearance with her features squeezed into a tragic expression and with sunken eyes. At first, he did not even recognize the sorrowful figure as his mother-in-law, but when he did, he cried out, "Have they taken Father?"

It was the first time he had used that name for his scientific mentor of many years.

Mary gulped at the air, put her hand over her heart, then clutched at the lintel, swaying. "Even worse, Savvushka—they took away Veronika."

At that moment Nina came running up and, seeing her mother, weakened, seemingly turning blue before her eyes, she shouted, "Well, don't just stand there like a dummy!" She took Mary by the arm and dragged her inside.

After a sleepless night, Mary Vakhtangovna had taken the first streetcar in order to catch her relations in Bolshoi Gnezdnikovsky Street before they went to work. Trembling for nearly an hour in the stuffy crush of bodies, she was afraid she might die. Perhaps it was only her bitter thoughts that had saved her, pulled her away from slipping down into the depths. After a time, though, no longer thinking about anything, in a state of grief, she began the slide once again. One woman passenger even asked her, not indifferently, "What's wrong with you, citizen? Where are you from?" but then the car arrived at her stop and she began to push her way through to the exit.

Savva and Nina laid Mary down on a cot in the kitchen, opened a small hinged windowpane, and fetched cushions and blankets. After taking a large dose of Zelenin's Magical Drops, Mary began to come back to life. Her features softened, and her bluish hue began to give way to her normal color.

She had come to see Nina and Savva in order to ask their advice. "We can't wait any longer," she said, "or else we'll all be destroyed. Of all our children, only you and Celia are left, but Celia won't be of any help: all she does anymore is write one memorandum after another to the Central Committee explaining how correctly Kirill had always interpreted the various adjustments in the official Party line. I've decided to act. In the end, I can't just sit here with my hands folded and watch as my children disappear into the dungeons one by one. What can I do? Perhaps nothing, but perhaps quite a lot. I'm a Georgian, after all, and Stalin is one, too, you know. I'll get through to him!" Mary had already forgotten about her own condition. Her eyes were burning, as though she were approaching the finale of a bravura Rossini overture. She would go to Tiflis, raise all her old connections, all her relatives and friends, establishing a chain along which she would be able to make her way to where she could knock on Stalin's door. "We're all Georgians, all relatives, are we or aren't we? What do you say, Ninka? What do you say, Savvushka?"

The astounded Savva was silent. The idea of forming such a Georgian "chain" leading to Stalin sounded to him like someone begging relatives to get him in to see a fire-breathing dragon. He had never before thought of Stalin as a Georgian, or even as a *Homo sapiens* at all. He could not, for example, imagine him as one of his patients, with the anatomic structure common to all human beings.

Nina sat for several minutes in deep thought, since she knew Tiflis the best of the three of them, and then said, "You know, Mama, there might be something in your idea. There isn't much hope, of course, but somewhere out there may be a way out. There's enough beastly behavior in Georgia, but sometimes, every so often, and at times most unexpectedly, people suddenly revert to their nature. Here only the beast reigns."

Mary sighed. "Of course! Just take, say, my brother Galaktion—he knows the whole city, and everyone knows him! He'll go to a party somewhere, have a chat with someone, who will whisper to somebody else. It's almost certain he'll find me a way to see Beria, and through him . . . There are other possibilities as well. I've heard, for example, that my nephew Nugzar Lamadze has made quite a career for himself . . .

Nina seized her arm. "Whatever you do, Mama, don't go near that one. He's a terrible person, he—" She stopped short.

Mary looked at her intently. "Well, I only mentioned Nugzar as an example. It's possible to get along without him . . ."

Elenka came dashing into the kitchen. Over her head she held a doll on which she had drawn a beard and mustache. "Mama, Grandma, look! This was Greta Garbo, now it's Doctor Karpov!"

Mary had not been in her native city for more than . . . ten years? Eleven? Twelve? In a word, since 1927, when she had accompanied her "rootless leftist"—she had never been able to wrap her tongue around "headstrong Trotskyite"—to Uncle Galaktion's secure pharmaceutical haven. Since that time the city's name had been changed to Tbilisi in order to remove all undertones of colonialism. Tbilisi, Tbiliso . . . it really did sound more Georgian, she had no objection to that, though she herself preferred to call the city by its old name. For her, "Tiflis" had connotations not of colonialism but rather of cosmopolitanism, the city that was a bazaar, a carnival, the gateway from West to East.

As the train approached the city, she began to fix herself up: she arranged the braids of her graying hair into a bun, put on good lipstick, and put on a hat of Veronika's that had not made it into the NKVD's inventory. She looked at herself in a mirror—the "international" cars were well provided with them—and was satisfied: a distinguished, striking middle-aged lady in a hat and a fur jacket bought at Mure & Merilise in 1913: the furriers of old Russia knew their trade!

She sat that way, in her hat and jacket, silently watching through the window as Tiflis swam toward her across the gentle hills with their autumnal hues. She suddenly found herself recalling the short years of Georgian independence. At the very beginning of the Civil War, she had managed to get out of hungry Moscow with little Ninka and go south. Sixteen-year-old Kirill had refused point-blank to go with them. To seek refuge from the Revolution, the very idea! The only thing he had promised was that he wouldn't join Nikita's regiment until he had finished school.

The Civil War, a conflagration extending over thousands of miles, had cut Tiflis off from Moscow completely. An independent republic had sprung up in Georgia, led by the Liberal Menshevik Noi Zhordania. Iniquity raged everywhere, famine and pestilence reigned, but on the other side of the peaks of the Caucasus free Georgians, together with Armenians, Persians, Russians, Greeks, and Jews, sat beneath chestnut trees, drinking wine and Lagidze mint and eating fresh lavash bread, radishes, herbs, shashlik that wasn't bad for the times, and, as always, the exceptional satsivi chicken with nuts, lobio beans, and tskhvali fish.

Tiflis had witnessed an amazing flowering of artistic life. Even as war was raging on the western front, poets and artists were racing south in order to avoid the call-up, and later they came fleeing the Reds, the Whites, the Greens . . . in short, anyone who did not understand that only a revolution in art would save the world, not banal artillery, not vulgar sabers, and not those supremely indecent mass killers, machine guns.

Small theaters and bohemian cafés opened all over the place. The Futurist poet Vasily Kamensky read his epic *Stenka Razin* from a white horse galloping around a circus ring. Sergei Gorodetsky gently made fun of the Provisional Government in his Symbolist journal. Noi Zhordania was depicted on the cover of one issue as a loathsome, disgusting goat. In reply to this mockery, the premier smiled and said, "They're poets!" Titzian Tabidze, a member of a group of poets called the Blue Horns, ran across the mayor of Tiflis one day on Golovin Prospekt.

"Listen, Titzian, why do you walk around my city with your young wife looking so down in the mouth?" asked the mayor.

"We have nowhere to live, Mr. Mayor," complained Titzian. "We have no money to pay for a flat." The mayor took a key from his pocket.

"Titzian, I've just requisitioned the mansion of the Businessmen's Club. Go and live there with your young wife, work there. Only don't deprive Georgia of your verse."

So there was a feast and a ball every night at the Businessmen's Club, all artistic bohemia gathered there! And Mary went, dragged there by her brother-in-law, the tempestuous young artist Lado Gudiashvili. He introduced her to everyone—to the Blue Horns, that is, to Titzian himself and his friends Paolo and Grigol, young people from Moscow and Petersburg, the Futurists who had just closed ranks as the group 41 Degrees, the brothers Zdanevich, Igor Terentiev, and the scandal-loving Alexei Kruchonykh. The wandering chief of the Futurists' Slavophile wing, the brilliant "Chairman of the World" Velemir Khlebnikov, also put in an appearance that night. He was barely alive, dressed in rags, and wearing boots that were full of holes. It turned out that he had made his way from Astrakhan through the lines of the warring armies. An announcement was immediately made that a collection would be taken up for Khlebnikov. Mary removed a ring from her finger. He looked at her and gasped: she was bare-shouldered!

Yes, back then, that still happened to men at the sight of her: they gasped—

oh, Mary! And that in spite of the facts that Tiflis was full of young and beautiful poetesses and artists and that she was already thirty-nine.

The Armenian Futurist Kara-Dervish began to court her furiously, inviting her to readings at the Fantastic Dukhan* and the Peacock's Tale and to the productions of Ilya Zdanevich's absurd dramas at the miniature theater. He was closer in age to her than the younger people but surpassed even the boys with his idiosyncrasies: sometimes he would draw a dragonfly on his cheek, sometimes a large "third eye" on his forehead. Mary always took twelve-year-old Nina with her on these evening outings, above all, of course, in order to underline the purely platonic nature of her relations with Kara-Dervish, that is, the absence of any intimacy in these relations: gentlemen, gentlemen! It's comradeship, nothing more.

Oh, what evenings those were! Ilyusha Zdanevich was particularly memorable, such a dandy, always in brand-new clothes, pale from his mad love for Melnikova. A fervent Futurist, a foe of all "Blok foolishness," he experimented in obscene Trans-Sense poetry having an anal theme, all the while gazing at Melnikova with a reverence worthy of one of Blok's heroes looking at the Beautiful Lady. What were his plays called? One, it seemed, was called *Yanko, King of Albania*, another *Asshole for Hire*. During one of them they glued someone to a stool so he couldn't get away. The most wonderful nonsense.

Nina looked at everyone with eyes open wide as lakes, particularly the poetic girls like Tanya Vechorka and Lali Gaprindashvili. Perhaps it was these evenings that had drawn her into poetry.

There was Khlebnikov, brothers, the great Velemir had apeared, draped in his usual rags and reading something prophetic: "Graka khata chrororo, linli, edi, lyap, lyap, bem. Libibibi niraro Sinoacho tsettserets!"

They asked Mary to play. Play something atonal, Mary! Play something from "Victory over the Sun," there's a few notes for you! Mary sat down at the instrument—if one could use that proud word to describe the upright piano in the Fantastic Dukhan—and instead of Matyushin played Beethoven. The gabble of voices was hushed, the shuffling of feet shushed, sniffling and sneezing were snuffed—as the poet would say. The young people were clearly in no hurry to "throw Beethoven overboard from the steamer of modernity." Mary saw traces of genuine excitement on the faces of some.

Everything was so wonderful in Tiflis during that three-year springtime, Noah's ark Jordania floated like a prospering block of ice in a sea of blood and muck, in the sea of the typhus epidemic of the Civil War, and looked as though it might sink or split at any minute; maybe it was so wonderful precisely because it was so fragile; all present felt as though their heads were spinning.

*"Dukhan"—wine store in the Caucasus.

Mary's head began to spin, too, when her eyes met his. No, not Kara-Dervish—and may his name never be learned, the name of the man who was fifteen years her junior and wrote poetry, of course, the only one with whom she had ever cuckolded her Bo. In 1921, when everything ended, he managed to flee abroad, and then he dropped out of sight. Neither people nor their names ever came back from over there. And why should she remember this now, on the threshold of being an old woman? Even in remembrance it's not necessary to say his name, so let's just call him Tiflis. Moreover, it's not worth it to recall the tragicomic aspect of that brief romantic upheaval, of those little mockeries of Venus: at the time that sort of thing was difficult to avoid. Everything had passed, everything had been washed away and thundered off like the purest spring water into the pianissimo of a dark blue night.

By the end of 1920, all of this Silver Age that had been transplanted to the South had vanished, perhaps flown back to its sources, to the Greek islands. The Georgian Republic was in its death throes. In 1921 the Red Army burst in, freedom came to an end, and Mary and her daughter returned to Moscow, where, it seemed to her, there still remained one last scrap of independence, the dacha with its grand piano and her loving Bo.

Tiflis, though, soon returned to life—with the coming of NEP, its Caucasian guitar began to ring out again. It proved to be difficult to transform the ancient human habitation into a lice-infested barracks. Somehow or other, within ten years my daughter, too, received her share of the Silver Age. These were the thoughts of Mary Vakhtangovna Gradov as she approached her native city.

For some reason no one met her at the station. Her telegram had probably not reached its destination, otherwise her brother's voice would be ringing out here, armfuls of flowers would be dragged along in their wake, and toasts would be proclaimed right here on the platform.

There were no more horse-drawn cabs in Tbilisi, and it was impossible to get a taxi. Confused, Mary was at a loss over what to do—one could hardly drag oneself along on a streetcar with a heavy suitcase. Finally, she saw a checkroom, left her baggage there, and went into the city center empty-handed. She eagerly looked from the windows of the streetcar at the streets rumbling by. On the whole, the city had not changed, except for the addition of a huge quantity of red banners bearing the slogans of socialism to its blue-gray rooftops, pink façades, and deep blue shadows.

She got off the streetcar in the city center and walked along Rustaveli, formerly Golovin, Prospekt. It was difficult to object to such name changes—why should the main street of the Georgian capital bear the name of a Russian general and not the 800-year-old name of a knight of Queen Tamar, who had been keeper of the imperial treasury and a poet?

Alas, in addition to Rustaveli, every intersection was adorned by two other Georgian personalities—Stalin and Beria. "Long live Comrade Stalin, the great leader of the workers of the entire world!" "Long live Comrade Beria, leader of the workers of the Caucasus!" written in some places in ornate Georgian script, in others with the Cyrillic alphabet of the Party in the Supremacist style. Then again, how could there be any Supremacism in this case? All of the Slavophile Futurists had long ago been shunted into the darkest corners and now sat there afraid to utter a peep, while many of them had altogether left a world so inhospitable to their cosmic experiment. Art belongs to the people and must be understandable by the people! Just look at what primitive examples of Socialist Realism are displayed in the windows, at the sculptures of Young Pioneers with gliders, of a border guard with a rifle, of a girl with a paddle in her hands!

Mary looked around avidly. The people seemed to have remained the same: careworn, serious women, children carrying music folders and violin cases— every "decent" family in the city considered it its duty to give its children music lessons—and the men were the same, roughly divisible into the lazy and the crafty. Fewer people wore the national dress, hardly a native felt cloak was to be seen. On the other hand, the police had increased in number. Horses had almost disappeared, trolleys were running, automobiles rolled along, boys whirled madly along on bicycles. Something was still missing . . . what could it be? Ah, that's what it was—Tiflis' constant hum of voices, the age-old screech of our strange language, which at one time had clutched at you from all sides as soon as you came out onto the street. Was it drowned out by the sounds of engines, or had people begun to speak more softly?

The restaurants, dukhans, cafés, cellar taverns, and table-lined terraces that had once lined the main street were now fewer in number, to the point where they had almost disappeared. Something of them, though, still remained. Here, for example, was Lagidze Waters, which, though it no longer bore the despised name of the exploiter, still displayed its syrup-filled glass cones, familiar since time out of mind, containing bright liquids in shades of maroon, lemon yellow, and dark green.

Mary went into the capacious hall and ordered a drink. In one corner a vendor was selling a khachapuri, a melted cheese pie. The aroma was enough to make one's mouth water. After a moment of confusion, she ordered a pair of them in her native language. The vendor gave her a rather strange look and replied in broken Russian. After finishing her khachapuri, she moved on.

She came to where she usually turned off Golovin Prospekt on her way to her brother's home. The streets were now winding ever more sharply upward, and soon she found herself in the old section of the city, where nothing seemed to have changed: covered balconies, squeaking shutters, heavy cobblestones underfoot. From a distance, somewhere over her head, came a sort of singing, of which she could not as yet distinguish the words. Soon she would arrive on her native ground, the small square, and see the pharmacy with its two large opaque spheres above the entrance. Another few minutes and she would see her brother, her own "bubbling and boiling" Galaktion, who of course would come up with some idea, would find a way to help her devastated family, and would in any case ease her sorrow.

The singing was coming nearer, she could now make out a group of voices performing a *kremanchuli*, an ancient polyphonic Georgian melody. It was a strange, gloomy, disturbing song that had probably survived from the time of the Persian invasion. The voices were those of elderly people. Peering into a courtyard, she saw four old men sitting around a table beneath a plane tree. Obviously they had been playing dominoes before beginning to sing. They closed their eyes and went off to distant worlds, into their age-old polyphony.

Unsettled by the singing, she suddenly felt that the sharp climb had not been without cost to her, that her heart was beating resoundingly and irregularly, and that there was a numbness in her legs. Now, at last she could see the gauzy spheres. The "Gudiashvili Pharmacy" sign was now so smeared and dirty that it was illegible. But what was all this? For some reason the windows were covered with white paint, nothing on the inside was visible, and the doors of the pharmacy were barred by two boards in the shape of a cross. It looked as though the establishment was closed for one reason or another. Renovation? Inventory? Why would the door be blocked off with boards? Passing the main entrance, a bewildered, if not actually panic-stricken, Mary went up to the door behind which was the staircase leading to the second floor, to the pharmacist's flat. She rang the familiar mechanical bell and then abruptly noticed that two new electric buzzers had been installed. Beside one of them was a small piece of wood with the words "Two times for Bagramyan, three times for Canaris" written on it with an indelible pencil. Beside the other was written simply "Bobko." Had they crowded more people into the place? Unthinkable! Would the authorities really make the acclaimed pharmacist, known throughout the region as "noble Galaktion," give up part of his living space?

Again she pressed the spring of the old bell. She heard a stamping of feet inside and saw one of the window blinds go up slightly. Then someone looked through a small peephole in the door. An unpleasant voice, a woman's, that sounded like someone sprinkling metal shavings, was heard: "Who do you want, citizen?"

"I've come to see Gudiashvili!" said Mary loudly, but with great dignity, to the closed door.

"No one here by that name," answered the voice on the other side. A minute or two passed in silence. "No one here by that name"—it sounded like a terrible absurdity. That was like asking the way to Mount Elbrus anywhere in the Caucasus and receiving the reply "No one here by that name"!

"Excuse me, but how can that be, that he's not here?" Mary's voice was already trembling, going to pieces, uncontrollably, muffled by the tears welling up within her, by the lump rising in her throat. "I'm his sister. I've come from Moscow to see my brother, his wife, Gyuli, my nephews . . ."

Metal-sprinkled laughter rang out in senseless reply. Then a deep male voice said, "They don't live here anymore, citizen. Go and ask at the Fifth Police Precinct."

The door never opened. The window blinds went back down. The eye disappeared from the peephole.

Bowed over, trying not to fall, Mary hobbled away from the door into the middle of the square and began to tremble, tossed about by a staggering feeling of being unable to recognize her surroundings. She would have collapsed if someone had not taken her strongly beneath the arm and helped her to descend the cobbled hill to a dreary side street. Here she lifted her face and saw the stout figure of Avessalom, her friend since childhood.

"Mary, dear," he whispered, "you shouldn't have come. Right now, I'll take you home with me to spend the night, but tomorrow, the earlier the better, go back. You have no business being in Tbilisi now, no business at all being here, dear Mary."

The thing that NKVD Lieutenant Colonel Nugzar Lamadze wanted less than anything in the world was to be in charge of his own uncle's case. It was the sort of thing that happened only in nightmares—to sit opposite the swollen, suffering Galaktion in the role of the implacable investigator, to shine the blinding light into his eyes. It sometimes seemed to him that the case of the pharmacist Gudiashvili and the underground Trotskyite group that had used the sign of Pharmacy No. 14 as its cover was a scheme to undermine his position, an attempt to knock his rapidly rising star off the horizon. From the very beginning, as soon as he had heard in the office that Galaktion was about to be arrested, he had tried to distance himself from the affair as far as possible, pretending to pay it no attention, since even without it he had more cases than he could handle. One day, however, after a meeting about the presentation of a red banner that was making the rounds of the country to the republic, his old friend Beria, now almost a dweller in the heavenly firmament and "Leader of the Peoples of the Caucasus," took him aside in the garden and asked him what he knew about the case of the pharmacist Gudiashvili.

"I know, Nugzar, that he's your father's cousin, and I understand how hard it is for you, but all the same I want to warn you: some of our comrades are beginning to have doubts. This is natural, you must agree: you're the nephew, he's the uncle. Everyone knows that Galaktion has always made fun of our Party, of our ideas themselves, and in connection with this—" Here Lavrenty Pavlovich paused, walked up to a fountain adorned with mermaids, put his hand under one of the streams—it was said that the Leader of the Peoples of the Caucasus imitated the pauses of Stalin himself—and played with the gushing water for a long time, smiling quietly. It even seemed as though he had forgotten what he was saying—Nugzar stood silently behind him at the distance prescribed by protocol—and then he returned to his thought: "—and in connection with this, the fact that he joined the Trotskyite mongrels, the last of Lado Kakhabidze's holdouts, surprised us not at all. Therefore, Nugzar, as your old comrade, your longtime drinking companion and accomplice in your younger days . . ." He smiled mischievously. "Do you remember the Packard with the three silver horns? In a word, I would advise you to take the whole affair upon yourself, to conduct the investigation personally, to demonstrate to everyone that you are a genuine knight of the Revolution, fearless and above reproach."

He's having me on, thought Nugzar for an instant, and then it occurred to him that right now he could stun Beria with a blow to the back of the head and then throw him headfirst into the fountain. Either he's pulling my leg, which is not very likely, or else he's testing me. Maybe he's trying to make me into his most devoted underling. He's getting ready to go places, and he needs one absolutely devoted man, and that man has to be broken first.

Somehow or other, Lieutenant Colonel Nugzar Lamadze, who was already chief of his department and a rising star in the national security apparatus, became the investigator in the case of the ordinary pharmacist Gudiashvili. Throughout the investigation, he permitted no familiarity, did not call Galaktion "Uncle," always addressed him according to regulations, unfailingly gave orders to use the "conveyor," a method of torturing a stubborn case with sleep deprivation and thirst. The only departure from regulations he allowed himself was to leave the interrogation room when two sergeants appeared at his command to knock some sense into the old stinker.

If he doesn't sign today, I'll call in the sergeants and then leave the room for half an hour, thought Nugzar, looking from the darkness as the old bag of shit who had once been his loud-voiced, jovial Uncle Galaktion squirmed in the bright light.

"So then, Suspect Gudiashvili, cat got your tongue again? I advise you to stop playing this stupid game—after all, we already know almost everything about how you turned your house and Soviet establishment, Pharmacy No. 14, into a hideout for the Trotskyite underground. Moreover, we know exactly when it happened; it was that day in 1930 when the spy Vladimir Kakhabidze, a friend of Trotsky's, came to see you. So, how about it, Gudiashvili, cat still got your tongue?"

With difficulty, Uncle Galaktion managed to separate his split lips beneath his once luxuriant, but now drooping and yellowed, mustache. "No, today we'll have a talk, dear nephew, today I have something to say to you."

Nugzar slammed his fist down on the table. "Don't you dare call me 'nephew'! No Trotskyite toady is any uncle of mine!"

"That's just what I wanted to talk to you about, Nugzar . . . that is, Citizen Investigator," continued Galaktion, paying no apparent attention to the outcry. He gave the impression that he had decided on a course of action from which there was no turning back. "You say I'm in bed with the Trotskyites, as though you've forgotten that Trotskyism is a faction of communism. As though you've forgotten that all the factions of your accursed communism always made me sick. Your whole dirty business! Do you understand me, you jackal?"

Galaktion was now sitting erect in his chair, looking directly at Nugzar, his eyes flashing. A wave of rage swept Nugzar out of his chair. Without understanding what he was doing, he snatched up a heavy marble paperweight from the table and smashed it into Galaktion's temple with all his strength. With the frozen lightning still in his eyes, Galaktion crumpled to the floor. His arms and legs twitched briefly, a viscous substance flowed from his mouth, and then he was quiet, that is to say that he turned into a sack of excrement once again. Nugzar stood over him. The damned swine, he thought, you always made fun of me. You old bugger, you always took Otari seriously—oh, what a poet!—but you thought of me as a puppy and a jester. You, the Gudiashvilis, were always condescending toward us, the Lamadzes. You blue-blooded bastards always look down on us. You old idiot, you don't even understand that I'm saving you from the firing squad, charging you with complicity and not actual participation . . .

The door of the office opened. Using her special privilege, Second Lieutenant Bridasko, Nugzar's secretary, flew into the room like a nanny goat without knocking, her heels clattering on the parquet floor, skirted around the body lying on the floor—good work, that!—and whispered hotly to her wonderful, handsome chief, "Oh, Comrade Lieutenant Colonel, such a call just came in for you, such a call! It was directly from him, from Lavrenty Pavlovich's office! They said he's waiting for you right now! Can you imagine?"

Nugzar nodded glumly to the delighted Komsomol girl. The silly fool doesn't know how much we shoot the breeze with "the man himself," with Lavrenty Pavlovich, with the Leader of the Peoples of the Caucasus. He poked the prone body with the toe of his boot. The body did not reply to the nudge in any way, as though it were in fact a bag full of something. Nugzar was covered with perspiration, scarcely able to conceal the horror that gripped him. With a wave of his hand he put a stop to the rather unseemly swaying of Second Lieutenant Bridasko's hips.

"Call the doctor," he said to her. "It looks like the suspect Gudiashvili has had trouble with his heart." Having said that, he walked around the "bag of something" and quickly walked out of the office.

He had always been afraid of Lavrenty. His every meeting with the scoundrel—and that was exactly the word Nugzar used when he thought about the matter—reminded him of a visit to the cage of a beast of prey, and not one like that befuddled grizzly Nina had kissed once, way back on that day that had been starry from its first light. True, after several minutes in his company, this image of senseless, inevitable danger vanished and more benign metaphors began to suggest themselves—a pig, a gorilla, simply a despicable human being. Anyway, Lavrik could be a real pal during a drinking bout, no more hateful than you yourself, the same kind of gorilla or pig that you were.

Beria now had a new office in the Central Committee building in which Nugzar had not yet been. It was a suite of rooms rather than an office, beginning with a vestibule, continuing on into an office with what seemed to be a bedroom at the far end . . . or perhaps a jaguar cage. Everywhere there were rococo chairs, lavish chandeliers, heavy silk window blinds. The three invariable portraits were there as well—Lenin, Stalin, Dzerzhinsky.

Nugzar was led directly into the office and then left by himself. A few minutes later, Beria came in, exchanged a friendly handshake with the lieutenant colonel, and then, after looking around as if to make sure that there were no intruders present, gave him a bear hug. A billow of warmth flowed over Nugzar, washing away the accumulated filth in his soul, including the recent business of the paperweight, the motionless body of his once-favorite uncle. . . . Revealing a trusting nature that was a surprise to himself, Nugzar responded to the embrace—here's a friend, he thought, who won't let me down.

Beria took a magnificent decanter of cognac and two crystal goblets from a small mahogany cabinet. After the first swallow, Nugzar's inner warmth became even greater.

"Sit down, Nugzar," said Beria, indicating a couch with legs in the form of a griffin's claws and sitting down alongside him. He had changed little over the past few years—these prematurely bald fellows never changed much with the years, they only became a bit rounder, of course, or acquired solidity, as they say. The curves of his mysteriously shiny pince-nez somehow reminded Nugzar of everyone's archenemy, Trotsky.

> *Trotsky's on the wall,*
> *Glasses on his nose,*
> *Just have a look and see*
> *All you dirty bourgeoisie*

"Ohh," sighed Beria. "The more power you get, the less freedom you have. Do you remember, Nugzar, how we used to get a few broads in the Packard and stay out at the dacha until dawn? Those were the days! And political problems were handled decisively, the revolutionary way . . . do you remember, Nugzar, how we resolved political problems?" He suddenly removed his pince-nez and looked into the eyes of his friend with a glance that was anything but nearsighted, as if reminding him of that moment when, pistol in hand, he had thrown open a door and seen two readers, Lenin on the wall and Kakhabidze beneath him behind his desk. "And a man's business was taken care of cheerfully, eh, Nugzar?" continued Beria, giving the other man a nudge with his roundish knee. "Then again, we're still a couple of studs, don't you think, Nugzar? C'mon now, listen . . . to hell with it, let's forget about work for five minutes and talk about our common passion, about women, eh? You know, Nugzar, I want to make a confession to you: I love Russian women more than anything in the world! I'd much rather take a Russian broad than any of our Georgian princesses. When you fuck a Russian woman, you feel like a conqueror, eh? You can't help but feel that you're fucking a slave, or some bitch you've paid for, am I right? Do you agree with me, Nugzar? An interesting phenomenon, isn't it true? I wonder how it would be with a half-breed. Unfortunately, I've never tried it with one, I mean with a half-Russian, half-Georgian. You wouldn't happen to have had doings with a half-breed, would you, Nugzar? Won't you give a comrade the benefit of your experience? What's wrong with you, Nugzar? Well, don't talk about it if you don't want to, no one's forcing you."

Assistant to the chief of the Investigative Division for Especially Important Cases NKVD Lieutenant Colonel Nugzar Lamadze felt at that moment as though he had been plunged simultaneously into a boiling cauldron and an ice bath. Scalding and freezing waves washed through his body not sequentially, but simultaneously. He felt as though his body were turning to stone at the same time that his nerves and blood vessels were going into a furious dance. On the point of fainting, he slipped down from the leather surface of the couch and fell before Beria on one knee.

"Lavrenty, I'm begging you! Since that one night in 1930, I've never seen her or heard anything from her again!"

Beria rose from the couch, walked away to the far end of the office, and busied himself with refilling the glasses. Nugzar, not getting up from his knee, watched his back, waiting to learn his fate.

He was lying, of course. In 1934 he had gone to Moscow and met with Nina. He knew everything about her: she had been married for three years to a doctor, she was a member of the Writers' Union, a well-known poetess. And still, he told himself, she could hardly have forgotten that night. For him, the idea of "that night" contained nearly all of his youth, and in any case that entire day in the early autumn of 1930 represented the culmination of the adventures of the young *abrek:* saving Nina from the paws of a gigantic bear, the assassination, the murder of the obtrusive "reader," a lie, theater, a game, blackmail, and finally, his full and undivided mastery over Nina—in short, "that night"!

When he arrived in Moscow, he dropped everything else he was doing and tracked his prey for two days. He saw her coming out of her father's house with her husband, saw them walking along, laughing and kissing, to the streetcar stop, parting in the city center; saw Nina walking alone, seemingly absorbed in her thoughts, paying no apparent attention to men's glances; sitting on a bench on a boulevard, moving her lips, probably composing poetry, then making a sudden decisive, triumphant gesture followed by soundless laughter; standing in a queue at the box office of some theater; going into the offices of the magazine *Znamya* on Tverskaya Boulevard; running into an acquaintance and beginning to chirp like a schoolgirl; having a joyful lunch at the Writers' House, to which he gained access with the help of his red identification booklet and where he continued his surveillance, remaining unnoticed, all the more so since she did not look around herself with particular frequency.

She was just as attractive as she had been in Tiflis, if not more so, and he, as they say, was smoking with desire, or as Lavrenty would crudely put it, "was holding himself by his business end."

Once during these two days of surveillance, pursuit, or, let us say, romantic languor, he thought, maybe I shouldn't approach her at all, just leave everything the way it is, such a colossal love at a distance, such romanticism? He had to laugh at himself. What an *abrek*! Fragments of "that night" flashed through his mind. On the second day, he approached her at a book sale on Teatralny Lane. She had bought several books and was already preparing to run across the street to a bus when she discovered she had something in her shoe. She shook it out while balancing against the column of a streetlamp. Standing behind her, he coughed and said, "The organs of the dictatorship of the proletariat greet Soviet poetry!" He had to admit that he hadn't expected such a strong reaction to his rather lame joke. A shudder, if not a convulsion, passed over her body. She turned around, and he saw her face twisted by fear. The tremor passed, though, and the grimace of fear disappeared even before she realized who it was in front of her. Bravery had prevailed. So that's who it was standing before her! Now she was already having a fit of laughter. Obviously, she, too, had immediately been reminded of lots of things.

"Nugzarka, is that you? What a way you have of making a joke! We should send you straight to the Kashchenko loony bin!"

He gave her a friendly embrace. He liked it so much when she addressed him that way: Nugzarka—as though they were just old friends who had once had a dalliance together.

"Eh, Nina, I already know everything about you, my dear!" he laughed. "Who you sleep with, who you have lunch with—the vigilant watchmen of the Motherland know everything!"

"You know, for two days now I've had a feeling someone was following me," she said.

They continued down Teatralny Lane, chatting, in the direction of the Hotel Metropole, where he had just taken a semiluxury room. She complimented him on his new suit—wide shoulders, narrow trousers . . . real Oxford chic! Outside the hotel he took her by the hand and stopped.

Just as she had "that night," she glowered at him and asked quietly, "Well, what is it?"

"Come up to my room," he said with a superfluous gravity, an unnecessary note of drama.

She immediately laughed and shrugged. "Well, let's go!" She walked on, swinging the bundle of books she had just bought in a carefree manner. Everything was simple this way—a child of the twenties, the fruit of revolutionary anthroposophy.

What happened next was not at all what he had imagined hundreds of times in his isolation beyond the Caucasus. Everything had changed, there was no way to get "that night" back. He was no longer the same young bandit, and she was no longer the same girl she had been then, drunken, desperate, driven into a corner, in other words, a hero's plunder—on the contrary, she was happy in both her marriage and her career, sure of herself, and allowing herself simply to sprinkle a bit more pepper onto her daily bread.

Everything could have gone differently, taken a turn in the direction of "that night," had she not flatly refused at the beginning and only later yielded out of fear, under threat of the exposure of her Trotskyite past. He himself spoiled everything by his joking tone. She immediately snatched up this tone with unusual agility, and there he was—Nugzarka!—looking like a fool. It did not turn out to be "that night," there was no sweet act of violence done to a "thirsting victim," as he had defined the event many times in his mind.

And yet there was something undefinable that made her an independent and invulnerable person. It was only six months later that the vagueness became clear to him, when the news that Nina Gradov had given birth to a daughter reached Tiflis. She had been already well into her pregnancy at the time of their meeting. Mademoiselle Kitaigorodsky had already been asserting her rights to her womb.

The preoccupation of his cousin angered and frightened the lieutenant colonel. All around, they're arresting thousands of people who have nothing to do with Trotskyism, while she, Nina the snake, who had actually been a Trotskyite at one time—something he knew full well—she had been a fixture in the underground of the émigré Albov.

Knowing the specifics of the work of his beloved "organs," Nugzar understood that in those days it was not at all necessary for someone to have been accused of a real crime in order to be hauled off to Kolyma or even stood up against a wall. And still it gnawed at the pit of his stomach, the idea that everything could turn, the matter could come to light, and the girl of "that night" would be whisked away—to imagine her in a camp barracks was unthinkable!—and he himself, to the joy of all those envious swine, would be broken from the ranks, then crushed and destroyed.

In 1937 the situation worsened still further. Following the arrest of her brothers, Nina could have been arrested simply because she was a relative. For all the blindness of the machine of retribution, it had retained its sense of smell, and it didn't do a bad job of sniffing out those who did not belong.

That was what happened. Six months ago, her case had come from Moscow for the "finishing touches." The Moscow city directorate of the NKVD was gathering evidence against Gradov, N. B., relative of two condemned enemies of the people, who was now accused of having ties to I. G. Ehrenburg, agent of French and American intelligence. There was no mention of the Trotskyite circle. The old case file with the reports of Stroilo had obviously gone to another department, meaning it was buried for good somewhere in a filing cabinet among millions of other folders. The new case, then, had been sent to Georgia for clarification of the available information about the ties of Gradov to the recently unmasked enemies of the people Paolo Yashvili and Titzian Tabidze. The most remarkable thing of all was that Ehrenburg at that time was regularly going abroad and publishing thrilling reports from the theaters of action in Spain in *Pravda*.

Nugzar took heart from this circumstance and thought that with the help of a little cunning it would be possible to try to save Nina and her family. Well, at least in memory of his youth, if for no other reason. After all, everyone has his own version of "that night" in his soul, that "golden cloud on the gaunt cliff's breast," as Lermontov would have it, and his was that of a cursed Nina with her luxuriant mane of chestnut-colored hair and the stormy weather that never subsided from her deep blue eyes.

He handed her file along with a whole armful of other cases to the laziest of his colleagues and acted as though it, the file in question, were insignificant. Several weeks passed, after which Nugzar picked a quarrel with the sluggard, arranged an assignment for him in some godforsaken place, and had him transferred there with a demotion in rank. He assigned his cases to more efficient comrades, and as for the secret folder, he simply tossed it into the bottom of a box destined for the archives. It could remain there until the end of the century, unless, of course, Moscow suddenly woke up, and then, well . . . farewell, blue-eyed night and cloud! The blame for the confusion could be shifted onto the lazy agent. Then again, all indications were that the disorder reigning in Moscow in the fever of mass terror was no less than it was here, and all sorts of confusion could emanate from the center. Nugzar, meanwhile, kept track of what Ehrenburg published, read it all with great attention, and nodded approvingly: a very good commentator, a mighty man of the pen, a genuine anti-Fascist columnist!

And now today such a stunning blow from an unexpected direction. Lavrenty himself knows about this business with Nina! Maybe she's already under arrest, and now he's going to propose that I take charge of the investigation in order to "scotch the rumors circulating among the comrades"? And maybe he'll catch me in the lie right now, fly into a rage, take up his lacquered parabellum, which he always carries in the inside pocket of his jacket right over his spleen, and shoot me here on the spot, down on one knee like a Polish Catholic? This sort of thing happens with him—why, everyone knows that several men have been knocked off right here on the carpet in his office. Afterward, he would call his aides and say, "An unexpected finale, his heart gave out. Take him away and change the carpet!" Well, it serves me right! The only pity is that it will be with a bullet and not a marble paperweight, but at any rate, I'll have gotten the same treatment as Uncle Galaktion, and I won't have to run the investigation of my night and golden cloud . . .

Beria walked up to him with two wineglasses filled with Gremi brandy, a liquid of a remarkable shade, dark oak with a hint of cherry.

"Stand up, Nugzar, enough clowning around!" Nugzar leapt to his feet, took the glass from the hand of the Leader of the Peoples of the Caucasus, clinked it against the other's glass, and downed the contents in one gulp. Beria roared with laughter. "I love you, you bastard!" Then he put his glass down, laid his hands on Nugzar's shoulders, sat him down on the couch, and looked deeply into his eyes as though he were drilling into them.

"I'm glad you always understand me correctly, Nugzar. Listen to the news, now. The days of Marshal Yezhov are numbered. I'm being transferred to Moscow—to what post, I'm sure you understand. To be the right hand of the Master himself. You're coming along."

CHAPTER TWENTY

Marble Steps

☆

Gloom and numbness reigned in the Gradov house, as though the remaining members of the family were afraid to make any superfluous movements so as not to squander what warmth remained. It was reminiscent of war communism, when there had been nothing with which to heat the house, even though they now had old-fashioned tiled stoves in all the rooms and delicious smells often wafted out from the kitchen. Of all the inhabitants of the house in Silver Forest, only Agasha was in a state of heightened activity: constantly bustling about with piles of clean linen, putting up jars of salted and pickled preserves, making dough, cleaning the old quilts and window blinds, giving orders to Boris Nikitovich's chauffeur, going to the Invalids' Market herself for fresh provisions. This was how she spent her days, and by evening new tasks had accumulated for her: calling the children to dinner, checking the beds, serving the meals, taking the dishes away, and only then nestling up somewhere in the study next to her dear Mary, billing and cooing to the music of the magnificent composers of the past.

Agasha had already begun the transformation from a little citizen of an indeterminate age from the countryside outside Moscow into a woman of an indeterminate age, the sort one marvels at: how is it they're able to get everything done? Once upon a time, when Agasha was still a woman in a small-business guild, she had caught a terrible cold at a Shrovetide celebration that had developed into an ovarian inflammation. From that time, she had been childless and without family—who would want someone like her? she thought—and the Gradov household had become her family, her only haven amid the "kaos," as she spelled it, of the world. Now, though, feeling as though the house were collapsing, struggling with an inner trembling, Agasha was always on the run, wiping or scraping something clean, in order to, as she put it, "legitimate" it. A house that was so well looked after, so warm and cozy, so "legitimated" could not possibly crumble! What else could one think of, what more could anyone do so the house's residents would not shiver all the time walking through its rooms? Nevertheless, everyone did feel cold, prickly, uncomfortable. Mary was not at all herself when she came back from Tbilisi, she had no more bold ideas. She had, so to speak, tuned herself to a tragic key, and now simply waited—who would be next, Celia, Savva, Bo, or Nina, her only remaining child? Or maybe the pitiless, self-assured villains who were so convinced of their infallibility would come for her grandsons?

Nina came with Savva and Elenka for some fresh air and could not bear the tragic expression frozen on her mother's face. She began to rage: "Stop looking at me like that!" Mary muttered helplessly, "Ninochka, I'm so afraid, with your past, you—"

Nina began to laugh, then sat down near her mother and kissed her. "Mama, we can't live this way, just sitting and waiting. . . . We want to live! And the past . . . well, what about it? Do you mean you don't understand that they don't arrest people for that now? Back then, they arrested you for that, but now they take you away for nothing at all."

Looking at her, so confident, seemingly almost fearless, full of humor and defiance, Mary calmed down a bit: maybe it's really true that they don't arrest the cheeky ones these days? On the other hand, Cecilia Rosenbloom, with her incoherence, her state of near collapse, and her obsession with Marxism-Leninism, was, it seemed to her, absolutely doomed. Her every visit to Silver Forest had for Mary the aspect of a miracle: how is it that she hasn't been arrested? She's still writing her petitions and appeals, her memoranda to the Party authorities in high places, still trying to prove Kirill's innocence, his adherence to the Party line, his loyalty to Stalin. Cecilia too reassured her: "Mary Vakhtangovna, you don't understand, we are now going through an unavoidable and necessary historical cycle. In the conditions of the building of socialism in one, separately considered country, there periodically arise conditions of the sharpening of the class struggle. This cycle is presently approaching its close, the time of reckoning, of the summing up of the results, of the correction, you understand, I emphasize, correction of the measures that have been taken. And as a result of this correction, I'm sure, Kirill Gradov will return to normal, fruitful labor. We cannot allow ourselves to squander such unimpeachable cadres!"

"Who's this 'we,' Celia?" asked Mary sadly.

" 'We' means the Party," replied her daughter-in-law with certainty.

The devil take you, thought her mother-in-law and went off to her only refuge, the piano, to run her fingers over the minor keys.

The rare occasions when a semblance of a major key was struck in the house followed particularly complicated and successful operations performed by Boris Nikitovich. Then they would open a bottle of wine from the so-called "Moscow collection of Uncle Galaktion." Agasha would immediately remove a pie from the oven, as though it had been sitting there waiting for some time, and everyone would come to life, chatting gaily, not thinking about the family members who had disappeared, and after dinner, the professor would ask his wife to play something from "her old repertoire," and she would grudgingly play.

On the one hand, it was as though nothing in the life of Boris Nikitovich had changed. As before, he delivered lectures, operated, directed an experimental laboratory, and examined patients, including those at the Kremlin polyclinic. As before, he had to interrupt his meals or get up in the middle of the night from time to time because of an urgent summons. It must be said that he never grumbled about these emergency calls and always went where he was needed, because such extreme moments entered into his "philosophy of the Russian doctor," a legacy passed down within the family. Now, it seemed to Mary, he rushed off on these calls with a certain increased haste, going out to the front gate even before the car arrived as though the house were oppressive to him and he were taking advantage of any opportunity to leave it as soon as possible.

Old Pythagoras still considered it his duty to accompany his master to the gate. Now he was sitting next to Bo, waiting for the car. His collar turned up and his hat pushed down, the professor was looking down at the end of the street, sometimes lowering his hand to Pythagoras' head and saying for no apparent reason, "That's the way, Pythagoras, that's the way." The dog would look at him with a loving but nonetheless uncomprehending glance: for all his intellect, he could not fully understand what was happening.

Working at night always inspired Gradov. Night duty ennobled his work twofold. For some reason, a night patient was particularly dear to him, even though nowadays the strangest things sometimes happened. One recent instance had plunged the professor into a state of the deepest perplexity, occasioned tormenting thoughts of a practical as well as of a philosophical order, and yet . . . and yet, let us tell the story of these meditations later and for the time being say once again that, from a strictly professional standpoint, the life of Boris Nikitovich Gradov had not changed at all.

The public life of an eminent leader of Soviet medicine was another matter. In earlier times he had had to elude invitations to speakers' platforms, conversations with journalists, and receptions for foreign delegations of friends of the Soviet Union. Now it was as though he had been excluded, an ominous sign of his alienation from so-called public, utterly phony and idiotic, Soviet life. There were also other signs of heightening danger, above all, of course, the glances of his colleagues at the institute, at the clinic, in the laboratory. Most often, he would catch furtive and curious glances—how is it, they seemed to say, that he's still here, and not "there"?—and frequently he would notice the absence of a look, an averting of the eyes, a quick diversion to another object, eyes that seemed blinded by thought—what can you do, these people are learned, introspective—while at still other times he would notice gazes filled with silent sympathy, which also rapidly faded away and which he thought of as "frightened gazelles."

The constant sensation of gathering danger finally exhausted Boris Nikitovich. He felt as though he were caught in a trap. If there were only me, he thought, I would throw down the gauntlet, abandon all my honors and posts, and go away to the country, to a village hospital, or even to a mountain village in Central Asia. But I can't allow myself to do that: it's not only I who would suffer but everyone who depends on me as well, my beloved family, and of course it wouldn't do the ones already in jail any good, either.

One of his Kremlin patients advised him to write a deeply felt letter to the highest address of all and even gave him to understand that he would see that it was delivered. Boris Nikitovich heeded the advice, sat down to compose the letter, slaved over it, struck things off, crossed them out in search of phrases that were convincing and those of a loyal subject and yet at the same time dignified. He was even thinking of bringing in professional literary help—the poetess Nina Gradov, that is—but then it turned out that his patient and benefactor had just disappeared, catastrophically plunging beneath the surface of life, which immediately closed over him.

So everything continued in a terrified stupor, with shortened strides and muffled sentences, until one day the telephone in his office at the clinic rang and a woman's voice, in a resounding fanfare bursting with enthusiasm, said, "Boris Nikitovich, dear Professor Gradov, I'm calling from the Krasnaya Presnya District Party Committee! The textile workers of Krasnaya Presnya have just nominated you as a deputy to the Supreme Soviet! We would like to know if you would agree to run for office in the highest body of power in our country, to represent our marvelous Soviet medicine there?"

"I beg your pardon, but it sounds as though you drew my name out of a hat," muttered Gradov.

The voice laughed affectionately, cordially, just like something out of the movie *Volga, Volga*. What an absent-minded professor, it seemed to say, a learned man isolated from life. He doesn't know a campaign to nominate candidates is going on all over the country!

"Why, what do you mean, Professor, 'drew'? We're on our way to your office now, from the District Committee and the Executive Committee, loom operators and journalists both. It's such a joyful and unique event, after all, loom operators nominating a professor of medicine!"

Gradov put the receiver down and became flustered to the point of growling. What a country of imbeciles! They throw the children in jail and elect the father to the Supreme Soviet! Time to escape! Without even realizing what he was doing, he was already getting into his coat—home, home!—driven by a single instinct, to seek the shelter of his own roof. But the secretary of the institute's Party Committee, an utter abomination, an accumulation of base emotions, who had eyed him all this time like a wild boar, rushed to him.

"Boris Nikitovich, my dear man, what an honor for the entire institute!"

The rest of the day passed in an unimaginable, truly absurd whirl. The "shy gazelles" came running up to him with delight and reverence in their eyes: my, my, does this mean that it's all over now, it's behind you, it's in the past? The curious also came out of the woodwork with the question in their eyes—does this mean the Gradov sons will be set free now? Pencils in hand, reporters from *Moscow Pravda, Medical Gazette,* and *Izvestiya* were all over the place: "What was your reaction to such a surprising piece of news, Comrade Professor?"

Having planted himself in his chair and not stirring from it, he mumbled in reply, "Very flattered, but hardly worthy of such an honor . . ."

Everyone present laughed delightedly: Look at that, what a grump—what can you say, he's a real man of science!

The initial astonishment had passed, and he began to think about this unexpected nomination, which had undoubtedly come on orders from above, from great heights, and seemed more and more cloaked in darkness; there's something shady about this deal, better to think twice, even three times, before snatching at this life preserver.

That evening, Mary reacted unequivocally to the news: "Are you really going to join those idiots, Bo? You're going to take part in the charade of those elections? Lend your name to the executioners?" He didn't answer and went to their bedroom, slamming all the doors on the way. Outside, a car was waiting to take him to a rally of enraptured loom operators. He came out of the bedroom in full regalia: dark blue suit, diagonally striped tie, an entirely irreproachable gentleman if not for the three barbaric medals on his chest.

"Some people can afford angry outbursts of rhetoric—I can't," he said, speaking to his bust of Hippocrates, as he always did during quarrels. "Unlike some irresponsible and frivolous people, I can't refuse degradation and shame. I have to think about those who are in trouble and about the families I might be able to save by my own disgrace. I also have to think about the institute and its students!" he said, raising a fist with restrained fury, looking around to see where it would be better to strike, and bringing it down on the dinner table, which gave a good rattle. Then he cried, "And last, I have to think about the sick, damn it!" and walked off. At the last minute, just before slamming the door, he noticed that Agasha was crossing herself and Mary was following her example. They're both satisfied, he thought. Very satisfied, if not happy. It may only be temporary, but the principal catastrophe has been averted, the bulwark has not collapsed.

"Life has become better, life has become happier!" said the short adage, or rather assertion, or even better, accurate observation, set out in red letters nearly three feet high along the windows of the Central Telegraph Office and bordered with electric lamps. Then followed the name of the accurate observer, I. Stalin, and his gigantic portrait. Everything was ascribed to him—the improvement and future happiness of life. This was particularly true of the shop windows on Gorky Street. As they wrote in the newspapers, "Moscow gourmets have something to boast about in these days before the New Year's holiday!" Here there were garlands of sausage and fortresses of cheese, pyramids of canned anchovies, a generous spread of candies, bottles with their necks wrapped in silvery foil—a parade of imperial cuirassiers would hardly have had anything on them. And that was why the blush on people's cheeks flashed even more brightly through the gentle snowfall, and laughter had somehow become heartier and eyes even more lively: "Soviet violins sound better than any others in the world, and the smiles of our Soviet girls are brighter than any others . . ."

Alas, there still remained some monsters in our nation-family whom nothing gladdened. Three of them were walking up the main thoroughfare of the capital, two of them outwardly decent men and one of them even an attractive woman. All three smoked as they walked—there's the intelligentsia for you. It was Savva Kitaigorodsky, Nina Gradov, and her old friend from her Tiflis days, the artist Sandro Pevzner.

He had just come from beyond the mountains and had immediately dropped in on Nina, whom he had longed for so many years to behold in the flesh and whose image had been clouded neither by wine, nor by other romances, nor by painting. He had been quite anxious about how the married Nina and her doctor spouse would receive him, but they had given him a wonderful greeting, almost heartfelt, showing right away that he was "one of theirs," that is, someone in their circle whom they trusted and from whom they expected reciprocal trust. Savva had been getting ready to go out to "fuel up" the dinner table, and naturally, Sandro, as a Georgian, could not let Savva set out on this noble expedition alone, and Nina followed right behind them, so they had decided to take a sort of stroll to show the southerner the new center of Moscow.

In the stores, however, a rather disagreeable scene arose. Sandro would not let them pay for anything. No sooner would he see Nina at the cash register than he would rush to her with a pack of bills, and no sooner would he see

Savva preparing to pay than he would pull him back by the shoulder and throw money at the cashier, yelling, "Keep the change!" In a word, he was a Georgian, a rich and generous guest, a merchant from the East—even though his painting earned him scarcely a kopeck and he was working for a miserable salary making deliveries for the Artists' Fund, distributing busts of the leaders and canvases to various enterprises. He was a typical Georgian, this Pevzner, he even looked like a Georgian with his mustache, his large cap, his belted raglan overcoat. The ability of Jews to take on the features of the people among whom they happen to live is remarkable. The Russian Pevzner could immediately be distinguished from a Pole, while the Georgian and Turkish Pevzners had nothing at all in common. Somehow or other, loading their pockets with bottles, the threesome managed to leave the *gastronom* and slowly head up toward Bolshoi Gnezdnikovsky Street. Evenly, constantly, swirling slightly around the corners, a soft snow was falling. Here and there in the crowd people could be glimpsed with Christmas trees on their shoulders. In many store windows a Santa Claus stood alongside the father of the workers of the world, providing the workers with an immutable reminder of how fast this annual idyll passed and the fact that the Five-Year Plan was eternal. Sandro was recounting the terrible news from Tbilisi to Nina and Savva: "Titzian was arrested and disappeared, Paolo was taken away and disappeared . . . The Blue Horns were declared a Menshevik subversive organization. Styopa Kalistratov has been arrested and convicted of being a Trotskyite. It seems he got ten years and has been stripped of political rights for an additional five years. Otari, according to the rumors, was ripped to shreds at NKVD headquarters . . ."

Nina removed one of her gloves and for a second put her hand to Sandro's cheek. Rumors of terrible arrests among the Georgian intelligentsia had reached Moscow some time ago. Sandro had only confirmed the worst of them. In this case, no sort of gallows humor could be of any help—the lives not only of those arrested had been destroyed, but also of those left at liberty, the past was beginning to yawn like a vast emptiness, and the most terrible thing was that they were trying to disguise the emptiness with a veneer of "business as usual."

"You're not married, Sandro?" she asked.

"How could I be?" He sighed. "Your friends are disappearing, you yourself expect to be taken away at any minute, who can think about marriage? It's difficult even to have a mistress in circumstances like that."

"Aha, a mistress!" said Savva.

"Yes, yes," nodded Sandro. "My eternal tormentor. Nina knows her."

"He's talking about his painting," Nina explained. "What are you working on now, Sandro?"

"I'm drawing fish, birds, miniature deer figures, bits of landscapes, table objects, always in fantastic combinations, you understand. On the whole, it would be enough to get myself charged with Formalism. I—you know how, don't you?—sometimes take two or three canvases to my aunt's place in Baku. Maybe something will be saved."

"Still, it looks as though the wave is receding," said Savva. "When you live in a multistory building, you notice it."

"Listen, friends!" When Sandro spoke, his accompanying gestures sometimes had a bit of the theatrical marionette about them. Thus he was now speaking to both his left and his right, that is, to both Nina and Savva, his arms bent at the elbows and his palms facing upward.

"Listen, the artist is always a stupid, intellectually backward person. I don't understand what is happening. Historically, philosophically, I can't find any explanation for this business. Can you explain it to me?"

"Savva can explain it to you, he has his own theory," said Nina.

Savva undertook to explain: "All of modern Russian history looks like a series of breakers—waves of retribution. The February Revolution was retribution for our ruling aristocracy's arrogance and narrow-minded immovability in relation to the people. The October Revolution and the Civil War were retribution against the bourgeoisie and the intelligentsia for their obsessive summons to revolution, for the stirring up of the masses. Collectivization and the campaign against the kulaks were retribution against the peasants for their cruelty in the Civil War, for beating up clergymen, for the bloodthirsty anarchism. The current purges are retribution against the revolutionaries for the violence they wreaked upon the peasants. . . . As for the future, it's impossible to predict, but logically we can suppose that there will be even more waves, until this whole cycle of false aspirations comes to an end. . . ."

Lost in thought, Sandro walked on a few more steps and then turned to Savva. "You know, Savva, I'm ready to accept your theory."

"Yes, but it's metaphysics, you see," said Nina somewhat craftily.

"That's just the point!" exclaimed Sandro.

Several passers-by looked at him. A man with a walking stick and with a pipe between his teeth standing beside a poster, obviously a foreigner—they now rarely visited Moscow and therefore could immediately be distinguished from the crowds—took the pipe from his mouth and looked on with great interest.

"I think we've made a scene," said Nina. "Have you forgotten:

> *We don't know the land we live on,*
> *We amputate our speech*
> *And fear our own unending whisper*
> *Of a Kremlin mountaineer.*

"That was by Osip, wasn't it?" asked Sandro.

"Yes, and they say it cost him his life," replied Nina.

"Osip? Really?"

"No one knows for sure, but in any case, he's there."

Sandro crossed himself quickly.

"You cross yourself, Sandro?" asked Nina softly.

He became disconcerted and did not answer.

The foreigner was the American journalist Townsend Reston. He watched the backs of the threesome for a long time until they disappeared in the snow and gazed at the snowflaked crowds flashing by. He had just arrived, had left his bag at the National Hotel, and was taking his first evening stroll. On his earlier trips, these strolls had usually provided the keys to his best articles. The atmosphere of falseness struck him, even though he had expected it, because it had obviously acquired solid and reliable characteristics and seemed phony to no one but him. It was all the more improbable, therefore, to see three comparatively young people in the midst of this universal and sinister theater walking slowly in the current of the crowd, absorbed in a serious and melancholy conversation that was divorced from the falsity around them. Over the years, Reston had never learned Russian and as a result could not make any sense of their discussion, yet the appearance of this threesome worked like an epigraph on his as yet empty pages.

The newly elected Supreme Soviet was scheduled to convene in the Great Kremlin Palace several days before the New Year. After a near scandal at the All-Union Society for Cultural Ties with Foreign Countries, Reston had been accredited to attend the first session. He knew he wouldn't be able to see a thing from the little balcony provided for the foreign press except for the presidium, the calmly applauding leaders, and the exultation in the hall. Then again, said his colleague, the regular correspondent of *The Times* of London, there won't be anything but calm applause for the leaders and exultation in the hall. Yes, thought Reston, everything is tight as a drum here. It's quite wrong to curse the Bolsheviks as "Red Fascists," as people sometimes do—they're far more severe than those comic Italian scoundrels. It would be more accurate in a heated moment to call Mussolini "the Black Bolshevik." Iosif really had only one equal in the world—Adolf. Two captivating forms of socialism have flourished in the twentieth century, he thought—class and racist.

Reston had decided not to express these thoughts directly in his articles. His

pronouncements on the Soviet regime had long ago earned him the reputation of a "reactionary" in the liberal and left-wing circles to which he had
once belonged. The Western intelligentsia rejected the racist variety of socialism but had easily taken the bait based on class. If only by means of hints and
the introduction of parallels he tried to communicate the idea of the entirely
identical character of the two regimes. Alas, this simple idea was given no
consideration by the liberals. Even Feuchtwanger, who had fled the Nazis,
applauded the Bolsheviks. He had let himself be taken in by the "open trials."
Of course, for the time being Stalin was not crushing the Jews, but he'd get
around to it eventually. The writers, with rare exceptions, didn't see that
essential, yet terrible events were approaching. Despite the fact that the two
regimes now anathematized each other, there would be a rapprochement
between them in the very near future. Before very long they would strike at
the West. The Atlantic civilization would never be able to stand the combined
blow of German industry and Russian resources. A regime would be established in the world in which there would be no more liberals, either on the
right or on the left. The Cheka and the Gestapo would use the word "liberal"
to wipe their asses.

What the hell did I come here for? thought Reston. Didn't I know all this
even without coming to Moscow? What the hell am I always wandering
around this country for? What draws me to this place? I don't have a girlfriend here. Women take off as soon as they find out I'm an American. It looks
like purges, executions, and concentration camps have already finished off
any signs of life here. Even the trees in this country seem frightened out of
their wits. Before, it was still possible to have a conversation with someone
on the street and to be able to rely at least partly on your interpreter. Now
all of the All-Union Society for Cultural Ties with Foreign Countries interpreters are watched every minute by the unblinking eyes of the secret police.
Ordinary people do not try to hide their feeling that these interpreters are
out-and-out agents. What are they interpreting, and what will be the consequences for the speaker? Damn it, I never got around to learning Russian
during all these years, lazy boozer that I am. Why the hell did I come here
again to walk around the streets like a deaf-mute, and not alone at that, but
always tailed? It's only now, it seems, that I begin to realize this, when
everything seems to be opening up all around . . .

With these thoughts, Townsend Reston emerged onto the paving blocks of
Red Square, along which he had strolled at the very beginning of our story
with Professor Ustryalov of the Change of Landmarks movement, who had
now disappeared without a trace along with a whole fenceworth of unchanged landmarks. The entire square had been scrubbed clean down to the
last speck of dust, and swept so that one would never know it had snowed not

long before. Illuminated by powerful lights reflecting off its crenelated walls, the Kremlin's towers, a flag streaming from every modulation, stood out in sharp relief against the clear, deep blue sky. As always, the huge portraits of the leaders lent a surrealistic impression.

All over the square, people were strolling, both alone and in small groups. All were going in one direction—toward the gates of Spasskaya Tower. Before, they had usually queued up timidly here, stood in line to see Lenin's body, Reston recalled, but now there was no one at the Mausoleum except the sentries. What was happening? Aha—they're all going to the session. These are the very deputies themselves walking along, the "masters of their country and of their fate," as they had explained to him at the All-Union Society for Cultural Ties with Foreign Countries.

It was a densely packed, cheerful crowd, warmly dressed, perhaps even too warmly. There were quite a few Asiatics, who were just the ones moving in small groups. In the middle of the bodies and faces reflecting the simplicity of the people's elected representatives, Reston suddenly noticed the face of an intellectual—an elderly man in a soft hat and a beautiful old overcoat with glasses, a small beard, a walking stick in one hand. Well, why not talk to this gentleman, thought Reston. He might know foreign languages . . .

The man was Boris Nikitovich Gradov, deputy to the Supreme Soviet of the USSR from the workers of the Moscow Krasnaya Presnya district. He was on his way to the ceremonial session in the Kremlin and recalling his conversation of that morning with his wife.

The boys had been at school, Verulka at her kindergarten. Mary and Agasha were preparing a surprise for them—they were going to decorate a fir for the holidays. Slabopetukhovsky had as always brought an excellent tree. It goes without saying that there was an abundance of toys beneath it. The children would come home, squeal with delight, and dance around. Orphaned children of still-living parents, they particularly needed holidays like this.

Suddenly, Mary buttonholed her husband and drew him into his study. "Listen, Bo, perhaps we should tell the children about what a Christmas tree is, what the holiday is for, where it came from . . . basically, about all that?"

Boris Nikitovich reacted to this proposal by immediately taking offense to the point of tears, as had begun to happen lately.

"Forgive me, Mary, but I have the impression that you're always putting me to a test! What does this mean? Do you want to show once again that I'm a shit, that I can never say 'no' to what I hate and never say 'yes' to what I love? Is that what you mean to say?"

Mary clutched her hands imploringly to her bosom. "Why, Bo, my dear, how can you say such a thing? Who knows what a cross you have to bear if not I? How could I test you? I simply asked you the question because you're a wise man who is very close to me. Myself, I don't know. I'm just afraid we might do the children harm if we tell them about Christ . . ."

Boris Nikitovich immediately understood everything and immediately was ashamed of having taken offense. He caressed the cheek of his old friend, felt a warm tenderness inside him. "Forgive my outburst, Mary, dear. It's the emotional pressure we're living under. . . . You know, it seems to me that this isn't the time to introduce the children to religion, we ought to put it off. They're very open, easily aroused; in their position it might cause them trouble. I know you've grown closer to religion and that it helps you. Believe me, even I sometimes feel drawn to some secret temple."

Now every temple was secret, and there was one in front of him. Saint Basil's Cathedral was lit up on this solemn evening of the session and seemed to have acquired a broader expanse in the clear night. Or, as they now wrote of it in the papers, it "is part of the historical ensemble of Red Square." Obviously they had given up on their plans to pull it down. It was said that after the Church of Christ the Savior had been blown up, then shelled with artillery, the fate of Saint Basil's had been decided, when suddenly the city's chief architect had rebelled, supposedly saying, "If you want to blow up Saint Basil's, then blow me up with it." The synod of leaders, rumor had it, had been embarrassed, a delay had cropped up, and then directives had been changed to provide for the preservation of "historic architectural ensembles."

Boris Nikitovich felt an irrepressible urge to cross himself before the cathedral—like the architect, to issue a challenge to everyone, to take off his hat and cross himself. He removed his fedora as though he felt hot for a second and crossed himself beneath his coat, in small movements, but three times. It was not only Soviet fear that was nesting in this modesty, but also Boris Nikitovich's entire positivist upbringing, which his father, Nikita, had given him with the approval of his grandfather Boris. Now it seemed as though the end was coming for this education. The Red sabbath that emanated from behind those battlements had undermined the people's faith in rationalism, in the triumph of human reason, even in the theory of evolution. Philosophy was swaying at its moorings, passionately desiring to break through to some other, precious shore.

Suddenly a man standing slightly in front of the professor tipped his hat and spoke to him in English:

"Excuse me, sir, by any chance do you speak English?"

Boris Nikitovich was taken aback. It was so unexpected that he became slightly unsteady on his feet and planted his walking stick firmly on the cobblestones. An Englishman here, beside these walls, beside . . . Stalin? It seemed to him that the air here ought not to permit such sounds.

"Yes, I do," he lisped like a schoolboy. The stranger flashed a friendly smile. In reply Gradov smiled in bewilderment. Oh, God, what a strange stranger was in front of him, what a staggering foreigner!

"Would you be so kind, sir, as to give me a few minutes? I'm an American journalist," said Reston. He was very happy: what luck—to have a chat with a Russian intellectual of the old-fashioned mold without the help of those interpreters from the All-Union Society for Cultural Ties with Foreign Countries!

Without saying a word in reply, Boris Nikitovich lurched off to one side, then strode away sharply, almost running—in fact, yes, he was running. An American journalist! What is this, again I'm being put to a test, and a terrible one at that! To speak without an intermediary to a foreigner, and what was more, with a journalist, when your sons are in prison, when you yourself are going to be pilloried, when Stalin is practically two feet away. . . . No, that's just too much!

He was moving with determination toward the throat of the Spasskaya Tower as though he were seeking refuge beyond its portals. He had to stop in front of the gates, however, since soldiers were checking the deputies' credentials. Then he came to his senses, brought his breathing under control, wiped the perspiration from his brow. You're a coward and a slave, he told himself. A disgrace. Behind him, right over his shoulder, a man's voice said thickly, "Well done, Professor. That's the way to behave. You never know who is going to come sniffing around here." Gradov passed beneath the arch without turning around. The shadow of an owl flickered over him in the short tunnel with its resounding acoustics.

Slowly—they were told: slowly, comrades, solemnly!—the deputies mounted the marble steps inside the Great Kremlin Palace. There were reporters, photographers, and newsreel cameramen all along the first flight of stairs and on the landing. Photographic lights were glaring in their faces. An expression of solemn happiness showed on the faces of the deputies. The effect was produced with particular success by the skullcap-wearing Central Asians, whose faces shone with sincere reverence for those who awaited them upstairs. There, at the top of the steps, gently applauding and smiling at the envoys of the people, stood the members of the Politburo, and in the center of the group, in a light gray military shirt and high kidskin boots, stood Stalin. He was at once applauding everyone and each individual, and some of the deputies halted before him in order to say and listen to a few words.

Gradov was ascending the stairs in the company of a young aircraft engineer whom he had met in the vestibule. They knew each other from the

House of Scientists; he was reputed to be an aerodynamics genius, and besides, he had once courted Nina. In contrast to the guests from sunny Uzbekistan, the engineer for some reason was constantly glancing at his watch and continually talking to Boris Nikitovich about the possibility of using rockets to probe the upper atmosphere. Gradov was not listening to him; he was only watching to see how, with every step, the dimly shining boots of an excellent black color came closer. Trembling inwardly, he remembered those legs without the boots, their terrible secret. The secret was so profound and fetid that he would have been happy to forget about it once and for all.

"And here, Iosif Vissarionovich, comes the eminent surgeon, Professor Gradov," said Molotov without stopping his tepid applause. All of Stalin's old friends now called him by his given name and patronymic in public, while he still addressed them as he had in the old days—Vyacheslav, Klim . . .

"Which one? The elder or the younger?" said Stalin, squinting. Koba is pretending, thought Molotov. He knows both of them perfectly well. And you're pretending yourself, Scriabin, thought Stalin. You know perfectly well that I know Gradov.

"The elder, with three decorations," said Molotov. Stalin shot him a sidelong glance that was meant to be humorous. "Introduce me to him, Vyacheslav!"

Yes, Stalin knew Gradov, but he did not have the slightest desire to reveal a state secret even to those few who already knew it, especially Molotov.

Approximately three months earlier, the general secretary had begun to have convulsions at his dacha in nearby Kuntsevo. He had even thought for a moment—am I dying? It was not for himself that he feared, but for the cause. History cannot be stopped, of course, but it can be held up for a long time: it's not every day that leaders as consistent and resolute, men with so colossal a range of vision as this convulsion sufferer, appear, the poor lad Soso;* his mind even became a bit confused. . . . The convulsions had not come from out of the blue. Everything had started with a large banquet in honor of the conquerors of the Arctic—he must have eaten too much there. From there he went to the dacha of the newly appointed Commissar for Internal Affairs, his countryman Lavrenty. There, in more intimate company, they drank a great deal and danced with some women friends. He found that he had an appetite once again, though he'd not had a bowel movement. Toward morning Beria covered a table with delicacies from the Caucasus, and

*Stalin's nickname.

Stalin was unable to restrain himself from a new fit of gluttony. A combination of walnut satsivi chicken and shashlik in tkemala sauce had always contributed to constipation, but in the past Stalin had managed to cope with this annoying, "ridiculous," as they used to say at the seminary, nonsense without outside assistance by the method of his ancestors, with the help of his two fingers. This time, his ancestral method didn't help. Day after day passed, but no relief was in sight. Stalin put on weight, became sullen, and constantly flew into rages at meetings of the government, demanding the immediate purging of all, *all* the enemies of the people! He could not bring himself to tell the NKVD doctors who were always on call what was tormenting him: he had no desire to say the word "constipation" in front of those dunderheads, to put the leader of the laboring masses into a ridiculous position. The doctors in turn trembled with fear, dreading to make such a shameful suggestion to the great leader. Day after day, Stalin struggled heroically with the ordeal that had descended on him. He would retire to his personal rooms, which no one was allowed to enter, and sit on the toilet for hours, reading old newspapers with pictures of his now-arrested comrades in arms, convincing himself of his rightness—it had been right to have these comrades arrested!—waiting for the blessed moment. But the blessed moment had not come; his stomach felt like a container full of lead, or rather a solid piece of lead. His head became muddled—he had begun to have thoughts about his mother, which meant his head was muddled. The lead had begun to rise into his throat—he wanted to divide it up into nine-gram bullets and send them swarming out into the world. In other words, there is no doubt, comrades, that you see before you the symptoms of lead poisoning, which the Bolsheviks warned us about not long ago. At just such a moment, he flung open the door, shouted "Doctors!" and collapsed onto an ottoman.

The NKVD doctors came on the run. "What's wrong, Comrade Stalin?"

"Lead poisoning," came the reply.

The doctors began to fidget in confusion. One of them was rolling two laxative pills in the palm of his hand. "Maybe we should give him . . . these?" he asked the second.

"What are they?"

"You know what they are!"

"Well, fine, give him those, otherwise . . ." The pills might have worked had Stalin taken them five days or so earlier, but now they only produced attacks of agonizing convulsions.

He was dripping some sort of liquid, the leaden wall stood firm. One day, in the throes of these convulsions, Stalin evoked the name of Gradov. "Bring Gradov, you bastards! A real doctor, Professor Gradov!" Gradov's name had remained in his memory since the twenties—even before that important

Party measure in whose implementation Gradov had partly participated,
Stalin had known of this celebrated Moscow professor, and somewhere in the
back of his mind had always kept in reserve this good, profoundly Russian
name—not just some weird foreign borrowing—as the name of a healer, a
real doctor. Since then, of course, life had grown ever more complicated and
the class struggle had increased in ferocity, all sorts of things happened to
people, you couldn't keep track of them all, but here at this fateful hour of
convulsions, the name suddenly sprang from its hiding place—Gradov! Gradov!

Boris Nikitovich was on his way home after an operation at a wild and
piercing time of night, in the dank and droning witching hour, when two
secret police vehicles intercepted his car on the highway. He immediately
realized that it was not just a run-of-the-mill arrest but something a little
more serious. The senior officer of the group said to him in a metallic voice,
"Get into our car, Professor. It is a matter of supreme importance to the state."
In the car, he added in the same tone, excluding any possibility of establishing
a dialogue, "Take care, secrecy must be one hundred percent. If you divulge
even the slightest detail, you will bear the responsibility in its severest forms."

The patient, that is, Stalin, he saw lying on an ottoman in his office. There
was an overpowering stench in the air. The patient was semiconscious,
muttering something in Georgian. No one had been able to summon up the
courage to approach him, even to unbutton his constricting military blouse.
The NKVD doctors were cowering in a corner of the office.

"Undress the patient!" Gradov ordered immediately and began to unbutton
the blouse himself. The bodyguard quickly pulled Stalin's boots off. "Remove
his trousers!" His officer's trousers slipped down. His long johns were of
surprisingly poor quality. "Gauze! Cotton! Warm water! Oilcloth! Bedpan!"
The professor, continuing to give orders, turned to the NKVD physicians.
"Doctors, come here!"

Not without interest, he looked at the two medical men of the invisible
army. It didn't appear as though they were used to doctoring—they must
have practiced more in other fields.

"The anamnesis!" he said to them. The doctors, perplexed, muttered,
"Complete absence of peristalsis . . . intestinal stenosis . . . didn't want to do
anything until you arrived, Professor . . . the picture is atypical . . . Comrade
Stalin did not consult . . ."

"Remove his undershorts, too!" barked Boris Nikitovich to the bodyguard.
Stalin now lay before him nude. He began to palpate the stomach, absolutely
stone hard under its layer of fat.

Just at that moment, the next convulsion began. A small amount of liquid trickled along the oilcloth beneath Stalin. The sixth toe on his right foot was twitching independently of the rest of the body. The patient's pain-filled eyes looked out from behind the pockmarks and wrinkles. Stalin said hoarsely, "Help me, *katso*,* and ask anything you want."

"How many days has it been since your last stool, Comrade Stalin?" Boris Nikitovich asked gently. He knew that the very sound of his voice had a beneficial effect on the sick. Sure enough, Stalin sighed with evident hope.

"It's been ten days," he moaned. "Maybe two weeks."

"Right now we're going to help you, Comrade Stalin. Be patient a little while longer." Gradov encouragingly clapped Stalin on the arm, catching himself in the thought that this was no "leader of the peoples" before him but simply a patient. He would have patted any patient on the arm in this way. Then he asked to be shown to the telephone, and he phoned the Kuntsevo Kremlin Hospital and began to give orders. The three men standing alongside with faces like borzois were listening to every word. Twenty minutes later, two nurses arrived from the hospital, bringing everything the professor needed. Boris Nikitovich put an enema into place and gave Stalin several injections: Euphilin directly into a vein, camphor beneath the skin, and intramuscular magnesium. Stalin's blood pressure dropped, his breathing and pulse became more regular. The enema did its work as well: in a few minutes, the lines of defense were broken, the walls of Babylon crumbled—call it anything you please, just don't call it the exit of Stalin's shit. Meanwhile the feces continued coming and coming, the nurses could not change and carry out the bedpans fast enough, the gas bubbles popped with a triumphant roar like a distant avalanche, peristalsis had been awakened. The stench came in uneven waves, since each layer of excrement brought its own. There was no way of getting used to it, one had to simply tell oneself that that was the way things were.

Stalin lay with a beatific smile on his cunning face, which had regained its acuity. Never, never, never in his life had he known such staggering liberation of flesh and weary spirit. Not even when he had escaped from exile, not to mention the Revolution of 1917. The occasions of liberation of those days had only made him shake himself like a dog and thirst for immediate activity. Only now, after this "breakthrough"—in his mind, it was the word "breakthrough" that he used to describe all of this—did the trembling pass away, gently sloping hills and expanses of various shades of blue opened before him, and he felt himself a part of this blessed abundance, almost dissolved in it, as though he had not begotten and would not beget all these revolutionary

*Georgian for "man."

horrors. And into these waves of warmth and disavowal now and again swam a bearded visage with eyes that were indeed mirrors of an unsullied soul. "How do you feel, patient?" the face asked. It was interested in its patient, was interested in someone out of artless humanity—well, why try to be clever? It was interested in Soso.

"Thank you, Professor, I feel fine, just fine . . ." The human face surfaced and trembled nearby. Ask for anything, Professor, and it's yours. Ask me for your sons, and they'll be with you in two days. Ask me now, Professor, while I want to thank you; later on it will be too late."

No, I can't ask you for anything right now, you tyrant, thought Gradov. A doctor cannot ask his patient for anything at the moment when he is helping him, and right now you're still my patient, and not a dirty tyrant, you tyrant!

Going down one step, Molotov shook Gradov's hand. "Congratulations, Professor Gradov, on your election to the Supreme Soviet! I'd like to introduce you to Comrade Stalin!"

Stalin shook the hand of Boris Nikitovich. He was now in excellent health. His whiskers had been washed in eau de cologne and his hair gave off a dark red shine. "Congratulations, Professor! It's very good that representatives of Soviet science, and in particular of our progressive medicine, are going to sit in our Soviet parliament alongside workers and collective farmers."

They looked each other in the eye for several seconds. If he asks me about his sons now, I'll destroy him, thought Stalin.

"Thank you, Comrade Stalin," said Gradov and tactfully moved off in the direction of the stream of deputies.

Stalin followed him approvingly with his eyes. The next instant, it suddenly seemed to him that the skylight above the marble steps was filled by the gigantic eye of an owl. Then it was over.

SEVENTH INTERMISSION
THE PRESS

Heroes of the Soviet Union in Washington. It has been a long time since a major aviation event has received as much press coverage as the flight of Chkalov, Baidukov, and Belyakov. "Heroes of the air," "Victors of the magnetic jungles at the top of the world," "The Soviet capital is closer to us than we thought"—the American press has used phrases like this in its estimation of the Soviet heroes' feat. The president of the United States, F. D. Roosevelt, is expecting the pilots at the White House.

. . .

The Moscow police have arrested Burtseva, who was performing abortions in the apartments of her patients and in rooms at public baths.

> Radio. The North Pole.
> Moscow, Central Committee RCP(b), to: Comrade Stalin, Comrade Molotov.
> Dear Iosif Vissarionovich and Vyacheslav Mikhailovich! Our group of four was delighted to hear the news of the highest award of the Motherland. Much labor awaits us, but we are firmly convinced that we are surrounded by your love and concern, and by the attention of the entire country. We will expend every effort to justify your confidence and to preserve the honor of our Motherland in any circumstances.
>
> Papanin, Krenkel, Shirshov, Fyodorov

The laboring masses append their signature in friendship to the loan issued for the strengthening of the defense of the USSR.

After a long silence, the Union of Soviet Writers of Karelia has finally decided to discuss the question of the harm done to literature by Averbakh. The debate showed the devastation wreaked upon Karelian literature by the diehards of the infamous group RAPP—the Russian Association of Proletarian Writers. The bourgeois nationalists Luoto, Onnonen, and Raitunainen oriented writers toward founding a pan-Finnish (clearly bourgeois) literature. These small-minded Trotskyite-Fascist ideas led to the attribution of the Karelian national epic, "Kaleval," to Finnish authorship. The nationalists have been expelled from the Union of Writers.

The Central Committee of the RCP(b)—the Communist Party—with great sadness announces the death after an extended illness of the old Bolshevik, prominent worker in the fields of agriculture and heavy industry and member of the Central Committee of the RCP(b), Iosif Vikentevich Kosior.

. . .

In recent days, several political prisoners in Germany have died from the beastly tortures of the Gestapo. The newspapers have given the names of the well-known German sports figure Willi Grossein and Walentin Schmetzer, among others.

The greatest project of the Second Five-Year plan is complete—the Moscow-Volga canal, begun at the initiative of Comrade Stalin! Greetings to the builders of this remarkable construction of the Stalinist epoch.

According to preliminary data, Irina Vishnevskaya (pilot) and Katya Mednikova (copilot) have broken the women's world altitude record of 19,800 feet.

The English Caledonia amphibious airplane and the American Sikorsky 42-B amphibious airplane have completed the first round-trip transatlantic flights. Regular transatlantic flights carrying both the mails and passengers are planned.

The masters of the liquidated Fascist band of Tukhachevsky and Co. cannot get over their severe and unexpected defeat. Even now they are still lamenting their faithful agents. And why not? One of fascism's most important military espionage groups has been put out of action. The grand collapse of their intelligence agencies is obvious to the entire world.

With artificial indignation, the author of an article in the military newspaper *Deutsche Wehr* tries to challenge the espionage charges against Tukhachevsky but at the same time is forced to admit that he was the organizer of a counterrevolutionary conspiracy: "Tukhachevsky wanted to become the Russian Napoleon, but he tipped his hand too early or, as usually happens, was betrayed at the last minute."

Among the judges, continues *Deutsche Wehr*, "were the military proletarians Blücher and Budyonny." Our country, along with the laboring masses of the entire world, takes pride in these "military proletarians." *Deutsche Wehr* betrays wholesale Fascist military intelligence.

Clients of barbershops, demand that your barbers wash their hands!

.   .   .

From the speeches of Prosecutor of the USSR Alexander Yanuarievich Vyshinsky: "We all remember great Stalin's words to the effect that 'The new constitution of the USSR will be a moral aid and a real help for all those who are presently carrying on the fight against Fascist barbarism.' This is why our foes are in such a rage.

"In the USSR, where socialism has triumphed, where genuine culture and democracy have been unshakably secured, legality is a mighty weapon for future progress in the future struggles for socialism.

"Comrade Stalin has indicated the dangers of the 'idiotic sickness' of unconcern and the necessity of overcoming this sickness so as to recognize and defeat the enemy. The forces of anti-Soviet counterrevolutionary agitation are presently resorting to the most varied devices and doing a very bad job of masking their anti-Soviet undertakings. For example, not long ago in the city of Kuibyshev, a 'deaf-mute' was detained in a marketplace with a board around his neck bearing a counterrevolutionary inscription: 'Help a deaf-mute, they took my job, took my clothes, and won't give me no food.' At the police station it was discovered that this 'deaf-mute' was neither deaf nor mute at all. He turned out to be a de-kulakized kulak who had chosen to carry on his struggle with Soviet government in this form."

Spartak scores a major soccer victory over the team from the Land of the Basques. Score 6–2.

On Red Square, 40,000 physical fitness enthusiasts from eleven republics demonstrate their strength, vigor, courage, ardent love for the Motherland, and boundless devotion to the best friend of Soviet athletes, Comrade Stalin. Dances, human pyramids, flowers arranged in the shape of tanks!

> *Hunger of youth,*
> *Wealth of maturity,*
> *Days of Stalin, age of beauty,*
> *Legends of Hellas revived.*

> *Our sky—clearer,*
> *Our sun—more loving.*
> *Our joy—decked in live flowers,*
> *Our proud children—October's victory.*
> *—Alexei Surkov*

We saw Stalin, saw his smile—affectionate, fatherly. . . . At the first summons of Stalin our whole country will pass before the leader—an entire valiant people of horsemen, mountaineers, cotton farmers. We return home inspired by Stalin.

> —Leader of Physical Fitness Delegation of the Tadzhik SSR Kornienko, Commissar of the delegation Kuzi Akilov, physical education teachers Aslan Shukurov, Amito Yuldasheva, Vali Malakhov

Decree of the Central Executive Committee of the USSR: For distinguished service in the direction of the organs of the NKVD charged with the fulfillment of government tasks, Comrade N. I. Yezhov is awarded the Order of Lenin.

Comrade Yezhov personifies the image of the Bolshevik whose word is never separated from his deeds. History has appointed the organs of the NKVD to be, in the words of Stalin, "the scourge of the bourgeoisie, the unflagging sentinel of the Revolution, the unsheathed sword of the proletariat." The despicable traitor and enemy of socialism Yagoda tried to dull the sharpness of our sword. The iron hand of Comrade Yezhov, the emissary of Stalin and the Central Committee, has reestablished Bolshevik norms.

The people hold this sword in hand. Thus the NKVD already has, and will increasingly have, millions of eyes, millions of ears, millions of toilers' hands —all led by the Bolshevik Party and the Stalinist Central Committee. Such strength is invincible!

The development of the collective farm system in Tadzhikistan was impeded by a band of enemies who had ensconced themselves in the leadership, and they were all given refuge by Chairman of the Council of People's Commissars of Tadzhikistan Rakhimbaev. The bourgeois nationalists of Tadzhikistan under the leadership of Rakhimbaev, Ashurov, and Frolov have gotten out of hand. Time to shorten their reach!

Slander of Ukrainian reality.
Odessa: An exhibition of paintings and sketches from Soviet Ukraine and Moldavia has opened at the Odessa State Art Museum. The paintings and sketches have been selected and displayed in such a way that the Ukraine and Moldavia are shown in a completely distorted light. Here are three down-

trodden beggar women trudging along a road. Here is another painting—a sickly cow, two roosters, an overturned washtub, and a thin, unattractive woman . . . the painting is called *Milkmaid on the Collective Farm.*

. . . And where are the Ukrainian collectives, the handsomely arranged streets, the freshly painted houses? Where are the prosperous Ukrainian collective farmers? Where have the wonderful Moldavian dances and songs gone? Where are the Stakhanovites? There is none of this at the exhibition!

It is impossible to regard this exposition as anything other than an impudent sally by Ukrainian nationalists. Trotskyite-Bukharinite enemies and wreckers active in the Directorate of Artistic Affairs of the Ukrainian Soviet of People's Commissars knowingly directed the hand of certain artists along a hostile path.

The Central Committee of the Communist Party of Armenia was long headed by an enemy of the Armenian people, the despised traitor Khondzhian. After the unmasking of Khondzhian, his post was occupied by Amatuni. The new leader has often boasted that the credit for the unmasking of Khondzhian belongs to him. Yet it now turns out that Amatuni was in fact a savage henchman of Khondzhian, a continuer of his counterrevolutionary activities.

Amatuni has been betraying the interests of the people for a long time, ever since he sided with the Trotskyite opposition. He made the Dashnak* agent Akopov his right-hand man, promoting him to the post of deputy secretary. The post of chairman of the Soviet of People's Commissars was occupied by Gulaian, an arms bearer of the executed enemy of the people Kamenev.

The recently held plenum sent a Bolshevik message to Comrade Stalin to demand that all enemies of the Armenian people be crushed.

Drink tasty and nourishing Extra Cocoa!

The drama club of the Aviakhim Factory has staged a production of W. Shakespeare's *Romeo and Juliet*. In the role of Romeo—Comrade Drozdenko, cab dispatcher. In the role of Juliet—Comrade Kriuchkova, stock clerk.

The western frontier of the Byelorussian SSR: The night was dark. From their concealed night post, border guards Vasily Nikishkin and Nikolai Oskin noticed a man making his way into Soviet territory. Nikishkin shouted,

*Armenian nationalist party.

"Stop!" The man fired his gun in reply. The border guards shot the violator. A search of his body uncovered a pistol with five rounds in it, 300 Soviet rubles, a small wooden box containing a toxic powder, and a bottle containing an unidentified liquid. The dead man was an agent of a neighboring state.

An enemy foray: Someone's hostile hand is active in the City Soviet of Kemerov. Certificates granting the right to compile electoral rolls and filled out in a hooliganish, counterrevolutionary fashion are being issued over the signature of Deputy Chairman of the City Soviet Gerasimov and Senior Secretary Volokhov.

Soviet perfumes—the best toilet soaps, Pond's cold cream.

Readers who received the latest issue of the journal *Pacific Ocean* were amazed to see that the editorial board had passed over in silence the resolutions of the February-March plenum of the Central Committee of the RCP(b). There is no indication that the editors drew any conclusions from Comrade Stalin's speech. A large amount of material has been dragged into the journal by the hand of the enemy. The author of an article on Japan, for example, writes, "For the time being (!!), Fascism in Japan still has no significant (!!) power of attraction for the masses . . ." What does this "for the time being" mean? Perhaps fascism will have "significant" power of attraction for the masses in Japan in the future? . . . Enemies have become so firmly established at the journal that they print reactionary articles from the Japanese press on its pages. In whose interests is the journal's editor, G. Voitinsky, acting? He scarcely puts out a single issue containing no enemy contraband.

Unmasked enemies of the people, who had occupied posts in the Academy of Agricultural Science and the Grain Directorate of the People's Commissariat for Land of the USSR, have taken no small pains to throw the grain industry into confusion. It would be an act of unforgivable leniency to consider that all is well on the plant cultivation front after this unmasking. The roots of wrecking have undoubtedly survived.

Children from Spain have arrived in Leningrad. The steamer *Cooperation* approached the floating welcome lighthouse with more than six hundred children of the heroic combatants of Asturia, Bilbao, and Santarena. Several hours later, the steamer *Felix Dzerzhinsky* sailed up, bringing several hundred children. The voices of the children could be heard ringing out: "Viva Russia! Viva Stalin!"

> *The names of heroes march in ranks*
> *Straight unto history's lustrous banks,*
> *The Soviet land does joy bring,*
> *Just like a garden in the spring.*
> *Oh, twentieth anniversary—such a bounty!*
> *Ring out, bright days of our native land,*
> *Call out in joy for one man!*
> *Feats of glory, days of fame,*
> *We find your path in Stalin's name!*
> —*Alexei Surkov*

According to data collected by the Party Committee of Bashkir Province, 377 Party cards of the new type have been lost by the Communists of the republic, and this circumstance was exploited by enemies of the people, spies, and saboteurs. A considerable number of Party cards have fallen into the hands of the enemy.

A meeting of Stakhanovites and pace-setting miners from all across the Don basin. In his speech, Comrade Nikita Izotov said, "Root out every last one of the wreckers!"

A live report of the writer Vsevolod Vishnevsky from a preelectoral meeting of textile workers: The name of Stalin is on everyone's lips. Almost every orator with passion and at the same time with deep intimacy has been speaking of his personal attitude toward Stalin. In nominating Stalin as a candidate for the Supreme Soviet of the USSR on behalf of the laboring masses, textile worker Zverev said, "Comrade Stalin scrutinizes every trifle, every detail of daily life, work, and the workers' salaries. Comrade Stalin has introduced so many improvements into the textile industry!" Four thousand hands erupt into the air as one in favor of the candidacy of Comrade Stalin.

EIGHTH INTERMISSION
THE LEAP OF THE SQUIRREL

He had never imagined that he would so quickly find himself in his former domains or that he would be able to recognize anything here. At that moment, not long ago, when Gorki Village with its cozy little palace and park had begun to fly away rapidly behind him, Ulyanov was convinced that he would be totally blown away, tumbling down into Hell, into Tartarus, though it had seemed to him at first that the hillocks were below him and he was flying upward. Tartarus, Tartarus—that was the one and only word that still remained in his once-rich vocabulary. Soon all this nonsense about upward or downward, leftward or rightward, disappeared, and Tartarus actually stretched out before him. In some part of himself he still sensed that something had been here sometime in the past—coffee and hot rolls, for example—that something was still here somewhere even now, something measured and ecstatic, musical, now inaccessible, but he also understood that in another instant, there would never again be anything anywhere except for Tartarus. Least of all did he think, at that moment, of course, that he deserved his fate, either because of cruelty or treachery, for ideas such as "retribution" had disappeared and even such favorite subjects as "How we can reorganize worker-peasant inspections"—that is, those things that had shone almost to the very end—were swallowed up by the steadily approaching Tartarus. Suddenly something seemed to give a lurch, as though a brake had been applied or a parachute had opened, and Tartarus, implacably transforming all of Ulyanov's being into the essence of torment, suddenly came to a stop and began to fall away into the background. Ulyanov, on his little parachute, began his unhurried descent or ascent, crossing enormous expanses of air in which scraps of worker-peasant inspections flashed by from time to time and, what was more, abandoned notes of that same "inhuman music" by Beethoven that had forced him one day to forget for a moment his revolutionary calling.

In his tree hollow amid the stirrings of other creatures as small and furry as he, he again felt the presence of the air and the moisture suspended in it. He stuck his head out from underneath Mama's belly and was staggered by the smells of the world. Bark, Mama's secretions, a wisp of smoke, decaying bones, leaves, buds, ants, worms, the thick, intoxicating odor of the thawing earth, everything was still unknown, unrecognized, but it was the future that made him suddenly emit a peep of joy and jump up in the manner of a stupendous, long leap with a giggle, fingers nesting in his vest pockets—heh-heh, my goodness!

He grew quickly, and by the mid-thirties some observant nature fanciers in

Silver Forest could distinguish a remarkably large male among the sizable squirrel population. It ought to be pointed out that Ulyanov's appearance gave him an authority among his fellow squirrels. Naturally, he no longer wielded his hypnotic intellectual powers, but on the other hand, by virtue of some unknowable game of nature, this robust he-squirrel had acquired phenomenal capabilities of reproduction. To this, then, he devoted himself. In this he found his calling. From the first glimmer of dawn to the last rays of the setting sun he flew from tree trunk to tree trunk, executing colossal leaps from branch to branch, rushed along the fallen pine needles, down paths, over rooftops and dacha fences in pursuit of his latest fluffy-tailed temptress, who thirsted to be caught, which was why he ran as fast as his paws would carry him. Having caught up with his Jezebel, he would subject her to a magnificent act of copulation.

It was only at night that he permitted himself to rest, to rock back and forth in his sleep on a reliable pine branch, feeling secure and comfortable amid the play of the shadows and moonlight. Sometimes, though more and more rarely, he was afflicted by illuminating visions that seemed to come from nowhere—visions in which more often than not there arose walls with swallow-tailed crenelations—but he chased them off with sweeps of his mighty tail.

It must be said that other Silver Forest males recognized his primacy. They did not, however, gather around, as others had done in his previous life, but rather tried to keep their distance, timidly scavenging on the periphery of his innumerable harem. Displaying a magnanimity known only to the mighty, he paid no attention to the timid, and as for those few who dared issue him even the slightest challenge, he dealt with them immediately and severely— he would watch for his victim, then rush at him and, in the blink of an eye, snuff out his life with a bite to the throat. Visions of the past appeared to him in these triumphs.

After a few years had gone by, though, he became more sedate, having already fertilized several generations of female friends—that is, his daughters, granddaughters, and great-granddaughters. A certain harmony came over him, and he even began to allow himself to let the illuminating visions of his now almost impenetrable past linger a bit and on occasion even asked himself the question: do you suppose there is a certain big walnut hidden behind those battlements?

One day toward dusk, resting after his latest coupling on the top branch of a mighty pine, he looked down and saw a woman sitting on a bench in a pose of sad contemplation. This female of the human species, usually gleaming with all the colors of the spectrum, had attracted his attention before. In earlier times she had not been so quiet—on the contrary, she had spoken loudly, laughed often, quarreled noisily, and played lovers' games, for the most part with the same man. Now she was sad, absorbed in sorrow. Her shadow was enveloped in smoke, and the flowery smell that had always accompanied her had faded a bit. Could he have imagined her like this, sitting alone in a wood? Ulyanov was suddenly struck by an otherworldly thought: with a woman like that I would not permit the schism of the Party, I would not descend to dictatorship . . .

He slipped down the tree, hopped onto the bench, and struck his favorite pose. She sensed his presence, raised her head, and turned toward him.

"My God, how big you are!" Veronika said with a laugh that sounded almost like the old days. "We should show you off to the Young Pioneers, Grandfather Lenin!" She cautiously extended a hand to the illustrious squirrel. Ulyanov did not hop away. He saw above him a soft, small stream pulsating with a melancholy rhythm. It would have been easy to bite through it in a single flashing leap. The hand descended upon his head and went down along his back. "He's not afraid," said Veronika in surprise. "Come along with me, come to our house, I'll give you some nuts."

She walked away down the path. Ulyanov, sitting beneath the pine, shuddered in orgasm. He had spent that night near the house where the woman lived. The house was full of light, shadows could be seen flickering here and there through the chinks in the shutters, and from time to time hers passed as well. Ulyanov had slept blissfully.

That night they had taken her away. Ulyanov, though he could not make sense of what was happening, had a feeling it would be forever. At the last moment, before they put her into the car, he managed to race across the yard and stand in front of Veronika on the crown of one of the gateposts. As she scanned the sky, her glance fell upon him. Her face was twisted with terror. The door of the car slammed. Since then, Ulyanov had thought of her from time to time, for some reason always in conjunction with the indefinite curves of the crenelated walls, as though in that moment of space and time the irretrievable had come together with the robust smell of fresh coffee, comrades.

One day, an exceptionally clear day when the skies were a bottomless shade of blue, Ulyanov the squirrel looked above him and, seeing a black dot at a great height, knew right away that it was the end. Just before it began to dive upon him, he had time to experience one more flicker of revelation and to understand that his short squirrel's life had been given to him only so that he might cool down at least a little after all his previous satanic agitation.

VOLUME II

——— ☆ ———

War and Jail

The human mind cannot grasp the absolute continuity
of motion.   —Lev Tolstoy, *War and Peace*

PREFACE

Sometimes when a writer prefaces a narrative with an epigraph, he forgets about it entirely after one or two pages. In such cases the quotation hung above the entrance to the novel ceases to cast a light on what lies within but serves as a sort of brass plaque or token attesting to the intellectual accomplishment of the writer, of his membership in the club of thinking people. At the end of the day it ceases to exercise even this function, and if the reader upon completion of the book takes the time to glance back at the beginning, he perceives the epigraph as a ludicrous makeweight, a hood ornament from a Jaguar welded onto a decrepit Moskvich. In expressing these ruminations, we understand that we are placing ourselves in the line of fire of a critic from a hostile literary group. This mudslinger will seize upon our elegant Tolstoyan epigraph and say with a grin—there you have it, he'll say, that's just it: a "Jaguar" on an old Soviet jalopy! Being able to foresee such an episode in a literary struggle, we must refute this argument straightaway, declaring on the spot and without false modesty that we have had cause over many years of belletristic experience to take pride in the harmonious connection between our epigraphs and the texts that follow.

In the first place, we never abuse the practice of using epigraphs, and in the second place, we never employ them as ornaments. If at any time we do resort to vague pieces of folk wisdom, then it is for the sole purpose of increasing the power of artistic obscurity. So, that's that, and that epigraph of ours which we left just back there, that very one—well, those engraved words of Lev Nikolaevich himself, that idea about the incomprehensibility of "the absolute continuity of motion," were taken by us not only because we wish to join the flock of the intellectual bigwigs (to make perfectly clear that we are not up to any tricks), but, most important, in order to begin our journey through the Second World War. This epigraph will be something similar to one of the peasant stoves at Yasnaya Polyana, which will serve as our intellectual points of departure, developing, and at times impertinently contradicting, the great dead-end thoughts of the national genius. We will go further, then, in the direction of the war, in which among the suffering millions we will discover the faces of Professor Gradov's beloved family. Their contribution to the thunderous collapse of time was not at all insignificant if one considers the point of view of Tolstoy, who said that "the sum of human acts of will created the revolution and Napoleon, and it was only the sum of these acts of will that sustained and destroyed them."

Consequently, the old doctor B. N. Gradov, his wife, Mary, who so loved Chopin and Brahms, their domestic, Agasha, and even District Constable Slabopetukhovsky in the gigantic pandemonium of human arbitrariness exercised no less an influence on the course of history than did de Gaulle, Churchill, Roosevelt, Hitler, Stalin, Hirohito, or Mussolini. Not long ago, we were reading *War and Peace*—for the first time since childhood, we must admit, and not at all in connection with the beginning of *War and Jail* but for pure reading pleasure—and came upon a number of Tolstoy's thoughts on the riddles of history, which sometimes touch us joyfully by their similarities with our own thoughts but which at other times lead into a blind alley.

In denying the role of great men at historical turning points, Lev Nikolaevich adduces several examples from practical experience. For example, he says, as the hand of the clock approaches ten, the bells begin to ring in the local church, calling everyone to prayer. This does not mean, however, that "the position of the clock hand is the reason for the movement of the bells." How can it not mean that, queries in surprise the modern mind raised on anecdotes. Why, isn't it just the other way around? After all, it isn't the bells that move the clock hands. The ringer takes hold of the bell rope only after having looked at the clock. Tolstoy, however, had something else in mind in proposing this example.

Hearing the whistle and seeing the movement of steam engine wheels, Tolstoy denies himself the right to conclude "that the whistle and the movement of the wheels are the basic reason for the movement of the boat." The whistle, it goes without saying, does not enter into the list of reasons, but permit us to have our doubts regarding the paddles—after all, it is precisely these paddles that occasion the movement of everything piled up on them, by going either forward or backward. Here again we are left with no choice but to suppose Tolstoy had something else in mind for the illustration of historical processes.

The last example, advanced in the third part of the third volume of *War and*

Peace, throws everything into confusion, unless one shifts the blame onto the Pravda publishing house, which issued a twelve-volume set of Tolstoy's collected works in 1984. Peasants think, Tolstoy writes, that strong winds blow in the late spring because the buds on the oak tree have opened. We quote, adding ambiguity to our epigraph, "though the reason for the blowing of strong winds during the time of the opening of the oak buds is unknown to me, I cannot agree with the peasants that the unfolding of the oak tree is the reason for these winds, precisely because the force of the wind is beyond the influence of buds."

Here, the question of what would happen if events were reversed fairly begs to be asked, that is, if the buds opened because of the influence of the cold wind. Tolstoy, however, does not deal with this, and we suppose that that which is on the surface is not what he has in mind at all, that his thoughts and deepest religious feelings dissociate themselves entirely from the positivist theories of the nineteenth century and move off into the sphere of metaphysics. In other words, his thought throws wide the door leading to the unfathomable depths of the unnameable and unknowable, where before our eyes stand all these staggering things that exist as self-contained entities.

Alas, a few lines on down the page, the count suddenly renews his ties with his age of "great scientific discoveries" in order to state, "I must change my vantage point entirely and study the laws of motion of the steam, the bell, and the wind. History must do the same. Such attempts have already been made."

On the whole, Tolstoy, as a result of these abstract and unanswered (in his view, only for the time being!) questions, arrives at the conclusion that "for the study of the laws of history we have to change completely the object of our observation, leave czars, ministers, and generals in peace, and study the uniform, infinitely small elements that motivate the masses."

This is nearly Marxism. It is obviously this thirst for knowledge that Lenin had in mind when he conferred upon the count the title of "mirror of the Russian Revolution." The leader, however, should have known that things were not always so simple with Tolstoy, that he was not only occupied with the reflection of the "sum of human acts of will" but added his own not insignificant will to this sum, and above all supposed that the movement of these endless wills was directed from Above, that is, not by economists' or anthropologists' theories, but by providence.

Nonetheless, it sometimes happens that certain theoreticians and practical people come to stand out from the sum of these acts of will and send millions to their deaths and billions into slavery. Consequently, there are acts of will, and then there are acts of will, and despite our desire to do so it is difficult for us to adhere to the image of the swarm, however impressive it may be, and to deny the role of the individual in history.

All of these reflections on Tolstoy's themes, which would seem to provide full justification for our epigraph, were needed in order to approach the beginning of the forties and to peer through the magic crystal into the next expanse of that same "free novel" of world history, of which there is only one, and of which we would like to see our narrative as being a part, and there to survey that grandiose spectacle of "human acts of will" known in history as the Second World War.

CHAPTER ONE

Listen—the Thump of Boots

☆

A column of new recruits, several hundred Moscow youngsters, was moving in a disorganized mass down Metrostroevsky Street, formerly Ostozhenka, by night toward the Khamovnichesky barracks. Despite an order of "No smoking in the ranks," tiny glows could be seen here and there in the dark human mass, illuminating lips, palms, and the tips of noses. This was not the first time that these young men, who had been schoolboys the day before, had smoked on the sly, "into their fists." In fact, they were marching directly from a school in the Sivtsev Vrazhek district that had served as their assembly point—in other words, they were coming directly from their habitual environment. Civilian boots shuffled along, one occasionally even glimpsed fashionable white shoes that the day before had been rubbed with toothpaste, and cloth sneakers flew by noiselessly.

Though it had not been announced where they were marching, everyone already knew: to the Khamovnichesky barracks for disinfection, medical examination, and distribution of gear. Moscow was deserted, the street lights were darkened, windows were tightly shuttered closed for the obligatory blackout, but the sky was lit up. There was a full moon, but it was the searchlights, cutting across the starry firmament in different directions, now crossing, now forming giant chevrons, that were the main source of illumination. Only sausage-shaped aerostats from the Air Defense Corps were seen in the lights, yet everyone knew that at any moment something else might appear. Muffled rumors were going around the city that German reconnaissance planes had circled over the capital more than once.

In the midst of the formation, nineteen-year-old Mitya Gradov-Sapunov was marching with his peers. Over the years he had become a fairly tall lad with broad shoulders, a strongly developed torso, longish arms and shortish legs, a good forelock, a jut-jawed, high-cheekboned face, strong and mysteriously shining eyes; on the whole, a magnificent specimen. He had finished school just three days before the start of the war and had been preparing to matriculate at the medical institute (on the advice and under the protection of Grandfather Boris, naturally), but things had turned out differently: barely six weeks had passed after school completion before he was called up.

Someone in the ranks had already begun singing: "Let noble fury soar up like a wave! This is a people's war, a holy war!" This song had begun coming out of loudspeakers quite recently and had immediately become part of common usage. Something in it stretched out mightily, not allowing any doubt. Even to Mitya, who had always felt himself an outsider in Soviet society, the heavy march rhythm and nightmarish lyrics ("The sightless Fascist scum will get a bullet in its brain / For the mongrels of humanity let's dig a mighty grave") filled him with a powerful, though not very clearly directed, rage. Then again, it was not the song that disturbed him, here in the ranks, in the night, on his first wartime march, but the presence in that night of Cecilia Rosenbloom. A knot of mothers was seeing the column off, and Cecilia was tripping along with them. Who had asked her to come, who needed her mushy affection? The mother in her, you see, had been awakened! "What tactlessness!" thought Mitya with words that were strange to him, that he had borrowed, naturally, from the lexicon of his grandfather Boris. In all these years, the adopted son had never once called Cecilia Rosenbloom "Mother." He not only gladly called her father, Naum Matveevich, "Grandfather," he considered him almost his natural grandfather, just like "Grandpa Boris." His adoptive father, Kirill Borisovich, who had disappeared into the Kolyma tundra long ago, he still remembered as his father, perhaps as even more than a father, since his memories of his real father, Fyodor Sapunov, a cruel and uncivilized peasant, had not entirely disappeared. He often remembered as one of the most treasured moments of his youth an occasion when Kirill, about a year before his arrest, had sat down next to Mitya's bed, thinking he was asleep, and had looked at him with gentle love. Pretending to be asleep, he had looked at the face of his "father" through his eyelashes as though through the branches of a pine and thought: what a face my father has, what compassionate eyes! And now, whenever he thought about Kirill, he always called him his father: how is my father out there, have the fiends killed my father yet? He could not remember clearly whether he had ever called him "Father" aloud or if he had maintained his original "Uncle Kirill" right up until the end. He told himself over and over, though, that he had said it, and on more than one occasion, and in the end convinced himself that he had called the man who had saved him from exile in Kazakhstan, where three quarters of the people of his village had died, not "Uncle" but "Father." As for his father's wife, who was, after all, also his rescuer, he could not even in his most faraway thoughts call her "Mother." She seemed to be a good-natured aunt, sometimes even extremely kind, but she was not cut out to be a mother. This muddled, absent-minded woman, who always dressed utterly absurdly and was not always ideally clean (he sometimes noticed that in the mornings when, in her ceaseless muttering, cursing, and looking for cigarettes and books, she would forget to bathe), this learned Marxist woman with the not entirely agreeable odor, whose only pedagogical method was slapping him and grabbing him by the ear, could not take the place of Mitya's emaciated mother in Gorelovo. Mitya did not have a clear recollection of these annoying, painful pinches; he remembered something else instead: sometimes his real mama would also grab him by the ear in order to punish him, to hurt him, but sometimes she would suddenly cover his ear with her entire hand and caress it as if it were a small bird. That was what remained of her, of his mother consumed in the fire.

Mitya's draft notice had been delivered, of course, not to Silver Forest, where he lived nearly all the time, but to Cecilia's apartment, his official address. Therefore his assembly point turned out to be not on the outskirts of the city but right in the center, on the Ring Road. They kept them in the school for almost twenty-four hours, and a field kitchen was sent there from the Khamovnichesky barracks. Every time he had looked out the window, beyond the iron railing surrounding the school, he had seen Cecilia in the throng of mothers. Oh, my God, so now the mother in her has awakened! Now she was walking quickly to keep up with the column, occasionally breaking into a trot. Her skirt nearly trailed along on the ground behind her, while in front it was lifted up at an angle, revealing her left knee in a thick, wrinkled stocking. He was suddenly reminded of something quite shameful—Cecilia's tits, how Kirill had grabbed them, how he had caressed them during their first tryst in that barn. Mitya had always tried to forget that scene, which he, a peasant boy exhausted by hunger, had secretly watched through the spaces between some rotting barrels. He thought he had forgotten it, but now it came back to him. It was hard to imagine that that red-haired girl with the white freckled body and this old Jewess were one and the same person. Well, how can she be such a frightful old Jew, such a . . . you can say it, such an appalling old Jew, Mitya thought, and he shuddered in revulsion: not at "Aunt Celia," but at himself. For the first time the thought crossed his mind that he, perhaps, did not call her "Mother" because she was too Jewish, that maybe he was ashamed of her. In the Gradov house, there was nothing more hateful than anti-Semitism, and Mitya had been brought up in that spirit, and yet it seemed that some sort of flue had suddenly opened a crack somewhere in the depths of his being, and he realized that at that moment he was terribly ashamed of Cecilia, ashamed before the recruits who were his new comrades lest they think she was his mother.

The column was already crossing Sadovoe Koltso when Cecilia, noticing that the accompanying sergeant had gone on ahead, broke into the ranks with a small bag for her Mitya. "Take this, Mitya—there's a package of strawberry cookies, a pound of Belka chocolate, which you always loved, a half-dozen eggs, and a tin of cod liver oil—now, see that you drink it!" The cod liver oil had begun to leak out of its container, and probably some time ago, since yellow stains were spreading along the bag, giving off a stench.

Mitya pushed the sack away with his elbow. "I don't need it. I tell you, I don't need it, Aunt Celia!"

It wasn't the smell he feared, of course, but rather the idea of being involved with a Jewish woman, who on top of everything was thrusting a stinking sack in his direction, as though it were done on purpose in order to make a funnier anecdote. What the hell is this, she put cod liver oil in it, too? She must have remembered that children are supposed to be given cod liver oil. . . . Oh, what a swine I am, he thought crossly.

"If they ship you out right away, Mitenka, write immediately. As soon as you arrive, write, otherwise we'll all go out of our heads with worry," muttered Cecilia, bringing her face closer to his. Her upper lip with its mole beneath her left nostril was protruding noticeably as though she wanted to kiss him.

The lads around him looked on, snickering. Mitya broke into an embarrassed sweat. "Okay, okay, Aunt Celia. I'll write, Aunt Celia. Go home, Aunt Celia!"

She interrupted his mumbling with an almost desperate cry: "What do you mean calling me 'Aunt Celia'! Why, I'm your mama, Mitenka!"

The sergeant, having returned to the middle of the column, suddenly saw an outsider in the ranks. He grabbed Cecilia by the sleeve. "What's your problem, citizen, are you crazy? Breaking into a military formation? Do you want to be arrested?" The sleeve of her rayon sweater stretched further than it was designed to, forming a shape like a bat's wing. Cecilia stumbled. The package dropped from her hands, and books began falling out of her straw bag. The column left her behind, and in the ranks furthest to the rear a few laughed. "Look at the Jewess crawling around after her books!"

Goshka Krutkin, thin and gaunt, a construction worker from the Palace of

Soviets project, was marching alongside Mitya. He nudged him with an elbow and asked rather indifferently, "So, Mit, your people are actually Jews, eh?"

Mitya exploded. "I'm a Russian! A one hundred percent Russian! Can't you see, or what? I have nothing to do with those . . . with those . . . Nothing! And that . . . that . . . well, she's just a neighbor!"

They were already passing beneath the archway of a long yellow barracks building when sirens suddenly began to wail and an antiaircraft gun thudded to life right next to them. From the windows of the barracks the new recruits saw the glow of fires over the rooftops of the outlying districts of the city. That night, Moscow was bombed for the first time.

The alarm continued for several hours. Dawn glowed on the horizon, but the sirens were still howling, antiaircraft guns were firing here and there, though by now into an empty sky. A fire in Shabolovka was finally put out. Clearly the Germans had been aiming for the radio tower but had not hit it, succeeding only in setting fire to a few residential buildings.

That morning the streetcars began running two hours later than usual. They were stormed by such huge crowds that Cecilia could not summon up the courage even to approach them, and so she set off for Lefortovo on foot. When she got there, though, it turned out that the line to send parcels that day was not to be believed. Someone passed her a stub of an indelible pencil, and she, following the example of the woman standing in front of her, wet it with saliva and wrote her five-digit number on the back of her hand. The number meant she would have to stand there all day, until dark, and maybe even then she would go away unsuccessful in her mission. "You have to count on being here all day, citizen," her neighbor said to her. Prepared for this eventuality, the woman had brought her knitting along. The public knew that in the NKVD's Lefortovo prison there were only three windows for the sending of food parcels and that sometimes only two of the three were in service—or one—and that all of them closed for two hours at lunchtime.

Cecilia had a great deal of experience at waiting in prison lines. Usually, she brought a book with her—*Questions of Leninism* by I. Stalin or some other fundamental work—and made notes in the margins and wrote down quotes, which greatly helped her in lecturing. Books, her age-old friends, reliable Marxist books, also helped her to struggle against the miserable panic she always felt when standing in these lines. The problem was that her packages addressed to Kirill were not always accepted. In his case, there had obviously been some sort of snafu, some kind of bureaucratic mistake. Sometimes, after a whole day of standing, they would throw her parcel back at her from the little window, saying that Gradov, Kirill Borisovich, was not on the list of names of those authorized to receive packages. This might mean the most terrible thing of all. . . . No, no, anything but that, not the most terrible thing. Almost anything less horrible might have happened—he might have been, let's say, temporarily deprived of the right to receive parcels for some misdeed out there, on the inside. Given his attachment to principle and his stubbornness, frankly speaking, he could have angered some comrades in the administration, couldn't he? After all, sometimes they accepted her packages without any discussion, only having her sign some official register, and that was all. Obviously this meant he was on the list of people authorized to receive food parcels. Wasn't that logical?

The line leading to the small windows wound outside the prison into the side streets around Lefortovo, where there was neither a war nor, for that matter, any twentieth century at all. Small fences, dovecotes over narrow roofs, mignonette in the windows, mushroom extract, alley cats, a kerosene shop on the corner, reminiscent of desolate times, like the stagnant years of Alexander III's reign. It was only when one came quite near that one could see a modern structure arising, an endless, faceless concrete wall to which newspapers or propaganda posters were sometimes affixed.

The infrequent passers-by, the inhabitants of the adjoining quiet streets, tried to walk past as if they did not notice the ever-present, softly murmuring line of relatives of the "enemies of the people." Perhaps some of those passers-by were themselves related to "enemies of the people" and stood somewhere else in similar lines. Here, however, none of them showed any sympathy for the tired "senders," all the more so since here and there in secluded corners of the side streets one could see women squatting or men with their heads lowered in concentration, thereby disrupting the idyll of the Lefortovo streets and courtyards.

Books helped Cecilia not only to kill time in the lines but also to wall herself off from those around her, that is, to avoid equating herself with them. After all, who knew what kind of people surrounded her? Surely our bodies of law and order couldn't have made so many mistakes, the same kind they had in Kirill's case—could they? Could it really be that all these women found themselves the wives, sisters, mothers of condemned political criminals by a mere twist of fate? Might they not be undiscovered accomplices? There was no way to be sure.

She had to shield herself from the conversation around her as well, conversations that were carried on quite irresponsibly, sometimes bordering on sheer provocation. This was the hardest thing of all for Cecilia. Even though she herself took no part in these discussions, she could not help overhearing them, because time and again something would slip into them that had to do with Kirill. Right now, for example, two women behind her were whispering about sentencing "with no right to correspond." "My husband was sentenced to ten years without the right of correspondence, but I'm still hoping . . . ," muttered a weeping voice that seemed to be begging for consolation. "Forget your hopes, my dear," answered another voice, which, even though muffled, sounded a note of challenge. "Better look for another husband. Do you mean you don't understand what this 'no right to correspond' means? They've been shot, all of them!"

Through suppressed sobs, the first woman said in barely audible tones, "But they sometimes accept my packages . . . sometimes they accept them . . ."

"Stop it, why do you insist on fooling yourself?" said the second woman, parrying the argument mercilessly.

Cecilia's temper flared, and, unable to control herself, she turned around. Two women were leaning against a lamppost, one of them young, thin, and crying soundlessly, the other round-faced and middle-aged with closely cropped hair under a beret and a cigarette in her mouth. Cecilia, forgetting her own rules, flew at her like a whirlwind.

"What's this rubbish you're talking? What kind of crap are you thinking up? Who's supplying you with this stinking information? If someone is sentenced with no right to correspond, that only means that he's not allowed to write and get letters, nothing more! But you, citizen, don't listen to anyone! If they take your parcels, that means your husband is alive!"

The young woman stopped crying, nodding to Cecilia rapidly in fear, as if saying, "Yes, yes, he's alive, only please don't raise your voice!" The round-faced lady bit down on her cigarette defiantly and looked away in silence; one could sense an enemy in her.

Several women approached, exchanging understanding glances. One kind old woman took Cecilia by the arm. "Don't grieve yourself, my darling—if he's alive, then he's alive, it's all God's will." She turned to those around them, who were looking at the learned Jewish woman who had become so excited, and explained, "They're not accepting her parcels, that's the problem."

Cecilia withdrew her arm from the woman, more indignant than ever: that means the habitues of these lines have already noticed her, that means they already know . . . Oh, what shame, to be in the same class as these women who virtually live here—what a disgrace!

"If they don't notify you that a relative has died, that means he's alive!" she cried out, still trying to maintain her aplomb. "There are laws, there is order, and you shouldn't spread harmful gossip!"

.   .   .

Several hours later, having made her way through the twists and turns of the side streets, she emerged into the shadow of a kilometer-long stone wall, at the very beginning of which was a poster showing a huge fist raised over a horned Fascist helmet. Large black letters brought the confident Stalinist utterance to the people: "Our cause is just, the foe will be smashed, victory will be ours!"

You could always feel so much strength in his words, thought Cecilia, so much weight! What a happy day it would be if Kirill's case could come before him—he would wipe out Kirill's shameful sentence, and my love and I would go together to the front, where our Mitenka is already fighting, to defend the Motherland and socialism!

A megaphone attached to a loudspeaker above the wall was singing as it had in peacetime: "The morning with its gentle light bathes the Kremlin walls / All of the Soviet lands awaken to its call!" It was not dawn they were dealing with now, though, but dusk. It was quite dark beyond the wall, and the women were growing weary. Pangs of hunger gnawed at Cecilia: as usual, she had forgotten to bring anything to eat with her, and as usual some kind person turned up to offer her something, a piece of bread or a biscuit. This time it was that same unwholesome round-faced woman in the beret. Unwrapping a strawberry-filled cookie, always one of Cecilia's favorites, she extended it to her on her open palm.

Cecilia took three pieces of the wonderful, crumbly product one after another and looked at the woman with awkward gratitude. "Excuse me, maybe I was a bit overexcited, but—"

The woman dismissed the apology with a wave.

"Oh, I understand, we're all a bundle of nerves here. . . . Take another cookie. Do you want a smoke?"

Cecilia suddenly realized that she knew this person, that she might even belong to her own social class. "Pardon me, but is your . . . your husband here?"

"Well, of course. I'm Rumyantsev—you know me, Celia."

Cecilia gasped in surprise. And indeed it was: Nadia Rumyantsev from the disbanded Institute of Red Professorship! Her husband was an eminent theoretician—what was his name? Rumyantsev, Pyotr . . . Vasilievich, it seemed. He had been known in discussion groups as "Thunder and Lightning Pyotr"! As she chewed the remains of the cookie, Cecilia caught herself in at least three mistakes: first of all, she had come into contact with the line, even though she had sworn never to do so; in the second place, she thought of Pyotr Rumyantsev not as an enemy of the people but simply as a decent Marxist-Leninist theoretician; and in the third place, she thought of him only distantly, and in the past tense, as though a man who entered these gates no longer fully existed, which meant that Kirill, her beloved, her only light in the world, her "boy," as she always thought of him, did not fully exist anymore either, unless . . .

She reached the window just before closing time. A female officer in a military blouse bearing the insignia of a lieutenant was sitting there. "Last name! First name! Patronymic! Article of the Penal Code! Sentence!" she barked in an automatic tone. "Gradov, Kirill Borisovich, Articles 58-8 and 11, ten years," muttered the trembling Cecilia, pushing a small bundle across the window.

"Speak up!" shouted the police agent.

In a louder voice she repeated the cherished name with its revolting appendage, the article of the penal code pertaining to counterrevolutionary activity. The agent slammed down the window: that was the way it was done, so that no one would see the procedure for checking names. The seconds ticked by agonizingly. Less than a minute later, the window opened again, and the bundle was pushed back.

"Your parcel cannot be accepted!"

"How can that be?" shrieked Cecilia. Her white skin flushed, and her freckles imparted an additional, crackling fire to the blaze. "Why? What's happened to my husband? I beg you, comrade!"

"I have no information about him. Make inquiries with the competent authorities. Don't linger, citizen! Next!" the woman shouted with routine impassivity.

Cecilia lost her head completely, continuing to shout something entirely inappropriate to the circumstances. "How can that be? My husband isn't guilty of anything at all! He'll be freed soon! He'll go to the front! I protest! Soulless formalism!"

"Go on, citizen! Don't hold up others!" a young woman behind said in a sharp, angry voice. It was the same woman who that morning had been sobbing about "no right of correspondence." The women in the line were making noises now, pressing forward. By now Cecilia had lost control of herself, grabbing the counter in front of the window and trying to hold on, screaming, "He's alive! Alive! No matter what, he's alive! A curse on you all!"

One of the two potbellied sergeants standing on duty at the doors outside came in at the sound of the disturbance. He grabbed the clamoring Jewish woman by the shoulders, yanked her back, and dragged her away from the window.

It was already quite dark when Nadezhda Rumyantsev left the prison receiving room, still carrying the food parcel for her husband.

Silently cursing the "Communist swine" (only yesterday she had been a member of the Komsomol, and now that she had become a victim of the regime, she did not even notice how quickly she had sunk to using the words of the White Guards), she was trudging toward a streetcar stop when she suddenly saw Cecilia Rosenbloom sitting on a bench in a little square in a state of collapse. On her knees were sheets of paper covered with smudged ink—the only letter she had received from Kirill in all the time since his arrest.

Nadia sat down alongside her. For some reason she sympathized with this "rabid Marxist" (again she had dredged up an anti-Soviet expression—from where she didn't know), though she had been offended that the woman had never looked her in the eye at their previous meetings in the Lefortovo line.

"You're lucky, still," she sighed. "At least you're getting letters."

Cecilia shuddered, looked at Nadia, then suddenly put her head on the shoulder of this woman whom she hardly knew. "It's from thirty-nine," she murmured. "The only letter. Just some ordinary phrases."

"You're lucky, still," Nadia repeated, though she was dissembling: she had received three letters from "her man" in three years. Surprising even herself, she began to stroke Cecilia's hair. Why was she acting with such childish tenderness? The two women embraced each other and burst into tears.

"Why won't they accept packages sometimes, Nadia?" Cecilia asked after a time.

By force of habit, Rumyantsev looked around—in those days, any Soviet citizen looked around before uttering a more or less energetic sentence. "Oh, Celia, maybe they just don't know where these people are. I wouldn't be surprised if things are just as fouled up in their business as they are everywhere else."

They rose from the bench and plodded heavily toward the streetcar stop like two old ladies, even though they were still young, perfectly healthy women. Quite apart from everything else, the system had completely destroyed their sex lives.

"They'll have to reexamine their relationship with the people," said Nadia. "The war will change everything."

"Maybe you're right," Cecilia replied. "And the first thing we'll have to reexamine is our relationship to Party cadres."

They were speaking in a quite friendly manner and did not notice that one of them said "they" while the other said "we."

"And the ones with 'no right of correspondence' have all been shot."

"Is that really true?" whispered Cecilia in a barely audible voice. Then she began to speak a bit louder. "Pardon my outburst, Nadia. My nerves were on edge. Kirill, however, did not have that formulation added to his sentence, and there is, after all . . . this letter . . ."

"Yes, yes, everything will be fine, Celia," said her new friend encouragingly.

They turned a corner, and from a low open window immediately over their heads a radio announced, "From the Soviet Information Bureau: fierce fighting is going on in the Smolensk sector. The enemy's losses in men and materiel are growing—"

"Do you hear that?" Cecilia exclaimed in a panic. "The Smolensk sector! They're getting closer! What's going to become of us?" The Moscow sky with its new aerostats and searchlight beams contrasted wildly with Lefortovo and its atmosphere of a provincial settlement, while the old Kukui neighborhood, which in the seventeenth century had been a German ghetto, shuddered in horror as it awaited the arrival of its tribesmen.

CHAPTER TWO

Fireworks by Night

*

In the ten or more years that have passed since our first visit to the Byelorussaia Station, it has changed fundamentally. Not, of course, in the sense that its pseudo-Russo-Prussian architecture has gone anywhere or that its sooty glass roof—a covering that makes it part of the family of great European stations—has disappeared but rather in the sense that instead of the peaceful, though basically militarized atmosphere of 1930 in which we contrived to entwine the flourish of a romantic intrigue into our story, we find ourselves now in August 1941, at one of the war's transfer points, a base for shipping soldiers to the front and evacuating civilians from the burning western regions.

At the very moment when the surviving Gradovs had gathered for the send-off of everyone's favorite—Savva—a train from Smolensk began pulling in on one of the long-distance tracks. Several of the train cars looked more like the burned-out skeletons of cars. There could be no doubt about it, the train full of refugees had been attacked by German bombers along the way. The windows of the surviving cars, filled with the pallid faces of refugees and wounded soldiers, drifted slowly along the platform like an ancient art show, while people still stirred in the charred cars, on the floors amid the ruins, creating a positively eerie impression.

The platforms and waiting rooms of the terminal were filled with a ceaseless movement that resembled boiling porridge, as though a cook were stirring the human swill with an unseen ladle: some people were pushing others with their bags, collapsing onto the tiled floors together with the contents of their sacks, leaping to their feet and rushing around, making their way through the seething mass, urinating in corners because there was not enough room in the toilets for everyone who wanted to use them. Military patrols brandished rifle butts, clearing a path for themselves. There was a hubbub of howling women, sobs, shrieking children, incomprehensible orders over the loud-speakers . . .

The Gradovs felt bewildered after the quiet and absence of people in Silver Forest. Only Nina seemed to take no notice of it all, cheerfully poking fun at her husband, who was attired in a baggy uniform with fresh major's stripes.

"Look at Savva!" she sang out. "Well, what do you think? See how he wears his first-class uniform like a carefree dandy! I never suspected I would marry a man in the cavalry guards!"

Major Kitaigorodsky of the Medical Corps tried to play along with his wife's joyful mood. He threw out his chest, combed an imaginary mustache, and walked along beside the train with the long, springy gait of a guardsman, jingling his make-believe spurs. Seven-year-old Elena unself-consciously laughed aloud at her papa, ever the comedian. The others maintained a baffled silence.

Nina, a very lively thirty-four-year-old—from a distance of only a few feet she still looked like an adolescent girl—danced around her husband, tugging at his short military shirt. "You know, there's still something missing, we haven't thought of everything. No shoulder braids, for example!"

"A rusty kopeck we won't trade / For your goddamned shoulder braid!" Savva sang the line from a popular song in a bass voice. He was clearly sick at heart, but he could tell from Nina's antics that she was feeling even worse, and he continued to play along. He took her by the arm and whispered hotly in her ear, "You're mistaken, my dear, taking a hussar for a guardsman, a battle steed for a cart horse!"

In the end everyone laughed. Even Mary Vakhtangovna, on whose face an expression of frozen tragedy had begun to appear more and more often, smiled: how can they clown around like this when they're on the eve of parting? she wondered. No, I don't understand them, but maybe it's easier that way?

She had not yet recovered from Mitya's departure when Savva called and told her he was leaving for the front: he had been assigned as chief surgeon to a divisional field hospital. Even the head of the family, even Boris, despite his age—he had just turned sixty-six—was now immediately connected to the war, having been promoted again, as in the twenties, this time to the upper echelons of the Armed Forces Medical Corps with the rank of major general. He was constantly at conferences or on the road inspecting medical facilities at the front. Mary hardly ever saw him anymore; indeed, hardly anyone ever saw him. Today, for example, he had promised to come to the station to say good-bye to Savva, yet he still hadn't arrived and the train was going to pull out at any moment.

The train could indeed leave anytime, yet it looked as though it might also depart in several hours, or perhaps even not at all. Savva's entire family was there—his mother and stepfather, those miraculously surviving remnants of the past, philologists from the Silver Age (if one could say that the fragments of a vessel smashed to smithereens had survived), Mary, and Agasha, the unsinkable dreadnought of the Gradov family haven. Boris IV, a manly adolescent, looked at him with the clear eyes of his family, inherited from his father and grandfather, expressing with his powerful, lithe figure a mighty, youthful desire to go away with him, all the while holding his younger sister, Verulya, by the hand. In the girl's eyes the soft night of the Transcaucasus seemed to have found a resting place, and the two of them formed a most touching pair—"orphans" of parents hauled off to the camps. And, of course, there was his perfectly impossible sister-in-law Cecilia Rosenbloom, who would have been well cast in the role of "the comical old woman," despite the fact that she was thirty-seven, and also her oh-so-positive father, Naum. Lord, how Savva loved them all, and how much he feared for them! Savva urged them to leave the station, but they stubbornly refused to go, resisting the waves of the crowd and milling about on the platform.

Everyone was quite exhausted, and no one knew any longer what to talk about or how to express his feelings to the man who was leaving. Only Nina continued to pester Savva, now leading him off to one side, where they whispered and laughed together, now coming back to their family and continuing to make fun of the "cavalry guardsman." The further she went on, the more threads of desperation began to weave themselves into her jokes.

"Well, go on, go on home already!" Savva called out. "I'm tired, I'm going to get in the car and lie down. The viewing of the body is over!" No one, however, went away. What was more, Mary Vakhtangovna declared that Boris was going to arrive at any minute.

The head of the family appeared, very animated, in an overcoat with a general's insignia on the lapels and accompanied by an adjutant. He walked with a confident, vigorous stride, and the crowd parted at the sight of the authoritative figure of a general in the medical service. Mary Vakhtangovna did not immediately recognize her husband: Boris Nikitovich had changed radically since the beginning of the war. The sadly withering, philosophically inclined professor had disappeared, and an energetic leader of the defense of the country, always in an elated mood and with fire in his eyes, had appeared in his place.

"Well, where's our major?" demanded Gradov.

"I wish you health, Your Excellency!" Savva barked, snapping to attention. They embraced, then stepped apart a few paces and looked at each other warmly.

"Off to great things at a trot!" exulted Nina.

Suddenly, several heavyset soldiers came running along the train, and a conductor with a strangely contorted face jumped out. "We're leaving in five minutes!"

Without a word Nina rushed to her husband and threw her arms about his neck, pressing her whole body against him as though she were demanding that they make love immediately. Everyone half turned away in embarrassment. The moment of parting was at hand.

The stern young man Boris IV, meanwhile, was vexed: he had not had time to ask Savva several important questions. Would the new units be able to stop Army Group Center? Why aren't our parachutists and airborne units doing anything? Is it true that the T-34 tank has no equal in the world, and when, in Savva's opinion, would it be deployed in the theaters of operations? And, most important of all, why are we retreating so quickly, surrendering city after city? Perhaps they were implementing a strategy along the lines of Kutuzov's in 1812—luring the invader deep into the country, extending his lines of communication, so as then to strike a massive blow at his flank? His father could have answered these questions better than anyone else, but he was not there, he was "growing a hunger belly," as the kids from the streetcar turnaround would say, in the camps instead of fighting the war. Uncle Savva, though, was a serious person, and more than once he had discussed questions of world military strategy with him, but just now Ninka—Borya, following family tradition, called his aunt by a diminutive—would not let anyone even get near him.

All of a sudden, without any further warning, without a bell or a whistle, the train moved off. In a panic, Savva pulled free from his wife and raced toward the car to grab the railing. He jumped, caught it, and hung there with his legs dangling, then took hold of someone's leg and pulled himself up. Fortunately, some of the officers moved into the car, and Savva hastened to take up a position on the running board in order to be able to look back at least one last time to see everyone, the faces of those dear to him and that of his beloved; he had a strong feeling that just at that moment he was rolling away into another world—another instant, and an iron trapdoor would slam down over his youth. . . . As he turned around, the train was already reaching the end of the station platform, and someone was running alongside, arms waving. He felt someone's warm, alcoholic breath on his cheek. Suddenly he caught sight of a youth with burning eyes—why, it's Borya! And who's that he's dragging by the hand? Yes, it's her . . . how grateful I am to you for everything . . . her hair falling over her

eyes . . . I'll remember every moment with you to the end, everything, beginning with the little ice-covered puddles at Silver Forest, the first touch of
your cold hand . . . she's still running, can't see her eyes, her bitter mouth,
the dot of her face disappears, then appears again for a moment behind some
other heads, sweet mouth in a bitter grimace, good-bye!

"Come on, Major, come into the compartment," said a captain of artillery.
"We've got six bottles of vodka. We're going to live it up one last time."

Boris Nikitovich and Mary Vakhtangovna threaded their way through the
waiting room to the square, where a car awaited them. The adjutant walked in
front of them, as if he were clearing the way for them. Agasha brought up the
rear, leading Boris IV and Verulya by the hand. The boy, whispering curses,
tried to free himself, but the nanny was implacable, though she tried to make it
appear that it was not she who was leading him, but rather he her, an old
weakling, with a little girl on her hands as well, and that he was the chief of the
little group—the man. In the end Borya resigned himself and turned his
attention to the gypsy band around them. Most of the older people here were
chewing furiously, as though afraid that somewhere in the indefinite "out
there" they would no longer have the opportunity to chew. A woman from
Smolensk with a regional accent was recounting some horror, her eyes
growing wide, her cheeks quivering. "They dived right straight at us howling,
couldn't move your arms and legs—Lord Jesus, I'll never forget those bullets
ripping into the roof, there was smoke and fire, and everything was going up like
a candle . . ." Borya guessed that she was talking about a Stuka dive-bomber
attack. Not far away, someone had contrived to set up a samovar on the floor,
and there tranquillity reigned. Two girls of Borya's age cranked up a phonograph. A song began to play: "Come on, Andrusha, are we going to live in grief?
Play, accordion, play full blast! Look how the stars are twinkling, hear the rustle
of the gardens green!" Borya frowned: the ditty, saccharine yet somehow
strangely rousing, came flying out of the past, from supposed "peacetime," from
the pastoral days of the NKVD, when no one resisted the bastards and everyone
was submissive to them. You know what you can do with that kind of
peacetime! The war had flung open the door to a huge new world before the
boy's eyes, a world in which the image of the "bastard" assumed the form of the
German Nazi, with whom one could and must fight, as is fitting for a man!
Borya, naturally, was madly envious of his cousin and closest friend, Mitya,
who had already gone to the front—strangely enough, without much enthusiasm—while he, Borya, still had to go to that school that he was sick and tired
of for who knew how much longer. All the teachers knew he was the son of an
"enemy of the people" and viewed him either with sullen suspicion or, what

was worse, with ill-concealed maudlin sentiment. What Boris feared most of all was that the war would be over too quickly and he would miss his chance.

Boris IV's grandparents were talking to each other quietly as they walked through the station. "Oh, Bo, I've no more strength for these endless farewells, partings, arrests. . . . So many of our loved ones have disappeared from our lives: Nikitushka, Kiryushka, Vikulya, Galaktion, Mitya, and now Savva. . . . Who will it be tomorrow? What will be left of our family?" Boris Nikitovich suddenly kissed his old friend on the cheek and looked at her with a sly expression: "And what would you say, Mary, if for a change I were to propose to you that we organize a meeting instead of a send-off?"

Stunned, Mary Vakhtangovna stopped and put her hands to her face. "What are you talking about, Bo? What is this strange joking tone you've started using lately?"

With the same joyful expression as before, Boris Nikitovich clapped a hand to his mouth, then clenched his fists beneath his chin, as if to hold in the secret. He hunched his shoulders playfully. "I'm not going to tell you, it's too early!"

"What's all this?" cried Mary Vakhtangovna. "Did they tell you something important? Where were you today? At the Central Committee, at the commissariat?"

"No, no, it's not time yet . . ."

"My God, my God . . . ," muttered Mary Vakhtangovna. "Maybe they're going to release Vika, at least? You're right, Bo, don't tell me until it's time . . ."

Afraid even to think about her sons, she would admit only Veronika into her thoughts, and here she caught herself in the realization that if she had mentioned Veronika, then that must mean that she was less afraid to make a mistake where she was concerned, because Veronika was less dear to her then her own flesh and blood, that she had let her go forward as a means of protection, as the hostage, as it were, of her hopes. She felt ashamed and stopped talking altogether.

They were already on the highway going in the direction of Silver Forest when the sky behind them, over Moscow, was split by huge flashes and the thunderous din of engines could be heard; another group of bombers must have broken through to the capital.

Colonel Kevin Taliaferro, aide to the military attaché of the United States of America, was looking at the Kremlin through a chink in the blackout shutters. The embassy was located in a solid seven-story building built in the Soviet empire style with columns halfway up its front. Just across enormous

Manège Square from the fortress and next to the National Hotel, it had witnessed no small part of history over the years.

As was usual by night, the Kremlin was completely dark. From time to time, however, the sky was brightly illuminated by flares dropped from the bombers, and then the toothlike battlements and the openings of embrasures and windows could be distinguished clearly, and the towers threw sharply outlined, flickering shadows across the cupolas. Then a barrage of covering fire would rise into the sky, shells bursting among the clouds. Somewhere in the distance, a heavy bomb dropped at random split the night. The German planes were circling at a great height, beyond the range of the antiaircraft guns, but the latter did prevent them from descending to an altitude where they could aim their bombs. From all indications, the Germans were trying to damage the main government buildings, and even the ideological center of the Communist empire itself, the Kremlin fortress. So far, they had not been able to accomplish that goal and were forced to drop their bombloads blindly over Moscow, hitting residential areas. The other day, however, according to very reliable sources, a bomb had landed right next to the Central Committee building, killing the well-known playwright Alexander Afinogenov, who had happened to be on the street at the time. Strange as it might seem, his wife was American.

Taliaferro lit his pipe. A flare burned out in the sky over Kitai-gorod. The Kremlin was again submerged in darkness. Where was Stalin, then? Was he really sitting in the fortress, watching the bombing through a crack like me? It was said by some that he had left Moscow a long time ago. If that was true, then they must have abandoned the hope of repulsing an attack on the capital. Could it be that 1812 was repeating itself?

"Listen, Taliaferro, get away from the window with that pipe," Geoffrey Penn, the ambassador's aide for political affairs, said from the depths of the room.

"Are you afraid some Luftwaffe ace will notice this little fire?" the colonel asked with a grin.

Penn laughed. "I'm afraid a patrol will spot you from the street and we'll have to take our drinks down to the air raid shelter."

Several diplomats and a guest, the celebrated journalist Townsend Reston, were whiling away the time in the darkened sitting room. A single weakly shining bulb beneath a cream-colored lampshade gave the room that coziness peculiar to besieged luxury hotels. A battery of Scotch bottles, soda siphons, and an ice bucket—in a word, everything without which one cannot get a political conversation among gentlemen started—also contributed to the atmosphere.

"Well, Kevin, did Stalin wave to you from the Kremlin?" asked Reston when Taliaferro had moved away from the window and closer to the small bar so as to make himself another drink. They had been friends since Harvard, and their paths had crossed several times during the conflict that until recently had been known as "The Great War" but that henceforth, it seemed, would be known as the First World War. Then they had gone their separate ways, and Reston, coming to Moscow immediately after the opening of the eastern front, had been very surprised to find Kevin Taliaferro on the embassy staff, and in a colonel's uniform at that. It turned out that Kevin had been working all these years in an exclusively theoretical department of the Pentagon, had become a great expert on Russia and Eastern Europe, had defended a dissertation on Russian history, and had mastered the Russian language with its beastly declensions and moods. The last circumstance filled Reston with "black envy," as he put it: for all the times that he had come here, and even though he had in fact made a name for himself by writing about Russia, to this day he could not put ten words together in a clear sentence. Taliaferro, clinking the ice cubes in his glass, approached the group and sat down in a deep armchair, his lanky knees protruding.

"Stalin dropped out of sight," he said, "after that speech he made on July third, after his—well—biblical appeal to the people, 'Brothers and sisters . . .' Since that day, nothing has been heard from him, and no one in the outside world has seen him. It's terrible."

Reston smiled. "What's so terrible about it, Kevin, if you don't mind my asking? The people don't see their dragon, so there's no one to bring sacrifices to?"

"That's beside the point," Taliaferro countered. "One way or another, that dragon ended up as the leader of this country, of all of Russian civilization. For millions of people he was the symbol of the country's might, and right now, when the nation is collapsing, the symbol has disappeared. I have a feeling he's simply a coward, he fears for his own skin. It's a tragedy!"

"As far as I'm concerned, these Nazis and Bolshies are all one of a kind. I have no pity for them," grated Reston. "Of course, the people are suffering, but if the result is the ruin of both of these criminal bands, I won't weep."

"Excuse me, Rest" (everyone had called him that at Harvard, so that they wouldn't have to fuss about with the awkward "Townsend," which by way of abbreviation yielded only "town" and "sand"). "Excuse me, but there is a difference between the Nazis and the Bolshies. Unfortunately, they can't both go to ground at the same time. The Nazis are right outside Moscow, not the other way around. That's where the difference lies."

Meanwhile, the diplomats in the other chairs were discussing the catastrophic situation at the front. Geoffrey Penn was relating the contents of the latest summaries received by the ambassador. Under the command of Field

Marshal von Bock, Army Group Center was concentrating its forces for the final assault on Moscow. Made up of nearly two million soldiers, two thousand tanks, and a huge quantity of artillery, it was opposed by Russian armies that were scattered, demoralized by retreat, and at about half their regular strength. For all practical purposes there was no front line, many divisions having been caught in pincer movements. The Germans didn't know what to do with enormous numbers of prisoners. Rumors circulated of entire divisions surrendering, generals and all. The air superiority of the Luftwaffe was absolute. The Reds' tanks were unable to stand up to the slightest contact with the German armored fists, which were burning them by the hundreds. The operational incompetence of the Soviet line officers was striking. "In a word, it's utter collapse. We may have the occasion, gentlemen, to watch the Wehrmacht parading right under our windows!"

Reston did not respond to Taliaferro. He had been listening to Penn's accounts with half an ear and had wanted to join the other group, where the most important information was being reported. Kevin, though, was obviously in the mood for a discussion of a more general sort.

"On the whole, Rest, I have to tell you that I wouldn't be at all delighted to see the red flag over the Kremlin replaced by the red flag with a white circle and a black spider in the center," Taliaferro continued. "Quite apart from everything else, you know I've never made any secret of my love for Russia, for its literature and history, and in no way do I wish for its people to be turned into a herd of *Untermenschen* as prescribed by the Nazis."

"Kevin!" Geoffrey Penn said loudly, turning to him. "Is it true that Stalin wiped out a lot of his generals a few years before the war?"

"Absolutely," answered Taliaferro, but here Reston was roused to action, gladdened by the fact that the discussion had once again been taken up by all.

"I can tell you about that better than Kevin. I covered the Moscow show trials in 1937."

He began to talk about events that were only four years old, about how he had arrived in Moscow, unable to understand anything before coming to the simplest of solutions, which he began to apply to all complicated Soviet situations. Then everything had come together. The solution consisted of the idea that if the country was being run by a band of thieves, anything that was unclear could be explained by simple criminal logic. He captivated his audience, but at that moment Ambassador Lawrence Steinhardt's secretary, Mrs. Swenson, came fairly running into the room, bringing a sensational bit of news: "Just imagine, gentlemen, at about nine this evening, the ambassador received a call in his 'refuge' from the Commissariat for Foreign Affairs. They told him that, as a result of the increasing complication of the situation at the front, some government institutions and foreign embassies might be evacuated to Kuibyshev. Kuibyshev, gentlemen! That's eight hundred miles to the east, in the steppe beyond the Volga, something like Nebraska, but out there, I suppose, there are still nomads wandering around. The commissariat has suggested to us that we prepare without delay for moving out. Also, and I ask you to forgive me for barging in on your cozy 'men's club,' but a man from the commissariat—his name is Mr. Tsarap, I think—urgently requests, or if you like, demands, that you go down into the air raid shelters when the alert is sounded. In connection with that, the ambassador would like to underline the fact that the orders that he has already given on the subject are compulsory."

"Shall we drink to that, Liz?" asked Geoffrey Penn. Just then, however, the antiaircraft guns began pounding again, this time quite nearby, perhaps from the roof of the National Hotel or from the university courtyard, and even through the blackout shutters one could see the sky filling with ominous flashes of light once again.

The diplomats unwillingly extricated themselves from their comfortable armchairs. Now they would have to hang around for several hours in a cellar, "though the chances of getting hit by a bomb, guys, are really almost nil. About as likely," offered Geoffrey Penn, "as German parachutists landing in the forest clearing where the 'refuge' is." Penn, like many others on the ambassador's staff, almost openly ridiculed the exceptional prescience of "our lawyer," as they called Steinhardt, a nonprofessional diplomat. The war between Germany and Russia had scarcely begun when the ambassador had set about constructing a comfortable shelter some twenty-five miles from Moscow on the Klyazma River. The ambassador's functions had practically ceased. Obviously, he had decided to sit out these troubled times behind a high fence in the style of Old West forts—"just as long as paratroopers don't land on it," joked other diplomats. "And as long as Indians don't break in," added a particularly malicious tongue.

One way or another, they had to obey. Someone displayed remarkable foresight, slipping a bottle of Johnnie Walker into his pocket. Kevin Taliaferro ran to his office to grab some reading matter. Reston waited for him in the corridor. Taliaferro popped out with a small pile of old books under his arm. They looked at each other, and both at once thought the same thing: "This guy still looks pretty good."

Reston looked to see what books Taliaferro was dragging along with him. Mostly poetry—Pushkin, Tyutchev, T. S. Eliot . . .

"You're the strangest colonel I've ever met," said Reston with a smile.

"Blessed is he who visited this world in its fateful moments," replied Taliaferro in Russian, clearly to show off with a quote from the nineteenth-century poet Tyutchev.

Of the entire sentence Reston had understood only the words "world" and "moments." What a confounded language!

They caught up with the others on the stairs. Regulations prohibited the use of the elevator during alerts. On the bottom floor Reston noticed a small door with the inscription "Exit." He dropped back a few steps, and when the group had disappeared around a corner, he turned the knob on the door, which opened easily. A moment later the old adventurer found himself out on the street, or rather beneath the arch of the passage connecting the courtyard of the embassy to Manège Square.

For an instant, it seemed to him that he had emerged not in Moscow, but in some carnivalesque, not entirely real city. The sky was trembling with bursts of light, magnesium, and high explosives. Air and fire were mingling together. The Kremlin towers appeared suddenly, as if on a photographic negative; there was a storm of noise, in which the bass voices and descants of instruments of destruction were heard. From time to time there were moments of utter silence in the midst of the hurricane, and, like the absence of anything, these were even more striking than the tumult.

Reston tried to time his footsteps to the thunderous clamor of the air raid and to pass a nearby police station during the moments of darkness. He succeeded in emerging unnoticed from beneath the arch, passing the darkened National, and turned onto Gorky Street. For a long time he had stubbornly continued to call the street by its old name of Tverskaya until he translated the name "Gorky" into English. Gorky's real name had been Peshkov; "Gorky," meaning "bitter" in English, had been his pseudonym. Since then he had begun to call the main thoroughfare of socialism triumphant by his own name for it: Bitter Street—*Gorkaya ulitsa*—which, in his opinion, sounded perfectly appropriate.

Reston loved these unexpected departures from the schedule of a respected journalist with its receptions, cocktail parties, planned interviews, and press conferences. It was extraordinary moments just such as these, these bursts of impressions tout-à-coup, which had made his reporting an unusual phenomenon in journalism. This evening's spontaneous departure had made him simply ecstatic. I must not be getting old if I can still permit myself to do things like this, he thought as he strode quickly up Gorky Street. The soles of his shoes seemed to be flying, his muscles rang with joy; it was as though he had been waiting for some enchanted meeting he had dreamed of all his life and that each step was bringing him closer to it. Near the telegraph office, an expended antiaircraft shell fell at his feet, still smoking.

Suddenly a piercing blast from a police whistle cut through the air, and then he heard a cry of "Stop!" followed by a motorcycle approaching with its headlights blazing. Reston decided he would not give himself up no matter what happened and broke into a run. Otherwise, he thought, they'll herd me into another bomb cellar. He didn't pause to reflect that in a situation of this kind—night, alarm, an air raid, a patrol, a man running away—it might be a question of something else entirely, to be precise, a bullet in the back. He did not know that for several weeks now, calls had been issued everywhere in Moscow for greater vigilance, that everyone, even schoolchildren, had been seeing "German spies" who supposedly guided the bombers from the ground with signal lamps during air raids. Reston did not know this and ran from the motorcycle with even a certain playfulness. He dived into a courtyard, ran into a darkened doorway, watched the motorcycle roar past, then jumped back out onto Gorky Street. There were no further alarms, and he walked along calmly for several minutes, even stopping for a bit in Pushkin Square, watching as a rather pompous sculpture, a socialist angel soaring above the roof of a corner building, was lit by the fires.

The firing of the guns increased, the beams of the searchlights tossed back and forth across the entire expanse of the sky. In Mayakovsky Square, he suddenly saw high in the sky the crosses on the wings of the Nazi bombers floating slowly by, caught in the intersection of the beams. It was impossible to tell what sort of planes they were, but he told himself they were Heinkels and Dorniers and quickly scribbled in his notepad, "Heinkels, Dorniers." Then, quite nearby, there was a terrible explosion that immediately turned into the sound of a building collapsing. He realized that the peacefully floating crosses had begun to drop their load.

He already knew that the Moscow subway was used as a civilian air raid shelter and quickly made for the familiar Mayakovsky Square station. Some lads in paramilitary uniforms standing guard in the entrance hall spotted him, rushed at him, and, shouting, "Are you crazy, buddy?" dragged him inside. Reston could not wrap his tongue around the cursed Russian word *bomboubezhishche,* meaning "bomb shelter," but managed more or less to pronounce it.

"Some crazy Englishman is knocking around up here!" one of the guards shouted to someone. He pushed Reston toward the escalator. "Go on, get down there!"

The escalator, naturally, was not running, and Reston walked for a long time, marveling at the depth of the shaft. It was not too far-fetched to suppose that someone had already been thinking of future bombardments when the subway was designed at the beginning of the thirties, he thought.

Like all foreigners, Reston was amazed by the Moscow subway's lavish decoration, in which Russian modernism, now brought entirely to bay, still shone here and there through the nascent Socialist rococo. Why had they gotten it into their heads to embellish an ordinary urban transport system so luxuriously? In all probability, it was the idea of Stalin himself—nothing here was done without his approval—but still, what could he have had in mind? Perhaps in these palaces he wanted to show the features of approaching communism to the masses? Amazing that ideal communism should make its first appearance underground!

The stairs ended, and from the gloom there emerged two rows of steel columns, polished and rust free. There were marble-faced walls, a cupola with mosaic panels in which a certain formalism gleamed through the joyful Socialist subjects. The hall's main floor, which Reston remembered for its geometric design, could not be seen, since every square inch of its area was covered with people sitting or lying in huddled positions.

Reston stopped in confusion, then tried to move forward, balancing himself. It's not very likely I'll find a place to sit my ass down in this temple of socialism, he thought, but you really can't sit on people. Just then someone called to him, "Hey, sit down, citizen!" He looked around and saw that someone had managed to move over, freeing a piece of floor large enough for one and a half of his buttocks. Sitting down, he thought, I probably won't get out of here without sciatica. The next moment he felt terribly awkward, when he realized he was huddled up against a woman. Another moment passed before Townsend Reston realized he was damned lucky: the woman was enchanting. She had thick, dark hair and clear blue eyes, a combination one saw sometimes—infrequently—in northern Italy. Had he not met her there? He was dogged by the sensation that he had seen the woman somewhere before. Meanwhile, it was as though she were sitting not on the floor in an air raid shelter, surrounded by people on all sides except for her back, which occasionally had the good fortune to make contact with a column, but rather in a comfortable armchair by a fireplace. Her legs were covered with a checkered blanket. Reston did not fail to notice the sweetness of their contours. On her knees she had a notepad, on which from time to time she wrote things down. Had the old bandit of the pen happened on a journalist? A little girl of about seven was curled up against the woman's left side, sleeping serenely, breathing heavily through her nose. On her right, alas, towered a strapping American smelling of pipe tobacco and Scotch whiskey. She smiled at him supportively: make yourself more comfortable, she seemed to say.

"I'm awfully sorry, ma'am, for such an inconvenience," he murmured.

She raised her eyebrows in surprise, if not amazement. A foreigner?! Here?!

"Not good Russian," said Reston. "Est-ce que vous parlez français, madame?"

It turned out that her French was not bad at all, though she kept laughing at how she stumbled over words and her own bad pronunciation. "Lack of practice," she explained, "or rather an absence of practice." She sometimes chatted in French with her husband for a laugh, but he had gone to the front almost a month ago.

"Your husband is a soldier, madam?"

"No, he's a doctor, a surgeon, but as you understand, surgeons are in great demand just now."

"Your French, madam, is not much worse than mine, and I lived in Paris for more than twenty years. Are you Russian?"

She smiled. "Half Russian, half Georgian."

In asking the question, Reston, like all Americans, was thinking more of her nationality than her origins. His interlocutor, though, had answered in a typical local vein: multinational Soviet citizenship was something that was understood. Georgians—they're somewhere in the south, he remembered. That's where this remarkable combination had come from, the Mediterranean and the North, an echo of Scandinavia, which has also always been present on this plain, if one is to believe history.

"Pardon me, madam, but I cannot help but feel we've met before," he said. Because of the way they were pressed together, she had been talking to him the whole time more or less over her shoulder, and this pose of hers was beginning to make Townsend's head spin.

"Strange," she said, "it seems to me too that I've seen you somewhere, but that's impossible, isn't it?"

"I'm an American, but I come here often. Allow me to introduce myself, I'm Townsend Reston." Having said his name, he instantly regretted the fact that he was putting her in an awkward, not to say frightful, position. After all the horrors of the thirties, it was entirely understandable that the Soviets were afraid to associate with foreigners. It seemed to him that she was taken aback. "Don't worry, madam, I understand everything."

She laughed. "If that's so, then I envy you. For my part, I understand nothing at all. My name is Nina, Nina Gradov."

Nina was struck by the accidental nature of this acquaintance. Of the thousands upon thousands of people who had taken refuge from the bombing here, it was next to her and no one else that possibly the only foreigner in the whole crowd had ended up, as though by the whim of a novelist—a real "Hemingway," an international gentleman, an American from Paris, at that! Moreover, he turns out to be a journalist, a commentator on European events for the *Chicago Tribune* and *The New York Times*, who came here via Teheran on an English plane to write about the Battle of Moscow. She was almost certain she had encountered the name in the Soviet press in the context of ferocious ideological counterattacks: "the not unknown Townsend Reston with his habitual anti-Soviet viewpoint" or something of the kind. Well, that's that, she thought, they'll arrest me going out. Then again, no one seemed to be paying any attention to him. There's a war on, after all, bombs are falling on Moscow, houses are falling in, people are dying, the NKVD seems to have called off the hunt for its own people for a time, and America might become our ally in this war.

Everyone's attention was attracted by a row that seemed to be developing near the escalator, one that was difficult to understand. There was shouting, a waving of arms, people rushing about, restraining someone. A sense of alarm ran through the gigantic air raid shelter like lightning. Maybe we're trapped down here, thought Reston calmly. He had been in a similar situation once before, in Spain, but not at this depth. The panic, meanwhile, reached his neighbor as well. She closed her eyes for an instant and covered them with her hand, whispered something soundlessly as if she were saying a short prayer. Reston understood none of the cries that were raised around him except for "Be calm, comrades!" and "Comrades, don't panic!" Everything else, like "Fuck off!" and "Let me through, you bitch!" was lost in the general chaos.

"What's happening, Nina?" he asked.

"The people are frightened," she answered. "There are rumors that German paratroopers are landing in Moscow, that the city is already partly occupied."

"Are they really that afraid of the Germans?" he asked. This question had interested him since the beginning of the war in the East—are the ordinary Russians afraid of the Germans' arrival?

"Well, of course!" she exclaimed, looking at him in surprise. What did you expect? her expression said.

"You, too, Nina?" he asked cautiously. "Do you think the Germans will be—" He did not dare finish the question.

"Ah . . ." she drawled. "I see what you mean . . ." She thought for a minute, then tried to do a makeshift translation of a brief poem she had recently heard from a tipsy author named Kolya Glazkov: "Dear Lord, stand up for the Soviets! Protect us from the master races, because Hitler violates your covenants more often than we do."

"More often than we do," she repeated.

Reston was about to ask "Are you sure about that?" but checked himself. He looked at Nina's profile and began to have thoughts he had rejected in contempt all his life, ever since his student days, when he had parted with his romantic illusions; thoughts that were entirely inappropriate at a depth of half a mile beneath the Soviet capital under Nazi air attack. I've finally met the woman of my life, he thought. Finally, at the age of fifty-two, I've met the right woman. All my life until now, my egotistical bachelorhood with my habits, with its so-called freedom and so-called sex, was just squalor, because this woman was not a part of it. I need to live with this woman, and sex is not the main thing—I just want to take care of her. I need someone in my life to take care of, and here she is, this Nina and her daughter. No, I have to change everything in my musty, empty life before it's too late, in spite of the war consuming everything, or maybe because of it. She's just the one to throw all of my foolish habits and fetishes of caste onto the trash heap, she will clean out all the empty spaces and fill them with her obvious artistic qualities, with her light step, which I haven't yet seen but which I can imagine from the outline of her hips and legs beneath this checkered blanket. She and I and her daughter will run away somewhere, say, to Portugal, to that strip of coastline north of Lisbon, and from time to time I'll go away to warring countries and then come back to her.

This sort of dream, so unusual for Townsend Reston, went through his mind until he suddenly discerned that he was swimming with rapid, magical strokes toward a large underwater stone. The husband, damn it! She has a husband, after all, in the active army. Why did I decide so quickly that she was destined for me when in fact she's destined for her husband? Now his imagination was plagued with vile thoughts. The husband is at the front, under fire, with a good chance to become a German sniper's prey. What's some Russian sawbones next to an internationally renowned journalist? How can their pathetic Moscow communal flats compare with the Reston family house on Cape Cod, not to mention all the possibilities my bank account will open for her? That's sickening, he thought, interrupting himself. None of that means anything to her, otherwise she wouldn't be my woman, and she really is just the one I dreamed about even in my young, so shameful romantic period, which I've been trying all of my life to forget . . .

In the meantime, while he had been indulging in these dreams, which were so out of place, the mood of panic in the underground station had grown. Rumors were going around that German tanks had broken through, that the Tushino airfield was already occupied, that the Kremlin had been bombed into rubble, that the city was in flames, that gangs were looting stores and robbing houses, and that military detachments, maybe Russian, maybe German, were releasing poison gas into air raid shelters. Suddenly, piercing howls went up: "Make for the exits! Every man for himself!"

The people in the crowd jumped to their feet and began shoving chaotically, some heading for the escalators, others halting before hopeless snarls of bodies. Small boys tried to crawl between legs or along a carpet of heads, and people kicked them and pulled them from their shoulders. Everywhere there were deafening squeals and old women weeping, here and there fistfights broke out. Everyone seemed to have been seized by the horror of claustrophobia, and fear alone motivated them, a blind desire to get out of the underground trap.

Nina was trembling as though she had a fever. She took little Elena by the shoulders, pulled her to herself with a single concern—not to let her daughter be torn away from her, not to lose her in the mob. She had already forgotten about her pleasant neighbor, and when Reston yelled at her to hold on to him, she looked at him with an expression showing that she had no idea who he was, which staggered him. Suddenly, as though someone had removed a plug, the crowd surged forward. Reston, though he was trying hard to stay next to Nina, was hurled onto another escalator. For some time he could see her disheveled mane among the heads rushing upward, and then she vanished. He still hoped to find her once above ground, and when he reached the entrance hall, he began shouting. "Nina, où êtes-vous? Répondez, s'il vous plaît! Répondez donc!" He received no answer, though. Finally, after another terrible crush, he was carried out onto the street, and here, too, he saw nothing but gloom and figures running off in different directions, heard nothing but curses and wailing sirens, felt nothing but cold rain trickling down the back of his neck, rain that filled him with sadness, desperation, and shame for his strange underground fantasies, which were undoubtedly the result of the beginnings of male menopause. The air attack was apparently over—there were no more explosions, there were fewer flashes in the sky, and the searchlight beams cutting through the clouds seemed to become languorous.

He turned up his collar and headed down Gorky Street in the direction of the embassy. "Nina, Nina," he was muttering. "She's an interesting person, isn't she? Should I try to find her? Nina . . . I've forgotten her last name . . . Nina who?"

CHAPTER THREE

Underground Bivouac

★

The first wave of panic that seized Moscow subsided, but a second was to follow, as crushing as a ten-story-high tsunami, one that would be remembered long after October 16, 1941. In the interval between the two waves, on a comparatively calm night, our story has brought us again to the Mayakovsky Square metro station.

This time, though, all the approaches to it were guarded by military patrols.

The people of Moscow, who had already gotten used to going there to spend the night, were being turned back. "Citizens, the Mayakovsky Square station is closed this evening. Use other shelters." Must have been some sort of explosion, thought the Muscovites, a burst water main or sewer pipe.

The station, however, was in perfect order. Moreover, that night it shone with an intimidating cleanliness. One of the escalators rolled slowly and reliably downward. Lamps that resembled chalices in a pagan temple flickered dimly but steadily along the walls. As though it were peacetime, the usual signs reading "Stand on the right, pass on the left!" and "Hold on to the railing" were illuminated, along with the names of the other stations on the line: Byelorusskaya, Dynamo, Airport, Sokol, in one direction; Sverdlov Square, Okhotny Ryad, Lenin Library, Palace of Soviets, Gorky Park in the other.

Shortly after midnight, several stubby armored cars carrying the commanders of the army fronts and their accompanying staffs drew up to the station. Zhukov, commander in chief of the western front, Yeremenko, C in C of the Bryansk front, along with generals Konev, Lelushenko, Govorov, and Akimov, descended from the cars and made their way inside.

Ahead of the others went Zhukov, short, bandy-legged, his leather overcoat covering his prodigious backside and drooping shoulders; the reflection of the gloomy fortifications that were his features was seen for a moment in the glass doors leading to the subway. The generals rode downward in a silence disrupted only by the faint rhythmic knocking of the escalator mechanism.

On this occasion, all the ornamentation on the floor was clean, shining dully beneath the dim illumination of the decorated ceiling. Far away in the huge expanse of the station one could make out the white bust of the poet. Did Vladimir Mayakovsky, the "handsome man, twenty-two years old" wearing a yellow jacket and a monocle, ever imagine he would end up as an idol in a subterranean pagan temple?

The generals strolled slowly among the steel columns. No one spoke. Zhukov continued to walk ahead of the rest of the group. From time to time he would raise his left arm, push back his coat sleeve with his right hand, and glance at his luminous watch. Then the other generals would look at their watches as well. It was at least ten minutes before the faint noise of a train approaching from the city center sounded in the tunnel. An ordinary passenger train pulling empty, or nearly empty, cars emerged from the tunnel and halted alongside the platform. In one of these nearly empty cars sat Politburo members Molotov, Kaganovich, Voroshilov, Beria, Khrushchev. Along with them arrived the commissar for defense, Marshal Timoshenko, as big as a dray horse. If the generals, who had not used public transport for some time, did not find anything particularly extravagant about the method chosen by the leaders to arrive at the rendezvous point, their adjutants were struck by how incommensurate the two concepts were: an ordinary metro train carrying the mythic "portraits"!

The doors opened with a pneumatic hiss. Zhukov looked morosely at the emerging men. Stalin was not among them. Unable to contain himself, he said aloud, "Comrade Stalin is absent again." Yeremenko looked at him silently. In case Stalin appeared, Zhukov had been preparing to give the command "Attention" and then to mark off several crisp steps and report "All present" in the name of everyone there. He was, after all, the newly designated commander of the western front and was recognized by everyone as the senior officer. Now, though, he did not give the command, and all the generals remained in the positions that pleased them.

Now they're smiling paternally, thought Zhukov in disgust. If there's one thing I can't stand, it's their paternal smiles. The bastards, he suddenly thought, surprising himself, and then saluted—quite casually, not at all according to regulations.

"The high command of the western and Bryansk fronts have arrived as per the orders of the Politburo of the RCP(b)," he said, again without the slightest warm feeling toward the idols of the people. In peacetime I would have been sent flying out of here head over heels just for speaking in that tone, he thought. Now, though, there's a war on. Right now they need me more than I need them.

This time there were no fatherly smiles. Molotov shook his hand. Let's get to work, comrades! He walked on into the depths of the hall, where somehow a long, wide table had been set up for the conference along with two dozen chairs, portable lamps, and military map stands.

Everyone took his seat. Molotov and Zhukov eyed one another across the table, two faces set in stone with not even a hint of emotion showing.

"Comrade Stalin has asked me to send you his warm greetings, comrades," said Molotov. "He is following the development of the situation every minute and is preparing for a key meeting of the Defense Council and the commanders of the fronts and armies. In the meantime, we must resolve certain current operational problems."

He's lying, the swine, thought Zhukov. Not a wrinkle on his face betrayed any change from the general's stone-hard disposition. Why don't they tell us what's really going on with Stalin? Maybe he's already been in Kuibyshev for a long time? Current operational questions—what rubbish! Why hold the conference in the subway, then? Why keep those who most need to know in the dark? Everything now depended upon these operational questions. No one would escape.

"Georgy Konstantinovich, the members of the Politburo would like you to give a report on the situation," said Voroshilov. Zhukov turned to him slightly. This blockhead is trying to be clever, he thought. Give them a report, he says, I know everything, he says. And who has ever seen you at the front, the "first Red officer"? He nodded, stood up, and with crisp strides went over to one of the maps. A rustle seemed to run through the members of the Politburo: the map he had approached showed not the Center West regions but Moscow and its environs, that is, the nearest approaches. The dazzling reflection of Beria's pince-nez followed the marshal's pointer, which settled on Mozhaisk.

"Following the capture of Kaluga, Guderian's tanks are advancing on Mozhaisk," Zhukov announced with perfect coolness, as though he were giving a lecture at a military academy. "We have succeeded in consolidating a group of forces from the Forty-third Army in the Maloyaroslavets area. The force is composed of the 110th Rifle Division, the Seventeenth Armored Brigade, cadets from the Podolsk Machine Gun and Artillery School, and two reserve regiments. We are still holding on here, though the state of troop morale leaves something to be desired. The soldiers have been demoralized by the nonstop Stuka dive-bomber attacks."

At these words, Kaganovich's brows rose momentarily and his small mustache, of a style that had been fashionable among European heads of state in the thirties, seemed to push forward slightly. This movement of his facial hair might have been a sign of comical surprise if not for the heavy stare of the Iron Commissar. What was he unhappy with—the howling Stukas diving on our foot soldiers, abandoned by "Stalin's eagles," releasing their lethal cargo of lead and high explosives, and then climbing sharply upward, or the old-regime word "soldiers," which the commander had used instead of the term "Red Army men," so dear to the heart of a Communist, a term wrapped in the glory of the Revolution?

Zhukov said a few more words about the Germans' crushing air superiority. Perhaps they already know it, Zhukov thought, just like every soldier at the front and millions of people in the occupied zone, or perhaps not, in which case it would be useful for them to know.

He continued to trouble the leaders with candid remarks, relating details they might not otherwise get around to learning because of their grandiose tasks. Our tanks cannot stand up to the German Mark IIIs, not to mention the Mark IVs. For the time being, there are not enough T-34s, and the KVs burn like plywood training mock-ups. This observation was a direct stab in Voroshilov's back: the KV tank—for "Kliment Voroshilov"—was, naturally, his beloved brainchild. The most terrible thing, Zhukov continued, is the severe shortage of officer cadres. The insufficient training and complete lack of combat experience of many commanders is leading to countless wrong decisions at the regimental level and, in conjunction with various factors, to the collapse of the front, the formation of enemy pincer movements, incidents of mass surrender, and outright treason.

How he goes on, thought Beria, looking at the rather disagreeable Russian peasant in a general's uniform. He never seems to shut up. That's war for you, people run off at the mouth. "Have I correctly understood you, Comrade Zhukov, that the most important question before us is how to stop Guderian's tanks?" he asked.

Zhukov turned to face the shining pince-nez. He felt like laughing right into the frightful little glass ovals, but on the whole, he was not much given to laughter. The most important question is not before us, he thought, but before Guderian. Does he have enough fuel for another two weeks, long enough to take Moscow? As a military man, he understood that in theory the only thing that could stop the Germans before Moscow would be an unfortunate—for them—combination of circumstances, some sort of collapse on their side, but certainly not the disorganized Red Army. He did not say this, however, or he would have immediately been branded a defeatist, and that could get him in the Devil-knew-what kind of hot water, like in '37.

"As far as our tactical deployment is concerned, Comrade Beria," he said, "we have to try to put ourselves in the shoes of the enemy and imagine what difficulties face him. And difficulties he has, in particular his greatly extended lines of communication . . ."

Zhukov continued to talk for a while and used the pointer as though he were looking at things from the perspective of Field Marshal von Bock, until he realized he was inspiring even more fear in the leaders.

"On the whole, comrades, our position is very serious, if not desperate." He put down the pointer and tapped out six steps on the stone floor in returning to the table. He sat down and added, "Nevertheless, it is not yet hopeless."

Silence prevailed for a minute or two. The members of the Politburo were, as always, afraid of one another. Voroshilov sat as silently as if he had swallowed a toad and was not about to let on. The generals were also afraid of one another, as well as of the members of the Politburo. To a man, however, they felt that this inner fear had lessened thanks to the approach of a pitiless enemy from outside, an enemy who could not have cared less about their Byzantine intrigues and the fine points of Kremlin court politics and was simply preparing to put an end to them and all of their Soviet Byzantium with one mighty blow.

"What about the people's militia?" asked Kaganovich. "Does it have any role to play?"

The generals traded glances. The people's militia, thousands of greenhorn civilians with no training and one rifle for every ten men; it would be better to stop getting people killed just for the Germans' amusement.

"You can't be serious!" Colonel General Konev interjected in a soldier's voice. "This time we're not going to be able to have another Battle of Borodino."

The Party leaders sat frowning. Even if they did manage to arrange another Borodino, that event, for all its historic glory, hardly suited their purposes, for it had led, like it or not, to the fall of Moscow. At that time, in 1812, it had not been such a terrible thing, since Petersburg had been the seat of government and had not been threatened; now, however, the threat was directed right at them, the highest councils of government!

Zhukov suddenly felt a jolt of somber inspiration. Perhaps the mention of Borodino was the source of it, or maybe it was everything that had accumulated in the last few weeks, all the humiliations before a foreign army and a terrible desire to avoid the inevitable. Whatever the reason, he suddenly discarded all of the circumlocutions through which one always had to pass in meetings with the senior members of the Party, decided to take the entire conference into his own hands, and began to speak in an almost dictatorial tone:

"We have very little time left. It is impossible to regroup our forces in the face of a constant hail of fire. The only thing that we can possibly do to stop desertion and surrender is to station punitive units with their weapons trained on the backs of the men in the front lines, and those men in the rear ranks will have to act without mercy."

At this point in Zhukov's discourse Beria nodded approvingly. The marshal went on, "We must provide for the deployment of fresh divisions from the Urals and Siberia as soon as possible. However, as far as the organization of these divisions into battle-ready units, both for now and for the rest of the campaign, is concerned, I emphasize that we must sharply and immediately increase the complement of upper- and middle-level officer cadres. I request that this be reported to Comrade Stalin immediately."

The higher-ups immediately understood what Zhukov had in mind and suddenly found themselves engrossed in their folders and documents; only Voroshilov exclaimed, with his habitual cheap theatricality, "But how can we do that right away, Georgy?"

Zhukov looked at him unsmilingly. I'll never figure out whether this man is only playing the fool or if he really is one. Maybe that's what has saved him all these years? "You should know more about that than I do, Kliment Yefremovich!"

The words seemed to reach Voroshilov, and he opened his mouth halfway in apparent astonishment, as if this strange factor in the stunning defeats of the Red Army had never managed to enter his mind, but then he closed his mouth and delved into his empty folder as well.

Molotov suddenly parted his claylike lips. "Well, Comrade Zhukov, we shall give a report on your ideas to Comrade Stalin without fail. For my part, I would like to say that in circumstances as extreme as these, the most extraordinary measures are possible. The fate of socialism as a whole is being decided."

Zhukov nodded, again without the slightest emotion, simply with the determination of reinforced concrete, the last line of defense. "I'm glad you've understood me, comrades. It is the fate of our whole Motherland that is being decided."

The conference went on for another two hours, if it was possible to count the passing of the minutes in this hermetically sealed expanse swimming in the obscure depths of the Russian earth. An outside observer—the author of this novel, let's say—would be surprised at the mingling of epochs that was manifested in this gloomy spot in a sea of darkness. Blind-eyed, rotund Roman antiquity was represented before us by the head and shoulders of Lavrenty Beria. The army leadership was a bivouac for dull-witted noncoms. Molotov and Voroshilov were like two characters from a Gogolian comedy. The Iron Commissar looked as though he were about to jump out of the wings in the leather apron of early capitalist days with a sledgehammer in his hands. Meanwhile, the head of the Futurist poet Mayakovsky loomed over the whole gathering, the steel columns of the Soviet utopia rose toward cupolas barely distinguishable, and occasionally the Valkyries of German socialism seemed to penetrate all of the strata of earth and concrete to hover soundlessly over the table. Sensing their presence, the Politburo leaders now and again went numb with horror.

FIRST INTERMISSION
THE PRESS

The New York Times: London, June 12, 1941:

The governments of the United Kingdom of Great Britain and Northern Ireland, Canada, Australia, New Zealand, South Africa, Belgium, Czechoslovakia (in exile), Greece, Luxembourg, the Netherlands, Norway, Poland, and Yugoslavia, and representatives of General de Gaulle, leader of the Free French, together drawn into the struggle against aggression, have reached an agreement that they will continue the resistance to the German and Italian aggressors to a victorious end.

June 20, 1941:

Former ambassador John Cudahy on his meeting with Hitler: The dictator's dyspeptic appearance reflected tension and extreme fatigue. His hair is rapidly going gray. The pallor of his face and the lifelessness of his hands are striking.

Time **magazine, June 20, 1941:**

Italian newspapers report Benito Mussolini as saying, "This war is taking on the aspect of a war between two worlds."

We see that the totalitarian world is organizing itself for a decisive battle, of which Russia will be an integral part, despite the reports that are appearing to the effect that Hitler has an armlock on Stalin.

June 30, 1941:

While the rest of Russia, pressing close to its cannons, awaited the conqueror from the west, scientists in the east, in Samarkand, penetrated the burial vault of the mightiest conqueror of all time, Tamerlane the Great. An ebony coffin, in which the emperor lay in his gold-embroidered raiment, was discovered beneath a three-ton marble slab and two other unpolished slabs of granite. With the exception of the head, the skeleton was well preserved. The scientists confirmed a scholarly conjecture: his right leg was shorter than his left.

July 7, 1941:

Our correspondent, who has just returned from a six-week journey through Russia, tells of a bearded peasant collective farmer in a village near Moscow asking him when the Germans would "finally come to put things in order."

The Finns are unhappy that Russian phosphorous rounds incinerated the forest around Khanko Lake, in which they loved to relax in the summer . . .

The Romanians, though delighted with the prospect of stealing a piece off of Russia, are deeply concerned by the landing of Soviet paratroopers in the Poleşti oil fields. As a reprisal for this landing, the Iron Guard put to death 500 "Jewish Communists."

Both sides are careless about reporting casualty figures. The Germans announced that they had killed 600,000 Russian soldiers. The next day, the Russians, not wanting to lag behind, declared that 700,000 Germans had been killed. The Germans immediately raised their figure to 800,000. The Russians replied to this with a figure of 900,000 . . .

.   .   .

In the center of Madrid, in front of the Prado, stands a statue of Neptune with a trident. One of the ever-hungry Spaniards has hung a sign on it: "Give us something to eat, or take away the fork!"

The Daily Mirror, column by "Cassandra," July 20, 1941:
If there was a man who raised the starter's gun and signalled the beginning of a new world war, then that man was Comrade J. Stalin. . . . How would we get along with this hypocrite?

Albania has declared war on the Soviet Union. The old Bolshevik Solomon Lozovsky, deputy commissar for foreign affairs, joked, "The hunter cries, 'I've caught a bear, but he won't let me get away!' "

Il Telegrafo (Italy), August 1941:
Women's trousers made their first appearance in Bolshevik Russia. Snobs at resorts in Britain and America have found the fashion attractive and given it a certain luster. . . . Yet another example of how much communism and plutocracy have in common. . . .

German Press Agency DNB:
The Stalin line has been breached in several places. Soviet forces are retreating in complete confusion, the leadership is incapable of restoring order. . . .

Soviet Information Bureau:
The results of the first three weeks of the war testify to the undoubted failure of Hitler's plans for a blitzkrieg. . . .

Time magazine:
Much attests to the fact that the Germans, as well as the Russians, are lying. . . .

Stalin has entrusted Leningrad to Kliment Voroshilov, Moscow to Semyon Timoshenko, and Kiev to Semyon Budyonny. . . .

The German forces have proudly announced the capture of the mammoth 120-ton tank *Glory to Stalin*. The behemoth could develop a speed of four miles per hour. . . .

SECOND INTERMISSION
THE INDOOR MAGNOLIA

The ficus had a masculine contempt (though one might have guessed that the tree was feminine and had an equally good chance of being right) for the pot of geraniums that lived next to him. Well, obviously not for the pot, but for the plant growing from it. The geranium, whose gender was also in doubt, though it appeared feminine to him (her), seemed lacking in inspiration, a thoughtless creature. He received no signals from her (him). Sometimes he put his coarse leaves almost right up against her, but it was all for naught, there was no response. Touching the lace-covered chest of drawers would have brought better results. Both plants stood by the window of the apartment of a guard named Kolymagin who lived in the Petrovskaya Sloboda. Both of them had yet another neighbor on the windowsill, a slimy, utterly repulsive jellyfishlike substance in a gallon jug. They called it "the mushroom." It had only one occupation, the production of a dubious "juice" that Kolymagin drank when he had a hangover. The ficus refused to acknowledge the existence of "the mushroom," just as his kindred souls the Paleologues had renounced the flies that came into the windows of the palace from the Moslem bazaar.

The ficus had learned to look out the window over the mushroom and to see there something that nearly always pleased him: a small brick path leading to a gate with broken boards, two buckets upside down in the yard, a zinc tub full of moldering rags, a barrel of sand for cheerless firefighting purposes, green tomatoes, their withered shoots bent by their eternal unripeness, dirty little mice scampering by—the whole atmosphere of everyday life, the desolation of middle earth, in which once upon a time, for reasons that no one knew, a magnificent column of fire suddenly blazed up, whereupon there occurred a fusion of its two origins: the semitropical and the semiarctic, that is, the Greeks and the Varangians.

The former were recalled at sunset on evenings when something that was a rare phenomenon in Moscow occurred, namely, when the horizon to the west was clear. Then, something from deep in the distant past resurfaced: the despondent pride of a czarina at the window of a convent, abandoned by all, waiting for a dagger; then steps along the cobblestones by the door; a sunset reflected in the cuirass of her beloved returning in triumph from a victory near Azov. Even if it were from a defeat, what would it matter? The important thing was the tightness under the tits. She would forget the kingdom, only to throw herself open before this son of Rurik, to carry on the line. Liberate me, my prince! Surely you don't want my Byzantine hips to run dry in a monastic cell, to watch my living body be transformed into a barren indoor magnolia— that is, a ficus.

The Varangian beginnings of the plant naturally rejoiced at the first snowfall covering the path and the fence, and the flat crown of the amusing palace that was uncovered after the falling of the leaves.

"Well, what do you know!" would exclaim at these times the guard Kolymagin, who, even though he put out his hand-rolled cigarette butts in the soil at the foot of the former magnolia, was still a favorite. He reminded the tree of some of his relatives and forefathers, emerging from beneath the snow, sometimes with the sharp squint of a Tatar.

"You should stop sticking your disgusting cigarettes in that pot," said his landlady in a voice quivering like the rustling of dried locusts.

"Too bad they don't let us take the weapons home with us," answered the gunsmith Kolymagin. "I'd finish you off, you bitch!"

"You're going to turn into an alcoholic!" whistled the locust.

"I'll set fire to your goddamned hovel!" snarled Kolymagin, driving the landlady into a corner, twisting her arms and legs. "I'll take care of this dump! Even if it means giving up my Party membership."

Sure enough, one day the house did burn down, and the indoor magnolia along with it. The fusion of pretropical and prearctic had deprived her of the capability to germinate, though she—or was it he?—burned magnificently.

The whole house was crackling, cats were howling at the top of their lungs, the locust was shrieking like a circular saw, and Kolymagin was hooting joyfully like Mongolian Marshal Choibolsan.

The leaves of the ficus at first yellowed, then withered, and finally burst into flames. Suddenly, the fire consuming the geranium shot toward the ceiling in a column. The ficus heard her cry. "Can't you hear it now? Can't you hear it, even now?" the geranium called out in desperation.

"Oh, it's you!" the ficus finally guessed, and burst into flame.

CHAPTER FOUR

Dry Rations

☆

One hundred twenty miles up the Kolyma highway from Magadan, winter had already set in. While hauling his third wheelbarrowful of ore from the mine that morning, Nikita Gradov was struck by the intense sunlight. Wake-up hour and the march to work in total darkness had promised nothing but an ordinary cloudy, snowy, bone-chillingly cold and absolutely typical day in the prisons of Kolyma, and suddenly the sugarlike vistas of the "planet of wonders" opened on the third trip from the upper level of the quarry, along with shadows dense and dark blue like wrapping paper, the taiga stubble of the gulleys and the immense sky of the land primeval. If he could distract himself from the revolting spectacle of the convict quarry, he could forget about human history beneath such a sky and feel as though he were free. Nikita stopped for a moment on the hump of a hillock as though he wanted to give his hands a rest and breathe deep of the frosty air. If I still have such thoughts, that means I'm still holding on, he thought. For some time now he had been observing himself from the outside, applying this formula to any manifestation of his mind or body: "If I can still ..., that means I'm still ..." His experience in the camps had taught him that the moment to be feared most of all was when that "still" was broken off and a man began to turn rapidly into a "goner." Once, in the bathhouse on disinfection day, he had glimpsed in a murky window the reflection of a youthful figure with a sunken stomach, square, angular shoulders, and bones protruding at the narrow hips, and it was only sometime later that he realized he was staring at his own image, having become, strangely, so much younger. The forty-one-year-old former corps commander looked like a twenty-year-old soldier; the slightest memories of "Socialist fat accumulations" had vanished from under his skin, replaced by the figure intended at birth. This spectacle gladdened him not at all; in fact, it frightened him. He already knew that this unexpected youthfulness appeared only in the obscurity of dirty windows, that it was as fragile as a dry, frozen branch, that the ever-present, debilitating hunger and exhaustion could at any moment bring him to the breaking point and to a rapid descent to the very bottom, where the parting words of the secret police investigators would be realized: "You'll be ground down into dust in the camps!" Thus he always kept an eye on himself every time he tried out the convict formula "if—still, then—still." If from time to time he still had erotic dreams in his bunk, visions of Veronika and her caresses, and he woke up in a heat of magical tension and ejaculation, he was still alive. If he still had the will to run out of the barracks in the morning, cast away his padded jacket and rub himself with snow, he was still alive. If when he was sitting by the stove in the barracks after his shift, instead of flopping onto his bunk and shutting out the world he argued with the idle philosophers about whether or not positivism was in a full-blown crisis, that meant that he was indeed still alive and that he needed to do all of these things persistently: to daydream about Veronika, to masturbate, or "wank off," to rub himself all over with snow, to do stretching exercises and even handstands, to defend the positivist philosophy of the Gradovs that he had inherited. Not infrequently, though, he had the "final thought," as he called it: why prolong things, there's no way out of here; stop making a fuss, finally—your youth doesn't have much time left. This was a sign that he was beginning to think like a "goner." Terrified, he tried to pull himself together, began to breathe deeply, puffing out his stomach, closing first one nostril, then the other, allowing a stream of cosmic energy to pass along the unseen passages of his body in accordance with the principles of Indian Hinduism. He had been taught this method of breathing by his bunkmate, a teacher from Kharkov who had received his ten-year sentence because of his devotion to "the idealistic teachings of the East and attempting to disorient Soviet youth." Nikita was sure that this system would help, telling himself, of course, "If I can still breathe by the Pranoyama method, I'm still alive."

In these attempts at self-preservation, Nikita was for some reason filled with a feeling of aloofness where his family was concerned. He tried to drive away the warmth of the house in Silver Forest, along with the faces of his parents, his sister, the children, their nanny. . . . Even in his dreams he tried to chase away his memories of that irretrievable warmth, and he succeeded—Silver Forest disappeared, except for the image of a hefty male squirrel springing back and forth.

He knew or, more accurately, almost knew that his wife had been arrested. In one of the letters he had received here at the Kolyma camp two years or so before, Mary had written, "Veronika had to leave us unexpectedly, and she has vanished. Bobochka and Verulya are with us, they're well." It went without saying that this was news of her arrest, but instead of fully realizing the horror of his delicate girl in the NKVD hell, perhaps in a barracks just like this one, in a quarry, behind a wheelbarrow, he carefully pushed those thoughts aside, then allowed himself others that were almost absurd: maybe it was just that some man had turned up, maybe an actor had spirited her away, or one of the polar air explorers. . . . Jealousy then shook him mightily, and he noted, not without satisfaction, "Well, if I can still feel jealousy, I must still be alive."

In the barracks they knew there was a war going on, but they had no idea as to its character and scope. In the beginning, when the first rumors had filtered through to them, Nikita was often asked, in his capacity as a military specialist, if it would be long before Berlin fell. He would throw up his hands: unless there has been a radical improvement in military technology during the years I've been inside, taking Berlin is out of the question. Most likely, the front line runs through the middle of Poland, and the Red Army will have its work cut out for it just to hold that. The war between Germany and the USSR could go on for an indefinite period of time, depending on relations with the Entente powers. Most likely, Stalin and Hitler will conclude everything with a truce, with long negotiations, and then, possibly, strange as it may sound, with an agreement on cooperation. In the special contingent of particularly dangerous state criminals to which Nikita still belonged two years after his transfer to Kolyma from a prison in the interior, isolation from the outside world was one of his chief prerogatives. No new zeks—prisoners—came here to this small, sealed system, vaguely known by the fear-inspiring name of Greenery Camp, and no one here knew that Hitler and Stalin had concluded a pact back in 1939, that the new allies had immediately divided up Poland, that a war had begun in the west, that France had collapsed. Finally they had gathered from snatches of the guards' conversation that there was in fact a war on the western frontier of the country.

Not long ago, a sensational event had taken place. Nikita's neighbor in the bunk below his, a man named Zem-Tedetsky who had once been an important functionary in the Comintern, had managed to hide a scrap of newspaper beneath his shirt in the camp infirmary and carry it back to the barracks. The brash Polish Jew had literally risked his life for the sake of his political curiosity. It was rumored that Aristov, the camp commandant, personally dealt with those who violated regulations, and that precisely for the theft of a newspaper he had led a zek from the Serebrany mine out beyond the barbed wire and bumped him off with his Browning, just as in the glory days of the Civil War. Somehow or other, after their shift, sitting around the stove in the presence of those they could rely on most, they cleaned the filth off the scrap of newspaper, smoothed it out, and suddenly, by the reddish, flickering light, saw the announcement by the Soviet Information Bureau concerning "fighting in the Smolensk sector." Was it possible? That the Red Army, "invincible and legendary," was retreating? That Byelorussia had already been surrendered, along with half of the Ukraine? That the Baltic republics were occupied by the

Germans and Leningrad was threatened? "Byelorussia, land of old, Ukrainian
steppes, golden land! Your young happiness with steel we'll defend..." So that
was what they meant in that snatch of the song that drifted into Greenery
Camp from loudspeakers outside the wire!

Nikita moved away from the stove then and lay down on his bunk facing
the ceiling, which like the entire barracks was covered with snow and ice that
for some reason was yellow, as though it had been urinated on. The names
he had glimpsed in the news report meant nothing to him, with the possible
exception of Major General Kolesnik, who commanded a motor-rifle division.
It seemed to him they had met during some general staff training exercises;
he was someone's adjutant—Gamarnik, wasn't it? So everything he had
dedicated so many years of work to in the Western Military District had been
swept away, smashed into a million pieces, if the Germans were already
outside Smolensk—that is, if they weren't already beyond Smolensk. It was
an old newspaper, after all. He lay there for a long time, trying to get himself
into a military frame of mind, to imagine what he would have done during
such a frightful invasion; to picture himself at a battlefield command post or
at the front leading a division, a regiment, even a company; to see himself as
even an ordinary private under German fire. But nothing came of it. Everything was clouded by an uncontrollable fatigue that seemed to emanate from
within his cells, by indifference, and most important, by the ravages of hunger, by visions of the few crusts of bread he managed to sweep off the table
during meals and hide in the lining of his padded jacket. He passionately
dreamed of one thing only: to cover his head with his jacket and instantly to
devour those sweet bits of crust that looked as though they might be crunchy.
But he had made himself a promise that he would exercise willpower, save
them until morning and then eat them before he went to the mine. Then
again, what was the point of having willpower, of dragging things out, of
trying to maintain one's dignity? Why not, finally, just lick the plates the way
the goners did? What has the war changed for us? The Germans aren't going
to reach Kolyma, after all, we won't have the chance to die for the Motherland
on the field of battle.

All around, former theoreticians and practical workers of communism who
were knowledgeable about world politics were having discussions in heated
whispers across the bunks. Nikita said nothing and no one spoke to him,
which demonstrated a dramatic tact, an understanding of the sufferings of a
high-ranking officer of the Worker-Peasant Red Army at this fateful hour. As
he told himself, all these men around him were real survivors. They viewed
survival as their basic task and never let pass the smallest chance to bolster
their bodies and minds, which they would need for any tasks in the future.
Whenever they felt the twig of a dwarf cedar beneath their feet, they would

gobble it down to the last fiber, needles, bark, and all—that was how they got the invaluable vitamins. Peeling potatoes was also considered an extremely useful job, and from time to time they would manage to get themselves assigned to kitchen detail. A tiny lump from a damp, rotting potato was counted as a gift from fate and would provide enough fuel for, say, another week. One man had come up with the idea of drinking his own urine: not only did it help to keep up muscle tone, it could also cure many camp illnesses. Some came to believe so fervently in the powers of urine that they felt immune to everything. Nikita, too, had taken to drinking his urine when ulcers began to appear on his legs, and it seemed to help—the sores had gone away. Into the category of "survival measures" and the preservation of "human dignity" also entered these endless political discussions, the rehashing of old Party congresses, oppositions, groups and platforms, international agreements and intrigues, the formulation of every possible hypothesis both internal and geopolitical. Nikita was certain that the passion with which they were now discussing the scrap of newsprint had as its basic aim that same formula "If-I-still-then-I-still."

Meanwhile, he lay there in desperation, thinking not about the war but rather about his indifference to it. In the end, a note of salvation emerged from the dead-ends in his thoughts: "If I still think about my indifference with despair, I'm not indifferent and I'm still alive." He pulled his jacket up over his head, chewed his crumbs of bread with his scurvy-racked teeth, then drifted off into a deep sleep. He did not dream. His glands were quiet, as though the terrible permafrost of Kolyma had penetrated his body and encrusted it. That day, at the beginning of his third trip to the quarry, he had already begun to feel hopelessly tired, almost entirely cut off from the face of the earth, even from that face disfigured by the gash of the quarry. One after another, the zeks pushed wheelbarrows filled with rock from the hillside mine upward to freedom, rolled them out onto a knoll, from where the surrounding world flickered into view for an instant, then straightaway began the agonizing descent to the bottom of the pit, where a bowlegged, hideous dredge, which for some reason did not dig but howled bestially, bellowing and whistling, reworked the stone.

If I'm already so tired after only the third load, Nikita reflected gloomily . . . but he did not complete the thought: sunshine suddenly splashed over his face, vast distances flung themselves open before him, air entered his chest and momentarily gave his frozen constitution a good shaking; his fatigue left him. "If-I-still-then-I-still . . ." He was being jostled from the rear, making it impossible for him to remain on the hillock, and he began the descent, yet in a different mood, with the hope of seeing the sun again on his return trip to the mine, and then again and again until sundown, and night, when it falls, will be different, not with its usual absolute blackness, but with stars, perhaps even with a moon. All of today's shift, he thought, will pass that way, all thirty-four trips with the wheelbarrow, and maybe I'll be able to hold out, maybe. . . . And if I still think "maybe," then I'm still . . .

At the sharpest point of the curve in the road, where he had to pull on the wheelbarrow with all his might in order to keep it from getting away and overturning, there were two thuglike guards in sheepskin overcoats.

"They're checking out cadres," said Zem-Tedetsky behind him. "As Comrade Stalin put it, cadres are decisive during the period of reconstruction."

"Hey, Gradov, stop!" the guards suddenly said. "Get rid of that wheelbarrow! About face—march!"

One of the functionaries headed back down the road, and the other slung his "shooting iron" over his shoulder and followed behind prisoner Gradov, L-148395.

Shaken by the unexpected turn of events, by the disruption of his routine, stunned by the breaking of the monotony of the trips to and from the quarry, Nikita now walked toward loaded wheelbarrows and right alongside empty ones, but without a wheelbarrow himself. Some of the zeks cast surprised glances at him, though most of them paid no attention, absorbed as they were in their own "survivalist" processes.

"Get a move on! Stir your stumps!" the guard at his back snarled.

They came to the top of the hillock. The sun struck Nikita in the face so fiercely that he took a slight step back. His legs turned themselves to go back down into the black hole of the pit.

"Take a left!" shouted the jailer.

"Where are you taking me, boss?" asked Nikita in zek fashion.

"Shut your fucking mouth! Take a left!" barked the guard. Nikita sensed he had removed the rifle from his shoulder and was now carrying it at port arms. It was all in accordance with the way things were done in Greenery Camp, except for this unexpected stroll down a narrow path winding through glistening snowbanks.

A quarter hour later, they came up to the camp administration building, a barracks with plaster walls and genuine windows, through the panes of which could be seen, wonder of wonders, the faces of women—taken from among the prisoners, naturally—who served in the orderly room. A military all-purpose vehicle was parked by the porch, on the railing of which sat two army lieutenants who seemed to be basking in the sun. The camp commandant, yes, indeed, the omnipotent Major Aristov himself, was chatting with them, laughing and smiling, clearly trying to be likable. The army officers were barely listening to him, and when they did occasionally look at him, it was with unconcealed disdain, though they were both only lieutenants.

"This one?" One of the lieutenants pointed a bulky index finger in the direction of the approaching Nikita. The second man only gave a low whistle, visibly impressed by the appearance of the "particularly dangerous enemy of the people."

On the porch next to the major's shiny boottop, Nikita saw his rucksack, packed and tied shut. They're taking me off somewhere, obviously to reclassify my case and to have me shot, he thought, and he was not afraid. Then again, why are they military and not from the NKVD? Why, it all makes sense—a military tribunal sat in judgment on me, so now military men are taking me away to review my case in order to have a dangerous enemy shot in view of the military situation. Suddenly his mood soared as a result of these reflections, he even felt a sort of exultation—the sun, the sparkling snow, army officers, a firing squad!—anything was better than the slow ebbing away of life, day after day, as he grew to be one with the permafrost.

"Get in the car!" one of the lieutenants ordered him.

"Where am I being taken?" asked Nikita. The impending execution filled him with a sort of pride, of the sort he had felt in the old days, for the first time since his entry into Greenery Camp.

"Get in, get in, Gradov! Or don't you want to leave our resort?" Aristov guffawed.

"They'll explain later," said the other lieutenant in a colorless, martinetlike tone that had, however, nothing of the NKVD agent about it.

Then he sat in the front next to the driver, while Nikita took his place in the backseat next to the other lieutenant. From time to time during the journey the latter wrinkled his nose and edged away from the zek. Class hostility, Nikita thought at first, but after a while he guessed that it was because he stank, reeked disgustingly of the barracks, and that the rosy-cheeked lieutenant, wearing aftershave that he had put on that morning, found it difficult to bear.

The car proceeded slowly along a winding road past a gorge, and in one place where the wind had formed snowdrifts it lost traction. The two lieutenants got out and began to push. Nikita offered to help, but they cut him off sharply. Shortly afterward, they came out onto the broad highway used by truck convoys. This was the notorious "Kolyma trail," built literally on the bones of prisoners, extending almost a thousand kilometers north from Magadan.

Nikita's head was spinning, over and over he closed his eyes: the spectacle of the free highway rushing by was too much for him to take. Soon, however, they turned off of the "trail" onto a side road that ran along the bottom of the gorge, between the lifeless hills overgrown with dwarf cedar. Then the gorge began to widen, and they were passing through some sort of narrow "zone" with guard towers and barbed wire, followed by a few scattered barracks and a scanty village of guardhouses. Suddenly they emerged onto a small airfield, where the car came to a halt.

The lone craft on the field, a TU-2 with rippled aluminum sides, began turning over its propellers as soon as they appeared. They took Nikita out of the jeep and led him toward the plane. The rucksack on his back seemed heavier than any wheelbarrow. His joy at this unfolding, improbable change almost robbed him of his strength. He was thinking about nothing except greedily catching perhaps the air, or perhaps the moment of the change, with his mouth, as though he were trying to drink it in to the end and not to forget any of it.

In the plane, the pilot, dressed entirely in fur-lined leather and wearing fur boots, tossed him a huge pair of trousers lined with cotton batting, two jerseys, a sheepskin coat, felt books, and a fur hat.

"Put them on!" the pilot shouted. "Otherwise," he added with a laugh, "you won't make it."

The engines were already roaring at full throttle. The plane began to taxi toward the runway. Nikita was sitting in a corner on a pile of sacks, all alone in the spacious fuselage with its two small rectangular windows. He knew these airplanes, which even in his time had begun to be withdrawn from the bomber forces and reassigned to transport duty. A few minutes later, a flyer emerged from the cabin and offered Nikita a bulky package.

"There are orders to give you dry rations," he said and then handed him a can opener and a spoon separately. "And you have orders to eat." Then he produced some sort of manifest and a stub of a pencil. "Here, sign this receipt."

Then he left Nikita alone with his "dry rations" and returned to the cabin. Right away the airplane lurched forward; huts and the bristly cheeks of the gorge raced by, and then the craft took off. Now the revelation of the contents of the "dry rations" was made to zek L-148395: a section of smoked sausage, one tin of some stewed meat and another of sprats, a piece of Gouda cheese, a package of butter, a small jar of condensed milk, a container of pear jam, two chocolate bars, a large, coarse bun, and three pieces of zwieback. All the mysteries of love, war, and prison were forgotten, there was only the moment; the strongest impression of his life lay unwrapped before him on a sackcloth in the form of the dry rations of the air force officer corps.

Almost unconsciously he snatched a chocolate bar, began breaking it up and shoving the pieces into his mouth along with bits of the wrapper, while simultaneously digging his spoon into the butter, which meant he was eating buttered chocolate. Then he tore at the hard, unheard-of, fantastically deli-cious sausage with his teeth, crumbled the cheese and stuffed it into his mouth, then the bun, went back to the chocolate and the butter, until it all mixed together on his tongue in a sweet-and-salty, fatty-cheesy mass of food, which went down his astonished gullet in fits and starts until it reached his flabbergasted stomach, which was virtually dry of gastric juices and suffering from small bleeding ulcers. In no time he had polished off everything except for the contents of the tins. He had been about to take the can opener and continue the feast, but he was not strong enough: a drugged feeling of satiety that felt almost supernatural came over him. The plane was tossed about by air pockets as former Lieutenant General Nikita Gradov tumbled down into a hole somewhere in his consciousness, emerging only occasionally into the trembling metallic sphere, its three engines roaring. During those moments he tried to hide the tins of meat, sprats, and jam in his rucksack, muttering to himself, "They won't give you any more there, there won't be any more" as he loosened the cords, puttered about weakly, cursed, moaned, struggled against nausea, until he finally managed to forget the whole situation of flight.

One of the flyers who had come back to check on him returned forward with a joke: "We have a fourth engine, our passenger is snoring like a Junkers." The crew had not been told whom they were ferrying from Kolyma, but the airmen had guessed, of course, that it was a V.I.P.—whether friend or foe didn't matter, he was still a creep. Judging from his looks, must be a Fascist we're taking for trial. Wouldn't want to meet that one in your sleep—wide awake, all right, but not in your dreams . . .

An hour before their landing, Nikita was awakened by a terrible pain in his stomach. It felt as though a ball of barbed wire were tearing at his insides. He tried to stand and fell from the sacks onto the duralumin floor; then with a howl he staggered toward the tail of the airplane. A stream of gastric juices mixed with blood and the undigested delicacies gushed from his mouth.

He was unconscious when they took him from the plane at the military base near Nikolaevsk-na-Amure. "What do you know," said the pilots, scratching their heads. "And they say that grub never killed anyone."

"Idiots!" a doctor, a major in the Medical Corps, said to them. "Do you think you give that much food to a starving man unless you want to kill him?"

"What does that have to do with us?" objected the flyers. "They gave the orders, we carried them out." Then they scattered to their homes, distracted: they had managed to take a liking to their ghastly cargo.

He did not die, though—on the contrary, after a week in the base hospital on a diet of chicken broth and rice kasha supplemented by injections of glucose and vitamins, he was himself again and became stronger.

He had a single cell and clean sheets. In the spruce tree outside his window, crows hopped from one ice-coated branch to another in the punishing November wind. Why are these people making such a fuss over me? he wondered. Maybe they're preparing some sort of show trial of military "wreckers" in order to justify the defeats at the front? One could hardly condemn to be shot a man from the camps who was on his last legs; it was logical that they would want an enemy in the full bloom of health.

Every morning a hospital orderly brought him *Izvestiya* and *Red Star*, the armed forces newspaper. At times it seemed to him as though someone was taking great pains to see that he was up to date on current events. Using his well-developed ability to read between the lines of the newspapers and their arsenal of circumlocutions, half-completed statements, and hackneyed double entendres, Nikita had no trouble in understanding that the situation at the front was desperate, that any day now a catastrophe could occur, followed by the fall of Moscow. For the first time the military disposition began to affect him. He asked for a pencil and started scribbling tactical calculations in the margins of the newspapers. The efforts of the Soviet high command were coming apart like a coat of rags. The thought of Hitler entering Moscow was unbearable to him.

In a strange way, he had almost no memory of Greenery Camp, and it was only sometimes in a nonsensical nightmare, in which all of the terrors of his life, including the Kronstadt sailors, appeared, that he had visions of a wheelbarrow advancing monotonously along the infinitely familiar path, the descent into the quarry, repeated over and over and over, as though life had no sense outside of this repetition, as though he had lived a million lives and each of them contained the ponderously turning wheel of that wheelbarrow.

Suddenly he caught his eyes ranging over the curves of the back of his nurse, Tasia, wrapped in a white hospital gown. One day, apparently sensing that he was watching her, she glanced back over her shoulder intently. At that moment he was shaken by an uncontrollable desire that had nothing to do with any of his "If-I-still-then-I-still" formulations; it was simply a thirst for immediate and decisive action, namely, ripping all her clothes off, raising her legs, spreading her petals, to shake all over, to spew his sperm into her. . . . After this exchange of glances, Tasia began to come to his room accompanied by another nurse.

Each day after examining his patient, Major Gurevich sat on the edge of the bed, engaging him in philosophical discussions and addressing him as Nikita Borisovich. "Sometimes I have the strangest thoughts, Nikita Borisovich. I'm a confirmed materialist, you know, yet if we appeal to a man to sacrifice himself, isn't that a remnant of idealism?"

"What's in store for me, Mikhail Yakovlevich?" Nikita asked him.

The major shrugged. "That's not our department."

One day the doctor suddenly appeared with a careworn expression, quickly took Nikita's temperature and blood pressure, read the results of the latest tests, and said, "Congratulations, Nikita Borisovich, you're in great shape again today, and in fact I've come to say good-bye."

An officer's service cap was already in sight in the corridor outside the glass door. Well, that's it, thought Nikita, the story is coming to an end. I won't put myself through any more torture, I'll sign anything they want and say anything they want me to say at the trial. Our resistance means nothing to them, nothing at all.

He was given the same flight jacket to wear over his hospital pajamas and then put into a staff car. There were no blinds over the windows, and he was able to see the small village and the surrounding hills. Kolyma couldn't hold a candle to the taiga here, where huge spruce and larch trees rose into the foggy heavens like a mythical army.

The journey was not a long one; some fifteen minutes later they drove up to a small cottage, which, if not for its damp plaster walls of a grotesque shade of pink, might have been something out of an idyllic Alpine scene. The interior was well heated, and the atmosphere that prevailed was that of a hotel with carpeted hallways, plush curtains, the invariable painting *The Fallen Trees* by Shishkin on the wall, and a bulky radio. The lieutenant who was leading him clicked his heels, saluted, and took his leave. The door to the next room opened, and on the threshold stood none other than Nurse Tasia. This time she was dressed not in a white hospital gown but in a silk blouse that attractively shrouded her shoulders and breasts.

"You have to change your clothes, Comrade Lieutenant General," she announced in a most tender, feminine voice. He looked past her and saw a room with a wide bed on which lay a general's uniform with three medals— the same medals they had confiscated from him earlier. Next to the uniform stood a high pair of stiff boots.

Without fully understanding what was happening and without asking any questions, he rushed into the bedroom, seized Tasia, and began to remove her clothes; then his patience ran out and he cast her onto the bed with her skirt lifted.

This time, the carnal feast brought him none of the sufferings he had experienced with the "dry rations," if one doesn't count the fact that his member was raw from rubbing away at his omnipresent and ever-growing desire.

He spent the remainder of the day in the sweet captivity of Tasia's care. She gave him a shave and a haircut, outfitted him in underwear of the best quality, riding breeches, and a shirt of finely spun cloth, and sang several tuneful Ukrainian songs. The young woman was clearly a master of the art of teaching a man to live in the world again.

"We're having a guest for dinner this evening, Comrade Lieutenant General," she said in a sly voice. "No, no, don't ask—it's a surprise."

The guest turned out to be Major General Konstantin Vladimirovich Shershavy, whom Nikita had known as "Koka from headquarters" in the days when he had served in Byelorussia. In those days Shershavy had been a good fellow, an unfailing participant in the bacchanalia organized by the C.O., a guitarist, a connoisseur of the female contingent of Minsk and Vitebsk, in short, the epitome of the well-known "Russian hussar" who rode at the head of the proletarian forces and even in the ranks. Now he had taken on a mature, heavy-cheeked appearance and under his shirt rippled not only muscular shoulders, but also hips like sandbags in the area of his upper backside; his eyes, however, were still the same, friendly and of a cheerful salaciousness; all in all, he seemed to say, in spite of my high rank, I'm still the same old "Koka from headquarters"!

He ran straight from the door with outstretched arms, which he wrapped around Nikita's upper body, which was still emaciated from the camp. Then he covered Nikita's face with wet kisses—on his cheek, his ear, his eyelids, and finally, even on the mouth, in the name of the Communist Red-Banner-Bearing Hussar Guards!

"Nikitushka, you're back! What luck, what joy for the whole army! After all, you were always our showpiece, the favorite of the officer corps! We all simply gnashed our teeth when you were. . . . Personally, I gritted my teeth and said, well, gentlemen, I think it's all a mistake. Then they raked me in, as well . . ."

"What, you did time, too?" asked Nikita. He could imagine almost anyone but Kostya Shershavy in a convict's jacket.

"And how!" the other sang out. "They picked me up in thirty-nine, when I was stationed in the Caucasus—in our sector, everyone was purged right down to the battalion commander level. What do you think, Nikita? I got out of the camp only six months ago!"

Standing at the table, raising his glass of cognac almost to the chandelier, Shershavy proposed a toast: "I drink to the return of the legendary commander Nikita Gradov to the officer corps of the Red Army!"

The cognac resounded inside Nikita with such ease that one might have thought that instead of vital organs he had simply a capacious container designed to receive liquor.

"The Far East Army is a steadfast foothold!" Shershavy yelled a soldier's song. Then he sat down, genuinely happy, having eaten and drunk his fill, a sort of perpetual loafer but one of the kind every enterprise needs to get off the ground.

"Just the other day at headquarters, Nikita, see if you can guess whom I met—my namesake, Kostya Rokossovsky! That's right, he's out, too, all his medals have been returned, and he's already been given a hell of a promotion!"

Suddenly he turned to Tasia, who was plying both generals with hors d'oeuvres and beaming maternally. "My dear girl, take a walk for half an hour or so, won't you, sweetheart? I have a few secrets I need to discuss with the lieutenant general before they come to pick us up."

Tasia did not have to be asked twice. She threw on her fur coat and went off on a stroll to the army-navy store to buy the general a pullover to wear underneath his shirt, socks, and a shaving kit worthy of his rank. There was no need for her to eavesdrop on them, as it was not required of her.

"I've come to you with a mission, Nikita," said Shershavy, "only don't think it's from . . ." He looked to the left, to the right, and behind him at *The Fallen Trees.* Then he glanced at the ceiling. ". . . from them, you know whom I mean. I swear, it's from the commander in chief of the western front—yes, that's right, Georgy Konstantinovich himself.

"You know how things stand, even from the papers it's clear that the situation is actually ten times worse. Zhukov has a lot of respect for you, in a professional sense, and he wanted you to be told that it is now a question of the fate of the Motherland at the most basic level. If Moscow falls, everything will collapse, and that means we'll be a German colony for many decades to come."

At that moment, Nikita, who had been turning his glass in his hands and staring at the tablecloth, raised his head sharply and looked at the messenger. Major General Shershavy nodded dramatically. "Pardon me, Nikita, but I'd like to add a personal note. At times like this you have to forget personal resentments. The Motherland is bigger than . . . well, you know what I'm saying. To make a long story short, they're offering you the command of a special strike force that's being formed out of fresh units from Siberia and the Urals.

"It goes without saying that the 'Blücher affair' has been forgotten and that you are completely rehabilitated. Moreover, an order has already been drawn up to give you the next rank up, that is, colonel general. So what do you say?"

"Has Stalin agreed to all of this?" Nikita asked softly. Something vaguely resembling the nausea that he had felt in the airplane began to rise within him—was it from the depths of his soul or the pit of his stomach? Maybe he had just had a bit too much cognac, or maybe it was a result of the avalanche of official favor.

"It comes straight from him!" exclaimed Shershavy. "I'll let you in on a secret—Iosif Vissarionovich personally offered you the rank of colonel general!"

Nikita looked the bearer of the message straight in the eye, where he saw splashes of Stalinist euphoria, Dzugashvilian delight, hypnotic gladness at the chance to be connected to the *pakhan*.* To fight for the Motherland and thereby defend those criminals in the Kremlin, what a terrible, primeval fate! To take up arms against Hitler's racist hegemony and in favor of Stalin's class hegemony, for *his* criminal band!

Shershavy could see that his joy found no answer in Gradov's eyes and became worried. Once again he picked up the bottle of first-rate cognac.

"Well, I can understand that you need time to mull it over—it's all so unexpected, you need to work it out in your mind both for yourself and for the good of the cause. . . . I understand, Nikita, so let's resume this discussion again tomorrow, all right?"

He tossed down another glass of the dark amber liquid and picked up a piece of smoked salmon with his fork.

"You'll have to decide by tomorrow, though, Nikita. Every hour is precious. Guderian could smash through our front at any minute, and, according to our intelligence, the only thing preventing him from doing it right now is lack of fuel."

After finishing this sentence, the major general was abruptly overcome by a bout of sentimentalism. In the best tradition of barracks carousing, he planted kisses on Nikita's cheeks, bellowed about the connections Nikita had at headquarters, bragged about his courage, his strategic foresight and tactical shrewdness, swore they would fight together "on the last redoubt of socialism," endlessly proposed toasts to victory, to Russian weaponry, to women, who "truly turn our lives into an attractive adventure . . ." Just then Tasia returned, and Shershavy, as though he had only just espied her, expressed in florid language his delight at this "ideal frontline companion," as he put it, and began to propose toasts to her, envying Nikita's success with her while unambiguously hinting that he had played a part in this conquest—"Alas, I know only too well what the absence of female companionship is." He asked for a guitar—strangely enough, there was in fact a guitar in this remarkable little house—and sang, "My heart, you do not want to be at peace" in a pleasant, albeit drunken baritone. Then, already quite far gone, he asked Nikita for permission to retire to one of the bedrooms for an hour or so with Tasia, simply in order that she might know true feminine happiness at least once in her life. After that he "pulled the plug on himself," as it were, his left jowl plowing into a saucer of red caviar.

The guitar now passed into the skillful hands of Tasia, who sang, "My campfire shines forth in the mist" in resounding, romantic tones. This is

*Criminal slang for "leader."

some woman they came up with for me, really some woman, thought Nikita drunkenly as he stroked her spine firmly and then went out onto the porch to seek the sobering effect of the icy wind.

There he found his old chauffeur from the Special Far East Army, Sergeant Vaskov, who by now, of course, had attained the rank of sergeant major. His mug had become even more wily and impenetrable with the years and seemed to say, "Keep your distance." Vaskov immediately saluted and barked, "At your orders, Comrade Colonel General!"

Aha, so he already knows about my third star! Nikita skidded slightly on the porch and received the support of Vaskov's reliable shoulder. The notes of Tasia's song continued to flow through the open door, while the high-ranking messenger was muttering something incomprehensible into the caviar.

There's a lot that I need to make sense out of here, Nikita thought. He vigorously wiped his face—once, twice, three times; after the third time, he emerged from his hands as the commander of the Special Strike Force. Tomorrow we'll begin sorting things out, immediately and inflexibly, in their most minute details. It was only then that he suddenly realized that he had come of age, truly, mightily, and intransigently.

The next morning he submitted a list of two dozen officers' names to Shershavy. The major general, wincing from an aching head, read the list, pausing by each name with a pudgy, hungover finger. "Colonel Vuinovich, Lieutenant Colonel Bakhmet, Major Korbut . . . I know them, first-class officers every one . . ."

He drew a snot-encrusted handkerchief from his pocket and blew his battle-hardened nose—"Nuts, I caught a cold on the plane"—and looked gratefully, though not without mischievousness, at Tasia, who had brought him the glass of vodka so indispensable on mornings like these.

"As far as I know, all of them are still alive," said Nikita harshly. "They have to be gathered together from the camps immediately. I won't take command of the Special Strike Force without them."

"Thank you, Nikita," said Shershavy, looking at him with brimming—he'd had his morning drink—eyes. "This is exactly what's needed now. To build up a cadre of officers. Thank you, Colonel General! I ought to tell you that they have empowered me to agree to all of your demands."

Powerfully and inflexibly mastering the waves of emotion that were rocking him and filling him with the desire to burst into tears, Nikita walked around the room, gently, even tenderly, pushed Tasia into the kitchen, then stopped at the table across from the envoy. "Well, in that case you ought to be able to guess what my principal demands are. Where is my wife?"

"She's fine! She's in an ordinary-regime camp in the northern Urals, and

I suppose she has already been notified of your rehabilitation. Which means that you'll soon be seeing your beauty in Moscow, Nikita Borisovich. Oh, she was fine, your Vikochka—as I remember, the whole garrison was in love with her. Flirtatious and inaccessible, a rare combination . . . and what a tennis player! All in all, she's not a woman, but a sort of personification of the twentieth century . . ."

"Hold on, enough chatter," Nikita interrupted. "What about my brother?"

"Now—that's a more difficult question, Nikita. So far, we haven't been able to find a trace of him. After all, Kirill was sentenced with no right of correspondence, and you know what that—"

Not waiting to hear the rest, Nikita retreated to a corner and stood there with his arms propped against the walls at their meeting point. The bastards killed my Kiryushka, my "stern youth," the utopian Marxist, put a lousy stinking KGB bullet in the back of his head . . . the swine—into the latrine bucket with the whole damned bunch of you! Well, all right—if, God willing, we stand up to Hitler, we'll remember all this later!

Major General Shershavy looked with concern at Gradov's gaunt back, clothed in dark green cloth, his vertebrae standing out like the Maginot line. Just don't let him change his mind, don't let the mission fall through! Once again he began muttering something about Guderian's tanks and the wheel of history, about the fact that all hope of finding Kirill was not lost, that he had been through it himself and knew what was what, and about how not long ago he had been drinking and reminiscing with his namesake Kostya Rokossovsky—but just the same, we're soldiers first and foremost. Who will defend the Motherland if we don't? Certainly not the NKVD. He had the feeling that Nikita was not listening to him, an impression that was confirmed when the latter turned sharply, strode by, opened all the doors, and called Tasia and Vaskov; he took the telephone himself, called the airfield, and asked when Colonel General Gradov's plane would be ready. It turned out that his plane had been ready for some time and was waiting for him.

He embraced Tasia, who clung to him gratefully.

"Well, good-bye, little lady with the big house," said Nikita with a tender smile.

"No need to say 'good-bye,' Nikita Borisovich," she murmured. "Let's just say 'so long.' "

Then the three of them—two generals, one clumsy and corpulent, of the hungover Soviet variety, the other lean and almost in the White Guard mold, and the woman, sniffing sentimentally—went out onto the porch. Vaskov was turning the crank of a staff car's engine.

"Oh yes, there's one thing I forgot to tell you, Nikita," said Shershavy. "They had me in mind as your chief of staff. I trust you have no objection?"

"I object," Nikita replied immediately, with an unheard-of, almost frightening clarity in his voice.

The staff car roared to life with unexpected power, like still-unvanquished Russia.

CHAPTER FIVE

*Le Bémol**

★

One day in November 1941, the Soviet Information Bureau informed morning newspaper readers and radio listeners that air force units under the command of Major Delnov had destroyed 80 German trucks, more than 20 armored cars, four tanks, and 20 antiaircraft guns. Meanwhile, flights commanded by Major Komarov over the last ten days had destroyed 60 German tanks and 420 trucks, and inflicted heavy losses on three infantry regiments and one cavalry squadron.

That same day, Hitler's headquarters announced that offensive operations in the Ukraine were developing successfully. A tank unit had encountered a Russian armored column on the outskirts of Kharkov. Thirty-four of the 84 enemy tanks were knocked out, with the rest retreating.

German bombers were continuing to attack military installations in Moscow.

Five English transport ships with a collective displacement of 25,000 tons were sent to the bottom by submarines.

On that day, the Finnish high command issued a communiqué reporting victory in engagements to the south of Petrozavodsk. The encirclement of a large enemy unit was complete.

The British Ministry of Aviation reported consecutive attacks on targets in Hamburg and Stettin. Industrial objectives and docks in both cities were on fire. Only one bomber was lost.

In Libya, a sandstorm halted all surface operations. The situation there remained unchanged.

That same day, the Italian high command informed the curious that a

*French for "B-flat."

British convoy, following a successful attack by Italian airplanes, had also been attacked by Italian submarines further along its route to Gibraltar. Two ships had been torpedoed. Three Hurricanes had been shot down in the air engagement.

In short, a lull prevailed that day on all the fronts of the merrily raging world conflict. That is the conclusion that would have been reached by anyone reading all these communiqués—anyone, that is, but Major Savva Kitaigorodsky of the Medical Corps. For him, that day was simply a continuation of the endless fiery nightmare that had engulfed him the moment he began serving at the front; there was no lull. The hospital was constantly packing up and moving. No sooner would they manage to set up an operating room than an order would come down to move out again, or the roof would catch fire, or the walls would cave in: supposedly stationed in the rear, they constantly found themselves right in the thick of the action. Just last week, the hospital personnel had had to defend themselves from a platoon of German motorcyclists who had broken through the lines. The worst thing about it all for a top-flight surgeon such as Savva, who in his clinic at home had performed the most complicated anastomoses, was the constant necessity of doing the crudest sort of "meat cutting," and in an ever-increasing volume at that. The hospital was treating three times the number of wounded it was equipped to handle. In keeping with secret instructions, the division's chief of medicine, Colonel Nazarenko, insisted that first priority on the operating table be given to those who could return to action. Savva clung to remnants of the outmoded Hippocratic oath, operating on whoever came in. As a result, he did so many amputations that his statistics for the number of men who might be returned to action were lamentable. Add to that the constant shortage of elementary disinfectants; instruments, equipment, and materiel lost in hasty retreats; add to that the relative—to put it mildly—asepsis in the operating room, the utter exhaustion of the personnel, and the fact that three of the ten surgeons under his command had themselves been wounded; add to that the thievery of the medics, who stole not only from wounded men but also from the stocks of alcohol, even under threat of the death penalty . . . well, then, just try to imagine the statistics of the division hospital run by Major Kitaigorodsky, statistics reflecting the real state of affairs, not the ones Colonel Nazarenko wanted to see on his desk.

Several days earlier the hospital had redeployed to Klin, a little town not far from Moscow at the meeting point of the Sixteenth and Thirtieth armies, where nothing more nor less than an entirely untouched high school building was assigned to them. The doctors and nurses hoped that here, at least, they would be able to establish a more or less stationary position; after all, after Klin there was apparently nowhere else to retreat to. Savva remembered how he had once gone to Klin for a celebration, a concert in honor of Tchaikovsky; the national genius had been born in the town, and his personal grand piano was still preserved there. Everyone on the bus that day had been in a cheerful and talkative mood for some reason, and none of them had even noticed how they had gotten to Klin.

Passably constructed cots for the wounded had been set up on all three floors of the building, while in the separate one-story building that had been a gymnasium they had set up the "sorter," or, as it was known in normal medical parlance, triage, along with the "meat cuttery," as the young surgeons under Savva's command, with the black humor that was their special trait, called the operating area. Here they worked for whole days and nights, cutting through skin and muscle fiber, sawing through bones, tying off blood vessels, throwing away gangrenous limbs and scraps of saturated tissue, sewing muscles and skin, over and over . . . and then again and again, as though all humankind had suddenly decided to rid itself of its superfluous flesh.

The method of local anesthesia that Professor Gradov and his assistant, Kitaigorodsky, had developed once upon a time was in use everywhere. It turned out to be enormously useful in field conditions, where there was practically no possibility of general anesthesia. The young doctors of the hospital were immensely flattered that their chief was that same Kitaigorodsky whose system of anesthesia they had recently studied at medical school.

Meanwhile, there were ever more wounded, and the roar of battle, never subsiding for a moment, was coming ever closer. Welded structures of flying metal that flamed up in an instant were seen more and more often over Klin.

"The patients are in a rage again," Dod Tyshler, Savva's favorite student, would usually say as they glanced up to watch the Hawks and Messerschmitts racing from cloud to cloud. They would see one, then the other; more often than not, naturally, it was the snub-nosed, old-fashioned Hawks that seemed to stumble in the air as though lame in one wing and then began to smoke, leaving a trail of black and tongues of fire that became wider and wider, then rushed toward the earth with such determination that one might have thought it had been created for that purpose. Sometimes a dark spot detached itself from the mass of burning metal, followed by a parachute opening above it.

"He knows how to fight for his life, a good sportsman," said Dod Tyshler, who himself had recently played on a university volleyball team. "Welcome, parachutists of the warring armies!" he went on and then immediately had to be brought up short; you never could be sure an NKVD informant would not overhear a joke.

Strangely enough, no pilot from a downed Messerschmitt had ever ended up in their hospital. Either they were shot on the spot, or they were sent off to some special medical detachment.

Savva's third patient that day was Captain Ostashev, a famous ace, who, it was reported, had shot down no fewer than ten enemy planes. He had been shot down trying to intercept a formation of German bombers on its way to Moscow. Even if it was impossible to imagine Prince Andrei Bolkonsky in the ranks of the Red Army, Captain Ostashev nonetheless bore a strong resemblance to him, all the more so since suffering, endless excruciating pain and resistance to it, and a determination not to lower himself to moaning, howling, and cursing imparted a look of stern nobility to his features.

To tell the truth, Savva could not understand what reserves the flyer was running on in order not to lose consciousness and to answer questions. He even held out during the removal of his bandages, only grinding his teeth as though he were chewing broken glass. After an injection of morphine he drifted off, and everything "princely" and heroic left his face, which now showed only the expression of a lad from the outskirts of the city, like a decal. "Aunt Lidia," he muttered, "yes, it's me, Nikolai . . . Mother sent me for some s—soap . . ."

That morning the captain had been dragged from the wreckage of his airplane, which had crashed about a quarter of a mile from his forested airfield. He had lost a lot of blood en route to the hospital, in spite of competently applied bandages. The first thing that Savva saw to was the preparation of the medical drip. The recently synthesized glucose was considered almost a panacea. It was only afterward that he proceeded to examination of the wounds, the sight of which would have plunged anyone into gloom—anyone, that is, but the chief surgeon of a divisional hospital after three months of work in conditions of retreat all along the line. The captain's right leg and left hand were shattered, and there were numerous small wounds on his chest and shoulders. His most serious injury, though, was a gaping laceration over the peritoneal cavity, which at present was stopped up tightly, though there had still been some seepage, giving off a foul odor. Interesting how even his wounds remind me of Bolkonsky's, thought Savva. He examined the captain's head, probing with his fingers. The skull seemed intact, though the bruises on his temples were undoubtedly indications of very serious contusions, which were perhaps the cause of his strange, combative stability.

"This one, I think, can still be saved," said Savva.

"Yes, but we don't know whether or not he'll be grateful to us," muttered Dod Tyshler.

"Nevertheless, we're going to save him," said Savva.

He gave orders to prepare everything for a major operation, after which he and Tyshler went out of the gymnasium into the schoolyard to have a smoke before beginning the long job.

Their ears were immediately struck by the fact that the noise of war had moved sharply closer. Clouds flew past in the pale blue sky, and bare trees and patches of snow worked in concurrence with them to present a picture of the classic Russian patriarchal landscape; a hideous plaster statue of a Young Pioneer with a bugle added a touch of Soviet provincial taste to this tableau, while the thunder, grinding, and shrieking of some terrible nearby and approaching battle imparted the aspect of a nightmarish grin to the peaceful scene.

"Don't you think it's time we bugged out of here, Chief?" asked Dod Tyshler, crushing out his cigarette.

"There's been no order yet, Dod, so we have to go to work," said Savva.

"Quite right," the young doctor replied. He stretched, made a few volleyball motions to loosen his limbs, then whistled a few bars of a popular tune called "In the Distant North."

Suddenly, three flights of ground-attack planes with red stars on their wings flew over in a westerly direction, so low they were almost scraping the treetops, the roar drowning out everything else.

"Aha, the armored Ilyushins have shown up!" exclaimed Dod. "You see, the new technology is already coming onto the scene!"

Savva looked at him and for the first time thought, "Dod's Jewish." If they were encircled . . .

"Listen, Dod, if you don't want to assist on this captain, take care of someone else, and I'll bring Stepanov in on it," he said. Then he was immediately afraid he had put his foot in his mouth.

Tyshler spoke up with cheerful indignation. "Whatever for? Refuse to work with Kitaigorodsky himself? Even yesterday, I couldn't have dreamed of it!"

Fortunately, he seems not to have understood me, thought Savva—he didn't understand that I wanted to give him the chance to take the first opportunity to get out of here because he's a Jew. Well, we need to get to work, not sit here waiting for the order to take off. There's a thundering racket somewhere nearby, but it doesn't sound like the breakthrough yet. A German breakthrough was usually preceded by a bombardment, a fierce shelling, retreating, or, more often, running troop columns; just now, there was none of that to be seen.

As though in response to his thoughts, a grove deep in the woods was suddenly illuminated by a violent flash. Two medics taking care of the less seriously wounded were walking across the yard. They turned in the direction of the blast and laughed. "It was a stray bomb, she went off!"

"What do you think, one of ours or one of theirs?" Dod Tyshler asked the soldiers.

"Who knows, Comrade Doctor, ours or theirs?" the soldiers answered.

What made them think it was a "she"? thought Savva. Why, it was obviously a shell that had landed, and there they were calling it a bomb. Maybe it was a subconscious connection with the word "death," which was a feminine noun in Russian? Was she ours or theirs?

Captain Ostashev was already wheezing beneath the chloroform mask when they came into the operating room, where gymnastic rings and climbing ropes hung lazily from the ceiling.

"He mustn't be kept under chloroform for long after losing that much blood," said Savva. "Begin local anesthesia, Dod."

The first thing that had to be done was to take care of the abdominal wound; otherwise irreversible peritonitis and intestinal necrosis would set in. His limbs would be a second priority.

The operation began, and Savva, as usual, was "in his element." He worked almost automatically, one eye following Tyshler's deft, almost stylish movements and the other managing to keep tabs on what was happening on the five other tables. They took the mask from the captain's face. Completely unconscious, he breathed deeply and heavily, almost like an old steam engine. From time to time he began to mutter something unintelligible, the same words about some Aunt Lidia, from whom a boy named Nikolai—Captain Ostashev himself—asked for something, sometimes soap for Mama, sometimes a pat on the head for himself.

Opening the peritoneum, draining it, clamping off blood vessels, Savva caught himself mechanically reciting Nina's latest verses, which she had sent him the other day not through the normal field post but with a frontline photographer from *Izvestiya.*

"I descend into the murky depths and polished walls, the mirror has been covered with plywood, I hear a belching and smell the stench of prewar sardines, thousands of the same Persephones, three or four reeking buckets, my poor slack-spined people, farewell, nightly geometry lessons, stream toward the subway from all sides, the cube of the hypotenuse with three sides smashed by shrapnel, how much suffering still remains in these cellars?"

"The age is extinguished, silver candlesticks, a long list of privileged 'Letter V' ration coupons from Evakua Island, melt in hideous idols, you, grand master of joyous torture, there are no domestic animals except for the dry, black cats, hit them as hard as you can, no beating about the bush, don't open the doors, signal immediately!"

"Perish, my literature, give me your palm, with an indelible pencil on the mons veneris, Lancelot, Onegin, Don Quixote, you shall never hear the roll calls at the monasteries, cubic capacity suffers terribly, a filthy snake crawls toward me, into my mouth, to stand there like muscular bas-reliefs with bunches of falsehood on my shoulders, with a banana of deceit in my right hand."

"Only you have remained free, until the final bombardment begins, plowing up the impudent *le bémol*, the slow crumbling of façades, the completion of elementary photosynthesis, you alone are in my favor, the speeding up of centrifugal force, bright-eyed northern king, from the Varangians to the Greeks with no intermittent halts . . ."

"You see," wrote Nina, "what simplicity I'm falling into. Take the modernist prose away, it nearly comes out as a normal poem . . ."

This was what he did, then, from that time forward constantly muttering her "nearly normal poem" to himself. The only difficulty was in the "impudent *le bémol*": he could not understand what he had to do with it—it wasn't there just to make a rhyme, after all—until he suddenly remembered an old family *khokhma*. One day, Savva, a virtual musical illiterate, had used the term *"le bémol"*—B-flat—for no apparent reason whatsoever, much to the boisterous delight of Nina. She simply couldn't get over it and for several months afterward teased her husband with this ill-fated *"le bémol."* Professor, how is your *le bémol* today? You've got everything, Savka—you haven't forgotten your *le bémol*, have you? I love you, my friend, but most of all I love your *le bémol*. . . .

The silly, contagious joke, turning up unexpectedly in a line of Nina's serious and clearly tragic poem, turned his thoughts in an unexpected direction. It seemed to him that by taking hold of her, he could untangle the web of his feelings and explain to himself why he, a professor and department chairman, had wound up at the front, in almost the front line.

This tone of infinitely charming mutual mockery, with which they had often jostled each other in the early days of their marriage, had long since worn itself out, and she did not understand this—forgetting to change the record, she had put on the same tune. For that matter, he himself could now understand where this sudden irritation he felt with his one and only beloved had come from, the slightest, most fleeting annoyance imaginable. Behind the endless jokes, he now suddenly realized, lay something else—irony, condescension. To her, the poetess and on the whole bohemian, he, the surgeon, neat, athletic, had clearly always seemed the embodiment of contemptible common sense and, as a result, her partner in mésalliance. There was no doubt about it, Ninka loved him madly; when she was in bed with him she forgot about everything else in the world; their orgasms brought her a feeling of romantic soaring. Apart from that, he was for her a source of steadfast support, a man who did not compromise with himself. She admitted sometimes that he was what saved her from depression, maybe even alcoholism. Yet, in spite of all that, she always maintained a sort of emergency exit for herself, a hypothetical possibility of slipping away from their marriage— through irony. Alas, he knew all too well that these hypothetical possibilities from time to time became reality. At times he could see her head beginning to spin. On days such as those she lingered somewhere, often taking off on "assignments," either real or imaginary, and she would come home with a distracted look about her, suffering from the flu or tonsillitis, once with real pneumonia; she would wrap herself in sweaters or blankets and sit in a corner, scribbling away in a little notebook, joking guiltily, though she always joked anyway. As a result of these attacks, naturally, poetry appeared. Everything happens for some good reason, as they say. The causes of her "lofty maladies" appeared before him everywhere. He caught people directing sardonic glances at him at writers' meetings and poetry readings. On one occasion some decadent creature, seizing the moment, asked him with a smirk, "Savva, are you really that attached to this Nina Gradov?" Perhaps she was hinting at Nina's infidelity, or perhaps she wanted to go to bed with him herself—in any case, she asked the question as though he were not the husband of "this Nina Gradov" but rather one of her, let's say, "lyrical heroes."

By the way, about her lyrics. Reading her poems attentively, line by line, he could not see himself in them. Oh, well, that's my lot, I get only her day-to-day irony, and I have to reply to her accordingly. Elena was so influenced by her mother that she had gotten used to seeing her father as the court jester of the house. That's how I seem, then. Good evening, mesdames, the house jester has arrived. What else can I do for your amusement? Wouldn't you like to see Papa hang from the chandelier? Pas de problème, mesdames, only I must ask you not to swing him. He never lowered himself to jealous scenes, that was definitely not on. I'll never ask her about her "lyrical heroes," though it would be interesting to know who it is that has such an effect on her poetic inspiration. Maybe it was one of these Soviet

Hemingways who were so much in vogue and in whose company Nina had been spending more and more time recently? They all wore mustaches and had some experience in Spain under their belts, like the Khalkhin-Gol battle in Mongolia. They wore their Orders of the Red Banner pinned to their Oxford jackets, had their own cars, had apartments in new, ponderous stone buildings. Young, hard-drinking travelers, in the first days of the war they had donned idiotic leather jackets and begun showing up at the writers' club with soldiers' rucksacks. . . . What is it if not a lapse in taste, my dear Komsomol girl-decadent, when you dedicate a poem to a transparent set of initials and write, "He has flown away again, making his wings the likeness of the Motherland, slipping through the cold, empty clouds like a shadow"?

At a faculty meeting of Savva's institute, a representative of the Commissariat for Public Health had informed those in attendance that all professors and teaching assistants were to receive an exemption from the draft. The Party and the government were sure that these highly qualified specialists would make a contribution to victory over the foe by doing examinations and operations in hospitals behind the lines. Moreover, the problem of the preparation of medical cadres for the army was becoming more complicated. We must guarantee horizontal, as well as vertical, medical care for the active army, they were told. Suddenly, Professor Kitaigorodsky had mounted the speakers' platform and said that in fact, in connection with the horizontal, and chiefly with the vertical, aspect of medical care for the army, he intended to go to the front. He had also laid stress on the fact that ever since he had taken his first steps under the aegis of Boris Nikitovich Gradov, his medical research had always had a military aspect to it and that it would make no sense for him to let the chance to try out this research in field conditions slip away.

Several of those at the meeting had followed his example, and Kitaigorodsky was declared to be a man who had started a patriotic initiative. The institute's well-wishers said of him, "Savva demonstrated true patriotism. There's an example for you—not a single high-flown word, even slightly ironic, and there, if you please, you have the Russian intelligentsia!"

Savva himself did not understand what had inspired him at that moment to mount the rostrum and announce his decision, about which he had not had any idea a minute before he took the floor. Was it a burst of absurd quixotic enthusiasm? Perhaps it was unconscious patriotism, pure and simple, that had prompted him to take this not-very-rational step? After all, he really had been cut to the quick by the advance of a foreign army on his own people. Be it Hitler or Stalin, Nazis or Bolsheviks, nevertheless, an alien baseness was assaulting his native land in its hour of need, and his soul urged him to go be with his people.

Even if I can be of any use at the front, he thought, it won't be the same usefulness that I bring to the cause here, behind the lines.

Nina had not asked for any explanation. She had simply sat down on his lap, kissed him and smoothed his hair, then bitten down gently on the tops of his ears, which over the years had become hardened almost like antlers. Both of them had had the feeling that something that could not be put into words was happening between them at that moment. Now that he had done what she least of all expected from him, he seemed almost like a poet to her.

Just then, he now thought, muttering the "nearly normal poem" about a descent into the murky depths, it was just then, on that night, that she suddenly seemed to see me as an equal, for the first time, and that was the principal reason I took off for the front—to prove to her that I was not at all the man she had taken me for all her life.

The foolish *"le bémol"* looked all the more odd, reducing the final stanza almost to a silly verse, all of which again was related to her habitual, almost hardened irony where he was concerned, the man who was, of course, her one and only love, even if quite ordinary and un-Hemingway-like. . . . These thoughts did not leave Savva, even while he precisely and expertly worked, without wasting a second, on the peritoneum of the famous flyer Ostashev.

Meanwhile, the situation around the division hospital had become more than unclear. The school building was already being subjected to a rather chaotic artillery barrage. Through the large windows of the gymnasium, one could see the shell bursts, lifting clumps of frozen earth and bits of trees high into the air. Tanks with their turrets pointed in the direction of the enemy regularly came into view among the trees in the park as they moved rear-ward. One tank appeared trailing smoke and with a number of small fires blazing on its armor. It plowed into a large tree and came to a halt. Two of its crew jumped from the turret in a hurry, while a third managed to get only halfway out before falling to one side like an oversized black doll. A moment later, the gas tank exploded.

Scattered companies of infantry were running by quickly. Men from a mortar platoon jumped up onto the hillock, where a plaster of Paris trumpeter stood, and in an instant deployed their absurd weapons. The mortars began spitting fire. Their range was not great, which meant that the enemy must have been quite close, otherwise there would have been no point in firing with these pipes. Not ten minutes had passed before the mortarmen were swept from the hillock by a firestorm.

Savva did not see any of this because he was working with his back to the windows, but the howling roar raging outside left him with no doubt that the hospital was in the path of the German breakthrough and that it might be too late to retreat.

The panes of all four windows in the operating room had long ago been shattered. A shell had come through a wall and torn away a basketball backboard. All the lights in the room went out. A dangling transformer shield was visible through the breach.

"Everyone who has finished with the operation, retreat!"

"But what about an order? There's been no order from headquarters, Savely Konstantinovich!" the hospital's political commissar, Snegoruchko, wailed hysterically from the anteroom.

"There's probably no one left to give the order!" Savva shouted to him in reply.

Snegoruchko suddenly burst into the "holy of holies," the operating room. He put his hand to his holster, his eyes gleaming like copper coins. "Don't panic, or I'll shoot!"

"Get that idiot out of here!" Savva commanded the orderlies.

The next explosion, the closest yet, shook the whole building.

"You join the retreat as well, Tyshler!" Savva said harshly to Dod. "We'll finish up this peritoneum without you. Thanks for your help."

"But his legs!" Dod whispered heatedly, also not quite himself. "What about his legs, what will happen to them?"

"We'll take them in hand." Savva smiled. "If we manage to get out of here, we'll see to his legs tomorrow." For some reason he was perfectly calm without any pretense at all, as though his recent thoughts about Nina had helped him to cut himself off from the danger.

"I know what you mean," continued Dod in the same impassioned whisper. His hands, though, were not trembling at all—they continued as before, forming stitches with the catgut thread and tying ligatures. "I'm not going anywhere!" he blazed.

"Don't be a fool!" said Savva. "Carry out the order! I'm designating you my adjutant to supervise the withdrawal!"

Suddenly, the thunder and roaring and whistling and howling and crackling—everything—around the hospital ceased. In the ensuing silence the hum of the engines seemed almost idyllic after the preceding symphony.

Broken it off, have they? Wonderful. Congratulations on your new denunciation, Comrade Snegoruchko, Savva thought. He made a gesture to Dod that said, "All right, let's close." At that moment, Dod looked back over his shoulder at the smashed window. He shuddered, said nothing, and came back to the stomach of Captain Ostashev, who had now returned from his childhood travels to his Aunt Lidia and lay silently, gritting his teeth, again in the image of Prince Bolkonsky, hardened in the ranks of the Soviet Air Force. The surgeons had already closed his peritoneum and sewn the last stitches, leaving an outlet for drainage. Savva worked without raising his head until he suddenly realized that in the surprising silence something still more surprising had happened. He cast a glance over the gymnasium, or rather the operating area, and saw all the other doctors and nurses looking in his direction—not at him, but beyond him. Then he understood that he would need to turn around in order to learn the latest war news, news that concerned him.

He turned around and saw three strangers, so stunning in their foreignness that they might have come from another planet, standing directly behind him. Nearly a minute went by before he realized that they were members of a German tank crew and that an entire small unit of German armor was already stationed in the courtyard.

The unit commander was standing immediately behind Savva with two younger officers. The three pairs of eyes of differing shades of blue produced a striking effect. They reminded Savva of his own eyes. The commander raised an arm in a heavy leather sleeve and pronounced some combination of coarse words from which Savva immediately understood that he could finish the operation. Savva and Dod bent over their stitches. They each had something they wanted to say to each other, but they were unable to utter a word. The Germans at their backs continued to converse loudly. Savva suddenly realized that he could understand them, though he had always entertained feelings of disdain for his schoolroom German, as opposed to the French that he had acquired later and that he liked to show off. They seemed to be saying that everyone else in the school building, *Scheisse,* ought to be chucked out, *Quatsch und Scheisse,* and that they could bugger off anywhere they wanted, going back home or crawling up Stalin's sleeping, cobweb-covered ass. They couldn't take them prisoner, they had no time to fool around with prisoners, they had too much of that shit already, there was no getting away from this *Scheisse.* They were getting too much food, the mongrels. Better just to kill these prisoners—well, not by our hands, we're tank drivers; let the people whose job it is kill them, we have enough to do already.

When is this doctor going to finish sewing up his Ivan? *Er ist sehr gut! Sehr, sehr gut! Ein sehr guter Artz!* He'll finish soon, and then we'll drive them all out of here. Right up the ass, ha, ha, ha! Right into Stalin's turds! Hey, are you done, Herr Artz? *Wunderbar!* Everyone out of here now! *Raus! Los, los!* To Stalin! *Quatsch und Scheisse!*

The medical personnel still did not understand that they were to be let go. Commissar Snegoruchko continued standing as before with his hands in the air. One of the young tank soldiers nudged him in the backside with his knee, discovered the commissar's holster on a belt, and tore it off him together with the holster, which he threw over his own shoulder, promptly forgetting about his "captive."

Savva, in utter bewilderment, was giving orders. "Everyone who can walk, move at your own pace! We'll carry the seriously wounded! Move it! Faster! They might change their minds!"

He bent down to Captain Ostashev's face. "How do you feel?"

With a sly wink the latter whispered, "Give me poison, Doctor, poison!"

"You and I will live to drink vodka together, Captain!" said Savva, replying with the phrase that was customary in such cases.

Dod Tyshler produced a stretcher. Then they began moving the captain. Two Germans watched the scene with great attention. Tyshler's clearly Jewish features did not seem to interest them. Then again, Dod, with his appearance, could have easily passed for someone from the Caucasus or even one of their Italian allies, one of Mussolini's foot soldiers. He was not the one who interested them; rather, it was the one who looked particularly Slavic, Major Kitaigorodsky. The tank commander beckoned him over and asked if he spoke German.

"You will remain with us, Herr Major," he said, not at all roughly. "Everyone will leave except for you."

"I can't!" shouted Savva. "*Ich kann nicht!* I'm chief surgeon here! *Ich bin Hauptdoktor!*"

"All the more reason," the German replied with an amicable grin. "The chief is just what we need. My friend is wounded. I want you to help him. You're a good doctor, you will serve Germany."

Savva jumped back in horror. A young tank crewman poked him in the chest with the muzzle of his Schmeisser. The personnel and the wounded left the gymnasium. Savva caught Tyshler's glance for the last time. The latter shrugged his shoulders before vanishing. Nothing was going the way anyone might have predicted. Savva was speechless. He sat down in a corner on some broken glass and put his head in his hands.

The front line, that metaphor of final, irreversible, biological, and ideological ruination, had now been closed off for him for good. And the only people in the world whom he loved, two female beings, Nina and Elena . . . that which ten minutes earlier had been his family was now speeding away from him into a howling funnel . . . *le bémol, le bémol,* forever.

CHAPTER SIX

The Poor Boys

☆

The giant armies of Russian prisoners were indeed a headache for the German High Command. The German goal at the beginning of the war had been fairly simple: the destruction of the seven-million-strong Red Army as soon as possible. Making use of their tremendous mobility and air superiority, the German wedges sliced through the unwieldy, clumsy Russian units, enclosed them in pincer movements, then drove them into pockets for final destruction. The Russians, however, more and more often fled from head-to-head combat, retreating further into the depths of their boundless territory, intentionally or unintentionally transforming Field Marshal Keitel's exclusively military doctrine into a geopolitical one. The regiments, divisions, and armies that remained in the pincers threw down their weapons and turned into uncountable herds of prisoners of war, acting as a heavy ballast and slowing the German advance. Who knew why the "Ivans" refused to fight? Perhaps they were frightened to death by the Stukas howling down from the skies, or perhaps they had immediately come to believe in the inevitable destruction of Stalin and did not want to lay down their lives for the accursed *kolkhoz*. An enemy who does not fight can sometimes disrupt a carefully planned strategy just as well as a vigorous defense can. A German journalist who had wangled his way into the cockpit of a bomber on a mission wrote in his notebook, "Below I can see nothing except the most complete confusion." And so it went for several months, until the beginning of the Battle of Moscow. An analogy between Napoleon and the mechanized forces of the twentieth century insisted, impudently, almost insultingly, on being made. The German lines of communication, growing longer and longer, were constantly interrupted by fanatical groups of bandits appearing behind the lines in response to a summons from Stalin. The Germans' massive pincer movements had already been halted on several occasions by a lack of fuel.

And then there were still these gargantuan accumulations of prisoners, who had to be not only guarded but fed. A million of them had been taken by November 1941. They could not be released without creating numerous zones of banditry and anarchy. To exterminate such a mass of people would be an onerous task, not to mention simply murderous, so to speak, in terms of propaganda. The best solution would be to send them to the rear and use them for slave labor, but this again would demand time, detailed planning, and a huge quantity of transport and would disrupt the strategy of the blitzkrieg.

Meanwhile, camps had been set up in fields that were already beginning to freeze. It would be good if they could manage to erect some semblance of cover or sheds for shelter from the rain and snow; more often, men lay side by side beneath the open sky in zones that were largely a fiction, delineated by strands of barbed wire. Many perished from exhaustion and exposure, but the death rate nevertheless dismayed the German High Command.

In one of these camps, near the Pripyat marshes, there was a Red Army soldier—Mitya Sapunov. He had been a prisoner for more than a month and was suffering from a never-ceasing hunger that singed his insides. From time to time, but not more often than every other day, a field kitchen would roll into the camp, and the fortunate ones who had managed to keep their mess tins had them filled with ladles of so-called "soup," a lukewarm slop containing a few cabbage leaves and lumps of unwashed potatoes. On other days, the guards simply tossed a few ossified hardtack biscuits into a crowd of prisoners and then looked on with pleasure at the circus that resulted, while the Russians, having utterly forgotten their human dignity, fought with one another, thrashing around on the ground and, having seized the biscuits, stuffed them into their mouths, anything to avoid having to share them with their comrades. What more proof was needed of the inferiority of these people, the worst of the Slavs?

Mitya had had almost no chance to fight. When after a month of training, his regiment, two thirds of which was made up of new recruits, arrived at the front, the Germans had just started another stunning, paralyzing offensive. First came three waves of dive-bombers, one right after another. With howling sirens and carrying iron barrels with holes specially punched in them so as to produce a whistling sound, with their leonine paws spread apart, they dived out of the skies directly on Mitya and his friend Gosha, riddling the burlap cloth of their greatcoats and flattening the abbreviated dugouts that were all that remained of the line of defense. Just try to dig a trench in the midst of excitement like that, when all of your insides are shaking! No sooner did they manage to dig these pathetic slit trenches than the whole valley in front of them filled with German tanks looking as though they were on parade. Columns of infantry advanced calmly behind them. Frequent bursts of automatic fire shot from the belly of every soldier. The political commissars of the Red Army had told the men that the Germans went into battle either drunk or under the influence of some sort of mysterious anesthesia. This curious information, however, did nothing to lessen the Soviet soldiers' fear—on the contrary, it only made them tremble all the more in the face of the intoxicated conqueror, bursts of fire coming from his stomach, who had vanquished every army in the world, never mind poor boys like us.

A tank drove right over the trench containing Mitya and his inseparable friend Goshka, a frail, runty kid, covering them with clay almost to the waist as it passed. After the tank came soldiers jumping over the trench, displaying the durable wool expanse of the crotch of their uniforms. One of the Germans released a frightful tongue of fire from a container on his back, and then everyone from the platoon who was still alive stood up with hands raised.

In this deplorable fashion Mitya's baptism of fire came to an end.

Since that day he had done nothing but trudge along the roads in columns of prisoners, dragging himself along in an overcoat heavy from dirt or wallowing on the ground, embracing his friend as tightly as possible so as not to freeze. The lad tried not to get separated from him when, the next morning, new columns arrived and huddled together, as though he saw in Mitya's presence some chance to be saved. Mitya himself constantly looked around for the runt, wondering whether or not he had wandered off.

During one night's encampment, the runt thrust a hand into Mitya's fly and took hold of his penis. Instead of punching him in the mouth, Mitya took his flaccid, tiny penis in his fist. In this position, then, in their overcoats, beneath the frosty stars, they began to dream about some unknown girls, imaginary movie stars in crêpe-de-chine dresses.

Ten thousand Red Army soldiers had thus been waiting idly for more than a month in the Pripyat camp with no idea of what to expect. The most unbelievable stories were making the rounds. It was rumored that Hitler and Stalin had decided to make peace and had reached an agreement to exchange men for oil. That's it for us, lads, explained one disheveled officer, who out of hunger had devoured all of his leather sword belt. According to Stalin, all those who surrendered were traitors.

Suddenly, one day the field kitchen came to Mitya's section of the camp—and not just one with "soup," but three units serving real meat goulash. Then the "billy goats," as the guards were called, began distributing generous portions of sugar and soft bread. What could it all mean? Maybe they were all now to be shipped to Norway to work in the "steel mines." Everyone will kick off there, and soon, but at least we'll chow down on the way.

At that moment, a large frontline Mercedes-Benz carrying two V.I.P.'s—

Hauptsturmführer SS Johann-Erasmus Dürenhoffer and Standartenführer SS Hübner Krauss—was heading for the Pripyat camp. The car's magnificent springs protected the officers from the potholes in the road, which was in terrible condition; they also allowed them to carry on a significant ideological conversation. Dürenhoffer, who was pale and rather thin, though with a face swollen like a rabbit's, was proposing a fairly liberal solution to the problem of the eastern territories, while the broad-shouldered, square-jawed Krauss insisted upon a fundamental approach based on the race theory of the Party. Dürenhoffer reasoned, "Huge masses of human beings, defeated and turned into slaves, are always a threat. On the other hand, we can make allies out of these people and even, later on, citizens of a certain category of the Reich—second class, of course. In the eyes of most of these people, the eastern Slavs, my dear Hübner, the greatest evil is communism, perpetual poverty, stagnation, the absurd. Just think about it—they took away the peasants' eggs when they were thirty kopecks each and sold them back to them for a ruble. I assure you, my dear Hübner, that if we introduce the Russian *muzhik* to the market system of central Europe, if we give him the opportunity to buy shirts, bicycles, flashlights, shoes . . . we won't have any problem with these people. The most important thing is to let them know that communism is finished."

He smiled. His mother had neglected his teeth, which had grown too quickly, and had not had braces put on them, and now they protruded every time he smiled—which, incidentally, did not make him any less charming or intellectual. He liked to smile and was not ashamed of his moderate liberalism, which, after all, always had the best interests of the empire at heart. Standartenführer Hübner Krauss, by contrast, was not a man who liked to smile. Not that he was antisocial—he was simply very serious and always remained in the sphere of serious, realistic thoughts. Here, for example, is his riposte to the arguments of the man with whom he had regular discussions.

"Oh, my dear Johann-Erasmus," he said, puffing up his cheeks next to his wide chin, which, incidentally, did not make him look fat but only wide, wider still, a quite extraordinarily wide SS officer, "why do you think all the features of Stalinist communism ought to be done away with immediately? Your example of the eggs, my dear Johann-Erasmus, is not very apt. The collective farms were an extremely successful invention on the part of Stalin for dealing with such a population, and they should be preserved without fail. Individual farming is not for them, my dear Johann-Erasmus."

Dürenhoffer produced a bottle of Chartres liqueur from a portable wine cooler. The Mercedes came to a stop, allowing the officers to take a small glass each.

"It seems to me that it's a bad idea to constantly remind these people of their inferiority, dear Hübner," Dürenhoffer went on. "They will figure out for themselves what their place is."

"You think?" joked Krauss, though seriously, without a smile. "Oh, my dear Johann-Erasmus . . ." Then he raised his eyebrows quizzically, gesturing toward the front seat, where a Russian in a Party uniform and a Molotov-style gray gabardine hat sat next to the chauffeur.

"Don't worry, dear Hübner, our traveling companion doesn't understand rapid speech," said Dürenhoffer, his buckteeth protruding sympathetically.

Then again, to say that this Russian was the "traveling companion" of the two officers would be to use the term very loosely. Perhaps it was the other way around: he was the chief actor on the trip to the Pripyat camp, while Dürenhoffer and Krauss were accompanying him to lend more weight to the voyage. A former colonel in the Red Army, Bondarchuk was on his way to the prisoner of war camp as a representative of the Committee for the Liberation of Russia, which had recently been formed in Smolensk. Bondarchuk himself had been taken prisoner quite recently and before that—though not long before—had been a member of the RCP(b) and an ardent builder of socialism. When the Stalin line was breached in July, he had been surrounded in his dugout by a detachment of fierce German paratroopers. In the best Red tradition, he had wanted to put his gun to his head so as not to fall into the hands of the enemy. Just then, however, the entire dugout had been shaken by a grenade blast, his pistol had fallen to the ground, and Bondarchuk, tormented by a sharp pang of nausea, had fallen into the arms of the enemy bursting in upon him.

Later on, that is, in his first weeks of Nazi captivity, Bondarchuk began to undergo a profound transformation. Some of his secret wellsprings began to open, since there was no longer any point in concealing them. In particular, he discovered that he was deeply dissatisfied with the Communist system and that he was extremely skeptical as to the genius of I. V. Stalin. The SS officers who interrogated him did not conceal their pleasure upon learning that he was *Volksdeutsch*, since his mother's maiden name, hidden by her two marriages, was Krause and she was descended from German settlers.

This last circumstance conferred a major advantage upon Bondarchuk, the possibility of standing out among the captured officers of a patriotic bent, since he could manage to speak German, albeit badly, without an interpreter.

True Russian patriots, the anti-Bolshevik Red commanders had been much inspired by the creation of the Smolensk committee. Bondarchuk and a few comrades traveled to Smolensk, which was in German hands, joined the committee on the spot, and from there set out for the most awesome capital of the Reich, the city of the Stone Eagle—Berlin. Once they arrived, their proposals were coordinated. The most grandiose and paradoxical of all ideas, comrades—sorry, gentlemen, I mean—lies at the heart of this undertaking:

to prevent an inevitable national catastrophe by creating a pro-German, but at the same time patriotic, Russian army. Needless to say, this is no simple matter, and in the beginning we will have to limit ourselves to creating auxiliary units made up of volunteers. When they see they can rely on us, the Germans will give us the go-ahead.

Once this approach was agreed on, the officers scattered to sites where prisoners of war were concentrated—to explain and recruit.

Bondarchuk set out on his journey looking 100 percent Soviet, wearing a tight-waisted jacket and cap. Anyone would have taken him for a regional committee secretary. It seemed to him that, dressed that way, he would be closer to the soldiers than in a well-sewn German uniform without any indications of rank. They could see right off that he was one of theirs, a Russian and not some blue-blooded aristocrat who had emigrated after the Revolution. Indeed, it would have been difficult to suspect Bondarchuk of any blue blood, given his appearance of a typical middle-aged Soviet plebeian leader. Sitting now in the front seat of a Mercedes-Benz in front of two aristocratic SS officers, Bondarchuk thought over the situation for the hundredth time. Dürenhoffer was surely right: their "companion" could not follow fluent German speech, but not everything escaped him—chiefly the facts that during the long trip from Kiev the officers had failed to ask him a single question and that all his attempts to establish contact had led only to raised brows and condescending silence. They wouldn't even think to offer me a glass of schnapps, these fucking *Übermenschen.* But let it pass, once we have our own army, there will be more respect. And there won't be any need even to remember these Fritzes, who are nothing to us in any case. In the meantime we'll carry out their orders and later see what comes of all this. We'll see who will be the ones to receive the thanks of the Russian people. Even Alexander Nevsky and Dmitry Donskoy paid ransom to the Golden Horde. . . .

The entire enormous camp was guarded by a single platoon of bedraggled *Volksdeutsche*—no one was planning to run anywhere. And where could you run to anyway—to your own troops to be court-martialed and shot? That day another half regiment had arrived and begun to work with the people, breaking them up into columns. The runt almost got attached to the slobs from the Eighteenth Division and would have been separated from Mitya, but he disappeared into the crowd and managed to create some sort of diversion at the head of the column. By the time the guards came running up, the runt had crawled through a forest of legs and attached himself to Sapunov. "Mityai, did you see me make clowns of them?"

Some of the barbed-wire sector partitions were removed, producing a large open area. At the far end of the square, next to the gates, the carpenters were finishing some sort of wooden scaffolding.

"What's that, a gallows?" Mitya joked.

Goshka giggled nervously. "Sure looks like it. Top class! Right, Mitka? Let's take a swing! What do you say?"

Mitya gave him a light punch under the ribs. "It's worth being hanged if I can just get rid of you, runt."

It turned out that they had erected not a gallows but a speakers' platform, one that even had a good-sized, land mine–like microphone rigged up to it. A large number of Red Army folk were milling around happily, expecting some sort of miracle. Maybe Hitler's going to sell us to Turkey or Africa, going to drive us out there to fight for the Italians? Maybe that whore Stalin has hightailed it off to Georgia and they're bringing the czar to see us?

Finally, submachine gun–bearing guards formed a ring around the platform, which was mounted by a group of four: two German officers, one rather lanky, the other quite heavyset; a corporal wearing glasses; and finally, a plumpish old boy in a paramilitary uniform looking very much the Bolshevik. Maybe they really had made up?

The thin man spoke first. He would speak a few words, step back, and the corporal would interpret.

"Russian soldiers! You have fought bravely, and it is not your fault that you have been captured! Those responsible are the criminal Bolshevik leaders who dared to raise the sword against Germany triumphant, against mighty national socialism!"

Hauptsturmführer Johann-Erasmus Dürenhoffer was greatly enjoying this moment, listening with pleasure to the crackling sound of his own sturdy voice bringing the powerful and noble truth in German literary language to this huge formation of Russians. Fortunately, the gruppenführer had no idea that his speech was losing a great deal in the translation by the bespectacled corporal, who was of *Volksdeutsch* origin and whose Russian was a mixture of local dialect with *shtetl* overtones. He went on, "Our füher, Reichskanzler Adolf Hitler, would like to see you not as enemies, but as worthy laborers making their contribution to the New Order that he has established. Everything else depends only on you! The total destruction of bolshevism is nearing with every passing day! Long live the New Order! Long live Germany! Heil, Führer!"

All four on the tribune, including the high-level Bolshevik, clicked their heels and raised their right arms in the Nazi salute. Then the Bolshevik stepped to the microphone, smoothed down his uniform jacket, which was sticking up over his stomach and at the sides, and began to talk like a regular good old boy, almost like one of our own Soviet people!

"Dear Russian soldiers, officers and commissars! I, Colonel Bondarchuk, appeal to you in the name of the Committee for the Liberation of Russia. We are a group of patriotically minded, anti-Bolshevik officers who, having found ourselves behind the lines of the triumphant German forces, have broken decisively with the past and now issue a challenge to Stalinist tyranny! We are filled with deep gratitude toward the German High Command and toward Reichs Marshal Adolf Hitler personally for giving us the chance to join them in their noble struggle!

"Soldiers, brothers, the Committee for the Liberation of Russia summons you to join the ranks of fighters against the hateful Yid-Communist regime! You're exhausted, brothers, but what can you expect from the German command when Stalin refuses to recognize the Geneva Convention concerning the treatment of prisoners of war, when for him you are all traitors? I want to ask you, Russian people, how you feel about these bloodthirsty Bolsheviks, about those who knocked down your houses and drove you like cattle into filthy collective farms, about those who drove thousands and millions of your brothers away to Siberia and Kazakhstan, about those who never stop raping our long-suffering Mother Russia with their accursed Marxist-Leninist Yiddish theories. Listen to the voice of your own heart, and you will answer—we hate them!"

From more than a hundred yards away, Mitya Sapunov was peering intently into the open-mouthed block of a face. From time to time the block would freeze in a broad yawn, clearly in the expectation of responsive cries and applause. Shouts and noise came from one end of the square and then another, but clearly not on the scale the speaker was hoping for. Mitya then directed his gaze at the faces of his comrades. The majority of them were indifferent; quite a few were clearly afraid—of what, under the circumstances, he couldn't tell—and were averting their eyes. Little by little, though, particularly at the mention of the words "collective farms" and "Yids," the prisoners became more animated.

"Down with the Red abominations!" came the call from the platform.

"Down with them!" scores of voices around Mitya roared. "Bloodsuckers! Snakes! Down with the kikes! Down with the collective farms!"

An image that Mitya had almost forgotten during his years spent in the professor's "fortress" fluttered to life and swelled up within him: his crazed father with a bundle of burning straw in his hands, the last flickering glance he would ever have of Mama, her heartrending scream, and then his own unconscious flight into the darkness, into the forest, to get away from human beings, to become a wolf, and then spying, almost wolflike, on Gorelovo from a hillock; the arrival of the army detachment in the village, the shrieks of women that reached his lupine ears, the bellowing of cattle; the chicken he caught, killed by wringing its neck, and devoured. . . . All these terrible dirty things from the countryside were what would later cause the boy to wake up now and again in the night with his heart pounding and his stomach tumbling down into a bottomless abyss, to gulp for air and snatch at it with the fingers of his contorted hands, to suddenly find himself on the stairs in the moonlight, looking in bewilderment at the array of pictures with no understanding of what they meant until Grandmother Mary appeared to calm him with her warm hands, as though she were gathering under her palms everything that was running away and dispersing.

Again he heard the shouts of the speaker: "Russian soldiers, brothers! The monstrous Bolshevik empire is crumbling beneath the crushing blows of German arms, like a colossus with feet of clay. History has finally taken the path of just retribution! And yet we have to look ahead and try to envision what tomorrow will be like for Russia, our Motherland! For the sake of that day to come the Liberation Committee calls you to join the ranks of the support units, which in time will become the core of a new Russian army!"

Colonel Bondarchuk was satisfied: in the first place, he had not entirely carried out the Germans' orders—or rather, he had not entirely followed their instructions: he had spoken not for ten minutes, as he had been told, but for a whole quarter of an hour. In the second place—and this was the most important thing—he had managed to slip in a few thoughts that had not been agreed on, about the collective farms, for example, and about the future of Russia. In this way, one small step at a time, we'll consolidate our position.

The interpreter standing between Krauss and Dürenhoffer muttered to them in his fanciful German the contents of Bondarchuk's expostulations, and they applauded, as if to show that the speaker was a social leader, not a puppet but an independent quantity. A little while later, however, Krauss thumped him none too delicately on the back, as though saying, "Come on, time to finish up," and then stepped forward himself. The standartenführer's speech took no more than three minutes and contained not the slightest rhetorical flourish. He said that those who after the appropriate checks were enlisted in the new support units—neither of the German officers said "Russian army" or "Russian units" as much as once—would receive a new uniform, two changes of underwear, a weekly bath, an entirely satisfactory diet, cigarettes, and thirty-five German marks a month "for recreation." The soldiers must understand, though, that they would have to answer for the slightest infraction of discipline to the full letter of German law.

On that note the meeting ended. Immediately, lads in German uniforms with no insignia of rank sat down at tables made from planks and began signing up volunteers. There turned out to be a large number of them: it was difficult to tell what motivated them more—hatred for the Bolsheviks, Bondarchuk's entreaties for "the future of Russia," or the standartenführer's thirty-five Deutsche marks a month.

"For thirty-five marks, Mit, you can probably buy any whore and as much booze as you want," the runt said cautiously.

"Well, then, go sign up, Runt!" said Mitya casually, lightly, as though he were telling him to sign up for a football team.

"What are you saying?" Goshka Krutkin replied in fright. "Against our people, Mit? Aren't we Komsomolists, or what?"

"Since when do I belong to your Komsomol?" Mitya roared with laughter and headed for the recruitment queue. "A Komsomolist!" Suddenly rage exploded inside him, and he turned to Goshka, who was walking alongside him with mincing steps, seized the latter by his hardened chest, and drew him to himself like a folkloric warrior manhandling some sycophantic member of his retinue. "I'll hate your Komsomol, all of 'your people,' that whole gang of Red bandits, for the rest of my life!"

"Come on, Mitka, what are you saying?" whined Krutkin. "Well, if you think it's important, let's go sign up."

Mitya pushed him away. "What do you want to sign up for, Runt? After all, you're a Komsomolist, you shithead!"

Goshka seemed on the point of bursting into tears—in any case, he was wiping something wet over his dirty face as he looked spitefully at his friend around the fist he was rubbing over one of his eyes. His resentment, however, was only put on. Mitya suddenly had the feeling that everything around him was unreal, a sham, and that he and Goshka were doing pretty much the same thing, only playing out a scene for two actors.

"You're such a ham," he said to him conciliatingly.

Krutkin sniffled in response. "Dmitry, you don't give a flying fuck about me. All you do is call me names; you don't even think of me as a person . . ."

They were standing at the end of the line. The word was already going around that those who signed up would be loaded into trucks straightaway and taken to the bathhouse for disinfection and then to a warm barracks.

"Oh Mit, Mit," Goshka said with a sudden calm. "What about your aunt Celia, eh? You heard it yourself, didn't you, the speaker was shouting about 'Yiddish communism'? Jews, there you go, Mit! What are you going to do about your adoptive mama, about Cecilia Naumovna? Now, don't get angry, Mit, I'm just asking as a friend . . ."

So you're playing another scene, eh, Runt? thought Mitya. Maybe he's provoking me? The runt was looking at him with devoted eyes. He really seems worried about it . . . why didn't I think about Aunt Celia myself? Then he saw the main speaker coming down the line, shaking the volunteers' hands, answering questions. I'll ask the boss himself right now—he doesn't have a bad mug.

"Excuse me, Comrade Director, may I ask a question that might seem strange under the circumstances?"

Colonel Bondarchuk looked around in astonishment to see from what point in the faceless mass such an intellectually phrased question had come and singled out a strapping young soldier with a simple Russian face that had something of the romantic about it, that was even reminiscent of Esenin.

"What's your question, friend?"

"Well, you see, I come from a de-kulakized family. My parents set fire to their farm and themselves so as not to have to enter the collective, and my adoptive mother was Jewish. That being the case, what sort of treatment can I expect?"

Bondarchuk took Mitya by the arm, led him off to one side, and gave him an encouraging slap on the shoulder, despite the powerful stench emanating from the young man.

"Equal treatment, my friend, absolutely equal! In the first place, you—if I understand correctly—are one hundred percent Russian, the child of peasants who suffered; and in the second place, we have nothing against the Jews as human beings, you know. I myself," he said, lowering his voice, though only very slightly, "have friends who are Jewish. You see, we're only against alien ideas that have been forced upon the Russian people, namely, against Yiddish communism, not against the Jews as such. How do you feel about the Communists yourself?"

"I hate them with all my heart!" Mitya exclaimed sincerely.

"Well, then, that makes you a genuine fighter in the Russian Army of Liberation." Bondarchuk gave Mitya an affectionate shove in the direction of the line and made a mental note as he followed him with his eyes—must remember that lad, might give him a special assignment later on, a very curious young man.

Just then the interpreter came running after him. "Sir, Standartenführer Krauss sent me for you. It's time to go!"

Bondarchuk spotted the "aristocracy" on a hummock outside the enclosure. The lanky, ass-dragging Dürenhoffer was telling Krauss something smilingly and earnestly. Krauss, his hands behind his back in the pose of a noncommissioned officer, stood beside him with a stony, pensive expression.

Toward midnight, after their blessed disinfection and issue of new clothes—clean military underwear and the uniforms of the "Fritzes"—Mitya and Gosha were sitting on a staircase beneath the attic of a factory dormitory that had been transformed into a barracks. The blissful feeling of being well fed and clean, with the added and unimaginable pleasure of a sufficient tobacco ration, had aroused these young beings and would not let them sleep, as though future horizons of lives on which the door seemed to have closed had once again opened before them. Chain-smoking thick German cigarettes, Gosha Krutkin was reciting Esenin. Mitya was listening attentively. Suddenly he was pierced by the lines:

> *Cornflower words,*
> *My love for eternity,*
> *Melancholy heaped up like hay,*
> *Our cow . . . how is the old girl?*

So all of it had really happened, an appeal to an unknown sister, the eternal Russian cow, cornflowers in the ryegrass, everything animated and whole, not just dismembered carcasses. . . . All this would exist no more, of course, but it had been, which meant that it would always be—Esenin was a witness to it.

Goshka Krutkin, the "runt," went on, sounding like a carnival barker:

> *In the twilight gloom*
> *You dream*
> *Of a bar fight,*
> *Of a knife in my heart.*

The lad was extremely proud of his "friendship" with Esenin, which had begun a year before in a dormitory for subway construction workers, when someone had loaned him a small, semi-forbidden, well-thumbed volume of Esenin's verse from 1927 for three days. Goshka had copied the poet's most popular lines into a small oilcloth-covered notebook with an indelible pencil and later, having discovered that they worked smashingly with girls, began accumulating verses in his little book and learning them by heart. As a matter of fact, his association with his best friend, Mitya Sapunov, had begun with Esenin as well. Until then, every time he had approached the tall, handsome fellow, the latter had rumbled condescendingly, "Get lost, I'd piss in your pocket and not crack a smile about it!" But one day when Sapunov was offered the cloth-covered notebook with the words "Want to read some poetry, Mitya?" he had looked at Goshka differently.

As for Mitya, he had received a thorough grounding in poetry thanks to his aunt Nina. Of course, he had never called Nina "Aunt," and, to tell the truth, he fantasized about her during masturbation, just as he did about Aunt

Veronika. But Nina had frequently dragged the entire Silver Forest household to poetry readings; furthermore, Mitya had often heard various sorts of literary discussions and as a result had developed a quite disdainful attitude toward the hugely popular Esenin: "Well, Esenin is one of that gang who like to play peasant. . . . It's all as ridiculous as a cow in kid leather gloves. Just look closer, he's nothing but a balalaika player in a popular chorus . . ."

It was only in the army, then, at a time of sweat and cruelty, that he actually came to feel quite close to these verses from the "country of the birch trees." And right now, behind the lines of another army, in a uniform of gray-green cloth, each line penetrated everything alien around him like an X ray, imprinting itself on his skin, burning his heart, making his eyes brim with tears that his high-cheekboned face could hardly restrain.

> *Russia fearless,*
> *Lost in Mordva and Chud,*
> *Shackled on endless roads . . .*
> *And I too will be led away*
> *Down a winding road,*
> *Across the sand,*
> *A rope around my neck,*
> *To love my own despair.*

CHAPTER SEVEN

The Special Strike Force

☆

An air of excitement reigned at the Special Strike Force command post within a painstakingly camouflaged system of dugouts on a truly epic hill. The decisive preparations for the Red Army's first advance of the disgraceful summer–autumn campaign of 1941 were in progress.

In order not to give away their position, the stoves in the dugouts were not used during daylight hours, with the result that ferocious cold prevailed in every compartment of the command post. No one noticed it, though, or rather everyone pretended not to, in imitation of Commander Nikita Borisovich Gradov—as was always the case at headquarters.

It should be pointed out, however, that there was some "heating oil" there and that hands frequently drew out flasks from sheepskin coat pockets or boottops. As a matter of fact, in this regard too the staff was following the example of the commander, who from time to time was given a good shot of cognac by Sergeant Major Vaskov, the driver of his personal armored car.

The newly formed staff of the S.S.F. had not yet been corrupted by intrigue, and they idolized their young three-star general. Rumors about him surpassing one another in wildness were going around among the junior officers. It was said, for example, that he had been posted abroad for years at a time, directing an entire network of agents who had supposedly infiltrated the upper echelons of the German High Command. According to others, he hadn't gone anywhere, though he had been assigned to a top secret group of military advisers surrounding Stalin. The older commanders of the regular officer corps only smiled—the true story of the commander in chief of the S.S.F. was even more unbelievable than these fantasies.

For some half an hour already, the three-star general's retinue had been crowding around behind him in anticipation of further action and commands. The back with a sword belt drawn across it seemed to have forgotten the existence of its appendage, that is, its retinue. Gradov moved from one range finder to another, adjusting the lenses himself, observing the enemy positions without a word. What he could see in the snow-covered hills beyond the Istra River, only he knew, but he surely saw something, or else his men would not have continued to jostle one another behind his back.

The enemy was doing nothing to give itself away. Only once had Nikita noticed the slow advance of several round-headed figures along the bottom of a ravine among the drooping, repulsive locks of tree roots and through some abominable shrubberies. Obviously the signal corps stretching a line from the Fourth Tank Group to the headquarters of General Buch, he thought. We could use a system of communications like the one the Germans have. In analyzing the actions of the Wehrmacht during the first months of the war, Nikita Borisovich could not repress a feeling of admiration: a concentration of millions of soldiers that had the agility of a ballerina, something that had been achieved first and foremost by perfect communications.

In all other respects the hills beyond the Istra River kept their idyllic appearance, if one could say such a thing about a shapeless expanse where murky white dotted here and there with jagged grayish-brown patches was the predominant hue. The absence of movement for half an hour, though, might also speak volumes. There were no signs of life, only three steel helmets from the Fourth Tank Group moving slowly, almost imperceptibly crawling along the bottom of a gully among the snags. No puffs of smoke, either, so they must be freezing, warming themselves with schnapps. That means they've gone into hiding, they know about our preparations. They're waiting, and for the first time in the entire war, they're taking the possibility of a Russian counterattack seriously. In the early days, those tanks would already have pushed forward, smashing our defenses and giving us no chance to concentrate. So they must be out of fuel, just as before.

It was remarkable how exactly Hitler's advance on Moscow duplicated Napoleon's—they had begun on almost the same day, June 24, 1812, and June 22, 1941. The same mistakes had been repeated, particularly with regard to communications. How could one carry on mechanized warfare without having thought through the problem of the railroads, without making preparations for the change from the narrow-gauge European tracks to the wide-gauge Russian ones? They must have incompetents, too, their own Voroshilovs and Budyonnys—so Wilhelm Keitel isn't the cleverest man in the world.

Nikita Borisovich called his artillery commander, Colonel Skakunkov, over. "Ivan Stepanovich, give the order to Droznin's battery to shell that gully immediately. Five minutes of good concentrated fire!"

Continuing his observation, he marked the time on his special-issue "commander's model" watch, which at times seemed to urge on his blood flow with its stubborn ticking. Droznin's battery went right to work. Shells plowed up the ravine for the brief allotted period of time, raising geysers of dirt and wood detritus. Then all was quiet. Ten minutes later three Messerschmitts flew over the lines in the direction of Droznin's battery. Then Gradov gave an order to scramble a flight of fighters to engage the enemy planes in a dogfight. Everything was working perfectly—the diversionary artillery barrage had fooled the Germans, who had swallowed the bait, or, as they say in the gulag, "been bought like whores."

For several days Nikita Gradov had been trying to leave the Germans with the impression that the chief target of his advance would be this very unit, the Fourth Tank Group, which was partly immobilized by lack of fuel; the Russians would try to isolate and then pulverize them in order to remove the threat of the storming and capture of Moscow. In fact, it was just the opposite that was intended: to ignore the tank unit entirely and to pass significantly further to the north, reach Klin in one day, link up with elements of the Thirtieth Army, and take the city. Even if Buch did manage to put two or three dozen tanks in action in the next ten days, they would still make no difference, assault aviation would take care of them. In other words, the Germans would think the Russians were attacking within the framework of traditional defensive strategy, and then right before their eyes an entirely new concept would develop: the beginning of an offensive all along the line, the end of the blitzkrieg. Quite satisfied, Nikita Borisovich continued to observe the murky white valley, illuminated at its periphery by frequent muzzle flashes: the German artillery had opened fire on a fictional headquarters, set up and open to view five hundred yards further back in the defenses. The shells thus flew over the real command point.

In the retinue, some had finally figured out what game their commanding officer had been playing at during the past half hour, and some assessed the game very favorably, not from a tactical point of view but in terms of grand strategy—among them Colonel Vadim Vuinovich, deputy chief of staff for communications, who could not help but admire his old friend.

Vadim, of course, was perfectly well aware that he owed his liberation from the Karaganda camp to Nikita, though not a word was said about it. All things considered, there was no renewal of the old friendship, not even so much as a "manly conversation." Nikita let Vadim understand that his assignment to S.S.F. headquarters was only temporary and that after the campaign in progress was completed, he would be free to join another unit, if only so as not to feel restricted, as he would if he remained the immediate subordinate of his former friend and husband of the woman of his dreams. Of course, it would have been marvelous to open a bottle of vodka, lay out some food on a suitcase, and, sitting there like Cyril and Methodius, put the dots on a long rows of *i*'s, as it were, to tell each other about their interrogations, their time in the prisons and the camps . . . and yet, all these past events, which at the beginning had seemed like something that would naturally bring them together, now seemed almost unimaginable, an effect that was in no small part caused by the vast gulf between their ranks—it was almost a joke, a three-star general and a colonel—and they had tacitly agreed that now was not the time for these things, that right now there was not even any time to sit around; we'll make time to get away later on, they said. The main thing was that they could look each other directly in the eyes without blinking or blushing.

One day, however, in a rare moment when no one else on the headquarters staff was around, when there was only Vaskov sitting by the door with his accordion, Nikita suddenly raised his head from a map and asked Vadim, "Did you know Veronika was *there*, too?"

Vadim had not known and was shaken. To picture Veronika, the shining star of his life, *there*, among the tarts of the camps, was more than he could bear. They looked at each other for several seconds and then, behind their masks of sturdy military men, suddenly recognized in each other the shivering, half-alive prisoners they had been in the gulag. It was such an overwhelming moment that they nearly threw themselves at each other in an embrace and burst into sobs. At that point, fortunately, the quick-witted

Vaskov broke off the tune he was playing, and they went back to rustling their maps, speaking in strained voices, moving further away from each other—friend from friend, rival from rival—with each passing minute, returning ever more swiftly from the shameful state of nonexistence in which they had lived in the camps to their supposedly genuine existence as high-ranking officers of the headquarters staff, the supposedly real essence of the war in which their whole lives were bound up. At the end of this private audience, the commanding officer inserted into a series of technical questions put to his deputy chief of staff for communications: "She's just fine now." He could see that Vadim was grateful to him for these words, and Nikita himself was glad that the other man had asked no questions.

The general stepped back from the range finders, rubbed his hands, and winked at his staff officers in satisfaction. Every man, including Colonel Vuinovich, felt as though this friendly wink were directed at him. A mighty current of energy radiated from the commander, who seemed to have no doubt about what only yesterday no one would have believed, that victory would be theirs; there was no apparent ideological mysticism for him in the very idea of "victory," nothing akin to the agitprop incantations that came out of the newspapers and the radio. He saw victory in strictly military and professional terms, almost like a sport—perhaps this was what encouraged those around him most of all.

"Everybody back to work!" ordered Nikita. "Operations conference in Khimki at 0700. No more vodka, gentlemen!" Army Commissar Golovnya raised his eyebrows at this last form of address, as if to say, "What are we supposed to make of that?" It seemed at the very least a strange thing to say to men in a proletarian army. The commanding officer, however, switched to a joking tone. "And no card games, singing of romantic ditties, or dancing quadrilles! Think only of operational categories, prepare your thoughts on your respective areas of responsibility!" Golovnya's face broke into a smile along with those of the other men—just a joke, he understood, to keep up everyone's fighting spirit.

"Let's go, Vaskov!" said Nikita as he moved toward the door with a long stride.

Several minutes later, an armored car rolled out of its shelter beneath a moldering camouflage net and drove along a barely noticeable road that might have been better called a field heading for the operational area of the Eighth Aviation Regiment; the field was so overgrown and wild it might have been taken straight from Russian folklore. Behind the armored car lumbered the transporter carrying the commander's personal bodyguard; Captain Eryes, a strange type, was undoubtedly among them.

This Eryes has mischievous eyes, Nikita Borisovich remembered. He hides them. What the devil is he always following me for? Who assigned him to this detail? There was no need to guess; it was obvious.

Suddenly, figures of women carrying spades loomed up in the field; their fur hats with long flaps that could be bound around the neck stood out sharply amid the dirty snow. They were the civil defense workers of Moscow, digging trenches, ineptly hacking at the frozen earth with miserable shovels. The women followed the progress of the armored car with their eyes. They were in a lamentable state. Students and charwomen in pathetic "spring and fall" civilian overcoats, some even wearing elegant hats, were doing a great deal of work, which although in military terms was a useless diversion was very significant in terms of propaganda. "The entire people will hold out in a single spirit." Which reminds me, thought Nikita, I have a brigade of Home Guards made up of dentists and lawyers and the like on the left flank, a mighty force with one outdated rifle for every three men. Mustn't forget to get them out of the line of fire before the fight tomorrow.

They were already waiting for the general at the airfield, even though he had not notified the aviation chiefs of his coming. The commander of the regiment, Lieutenant Colonel Blagogoveny, together with his staff officers and squadron leaders, was already coming toward him. Now, there was an inspiring spectacle, a group of young, healthy fellows in flying jackets, bolstering one another with their assured steps, barracks swearing, and general military vigor.

The principal forces of the regiment, Hawks and Ilyushins, were camouflaged somewhat haphazardly in a nearby grove. They were supposed to look like U-2 two-seater biplanes, but there had not been enough materiel to finish the job, and they were now parked any which way on the summer field. After exchanging a few words with Blagogoveny about combat readiness, the commander headed toward one of the biplanes, which seemed like a bit of aviation history.

The plane's pilot came to attention before the army commander. "Lieutenant Budorazhin!" In the left-hand corner of his mouth was a gold tooth.

"Well, Lieutenant, shall we go for a ride?" asked the commander suddenly, much to the surprise of all present. Without waiting for a reply, he climbed into the passenger seat.

Everyone was dumbfounded, particularly the members of his bodyguard. "What do you mean, Comrade General?" said a flustered Vaskov.

Budorazhin immediately hopped up onto the wing and produced a fleece-lined flight jacket for the commander, who would remember to commend the pilot for his readiness to make immediate decisions. A few minutes later, the clattering old "corn grinder" rolled out onto the runway. Squinting, Nikita observed his bodyguards. Captain Eryes seemed to have lost his head at the unexpected decision, rushing up first to Vaskov, then to Lieutenant Colonel Blagogoveny, yelling until his voice was on the point of breaking, even grabbing at his holstered pistol. Vaskov was nearly on his knees before him, clutching his hands to his own expansive chest beneath a fur-lined jacket. That was Vaskov all over. The commander of the flyer regiment hardly even favored Eryes with a glance. The submachine gunners of the guard detachment were grinning, showing their thumbs. Yes, thought Nikita, they're good men.

Eryes could have blown his own brains out in desperation: he had been inattentive. To go over the front lines in the U-2 was a hop of ten minutes or so. If you don't keep your eyes about you, he told himself, you'll have a high-ranking defector on your hands. Gradov has reason to hate us, after all—he was an enemy of the people, he hasn't forgotten the skill of the secret police. And that would be the end of Captain Eryes and all his brilliant plans for the future.

That Eryes is too emotional, the general thought coldly, watching the lanky figure running to and fro among the officers. An excess of emotion in his line of work was not called for at all. A Chekist was supposed to have "a cool head and a burning heart." Eryes was simply a case of overheating all around.

Before the plane began to taxi, Nikita Borisovich gave orders to Lieutenant Budorazhin as to where to fly. Then he wrapped himself more snugly in the leather jacket and flopped back into his seat.

From an altitude of a thousand feet the earth seemed filled with a bleak drowsiness, as it often is in the area surrounding Moscow when the dreary days have settled in for too long. The sky at that moment was empty, there was no aerial combat, and there were no flashes of gunfire to be seen in the area. It appeared as though peace had returned to Soviet Russia. Then again, had she ever known peace? There, beyond the Yakhroma River, huge concentration camps had recently been set up; canal locks adorned with statues had been constructed with slave labor; and even if one didn't count that, the country had seen enough fear, enough despicable acts, and enough violence since the days of the great Revolution. Of course, there were other things to be found here as well—youth, love, rhapsodic evenings. . . . From that lake that just went by below, for example, a Russian princess had once emerged in a skin-tight bathing suit in the twilight, water dripping from every blessed curve of her body, at first in momentary currents, then in streams, then flying off in large drops that disappeared beneath the grandiose, symbolic sky.

.   .   .

After four years of separation—and what a separation!—they met in his father's house as though nothing out of the ordinary had happened, as if he were simply returning from an extended official voyage, as he had in 1933 after spending several months in China on a secret mission.

In Silver Forest, they knew he had been set free and could appear at any minute, so he wasn't expecting to send anyone into a faint, all the more so since Veronika had returned the day before yesterday. He rolled up to the house in a staff car, opened the gate, and walked up the path to the house, just as he had in days gone by. A pair of skis protruded from the snow on the front porch. The same old lamp with its base of Chinese porcelain was still in a second-story window. Nikita was suddenly struck by an ephemeral feeling of enmity toward it all, all of that which he had not even allowed himself to dream about, which he had always pushed further and further away from himself like a *ne plus ultra*, a mirage on the edge of dying. His father's house, "in the bosom of his family . . ." At that moment it all seemed like an importunate absurdity, an inappropriate embellishment to his unsentimental—to put it mildly—life, like the string bag packed with groceries suspended from the transom window of the kitchen. Another step, and all these vile thoughts were swept away. He opened the door and plunged into the warmth of what was near and dear to him, into a small, miraculously preserved bubble of peace and goodwill.

His mother still could not get to sleep without taking large amounts of valerian drops, and Agasha just wasn't herself anymore. A strapping adolescent, almost a young man—Boris IV, in fact, his own child—shouted into the telephone, "Grandpa, come home right away, Father has come back!" He was surprised by the large, heavy suitcases assembled in the library. What was all this, then? "We're preparing to be evacuated, Nikita!" Verulka hung on his arm, not wanting to let go, tugging at his chevrons. And then, seemingly straight from the past, driving the four terrible years from memory, the dazzling Veronika came running down the stairs.

Several hours later, when things had calmed down and they were alone, he asked her, "Listen, how is it that you're just as beautiful as you always were, still the same Veronika?"

She gave a little shudder and looked at his face, in which at that moment there was something frightening and unrecognizable. "Do you think so? Thank you for the compliment. You've changed somehow, though, Nikita. No, no, on the outside you've gotten even better, you . . . ha, ha . . . you're an interesting man, but something has appeared in you. . . . Then again, it'll pass, surely."

It was not difficult to grasp what she had in mind. In the old days, the first thing he had done was to drag her upstairs, even after only a week's separation, roaming around like a sexual somnambulist, literally unable to speak to anyone if he did not have his way. It was even ridiculous at times—at least wait ten minutes, for appearances' sake, you lunatic! And now, after having been apart for four years! He wandered around upstairs for several hours, refusing even to go into the bathroom—he explained that he'd already washed that day and that he was waiting for his father—he drank vodka with lunch, beamed at everyone, including her, but not the way he had before, not like in days gone by, when he had looked at her with eyes quite blinded by desire.

He sat her down on his lap and began to unbutton her dress. "Still the same perfume," he mumbled as if seized by passion, but his words rang false. Through the fragrance of "Madame Roche" the despairing Nikita sensed the corruption of the camp, the lingering stench of wet rags from the barracks, the slime of watery soup, the chlorine used to wash out the latrine buckets. He stood up from the bed so sharply that Veronika was jostled to one side.

She looked at him with an entirely new expression, that of a camp dog. "It's okay, darling, it's all right. Let's just sleep, then—you're tired, my love . . ."

"No, wait! First tell me how you managed not to become ugly—you look stunning, even without any makeup!"

She brushed the statement aside with a wave of her hand. "Makeup! By some miracle, I did find a jar of cold cream yesterday, and the perfume was left over from the old life . . . and I bought some lipstick from a passenger at the station . . . for your arrival, my lord . . . terrible stuff, 'Moscow Lights.' "

"Why didn't—why didn't you put it on, then?" he asked, feeling a sudden return of the old, powerful surges.

She sensed it as well and looked at him like a slut who knew just what he wanted. "I tried to put it on, but somehow it just looked too vulgar. Do you want me to put it on now?"

"Let me do it myself!" He took the lipstick, which smelled of strawberry soap, and with it began to paint the submissive face. She was behaving admirably, like a seasoned performer.

"You haven't even lost weight, Veronika! Did they feed you well?"

"Just imagine, I acted on the stage there!" She laughed in a way that made him quite lose his head. He turned her sharply so that her back faced him. She exposed herself with instantaneous willingness. "Just imagine, I was a hay mower in an amateur production in the camp. I played a role in the play *An Optimistic Tragedy*—just picture that!"

"I'm picturing it!" he said huskily and just then saw in the dark window the reflection of an officer with a half-undressed woman, a pornographic scene of the greatest intensity that stirred him to the depths. "I'm picturing it," he repeated, "picturing it. . . . So you're an actress, eh? Screwed the guards out there, did you? And it was the guards who fed you there, my 'optimistic tragedy,' right?"

By now she was even moaning, something she had never done before.

Afterward they lay motionless for a long time, he on his side, she with her face buried in the blanket. Melancholy and grief had burned them to the ground. There would never be a return of what they had had between them all their lives, pure, stormy, and tender; all their comical, childish murmurs, their whirlwinds of passion and gentleness; all that was gone—the only thing that remained was prostitution. And not only in her, he thought, but in me as well, nothing but prostitution. Not only in me, she thought, but in him as well, nothing but prostitution.

"There, you see, Nikitushka, I played the part of the whore for you," she said softly.

Nikita, who seemed to be asleep, did not answer. He had gone to sleep with his boots on, the way officers do in brothels.

She got out of bed, shook her shoes off, and began pacing around the room noiselessly and aimlessly, touching the shutters and books. Then, as if seeking an escape, she went to her wardrobe, opened it, and began to sort through the dresses hanging there. Some of them were even quite good, the few that had survived the plundering of the NKVD and the ones Ninka had brought last night—georgette, crêpe de chine, cashmere. . . . All at once she dissolved sobbing into a squall of anguish, shame, and hopelessness and sat down on the floor in front of the wardrobe. With her head in her hands, she raced back in time to her own yesterday, to the camp north of Syktyvkar.

Bedlam reigned in the large women's barracks toward evening after the end of the workday. The thieves—that is, the majority of the population— were running from bunk to bunk, clarifying relationships, demanding their rights, making mad scenes. One jealous commotion after another was played out between the "studs" and the "bitches." Everything ended up in shrieking and bodies rolling on the floor. Then they calmed down, their faces scratched and bruised, and everyone took their respective places, embracing their partners, singing popular songs or retelling the plots of novels about noble counts and their illegitimate daughters who had become thieves and prostitutes. Of course, the storytellers were prisoners with light sentences on charges of counterrevolutionary activity, who had mostly been arrested for being a member of a family of an "enemy of the people," a group that included Veronika. The third principal group of the camp population was made up of the so-called "women from the west," rural Catholics from Galicia. They stuck together, whispering prayers in their nearly incomprehensible language or sewing. The attempts by the thieves' gangs to wreck the solidarity of these women foundered on some strange, obstinate inviolability on the part of the Galicians.

It occurred to Veronika, as she observed the life of the barracks, that everyone here struggled for her human dignity in her own way: the Galicians with their stubborn, indissoluble, unceasing activity; the women from the Party and the "family members" with their memories of stays at sanitoriums for the elite; and even the thieves—who perhaps struggled more fiercely than anyone else—who shrieked and clawed one another and played out their scenes of jealousy as though this were their way of defending their right to scream and fight, to be jealous, and to have a sex life, and of expressing their desire not to turn into servile cattle.

So it was that Veronika one day raced in despair toward a saving gleam of light, the camp House of Culture (which existed there, as elsewhere, as an integral part of communism) and joined the drama club. The troupe was presided over by a first-class professional, the Moscow director Tartakovsky of the Vakhtangov school, who had recently been dragged away half alive from the mines when the authorities had suddenly decided to use him in this function. That had been the directive from the top: support the Houses of Culture! They pulled him out and spared no expense—all the bigwigs of the camp administration came to his shows. Tartakovsky began to give Veronika more and more prominence, as she seemed to him to be a person of his circle, and they did indeed have many mutual acquaintances in Moscow. One day, Major Koltsov, the camp commandant, appeared at a rehearsal of *An Optimistic Tragedy*. Someone had reported to him that among the zek actresses was a beautiful general's wife. What do you say, Gradov, would you like to drop by for an hour or so and talk about art? Koltsov was a man of whim, and her nauseating privileged status began at that moment. The commandant's pet, what a disgrace! Koltsov's aide, a self-styled Cossack in a high fur hat, a small lock of hair falling over his forehead, and the expression of a bored hooligan written all over his face, came to the barracks not less than once a week. "Gradov, let's go for a walk!" She walked down the rows of bunks. The thieves jeered after her: "Off to rehearsal, eh, Miss Artist? She and Koltsov are going to have their own private rehearsal! Climb on up here, pretty girl, we'll give you a better rehearsal than the commandant will!" An old woman from St. Petersburg named Kappelbaum never failed to snatch at Veronika's hand. "Vikochka, please bring me back something, anything! Please, just a scrap of something nutritious, my dear! Anything edible, I beg you!"

This went on for nearly a year, and then a room was set aside for her in the officers' club, thereby cutting her off entirely from the camp masses—in other words, she had become a tool of the camp administration, but in the highest category. Sometimes, however, before an inspection or after a row with Koltsov, she was sent back to the barracks, where the women of the thieves' gangs greeted her with an alley-cat serenade. Then she was back to Koltsov's good graces.

He was gangling, weak, and hysterical. In addition to his other charms, he also suffered from incontinence and was forever jumping to his feet and shuffling down the corridor to the latrine. The major's greatest pleasure was turning a zek into a lady. In fact, he himself loved acting, though it was difficult to understand just what absurd role it was that he was playing when alone with Veronika—perhaps it was something along the lines of the "count" of the barracks "romances." Wasn't she some sort of damned Eliza Doolittle, after all?

"Oh, my dear, I can't stand to see you in that awful padded jacket! Off with those dreadful boots! Please, darling, take off those nightmarish (pronouncing the word gave him unadulterated pleasure), nightmarish trousers! Look what I've brought for you. Here are new undergarments, stockings, a silk dress, shoes!"

He dressed her in these odds and ends that he had found in the Syktyvar army-navy store, and only after he had completed the spectacular metamorphosis did he throw himself upon her with something like a growl; perhaps he was capturing a trophy, or perhaps he was receiving payment for his magnanimity.

In sorrow and despair, with a feeling of revulsion for her benefactor and even more for herself, Veronika accepted her role in this stinking theater just as she did all the food parcels that went along with it. Just yesterday, when rumors that Nikita had been shot had reached her via the camp grapevine, it had seemed to her that there was nothing left to live for, and now today she had lunged forward again like a frog. It's just like churning butter, she told herself, for the sake of the children—anything to survive, to return to the children . . .

Koltsov made her sick to her stomach: a damp red mouth, a nose like a bird's beak, raven black bangs, greedy and sluggish extremities. One day, just to spite him, she said to his aide, Shevchuk, "Why don't you come along too, cossack?" The young boor lost no time showing up, and Veronika took to unburdening herself with him, avenging herself, as it were, for all the violence that had been done to a past as pure and ringing as the sound of a racquet hitting a tennis ball, for the whole "tennis" period of her life.

There will never be any more tennis for me, she thought. She was sniffling and whimpering, sitting on the floor beside the wardrobe, her appearance disheveled. All you have to do is raise your head a bit, and right away you see your ugly snout in the mirror, smeared with lipstick, streaks of mascara under your eyelashes; it was all slopped together like something out of Stendhal—the red and the black, a bad joke on the victims of the era. Everything is finished, Nikita will never come back to me—for that matter, he'll never be himself again . . . it's the end, the end . . .

Everything is finished, thought her husband, who was only pretending to be asleep. Veronika didn't come back, she no longer exists. Is it worth it, fighting the Germans for the ruins of my family?

A great deal of moving and shaking began the next morning. A five-room apartment was allotted to, or "unsealed" for, them. It had obviously been inhabited by some enemy of the people before it was "sealed." The flat was in the most aristocratic area imaginable, on Gorky Street itself, immediately opposite the Central Telegraph Office. Veronika forgot all her resentments and acts of self-abasement of the previous night: like it or not, war or no war, she would have to set up housekeeping in the flat, have the children transferred to another school, see to the provision of the general's ration, and so forth and so on.

What the hell, thought Nikita as he sat in the observer's seat of the antediluvian biplane, which shuddered through every air current. What can you do? As people say these days, "Chalk it up to war . . ." The pilot turned around, his young teeth sparkling. Is everything all right, sir? With a motion of his hand, Nikita indicated the direction of the location of his tank units.

Back on the ground, Captain Eryes was breathing a bit more easily; the biplane was flying away from the front lines. "Put a few escort planes in the air, Major," he said to Blagogoveny. "Otherwise they might lose their way." The powerful flyer simply directed a sarcastic sidelong glance at him. "Did you hear what I said?" said the Special Forces agent. "What are you, some kind of fucking idiot, Captain?" the commander of the regiment shot back most impolitely and walked away. People have quite a cheek when they go to war, thought Eryes. Must take some action. They really get cheeky when they get weapons.

Tomorrow, the armored wedge will decide the whole affair. Thirty new T-34s that just arrived from the Urals will break through the first German echelons with losses of around ten percent, the second with, say, five percent, and then the main force, crushing all in its path and sowing panic, will get to Klin in a day. Nikita looked down upon the new column as it approached a grove of birches. A good machine, the T-34, reportedly superior to the German Mark IV in all respects. We'll see tomorrow how it acquits itself in conditions of headlong advance. The commander of the lead tank waved to the passing biplane from his hatch. On the other side of a spruce-covered hillock, two dozen monster IS Stalin tanks, the pride of the prewar Red Army, were waiting in a ravine. There was no camouflage that could cover them, and what would be the point anyway? It would have been obvious. Slow, with a maximum speed of no more than eight miles per hour on good roads, these dinosaurs had been a favorite target of the Germans throughout the war, beginning with the battles on the Stalin line, as the enemy called the system of fortifications on the old western frontier. The Messerschmitt 109s hardly even considered them a "kill," and Fritz the foot soldier, the out-and-out scourge of the front lines who was used to coming to grips with the fighting tools of many nations, had immediately learned where the blind spots of the IS machine gunners were, calmly approached to a suitable distance, and only then drew a "potato masher" from his boottop. In spite of everything, though, the High Command still considered the remaining heavy tanks a vital reserve. Obviously Stalin had not been given any reports about the fate of his namesake at the front. The S.S.F. had been saddled with a division of them, despite all Nikita's efforts to refuse.

We'll send them in the direction of Sosnyaki to give the Germans the impression that the main blow is directed there. We'll have to move them right up to the front line during the night. Of course, the Germans will torch all of them in the first hour, but it is precisely that first hour that could prove to be decisive. An unexpected thought suddenly gave Gradov chills all over: did that mean that they might as well start making funeral arrangements for the tank crews? That's the way it goes, the commanding officer reflected, reining himself in severely: by sacrificing hundreds, we will save thousands. As for who ends up under one heading and who under the other, that's not our business anymore.

Below them there appeared a half-destroyed farm machinery and tractor station that had sprung up in its day near some desecrated churches. Among the twisted combines were parked harmless-looking trucks—three-ton vehicles with rails thrusting up into the sky at an oblique angle from the chassis, the so-called barrelless rocket artillery. It was nothing if not a serious weapon, able to generate an extremely rapid, dense fire. The word was that the soldiers had begun to call these strange cannons "Katyushas"—a woman's name. Not a bad little joke when you think about it, quite in keeping with the spirit of the war; jokes, a clever saying, and a cigarette, and then everything goes to hell in flames and explosions. However, if these Katyushas, so good at belching forth death, were not mounted on a suitable vehicle, there would be little sense in using them. They could not be carried far on these three-tonners, and yet they would have to be run back and forth between the lines of the front like fiery archangels, to be elusive on rugged terrain, and to follow up on breakthroughs. The army needed powerful, speedy trucks capable of hauling large objects, but there were none in sight. Tukhachevsky had talked about the possibility of such a vehicle in his day, but no one had heeded him. And yet without them, Nikita thought, it will be practically impossible for us to mount a serious counteroffensive. Military men can raise this question until they turn blue in the face, but there's no way out, the Americans won't build such a machine for us.

The soldiers manning the Katyushas were obviously already aware that their commanding officer was flying over them. Several crew members formed ranks and saluted out of the rubble of the tractor station.

Budorazhin, carrying out his orders to the letter, began to fly on a north-easterly heading after passing over the tractor station. Nikita Borisovich was surveying a huge area plunged into the calm that comes before a storm. There were nearly three hundred thousand people under his command here, and every one of them hoped to survive not only tomorrow's battle but the war as a whole, to return home to his own unique idea of warmth. It was an army almost equal in size to Napoleon's entire Grande Armée: infantrymen, artil-lerymen, tank crews, flyers, two cavalry brigades, even a brigade of marines (to be kept in reserve until the storming of Klin itself!), sappers, signalmen, paratroopers . . . and every one of them sure it would be someone else who would be killed. It's one of the mysteries of mass psychology, he thought, just as I have my own part in the riddle. Everyone assumes he'll survive, and yet at the same time we quite cold-bloodedly calculate the percentages of our losses without even considering the fact that these percentages, always more or less accurate when worked out by a well-trained specialist, are made up of a mass of instantaneous transformations of thinking, moving, and hoping human beings into shredded scraps of flesh. We have no choice, though, he thought, and he was suddenly filled with a sort of inspired, symphonic resig-nation. This is my shining hour, the great war—isn't this what I've been moving toward my entire life?

All of a sudden, the peaceful, snowy region was lit up with fire. Several German batteries opened up from behind the lines. The pilot turned around. He was a quick-witted lad. Nikita Borisovich gestured to him—back and down! What was the meaning of this shelling? Surely they're not preparing an offensive? Maybe I've overlooked something somewhere after all? The shelling stopped as quickly as it had started, as though it had not been the work of human hands but rather a passing phenomenon of nature, only a quick splashing-out of some magma. They were approaching the airfield in an empty, overcast sky whose whiteness was speckled here and there by blue—a formation of Dornier bombers, which the English had aptly nicknamed "Flying Pencils," was heading for Moscow at a great altitude. They were flying further and further to the east, where an aerial battle was shaping up, but all of that was already outside the boundaries of "Gradov's land."

THIRD INTERMISSION
THE PRESS

Radio Moscow:
German workers! They're making you work at a forced pace. Work slowly, in order to hasten the end of Hitler!

The BBC:
An anonymous London taxi driver said yesterday, " 'E's bitten off more'n 'e can chew!"
The celebrated Bernard Shaw declared, "Either Hitler is a bigger fool than I thought, or he's off his head."

Noticias Gráficas, **Argentina:**
The crushing of the Fascist putsch in which highly placed members of the army and government participated was carried out in conditions of absolute secrecy . . .

Time **magazine:**
Red "About-face." When Soviet Russia signed a pact with Hitler 22 months ago, the American Communist Party suddenly adopted a pro-Nazi orientation and pronounced the pact a "magnificent contribution to the cause of peace."
Party Chairman William Foster now declares that the new war is "an attack on the people of Germany, of the United States, and of the entire world. . . . The Soviet government is standing up for the vital interests of the peoples of the whole world . . . of all progressive humanity . . ."

Time **magazine. October 13, 1941:**
Last week Adolf Hitler said he had beaten Russia. Obviously he meant to say that he is beating Russia. . . . He still has much to conquer before he can lay a bearskin rug in the German living room. . . . He will still have to rout the Ukrainian armies of the mustachioed cavalryman Semyon Budyonny . . .

. . .

Lend-Lease negotiations. . . . The supplicants say: We need light bombers by such-and-such a date. The givers reply: That's impossible. Supplicants: In that case, Moscow will fall. Givers: We'll do everything possible . . .

October 20, 1941:
The last unscathed Russian armies, those of Marshal Timoshenko, are encircled in the Bryansk and Vyazma regions. . . . The southern armies of Marshal Budyonny have been routed. . . . Marshal Voroshilov's best troops are sealed in Leningrad . . .

The New York Times:
Novgorod is a terrible sight to behold. A cemetery of living corpses.

In the 13th century, this city called itself "The Great Lord Novgorod," and its Kremlin even then was much older than the oldest building in the United States is now. . . . Stukas, however, have no respect for relics. Only 56 of the city's houses are still standing.

Time **magazine, October 27, 1941:**
Stalin's life, jealously guarded by the fearful abbreviations OGPU and NKVD, is now threatened by TNT. Three of his Kremlin rooms have been directly aimed at. Last week, seven bombs fell inside the old fortress.

. . . the Lenin Mausoleum on Red Square is closed. . . . One supposes that his remains have been removed from the city . . .

Winston Churchill, November 17, 1941:
We vow to ourselves, to our Russian allies, to the people of the USA . . . that we will never enter into negotiations with Hitler . . .

Generalissimo Chiang Kai-shek:
This is a crucial time in our common struggle . . .

General Charles de Gaulle:
We have reached the very moment when the tide of battle has turned in our favor . . .

Selected by *Time* magazine as Man of the Year for 1942: Iosif Stalin, whose name in Russian means "steel."

Men of goodwill: William Temple, archbishop of Canterbury; Henry J.

Kaiser, industrialist, producer of Liberty Ships; Wendell Willkie, who traveled around the world as an independent political figure.

Men of war: Erwin Rommel, a great virtuoso among field commanders; Theodor von Bock, who reached the left bank of the Volga; the frog-legged Tomoyuki Yamashita, who drove the English from Singapore; the Yugoslavian general Drazha Mikhailovich, who carried on the resistance when resistance seemed impossible; General Dwight D. Eisenhower, who landed in North Africa; Douglas MacArthur, whose artfulness and bravery raised him to the level of a hero.

The Guardian, London:

Major Valentina Grizodubova is a 31-year-old pretty falconess of Red Aviation. She has a 5-year-old son whom she calls her "little hawk" . . . Female squadrons fly Hurricanes and even bombers. . . . Nina Lomako shot down a German plane a month before her daughter was born. . . . "Christmas crackers!" exclaims a pilot in Her Majesty's Air Force. "Nowadays a man can get the push from any job! I'd like to meet these birds!"

Time magazine:

Factory workers in the Urals wait for weeks for their turn to have a bath.

FOURTH INTERMISSION
THE ROSSETTE DOVE*

Appearing in the world once again, Alexandra Rossette would have liked to have been a "peace dove," that is, to fly, gliding and turning aerial somersaults, over the marble terraces of the Alexandrian Library, to perch, cooing gently, on the cornices closest to the windows of the philosophers and poets—in other words, to live in the so-called distant past. Instead, however, as that lovely man Alexander Pushkin put it one day in a bon mot, the Devil had come up with the idea to bring her to life in the same Russian land, and moreover in the so-called future, at the limits of incredible cold, where in the terrible, gloomy days of war and prison you don't know what to do with a talent for love and elegance.

Nevertheless, her little heart fluttered when she saw the façade of the Bolshoi Theater, so familiar she was on the verge of dovelike tears, with the façade of the Maly Theater alongside it, a chariot on the roof, the colonnade,

*Alexandra Rossette, a lady-in-waiting and favorite of Tsar Nicholas I. She interceded with Nicholas on behalf of Gogol.

steps down which her friends from Petersburg had once run on short visits, young men from the days of the beginning of Nicholas I's reign full of life, ideas, and poetry. Instead of them, the new era could be seen moving quickly here and there in different directions: closely cropped hair with faces protruding like tumors; and with strange eyes, maybe threatening, or maybe just scared to death. No, all these Delones, Rossettes, and Amalriks weren't running to these people from the bloodied Paris riffraff. Far were they, far indeed, from the bucolic scene that had sheltered the French royalists!

Nestling on the cornice of a huge, unknown house decorated with a faded lilac fresco that somehow clashed with the modern round-faced man, the dove dreamed about the Alexandrian Library, about the lads of the Arzamas circle, about the languid, trembling long sideburns of the sovereign, of polished floors, of ladies-in-waiting rustling their petticoats as they flocked down the triumphal steps. Someone scattered a few bread crumbs from a transom, and she pecked at them with gratitude as she looked through the dusty window into the depths of the room. A long-nosed man wearing a green uniform, a crew cut, and a determined expression on his face was sitting there. Suddenly she remembered: the balcony above Nice and on it, with his back to the sea, the same long-nosed, round-shouldered man, but with long, disheveled locks of hair that were not always in an ideal state—who is he? "Can it be you are in love with me, Nikolai Vasilievich?" It seemed he would now wave his coattails in horror, soar over Nice, and head for the blue-tinted hills of Provence to hide among the rocks somewhere, concealing his legs in stockings that were also far from ideal. Instead of this, though, he rushed by her, through all the rooms to the way out, his boots banging on the stairs, and did not appear again for two weeks. The crane and the dove turned out to be incompatible as lovers.

The dove cooed a few grateful words to the long-nosed humanitarian for the crumbs of a baguette, received according to category "A" from interdepartmental funds. Their friendship dated from that time. The dove simply took up residence on that cornice, where she could take shelter from the cold wind in the mouth of a ventilation shaft. The long-nosed fellow never forgot to sprinkle a few crumbs from his window three times a day. He smiled, showing his uneven teeth, thinking that there was no shame in showing signs of tenderness before a mute creature.

The dove came to love the solitary man, though she continued to offer herself to the king of the pigeon population of Teatralny Square. Then again, it never occurred to her that the one might have the slightest bearing upon the other. Flying across the square and landing on her cornice, the pigeon king pecked up all the remaining bread crumbs and only then began his mating dance, distinguished by its duration and courtliness. No sooner had the ritual finished than he began crowding his mate into a corner behind the stone column, where he took her to their mutual pleasure. Thus she had once been led down the darkened halls of the palace over the great water in order for him to thrust her into a velvet corner and to reward her with his most high favor. One day, in the middle of their ecstasy, the dove noticed the long nose protruding from the transom window and the fear frozen in the eye of her breadwinner.

Several weeks went by before the day when Alexandra, emerging from the ventilation shaft in the morning, found no bread crumbs upon the ledge. There were none again at noon, nor in the evening. In some confusion, she paced back and forth beneath the small window and trembled at the squeak it gave when it opened by itself. She flew up to the height of the transom and looked into the room. The man with the long nose was stretched across his bed, his back to the wall, wheezing. From his nose hung two leeches gorged with his blood. "A ladder!" he called as loudly as he could through his death rattle. "Give me a ladder!"

Caught up in the turbulence of the symphony playing itself out before her, Alexandra soared up into the sky, on which the shades of night were beginning to fall and where blinding rockets hung suspended, launched from the earth in the direction of the bomber squadrons.

To fly off forever and die somewhere far away was her passionate dream. Several months later, she crossed over warring Europe and came to rest on a tiled roof beside a mansard window in which a bald man in a sailor's striped jersey was visible. She surveyed the sharp curves of the roof and burst into tears of recognition. The bald, sharp-eyed man, meanwhile, sketched her with a few strokes of his pencil, her wings opened. In another few years, this drawing would become the symbol of peace and a source of no small amount of mileage for Cold War purveyors of disinformation.

CHAPTER EIGHT

Professor and Student

★

In March 1942, after five months of unceasing work in the divisional hospital, Dod Tyshler went to Moscow for new surgical equipment. To be honest, he had never thought a trip on an ordinary trolley would bring him so much pleasure. No sooner had he spotted the two-tiered means of transportation on Gorky Street than he rushed toward it, pushing his way through a crowd of pedestrians who also wished to become passengers, and with relish allowed himself to be squeezed inside and pushed to the upper level.

The trolley was going downtown. In Dod's eyes, impoverished wartime Moscow represented the epitome of what a capital city ought to feel like, of peace and a carnival atmosphere. A stream of enchanted springtime city air came in through a broken window. It passed along Tyshler's poorly shaven cheek, dived behind the back of the conductor—she's so typical, so Muscovite, so prewar! he thought—and into the wedged-open door and immediately made the return trip through the same smashed window to the same cheek. Bliss, lyricism, memories of Milka Zaitseva.

They passed Tverskaya Street, and there he was—the poet, Alexander Pushkin, still standing and, even though he was encased in a wooden box, still present. So even incendiary bombs couldn't reach Russia's love and glory. And there was the nymph of socialism still soaring in apotheosis over the house on the corner as she had always done, even though she certainly should have croaked before anything else in such a Vesuvius-like eruption. Even the cops were on hand—not a military patrol, the most ordinary sort of Moscow cops in felt boots with galoshes pulled over them. They may be thirty years older now, but they're still our people, our own Moscow cops! And among the military posters there were even scraps of an old prewar poster announcing a relay race on the Garden Ring . . .

He himself had run a five-hundred-meter leg in that race, for the "Medic" team—he had succeeded in overtaking three men before handing the baton on to—to whom? Why, what are you saying, "To whom?" It was to the unforgettable Milka Zaitseva herself, of course.

Dod Tyshler seemed to take no notice of the suffering on the faces of his countrymen; of the boarded-up main entrances to buildings and, by contrast, of the doorways that were now yawning black holes since the portals had been taken away during the winter and chopped up for firewood; of the long, hopeless lines of old women lined up for hours and days on end to see what ration coupons they could turn into goods; of the crowds of drunken war invalids outside Central Cinema; of the jackallike black marketeers who sold them cigarettes for a ruble each; of young girls with noses blue from the cold and wearing broken-down shoes, who were nevertheless making a pathetic attempt not to let their youth slip away from them. . . . Tyshler was a fellow singularly lacking in awareness, or rather, perhaps he was gifted with an excessive awareness: he did notice mass poverty, but he could immediately seize on anything that stood out in the slightest from the crowd: a bold glance, for example, or a pair of gorgeous polar pilots' boots, or three French officers walking calmly through the Moscow throng, or a stunning beauty in a fox jacket coming out of the ZIS limousine on the other side of the street. . . . Tyshler could not take his eyes off this last woman, but, alas, after a few minutes she was blocked from view by a convoy of military trucks. Naturally, Medical Corps First Lieutenant Tyshler could not know that it was Mrs. Gradov, wife of Colonel General Gradov, commander in chief of the western front, and the sister-in-law of his vanished chief, Professor Kitaigorodsky, major, Medical Corps.

He got off at Okhotny Ryad and headed for the Army Chief Medical Directorate on foot, once again experiencing an unheard-of feeling of pleasure as he passed the Moscow Hotel and the building of the Council of People's Commissars, walked by the Hotel Metropole, the Maly Theater, the Bolshoi Theater, and GUM . . . the stroll through the capital turned out to be an even greater pleasure than the ride on the double-decker trolley. A hard, even surface beneath his feet—that alone was worth the trip! No need to consider constantly where to sit down and where to flop on your belly, what bliss! It seemed as if Moscow were becoming its old self again after the repulsing of the invader's assault.

Arriving the night before, Dod had surprised his mother, Dora, with her lover. Well done, eternal Dora! In her letters to the front she had written that she refused to be evacuated to Sverdlovsk, chiefly to prevent her neighbors from snatching her rooms with the picture window right on the corner of the Arbat and Starokonyushenny Street, the bastards. I'm not afraid of bombs, she said, and if we survive and fight our way through this, Dodka will still have some place to bring his sackful of medals. Perhaps that was the basic reason, but the second, less fundamental reason, as Dod now guessed, consisted of this respected man with the unimaginable name and patronymic: Paruir Vagrichevich also either could not be evacuated or did not want to be.

At the sight of the tall, gaunt figure of her son, Dora, quite in the manner of the actress Faina Raneevskaya, cried out, "Pinch me, Paruir, I'm dreaming!" Her lover, without a word, threw a luxuriant fur coat over his expensive silk pajamas and disappeared into the mists of the Arbat. He returned almost immediately, however, with three bottles of port.

Moscow lives, thought Tyshler as he turned from Kuznetsky Most onto Neglinka Street. He could not believe his eyes when, looking into the window of a pharmacy, he saw a dense crowd of people lining up for little yellow spheres: vitamin pills. What do you know, Moscow is coming back to life, even though there are still air raids and the civil defense aerostats are still hanging in the skies. Outside the pharmacy, a woman was slapping a little girl in the face for swallowing three of the pills "without permission," but Dod did not notice this, either.

Even the elderly nurses at the Chief Medical Directorate were in uniform. A strict check of identity papers was carried out at the entrance. Walking down a corridor on the first floor, Dod heard the clatter of numerous typewriters making a sound like a platoon of machine gunners battling a landing by parachutists. Almost immediately, among the numerous military doctors scurrying from office to office, he ran into two men who had been on his course at the medical institute. It was Genka Mazin and Valka Polovodiev in the flesh, with lieutenant's bars and even sword belts! The two greeted Dod with delight: "Dod, where did you spring from?"

"Me? What do you mean, me? From the Thirtieth, *natürlich!*"

"The thirtieth what? The thirtieth hospital?"

"Why, the Thirtieth Army—the Devil take you, you two old whales!"

The lads, it turned out, were working in Moscow hospitals and envied Dod's "field experience." If only they knew, he thought, what it takes to get this field experience. They were obviously well known at the Chief Medical Directorate, especially Valentin Polovodiev. They began to take Dod around the offices, introducing him to sweet young things in army boots that made their lower extremities all the more attractive. "Any important affair must begin with a secretary, with a woman to expedite matters," Polovodiev instructed them.

"It should end with them, too," joked Mazin. Tyshler had clearly made a good impression. His manifests flitted rapidly along through the manicured fingers of the sympathetic female lieutenants.

"Now our business is to have a smoke in the corridor," said Polovodiev. They perched on a windowsill next to a marble staircase.

"Well, how are our classmates doing, on the whole?" asked Tyshler. "Where are the people from our class at the institute?"

"Are you interested in anyone in particular, Dod?" asked Mazin. "Milka Zaitseva, maybe?"

"Sure, for example. Is she married? Has she been evacuated?"

"Do you want to call her, Dod?"

"How would I do that?"

"Take this token, drop it in that iron box, and there you go. Ask for Dr. Zaitseva. Then Milka's yours."

Tyshler, concealing his embarrassment, straightened his gangly shoulders, his joints cracking as he did. "You know, boys, I could sure go for a game of volleyball right now!" Suddenly an attractive young woman in an officer's uniform came racing down the stairs. "Are you First Lieutenant Tyshler? Boris Nikitovich wants to see you!"

Her presence seemed so filled with meaning that Dod immediately leaped to his feet and straightened his uniform. Boris Nikitovich wants to see me! Did you hear that, guys? Mazin and Polovodiev were standing at attention, heads back, eyes wide open, expressing their absolute amazement, which might have been caused by either the message or the messenger. They were well known as performers, a comic pair, in the institute amateur revues. The girl snorted. "Stop clowning, boys! You probably learned surgery from his textbooks!"

As it turned out, it was none other than Major General and Professor B. N. Gradov, deputy chief surgeon of the Red Army, who wanted to see him. For Dod, this was a bit of news that was enough to make a man stop dead in his tracks. The surgeon Gradov was a long-standing legend in the medical world, as well as among his patients, that is, the general populace of Moscow; the kind of man about whom one invariably asks in discussions at parties: what, is he still alive? Not only had Dod studied Gradov's textbook, he had attended several of his lectures, which had often turned into cultural events in themselves, attracting a good number of humanities students. Dod had once even managed to slip into the auditorium when the great man was operating: the most complicated anastomoses under local anesthesia, unforgettable! How can it be, he wondered, that such a man would want to see me?

Gradov rose to greet him, indicating a leather armchair in front of his desk. "Sit down, please, Lieutenant!"

Dod was devouring everything with his eyes. I must remember all the details, he thought, someday I'll tell my children about this meeting. Boris Nikitovich had already gone quite gray, yet he still cut a powerful figure in his general's tunic. From time to time when speaking, he would thrust out his lower lip, giving his face the expression of an absent-minded intellectual rather than that of a general. This mannerism reminded Dod of someone, but just who he could not immediately remember. Certainly not a predecessor on the evolutionary ladder, anyway.

"So, Comrade Tyshler, you're from the Fifth Division hospital, Thirtieth Army, isn't that right?"

"Yes, sir, General." Both of them smiled, as if giving each other to understand that there existed between them a more natural connection than
military subordination—the relationship between a university professor and
one of his students, to be precise.

"And you held the post of chief surgeon there?" Gradov's light gray eyes
were fixed on Dod's face with unfathomable intensity.

"For a very short time, General, for only a month after my chief was killed.
After all, I graduated from the Moscow Medical Institute only last year."

"And your chief was Savely Konstantinovich Kitaigorodsky, isn't that so?"

Tyshler noticed then that the professor's right hand was twitching slightly
as it rested on the green fabric of the tabletop. All of a sudden he remembered
whom the professor's mannerism reminded him of. Savva used to protrude his
lower lip just that way from time to time. There was something oddly simian
and at the same time perfectly characteristic of the Russian intellectual class
in that expression. Now it all came back to him: local anesthesia by the
Gradov-Kitaigorodsky method. They must have worked together at one time.
"Tell me, David, were you a witness to his death?" asked Gradov. He was
clearly finding it difficult to control himself, and suffering that was most
ungenerallike was written on his face. "Please tell me everything you know."

His agitation was transmitted to Dod, who, stammering, began to recount
how they had been operating on a pilot during an intense artillery barrage,
when German tank soldiers had burst into the hospital and ordered everyone
to clear out—everyone but Savva. For some reason they'd kept him behind.
"And he shouted, 'Everyone out! Right away! Take out the wounded!' and
then sat down in a corner and put his head in his hands. That's how I saw
him for the last time, Boris Nikitovich. On the floor, in an attitude of despair."

"You mean he's alive after all?" Gradov exclaimed.

"At that moment he was still alive but . . . then . . . then those of us who
had managed to flee the hospital gathered on a hill about a kilometer from the
scene. We thought we were out of the combat zone, in a sort of no-man's-
land, so to speak, of a retreating army . . . but our side began a counterattack,
and one wing of Ilyushins after another began hitting the park and the school
where the hospital was located because the area was full of German tanks.
They were raising sheer hell, Professor . . . er, pardon me, Boris Nikitovich,
General. . . . Tanks were exploding, Ilyushins were catching fire, and the
school was simply leveled. On top of everything else, one of our planes that
was shot down crashed into the ruins. Then the counterattack was over, and
the park was back in our hands. I ran back down with several of our lads to
try to save at least some of the surgical equipment but . . . there was . . .
nothing but a jumble of bricks and . . . well, you understand. . . . And then
half an hour later another ferocious artillery barrage began, there was no

way of telling if it was our side or theirs doing it. . . . Then more Junkers came diving down on the park, and our forces had to retreat again. . . . In short, a wonderful day was had by all . . ." Dod's facial muscles began twitching at these reminiscences like a frog under the knife. "Forgive me, Boris Nikitovich, I've dreamed about it so many times since then. . . . It was just like Coventry, nothing but a heap of bricks . . ." He reached into a pocket of his tunic and drew out a pair of glasses. "I found these in the ruins. . . . I remembered them, they're his glasses. . . . He was wearing them during the operation . . . three and a half diopters . . . I kept them as a souvenir and use them sometimes when my eyes are tired . . . though I have my own, of course, so if you want them, Boris Nikitovich . . ."

Gradov held Savva Kitaigorodsky's thick horn-rimmed glasses in his hands, the spectacles that had always impressively crowned Savva's powerful nose. The professor was trying to drive away what he feared most of all, what in his mind he called "the old man slacking off," when he didn't want to look at anything anymore, wished only to cover his face with his hands and let himself go, become filled with sadness for the entire human race. "Thank you, David," he said. "I'll give them to my daughter." "Why your daughter?" asked Tyshler in confusion.

"She's his wife. You didn't know? It's quite a story . . . yes, quite a story . . ." Gradov muttered, directing incomprehensible and shamefaced glances at Dod. Gradov shrank into his chair, streams of sweat pouring from his forehead, his brows knitted together, his eyes moist. It was awkward for Dod to watch as the old man struggled against the sobs welling up within himself. Then Gradov suddenly straightened up and pulled several folders filled with documents to him as if demonstrating by these movements that he had control of himself again.

"Thank you very much for the information, Comrade Tyshler. All your requisitions have been signed, so that you can receive new equipment. Burdenko, Vovsi, and I are going to the front soon, and we will also be in the operational area of the Thirtieth Army, so I hope to see you again soon. I've heard you're a capable and innovative military surgeon."

Dod rose from the deep armchair and drew himself up straight. He felt like a louse. Of all the tricks the war had played on him, the Klin "meat grinder" had somehow etched itself with particular sharpness into his memory. Every time it arose before him, he wanted to tell everything to go to hell, to run somewhere and disappear into something.

"Forgive me, Boris Nikitovich, forgive me for that cursed bit of information," he muttered in a voice that was close to breaking, hoping thereby to show the professor that there was no need for him to continue to play the role of the general.

Gradov understood it and, filled with warmth, took Tyshler by the arm and led him to the door. "I never thought I would have to mourn Savva's loss," he said by way of parting words. Dod, in spite of his youth, immediately grasped the underlying meaning of the utterance.

Dod Tyshler spent the rest of the day with his old schoolmates. They managed to lay their hands on a volleyball and a net and then took off driving around Moscow in search of a playing surface. All the public gymnasiums were either closed or had been converted into hospitals, warehouses, or barracks. Finally, they managed to find a spot in the Wings of the Soviets building, which was more or less untouched, though unheated. They began to hit the ball back and forth, doing circle drills, and then one by one other "whales" turned up and by evening they had a respectable team together, the remains of the volleyball-playing circles of the capital. Even Slava Peretyagin, a sharp-featured volleyballer and the league deputy chairman, appeared. After briefly watching Dod play, he went up to him. "Tyshler, you need to get into training. After the war you could play for the national team. If you like, I can get you a deferral."

Dod laughed out loud, left Peretyagin, and went off to practice his spike. He had no tennis shoes, so he was playing barefoot. "Nothing to worry about," said Polovodiev, consoling himself. "We'll recoup our losses and then get boozed up!"

Suddenly the door to the gym opened, and who should appear on the threshold but Milka Zaitseva herself, Dod's childhood friend. Naturally, the boys had invited her to the "Wings," saying, "Dod Tyshler is dying to see you." She still sounded like a girl, all right, the dream of the active army! She was wearing a cloak thrown over her shoulders, a garrison cap over her mane of hair, gleaming knee-high boots, and a skirt that began just a fraction of an inch above them. Her eyes, of course, were mischievous: ha, ha, long time no see, Dod Tyshler!

Dod broke into a run toward the net just as she came in and at the end of his dash delivered a blow that tore through the formation on the other side of the net. Only then did he leave the court, to the sound of applause. "Ah, ha!" he said. "Who is that I see? As I live and breathe, it's Ludmila Zaitseva!"

"Enough clowning, Dod," she said. "Put your boots on and let's get out of here."

"Hey!" shouted the other players. "We're not giving up Dod! Where are you taking him, Milka?"

"Take it easy, boys!" replied the star of the Moscow medical schools. "You'll have a good time tomorrow at the wedding! Adieu!"

The next day they registered their marriage. Just to be on the safe side, she said—in case you get knocked off and I have a baby. That way, our little girl would have a name—there are all sorts of practical considerations like that, Dod, my beloved, my one and only, without whom I simply couldn't go on . . .

CHAPTER NINE

Clouds in Blue

☆

After Tyshler had gone, Boris Nikitovich stood by the window in his study for several minutes. He had more than once had the feeling that it was unlawful for him to be in this office. Several years before the Revolution, a well-known Moscow millionaire had had the building put up for his personal use, and right here where Gradov was standing, conferences of the board of directors had taken place, cigars had been smoked, well-aged brandy had been drunk . . .

There was turmoil in the branches of the trees in the small park outside: the rooks, which had come back quite recently, were squawking and flapping their wings as though they did not recognize the city. The sparrows that had spent the winter there flitted among them as if briefing them on what had happened there while they had been away. The saddest bit of news was that Moscow's trash had lost its power of nourishment.

Boris Nikitovich held Savva's spectacles in his hands. The lenses were not even broken. He remembered how proud Savva had been of these glasses. Ninka, as usual, had made fun of him, even though she herself had gotten him the French frames through some mysterious Moscow channels. "In those glasses, Savva, you look like a hundred percent enemy of the people, a bourgeois spy! They'll snatch you right off the street just because of those glasses, and quite rightly—if everyone goes around in spectacles like that, who knows what will happen?"

It sometimes seemed to Boris Nikitovich that Savva Kitaigorodsky was closer to him than his own sons, and that he was at any rate much more important than just as a pupil or even a son-in-law, the husband of his beloved Ninka. Despite his love for Nikita and Kirill, he had always, looking down from the heights of his bell tower, seen in them a certain imperfection, a failure to realize their potential, to become entirely sound; it was the feeling that in the past had caused him to say, "The boys haven't made it." There was no small amount of joking about this in the family circle, and though Gradov always laughed it off with a comical wave of the hand, he could not overcome his disappointment: they were not following the family path, they despised medicine, were drifting away . . . Even after "the tragedy," as he always referred to the arrest of his sons, this thought had not left him and sometimes appeared in morally questionable outlines: there you go, he would say, they digressed from the Gradov calling, and now they've paid for it. . . . Of course, Boris Nikitovich never allowed such thoughts to develop further.

As for Savva, in him he had always seen perfection, fulfillment, stability. Like them, the Gradovs, he was a hereditary intellectual of mixed class background and a doctor at that, making him the founder of a dynasty of the future and the indirect continuer of the Gradov tradition. In principle, Boris Nikitovich could see no more natural affair in the history of civilization than the business of doctoring.

He remembered Savva's father, Kostya, from their student days. They had not become friends, but they had been on good terms. Gradov and his girlfriend, Mary Gudiashvili, had even been invited to the wedding when Kostya Kitaigorodsky had married Olechka Pleshcheev. The marriage of the two people, which had come very early in their lives, had delighted everyone.

What a handsome young couple they had been, and how perfectly suited they were to each other. Several years later—that is, when the young Savva was around seven, in 1910 or 1911, rumors began to go around that Kostya and Olechka had split up, even with some bitterness and irreconcilable differences. Kostya disappeared soon after, traveling abroad to work—in Abyssinia, it was said. Savva had no real memory of his father: the man was a taboo subject in the large Pleshcheev family and later on in the larger family of Soviet peoples, inasmuch as having relatives in foreign countries came to be considered criminal. Supposedly, he did not even make any mention of foreign lands in any form that he filled out—in the space for "Father," he put "Died in 1911": just go ahead and try to check it out after the ruin brought about by the Reds. In a mysterious way, the time before the Revolution appeared so distant that a century seemed to have passed since the days when a subject of the empire might tranquilly travel to Abyssinia via Paris and Marseilles. No one among Savva's family and close friends remembered his father except for Boris Nikitovich and Mary Vakhtangovna. Even Savva himself, it seemed, was not terribly well informed about "Abyssinia." It was considered entirely improper to make mention of his father in the presence of his mother. Olechka Pleshcheev's lips, once so charming, would immediately tighten like a dried fig. The old wound was a deep one, very deep indeed.

Of course he saw a father in me, thought Boris Nikitovich. From the very beginning, even as a student, when he shyly began to get closer, he saw in me not just a professor but a sort of father figure. Then came his falling in love with Nina, and all his sufferings, and our ever-growing friendship, and finally their wedding, and his present legal status as son-in-law, almost a son . . .

And now it was all over, he had disintegrated in this hellish pandemonium . . . everything had been swallowed up by billowing flames, which were themselves swallowed in their turn by the fires of oblivion . . . and after all that one still had to continue the fight against the Germans . . .

He was just about to phone Ninka and arrange a rendezvous but found he could not bring himself to do it. Instead, he put his old civilian coat on over his general's uniform and left the office after telling his startled secretary that he would be back in an hour and that no car should be sent for him.

He walked along the same Moscow streets that Dod Tyshler had: Neglinka, Kuznetsky Most, Kamergersky, Tverskaya. . . . He rarely used the new names for these places that he had known and loved since his childhood—he would not permit himself such effrontery, and why, pray tell, should Sadovo-Trium-falnaya Ulitsa, the Street of the Gardens of Triumph, have become Maya-kovsky Street, anyway? Or, let's say, Razgulyai, Carouser's Walk, Bauman Street? Large, turn-of-the-century houses, at one time filled with light, com-fort, and the liberal worldview and now teeming with the spreading vegeta-tion that was the communal apartments, joined together in some places and in others opened holes in the sky of the approaching dusk. One day, outlined against just such a backdrop, a human figure wrapped in a bright cloud of a skirt had flown by before his eyes. He was in a streetcar when the woman, who had jumped from a seventh-floor balcony, slammed into the roof of another trolley. The streetcar on which he was traveling continued on. No one in it had noticed the form that had flown by, and he jumped to his feet, started to open his mouth, then realized he would be misunderstood and sat down again quietly. The only thing that remained in his memory was: these were the last, quite unusual seconds of someone's life. After that, silence. Are you getting off at the next stop?

He crossed Tverskaya Boulevard, or rather Gorky Street, and passed beneath the arched entrance to a new block of flats built not long before the war on Gnezdnikovsky Street, which at that moment, if one paid no attention to the plywood covering the doorways, looked just as it had before, down to a lady with a little dog out for a stroll. Both of them, though, were correspondingly older and more frayed around the edges. There was, however, a sign of the times pasted to the wall of the building where the Kitaigorodskys themselves lived: a "TASS window." The left half of the poster depicted a large-chested, insolent German advancing on some unfortunate Russian peasants. "By day, the Fascist said to the peasants, 'Off with your hats!' " On the right half, the same peasants had cut off the head with its animal snout from the barrel-chested body with a saber. "By night the partisans said, 'Off with your head!' " For some reason Boris Nikitovich stood there for a long time staring at the poster and stamping his feet. The exaggerated nature of the retribution surprised him unpleasantly. After all, the invader had only demanded that they remove their hats, and he had paid for it with his head. Clean off, all at once, all those muscles, arteries, tendons, and vertebrae in one blow—what a surgical procedure! Our allies the English would hardly put such a loathsome image on one of their anti-German posters. That's the way it's been done here in the past, though, kind gentlemen, remember? During the First World War, the celebrated cossack Kuzma Kryuch-kov had slashed off the Germans' vile tentacles. Finally, Gradov realized he had been marking time in front of the satirical poster for a long time. He simply did not have the strength to go into the house, to Ninka and Elena, bearing the news contained in the horn-rimmed glasses that now lay in his coat pocket. After all, Savva had been listed as "missing in action" until now, and Nina was still waiting every day for her vanished friend to suddenly send word to her, and for similar messages from similar cases to flow into her hands from all over the city, and then the disappeared would declare themselves. One day when he had called her, he had lingered over the receiver for a moment and had heard Nina's joyful voice: "Savka, it's you, finally!" I must tell her everything Tyshler said, thought Gradov. I won't say straight out that Savva is dead, but I'll tell her about all the circumstances of his disappearance and then give her the glasses. Was that necessary, though? After all, the glasses would do just that, tell them bluntly that Savva was dead. Then again, a wife and a daughter ought to find out about the death of their husband and father, and anyway, the Gradovs never try to hide from reality. . . . It would be immoral to conceal from her what you know, along with a final souvenir, these glasses. It would be a sin to conceal what you know from her. . . . A sin? Yes, precisely—a sin.

Suddenly the ugly plywood-covered door opened wide, and Ninka came out into the street. Boris Nikitovich spun back to the ridiculous poster. Nina passed without noticing him. She glanced at her watch—obviously late for her job at *Working Woman.* She passed beneath the arch and slipped out onto a path covered with well-worn ice, gracefully keeping her balance. He walked after her rapidly, almost running. Nina looked back into the Gorky Street crowd, obviously sensing someone was following her. At the corner she came to a stop and looked around in confusion. Then Boris Nikitovich waved his gloves at her. "Why, it's none other than the poetess Gradov! There I was, thinking, 'Who's that over there with such a fine figure, such a familiar face?' "

She kissed him on the cheek, then looked at him with alarm. "Were you following me, Bo? Has something happened? Is there some news about Savva?"

"No, no, I just happened to see you, I was just . . . er . . . at a conference at the city soviet . . . to discuss transport of the wounded . . . and then I simply decided to go for a stroll—it's such a wonderful day, the first after an awful winter . . ."

"You're dressed strangely, somehow," she said suspiciously.

"You know, I'm not sure why myself . . . I'm sick of those military duds and constantly saluting," he muttered.

"Then, about Savva . . . there's no news, like before?"

"Nothing comforting," he answered.

She seized him by the hand. "Well, is there anything discouraging, then? Tell me, Father! Don't you dare keep anything from me!"

He lost his nerve again. "Oh no, no, I only meant that unfortunately, communications with many units have not yet been reestablished. . . . The enemy has been repulsed, he has been thrown back, but many units are still inside his 'pincers.' We cannot rule out the possibility that Savva is in one of these troop concentrations and that everything will work out well. As I've already told you, though, you have to be ready for the worst . . . this is a war, after all, a large, cruel war . . . ," he said, uttering phrases that were already well known in the Gradov household.

They were standing on the corner of Pushkin Square, with the triumphant Socialist maiden soaring through the rays of the setting sun. Nina calmed down slightly—her father, it seemed, really had no news. In her heart of hearts she had known for a long time that Savva had been killed, yet both with herself and with her family she fiercely maintained a single attitude: if there's no news, that means he's still alive.

"Are you going to the office?" asked her father. "Let's go, I'll walk you there."

She took him by the arm, and they walked along slowly in the pitiful, gloomy crowd of Moscow's first wartime spring: military coats, padded jackets, and improbable combinations of civilian clothes.

"How do you feel, Bo?" asked Nina.

"Me?" said her father in surprise. "All in all, not bad for my sixty-seven years. Why do you ask?"

"I wasn't talking about your physical health," she said. "It seems to me you've become a good deal more chipper since the war began. I have the impression that the war has swept away all of your long-settled melancholy, driven away the eternal gloom in the skies over your head. Maybe I'm mistaken?"

He looked at her gratefully: what a clever, perceptive girl! In fact, she had hit the nail on the head. Just before the war, old age had come upon Boris Nikitovich like a roar out of a dismal cave. He had scarcely had the energy to struggle with the waves of depression washing over him. There was no shortage of reasons, naturally: the murkiness of his position in the medical hierarchy, having to say good-bye forever to his best friend, Pulkovo, the arrest of his sons, his constant fear for his grandsons. The principal reason, however, was obviously his advanced age, the approach of the inevitable, the breakdown of his habitual positivist philosophy of nature, whose ostensible function was to cheer him up when in fact it left him with nothing but the grin of a skeleton. Then, suddenly . . .

"Yes, you're right, Ninka. I have to admit that. You know, I never felt better than . . . well, than after a certain date. Believe it or not, I'm experiencing an élan of youth, something that reminds me of the days just after I graduated from medical school, a feeling of inspiration. I realize that it might sound blasphemous, but it seems to me that this war has come to our people as a sort of rite of initiation, as an atonement, a communion, call it whatever you like . . ."

Nina continued to hold his arm and broadened her stride as she walked to keep up with her father, looking at her feet and nodding as she did so. Her dark, well-washed hair fluttered from beneath the earflaps of her fur hat. All at once her father noticed streaks of gray in it.

"I think I understand what you're talking about," she said.

He went on, "I think it's not just a sensation that I have, but that everyone feels to one degree or another. After a certain date, we began to stop living in fear of one another for the first time. Indeed, it's only now in the face of a mortal enemy that we've really united. The enemy of not only those, well—" At this point, Boris Nikitovich, despite his "communion," markedly lowered his voice. "—of those who hold power, but of our entire history, all of our Russian civilization. . . . All of those old fears, worries, suspicions, acts of meanness and even cruelty have suddenly come to seem of secondary importance to people. And even if we are sacrificing ourselves today, at least we know that it's not for the sake of incantations but for our very being!"

"You're right, Bo," said Nina. "I have a feeling it's something like that. And it goes right alongside my constant sadness about Savva. A strange parallel. Here is Savva, and here is the war like a sort of symphony. Sometimes the two parallel lines suddenly intersect, and then everything becomes easier: Savva blends into the universal music. Do you understand? So now, tell me everything you really know. A bit more courage, Bo—you're a surgeon, after all!"

They had long since passed by the entrance to the building where *Working Woman* had its offices and were now walking down Strastnaya Boulevard, where old women, the angels of the simple Russian earth, sat chewing their toothless gums. In search of something to lean against, Boris Nikitovich went up to a lamppost, then sighed deeply, shook his head, on which his service cap with its red star was perched at a rather absurd angle, and finally handed Savva's glasses to his daughter.

Then she too needed to be supported and made her way blindly to a bench. Sitting next to some old woman, Nina's eyes brimmed over with tears. The old woman looked at her with noble sympathy. The tears flowed in streams, finally, liberating Nina by their presence. Boris Nikitovich, sitting alongside her, put his arms around her trembling shoulders. "She's my daughter," he considered it necessary to explain to the old woman next to them. The latter nodded sternly. He drew from his pocket a large handkerchief that had been ironed to perfection by Agasha and began to lift it toward Nina, who buried her nose and lips in his palm, that face that had been the object of so many preposterous terms of endearment from him in her childhood.

Then she took the handkerchief from him, dried her face, and commanded her father to tell her everything he knew, holding nothing back. Through her tears she had had a vision of the circumstances of Savva's death and the blood flowing from his wounds; of him slowly freezing in a splintered shed, its planks pulled apart, stars in the sky shining implacably through holes in the roof. She was surprised at how far removed the real circumstances were from what she had imagined. She asked for the details about Dod Tyshler, and the battle in the park, and about the end, when the surviving hospital personnel had returned to the ruins and First Lieutenant Tyshler, Savva's faithful assistant, had found his glasses there. "So he never actually saw the body?"

Her father understood that a new hope had arisen within her. "No," he said, "he didn't see the body." He fell silent, not wanting to add, "Fortunately, no one did."

Nina stood up. "Thank you, Papa, thank you for telling me everything. Well, so long, I've got to go to the office."

"Oh, forget about the office," he said. "Let me call for a car, you'll pick up Elena and come to Silver Forest to spend a couple of days with me and Mother."

"Another time, Papa, not right now. The latest issue is about to come out, and we have a meeting. And tomorrow I'm going to church to spend the day praying . . ."

They were going back in the direction of Strastnaya Square, Nina walking heavily, Boris Nikitovich tripping along lightly.

"What church are you going to?" he asked with difficulty.

"It doesn't matter which one," she said. "To the Yelokhov, I think. They say it reopened recently. Why should it be forbidden for me to go to church? After all, I was baptized, wasn't I? That's right, isn't it, Papa? Wasn't I baptized?"

"Naturally," he said. "In those days everyone was baptized."

"Even if I hadn't been, I'd still go to church!" she pronounced with considerable heat, and he looked at her cautiously. The paleness on her cheeks had suddenly given way to a blush of fury. Her face had the daring, young aspect of her days in the Blue Shirts.

"Where else would we go, if not to church?" she went on. "If Russians don't go to church now, after all of this, then what kind of people are they, Bo?"

"Fine, fine," he muttered. "If you want to go to church, then please go—there's no need to advertise it, though . . ." They parted at the door of the office. Boris Nikitovich headed in the direction of the administrative section with rapid strides. Nina began to mount the dilapidated staircase. Everything will be the same as usual, she thought: page proofs, galleys, idiotic headlines, articles riddled with clichés, optimism, faith in victory, holy hatred for the foe . . . can the words "holiness" and "hatred" ever fit together?

She entered the editorial section and immediately felt a bit more calm. For some reason she always calmed down when she came into these stupid offices. It was the mystical effect of stability, the illusion of activity, an exercise in self-deception. . . . It was here in 1937, right here, that they had taken away Irina Ivanova, but even so there was something fundamental about this office, the embodiment of reliability, even though she had been absent for several days.

Six women who worked for the newspaper, most of them more or less the same age as Nina, that is to say, in their so-called "Balzac years," were sitting in the large room. The ever-present kettle—the "bard of the commune"—was boiling in a corner. Everyone turned in Nina's direction and stared at her as though they were seeing her for the first time. "What's up, girls?" she asked tiredly and then walked over to her table. As usual, the office mascot, a cat named Anastasia Fillipovna, was sitting there. Nina sat down, quickly ran a comb through her hair, and pulled a stack of page proofs to herself. Anastasia Fillipovna was about to butt her with her head but turned away with her tail raised when she saw Nina's cigarette: she disapproved of women who smoked.

All the women continued to stare at Nina. "What's wrong, girls?" she asked in the same tired voice. "Have you heard some news? Let's have it then, spill it!"

"What an actress!" Glasha Nikonenko, a simple young woman with curly hair, peeped in delight. Everyone laughed. Nina looked them over, seeing an expression of simpleminded bliss on every face.

"You really don't know?" asked Tamara Dorsalia; surprise, like a half mask, occupied only a part of her expansive face.

"You could drive someone out of her mind this way!" Nina suddenly exploded. "Since when do I know anything? What makes all of you so smart?"

"*Komsomolka* has printed your 'Clouds in Blue,' and Sasha Polker has set it to music," said the assistant editor in chief, Masha Tolkunova, who always called celebrities by their nicknames, casually, as though they were her friends. "My goodness, don't you ever listen to the radio?"

Everyone rushed over to her to give her a kiss. It turned out that she really didn't know anything about it! "Shulzhenko herself is already singing it! You hear 'Clouds in Blue' everywhere you go. The whole country is already singing it, even at the front. You're famous, Nina! Look here!" They thrust a copy of *Komsomolka* into her hands. There, in the middle of the page, under the headline "The Secret of Success," were three pictures: Nina herself, the celebrated cabaret singer Klavdia Shulzhenko, and the composer Alexander Polker, a cheerful cynic, pool player, and dandy. The lyrics and music followed, along with a selection of letters from "frontline fighters and laborers in the rear," in which the writers spoke ecstatically about how much the new song was helping them to "crush the German serpent" and "forge the weapons of victory."

"I say, girls, 'Concert by Request' is on right now," Glasha chirped. "Can I turn it on, Masha? They're bound to play 'Clouds in Blue'! Oh, Ninka, it's just a wonder! And it's fabulous to dance to!"

The radio was turned on. Sure enough, right after the Pyatnitsky Chorale came the announcement that due to the number of requests that they had received, they were going to play Klavdia Shulzhenko's recording of "Clouds in Blue" by Alexander Polker and Nina Gradov.

An orchestra began to play, softly, with muted horns, a pensive saxophone, and the flowing notes of a grand piano—it might have been Sasha himself playing, virtuoso jazz pianist that he was—and then the low voice of the chanteuse loved by one and all came on.

> *Clouds in blue*
> *Recall that house by the sea*
> *Where the seagulls flew*
> *And that waltz in a minor key . . .*

> *For the third straight day*
> *Through the clouds, from the skyline*
> *The Junkers are flying away*
> *To strike at the forts on the front line.*

> *For the third day in a row*
> *I look down the barrel of a cannon*

At the sky, where planes fly in rows
Like a postcard panorama.

Clouds in blue
Recall that house by the sea
Where the seagulls flew
And that waltz in a minor key . . .

The Junkers will not fly
To your eyes from the postcard view
They will be knocked out of the sky
By my cannon true.

Clouds in blue
Will dance the waltz in a major key.
We will meet, me and you
Over a peaceful sea.
Clouds in blue,
Clouds in blue . . .

Nina was hearing the song for the first time. A week or so before, after a reading at the House of Composers, Sasha Polker had said to her insistently, "Give me a lyric, what will it cost you?" He demanded that she write him some words or at least give him the number of syllables and stresses right away, on the spot, because he had to deliver a new song—a lyrical one!—in two or three days for the benefit of the men at the front and planned to spend the entire evening at the piano to do it. A whole company of people gathered in a salon well removed from the frequented places in the building, one that had a grand piano, while someone turned up with several bottles of wine from old reserves. It felt like a get-together from the days before the war. Nina took a seat in a corner, and in about twenty minutes hammered out a lyric and gave it to Sashka, who immediately began to hum and murmur . . .

The "waltz in a minor key," naturally, turned into a "waltz in a major key," and the theme turned out to be quite infectious, even epidemic, one might say. Every line of the elongated second verse gave rise to a cautious syncopation, which was perhaps what distinguished this song from hundreds of others in the same vein, created a sort of mysteriously Soviet slow fox-trot, while the presence of the "Junkers" and the "cannons" lent a certain amount of definition, a clear image, to the rest of the blue-tinted mush. Finally, the sincere, romantic Soviet femme fatale Klavdia Shulzhenko had triumphantly struck this blow to the sentiments of the exhausted country: we'll surmount our difficulties, we'll get through it, we will return. . . . Clouds in blue are still accessible to everyone, to the hungry, the doomed, the wounded, even the dying . . . perhaps to the dying more than anyone else.

All the staff workers looked at Nina. She was sitting on the edge of the table, one hand holding a lit cigarette, the other for some reason over her eyes. Suddenly she felt a strange tugging in her throat. She threw away her cigarette and tried to conceal the convulsion with her hands, but she couldn't help swallowing. Glasha Nikonenko looked at her in utter amazement. Strange people, she thought—they ought to rejoice, jump high enough to touch the ceiling, and instead they twitch.

CHAPTER TEN

Guest of the Kremlin

☆

A gleaming throng of military men in spotless boots, their buttons and medals gleaming, was advancing through the deserted corridors and halls of the Great Kremlin Palace. The irreproachable parquet floor mirrored the movements of the crowd, whose boots, buttons, and medals in their turn reflected the marble panels, the bas-relief decorations, and even the dazzling chandeliers. It must have been difficult for the assembled commanders of various fronts to imagine that such luxury still existed anywhere in Russia at the end of the winter of 1942.

As it turned out, abundance did exist. It seemed to embody the unshaken bases of the society for which they had fought at the approaches to the capital with desperation, with all hope of victory gone, with their last breath. And yet they had held out, had not permitted alien boots to tramp across these parquets, had repulsed the threat. For the time being, a cautious man might say, Very well then, "for the time being"—that's not so bad. In a war you live minute by minute. They missed you this time, and again, and again . . . what the hell, not bad at all. In any case, an upbeat mood prevailed in the crowd of officers. The commendation ceremony for the generals who had particularly distinguished themselves during the winter campaign of 1942 was approaching. Some of these generals clearly had nothing to boast about and had distinguished themselves only by the fact that they had survived without being taken prisoner. This Kremlin reception had to say to them, too, along with the whole army, that the time of severe punishments had given way to an era when men under arms were to be given every possible encouragement. As for Three-Star General Nikita Borisovich Gradov, he stood out even in this group by his firmness of step and the determination of his facial expression. The smile that passed across his face regularly, like a sentry, contained perhaps at least as much meaning as the Mona Lisa's. In the days before the war, it would have been extremely unwise to appear at the Kremlin with such a smile, but now its chief premise engendered respect, displaying a certainty of success and an absence of fear. Everything else contained in this smile went unnoticed: it was no time to think about nuances. At any rate, the commanding officer of the Special Strike Force, having brilliantly carried out the January counterstroke that had taken Klin and cut off the enemy's Sixteenth Army from its supply base, could permit himself to amble through the Kremlin with such a smile, one possessing an abundance of meanings, in his eyes, on his lips, and in the lines around his nose. The generals, a striking group of powerful men, entered Georgievsky Hall and took their places along one of its walls. As usual, Andrei Vlasov with his serious, camellike expression towered over them all. On the other side of the room stood an inlaid czarist table, on which the medals in small boxes had been arranged ahead of time.

"Which would you prefer, Nikita Borisovich, the Order of Saint Anna or of Saint Georgy?" whispered Meretskov.

"Neither one would do any harm, Kirill Afanasievich," Gradov murmured in reply. "I suppose you're dying for a Stanislav with Oak Leaf Clusters?"

"You guessed it, Your Excellency," sighed Meretskov. These were the sorts of jokes the Red generals now indulged themselves in, instead of trembling reverently. The war dictated fashion, the army was moving ahead, and for the time being the Party and the NKVD had crowded together to make way for it.

The main doors opened, and the Party leadership came in to subdued applause. At the head of the group was the figure of obscenity personified, the "All-Union Wise Man," M. I. Kalinin with his crumpled beard. Stalin himself walked modestly behind, wearing a marshal's tunic. Then came the bosses, the "portraits," from whose company Molotov was conspicuously absent. At that moment he was in London, to which he had flown incognito in a four-engine bomber under the name "Mr. Smith from abroad." He was there to sign an agreement with Eden and Churchill, an agreement on a twenty-year period of cooperation between the Union of Soviet Socialist Republics and the British Empire (yes, twenty years!). And how much lexical energy had been expended since the time of Lord Curzon denouncing British imperialism? Was this not providence laughing at both the Bolsheviks and the lords of Albion? Lavrenty

Beria's pince-nez gleamed quietly in the first row among the leaders' round shoulders. He looked for all the world like a pharmacist of the old school. I wonder if he didn't kill our Uncle Galaktion with his own hands? thought Nikita, who continued to applaud vigorously in response to the leaders. The lights of newsreel cameras blazed up.

Stalin looked like . . . Stalin. What could one say about him? Human categories like "he had put on weight" or "he had grown thinner" did not suit him. He simply looked like the embodiment of Stalin, which meant in good form. I would have liked to see how he looked when he was panicking, Nikita said to himself. Hadn't he looked like a half-squashed cockroach then?

Stalin gave Kalinin a gentle push on the shoulder in the direction of the microphone. Fulfilling his role of "the elder," which he had entered into while still in his forties, Kalinin began as usual to mumble from a prepared text: "Dear comrades! In commemoration of the rout of the Central Group of the German-Fascist forces, the Presidium of the Supreme Soviet has adopted a resolution to decorate a group of leading Soviet military commanders . . ."

Three-Star General Nikita Borisovich Gradov was suddenly struck by a highly original thought: if I gave the order to my bodyguards to wipe out this whole group, would they obey? He looked to one side at the handsome Rokossovsky, several men down the row from himself. I wonder if Kostya hasn't had the same thought? After all, it wasn't long ago that he was pushing a wheelbarrow like me. In the name of and on a mission from all the zeks of Kolyma and Pechera? All at once it seemed to him that his thoughts and eyes had not escaped the attention of that blindingly gleaming pince-nez. He felt a cold shiver go down his back, but just then his name was called.

To him went the highest award of all, the Gold Star of the Hero of the Soviet Union together with the circular, weighty Order of Lenin. He strode across the parquet with crisp, resounding steps and accepted the precious boxes from the hands of "the elder." Another unpleasant thought flashed through his mind: what if this moron has mixed up the boxes? and then he was struck by the smiles of the leaders . . . Good people, fine people, very pleasant company again . . . He turned to the microphone: "I would like to thank the government of the Soviet Union and Comrade Stalin personally for this high honor, and I promise to apply all my energies toward the attainment of the common goal. In the name of the Special Strike Force I wish to express my absolute confidence in ultimate victory over the enemy!"

A wave of genuine, unfeigned enthusiasm suddenly washed over him, having its origins in his total attachment to everything that at that moment embodied his country, even to this collection of faces, to them especially and particularly, a group that just a few minutes before he had imagined as the targets of his loyal machine gunners.

After the ceremony, all the honorees were invited into an adjoining hall for a modest buffet banquet. War or no war, one still had to be a good host, or so Stalin obviously thought. Otherwise they'd think he was greedy. The table did indeed have his mark on it, that is, it had a Georgian motif: superb Caucasian wines, various cheeses, cucumbers and radishes from the Kremlin hothouses. Of course, there was no getting around the Russian traditions of caviar and sturgeon, which were present as well. No vodka was served, to the consternation of the frontline generals, who had become accustomed to it. "We all have a lot to do, comrades," said Stalin toward the end of the dinner. "However, I would like to share a few thoughts with you. Right now we are beginning Lend-Lease negotiations with our American allies . . ." He pronounced the last two words with a particular squint to his eyes, with a certain humor, as if on the one hand announcing a grandiose achievement—look at the allies we have, *American* allies—and on the other seemingly allowing for doubt as to the authenticity of such an alliance: what kind of alliance can there be, his expression said, between Communists and a capitalist regime?

"So," he continued, "large deliveries of military supplies can be expected. We must think carefully about drawing up a list of our basic needs. The orders Roosevelt will give to the American factories will depend on it. Comrade Gradov, what do you think our army needs most of all?" The question, or rather the person to whom it was directed, surprised everyone. Gradov was standing fairly far removed from the commander in chief, not across the table from him—that is, not in his line of sight but rather on the same side of the table.

This meant that in order to address none other than the man in question— putting yourself into Stalin's shoes—you had to have in mind that there were immediately to your right other, perhaps more important, figures than Commander of the Special Strike Force Nikita Gradov, with a glass of Rkatseteli wine in one hand and a fork in the other.

Everyone turned in the direction of Gradov, who, without the slightest confusion, as though it were entirely natural that Stalin should turn to him with the first question about Lend-Lease, laid his fork on his plate, stood his wineglass on the buffet table, and said, "I think, Comrade Stalin, that what we need above all are trucks. Large, powerful trucks with reliable chassis, capable of travel along any roads, to transport men and ammunition, to tow medium-caliber artillery, and to serve as Katyusha carriers. Quite frankly, without such a vehicle it is difficult for me to imagine how we can pass over to the second phase of the war, that is, the offensive phase, which is not far off, Comrade Stalin. To be sure, our industry is increasing its output of tanks, but it doesn't have the capacity to mass-produce such a high-speed, mobile, and at the same time powerful truck. The Americans, however, as I understand it, will be able to rapidly develop and expand this extremely important production."

In the interval that followed this statement, faces turned slowly in the direction of the leader. Stalin stood absorbed in thought for a full minute, stuffing tobacco into his pipe with his broad fingers; everyone already understood, though, that it was a favorable silence, that he was clearly pleased with the general's statement, all the more so since it had sounded a note of professional certainty that they would soon pass into the second phase of the war.

"An interesting thought," pronounced Stalin. "Comrade Gradov, I would like you to prepare a detailed report for the next session of the Defense Council. And now, comrades, allow me to propose a toast to our heroic army and its commanders!"

"Hurrah!" the generals roared. Glasses were raised and clinked together resoundingly. Lively, even exultant, conversation now began. Nikita was approached by Zhukov, Meretskov, and Konev, and they all took up the discussion about the trucks. "You're right, of course, Nikita Borisovich, we won't be able to pull ourselves out of this situation without trucks. We should order boots from America as well. Our men won't make it to Berlin in peasant sandals." These members of the High Command were clearly showing the newcomer, yesterday's "enemy of the people," that he was one of them, that no one considered him an upstart.

"It wasn't my idea," said Gradov, now very much in his element. "What was the secret of Brusilov's breakthrough? Brusilov was the first to put infantry on trucks."

"Really?" said General Konev, wrinkling his bald head as he always did when surprised. "You mean, in 1916?"

"Mechanization of infantry began in the leading armies of the world in the early thirties," said Meretskov. "In ours, too."

Nikita nodded. "Quite right. And it was already at that time that some people began saying we had no reliable vehicle. You remember, Georgy Konstantinovich—" He stopped short, having almost come out with "—Tukhachevsky was already talking about that." Konev and Meretskov averted their eyes, while Zhukov looked directly at him. All three of them, of course, had immediately understood whose name had nearly escaped Gradov's lips. It was whispered in the camps that while being questioned, Tukhachevsky had had his eyes gouged out by Cheka interrogators. Maybe it was just the usual camp scuttlebutt, maybe not. Zhukov had reportedly testified against Tukhachevsky. So had Blücher, whose name was also taboo. And what was Tukhachevsky? The butcher of Tambov and Kronstadt? You yourself were a Kronstadt spy, an executioner, a murderer of sailors, and now you're stuffing your face with sturgeon in the beast's lair! We're all stained, covered with crimes like a crust, like a Red leprosy. . . . He paused to take a large swallow of Rkatseteli, wiped his mouth with a starched napkin, then finished the sentence: "Well, comrades, you remember of course, that the Commissariat for War and the General Staff were already talking about it."

Zhukov nodded intently and gloomily. He remembered, all right. The conversation took another lively turn. "The second phase of the war," "Lend-Lease," the coalition of three great powers, it's all wonderful, boys (someone—Konev, it seemed—said just that, "boys"), but the fact remains that the Germans are still 180 miles from Moscow, and we still don't know what the summer campaign will bring. Most likely they will begin with an offensive to the south, more precisely in the direction of Kharkov, or perhaps even further south than that, toward Rostov and even the Caucasus. So until the coalition begins working at full power, our men will have to do the dirty work alone. So come on, boys, let's drink to him, to our dependable rock, the Russian soldier!

Once again, just as during the medal ceremony, Nikita felt possessed by the rising strains of some heroic symphony. He raised his glass and clinked it against those in the hands of the men around him, his comrades in arms. All of the slimy muck had been swept into the past by the mops of history, today we are as one, history has given us the chance to wash ourselves clean, whiter than the snow!

The gathering broke up just before nightfall. Searchlights were already beginning to range over the Moscow skies. The antiaircraft guns around the Kremlin churches and buildings were on a combat footing.

"Where to, Nikita Borisovich?" asked Vaskov. As was the case in almost all the wily peasant's questions, this one contained a subtext: Do you want to go to Gorky Street, that is, home to the children, most important of all, to Veronika Yevgenievna?

Of course I want to see them all, Borka and Verulka. . . . Veronika, however, probably already knows I'm seeing Tasia, a nurse from eastern Siberia, an FW—a "field wife"—as she charmingly referred to herself: a field wife with a large collection of bed linen, a buffet, a whole mob of orderlies under her command, a young thing with no complexes and only one, entirely worthy, desire—to serve her officer-prince. It was difficult to imagine how Veronika could not know about it; no doubt some do-gooder of a general's wife had told her out of sympathy. No, it would be impossible to meet his wife now, to have to turn his eyes away, overcome the false note in his voice. The split between them was too wide now, there was no repairing it. It turns out that the principal victim of the year 1937 was our love. . . . "What are you talking about, Vaskov? You know where—to the front! Tomorrow there will be a battle, everyone will be in the front lines!"

"Yes, sir!" answered Vaskov with apparently blind devotion, as though there were no "understanding" between them.

The commander's armored car, accompanied by two covering trucks carrying the platoon of his personal guard, rolled out of the Kremlin through the Spasskaya Tower gates and with a doubtful knocking in the engine proceeded along the paving bricks of Red Square.

"Do you hear that, Vaskov?"

"Yes, sir, General! We'll take the proper steps!"

They drove past the Historical Museum, a potbellied trunk with Gothic towers, onto Manège Square—on the right were two examples of the "buoyant" architecture of the thirties, the Moscow Hotel and the House of the Council of People's Commissars. Far off in the darkness, the columns of the embassy of the new ally, the United States of America, were faintly distinguishable in the twilight. The windows were darkened, but a narrow strip of light shone through on the upper floor. Who's sitting there? Nikita wondered. A diplomat, an intelligence agent, a mission liaison officer? They moved up Gorky Street, down a tree-lined street of darkened massive houses. There it is, he thought, my new "home," which I walk around to from the side, and there's the top floor, the seven windows of my flat; Boris IV is probably working out with the dumbbells now—body building is growing in popularity; Verulka is sitting in an armchair with a book; and Veronika is probably in her room sitting before her full-length mirror, enduring the suffering of her "Balzac years," even drinking cognac. They continued on up the street, gathering more and more speed, constantly increasing the distance between them and the "heart of the Motherland," heading in the direction of the fields and hills of tomorrow's battle.

Nikita looked at his chauffeur's profile. In reply, Vaskov shuddered, as if asking: are there any more details I should know about, General? Just keep your eyes on the road, Vaskov, there are no more points to clarify, I'm just studying the situation now. What is there to study, Nikita Borisovich—I'm yours entirely now, in the palm of your hand. Well, then, I'll take care that you're not swept away. Yes, sir, Comrade General!

After the disgraceful scene in the Eighth Aviation Regiment's sector in December of the previous year, Nikita and Vaskov had been alone in the dugout one day. Nikita had torn the accordion out of Vaskov's hands and literally put him up against the wall with a pistol to his throat. All right, now, Vaskov, spit it out, just as it happened—all your dealings with those Cheka creeps! What else was left to do when your whole life was bound to this extraordinary man, along with all of your modest worldly goods, as it were? No need to threaten me with a gun, Comrade Colonel General, I'm not afraid of a bullet—better just to ask me straight out how utterly devoted I've been to you these many years.

Yes, they made me inform on you in Khabarovsk, but I ratted on you in such a way as not to hurt you. Yes, they sent me to see Veronika Yevgenievna on a secret mission after your unjust arrest, but I acted only in a way that would help a lonely mother—not only did I not lay a hand on her, I frightened off anyone who wanted to. I admit, Comrade General, that the NKVD assigned me to you immediately after your liberation, but I acted in a way that confounded their plans. For example, I told the authorities about your supposed high opinion of Stalin.

"And you didn't tell them what an incompetent Voroshilov is?" asked Nikita, squinting intently at his irreplaceable stool pigeon. He had taken his pistol away from Vaskov's throat some time before but had laid it on the table instead of putting it back into its holster.

"How can you even ask, Nikita Borisovich, how could I!" cried Vaskov in a tone peculiar to the intellectual class that he had obviously picked up at Silver Forest. Nikita smirked.

"You made a mistake in not telling them, Vaskov. That was just why I said it, to be passed on."

Vaskov's jowls were trembling, his eyes were shining with delight like a puppy. "So you figured it all out a long time ago, Nikita Borisovich? You've been toying with me, is that it?"

"There won't be any games now," said Nikita in the "frontline" voice in which he had recently begun to speak, in tones that left those who disagreed with him no recourse. "Now we're going to be serious, Vaskov!"

Vaskov moved forward in trepidation, then understood that he was not going to be sacked, nor sent to feed the lice in the trenches. "Comrade General, I'm ready to do anything for you, anything at all!"

"We'll see." Nikita lit a cigarette, paced around in the director's office (the unit's headquarters was in the main house of a collective farm), then walked up to Vaskov, who was sitting at a table in a pose like an idol, and looked into the man's marshlike eyes. "Captain Eryes has no business being here. He tries too hard—to save his own ass."

"I understand," whispered the chauffeur in reply. "I understand, and I know what to do."

"Good for you, Vaskov," Nikita said with a grin. "You'll do it when I tell you."

Around three days after the beginning of the offensive, the commander arrived in the sector of the 24th Infantry Battalion, accompanied by his train of followers. The unit, or rather what was left of it, was trying to catch its breath among the cooling ashes of what had once been a large village. Having learned that the battalion had lost its commissar in the course of its advance and that unless he were replaced the unit would not be able to carry out its duties the next day, Nikita took the battalion commander, a man with shaggy eyebrows and tufts of hair protruding from his ears and nostrils, by the shoulders.

"Before tomorrow, Commander, you'll get two armored cars, a company of marines, and a commissar . . . I'll send you a commissar." He looked his retinue over briefly with the fleet pensiveness that was already well known to them all—a look that was usually followed by instantaneous and indisputable "Gradov decisions." "Here's your commissar! By special order, you, Captain Eryes, will be assigned to Major Dukhovichny as battalion commissar!" The men of the retinue froze in an exquisite wordless tableau. The agents of the secret police were special cases who were supposedly above ordinary subordination and whom everyone treated with kid gloves—and here was the force commander sending him into an impending murderous frontline attack! The commander allowed himself the pleasure of observing the play of the blood vessels on the face of his snooper for several seconds. Captain Eryes, swaying on his feet, plunged from unheard-of indignation into frozen horror and from there drifted into a zone where he felt as though he were turning blue from lack of oxygen and pure ruin and despair. That's for all the men you interrogated, for everyone you informed on, with best regards from those whose souls you warped by recruiting them. Now you can set a personal example, pistol in hand, "For the Motherland, for Stalin!" you son of a bitch!

On the way back from the front, Sergeant Major Vaskov, who was twitching everything it was possible for him to twitch—nose, eyebrows, and round chin that made him look like a Siberian boulder—whispered almost inaudibly: "I'll never forget you until the day I die, Nikita Borisovich. Allow me to remain as your faithful bearer of arms, you won't regret it!"

"Enough of this hearts and flowers crap, Vaskov!" said Nikita severely.

"Yes, sir, Comrade General," the "faithful bearer of arms" yelped joyfully.

This matter was now cleared up. The next thing to do would be to reinforce the headquarters staff with his own people, as well as the security and communication groups. One of his people had been his chief of rear services for some time, none other than Major General Konstantin Vladimirovich Shershavy. The force commander had to have a rather awkward discussion with him as well, from which the latter, known as the "miraculous messenger," emerged as one of the most devoted "Gradovites." Nikita sometimes chose his people, some of whom were genuinely "his," simply by the looks of them, fully confident that his eye never made a mistake. He promoted them to corps and division commanders and tried to permeate his entire officer cadre with them, right down to the regimental level.

In fact, all the bigwigs of the war, the army and front commanders, were doing the same thing. It was considered perfectly natural that a military leader should form the backbone of his army or his front himself. If Moscow did not encourage this practice, then it at least silently acquiesced in it. The only thing that was not known was whether or not the other upper-echelon commanders had the same aim as Nikita: to reduce "ratting" to a minimum, to eradicate the infectious sores that were the secret police from his entourage.

One way or another, Nikita had gotten what he wanted after six months in command of the Special Strike Force: he was surrounded by faithful—or so they seemed to him—"solid men," not "slobs." That they were not stool pigeons was understood—or rather, since one could not possibly have a Red Army unit without them, matters were arranged so that these indispensable informers worked for their own boss, not someone else's.

All of these "Gradovites" looked on their young chief—Nikita had not yet turned forty-two—with delight but not without a certain feeling of "hearts and flowers." They seemed faithful, decisive, and not cowardly. They all knew Gradov was going even higher, that he was already under consideration for command of a reserve front, which meant they would move up along with him, to new chevrons and bars, or maybe even to unknown stars, for there was already talk that the prerevolutionary rank insignias were to be returned to the army and navy, that the Red officer corps was to be turned into the "gold-trimmed officer class" that had been dragged through the mud a million times.

On the rare days of calm, the commander went skiing on a slope cleared ahead of time by a convoy. He refused any company, taking with him only his favorite dog, a lowbrowed, narrow-minded Labrador named Polk. Slipping down with ever-increasing speed, with an ever-widening sweep of his arms along the edges of the forest, Nikita tried to pay no attention to the "wolf-hounds" of his personal guard looming up here and there in the distance. He wanted to feel as though he were all alone, at least for a few minutes. The staff officers supposed, perhaps, that Gradov went off by himself in this way in order to think up new blows against von Bock and von Rundstedt, when in fact the all-powerful ruler of the 300,000-strong S.S.F. host was trying above all to drive the blood through his veins, to feel his every muscle, his fingers, neck, chest, the long muscles in his back, his stomach muscles, firm as a turtle's shell, the powerful lions beneath the skin on his shoulders, the dolphins playing rhythmically in his slipping, flying legs. In other words, what he was trying to do during these solitary training sessions was to shake off his "army commander" skin, to renounce the military-political significance he bore in his person and return to his essence, or at least to that most peculiar combination of skin, muscle, and bone that formed the engine driving his essence.

These vague feelings, which seemed so necessary to his sense of self-awareness, were constantly distracted by the sounds of the nearby conflict: when it wasn't tank engines rumbling on the other side of a birch grove or the sharp reports of an artillery duel in the forwardmost lines, it was the roar of aircraft in a dogfight, a roar that grew, faded into the distance, grew again. . . . War; thousands of collections of skin, muscle, and bone containing the human essence, each one a jumble of reflexes, hopes, and fears, rising every day and running in the direction of millions of pieces of burnished metal that accommodated no essence except for the high explosives flying toward them. Every minute there occurred thousands of tragic—or were they merely elemental?—combinations of circumstances, meetings of motion and stoppage, movements to the left or to the right, risings and fallings, concurrences with the unevenness of the earth, the coming together of seconds and instants, collisions of the living with the dead, flesh flying into steel or being caught by it, exploded by it. Now with a roar, now in silence, following right behind a sanguinary vapor that evaporated in a flash, from holes blown in the earth flesh wrested its personal, inimitable essence, which vanished straightaway in clouds of thick black smoke from a conflagration stretching as far as the sky could reach. Afterward, there is only the silence, he thought, unless, of course, you don't count the decomposing bodies and the revolting smells that cry out . . . to whom and to what? Strange, but even after having waved my saber about so much and having fired in every direction with every sort of weapon imaginable, after being an indirect—no, a direct participant in the execution of our brothers with the striped jerseys on their chests, after nearly perishing as a prisoner of the Red-Fascist band and devoting nearly my entire life to war, right up to this second Great Patriotic, disgraceful Stalin-Hitler war, I still don't understand the real meaning of this form of human activity. Perhaps the mass of theoretical literature that I read in the thirties, that I was always engrossed in to the point of being oblivious to everything else, is to blame. Was it a game of toy soldiers that had the appearance of a science?

Some Allied liaison officers had recently visited the headquarters of the S.S.F. and, having learned that the commanding general could read English fluently, had left him a pile of issues of *Time* and *Life*. With curiosity Nikita turned the glossy pages, filled with photos from all of the theaters of operation of the Second World War. Beyond the borders of Russia, the air and sea elements were prevailing for the moment. Throughout the huge expanse of the Pacific Ocean, the American Marine Corps was landing on scraps of dry land whose names sounded like the schoolboy dreams of the twelve-year-old Gradov: the Solomons, the Marshalls, Papua New Guinea. . . . Flying Tigers,

Tomahawks, Skyhawks, Cobras, bombers with sharks' teeth painted beneath their cockpits attacking Japanese positions in the Philippines. Japanese kamikazes aiming for giant carriers, while in the Atlantic the English were defending their convoys from the German U-boat pirates. There were many pictures of English rescue operations aimed at saving both their own men and the enemy. The crew of a submarine that had just been sunk was swimming in life vests through splashing waves to an English destroyer. Calm was reflected on the faces of the Germans, some of whom were even smiling; they were obviously sure the English would pull them out of the water instead of sending a burst of machine-gun fire across the tops of their heads. What a fascinating, almost childlike, sporting war! What does it have to do with our endless dirt, decay, and festering, the destruction of flesh that is mind-boggling in its scale and implacability? The land war in North Africa seemed quite diverting as well. Obviously there were no close quarters there: the huge desert horizons served as a backdrop for the attacks of the scattered tanks and riflemen in saucer-shaped helmets and knee-length shorts. Artillery crews operated their weapons stripped to the waist, which meant that one could simultaneously fight and get a tan. Patrols in open armored vehicles drove into ancient Arab cities: one could sense the presence of beauties, covered with chadors up to their eyes, on the other side of the crenellated walls.

Life presented a series of photos of the previous year's victorious campaign in Abyssinia. "The surrender of the Duke of Aosta turned out to be the culmination point of operations in East Africa. On the 19th of May, an Italian army numbering some 19,000 men laid down its arms at Ashba Alachi. The Vice Regent of Abyssinia and the Commander in Chief of the Italian forces in East Africa, together with five of his generals, were the last to surrender. Here you see the Duke of Aosta, led by several English officers, emerging from the cave that served as his headquarters. The defeated force was rendered military honors before a formation of the Scottish 'Transvaal' Regiment."

The Duke of Aosta was taller than all of the lanky Englishmen and looked rather absurd in his narrow puttees. He was walking alongside the beaming English commanding officer and intently explaining something, probably the reason for the defeat of his forces. A group of Italian and English officers were milling around behind them. Both were wearing light-colored summer uniforms. Many of the Englishmen were wearing shorts. A colonel stood in a classic pose with his riding crop under his arm. The Italians, as the losers, bore themselves somewhat more awkwardly than the victors, though it seemed that the role of local host should have fallen to them, with the English as the guests. The Duke of Aosta was holding a pair of gloves in his left hand. The idea that he was perhaps not particularly disappointed with the situation that had arisen was not out of the question: better, after all, to become a prisoner of the British colonizers than of the Abyssinian savages. Meanwhile, his troops marched between the ranks of the Scottish guardsmen. Then the Scots marched in front of his men. The difference was that the Scots carried their weapons, while the Italians gave their arms a rest. Scottish bagpipes and Italian horns were playing. Nikita showed these snapshots to his staff, and they laughed out loud. Screw the Geneva Convention! Nikita smiled too. That must be some civilized war that's going on there, the lucky devils! The match had been played out, the grand masters had stopped their clocks and exchanged handshakes.

Civilized wars, elegant butcherings. The nature of war, to which I, the child of a dynasty of Russian doctors, have consecrated my life, is manifesting itself here, where prisoners are driven around like dirty cattle and simply disposed of at the first opportunity, and we all know how; where civilian populations are terrorized; where we retreat, burning and blowing up everything without a thought to those who remain, and then return and see the fruits of our cruelty, as well as the infernal cruelty of the enemy, all of the rot and stench, the monstrous destruction of flesh . . . for the sake of what? The salvation of the Motherland or Stalin's triumph over Hitler? And now, when these magnificent Teutonic warriors have set about the mass extermination of Jewish children and old women . . . do you still insist on behaving like gentlemen, founders of the Convention?

He tempered his speed, then braked himself and finally came to a stop, hot and red-faced, in the midst of snow-covered pines and birches. He was also slightly bitter, as he had always been since his release from the camp. In the camp he had acquired a certain ferocity that, though it seemed almost imperceptible to him, was obvious to those around him. More than once he had caught people looking at him with eyes that were both understanding and fearful. Polk immediately came back and pawed at him, placing his sharply sloping forehead against his leg. Nikita gave the dog several approving taps on the ears. "Good dog, good boy—a bit thick-skulled, but there are soldiers like that, too . . ."

What I'm doing goes against my calling, he reflected. I was destined to become a doctor, just like my father, grandfather, and great-grandfather. I should have taken care of mankind instead of sending them to slaughter by the thousands. Still, if I'm doing what I'm doing, that means this was my calling, doesn't it?

Well, congratulations, you've done a brilliant job of leading yourself right into the pincers of a treacherous logic. Now try and get yourself out! Nikita looked at his watch and, powerfully swinging around first his left ski, then the right one, turned back. Immediately the "wolfhounds"—his submachine-gun-toting bodyguards—appeared from among the tree trunks or from behind the nearest hillock, where, of course, they had been all along. The "Prince of War" was returning to his domain.

It should be added here as well that at the age of nearly forty-two, Nikita Gradov had developed a considerable sexual appetite. There was no shortage of young women around him: nurses, telegraphists, secretaries from support units, lady flyers of the "night bombers" regiment. All of them knew of the weakness of their beloved commanding officer—ah, many of them had learned of it firsthand. His memories from the Far East, however, turned out to be indelible. A month earlier, Nikita had dispatched Vaskov to bring Tasia, and sure enough she had come, quickly adapting herself to the role of the frontline hero's principal companion, continuing to be entirely accommodating even in their most intimate moments, addressing him formally with his name and patronymic. Sometimes, though, at the most intimate moments of all, she permitted herself to utter the name she kept locked up inside herself: "Oooh, Niki-i-i-tushka-a Boriso-o-ovich . . ."

Thus lived our hero, the former zek and young military leader in a world conflict that was beginning to spread farther and farther. He had to keep positions, rears, and flanks in his mind all the time, along with the airspace over his head. In the same way the driver of an automobile comes to feel the machine as an extension of his body, Nikita had already absorbed the many thousands under his command, along with their mass of equipment and supplies, into his idea of "I," so that often to himself, and sometimes aloud, he would use expressions that went something like "My left wing will move out toward Rzhev, while at the same time my right wing will seize Vyazma."

There was only one small "detachment" that fell completely outside the reach of his wings—his own family. It seemed as though the three of them in the large flat on Gorky Street—Veronika, Bobka IV, and Verulka—had nothing to do with his present life, belonging rather to the past in which a phantom named Nikita Gradov moved, though not the real Nikita, the commander of the Special Strike Force.

The skies to the rear of the armored vehicle moving toward the front were growing darker by the minute, and the sunset, lying at an angle over the rooftops like a red-hot band, was fading. Moscow was retreating into the obscurity of a blackout. The Goddess of Socialism soaring over Strastnaya Boulevard was trying not to look to the west.

CHAPTER ELEVEN

The Master of the Kremlin

★

When the reception for the generals was over, Stalin went to his study, where his dinner was served. Only one man had received an invitation to his table that evening: People's Commissar, or, as was said more and more often in the capital, "Minister" for State Security Lavrenty Beria. Beria's aide, a young colonel, and three members of Stalin's personal guard, in the Georgian tradition, were invited as well. By the same tradition, Beria's men were playing at being coy, as though saying to themselves, "Look at us, just ordinary men, sitting right next to the great leader," but then taking their seats at the far end of the conference table with the greatest happiness.

Dinner was just the way Stalin liked it, in the simple Georgian style. They broke the churek, dipped vegetables directly into salt, picked at a fried chicken, poured themselves glasses of red wine. Stalin had developed a passion for Kindzmareuli, which seemed to pour all of the salubrious force of the Caucasian valleys into his sixty-three-year-old veins. He drank the first two glasses in one gulp, and immediately his fighting spirit, his historical optimism, returned. Then he took to sipping, at times imagining himself a shepherd on a hillside somewhere near Telavi; I'm sitting with a pipe by a cozy fire, my feet in woolen socks and galoshes, to hell with wars and intrigues. At times like this, he squinted shrewdly.

In the last two months Stalin had almost entirely regained his composure. It looks as though we're not going to lose. Adolf won't get the chance to lead me through Berlin on a leash. The historical situation is developing in favor of the freedom-loving nations of the world. The new set of people in the army isn't working badly at all. Perhaps future historians will reproach me for eliminating potential traitors, or perhaps they'll praise me. Maybe what they'll reproach me for is precisely the fact that I didn't get rid of them all. Still, there were enough loyal and reliable commanders left. Just take Zhukov, Konev, Vlasov. . . . Of course, there had been mistakes in the other direction, but that had to be expected—only a man without the slightest idea of how history works could not make occasional errors. It was good when one could correct some of these mistakes, as, say, in the case of Konstantin Rokossovsky, or Nikita Gradov . . . the latter, it seemed, was his doctor's son. Stalin smirked. My doctor, he thought. A good doctor, unlike that bastard Bekhterev, whom they had sent him in 1927, that lousy year . . .

Stalin smirked again.

Beria was sitting in a state of terrible tension, trying to decipher the enigmatic smiles of "the Tyrant," as he always called the beloved leader in his heart. Beria's aide, Colonel Nugzar Lamadze, breaking up the well-fried, crunchy chicken, was also following the slightest variations of light and shadow on the faces of the two leaders. In theory, he thought, right now I could change the course of history—in the blink of an eye. Two jumps from here to the end of the table, snatch up a liter bottle of Kindzmareuli and smash it over the head of Comrade Stalin. The men of Stalin's bodyguard, obviously, would not be able to react in time. Vast horizons of political considerations opened beyond.

"This Gradov," said Stalin, "what do you make of him, Lavrenty?" In a flash Beria reshuffled his thoughts. Therein lay the success of his favorably developing relationship with the "father of peoples"—his endless sequence of inward changes of mood. Before Stalin now sat the vigilant sentry of national and personal security.

"To tell the truth, Comrade Stalin, there was something about the look in his eyes that I didn't like," he remarked cautiously. Should I tell Comrade Stalin that "signals" have been passed about Gradov, and very serious signals at that? No, perhaps this isn't the place. Entirely inappropriate right now, of course, right after the medal ceremony. In the future, however, if a dossier were to be compiled, I'd be able to remind Comrade Stalin of my remark about "the look in his eye," that is, to underline my own perspicacity.

"He's a good soldier," said Stalin.

"Of course!" said Beria, "reshuffling" himself on the spot again. "A magnificent soldier!"

"The look in his eyes . . ." muttered Stalin. "The most unexpected things appear in the eyes of all people. Even in your glance, Lavrenty Pavlovich, I sometimes catch something unpleasant." As if seeking confirmation of his own thought, Stalin ran his eyes over the room and stopped at Nugzar Lamadze. "Something might even turn up in the eyes of this colonel. Just what do you mean by 'the look in his eyes,' Lavrenty?"

A wave of restructuring moves rocked Beria. Groping for something to say, he finally settled on something that seemed plausible. "I meant the 'Yezhov trauma,' Comrade Stalin," he said. "It's not easy to forget." The phrase seemed to hit the nail on the head! The term 'Yezhov trauma' obviously pleased "the tyrant." Beria had noticed long ago that the whole affair of the merciless dwarf was clearly to Stalin's liking, that he was even proud of it. To have done so much by means of that man's hands and then to pack him off with such elegance—he could even imagine Stalin's Georgian accent pronouncing the words—sending him right up history's ass! "Woe is me," Nugzar was thinking at that moment in Georgian. "Will I get home tonight?"

Stalin pushed his plate away and pulled at his mustache. "Very well, then, Lavrenty, what's the news from America?" Beria reconstructed himself yet again, changing from the watchful sentinel of internal security into a wide-ranging, strategically minded leader on the international scale, smartly directing all the intelligence-gathering services abroad. "The White House is already working on a plan for a colossal landing. That is the information that we have straight from England. Hundreds of ships, thousands of aircraft . . ."

"A landing in Europe?!" Stalin quickly drew a pack of Herzegovina Flor to himself with his healthy hand, then drew a pipe from his tunic pocket. "You're sure of this, Lavrenty?"

"The operation is a question of weeks, Comrade Stalin," said Beria with assurance. "The information comes from the most reliable sources. The only question is where the landing will take place. It will be in the south, in any case, Comrade Stalin, not in the north. Maybe in France, maybe in Italy in order to cut off Rommel's army at the same time. All the signs are that a unified operations command has already been created. It is headed by the American general Eichen . . . Eichenbaum, I think . . . some sort of Jewish name." The shine of his pince-nez now dull, he turned in the direction of Colonel Lamadze.

"General Dwight Eisenhower, Comrade Stalin," the colonel immediately and modestly reported. All of the remains of the meal had been removed. On the table before Lamadze lay a thin leather-bound folder containing the latest operations dispatches.

Stalin shot him a quick glance. It was like being stabbed with a dagger right through to the ribs, thought Nugzar.

A dense cloud of aromatic smoke rose over the leader's thick head of hair. "Aren't you getting things mixed up again, Lavrenty?" he asked in a mildly humorous tone.

At that terrible instant, Beria was unable to remake himself, and the drops of sweat that trickled down the crease beneath his right nostril like small glass beads betrayed him for a moment. Stun him with a bottle to the head, announce his tragic death over the radio, conclude a separate peace with Germany, give Adolf anything he wants, then expand our holdings at the expense of the British colonies in the Middle East, take Iran. . . . How would Nugzar react? See here now, what am I thinking about? Just a lot of fucking nonsense, must be going senile . . . "Why do you say 'again,' Comrade Stalin?" he asked almost plaintively. "What do you mean by 'again'?"

"Do you mean you've forgotten your errors, Lavrenty?" queried Stalin in the clement voice of a teacher speaking to a lackadaisical pupil. "Have you forgotten how you ignored the signs of the approaching German-Fascist invasion? How you had our agents executed for spreading panic? Quite a short memory you have, Comrade People's Commissar! Maybe you'd like to be reminded of something else, too? What about those fourteen thousand Polish officers we executed in Katyn, who would be so useful to us now in a common struggle with the beast?"

That's it, thought Beria. There's no way, of course, that I can escape the fate of Yezhov. Of course, it had all been suggested by Stalin, both the "sowers of panic" and the Poles. . . . All my life I've been able to figure out Koba's wishes, but what a fate now . . . and I've lived my life under the threat of exposure! And now this business of those anti-Soviet Poles. Sooner or later, it's all bound to come out, all the more since they're buried on occupied territory, and in that case there's always Beria as a scapegoat.

He found in himself the strength to offer no further objections to "the Tyrant" and only made a sign to his aide. The slender colonel immediately took the leather folder and brought it down the table to Stalin. The body-guards followed his movements with vigilant eyes. Stalin opened the folder, gestured to the colonel to return to his place, then released another cloud of smoke of a consumed Herzegovina cigarette. A pile of mouthpieces torn from the cigarettes lay before him on the table. What sort of a strange habit was this—breaking cigarettes in order to stuff his pipe? Couldn't he order the best tobacco in the world if he wanted?

"America . . ." Stalin intoned with pleasure, as though lifting a spoonful of honey from a jar.

Beria felt relieved: that means he's not going to develop the theme of my errors, he was only taking out a momentary flash of annoyance on me.

In fact, it was true that Stalin had been pricked by a sharp feeling of dis-contentment when the subject of an Allied landing came up. Why didn't they let me know? Does this mean they still don't trust me? Or maybe the capitalist lackeys still think I'm beneath them? Then again, he thought immediately, the plans are so secret they could not be transmitted by courier or by radio dispatch. The idea of a meeting of the "Big Three" had been put off for the time being. To meet on some doubtful islands, or in equally dubious Cairo, to travel there in a "flying boat," to suffer from fear and nausea. . . . Begging your pardon, but the leader of the Soviet Union considers it a bit premature. Churchill is preparing to come to Moscow, that's his business. It's surely this very information that he's coming with, and we'll dumbfound him with our information. Stalin's mood suddenly improved at this thought, and he forgot about the "errors" of his minister. America, he thought with pleasure, leafing through the dispatches. What a country, what productivity! Why did I get stuck with lousy Russia for the realization of my great ideas? In America we would long ago have built a Communist model for the world to follow . . . no luck. As Pushkin once said, "The Devil decided to bring me into the world in Russia with my soul and talent." Resources, industry, population . . . in short, real productivity of labor!

After having been coy with himself in this way for a short time, Stalin suddenly directed a penetrating glance at Colonel Lamadze. "Where are you from, *dzhigit?*" he asked in Georgian. It was so unexpected that Nugzar leaped to his feet, pushing back the table with a rumble and clicking his heels, and only when he understood that the question was an informal one asked in an informal tongue, the language of home and hearth, as it were, did he return to his former position beneath the smiling gaze of the guards.

"We're from Signakhi, Comrade Stalin. The Lamadzes are from Signakhi, Comrade Stalin," he said, as if making apologies for his excessive reaction to a simple question from a superior, and at the same time for the town of Signakhi, which lay beautifully suspended over the Alazan valley.

"Lamadze . . . the Lamadzes from Signakhi," muttered Stalin as he made an effort to remember. "You wouldn't happen to be a relative of the Borzhomi Lamadzes, the ones who are related to the Mzhavnadzes from Kutaisi?"

Nugzar beamed. "You're quite right, Comrade Stalin! My aunt Lavinia in Borzhomi was the wife of Bagration Mzhvanadze, the director of a state vineyard in Akhaltsikha."

"Aha!" Stalin exclaimed triumphantly. "That means that the Kiknadzes, the steamboat operators from Batumi, are related to you?"

"Absolutely!" said Nugzar joyfully, continuing to play up to the leader. It was already clear to him, of course, that this imaginary kinship with some Batumi capitalists would not hurt him; on the contrary, it would make things worse to deny it. "The Signakhi branch of the Kiknadzes are very close to us, Comrade Stalin. We lived right next door to Uncle Nikolai Kiknadze until we moved to Tiflis."

"I didn't know anything about this," said Beria in feigned bewilderment.

"Aha," said Stalin, quite satisfied. "I see that my memory hasn't let me down. So, *dzhigit*, you must be related to that fellow Gudiashvili from Tiflis, eh? You remember, don't you, Lavrenty, the famous pharmacy of Galaktion Gudiashvili?"

"I'm his nephew, Comrade Stalin," Nugzar replied, in another joyful transport of the search for pan-Georgian kinship, and it was only some time later that he felt a breath of cold, sepulchral air, a marble paperweight crushing the crown of a head. A vision of Uncle Galaktion's majestic expression just before he died flashed before Nugzar's eyes.

Stalin, fortunately, was not looking at him just then, having turned entirely to Beria. "I remember that wonderful pharmacy very well. I used to buy those—" He sneezed like a cat. "—those things for ten kopecks each, two to a package. Not always in my size, unfortunately . . ."

He guffawed, and Beria burst into laughter at almost the same time. Just a good-natured chat among men. Strictly speaking, we're all of a company, me, Klim, Vyacheslav, Lazar, Lavrenty . . . in short, all one group, those who hold power. Nugzar put his palm to his forehead and wiped off the cold sweat. All was well.

Stalin turned toward him. "And a *dzhigit* like that is still a colonel? What a disgrace, Lavrenty! I can see this scion of the Signakhi Lamadzes with a general's shoulder straps on his uniform, even though the army doesn't have shoulder straps yet."

All of those present smiled, knowing that one of the supreme commander's fondest dreams was a return to the old insignia of rank. Stalin was in a decidedly good mood this evening. And why not? He had encouraged his general staff, received good news from America, and had a good dinner in the company of two agreeable Georgians. Today, the owl, playing no tricks, perched as modestly as an unseeing gray stuffed bird on the chandelier beneath the high ceiling. Stalin rose from the table, and the others got to their feet as well. He shook the hand of the faithful Lavrenty and the newly promoted General Lamadze. Good wine always inspires good thinking. This *dzhigit* now has direct access to me, he thought, and I'll remember him in case the Commissar for Internal Affairs tries to pull anything.

He stopped Beria in the doorway. "By the way, who is the chief political officer in Gradov's outfit, the Special Strike Force?"

"Major General Solomon Golovnya," answered the commissar without hesitation.

Stalin frowned almost imperceptibly. There was something not very attractive about that name, not an ideal sound at all.

"We must reinforce that sector," he said. "Let's help Gradov get over his 'Yezhov trauma.' Think about a candidate and report back to me." As he descended the carpeted marble staircase, Beria, as he always did after his meetings with "the Tyrant," reflected upon the latter's exceptional capabilities. What a chess player, what a psychologist—he catches everything, never forgets anything! He didn't even forget Nugzarka!

He stopped in his tracks, and the beaming Nugzar nearly crashed into him. "It's good you didn't tell him everything about your relatives, Nugzar," the commissar for internal affairs said quietly but very distinctly.

FIFTH INTERMISSION
THE PRESS

Time, June 22, 1942:

The American ambassador to Vichy, the tall, balding Admiral Leahy, met with Marshal Pétain. These were his impressions:

1) The old marshal no longer believes the Axis powers can win the war.

2) Pétain desires an Allied victory.

3) Pétain is stubbornly resisting Nazi pressure applied through Laval, including a threat to starve more than one and a half million French POWs to death.

4) Admiral Leahy has great personal respect for Marshal Pétain.

Molotov visits London incognito. He emerges from the airplane in a quilted uniform and a pilot's helmet. The huge four-engine bomber is a surprise to the officers of His Majesty's Royal Air Force. The crew is so numerous that the English flyers begin to wonder when the parade of men jumping out of the craft will end. . . . A photographer from *The Daily Mirror* is arrested. . . . Molotov is referred to officially as "Mr. Smith from abroad." . . .

Mr. Wendell Willkie lands in Moscow in a Flying Fortress, an airplane the Russians have nicknamed "the monster." . . . The next day he goes with Ambassador Standley to hear Shostakovich's Seventh Symphony. . . .

He also attends a concert by Leonid Utyosov and his RSFSR jazz orchestra. . . . All of the Russians ask Willkie, "When will there be a second front?" Mr. Willkie dines with Stalin at the Kremlin. "Tell the Americans," says the leader, "that we need all the goods they can send."

The New York Times, February 1943:

Voronezh. Civilians are looking for their houses, soldiers for enemy mines.

Following a declaration by Ambassador Standley to the effect that the Soviet Union has been inadequately reporting on the American aid it is receiving, our reporter rushed to organize an inspection of Moscow grocery stores. . . . "Of course we're receiving American goods," he was told in one of the stores, which are called *gastronoms* over here. "Here are cheese—very good it is, too—lard, sugar, vegetable oil . . ." The salesgirls expressed calm satisfaction but not excited gratitude.

. . .

Half of all the tanks and forty percent of the tactical aircraft shipped under the Lend-Lease program are destined for Russia.

Maxim Litvinov, Soviet ambassador to the United States, contradicts Admiral Standley, saying that the Soviet people value American aid highly.

Newsweek, March 1943:

After fifteen months of what Hitler has called "Aryan Colonization," Kharkov looks like a city that has suffered an earthquake, an outbreak of the Black Plague, and the Chicago Fire. . . . As soon as the Germans enter the city, the bodies of hanged Russians are suspended from every balcony along Sumskaya Street. . . . Pretty Ukrainian girls are sent to Germany like a commodity. . . .

The Times (London), March 8, 1943:

Members of the French resistance attacked the Casino de Lille with hand grenades, killing 23 German officers.

The Times (London): April 1943:

The Bishop of St. Albans asks the government in the House of Lords if the production of contraceptive devices is a matter of state importance and receives his reply from Lord Manster: "No, sir."

Time, May 17, 1943:

A screening of the new film *Mission to Moscow* is held in Manhattan. The controversial film has produced a storm among intellectuals, while the Communists are absolutely delighted. *Daily Worker* commentator Mike Gold calls the film "patriotic and fearless . . . the best propaganda picture" he has ever seen. People whose Stalinist reflexes are less well developed react in different ways. Ann McCormick of *The New York Times* estimates that the film is "entirely unfair to Russia and presents an inaccurate picture of America. . . ."

Literary critic Edmund Wilson, a former Marxist, calls the film "a deception of the American people." . . . Philosopher John Dewey says that *Mission to Moscow* constitutes the country's first example of "totalitarian propaganda. . . ."

The film shows Marshal Tukhachevsky on trial, when in fact he was executed secretly without any trial whatsoever. . . .

Along with pride in their country's army, Soviet newspapers are filled with implacable hatred. "Kill Germans!" *Izvestia* urges solemnly. "To kill as many German soldiers and officers as possible—this is the sacred duty of every man in the Red Army, of every partisan, of every inhabitant of the occupied territory." . . .

Children ask their father, "Papa, how many Germans did you kill today?"

May 1943:

Robust Russian families have finally had the opportunity to taste American ham. The stores are distributing this rare delicacy at a rate of two pounds per person. . . .

In response to a question by Ralph Parker, correspondent for *The New York Times* and *The Times* of London, as to whether or not Russia wants to see a strong, independent Poland, Stalin says, "Of course it does."

Ambassador Joseph Davies has arrived in Moscow, where he has met with Dekanozov, Molotov's representative. Mr. Dekanozov resembles one of the Seven Dwarfs—certainly not Dopey, though, as he is one of the most intelligent people in the USSR. "If you see anything bad in our country, tell us. If you see anything good, tell the whole world," was Dekanozov's request.

Photograph of Davies and Stalin—two "Joes" beaming for the camera.

Newsweek, **August 1943:**

Lieutenant General Pyotr Sabennikoff, 6 feet 4 inches, tells the following story from his tent: "At Kursk we didn't see 'summer Fritz,' that is, 'the total Fritz.' Rather, there was a concentration of strike units of well-trained, tough young men less than thirty years old. . . . Yet even they began to surrender. . . . Those whom I spoke with said they had been greatly affected by the fall of Mussolini." . . . Bombers roar overhead, delayed-action mines are exploding. In a dugout someone is playing a Chopin waltz on the accordion. . . .

Russian flyers invite Captain Rickenbacker to visit them in order to test the effects of vodka on his steadiness. Returning home along the deserted Moscow streets, he proclaims, "I shot down three, another six were questionable, and God only knows how many got away damaged." The following morning he makes the following observation: "The Soviet Army's new epaulets, which are czarist in origin, show respect for rank and the reduction of the role of the commissars—this is the road to capitalism and democracy!"

SIXTH INTERMISSION
THE HORSE WITH A PLUME

The old circus gelding Grishka was whiling away his time in a stable on Tsvetnoy Boulevard. It had been a long time since he had put on a show beneath the big tent, even though he was sure he would be able to perform all the tricks in the program without any trouble: the circular run, when an acrobat leaps onto your back and stands up in the saddle waving to the crowd; the bow, where you bend both forelegs and wave your magnificent plume; and even the waltz on your hind legs while the brasses play "The Waves of the Amur." He missed these ceremonies. In his time as the Empress of Russia, Grishka had also loved anything to do with pomp and dazzling parades; the attention of hundreds of eyes riveted upon the full, splendid shoulders of the Little Mother Sovereign, her passing in review of a formation of six-foot guardsmen; the attentive selection of the best bananas, the most impressive bunches of grapes. It was said that only sizes were noticed, but that is untrue. More important, Monsieur Voltaire, was the overall harmonic development of these "simple folk" à la Russe: a powerful nose, a well-curled mustache, a sufficient, but not excessive, width of torso, the stomach drawn in, a throbbing still life protruding beneath their breeches; I do hope you're not shocked by this reverse play on words. So, the third, the seventh, and the eleventh to my bedchamber, right after receiving the Austrian ambassador.

Grishka could never remember what came after that, and if anything did appear from the depths of the sky, where the former empire now lay, it was only the swaying of high, powdered wigs, the sparkling of diadems, the ringing of weaponry, music—in other words, the same old circus.

One day his old friend and master, a groom who was also named Grishka, came to see him. Oddly enough, that evening he smelled less of vodka than usual. Grishka the horse did not know that the sale of alcohol had all but ceased in the besieged city.

The brute Grishka put on the bridle, pressed his cheek, rough like sandpaper, to the horse's nostril, and burst out sobbing. "Eh, namesake," he muttered. "The bastards have ordered me to lead you to the slaughterhouse because there's not enough to feed you. An artist like you, not a bad animal at all, under the ax! It would have been better for us to have run off to the Caucasus together in 1937!"

What nonsense the fellow is talking today, thought Grishka the horse and began to move his dappled white body out of the stall. The groom went out behind him, holding on to the bridle. It was night as they emerged onto the boulevard, over which a gigantic aerostat was suspended. And he says there's nothing to eat in this city, thought Grishka the horse. What nonsense this chap is talking! "What they'll use your hide for, I don't know," the brute said, continuing his mutterings. "Maybe they'll get a pair of boots out of you. And from your bones I suppose they'll make glue, another useful product . . .

"How fine you were, really, Grishka!" Grishka the peasant suddenly exclaimed heatedly, as though he had just had a glass. "You used to sail out wearing a gold-embroidered cloth like a peahen, like the greatest czarina there ever was! If only you were a stallion, I'd send you to a stud farm, you'd be able to stroke mares to the end of your days, and you wouldn't want for oats!"

They came out onto the Samotyoka, walking in the direction of some artillery units that were passing through the capital. Many of the gun carriages were drawn by horses. The soldiers took Grishka the horse from the weeping old man. Thus ended the latest incarnation of the great feminine-equine source. Like the Russian empress, Grishka the horse died with the name of Russia, that shining circus, on his lips. And was pecked clean by ravens, and was pecked clean by ravens.

CHAPTER TWELVE

Summer, Youth

☆

In July of 1943, the Zarya auxiliary unit, billeted in a barracks on the outskirts of Chernigov, was awakened before dawn to carry out a special assignment. The outfit was made up of former Russian prisoners of war and was essentially a subunit of the Russian Army of Liberation, commanded by Lieutenant General Andrei Vlasov, who had gone over to the German side the previous year. The soldiers were clad in gray German uniforms, with patches bearing the inscription "R.A.L." on their sleeves showing that they belonged to Vlasov's forces.

In these summer days many of the men had followed the German example of rolling their sleeves up to the elbow and opening their collars. Mitya Sapunov did not take to this foreign chic at all—the thing he wanted to look like least in the world was an Aryan conqueror. Take Goshka Krutkin, for example, ready to go to any lengths so the local tarts would take him for a first-class fellow, a *Herrenmensch;* he plastered a cigarette to his lower lip in the German fashion and loved to sprinkle his conversation with *"Scheisse,"* *"Schwein,"* and *"Quatsch"* and whistle *"Lilli Marlene"* and *"Rosamunde."*

For some reason he had grown noticeably in the year and a half he had spent behind the German lines. He was almost the same height as the powerfully built Sapunov and had begun in some respects to resemble Ideology Officer Johann-Erasmus Dürenhoffer, who frequently visited the Russian units to make speeches. He remained just as fidgety and restless as before, and with Mitya he still played the same role of mischievous sidekick and right-hand man. It was remarkable how he had always managed to stay close to Mitya despite their endless reassignments. He always managed to arrange things so they ended up in the same company, platoon, and even squad. Then again, Mitya was constantly looking around to see—is Goshka here? He was unable to get along without him and had come to feel as though the runt were almost a member of his own family. Only once in that year and a half had he held a grudge against his faithful bearer, all because of some lousy Communist broad, but he didn't feel like remembering that just now. It was a dirty business among outlaws, and there was no telling whose fault it had been. Better just to shrug it off, forget about it, wipe the slate clean. Chalk it up to war.

The only thing the Russian volunteers from the Pripyat Special Zone had done during these eighteen months was to be carted around the territory occupied by the Reich. The German High Command did not seem to know where to post them. Sometimes they were put on a strict regimen, while at other times they were left entirely to their own devices for weeks at a time. They were not entrusted with decent weapons. None of them, for example, had so much as touched a Schmeisser. They lugged heavy carbines of 1914 vintage, and even those were issued by the arms depot only with special authorization. They had been taught how to use German hand grenades, but as soon as the instruction was over, the grenades had been taken away.

It was not even entirely clear who was in command. Their German advisers constantly changed. Russians from the Committee for the Liberation of Russia like Colonel Bondarchuk would show up, make a few speeches, and then also fade from the scene. The volunteers were used only for supporting tasks like unloading trains and guarding the stations. One time they had been taken to Vinnitsa to prepare a sports stadium for a Nazi rally. They had set up benches and planted flagpoles for banners. They had had some difficulty raising a huge portrait of the führer in a leather overcoat with the collar turned up, above an inscription reading "Hitler the Liberator" in Ukrainian.

In the course of a year and a half, Mitya and Gosha had seen action two or three times at most, and only in engagements that were little more than jacking off. On one occasion they had been taken to somewhere in Poland as part of a recently formed battalion, then issued ammunition and dumped into a large field. Before them was a small village with a chapel, beyond it bluish hills shone in the summer sun. A pair of bombers was strafing the village and the surrounding forest over and over again. Then the Russian battalion was loaded into half a dozen armored transports, driven into the village, and let out to walk across the field. They fired their rifles at random, with no idea where the bullets were going. In the forest, however, there was a sizable number of men in four-cornered hats lying dead. On the edge of the forest the Germans were executing those they captured. Fortunately, neither Mitya nor Gosha had had to participate in the firing squads; they passed by as if the whole business didn't concern them.

They had fired their guns one or two other times, once near Bobruisk. Then, too, they had been smoking partisans out of the forest, but this time the other side was Soviet, their own people. It was there, in fact, near Bobruisk, that the disgusting incident with the girl had taken place, the one Mitya did not want to remember.

Then they had been reassigned again and taken to Germany, to a little town called Dabendorf. This time we really lucked out, they said to themselves, Europe doesn't get any more European than this—look at how the people live, how clean everything is! It was almost incomprehensible to them how people could live that way. The town was reminiscent of a dacha village like Silver Forest, only nicer. The houses were of superior construction, stone, some with columns and wrought-iron gates. A large munitions factory was located not far away, and the Anglo-American plutocrats, the Bolsheviks' accomplices, descended from the skies to bomb it nearly every day. The roar of exploding bombs could be heard in Dabendorf, the skyline was illuminated by flashes, but here everything was quiet, it sounded only like the rumbling of thunder. It even seemed strange to look at the pavement and see that it was dry.

Andrei Andreevich Vlasov himself came to Dabendorf. Quite striking in height, this fellow, no two ways about it. He certainly made quite an impression on the troops when he said, "Such is our historical fate, men. We will go through all kinds of battles, sufferings, and humiliations in order to turn a new page in the history of Russia!" Well said, that. Inspiring.

Mitya's feeling of desolate inspiration flared up again, though, to tell the truth, when he looked around he saw no such historical fate. Goshka probably had it right when he said that at least this was better than rotting alive in the camps.

Here they could even go to the pictures from time to time, sneak into the back row of the movie house with a few beers and some rubbery sausages to watch the magical German movie stars like Marika Rokk, Leni Riefenstahl, and Sara Liandra. As soon as these beauties appeared on the screen, Marika the blonde or Sara the brunette, the lads' hands would descend into their trousers, adding the play of their powerful, if somewhat monotonous, imaginations to the cinematic work of art. "We're both going to be shot here," Mitya said to Goshka one day after a beer.

"Well, to hell with it," replied Goshka. "Everybody gets shot sooner or later, goddammit, that's what a war is for."

"This is a dull life," Mitya said the next day over the barracks sink. He cupped his hands to fill them with water, which he threw over himself, and thought, what kind of a bloody mess of a biography am I making for myself?

Goshka was behind his back, reflected in the foggy mirror, pouting sadly, expressing his greatest sympathy, almost on the point of tears: I understand, Mit, I understand your needs, but what can you do, Mit, it's a war, a war that drives us, the young ones, like a herd of wild horses, like something out of an Esenin poem.

Goshka even tickled his friend a bit to rouse him from his melancholy mood. Mitya grimaced coarsely and punched him in the stomach, though it was obvious that he was glad of his sympathy and even filled with tenderness for Goshka: he's still a friend, after all, and everyone knows you shouldn't wipe your feet on a friend—we'll get through this war together yet.

Of course, if there had not been a war on, Mitya would have had different friends. He would have gone to the medical institute in keeping with the wishes of Grandfather Boris, would have donned a white cap, jersey, and white slippers, would have studied the most humane profession of all, would have attended concerts at the conservatory, as befitted any intellectual. He would have had a girl from an excellent family like his Gradovs, a girl like Aunt Ninka, only younger, of course. He would have gone for strolls with her in Neskuchny Garden, talked with her about science and art, and later their friendship would have grown into love. Here, though, in a war, everything humane is twisted into its opposing image, as though someone were mocking you—if you dreamed about something, you received it in its real form, that is, as banditry and piggishness, as though you had been inscribed once and for all on some sort of blacklist, as though it had already been decided somewhere that you were no longer human. That was what had happened near Bobruisk, where the battalion was posted before combing the woods for partisans. In the end it was impossible for him to drive the vile memory out of his mind; it returned like a stray dog begging for protection.

One evening, Mitya and Gosha had been slaving away at some detail on a rubbish heap next to the hut where they were billeted, when suddenly Larisa, the local librarian and the dream of fighting men on both sides of the lines, emerged onto the clubhouse porch. As a matter of fact, they found out her name and what she did five minutes later, though at first it seemed to Mitya that some sort of cinematic mirage had appeared before him: a hairdo of large ringlets, eyes like pools, a bright red mouth, a curvy figure in a marchioness dress, high heels.

"Well, come on, boys, come on in and make yourselves at home." Her voice was sensuality itself, arousing everything. Goshka all but neighed with delight and whispered hotly in his friend's ear, "Well, Mitya, it looks like we're going to add to our combat experience today!"

There was a curious triumph of humanism to be seen on Larisa's table: a bottle of German schnapps together with jugs of moonshine and homemade beer. Before long they were tipsy.

"So, how's life as young traitors to the Motherland?" coquettishly asked the librarian in all her intimidating beauty. She pulled out a phonograph from under the bed, along with a handful of steel needles of Ural manufacture and some records of songs from the movies. "A song helps to live and to build / Like a friend it calls and leads . . ."

"Hey, Mitya, how much do you want to bet she turns us over to the partisans?" Goshka whispered. Larisa was whirling around the room, her head thrown back in cinematic ecstasy, her light blue skirt rising to show that she was wearing no panties. A march was coming scratchily forth from the record player, but she was obviously dancing to her own music. "Which of you little boys wants to fuck me first?" she asked.

"Mitka, let Mitka go first!" shouted Krutkin. "Go on, Mitya, stick it to her! I'll stand guard to make sure the partisans don't burst in on us."

Larisa tousled Mitya's hair. "Well, come on, curlyhead!" In one movement, she sat down on his lap, face to face, and smeared her hungry red mouth against Mitya's lips. "Go on, give it to me like a goat, don't be shy!"

Mitya, however, was quite shy. He had a clear lack, not to say a total absence of, "combat experience" where female anatomy was concerned. To Goshka, of course, he had told any number of lies based on his own fantasies, when in fact he had touched a woman for the first time only a month before Larisa, in Poland, when some of the lads, giving in to temptation, had caught some chubby underage girl and gang-banged her in a dried-up fountain. When Mitya's turn came, he felt only nausea. It was a good thing it was dark, so that he didn't have to lose face before his comrades. He stuck his organ somewhere, probably in just any fold of skin where it made a sort of splashing sound, and pretended to make a mighty effort. The girl could only cackle something incomprehensible and wail at the same time. It was all obscene, a disgrace, but what could you do? There was a war on, what was needed was esprit de corps—if everyone around you becomes a jackal, then you become one, too.

With Larisa, though, everything was different. This was his real entry into manhood. He never would have thought he possessed such capabilities. The woman was singing, moaning, biting. "Mitya, my darling, you're so good! Come on! Come on! More! More!" Suddenly he fell head over heels in love with the undulating body writhing on his lap, with the face that was becoming keener, more intense, the embodiment of romanticism.

Goshka was sitting on the front stoop with his rifle, supposedly on watch for partisans, though in fact he was holding the door open a crack and was enjoying the spectacle. I'll kick his ass to kingdom come, thought Mitya as he went on with his most pleasant of tasks—I won't let him touch this girl. I'll close the door and stay with her until morning, and then maybe we'll run away somewhere together forever. To Argentina, "where the southern skies are so blue."

After a while, they arrived in Argentina, so to speak. All thoughts were forgotten, and a total outpouring of mutual delight began, a dizzying tango. It was only when these joys began to subside that Mitya heard loud laughter followed by the heavy tread of boots into the girl's room and Kravchuk's voice with its Kharkov accent: "Well done, Sapunov! They didn't pay him at the union hall, so he's paying himself in pussy!"

It was the so-called "inseparable six" of the battalion, who wandered the region by night looking for new gang bangs. By now they were so far gone that they seemed to have forgotten you could look for a woman for only one or two, or even not look for one at all. They shuffled along behind one another, peering around them with the eyes of jackals—just plain old collective farmworkers.

"Come on, Mitya, roll over! Take a walk, hand her over to a buddy!"

Into the midst of the lewd pushing and shoving flashed the face of his "bosom buddy," that traitor Goshka.

Mitya jumped out of the embrace of Argentina's southern climes. The last thing he noticed was a patch of moonlight swimming across the face of his beloved. "Get lost, you bloodsuckers! I've got a grenade in my pocket!"

Two of them immediately jumped on him and dragged him off to one side, and then Kravchuk threw himself onto the body sprawled on the ottoman. Mitya could not do up his fly because the buttons were torn off, and he moved along in jerks like a hobbled horse. They threw him from the porch into the mud and sent his boots and trousers after him, flying up into the night sky like a man's shadow. What sounded like the lowing of cattle, intermingled with the stamping of feet and Larisa's aroused shrieks, was heard from the house—"Come on, come on, sweetheart!" Mitya heard the strains of the "Rio Rita Quickstep": someone waiting his turn had turned on the record player. Mitya gathered his things and sat for a long time in the shadows, gnashing his teeth. If he had really had a grenade, he would have tossed it into the window to tear the pricks off every one of them. An old woman sloshed through the mud, looked over the fence, and said, "That new library lady has some fellers visitin' her." Finally, Goshka emerged with a rifle slung over each shoulder, Mitya's and his own. It took Mitya no more than a second to disarm the swine, and then he proceeded to thrash the creep with his feet and fists, striking him on the chin and in the stomach with his elbows. Then he took hold of his face and dragged him away. Not the slightest resistance was offered. It was strange, Goshka simply cocked his head over to one side with a dreamy smile frozen on his lips.

"Admit it, you bastard, you went in on it too, didn't you?"

"What do you mean, Mitya? Of course I went in on it! After Borovkov and before Khryakov, in my own way . . ."

"And what happened to her?"

"Who?"

"Larisa! Who else, moron?"

"What about her? She's fine, just a broad out for a good time. Don't hit me anymore, friend. I didn't call them, after all, they forced their way in."

That was the lousy business that had cast a cloud over the friendship of the two inseparable Muscovites for who knew how long afterward. Even much later Mitya still trembled all over when he recalled his "Argentinean adventure," even though some of the details of Larisa's rather complicated life story had reached him. It turned out, for example, that it would have been difficult to consider what had happened a rape, since the girl had always been insatiable. It was said that in '41 she had been through an entire platoon of Dovator's cossacks, and then it had gone on from there: she got all she could handle and more from Germans, from Italians, and from her own countrymen in the partisans; the woman developed nothing less than a case of "queen bee fury." So conclusions beg to be drawn, dear Mitya: at best, you and I picked up a case of the clap from the source of knowledge, and at worst, a victim of the war has rewarded us with syphilis. So we'll lose our noses, Sapunov, we'll walk together noselessly! Two noseless friends, ha, ha, ha! It turned out to be funny after all—two noseless friends! They'll never let us into Argentina like that, Goshka Krutkin. Well, fuck Argentina, who needs it? We'll go to Africa together and help ourselves until half the population decays while they're still alive. What, you say that half the population will die after their noses drop off? *Natürlich!*

As it turned out, they got off with only the first alternative, a simple case of a so-called "archbishop's head cold." The two lads squirmed in pain together, held on to their own business ends together, and had their rumps shot full of sulfanomides together; you wouldn't wish this sort of pain on a Bolshevik! It wasn't bad, though, for repairing the break in their friendship.

Mitya was no longer angry with Goshka, and he didn't give a damn about Larisa. Anyone could see that broad wouldn't have much longer to fool around. There was one thing, however, that he didn't forget—the ecstasy that he had felt with her, some sort of swirling fulfillment of a dream. He was stung by shame and sadness in the moments when he recalled these things. That means my love has been defiled forever by my cursed life, passed through a group rape of gonorrhea-infected louts. Will I never have the experience of real love if I felt this not with a woman but with a wartime apparition, a soldiers' whore?

It goes without saying that he did not share these melancholy reflections with Goshka; he suffered in solitude, and the rage within him continued to grow. The Gradovs' hearth and everything else about Silver Forest retreated further and further into the past: Agasha's almost soundless gliding in woolen socks, her faint murmuring that made the top of his adolescent head hum cozily; the peals of Mary's grand piano, which made everyone feel washed away and worn to tatters, like clouds flying by, while her voice remained steady in one vital, strong, Beethoven-like phrase. "Children, to the table!"; the dependable crackling of the parquet floor beneath Grandfather Bo's boots as he paced back and forth in his study, thinking; the small stone in one corner of the yard beneath fir trees and ferns, and in winter beneath a snowy hat looking like a huge mushroom, Pythagoras' tomb. All this, all that world of love and firmly established human habits where fate had suddenly deposited him after pulling him from the ashes, had been, it was now clear, nothing more than a breathing space, followed once again by the Russian's usual lot.

"Where are we going, Herr Linz? *Wohin fahren wir?*" Goshka asked the noncom, who that morning was issuing the ammunition, one full cartridge pouch per man. Four tarpaulin-covered trucks were waiting for the company at the gates.

The aging noncom, who resembled a shoemaker and who despite the earliness of the hour already smelled of something good, growled something absolutely incomprehensible to Mitya. Goshka, however, who had a facility for catching the important element in a mass of gibberish and immediately making sense out of it, understood immediately.

"He says he's sending all of us up the ass of the world, into a deep asshole, since wherever they take us is one, and right now they're taking us to a place called Garni Yar." Mitya was still yawning and stretching, his youthful vitality smothered by a generally discombobulated feeling. If it's up an asshole, then that's where it is. Where are they sending us now? Garni Yar? All right, let's go to Garni Yar. Probably to smoke out some more partisans or clear some railroad tracks . . .

"Garni Yar! Well, what do you know!" Goshka suddenly hiccupped, as though something about the name of the place rang a bell.

"So what do they eat it with, this Garni Yar?" asked Mitya. Without waiting for a reply, he climbed into the truck, found a place in a corner, put his head onto his friend's bony shoulder, and immediately nodded off. When after two hours of bumping and shaking they came to a stop and heard the command to dismount, the soldiers saw about them a desolate landscape, one that neither civilization nor its highest achievement, mechanized warfare, seemed to have touched. All around, as far as the eye could see, lay the uneven surface of the earth's crust, bare hills and wooded depressions; there were no telegraph poles, no burned-out houses or bomb craters to be seen. The modern age was brought to mind only by the dirt road by which they had arrived, a path covered from one end to the other with the tracks of tank treads and truck tires, indicating that it had been used by troop carriers. It was along this road that the Zarya team was to be deployed as guards.

Two riflemen were stationed approximately every hundred yards, the extent of each pair's line of sight. Their orders were to see that no one approached the road—and, more important, that no one wandered from it. If need be, they were to shoot without warning.

"Who are we waiting for, Lieutenant?"

"A column."

"What column?"

"A column on foot. A column of people. That's all. Repeat your orders!"

Mitya, naturally, was assigned with Krutkin. They sat down on a hillock. A wind with nothing to interrupt it was blowing. Fast-running clouds were scattering in all directions across the sky. Ancient Rus announced its presence at every moment.

"Eh, Goshka, Goshka," sighed Mitya Sapunov.

"Eh, Mitka, Mitka," replied his friend.

"We really fucked up, to be born in times like these—they're enough to make you sick."

"All times, all eras are enough to make you sick," Goshka countered cheerily. "Men have been nothing but criminals since time began."

"You've started to contradict me a lot lately, you little shit," said Mitya calmly to his underling.

"Let's have a smoke, buddy." Goshka sang a line from one of Utyosov's records.

"I wonder where the Germans get their tobacco from. I mean, it doesn't grow in their country," said Mitya, deep in thought.

"Probably from Italy." Goshka supposed. "It grows in Italy."

"Speaking of Italy, Goshka, things are really beginning to get hot down there. They say the English and the Americans have landed."

"Germany is invincible, Mitya," said Goshka. "Their new tanks just moved up to the front, didn't you see them? It was scary just to look at tanks like that!"

"And if they smash your Germany to bits, what then?"

"If they smash it, to hell with it! Good riddance, Mitya!"

"And where will we hide then, eh, Goshka? Are we just going to turn to ashes and fall to the ground like dust?"

"Where's that from? You don't mind if I write the words down?" came the ironic reply.

They were smoking and chatting in this way when suddenly the rustle of the free-blowing wind brought the noise of some commotion to their ears. It sounded as though the column was approaching.

"Listen, Goshka, what sort of a column is this, anyway?" Mitya asked.

"Probably some yids that they're taking to Garni Yar," replied Goshka with the same high spirits as before.

"What?" cried the flabbergasted Sapunov. "What are you talking about?"

Krutkin laughed out loud. "You mean you didn't know, Mitya? This is the road to Garni Yar. You didn't hear about Garni Yar when we were in Chernigov? That's where they're wiping out the yids—the Jews. They machine-gun them and push them over the embankment. Then they bring in bulldozers to cover them with earth and start a new layer. I hear the operation has been going on for two weeks now, it's an awful business. . . . What's with you, Mitya? Why are you shaking like that, friend?"

Sapunov jerked Krutkin up by his shirt. "You're lying, you bastard!"

Krutkin suddenly bared his teeth in a hyenalike grin. "Don't make yourself out to be such a virgin, Mitya! As if you didn't know what the Germans do with Jews! As if you haven't heard of Garni Yar! We were lucky, if you want to know, that they posted us on the road and not right up at the ravine."

Mitya still did not release Goshka, whom he was holding by the lapels, as if by pushing him around he wanted to draw out his denial of what he had been told. Suddenly Krutkin struck him on the side of the head so hard that they were both stunned. At that very moment, the lead armored vehicle in the convoy appeared from behind a coppice.

It was the ideal of the Wehrmacht armored transport vehicle, carrying two rows of steel helmets, a dozen machine-gun-bearing motorcycles following it. It was only after this inexorable epigraph that the endless procession began, a column of people who had nothing to do with the war, unless one counted the yellow stars on their clothes. Here and there guards were marching alongside them with their weapons trained forward. They were obviously the same sort as the Zarya team—Russians, or maybe Ukrainians. SS soldiers appeared, occasionally leading dogs. They were shouting something, undoubtedly "Schnell!" and gesturing with their arms: forward, to the target!

The whole column was humming in the same key: the roar of engines, the shuffling of shoe soles, voices that merged together in one vast buzz like a bumblebee. The closer it came, the more one could distinguish individual sounds, above all the wailing of children. My God, there were children, too! The younger children were being carried, while the older ones were led by the hand. Then the howling of the dogs began to cut through the din.

Mitya had already forgotten about Goshka. The column was approaching. It was the materialization of something awful, unnamed, and unrecognized, that had always been present in his life. Now it's coming right out of the field next to us, he thought, taking shape, getting closer and closer. Old men in winter coats. Midwives with their bags. Down kerchiefs that were slipping off. Possessions tied into bundles. Felt hats. Girls, lots of girls, many of them pretty, some of them even smiling. One was putting lipstick on. There were the Jewish mothers, many of them still bustling about and trying to keep track of their children, while others seemed to have freed themselves from their everyday cares, to have awakened to some new sense of life. The few middle-aged men who were there seemed already to understand everything clearly, and their faces reflected gloom and impotence. Many of them were smoking. One of them brandished his elbow in the direction of a young Ukrainian guard who had pushed him in the back with his rifle butt. The soldier jumped back and cocked the bolt of his rifle. The man spat onto the ground and walked on ahead. And the mass of Ukrainian Jews, all those skilled craftsmen, continued to stretch out endlessly: mothers mingled with children; children who had managed to hold on to some of their capriciousness; old men who had nothing left except for the biblical traits of their features, which represented the apotheosis of tragedy; and young girls, shaking all over, fearing the impudent pricks of the soldiers far more than bullets and in no way expecting mass death side by side. No, there was something not quite right about this scene. No one could go that peacefully to a mass grave; Goshka was probably just flapping his lips. There must be a railroad station at Garni Yar and they're being taken there for deportation, that's all. Why the hell would the Germans want to kill such a huge crowd of civilians, don't they already have their hands full at the front? And anyway, how could it be? Shooting these unhappy, gentle people would break an executioner's heart. Shooting into a child's face or its little belly. A heavy motorcycle with a sidecar carrying a machine gun drove along the side of the road between Mitya and the column, dragging a trail of dust. He saw three SS troopers sitting and talking to one another. From time to time their faces would turn back toward the column and contort in a squeamish grimace. Mitya remembered: the NKVD had had that same expression on their faces the night they came for Aunt Veronika. It was clear, then: the task would be carried out.

"Lousy Jewesses . . . it'll be a laugh, they're taking the Jew girls to the bathhouse!" Goshka's voice suddenly cut in over his shoulder. Mitya looked savagely at his friend, who narrowed his eyes and tried to smile cynically, but the cigarette plastered to his lip was quivering and his rifle barrel was shaking violently.

Mitya lurched off to one side and ran to the cover of a clump of shrubbery a bit further down the road. Goshka took off after him, caught up to him, and laid a hand on his shoulder. "Are you crazy, friend?"

"I can't watch this, Goshka! I can't stand it!" In a fury, he flung his weapon away into the grass. "The German monsters!"

"Shut up, Mitya, just shut your mouth! They'll squash you like a bug!" Goshka pleaded.

Mitya sat down sharply and crumpled into the grass with his head in his hands. His garrison cap with the Wehrmacht cockade fell onto his knees. His shoulders were trembling like a firing machine gun.

"Mitya, what's gotten into you? Enough!" exhorted Goshka. "It's not like you're a Jew yourself, Mitya, so what's your problem? Your aunt Celia adopted you, you're a one hundred percent Russian! Come on, Mitya, it's the war, just goddamned politics, forget it!"

Mitya wiped his damp face with his cap and stood up. Within a few minutes his features, even the locks of his hair, seemed as hard as stone, to Goshka's amazement.

"That's it! I've had all I can take!" Mitya said coolly. He picked up his rifle, slung it over his shoulder, and set off down the road alongside the column. Goshka caught up with him and after one or two skips fell into step with him. From a distance the two of them might have passed for a patrol professionally going about its business.

"What have you decided to do, Mitya?"

"I've had all I can take," Mitya repeated. "I joined up with the Russian army to fight the Bolsheviks, not to help the Germans kill Jews! Tomorrow they'll make us shoot children! To hell with you, you bastards!"

"Where are you off to now, though, Mitya?" said Goshka in desperation. "Where could we give ourselves up? Do you think we can just hide out in the forest and join the partisans?"

Mitya nodded silently.

"You must be out of your mind!" shouted Krutkin. "They're one hundred percent Reds, after all. Just the other day some of the boys were talking about one of ours from the Third Company who slipped away and found them. Know what happened? They tied him to the muzzle brake of a self-propelled gun and set it off. The guy was blown to bits!"

"Just the same, I can't stand this anymore," said Mitya, who came to a stop and put a hand on Goshka's shoulder. For the first time, he was acting like an equal speaking to a close friend. "You make your own decision, Goshka. My mind is already made up."

Krutkin was almost choked by love and gratitude. "I—where would I go without you, Mitya? I'd be so fucking lost . . ."

They continued on together.

"Where are we going?" asked Goshka cautiously. "If we're headed for the partisans, we have to bear left. Cross over those hillocks over there to that grove, then lie low until dark."

"That's what we'll do, then," said Mitya with a nod. "Before that, though, I want to see Garni Yar with my own eyes, so that I never forget."

The ceaseless hammering of machine guns came closer and closer. Then they began to hear cries. Mitya and Goshka were already a good distance from the road, but they could still see that the column had come to a halt. People were running around in horror, falling down in the dust, screaming. The guards threw themselves upon them, beating them with rifle butts. An officer standing in a truck bed was appealing to the agitated people in a most civilized tone, saying, "Ladies and gentlemen, you seem to have misunderstood," or words to that effect.

Mitya and Goshka slithered across an open hummock on their bellies and then plunged into some undergrowth. For almost an hour they crawled through shrubs that scratched and tore at them, orienting themselves by the pounding of the machine guns. Finally, a section of a gigantic ravine opened before them at the top of the sharp incline where they lay. An earthen surface scraped out by bulldozers extended the length of the sides of the vast gorge, and naked people were being herded onto it from several trenches. Almost all the men covered their groins with their hands, while the women held their breasts and children clung to the legs of the grown-ups. These were the last things they did in their lives. Bullets cut all of them down, and they tumbled to the bottom of the ravine. Mitya and Gosha could not see the bottom from where they were, but it was not difficult to imagine what was going on there.

From time to time, the machine gunners were given orders to cease firing, and then the maintenance personnel would appear on the earthen terrace with shovels, rakes, and hooks to toss the bodies that had lodged there over the edge. While this was going on, the gunners smoked, chatted, and looked up over their shoulders at the cloudless sky.

The machine-gun crews, two to a team, were posted along the near edge of the ravine. They were middle-aged men drawn from a support unit of *Volksdeutsch* soldiers. The crew nearest to Mitya and Gosha was lying next to its own truck another two hundred yards or so further down the slope. Both the men were broad-shouldered and had large backsides. When they stopped for a smoke, gold crowns gleamed in the mouth of one of them, the trigger man, in fact. It was this one that Mitya aimed his rifle at. The man was doing this job not out of fear but by conviction. He turned the barrel of his gun in such a way as to increase the area it could cover. In one sweep, no less than a dozen and a half people fell into the ditch. The soldier's shoulders were trembling like those of an industrious worker with a pneumatic drill. It was on him, just beneath the rim of his helmet, that Mitya Sapunov had drawn a bead.

"Oh, Mitka, what are we doing, what are we doing?" mumbled Goshka, who was drooling in horror while at the same time aiming at the gunner's comrade.

Mitya pulled the trigger. The head of the soldier firing the machine gun fell, quite unexpressively; he merely thrust his face forward, though his legs continued to twitch for another second or two. His partner managed to turn at least a quarter of the way around in an instinctive expression of alarm, but the shot Goshka fired cut off this quite natural motion. The two lads then turned and rushed up the slope, trying to get across the hillock as quickly as possible, not even watching as across the ditch from them the naked bodies began instantly to pile up in front of the silenced machine gun. Mitya's ill-considered act of revenge—later it would seem to him that he had been muttering "For Mama Celia, for Grandpa Naum"—had served only to increase the suffering of scores of people, to prolong their terror before the yawning abyss, until one of the neighboring gun teams, realizing that something had happened to Corporal Bauer, widened the scope of its work.

After several hours of making their way from one grove to another in short dashes, the lads reached a tract of land densely covered with trees. Exhausted, they lay down in the thickly matted grass on the edge of the forest. Around them, in the deep grass, intense, even interesting, life was going on: ladybugs crawled by, ants swarmed, velvety caterpillars swayed on stalks. As far as human activity was concerned, it was limited to the slow progress of a Fokker Wolf 190—a peculiar flying machine that Russian airmen called "the Frame" —across the empty sky. Dusk was falling. The land was untouched by civilization, without any sign of fires or human habitation. The Frame disappeared over the horizon, but returned soon after and flew over the forest.

"It can't be us that goddamned Frame is looking for," said Goshka.

"It could be," Mitya answered. "More than likely they're after partisans, though. The Germans probably think they killed the two machine gunners. Let's go, Goshka, we've got to get out of here as fast as we can."

Goshka whined, "Where can we go? We're done for, just done for!"

Mitya, though in a hurry, did not raise his face from the grass. How nice it is in this grass at this hour, he thought, and it's probably not bad here at night, either. If only you could live in this grass, shrink yourself down to the size of your own eye so that you wouldn't have to twist your neck and your ass all the time. He remembered how the German gunner had twitched when his bullet hit him, the first man he had ever killed. The first, in fact, at whom he had ever taken aim. Before that he had always fired in no particular direction, simply somewhere into enemy-held territory, but this time he'd gotten the bastard right below the helmet, blowing his brains out. Dejection and sorrow came over him, and he pounded the ground in front of his nose with his fist. An ant jumped from beneath his fist with its legs smashed, writhing in a mad hunger to save itself. Of the billions of ants in the world, it was on this one that something murderous had descended out of the universe turning peacefully to evening. Mitya crushed the kicking ant with a fingernail: his second killing of the day. "Come on, Goshka, get out of your clothes! If the partisans catch us in these uniforms, they won't ask any questions. It'll be right up against the wall!"

They took off their tunics with the R.A.L. patches on the sleeves, then their caps, boots, and trousers, tied them into bundles, and sank them into a bog. Wearing only their underwear, which did not appear to have any German markings on it, they plunged into the forest. They concocted a fantastic story about spending a whole year as prisoners and then escaping from the bathhouse just before they were to be transported to Germany . . .

For three days and three nights, perhaps a week—or was it a month?—Mitya and Goshka made their way through the woods without meeting a soul. One day, however, they saw flashlight beams and heard cursing in German not far away. Obviously it was a patrol on the hunt for partisans, or it might even have been our heroes they were after. The two young men then lay low in another bog, and at times, when the lights came closer, they would take a deep breath and sink into the fetid water over their heads. They continued to tramp onward, now in the natural camouflage of the swamp. "Swamp soldiers," giggled Goshka, recalling the title of a film from before the war. By now they were deep into the wild. All sorts of beasts scurried around them, and at night Mitya and Goshka had the feeling that eyes were following their every move. Wolves' eyes, of course—calm, lupine eyes. Goshka tried to catch some birds for food, but it was nothing doing. "We're a couple of pathetic products of evolution," Mitya joked. He was laughing about their ancestors among the apes. In fact, for some reason they were cracking jokes about all sorts of things. In theory they were leading a life of paradise, if one didn't count their hunger, swollen feet, and bodies covered with scratches. The days were hot, and the sounds and smells of their childhoods wafted from the warm pines. They felt as though they were playing a game of cowboys and Indians at a Pioneer camp somewhere on the Istra. The nights were lovely, with a fresh breeze rising to cool the two fugitives' bodies as if they had ordered it. They devoured everything they could find that was more or less edible—berries, mushrooms, grass, green nuts, the bark of young trees. They suffered terribly from diarrhea. Sometimes, with chattering teeth, they would gaze at far-off villages from the forest's edge. The sharply slanting rooftops of the hovels arched like freshly baked bread. Their stomachs would begin to convulse, and they would think about going down into the town to beg, maybe to steal something or rob someone. . . . And what if there were police there, or the Germans, or who knew what? There could be nothing good waiting for two young men of draft age. If they catch us, there'll be no getting away. They went on. One day Goshka howled, "Fuck, Mitya, we've already been on this very spot. Look, there's that 'Frame' over there!"

They came out into a large clearing, and sure enough, one of the ominous scout planes roared directly over their heads. Mitya butted his friend with his knee and laughed. "So now you're getting your bearings from a plane, Runt?" He understood, though, that Goshka was at his wits' end from hunger. Their flight was beginning to seem less and less like a Young Pioneers' adventure. This was just the sort of forest one might not have expected to spring up in the land of socialism, one that had no borders, no end, and no signs of human life.

"The Devil is leading us, Mitya, pulling us back into the swamp, only this time headfirst."

"Shut up, Runt, are you a man or a mouse?"

"What sort of a man should I be? This forest was made for partisans, just the place to find their miserable asses. And where are they anyway, your famous fucking partisans, that pack of dogs? Right now I'd surrender to anybody for a bowl of kasha. Let them shoot me, goddammit, as long as it's not on an empty stomach."

Suddenly, wonder of wonders, they emerged from the dense, nightmarish forest onto a barely noticeable path.

"Which way, left or right?"

"Let's go left, it doesn't matter where, left or right—if we run into nothing, we'll bear to the right. And if we run into a dead end there, then we'll split up because I can't stand to look at your ugly mug anymore."

"The feeling is mutual."

Every now and again the path disappeared entirely beneath a covering of twigs and ferns, then reemerged. Suddenly it turned onto a small clearing with a drop of sandy earth about ten feet high, from which long roots were hanging like witch's braids. There, underneath the precipice, goddammit, the remains of some sort of structure were to be seen: scattered planks, two or three burned-out stoves, even fragments of glass sparkling in the glare of the sun. A large animal jumped out of the jagged pit—maybe a wolf, maybe a wolverine, maybe just a devil—opened an angry, gaping maw at the bushes in which the lads were concealed, then took off.

"The pit, Mitya, it looks like a bomb crater."

"I'd say they bombed this place not too long ago, there are still a few smoldering embers."

"Yes, maybe the Frame came through here and dropped a couple."

"Or maybe the place was shelled by mortars. Maybe both."

"Anyway, it doesn't look like there's anybody still alive. There aren't even any bodies around."

"What do you mean, no bodies? What's that right at your feet, with his boots sticking out and the hand that something has gnawed at? Looks like they hit some sort of base here, no one was left alive."

"Listen, Mit, I'll bet you they left some chow here somewhere!"

"Careful, Goshka, you might blow yourself up!"

Goshka, not listening, was already racing through the shrubs to the destroyed dugouts. Mitya set off after him. They had visions of finding a package of moldering hardtack biscuits—they could not have asked for anything better. Now if only we could find a few biscuits to dunk into some swill or at least gobble down some bread . . .

There were more weapons lying around than you could shake a stick at: Soviet and German submachine guns, grenades, bayonets, but not a biscuit in sight. There was even a huge mess of dirty dishes, along with pots and pans. Obviously the swine had been feeding their faces; there were spoons strewn all around now, but no chow. Had they really gobbled it all down before they were killed? Suddenly a dizzying whiff of fried meat reached Mitya's nostrils. He jumped out of the ruins. A peaceful scene met his eyes: Goshka was cooking a slice of meat over some coals, five pounds or so of good meat with the fat still on it. "There was a horse lying over there, Mitya," the younger lad giggled happily, waving his arm in the general direction of the forest. "A horse that hadn't rotted a bit. I found a bayonet and cut out enough to make steaks for us. A man could live like this, eh, Mitya? If only we had a little salt, that's all we need!"

There was no salt to be found in the ruins, though they did not even bother to look, as hungry as they were. Next to the small fire, however, lay a napkin, actually a scrap of tarpaulin frayed around the edges, with a rhombus-shaped stamp reading "Supply Unit D-5AKU-I." They tore ecstatically into the food, ripping it with their teeth. They swallowed so much at once that they almost choked, and they laughed soundlessly at each other. Strength and optimism flowed into the young Muscovites' veins with every bite.

"What is this rag, Runt?"

"Who the hell knows, just some scrap that was lying around."

"Look, a Soviet laundry mark."

"How can that be, Mitya?"

"Because it's Soviet, obviously. Everyone here is Soviet, ha-ha-ha, ha-ha-ha, everything around is Soviet . . ."

No sooner had they gobbled everything down than the lads noticed a repulsive smell around them. The dead bodies, of which, as it turned out, there were at least ten, had already started to decompose.

"That's natural," said Mitya.

"Very natural," agreed Goshka.

They began to forage for other things they could use to live on. They found, for example, a broken shortwave radio and a German motorcycle. They did not pick up any of the firearms. Fuck the weapons! If they see you with a gun, they'll kill you first and ask for name, rank, and serial number later. They took a pair of Soviet cloaks. Some Germans were spread around as well, but they did not grab their clothes for reasons that are not difficult to understand. Now they would need something with which to cover themselves at night in the forest. Mitya pulled a pair of boots his size from a pair of legs protruding from beneath a bush. As he was yanking the boots off, the heavy fabric of the corpse's underpants stuck out, revealing the same stamp as the rag he had seen: "Supply Unit D-5AKU-I." He tried not to look under the shrub, but, as luck would have it, a strange absence of flesh on the left buttock of the dead man caught his eye. Suddenly Goshka Krutkin jumped out of the pit, his eyes nearly popping out of his head—he had just found an entire box of hardtack biscuits made in Dresden. If only we'd found them earlier, thought Mitya. They eviscerated the box and begun stuffing the biscuits into their mouths. What bliss! The appetizing bread pulp deadened the aftertaste of what they had just devoured. They walked on, chewing on the biscuits. They took turns carrying the box. We've got to keep going, what else is there to do? Sit around in the middle of a graveyard and go completely crazy?

The Frame came into view again in the scorching whitish sky. It was flying very slowly, surveying, its engine was inaudible, and anyone would have sworn that it was an animated being. All of a sudden, Mitya recalled the fat white maggot he had seen crawling along the edge of the pit. He began to feel a profuse wrenching sensation inside himself. He threw down the cardboard box he was carrying and hit Goshka on the back. "You bastard, what did you feed me? You gave me a piece of someone's ass, you shit-eating runt!"

He hit him on his blondish head, on the shoulder blades, beneath the ribs!

I'll drag you through shit, he thought, you son of a bitch! Suddenly Mitya caught sight of Goshka's paving stone of a fist, and realized it was flying toward his face. His jaw dropped as though it had been hit by a horseshoe, by the imaginary horseshoe of an imaginary horse. Mitya crumpled into the twigs and ferns. If only this were the end of it all! Krutkin, however, jumped at him with clenched fists. "You, you scum, you were everywhere with me, we did everything together, you cunt, you asshole! You got your kulak hide cleaned up at the professor's house! You and your fucking intellectuals! I hate you, you stinking goat! You're the runt, you are!" He raised his legs and hammered them into Mitya's sides—raise his head a bit, and you can give him another "horseshoe" to the jaw. Gathering as much strength as he could in his trousers, Mitya lashed forward with his boots. You prick! Krutkin crashed to the ground and was immediately pinned down by an onrushing mass. Now they were intertwined in a Greco-Roman embrace, rolling around on the ground in exhaustion, twisting each other's joints, until they were almost blind from rage. Krutkin puked right into his friend's face. Then he suddenly weakened and burst into giggles. "Hey, Mitya, that was quite a rigoletto we played! What a circus!"

In the end, feeling rotten and spent, they rolled away from each other and began snoring, bubbles blissfully forming on their lips. And the dragonflies of childhood hovered above them, trembling silently and gleaming, flashing all the colors of the spectrum, in the sun's rays that pierced the burlap of the forest. A few hours later the two sleeping lads were discovered by scouts from the Dnepr partisan unit.

CHAPTER THIRTEEN

A Sentimental Direction

★

By the autumn of 1943, they had begun to knock down the boards covering the statues of Moscow: the war front had been rolled back to a safe distance. Gogol's melancholy nose was once again suspended over the street with which it was associated, the former Prechistinsky Boulevard. At that moment, nothing on the earth nor in the skies threatened it. The monument would stand in absolute inviolability until 1951, when Stalin would look at it one day and snort, "What a disgusting anti-Soviet nose that writer has!" after which it would be immediately removed from its pedestal and tossed into the slammer, where its nose would gather dust and dream ceaselessly about escape as it suffered pangs of remorse, until 1959, the year it would rise again. The rehabilitated statue, pulled out of its jail, discovered to its surprise that its place had been taken by a new Gogol—a broad-shouldered, ever-so-manly figure that was the dream of his youth come true, with the same nose that had strolled so self-assuredly along Nevsky Prospekt in 1839, during the brief days of its escape.

For the time being, the residents of Gogol Boulevard noticed with delight that their beloved misanthrope had crawled out of his covering of planks and took up their old habits of strolling around the statue and sitting at its base. No less pleasure was taken from stopping here by those who were just passing through, in particular Colonel Vuinovich, just returned from a hospital at the front.

Vadim was already on his third cigarette. He was smoking them one after another, greedily, savoring every moment of peace, just as everyone at the front did. He looked at the bas-relief of characters, all sorts of Chichikovs and Korobochkas from Gogol's novel *Dead Souls*, forming a dance in the round about the base. Autumn in Moscow had always formed a particularly attractive tableau in his eyes: statues, streetcars rolling down tree-lined boulevards, the center of Russian civilization, the illusion of normalcy.

He had been wounded at the very beginning of the Kursk engagement. His artillery division had been moved up to the first line to repulse the attacking Tiger tanks. They had managed to set nearly a dozen of the mighty machines on fire, but others, maneuvering at top speed and belching forth a frightful rate of fire, had been able to breach the line of defense and break into the rear. That was not especially worrying to Vuinovich: in spite of enormous losses, he had managed to keep his division in order, and besides, it was Colonel Cherdak's forces that were supposed to worry about the tanks that had broken through, a fact to which the telephone receiver rumbling beneath his ear attested. Cherdak, his frequent drinking companion, who was not without his eccentricities—just the other day, they had downed a liter of pure alcohol at cards—was now sitting in his commander's tank reciting his favorite text: "Don't let any fucking thing scare you, Vadyokha. Right now I'm going to obliterate those shitheads with the biggest fucking boot civilization has ever known! So long!" With these words he closed the hatch of his tank and led the brigade off to intercept the Tigers.

In the meantime, six of the monstrous seventy-two-ton Ferdinand self-propelled guns manufactured by Porsche that were Hitler's newest hope had rolled out onto the hills in front of Vadim's position, crushing the remains of a village. At that moment Vadim, caught up in the excitement of battle and emboldened by Cherdak's rollicking curses, made an unexpected decision. Let's go straight for them, roll out our 75mm guns, carry them out if we have to! The Ferdinands stationed on the hills had begun an intensive shelling of the Russian rear to provide covering fire for the penetrating Tigers. Vadim's artillery crews, taking turns, were firing with great accuracy, but at the moment their shells were merely smashing against the thick frontal armor of the vehicles.

Closer! Closer! They hauled the cannons across a shallow stream. Meanwhile, Vadim continued to follow the Ferdinands' work attentively through his binoculars. The information that had recently come down from the reconnaissance units had proven to be accurate: the behemoths had no machine guns. So we'll transfer our fire to the escort vehicles while we continue to move forward, right at them! Prepare hand grenades, submachine guns, and pistols!

An assault company from the Second Panzer Corps, accompanied by what were obviously units of the SS Totenkopf Division, was formed up around the Ferdinands. They had first-class equipment, even mortars, with which they fired on the Russian artillery advancing in such an unorthodox fashion. Using artillery on the attack, what won't those damned *Untermenschen* think of next!

Vuinovich's guns were no longer shooting at the invulnerable Ferdinands, having switched to wiping out the escort unit. Taking up his sidearm, Vadim waved to his men and ran across a potato field in the direction of the approaching yellow-green hulks. Shoot into the observation ports, set fire to the fuel tanks, throw those grenades. Just then someone, some old goat, caught him across the stomach with a lead pipe.

The climax of the battle took place in his absence, in the sense that he did not see his artillerymen, carrying out their fallen commander's orders to the letter, put the new, ill-fated "wonder weapons" out of action. Vadim, in the meantime—if one could still talk about "time" where Vadim was concerned—was in a sort of parallel universe, now thrashing about like an insect before giant waves of red intermingled with lilac, now increasing in size by enough to absorb the full reach of all of the red and lilac, expanding to the point of exploding.

In the end, though, he neither drowned nor exploded; instead, the cheerful face of a young doctor—we'll call him David—flickered in the opening of the sky above him, saying, "Well, Colonel, better write the wife to tell her to light a candle in church for you!" Vadim was about to protest that his wife was a Muslim, but he did not have time before he was carried away into another contiguous universe, though this time one not as threatening or demonic; a land rather close to his own vanished youth, where for some reason the voice of the poet Alexander Blok repeated over and over, "The wind has brought a hint of spring from afar. . . . The wind has brought a hint of spring from afar. . . . The wind has brought . . ."

To make a long story short, he was saved by the surgeons' arts and a miracle drug from abroad called penicillin, the first shipment of which had just reached military hospitals. His improbable head-on artillery attack on armor was the subject of a great deal of talk. He had been recommended for the Order of Lenin for valor and initiative. Three-Star General N. B. Gradov, commander of the Reserve Front, saw his name when checking the decoration lists and changed the recommendation from "Lenin" to "Hero of the Soviet Union." He also proposed that Vuinovich be promoted to major general, but some high-level bureaucrat in Moscow put up vigorous resistance to the idea. Somehow or other, though, yesterday's "enemy of the people," an indistinguishable particle of "gulag dust," became a holder of the country's highest award.

In addition to this decoration, he had the benefit of another invaluable service from the doctors at the front: they sent him to recuperate in Samarkand, where his wife, Gulia, lived with their two sons, Valery and Rafik. His two months in the hospital in the rear turned out to be sheer bliss. First of all, the family was reunited out of the blue. Second, something else quite unexpected occurred, namely the disappearance of the sensation of a burden that Vadim had always experienced where his family was concerned, to be replaced by a new relationship.

Gulia had been eighteen years old at the time of their marriage. Distinguished by her stunning eastern beauty, she was from the family of a local Party functionary, a Soviet feudal lord of sorts. Her disposition was at once shy, brazen, and lazy. Her indolence connected her to the tradition of women in harems, but the similarity ended there. Brought up on a steady diet of Party stereotypes, she constantly tried to dominate her husband, a thoughtful sort, made frightful scenes for the silliest reasons, and even slapped him from time to time.

Suddenly, in place of the fury of old there appeared at the hospital a reserved young woman with well-combed hair, wearing a modest suit. She no longer even seemed as monstrously beautiful as before—now she was simply a girl with a kind face named Gulia. In the years following her husband's arrest, she had graduated from a pedagogical institute by correspondence and had read a vast amount of literature. Suddenly she buried her face in the hospital blanket and began to sob: "Forgive me, Vadim, forgive me!" In 1937 she had publicly disavowed her husband in speeches at Party meetings and forbidden her sons to mention their father's name.

"Oh, Gulia, my dear, there's no need for you to do this to yourself! You weren't the first, and you won't be the last!"

"Oh, Vadim, I know you don't love me. Even though you love another, forgive me—I'm the mother of your sons, after all!" Her interest in literature clearly stood her in good stead and was remarkable for its inclination to outright sentimentality.

The boys were delighted suddenly to have a Russian hero for a papa. Remembering the early days of their childhood, they constantly hung on his shoulders, bringing pain to Vadim's battered frame. Vadim, however, enjoyed the fuss they made over him. When he was given permission to go out, the boys would run straight to the hospital every day as soon as school was over, and he would accompany them home, limping, like an ancient ruler. That old goat in the Kursk salient had thrown not only his stomach into disorder, but his right leg at the hip as well. They walked past the Bibi-Khanum mosque, across Registan Square, scorching from the sun, toward the outskirts of the city, where the hills of the Zarevshan valley, covered with a lush carpet, were visible between the rooftops. Pyramids of all sorts of melons lay everywhere, sweet grapes were hanging above fences. Flour was rationed, but hot, brittle chureki were not considered a luxury here. The East, Sovietized as it was, could be seen everywhere, offering an unexpected demonstration of some inexplicable brotherhood, the feeling of belonging to a huge family, in the midst of brutal history.

When she was alone with her husband, Gulia cried, "All the same, you don't love me. You love Veronika Yevgenievna Gradov!"

Vadim kissed her without saying a word. In the darkness Gulia's lips parted like the petals of a tulip.

With regard to Veronika Yevgenievna Gradov, Gulia was probably wrong by now. The persistent image of the former had been entirely displaced during the years of separation by more recent impressions: the twenty-two methods of active investigation, the laying of railroad track in the Norilsk district, the ironlike game with the Ferdinands, and finally the fascinating other-dimensional trips. True, he had written her a letter, a friendly, energetic letter with good manly humor, with the requisite "subtle hint at obvious circumstances," to use a then-current phrase: if fate didn't bring us together in peacetime, he said, then in wartime anything is possible. Fortunately, he did not post this vulgar little note. Where would he have sent it, anyway? He had no idea what her Moscow address was. He certainly couldn't send it to headquarters at the front—"to the commanding general, for his wife." He could, of course, send it to Silver Forest, yet for some reason he immediately and firmly ruled out this possibility and pretended it had never even crossed his mind. In short, this Samarkand letter joined a scattered collection of letters never sent that, if gathered together, would have permitted some investigator to write an interesting report about the reveries of the officer corps of the Worker-Peasant Red Army.

In Samarkand Colonel Vuinovich very quickly regained his health. A second abdominal operation was not even necessary. Soon his leg was entirely mended as well. You're ready to grab your pistol and throw yourself at the tanks of the Reich again, Vadim thought. It should be mentioned that at the age of forty-three Vadim had reached the peak of manhood. Like his friends in high places, though unlike the skinny, round-shouldered Nikita, he presented a picture of the ideal of masculine beauty: graying temples, straight shoulders, and a walk that embodied all of the regulations of the Russian guard. Women behind the lines forgot wretched reality as soon as they laid eyes on him and even long afterward sighed deeply and tenderly.

Even now, as he sat beneath the Gogol monument with one knee forward and his map case resting on it, schoolgirls running across the boulevard stumbled and slowed to a walk as if they were waiting for the handsome colonel to call out to them, then moved off slowly, whispering to one another, giggling and looking back over their shoulders. Meanwhile, the colonel was holding a small letter folded into the shape of a triangle on his case, and he drew a circle around the address with an indelible pencil: "V. L. Shebeko, 7 Ordynka Street, Apartment 8, Moscow." The letter was made up into a triangle because envelopes had disappeared from the land of the living. It looked like an ordinary bit of correspondence, the kind that went back and forth between the front and the rear by the millions; this one, however, belonged to another era entirely. This was the very same letter that someone had thrown from a passing prison boxcar to land at the feet of Nikita Gradov. The reader who has forgotten these long-ago events is advised to go back to the first volume of our saga and return to the drunken, gloomy conversation of the two officers, at the end of which Nikita asked Vadim to deliver this letter. Before he ever got to Moscow, however, Vadim had had time to go home to the Afghan frontier, where he had been arrested right at regimental headquarters. And now in Samarkand, looking through Gulia's old photograph albums, he had come across that prison triangle: Strepetous, 7 Ordynka, Apartment 8. . . . The letter was already six years old. Even though at the time he had been keen to fulfill the wish of the unknown zek because he hated Stalin and "all of his gang," it was only now, after all that he had gone through himself, that he understood without any extraneous political emotions what this letter represented for that man.

On that fall day, alone with himself—though in the presence of Gogol—Vadim finally decided to go to the Zamoskvorechie region to deliver the letter.

Otherwise it would be lost again and forgotten, leaving only a vague feeling of guilt.

He walked down the boulevard as far as the Palace of Soviets metro station, then crossed over to Volkhonka Street and strolled on its right-hand side toward the city center, admiring the rooftops of buildings and the columns of the art museum. Almost everywhere he looked, he saw lines for rationed food stretching along the sidewalks. The people stood in closely packed, stable formations; old women had brought chairs and crates with them, establishing themselves comfortably with their knitting. There was also, of course, the figure without which no line in Moscow is complete, an elderly gentleman, an academic with round glasses, reading a large, dusty old volume. As he walked along the line of people, Vadim could not help thinking: how much more will you have to bear, friends? Think of the grief we've brought you by our ideas and our weapons. Even now, when victory is approaching, we have survived as a nation, but still as a nation of slaves, damn it! And as always, the accursed "cockroach" has left us with nothing but the impasse of standing in lines. You couldn't mount an uprising against this kind of war, after all! Who would follow you, anyway, when the laurels of victory were laid on the brow of the most hateful and criminal man in the country! The same filthy blasphemy was being instilled everywhere: "For the Motherland, for Stalin!" Now he sits there as an equal to—what am I saying, as the chief among—the leaders of the democracies! It was like a hallucination invented by the Devil!

Nevertheless, the mood in the queues of Moscow in the fall of 1943 was not at all hopeless—it was, perhaps, even somewhat elevated. For the first time in two years, one could really "cash in" ration cards: they were often good for oatmeal, sunflower oil, on occasion even for American tins of Spam and powdered eggs. Sometimes one could get a watery formula called "soufflé" for children's coupons. On the whole, things seemed to be looking up. Instead of the blackout, there were stunningly beautiful fireworks displays in the skies over the city! An element of reverie was added to the faces of young women. Men continued to become cripples, yet for all that—or maybe even because of this—they had begun to appear more and more often among the public. For example, the marvelous invalid Andrusha from Sivtsev Vrazhek. Play us a version of that marvelous waltz "Clouds in Blue" on a war trophy accordion. And he sings marvelously—like the great crooner Mark Bernes. The entire line of people was listening, enraptured, while girls from the Volkhonka neighborhood were dancing with each other on the pavement. Girls, just look at that marvelous officer passing by! Oh, I could just die, they don't make men like that anymore!

"We wish you health, Comrade Colonel!"

"Hello, girls!" Vadim answered with a smile.

"What would you say to having a quick dance with us?" asked the cleverest of the group.

"I'm only just out of hospital!" He laughed.

"Don't worry about it, Colonel!" roared Andrusha the cripple. "Go on and dance, the war excuses everything!"

Vadim, still laughing, suddenly caught up the bright girl and broke into a waltz with her. "Clouds in blue recall that house by the sea . . ." The girl, so happy she felt not the slightest embarrassment, lay her head on her partner's bemedaled chest. The crowd around them laughed and applauded.

"Whom did you give your leg as gift to, friend?" Vadim asked the accordion player. "Guderian or von Manstein?"

"I went ashore at Kerch, Colonel," said Andrusha with a wink, as though he were talking to a colleague. "I threw away my claw down there to fertilize the Motherland."

Vadim was about to take his leave of the girls, not without regret, and walk on further, when he heard a voice pronounce his name loudly. "Vadim Vuinovich? Is it really? It can't be!" Before he had even managed to turn around to the source of the voice, he felt a kind of instantaneous, remarkably keen awareness, right to the most trifling detail, of this autumn day as the day of his life when everything bore some relation to him and he himself was a part of everything—the cool breeze already with a hint of snow in it from beyond the Moscow River, the languorous din of the accordion, the girls with their hair flying in all directions—and realized that the event that was now taking place was more important than the whole world war, and that once again the triangular letter would not be delivered.

He turned around. Another "trophy accordion," this time a Mercedes-Benz limousine, was slowly rolling next to the sidewalk on the other side of the street. The driver's stone face was turned toward him with animosity. The second lieutenant's shoulder strap was twisted. Behind the driver the automobile's windows appeared like two black chasms. "Stop!" the same voice cried, this time not at him but at the chauffeur. The frame freezes for a second, and then a long, silk-stockinged leg ending in a leather shoe wrapped in intricate straps appears from the cushions of the backseat and through the door. The leg is moving a bit more slowly than the usual rhythm of a historical event, but then the dark opening of the car door nearly explodes in an abrupt, brazen, and bright flash as a beautiful woman is hurled out. In the midst of the poverty of Moscow, it indeed looks like a cinematic device: montage by contrast. The beautiful woman, dressed in a tweed three-quarter-length coat with a fur over her shoulders, dashes across the street like the embodiment of a celluloid fantasy, all the best qualities of Lyubov Orlov and Deanna Durbin crackling and multiplying as she approaches. "Vadim!" Another step closer, and one can see that the young lady is in fact no longer young. "Vadim!" But how splendid she is, my love! She stretches out her arms. He stretches out his arms. Their fingertips touch. They kiss each other on the cheek as friends do. The film ends, and startling real life begins.

"I knew I'd see you again some day!" she exclaimed.

"I was sure I'd meet up with you today!"

"Today?"

"Yes, today!"

"How could you be sure you'd run into me today?"

"I don't know myself, but I was sure it would be today!"

For the first time since they had known each other they were addressing each other in the familiar form. She burst into laughter, and a gold crown gleamed in the corner of her mouth like a small mushroom amid the pearly rows. She leaned on his arm. Well, come on, then, let's go! Where to? Anywhere you want, let's go to the river, I need to catch my breath!

Shevchuk the chauffeur, who had been ordered to wait, climbed out of the limousine in order to stretch his cramped legs. He gloomily approached the line. The old women got curious. "Who's the princess?"

"Marshal Gradov's lawful wedded wife, her Highness Veronika," responded Shevchuk with his usual sly thief's humor. He gestured silently to the cripple with his thumb and little finger extended from a fist, meaning an invitation to drink. What the hell did she drag me down here from the north for, he thought, if the first colonel to come along is already "Vadim" to her? Who needs these amateur theatrics?

The wind blowing along the Moscow River raised numerous layers of small waves on its somber surface. A huge portrait of Stalin looked down on them from the façade of the constructivist-style apartment building. Veronika allowed her hips to touch Vadim's for the first time, and her lips, stretched toward his ear, whispered, "You're a prisoner, Colonel! One step to the side and you'll be shot without warning!"

He had spent most of the days since his arrival in Moscow roaming the Arbat district. It seemed to him that it was somewhere in those side streets that Veronika must be living now. In his mind he pictured her, with her mane of long hair flying, somewhere near the Vakhtangov Theater, or on the Garden Ring. The Gradovs' flat must be in a building in the turn-of-the-century modernist style, in other words, closer to the sources of this whole romance of Vadim's, short in length—to speak ironically—and platonic. It turned out that the Gradovs had now set up housekeeping in the most prestigious area of the city center, in a solemn building with a marble base and with figures of laborers on the rooftop. If one went right up to the windows of the marshal's study, one could see the Kremlin walls and the two towers of the Arsenal. A portrait of the marshal in an overcoat bearing a general's shoulder straps graced the bookshelves. The photo had obviously been taken by some celebrated war photographer—Baltermants, let's say—at a moment when the military leader was at his command post observing the movement of his troops. The face with its narrowed eyes and sharp vertical creases on the cheeks spoke of nothing if not pugnacious concentration.

Of course, Vadim had known for a long time that Nikita and Veronika were estranged. Right at the start, even though he had only just arrived in the active army from the camp, Nikita had invited him into his dugout one day for lunch. They drank a fair amount and talked about all sorts of things, but every time the conversation came close to touching on Veronika, Nikita sharply, almost as though to prove a point, took it in a different direction. Sometime afterward a young beauty by the name of Taska Pyzhikov appeared at headquarters. The commander never made any secret of their campaign amour; on the contrary, he even regarded with favor those who happened to call Taska "the lady of the house."

Talk about all these doings among the higher-ups naturally reached the ranks of the artillery division. The men in the trenches loved to gossip about who was in whose bed. To say that these matters were always resolved in bed would be to use the term loosely, but at least these stories diverted them from the nightmarish business of the "destruction of men and materiel" for a little while.

For some reason Vadim was greatly affected by the presence of this "soldier's dream," Tasia Pyzhikov, at headquarters. Nothing of the sort would have happened to me, he thought. If I had acted more decisively in the twenties and lured Veronika away from Nikita, she wouldn't be in such an awkward position now. I would never humiliate her. Whatever happened, I would understand and forgive her. The romance between her and her husband was coming apart at the seams, something that had to be proved to her. It would be different with us. In nurturing his life in isolation from his image of ideal love, he had forgotten the emotions the living, passionate Veronika had once aroused in him, as well as the masturbatory fantasies over which her star had hovered.

And now here they were alone, Nikita no longer with her—all that remained was his picture on the shelf, a mere photographic artifice. She filled two tall glasses with a dark liquid the color of the oak cabinet paneling. Cognac. Genuine Yerevan cognac!

"Here's to our meeting!" she said, then added, in English, "Bottoms up!"

"Why did you say it in English?" he asked with a smile.

She swept across the carpet and turned the key in the study door, laughing over her shoulder.

"I'm learning it! For our relations with our allies!"

What happened next was so natural that the word "banal" fairly begs to be used. He began to unbutton her blouse. She helped him, raising her arms and turning her back to him. The hooks of her brassiere turned out to be too complicated for him, owing to the reverent trembling of his fingers. Smiles cascaded from her cracked lips when she had freed her breasts. At the sight of these two rosy creatures in the flesh, those two tender manatees he had dreamed about so many times, he fell to his knees and buried his face in the space between her legs. She shivered, ran her fingers through his hair, then began to raise her skirt and to pull down a sort of fantastic silken skin trimmed with lace. Alas, after that, something absurd happened. Vadim suddenly realized he was supposed to take his clothes off as well: one could hardly approach an idol in a military tunic and cheviot riding breeches so worn that they were shiny. He began to remove his boots. The damned leather was tight at the ankles and would not yield. He hopped around on one leg, tugging furiously at one of his boots by the toe and heel. She waited for him, sitting nude in the corner, trying not to look at her Kiplingesque hero but nevertheless casting disheartened glances at him from time to time.

One boot finally flew off, fortunately taking a sock with it. The second sock held out, but it would add nothing to the romance of our story to consider that the colonel possessed only two pairs. Vadim begin to take his trousers down but then remembered that underneath he was wearing underpants that were hardly an inspiring sight, yellow in the front with a string closure. Feeling cold all over with desperation, he started to pull off his riding breeches together with his underpants. In short, after these awkward, if not shameful, minutes had passed, only cognac could restore the earlier magical light-headed mood; to go for the bottle looking like this, though, would be awkward and embarrassing, and, as if desiring to show that he was just as hot, just as filled with passion as ever, he threw himself at her, grabbed her, threw her head back and pressed his lips against her skin. Still, everything turned out wrong.

He's doing everything wrong, thought Veronika. He could have just fucked me on the run, "officer style," as they say. This was, in fact, exactly how she had pictured the scene taking place in her mind: I'm alone in the half light, Vadim comes in, calmly unbuckles his belt. . . . Once one starts to do things gently, tenderly, though, one mustn't suddenly start to rush—one has to keep on with it, slowly, drawing things out to infinity, to total exhaustion. . . . "Oh, I'm so happy with you it's almost torture . . ." I suppose I did things wrong, too: I didn't draw the blinds, and for some reason I decided not to take matters into my own hands, or into my mouth, anyway . . .

Later they silently lay side by side. The leather couch was cramped, and Vadim's leg hung over onto the floor. Veronika quietly touched the palm of her hand to the scars on his stomach.

"You had a terrible wound," she said.

"They dragged me practically from the jaws of hell," he said. He was about to begin telling her the story of his wound but cut himself short: it might sound as though he were trying to justify his clumsiness.

"My dear," she whispered. As her lips began to wander lovingly over his face, his eyes moistened. She understands everything, he said to himself. She's a real woman, not a whore. It seemed as if something were drawing near once again. The "holy fire," as the dissolute classic romantic authors would have had it, was wandering anew in the dark labyrinths and might flame up at any moment, and then everything would be real. But just then she climbed quickly over him and hastened along the carpet, gathering up her scattered clothes. He had not even realized what was happening by the time she sat before him almost fully dressed on the edge of the table next to the bottle of cognac.

"Get dressed, Vadim! The children will be home soon!"

As he was getting back into his riding breeches, shirt, and leather boots, she downed a half tumbler of cognac in one swallow—"Bottoms up!"—and lit an American cigarette, a Chesterfield, that had come from her husband's abundant rations.

"By the way, Vadim," she said with worldly liveliness, "I'm going to hit forty tomorrow, you know. Can you imagine that? I can't!"

He raised his glass. "You'll be young for a long time to come, Veronika!"

"You think so?" she asked with keen interest.

Melancholy was sucking his soul out of him and taking its place. His bewildered soul, though, did not simply fade away but was splattered on the ceiling like the flags of the anti-Hitler coalition.

"Where's your family now?" asked Veronika. "What about Gulia?"

I don't remember ever having mentioned my wife's name to her, thought Vadim. Then he began to tell the story of how after his arrest Gulia had lived with a friend of her father's, a man who was a local Party bigwig, for two years in Tashkent. She was already preparing to institute divorce proceedings against the "enemy of the people" when suddenly something happened inside her, some sort of, believe it or not, moral change. She threw over her bigwig and moved to Samarkand to take a low-paying teacher's job. That was where she and her husband had met up again. The local echelons of command had notified her that her husband was in a local hospital.

"Was it a good meeting?" asked Veronika.

He began to mumble. "Well . . . you know . . . I forgave her everything . . . then again, strictly speaking, what was there to forgive? Right now I have a sort of . . . you know, Veronika . . . our whole scale of values has been turned around, confused . . ."

She nodded. "It's the war. It's turned us all upside down even more than the camps did. . . . You know, Nikita and I had an unpleasant reunion—"

"I know," he said.

"How?" she exclaimed. And from this cry, which burst out of her as though from a fire, he understood that the subject was presently the most important thing in her life, essentially the only subject of her life as it was now, and that within this subject there was a subheading, or a superheading, which was contained here in the expostulation "How?" How and by whom was the information being spread?

He shrugged. "I don't know, really. I just figured it out from the tone in your voice."

"Do you see Nikita . . . often?" Her hand hastened to pour out the remains of the bottle of Yerevan.

He did not have time to respond: far away, at the end of the flat, the banging of a door was heard, followed by crisp footsteps.

"Boris!" she cried and ran to greet her son.

Vadim followed her slowly. He caught a glimpse of himself in a mirror on the way. Everything seemed to be in order, there were no bands or strings showing.

The seventeen-year-old Boris IV was wearing a new navy pea jacket. His short hair was parted painstakingly. All his muscles were concentrated smartly, obviously to express the mien of absolute and definitive seriousness he had recently adopted.

"Just look, Boris! Do you recognize your uncle Vadim?" she asked in a playful tone that was at once sincere and forced, as though it were simply hateful to her to play the role of "Mama" for a boy his age.

"Unfortunately, I don't," answered Boris IV very seriously. With equal gravity he nodded politely to the fighting colonel with the red stripe over the left breast pocket indicating that the wearer had been seriously wounded.

"But he was with your dad . . . in the Civil War . . . they rode in the cavalry together . . . or rather, I mean they went together 'at a gallop, for a great cause,' as the song used to go!" she said, still merrily.

The young man's brow wrinkled almost imperceptibly at the drunken intonations in his mother's voice.

Vadim extended his hand to him. "Very happy to see you, Borya. You're almost all grown up."

They shook hands.

"Very pleased to see you, too," said Boris IV. "Now I remember—you're Vuinovich. Pardon me for not having recognized you." He opened the door to his room. "Excuse me."

"Why is your hair wet?" Veronika shouted after him. "Why don't you put a hat on?"

Without a reply, the boy closed the door behind him.

"He's taking karate lessons," Veronika said. "You know, I'm trembling with fear for him. Did you see how serious he is? I think he's decided to quit school and volunteer for the front."

"He has no business there," Vadim replied gloomily. "It's no good for kids like that to be crawling in the mud if we can get along without them."

They were standing in opposite corners of the large entrance hall, eyeing each other. An ever-greater awkwardness and embarrassment gripped them, as if what had happened earlier had not brought them closer together, but on the contrary had served only to scatter their commonly held castle in the air around the corners of the room.

"So, Vadim," Veronika said. "Well, now . . ."

The message was fairly clear: go away now, she was saying, get lost, the show's over.

"I'm flying to the front tonight," he said. He spoke the words quite matter-of-factly, and yet at the same time hesitantly: the scene was beginning to resemble something out of a film from the new Soviet sentimental school.

She sighed. "And Nikita is flying in tomorrow."

The same mood, no matter how you looked at it: from the evacuated Mosfilm studios.

"For your birthday?" Vadim asked.

She burst into defiant laughter that was clearly not addressed at him. "For an event a hundred times more important than some lousy birthday party! Come on, now, Vadim, get going." Suddenly, with some difficulty, she made the sign of the cross over him from across the room. "As they say, God protect you. Don't forget me . . ."

"Strange the way things turned out," he murmured.

"The war," she responded sadly.

She blew a tender kiss across the vestibule of the marshal's apartment. Further contact, then, was out of the question.

Coming out of the elevator on the first floor, he saw the bull-like figure of a second lieutenant leaning against a marble wall. A criminal mug with the obligatory cigarette plastered to his lower lip. A puff of Lend-Lease smoke. Vadim did not immediately recognize Veronika's driver. When he realized who it was, he turned around. The chauffeur, staying where he was, stared at him impudently. He looked more like a gulag guard than a thief: he had that official, overfed look about him.

When you think about it, Vadim said to himself, you see mugs like that everywhere. In a way, they form a very important ethnic group. The only place you don't meet them is among German prisoners of war. There you see a different ethnic type, the Gestapo agent. Aren't we all caught in a trap, though, those of us who are fighting for the Motherland? You come out of the battle, and right away all around you see these mugs, see the sort who tortured you beneath the picture *Above the Eternal Rest,* those who drove you into the salt mines with blows of their rifle butts. . . . So does that mean you're fighting for them?

"Why don't you salute?" queried Vadim, holding his hatred in check.

With a derisive smile, the flunky saluted without changing his posture. Rendering a military honor in such a way made a mockery of it. Well, don't get mixed up with a shit like that on top of all of the day's other absurdities. Vadim went out onto the street and was immediately hit by a strong wind from the west—that is, from the direction of the front lines. That sort of thing happens from time to time: you come out of a house where everything is close and stagnant, where you were feeling sad and listless, and the street suddenly changes your whole mood. The fresh air inexplicably boosts your spirits. It seems there's still some future out there after all.

That night, walking toward the Douglas at the airfield, his rucksack slung over one shoulder, Vadim was still feeling this unaccountable enthusiasm, a sensation of the fullness of life. White clouds passed rapidly through the dark blue sky. Their shadows ran across the airfield, along the parked rows of Douglases raising their dolphine noses to the moon. The moonlight produced a powerful effect on all sides. The colonel of artillery is going back to the front. The counteroffensive goes on.

During the flight, slumped against the vibrating wall, he repeated two lines of verse over and over again. He remembered neither who the author was nor the beginning and end of the poem. The only thing he could recall was that he had read them in one of Alexei Tolstoy's novels, perhaps in *Road to Calvary:*

> O, my unrequited love,
> A cooling tenderness in my heart . . .
> O, my unrequited love,
> A cooling tenderness in my heart . . .
> O, my unrequited love,
> A cooling tenderness in my heart . . .

CHAPTER FOURTEEN

We'll Waltz in the Kremlin

☆

Over the next few days, while Colonel Vuinovich was making his way to his division's position, feverish preparations were taking place for an important and festive event in the Kremlin, in the center of the Russian capital, atop Bronitsky Hill. At that very moment, when orderlies in the command dugout were beginning to hack up American Spam with German cutlasses and while the officers who had gathered to greet their beloved commander gleefully rubbed their hands over a gallon jug of strong drink, the doors to the Kremlin's Georgievsky Hall swung open smartly, and a crowd of guests moved with great animation to take their places along a huge, shining U-shaped table. This was that very event Veronika had estimated to be a hundred times more important than her own none-too-inspiring birthday: a Kremlin banquet in honor of the military delegations of the Western Allies.

The American and Free French delegations were represented by their ranking officers, among whom were the personal representatives of Generals Eisenhower and de Gaulle, while the British contingent was headed by Field Marshal Montgomery himself, the celebrated "Monty" who had outfoxed the "Desert Fox," Rommel, in the sands of Libya. "Monty" was tacitly considered the head of the Western side at the negotiations.

"So handsome!" The Soviet marshals' wives turned their eyes in the Englishman's direction. "Don't you think he's handsome, Veronika Yevgenievna?"

"Just another man," replied Marshal Gradov's wife with a playful pout.

"So who's your champion, Veronika Yevgenievna?" Mrs. Vatutin asked her.

Veronika slapped her hand to her hip. "My God, it's more than you can take in all at once!"

Wonder of wonders, there was a new fashion in the Kremlin court: the wives of the military leaders had been invited to the banquet along with their husbands. The spouses of generals and marshals eyed one another. Veronika Gradov seemed to interest them more than the Western Allies.

Joint negotiations had already been going on for two days at Supreme Headquarters. Front and fleet commanders were present. The principal subject, of course, had been the timetable for the opening of the second front in Europe. The Russians pressed: as soon as possible; how much longer will we have to bear the burden of this war alone? The westerners smiled: naturally, gentlemen, preparations are going forth at an accelerated pace, but the second front has essentially already been opened, Italy is out of the fight. The Russians replied with politely dismissive waves: for some reason they did not take Italy seriously. The Supreme Commander demonstrated a great command of the art of diplomacy: "We hope Hitler's Germany will soon share the fate of brazen Italian Fascism."

"Go on, Vikochka, who do you think is the best-looking one here?" Mrs. Konev asked in a whisper.

Nikita Borisovich winked at his wife, who was wearing a dress with a dangerously low neckline: don't give in to this provocation.

"Well, that one, for example." Veronika gestured with her chin in the direction of a graceful general in an unfamiliar uniform; he was a dead ringer for a foreign Vadim Vuinovich.

"That one there?" The woman looked at the marshal's wife's chosen one and was disappointed. "But he's a Frenchman!"

"A Frenchman by profession, but a real man by vocation!" Veronika countered.

It was said she had "danced in an operetta in Siberia"! Very good things, those Siberian operettas, whispered the wives of the military men. On the whole, everyone present was in a fine mood. The same upbeat mood must have prevailed at balls in Berlin in the autumn of 1941. In a way, this banquet had been arranged to mark the end of a year of successful battles: Stalingrad, the Kursk salient, the forcing of the Dnepr, El Alamein, the landing in Sicily, the development of the vast Pacific theater of operations. There was talk that the Big Three would get together very soon to sum up what had happened so far and to draw up plans for the concluding (concluding, I say, by God! Rejoice, ye peoples!) phase of the war. Where they would meet, of course, no one knew. Cairo, Casablanca, Teheran had all been mentioned, but Moscow could not be ruled out, since it was well known that Uncle Joe did not like to travel beyond the borders of his chosen country. So it was possible that Roosevelt would fly directly to Moscow in his "Sacred Cow" and Churchill in the pride of the Crown's aviation, a Sterling bomber.

Finally, everyone was seated: the Soviet hosts on the outside of the U, the guests and diplomats along with their wives (though there were a fair number of single men present as well) on the inside, in order to feel more snug, more at the heart of Russian hospitality.

The marshals were sparkling with medals. We're sitting here like Christmas trees, thought Nikita Gradov angrily, while the Allies wear only tiny little boards. We need to introduce little boards like that into our army, so that officers don't have to drag out these idiotic decorations everywhere they go. A new emerald marshal's star now propped up his chin.

The story of his promotion to the ne plus ultra military rank, which had happened quite recently, was a curious one. At Supreme Headquarters they were discussing the massing of forces for the drive to the Dnepr. Members of the Committee for the Defense of the USSR, that is to say, the Party-government bigwigs, took part as well. It was decided that the forces of Gradov's Reserve Front would strike the decisive blow. With his pipestem, Stalin indicated on the map the place where the mass of men and steel would pour out onto the foe. It was a narrow corridor between swamps and forests that were impassable for vehicles. The Germans, naturally, would turn this corridor into a real meat grinder. "Have you prepared a detailed study of the operation, Comrade Gradov?" asked Stalin in his Georgian accent. The rounded-off, complete sentences, occasioned, of course, by a less-than-ideal mastery of the language of an ideally subjugated people, had long ago acquired the hypnotic quality that can reduce things to ashes.

Nikita Borisovich unfurled his maps. According to his plan, only half the forces of the Reserve Front would hurl themselves into the ill-fated corridor, while the other half, following a swing to the north of more than sixty miles, would come crashing down on the enemy through another corridor formed by the topography. "In this way, Comrade Stalin, we will be able to bring more forces to bear and also deprive the enemy of the possibility of shifting reinforcements from one sector to another."

Those present were silent. General Gradov's proposal went against basic tactical doctrine, which called for the delivery of a united, massed blow at the beginning of any offensive; more important, it contradicted the ideas the commander in chief had already expressed.

Nikita is sparing with his grunts, he's trying to make himself popular, thought an irritated Zhukov, though he said nothing.

Stalin now pressed the stem of his pipe directly to the map. A drop of honey-colored nicotine residue left a distinct spot. "The defenses should be breached in one place!"

"We will gain many advantages if we break through their defenses in two sectors," objected Gradov.

Gradov objected! Objected to whom? Conferences at Supreme Headquarters had long ago acquired their own etiquette. After their successes in stopping the disgraceful flight of 1941 and defending Moscow, Stalin had begun treating his military commanders with greater respect. The dolt finally understood that these men were saving his beloved collective at the same time as their own country. Usually, he let everyone express himself freely and listened attentively, asking questions, but once he had spoken, all arguments came to an end. In this instance he had already spoken, and Gradov's plan now constituted—more accurately, was unavoidably interpreted as—an act of undermining the authority of the Great Leader.

"I see no advantages," Stalin grumbled in annoyance. Nikita noticed the glance Molotov and Malenkov exchanged and how Beria's unseeing lenses turned toward the light. Well, that's it, thought Nikita, not much chance of pulling out of this nosedive. The salt mines must be missing me terribly.

"I've spent three days thinking about this operation, Comrade Stalin," he said. Everyone was struck by the fact that the words were pronounced with a certain coldness.

"Then you've thought badly, Gradov!" The dictator raised his voice slightly. "Pick up your maps, and go off to think some more!"

His map rolls under his arm, Nikita went into an adjoining room, from the ceiling of which a perplexed cherub looked down from a chandelier. Adjutants came running along the corridors. Gradov's chief of staff immediately appeared, along with his chief of rear services, three army commanders, and a profoundly despised man, sent to him in the summer of 1942 to serve as the head of his political department, Major General Semyon Nikiforovich Stroilo.

Glancing at the completely bald, respectable-looking Stroilo, Nikita could not forget the contempt he had felt toward the man in their younger days. Naturally, he understood that in the person of this commissar he had on his hands someone who had been empowered by the higher-ups to act as a watchdog, but what irked him even more was the memory of the affair between his beloved, inspired, and erratic Ninka and this "representative of the proletariat."

All of the staff officers knew, of course, that their plan had been rejected and sent back for reworking, but they did not know that there had been a scene, that the front commander had contradicted the commander in chief. When they found out about it, they went limp. Nikita eyed his comrades in arms attentively. All of them seemed frightened, except for, it seemed, Pashka Rotmistrov. What is it that comes over people? At the front they don't flinch before shell bursts, while here they jump when a spring squeaks. They're eagles in the face of the other side, but when they're with their own they become rabbits. What was this dimness that tarnished the Russian subconscious? Some terrible idea of shame and the malicious insults connected with it? Does the fear of torture lurk in every one of them?

Five men melted down around him like thick wax candles. Only Pavel

Rotmistrov, commander of the Fifth Guards Tank Army, was calm, pulling slightly at his mustache, wiping his intellectual's glasses, and even, it appeared, faintly smiling. He had been the first to support Nikita's idea of dispersing the forces in the attack and did not seem about to back down.

Stroilo suddenly strode away to the window and drew out a cigar. "Shall we have a smoke, Nikita?"

The blockhead, thought Nikita, still wanted to draw attention to the fact that there was a special relationship between him and the front commander. As if he doesn't know that I've never stopped demanding his removal. Not for being a watchdog, of course, but for having no talent. These snoops, we have the usual respect for them in our country, but hacks we don't have much use for—at least not just now, while there's a war on. Stroilo the oak tree, the general thought suddenly, like a schoolboy. I suppose he thinks we'll step aside to the window now like the two closest friends in the company, vested with the Party's trust, the commander and the commissar.

"Why should I want to have a smoke with you?" Nikita asked with unconcealed enmity and haughtiness. "Stay over there and smoke by yourself, Semyon Nikiforovich."

Then he unrolled the maps before his staff officers and with his palm covered the accursed corridor in which his soldiers would have to lay down their lives. Their losses would be at least 30 percent.

When he was invited back into the "holy of holies," Stalin asked coarsely, "Well, General, have you thought about it?"

"Yes sir, Comrade Stalin," replied Nikita crisply and cheerfully.

There were smiles all around, particularly from the members of the Politburo. The fellow was a bit stubborn at first, but now he has realized he was wrong. The logic of the Party and its Leader are invincible. Even Zhukov wet his thin lips and said to himself, the little shit has decided to save his ass!

"So then, we'll deliver one crushing blow?" Stalin pointed at the corridor on the map with his pipestem. There was still a questioning note in his voice.

"Two blows would still be preferable, Comrade Stalin," Gradov replied with the same tone of a teacher's pet; it was as though he were challenging his favorite teacher to a fencing match.

The stunned gathering again withdrew behind impenetrable masks. Stalin stood in thought over the field map for two or three minutes. Nikita was not entirely sure that the Leader saw there what one needed to see.

"Get out, Gradov," Stalin suddenly said in a frightful, sepulchral voice. Then, as though coming around, he raised his head, looked at the pale young general, and with mere irritation dispatched him with a wave of his good hand. "Go out and think some more! Don't be so stubborn!"

Once again, Nikita rolled up his belongings and headed for the room presided over by the cherub, a room that seemed to him like the antechamber of a bathhouse. Molotov and Malenkov followed him. The latter, a eunuch of a young man, immediately pounced on him. "Have you lost your mind, Gradov? Do you realize whom you're arguing with? You're contradicting Comrade Stalin!"

Molotov took Nikita by the arm and led him aside to the window. The former's face, which reminded Nikita of a heap of paving stones, loomed silently before him for some time. Meanwhile, a flock of birds without a care in the world flitted about against the backdrop of a watercolor sunset. The paving stones finally opened. "How is your father's health, Nikita Borisovich?"

A strange turn, thought Nikita, as though he wants to show that he is not only "Molotov" the politician, but Scriabin, his real name, as well—a relative of the composer.

"He's very well, Vyacheslav Mikhailovich, thank you for asking. He's working in the army medical administration."

"Yes, yes, I know. I have great respect for your father as a doctor and as a Soviet man, a true patriot," Molotov added calmly. "You will have to agree with Comrade Stalin, Nikita Borisovich. There is no other way."

Shifting his eyes from Molotov's amicable paving stones to Malenkov's gloomily quivering jelly, Nikita reflected that even here in the country's highest body the same system had arisen as in the penal system: good investigator, bad investigator. And we're all still zeks, just as before, no matter what power we might have over other zeks.

Fifteen minutes later he was summoned to the "steam room" again.

"So, General Gradov, now do you understand that one strong blow would be better than two weak ones?" asked Stalin. He seemed to be in good humor again, beaming with unfathomable drollery.

"Two strong blows are better than one strong blow, Comrade Stalin," replied Gradov, throwing up his hands as if to signal that nothing would convince him of the contrary. I would like to do you a favor, gentlemen, the gesture seemed to say, but I can't.

"Well, which of your two—" Stalin's voice shot up toward the ceiling like that of a homegrown debater in a Caucasian tavern. "—of your two strong blows will be the principal one?"

"Both of them will be the principal ones, Comrade Stalin." With his hands Nikita covered the places on the map where his two "principal" blows would strike.

Stalin walked some distance away from the table and began pacing, puffing on his pipe and seeming to forget about all of those gathered in the room. Nikita sat down on a chair. The people around him watched not without curiosity to see how the drama would unfold, that is, in what circumstances the general would be beheaded, as it were, and would hobble to the door, carrying his unreasoning head beneath his arm.

Stalin walked behind Gradov and paced back and forth aimlessly for a while. In his day Zinoviev had had the sensation that a wildcat was passing. To Nikita, however, it seemed as though a real and stinking tiger was approaching him. Stalin's hand suddenly came to rest on the general's gold shoulder strap with its four stars.

"Very well, then, we'll trust Gradov, comrades. Comrade Gradov is an accomplished military man. Experience has shown that he has an exhaustive knowledge of the combat capabilities of his forces, as well as the potential of the enemy. Now let him prove that he's right on the field of battle. I like commanders of his sort, ones who know how to stand up for their point of view . . ."

The unexpected climax of yet another Kremlin spectacle created a feeling of catharsis, if not actual happiness, in those present. As an experienced director of these dramas, Stalin clearly realized that backing down at this moment not only did not shake his Tamerlane-like authority but on the contrary added something important to his aura of a master of startling finales. Then again, one could not rule out the possibility that he had recognized that the seasoned military specialist was right and believed in the man's theory of the development of Operation Kutuzov. It was also possible that he had a weakness for this general. He may even have forgotten that before him stood a former "enemy of the people," a plotter in a military conspiracy that, even though it had not actually existed, had in due course been uncovered. Or perhaps he heard something pleasant, reliable, in the very name "Gradov," perhaps for him it released humanitarian energy just as did the name of the man's father.

In any case, after the Reserve Front was split unexpectedly in two streams into the intersection of the Second and Third Byelorussian fronts, separating and sweeping away the forces of Field Marshal Busch and General Reinhardt and opening a huge expanse of territory for an almost unopposed advance, Nikita was rewarded in a manner unheard of up to that time: he skipped over "General of the Army" right to the highest rank of all, Marshal of the Soviet Union.

Sitting now at the Kremlin banquet, Nikita constantly sensed the marshal's star, a precious stone just under his Adam's apple. The jewel seemed to be attracting everyone's attention. Maybe I scrambled to the top too quickly? As our Agafia once said, quoting a bit of popular wisdom: "The higher you climb, Nikitushka, the harder you'll fall . . ."

Across the table from the Gradovs sat several Allied officers. The westerners were obviously looking at them and, equally obviously, were talking about them.

The banquet was opened, naturally enough, by the commander in chief, a man of the same rank as Nikita, Marshal of the Soviet Union Joseph Stalin. No sooner had his hypnotic voice begun to cut through the babble of voices around the table than everyone fell silent.

"Ladies and gentlemen! Dear comrades! Permit me to propose a toast to our glorious allies, to the armed forces of Great Britain, the United States of America, and Free France!"

All present rose noisily to their feet, the officers with a clinking of medals, the ladies with a rustle of silks and a whisper of velvet. The sound of glasses meeting across the table rang out. "That professor from the Change of Landmarks movement, Ustryalov, would be happy," thought the journalist Townsend Reston. Reston had arrived in Moscow again only that morning, this time via Murmansk, and had gone literally straight from the boat to the ball. Now, sitting together with his old buddy Kevin Taliaferro at the far end of the table, he grinned with the mordant capitalist humor that was his trademark. Very touching, the imperial splendor that reigns in this fortress! There are even beautiful women with nearly bare shoulders! What sort of dictatorship of the proletariat is this? And what is this nonsense of democracy and tyranny standing in formation together?

Kevin Taliaferro leaned over to his neighbor on his right, Major Jean-Paul Dumont, one of de Gaulle's flyers and now liaison officer for the French mission and know-it-all Muscovite who was up to date about everything. Incidentally, he was also the very same man in whom Veronika had discerned a "man by vocation."

"Who are they, Jean-Paul?" Taliaferro asked, indicating the Gradovs with his eyes.

"Oh, that's the brightest star in the Red generals' firmament," replied Dumont, eager to display his knowledge. "The commander of the Reserve Front, Marshal Gradov . . ."

"She's gorgeous!" exclaimed Taliaferro.

"Madame? Ha, ha! You know, they say here that she's a real lioness!"

"Stop it. . . . She looks like a romantic Russian aristocrat!"

"Particularly against the backdrop of the other women," Reston was unable to resist putting in.

In an adjacent hall, Leonid Utyosov's big band was thundering "It's a Long Way to Tipperary" in honor of Field Marshal Montgomery. Everyone was applauding and laughing: imagine, a Russian orchestra playing an English Tommies' march! Then the languorous sounds of the popular Russian waltz "Clouds in Blue" poured forth.

"Gosh, let the chips fall where they may, but I'm going to ask Madame Gradov to dance!" Colonel Taliaferro straightened his long, large-pocketed tunic and adjusted his tie.

"Kevin, Kevin . . ." Reston said after him.

For some time Veronika had been aware that she was the center of attention. The foreigners were gazing at her for all they were worth, talking about nothing else but her, as if unable to believe their own eyes. Maybe they think I was prepared by the Ministry of Internal Affairs as some sort of a lure? Now and again, from behind Stalin, the minister of the secret services himself turned his bald criminal's head and looked at her through his lenses. The exotic glances of a young general with Georgian features reached her regularly from the Soviet side of the far end of the table. There was something familiar in that look that she could not quite put her finger on. Of course, the generals' and marshals' wives—her friends—were all eyes. They're probably going on about how many of the men here have fucked me. How I'd like to get my hands on that list!

Suddenly she heard a voice behind her back: "Pardon me, Marshal Gradov. Will you permit me to invite your lovely wife to dance?"

The words were pronounced in flawless Russian, though the first sounds of the obviously memorized phrase gave the American away. She looked over her shoulder and saw a tall, thin colonel standing behind their chairs. Not young. Broad forehead. Something childlike about his face, of course. All American men had something boyish in their features, as though they did not begin to live until the age of fifty.

Veronika stood up with a rustle of skirts. "So long, Marshal, I'm sailing beyond the seas!"

Nikita followed the tall couple with his eyes as they walked away. Sad. How did all this happen? Why can't I love her anymore? Does she know about Tasia?

> *For the third straight day*
> *Through the clouds, from the skyline*
> *The Junkers are flying away*
> *To strike at the forts on the front line.*

Klavdia Shulzhenko herself on the stage! Then again, who else would be here, if not her? Everywhere one looked here, it was so-and-so himself. The bloodiest and the most glorious. The most beautiful woman in Moscow, too. That's me, of course, Veronika said to herself. The most beautiful woman around, but my husband doesn't want to sleep with me.

For the third day in a row
I look down the barrel of a cannon,
At the sky, where planes fly in rows
Like a postcard panorama . . .

That was Nina's song, her very own! Nina gets angry whenever anybody talks to her about "Clouds," but at the same time the whole country's singing it, along with the whole front, where they hum it groggily. Hell, even the Allies are purring it: "What a great tune!"

This colonel from the embassy . . . who had he introduced himself as? Delavero? . . . Hold on just a minute, he's looking at me like someone who was in love with me. . . . That's it—he's looking at me like Vadim Vuinovich did until yesterday, with that same adoration. Congratulations, zek U-5698791-014!

"Do you come here often?" asked Taliaferro in confusion. He was holding in his arms the personification of charm itself, gliding with her gently across the waxed parquet. The delightful creature sometimes touched his bony legs with her delightful knee, and at other times her delightful belly touched his sinewy stomach. He was trying not to look at her delightful plunging neckline, but nevertheless his head was in an absolute fog and he was at a catastrophic loss for anything to say.

"Come where?" asked Veronika in surprise.

"To the Kremlin," he murmured.

The charming creature burst into unrestrained, even delightfully vulgar, laughter and said in English, "Oh yes! We're here quite frequently! The Kremlin dance hall! Oh no, my colonel, I'm joking! This is my first visit here, very first! First Kremlin ball, ha, ha!"

"So, it's Natasha Rostova's first ball?" quipped Taliaferro, very happy indeed that he had so cleverly and resourcefully made a joke in Russian.

Veronika laughed even more loudly. "More like Katyusha Maslova's!"

Taliaferro was in ecstasy: a magnificent exchange of literary, "Tolstoyan" witticisms with a romantic Russian aristocrat!

"You like Tolstoy, then, do you, Madame Gradov?"

The charming woman was now beside herself with delight. "I like obvious hints at subtle circumstances!"

Even Kevin Taliaferro with his Russian Ph.D. did not quite get this "find," but he beamed anyway at the realization that his partner—why not call her his "chosen one"?—had a well-developed sense of humor and an easygoing, buoyant temperament.

All around them comrades in arms of the Atlantic Alliance danced by obliviously. It turned out that tables had been set for the entertainers in the adjoining hall and that there was no small number of beautiful women sitting at them.

"You see the kind of ball Uncle Joe can put on," Jean-Paul Dumont said to Reston.

"With his ability, there's a job for him at the Waldorf-Astoria," replied the incorrigible anti-Soviet in a hoarse voice. "He could be a ballroom major domo, don't you think?"

The horrified Frenchman took a step backward.

Meanwhile, up on the stage, a diminutive Soviet Jew named Sasha Tsfasman was taking an enchanting stroll down the keyboard while a virtuoso clarinetist tooted away beside him, pouring out waves of sound. The piece, played at jitterbug rhythm, was called "Concert for Benny" and was dedicated to an American Jew named Benny Goodman.

"Goebbels would croak on the spot here!" Colonel Taliaferro supposed.

In the pause, a brilliant, diverse group had gathered around the breathless Veronika. One of the men, a general from India, the pearl of the British empire, was even wearing a turban. This was indeed a stellar hour! Could she ever have imagined this when she was in the camp barracks, especially the day when three hags were pulling her by the hair—I'll rip out your clit, you bitch!—Shevchuk had saved her, dispersing the clustered harpies with a few kicks. He had taken her to the infirmary and then on the way back had had it off with her in the snow behind the water heater. Could she ever have imagined that one day she would be sprinkling English phrases around to the right and to the left, that she would even remember her school French, and that all around her would be gentlemen who would catch these phrases and delightedly understand them? The presence of the young Soviet general with the mysteriously familiar, Caucasian face on the periphery of the gathering worried her a bit. He seemed to understand very little English but was quite sensitive to Russian. Oh, to hell with all these "sensitive" types! Everything was changing, the war was breaking down the old order, Russia was moving toward democracy! How strange the bitter popular saying "One man's war is another man's sweet mama" sounded when refracted through this prism!

"Tell me, gentlemen," Veronika said in her most refined voice to the men around her, "is it true that permanent waves are forbidden in Germany?"

The men present looked at one another and laughed. "Where did you hear that, Veronika?" asked Taliaferro.

Veronika shrugged. "My husband told me. He read it someplace."

"So Marshal Gradov is interested in more than just tanks?" some Englishman cleverly put in.

Taliaferro put an arm around his shoulder. "On the other hand, my friends, the question is a serious one. I was in Stockholm not long ago, and I was reading the Nazi press. This is how the matter stands. After their defeat at Kursk and the landing of our forces in Sicily, the Germans, as we all know, declared a state of 'total war' in the country. Within the framework of this campaign, as Veronika rightly said, the devices used for permanent waves were forbidden throughout the Reich. Everything for the front, for victory, economize on electricity! At this point, however, certain romantic circumstances entered into the picture. The movie actress Eva Braun, who, rumor has it, is the close friend of the führer, went to him with a request that he not deprive Aryan women of the machines that they were so fond of, that they came out from under as even greater patriots. The führer, as a romantically inclined man—you remember that photo of him in the overcoat with the collar turned up—could not stand firm against such a request, of course. The right to a permanent wave was restored, but with one caveat: repair of the machines is strictly forbidden!"

"A sad tale," the Indian said unexpectedly.

"And how do they do permanents in Russia?" Jean-Paul asked Veronika.

"I'm not the one to ask, *mon cher*," she responded heartily. "My hair is naturally curly—like the waves of the Amur River. I don't know why the hair of decent people doesn't curl."

I'm perishing, thought Taliaferro, simply perishing in this woman's presence.

"Well," she sighed, "time to return to the Reserve Front deployment area."

Taliaferro led her back to the marshal's section of the table. "Will you give me at least one, at the least the slightest, chance to see you again, Veronika?" he asked her quietly and earnestly.

She now looked at him with eyes devoid of any fashionable wiles and lowered her voice as well. "I live on Gorky Street, *naiskosok* [diagonally across] from the Central Telegraph Office, but . . . I hope you understand, I cannot receive you as a guest."

At that moment he wanted to dive into his Russian-English dictionary to look up the word *naiskosok*.

After the banquet had ended, Marshal Gradov and his wife were already on the stairs when the well-built major general of the Caucasian features caught up to them.

"Nikita Borisovich! Veronika Yevgenievna! I've been hovering around you all night, hoping you'd recognize me, but you didn't."

"Who are you, then, General?" Nikita asked coldly. Veronika shot a quick glance at her husband and realized that the marshal was extremely surprised by this colossal breach of unwritten protocol: some run-of-the-mill major general was addressing him directly, and by first name and patronymic at that—speaking to him, one of the dozen or so most important men in the country, like that!

"Why, I'm Nugzar Lamadze—my mama, Lamara, and your mama, Mary, are sisters!"

Nikita's attitude immediately changed. "My cousin!" he roared and embraced Nugzar by the shoulders, shaking him. Nikita looked at his relative's shoulder straps. "So you're in the armored forces?"

Nugzar chortled happily. "Oh, no, Nikita, that's just a bit of camouflage, you know, for the Allies. I work for the 'organs of justice,' you know . . ." He then added with a note of pride, "But I have the same rank."

Nikita's mood changed once again, and he squinted disdainfully. "Aha, so you went down that path . . ."

Nugzar waved his hands in protest. "No, no, Nikita, don't think I'm one of those—" He lowered his voice and looked around furtively. "—one of the Yezhovites. It's just the way things worked out, you understand . . ."

"What the hell are you doing rotting away in the 'organs,' Nugzar, when you see what's going on?" asked Nikita sternly, as if he were thinking only about Nugzar's fate, "rotting away in the organs." "Your place is at the front! At least come to where I am, into the reserves! I can give you your own unit, at least you'd be at the front! If you want, I'll give you some tanks and you can lead an attack! Or would you like to be my chief political officer?"

"Excuse me, Nikita, but it seems to me that you have Semyon Stroilo as your commissar, don't you?"

"What the hell do I want with that piece of shit?" shouted Nikita. "Who is it you're sending me, in the active army? In the thirties, I used to throw out sacks of shit like him!"

"What does that have to do with us, *batono** Nikita? It was his political service that sent him to you, not us," said Nugzar in a soft voice, smilingly, almost openly inviting Nikita not to believe him.

"All right, all right," interrupted Nikita. "I know who Stroilo is. I'm not against the 'organs' themselves, just against certain members of them—those who don't know what the fuck they're doing!"

"When did you start using language like that, Marshal?" asked Veronika with a smile.

Nugzar beamed and gave his cousin's elbow a trusting squeeze. He was obviously pleased by the marshal's politically correct remark about the security organs.

*Georgian for "sir."

"Think about my offer, Nugzar," said Nikita in parting, and led his wife down the historical staircase. Nugzar accompanied them to the historical doors.

"You must come to see us some time, Nugzar," said Veronika. "One day before you go off to the Reserve Front, do drop in on your way from the 'organs.' We live—"

"I know where you live," Nugzar said modestly.

"How?" shrieked Veronika with histrionic amazement.

"Sometimes you know more than you want to," Nugzar responded, throwing up his hands again.

"Did you hear that, Nikita? He knows more than he wants to!" Veronika sang out. A strange feeling of superiority to these damned omnipresent "organs" that made a mess of whole lives made her head spin even more than the champagne she had drunk.

Nikita laughed roughly, self-assuredly, and slapped his cousin on the shoulder. "On my Reserve Front, Nugzar, you will know exactly as much as you want to."

The doors closed behind him. Nugzar stood frozen for a minute or two. Staggering thoughts about a change of master, of being defended by millions of troops, raced through his head.

It was three A.M. when Nikita and Veronika emerged from the Spasskaya Tower gates and headed diagonally across Red Square. Clouds were drifting across the sky, stars twinkling, and the moon appeared occasionally, unmasking the obscured city. The airways were traveled not only by bombers; winter was on its way as well. For the time being, a pair of ballroom shoes and the heels of the marshal's boots clattered across the stone pavement in the dry, frosty autumn.

He's probably imagining what it will be like to review a parade on one of Voroshilov's horses, thought Veronika suddenly with unanticipated bitterness. Nikita the conqueror! Everything is as it should be, everyone is obeying orders, I'm not afraid of anything, I'm advancing. His two wives are carrying out their functions perfectly—one for campaigns in the field, another for fancy-dress balls in the rear! I'll tell you right now, Alexander of Macedonia, I'm filing for divorce!

The huge area around them was deserted, and only the Kremlin guards and the crews of the antiaircraft guns stationed around the fortress were not sleeping. Only cars carrying the departing guests passed from time to time. Behind the glass surprised faces turned to look at the marshal and his wife.

"You know, Vika, something strange is happening to me," Nikita abruptly announced.

"Everything seems to be going perfectly for you lately," Veronika replied coldly. He took her by the arm in a trusting gesture that had something of the adolescent about it.

"No, I mean strange in a human sense. I've turned into some sort of command machine. I throw divisions into the breach, move up a corps as a covering force, and so on and so forth. People have become one giant collection of pawns to me. Percentages of losses, percentages of replacements. Not long ago at Supreme Headquarters I stood up for my own plan of attack and probably saved at least thirty thousand lives by doing it. That's good, you say? Yes, but understand that I thought about these lives only in retrospect, and in passing. The most important thing for me was to confirm the effectiveness of my attack plan! Of course I understand that an army group commander cannot be any other way in wartime, but just the same I sometimes take my head in my hands—why do I have to be like this, why has it fallen to my lot? The human element in me always survived, even in the camp. Now, it's flickering out . . ."

Veronika, not breaking away, was looking from the side at the marshal, who had said all of this without looking at her once, as though he had rehearsed it all both out loud and in his mind first, as though he were feverishly determined not to let this opportunity to say it all slip away; the opportunity, that is, to be with the only conceivable confidante of such revelations. Well, of course—whom else would he tell? That slut Taska? My poor boy, Veronika thought suddenly. What have those filthy Red bastards done to you?

"You understand, Veronika, it's as though my heart were covered with calluses . . ." he went on.

My poor boy, for whom I once dragged around bags filled with bottles of bromides from Ferrein's Pharmacy. They say that bromide reduces a man's "potential," but no such effects had been noticeable in him. On the contrary, after a bromide he wouldn't leave me alone. My poor boy, does he still remember his Kronstadt nightmares?

"It's a terrible feeling, Vika, when a scar forms over everything. I've lost my old fears and pangs of conscience. . . . You remember my Kronstadt nightmares—I don't have them anymore . . ."

"My poor boy," she said aloud. Shaken, he came to a stop. The moon now emerged from the clouds and illuminated the dark, lumpy hulk of the Historical Museum, making it look like a spur of the Karadag Hills in the eastern Crimea, where he had first met Veronika. Her father, a blustery Moscow lawyer, used to lead mountain climbing expeditions with an alpenstock and woven picnic baskets. They would sit in the hills until dark, until the moon came out. There, Kitka Gradov had lost himself in her young face illuminated by the moonlight.

Now that face was before him, once again lit by the moon . . . and she was calling him "my boy." "My poor boy" she says to a man who has a million armed men under him, whose plans are studied at the *Oberkommando des Heeres*, at Hitler's retreats. My poor girl, the mother of my children. . . . Nothing will tear me away from you . . .

He did not say a word, but she understood that something important was happening to him at that moment, as if a clump of dirt had been washed away. They walked on even more slowly, hand in hand like children. They went on toward Manège Square, passed the Moscow Hotel, and were preparing to cross Okhotny Ryad when, out of nowhere, Nikita's adjutant, Streltsov, appeared before them, standing stiffly at attention.

"Permission to address you, Comrade Marshal? What are your orders for now until morning? Would you like to cancel the plane?"

Veronika looked around and saw a group of officers approaching slowly. Obviously they had been following their commander right from the Kremlin gates. A Willys jeep, along with two Dodge trucks filled with "Gradov's wolfhounds," drove up and stopped. In short, his escort group did not sleep even during a moonlight stroll.

"What a delicate sense of timing your retinue has!" laughed the marshal's wife. The officers, swaying on their feet, smiled in reply. Why not, thought Veronika, we all know each other here: Shershavy, his chief deputy for the rear; his personal chauffeur, Vaskov, who has served long enough to have earned his first officer's star; and two or three others from the Special Far East Army—it looked like Bakhmet and Spritzer. The most remarkable thing of all was that there, marching with this group, comparing favorably with General Shershavy in height, roundness of chest, and significance of expression, was none other than the former Silver Forest constable, now captain, Slabopetukhovsky. Nikita had clearly surrounded himself with his own "organs"!

"Slabopetukhovsky, you're here, too?"

"Yes, ma'am, Veronika Yevgenievna! My life has found meaning under the colors of the Reserve Front and those of Marshal Gradov personally, more accurately in the quartermaster's offices at headquarters, at your service!"

Nikita looked somewhat embarrassed, and it was not difficult to understand why: whom should these people call mistress of the house? This was perhaps the first time his men had seen him in a state of indecision: should I cancel the night flight to the front?

She put her hand to his cheek. "Don't believe your calluses, Kitushka, you're still exactly the same. When can I expect you back?"

He sighed with relief and kissed her. On one cheek. Then on the other. And on the nose. Her lips were off limits, otherwise he would have to call off the flight. Anyway, we have to start redoing the apartment, really fixing things up, whitewashing the ceilings, scrubbing the floors, cleaning the carpets and . . . well, might as well send Shevchuk, what the hell . . . not send him to the front, naturally, but to any warm place, just to get rid of this. . . . "The way it looks now, not for another month at least," said Nikita.

"That's fine," sighed Veronika. "I'll expect you in a month, with another marshal's star, that way you can become a marshal two times over. Double Marshal of the Soviet Union, not bad, eh? What should I do about Borka?"

"Tell Borka that I am categorically opposed to his plans to join up. Let him finish school first, then we'll see. A hundred and thirty-three kisses for Verulka. So long!"

He jumped into the Willys. The motorcade moved off. Veronika crossed Okhotny Ryad in her fox stole and long silk dress. It was two steps from here to home. So that's the end of "Katyusha Maslova's first ball." Now I'm all alone. And he didn't even remember my fortieth birthday.

CHAPTER FIFTEEN

Officers' Candidate School

☆

We shall have to begin this chapter with a little scene that did not have the slightest desire to hang on the tail of the preceding one, even though it was directly related to it. The fact of the matter is that Marshal Gradov did not go straight to Vnukovo Airfield and the Il-4 bomber waiting for him after he said good-bye to his wife in Okhotny Ryad that November night in 1943; rather, he went in a large circle around the sleeping capital first. At that hour in the deep of night, when Moscow's flora, tired of trembling in the westerly wind, had let down its branches in the traditional pose of the Russian serf and its fauna made only a sound of somnolent chirping as they drove away their tumultuous dreams, all the cars in Nikita's train drove up to the old Gradov house in Silver Forest. Leaving everyone else outside the fence, the marshal opened the gate by the same old trick, the one he had known ever since childhood, that is, by pulling one of the fence boards back and thrusting his unnaturally arched hand inside. Then again, the gate was not infrequently left unlocked, and this picture of an apparently bolted, but in fact unfastened, gate did in fact defy the criminal imagination—unless one counts the NKVD men who had come here in the autumn of 1937 for Veronika.

Nikita Borisovich was hoping to see a light burning in his father's study or a lamp on by his mother's bedside, in which case he would go into the house; neither Boris Nikitovich nor Mary Vakhtangovna was suffering from insomnia that night, however. On the other hand, Father might be anywhere tonight besides the house, thought Nikita. As the deputy head of the Red Army Medical Corps, he did not so much sit in an office in Moscow as move constantly along the periphery of the front line from the Barents Sea all the way to the Caucasus. The previous summer, at the end of July, Nikita had quite by accident run into his father right in the thick of things, at the Lutezh bridgehead.

The famous "Battle in the Sunflowers" had only just finished. The sunflower seeds, it had to be said, had roasted nicely! Tens, if not hundreds, of Tigers, Mark IVs, T-34s, Shermans, Grants, and Churchills were burning and smoking low on the horizon, almost leaning against one another. Huge clouds of smoke rose from behind a distant hillock, covering the other half of the firmament: someone had just blown up someone's fuel dump there. There was the typical landscape of total war: endless black smoke mounting into the sky, tongues of fire, the remains of living creatures appearing here and there.

Meanwhile, a field hospital was being set up on the hill in the midst of the smoking wrecks. Soldiers hadn't even finished setting up the tents, but an operation was already going on in one of them. Nikita, passing by in his armored car, quickly surveyed the hospital and its "deployment efficiency"—must put them in for a commendation!—and was about to continue on his way when he suddenly saw his father coming out of one of the tents.

Boris Nikitovich was wearing a blood-spattered surgical gown. With that same expression of pride on his face that he always wore after a successful operation, he was removing his sterilized gloves. Someone, obviously at his request, had placed a cigarette, already lit, into the surgeon's mouth.

Nikita wanted to pounce on him and roar, "What the hell are you doing up here, in the heat of battle? You're sixty-eight years old, Boris III! You're a general, you should be leading by radio, by telephone—why the devil are you crawling under exploding shells?" Fortunately, he realized in time that this was not the right approach. He calmly dismounted from the vehicle, went up to his father, and embraced him. Two frontline photographers running by immediately recorded the touching scene.

"Just operated on Sergeant Nefedov," said his father. "You know, he's the stuff myths are made of. Where do people get that sort of fearlessness?"

Nikita had already heard about Nefedov's platoon, which had managed to repulse all attacks on its position on the upper bank of the Desna and to hold out until the 18th Division arrived.

"You know, sometimes the battlefield generates a peculiar sort of intoxication that drowns out the fear," Nikita said. "Take the tanks, for example, both ours and Fritz's, thrashing away at each other at point-blank range—no one escaped. What was that, then? They all seemed to be drunk. That's what saves us, and it's also the death of us, if you want to know."

"You may be right," his father replied in a reflective voice. "In fact, you probably are. You understand these things better, you're a professional . . ."

At that moment, German multibarrel mortars of the sort that the Russians called "Vanyushas" began hurling rocket-propelled shells into the sunflowers from their position on the other side of the hill. Neither father nor son paid them the slightest attention.

"We're all under the gas of war," said Nikita. "You and me both . . ."

His father nodded. It was evident that he was tremendously grateful to his son for this meeting as equals in the midst of battle. "So how are things going on the whole?" he asked, indicating the blackened horizon with his hand.

"We're crushing them!" whispered Nikita. Signal corpsmen and adjutants were already running through his thoughts. They embraced once more and then parted, without a word about Mother.

Now, in the dead of night, sitting on the stump of a pine tree across from the old Gradov nest, Nikita recalled this scene and immediately tried to drive it from his mind. He was sick of war. He thirsted after "nonwar." When he thought about it, he had come back to Silver Forest not for sentimental reasons but because he wanted to come into contact with something age-old, something that existed outside of the military situation, outside of history, and that was much more important, something that at once radiated and absorbed love. It wasn't even his mother and father personally whom he was seeking, but rather motherhood and fatherhood.

He remembered the builders of this house, his grandfather Nikita and grandmother Maria Nikolaevna, née Yakubovich.

He remembered himself at the age of seven or so. He would come here with his parents on holidays. Grandfather would come out to meet them, bellowing through his flowing mustache, a professor from out of the 1880s, a real Russian explorer and researcher. He had in fact been one at one time—he and Masha Yakubovich had met in Abyssinia, where they were working in a Red Cross mission.

Nikita's grandfather adored him and dreamed he would come and live with him in Silver Forest. Tests had shown that the air in Moscow was seriously polluted, while here there was pure oxygen and pristine Metchnikoff yogurt. He even offered the enticement of a pony. He placed the boy astride the little horse and proclaimed triumphantly, "the Georgian czar!"—an allusion to his heritage on his mother's side. Even without the pony, though, moving here, to the piney bank of the winding river, where there were mysterious ravines and the chillingly named Bottomless Lake, was all that Nikita-Kitka dreamed about.

Sitting now in the darkness and cold before the house, which, although it was sagging slightly at the corners, was still reliable and solid, Nikita tried to summon from memory scenes of childhood and of universal love that were not only distant, but nearly unattainable. Only patches of light flickered before his eyes and then were enveloped by a cloud of words, by the story of the family told and retold. Will these flashes of light ever unite again into a picture, at least when my time comes?

The "wolfhounds" peered from their Dodges across the fence at the hunched figure of their commander. They were armed with Kalashnikovs, Walther machine pistols, and all manner of hand grenades and cutlasses. No one in the sleeping household ever learned that such a flotilla had come close to them in the night, otherwise two of the sleepers would never have permitted themselves their youthful slumbers. These two were Boris IV and his best friend, the Moscow youth middleweight boxing champion, Alexander Sheremetiev—not, however, one of the Sheremetiev dynasty.

In the morning Boris and Alexander went for a three-mile run. In fact, that was why they had come to the dacha for the night—to go to the park in the morning to work on one of the programs for the modern pentathlon. Fencing was even more enjoyable when done on a pine tree–lined path, and as for swimming in icy water or running, one couldn't ask for a better place than Silver Forest.

They talked a bit about fencing as they ran. One might have thought it nothing but an atavism in the conditions of modern mechanized warfare, yet it was considered an indispensable element in the training of a young officer. Its benefits were many—agility, coordination, the ability to make split-second decisions.

At the firm insistence of Boris IV, they cooked only oatmeal and allowed themselves two hard-boiled eggs at breakfast as hardy sources of protein while they discussed the situation at the front. For all the recent colossal successes, it was still too early to rejoice. The enemy remained powerful. For example, the Third Guards Tank Army, which had just taken Zhitomir, had been forced to resurrender the city to the Panzer grenadiers of General Hermann Hoff and to retreat, as the Soviet Information Bureau announced, to "previously prepared positions." And look at the Atlantic theater of operations: Fascist Italy has collapsed, but the Nazis are throwing more and more forces across the Alps with the clear intention of driving the Allies into the sea with an armored fist. With an armored fist, I say! Add to that the outrages of the U-boats, their ever-bolder interceptions of the convoys on the northern route! In other words, "the most evil foe of the freedom-loving peoples of the world" is not about to give up.

"All things considered, Boris, we have our plates full," said Alexander Sheremetiev with a wink, lowering his voice.

"Then how do you like the Japanese, old boy?" Boris IV replied forcefully, trying to neutralize the effect of Shermetiev's hint.

"They were the first to violate the Geneva Convention on the treatment of prisoners!"

He gave the boxer's leg a shove under the table.

After the usual Metchnikoff yogurt—at the house they had managed to maintain the diet they had had before the war—Boris Nikitovich rustled through the newspapers.

"The focus of events, boys, is now shifting to the diplomatic sphere," he said, underlining with a fingernail a low-key communiqué concerning the meeting of Molotov, Cordell Hull, and Anthony Eden. "This is the most important thing happening today. It indicates that a summit meeting is coming up. One has to know how to read newspapers!"

Two elderly women lovingly watched the men—that is, the old man and the two boys—at breakfast. If only such a company would gather around the kitchen table every morning! Alas, more and more often Mary and Agasha remained alone in the creaking house, which at times even seemed to be making strange sounds of protest, recalling those who were gone: Kirill, Mitya, Savva, the mercurial Galaktion, whose heart had not been able to withstand betrayal and arrest in his native Tiflis, to which he had brought so much good. Quite often they remembered the angel of the house, who had assumed the form of a keen-eared dog with a perpetual sly smile on its toothy muzzle, Pifochka, Pythagoras. The dog had lived his whole sixteen years with them, and his death four years before had left them desolate and perplexed: how could the world, especially the Silver Forest world, continue to exist without him? For a long time, Mary was unable to play Chopin. The dog had loved everything about her piano, but the sounds of Chopin drew him into the study like a magnet. He would usually lie down behind her, resting his muzzle on his outstretched paws, snorting softly, obviously enjoying himself. Mary began to play an improvisation and looked around, expecting to see her beloved friend. Instead there was only emptiness before her eyes, and the sounds of the improvisation were stifled. Nina, gloomy and brusque, sometimes visited the house and asked her mother to play Chopin. No, please, anything else you like, Rachmaninov, Mozart, but Chopin, for some reason I just can't! She was ashamed to admit that it was because of Pifochka.

Cecilia came, disheveled as usual, her skirts billowing, the toes of her father's boots turning upward, always smelling of acrid soup. She was still carrying on the search for Kirill, but no longer with her old fire: the war had pushed the prisons to the rear of the stage like an unnecessary decoration. She now received not even so much as a formal reply to her letters to the authorities, and one day when she managed to get through to the Party Control Commission, she was told, "It's incomprehensible, comrade—the country is bleeding and fighting for its life, and you, a Party woman, are worried about the fate of some Bukharinite! Wait until the end of the war, then we'll sort it all out . . ." Sometimes, in her moments of irritation—and, it seemed to Mary, when she had had a bit to drink—Cecilia would begin to rush around in the Gradov family circle, hurling abstract accusations at those who did not even take the trouble to think about the fate of their nearest and dearest, and for whom nothing was more important than their own comfort. There were other people, she shouted, there were people who sacrificed everything for someone they loved; there were women who could determine their own fate, to whom men made direct propositions of cohabitation and even marriage, but they, these women, would renounce everything for the sake of an ideal, even for a falsehood—the myth of fidelity has seen its best years . . .

Mary listened patiently to these foolish insinuations, trying not to dwell on the subject. One day, however, when she tried to say that all of Bo's inquiries, and even the demands of Marshal Gradov himself, had been met by the reply that Gradov, Kirill Borisovich, was no longer on the lists of the living and that, my dear, it's time to get used to the frightful idea, Cecilia went into absolute hysterics. She raced around the dacha, ripping the shutters from the windows, shouting, "I don't believe it! I don't believe it! He's alive! When the war is over, they'll sort everything out, they promised me!"

"You're right, you're right, my child," Mary soothed her. "Maybe after the war some secrets will be uncovered. Maybe even Mitenka will come back. After all, any number of men came back from the First World War who had been listed as 'missing without a trace.' "

"Well, of course Mitya will come back," Celia said comfortingly. "There's no doubt about it, he'll come back with a medal, he'll atone for his kulak ancestry . . ."

"Atone for it?" Ninka would explode—if she were there, naturally. "What are you saying, Celia, you Marxist dimwit! It's all of us who will have to atone for our guilt before the people of that background, have you ever thought of that?"

"And you're a decadent! You play on petit bourgeois sentiments with your songs," said Cecilia, flaring up again and singing mockingly: "Clouds in blu-u-u-e . . ."

Then the former friends and Blue Shirts would run off to different corners.

Mary Vakhtangovna felt genuine bliss when her two granddaughters, Lenochka Kitaigorodsky and Verulya Gradov, met under the Silver Forest roof. In the same year at school, and both pretty blondes—Lenochka took after her father, Verulya after her mother—the little girls could spend hours together whispering to each other, looking at art books, pestering their grandmother to "play us the fox-trot 'George from Dinky Jazz,' please!"

The old feeling of trust toward Veronika had vanished again. Using her woman's intuition, Mary had guessed that there was conflict between husband and wife and, naturally, instinctively took the side of her son, though never, God forbid, did she bring up the subject. Veronika in her turn, as a person of reasonably fine sensibilities, had detected this almost imperceptible antagonism and with every word and gesture issued a nearly unnoticeable challenge in reply. The terrible vicissitudes of life, all these ups and downs and ups again have changed Veronika a great deal, thought Mary. Her entire life right now is a sort of challenge—to everyone around her, to impoverished Moscow, to the past. She goes around in chic outfits, wearing furs, earrings, all of which are daring, if not to say impudent. And then there was this constantly present chauffeur, who was forever accompanying the general's— now marshal's—wife.

Even though one might have expected her to have become accustomed to Nikita's constant progress up the military ladder ever since the twenties, Mary Vakhtangovna nevertheless seemed unable to fully grasp the fact that her son was one of the leading lights among those running this improbable war. One day a curious incident occurred in a streetcar. Once a month she went to the music conservatory for a concert to which she had a subscription. She boarded a trolley on the Ring Road and took a seat by the window. The car filled with passengers along the way, of course, but she remained by the window and observed the sorrowful appearance of Moscow all the way into the city center. A car from the Red Army Medical Corps head office usually came for her after the concert, and she saw no reason to refuse: after all, she was well over sixty. One day, on the way there—in the trolley, that is—one of the passengers asked in a loud whisper, "Do you know who that is sitting there by the window, folks? That's Marshal Gradov's mother!"

Mary pretended not to notice the curious, delighted stares, not to hear the murmurs: "Marshal Gradov's mother in a streetcar, just think! Marshal Gradov's mother, what a lady, what modesty—no, can that really be Marshal Gradov's mother here in a trolley with us?" The news passed endlessly from people getting off the car to those getting on, while Mary Vakhtangovna sat bursting with pride but not giving any indication that these discussions had anything to do with her, an upright, stern, humble Russian intellectual, the mother of Marshal Gradov, defender of the Motherland. "Look out, there, citizens, don't push like that—the marshal's mother is on board!"

Nikita, my little boy, she said to herself, I remember him as if it were yesterday in his little sailor costume, galloping along on a pony with his grandfather shouting after him so that his mustache billowed up: "The Georgian czar! Irakly! Bagration!"

Celia's hysterics, moreover, had something to do with family relations: her Kiryusha had never been the favorite. For some incomprehensible reason, he had been slightly—really, ever so slightly, by the smallest amount imaginable, an almost unnoticeable little bit—cheated out of his rightful share of his parents' love, the lion's share of which had gone to the older Nikita and the younger Ninka. Then again, maybe this was pure nonsense, maybe things only seemed that way now that Kirill was dead. She and Bo had suffered so much pain together, and of course both of them punished themselves where Kiryusha was concerned, though they never expressed these feelings aloud.

It was all so relative, so unstable, after all. For example, does it really mean that I love Elena and Verulka less than Boris IV, even if he is my favorite? Even Mitya, who is not even related to me, I loved no less, and he loved me as though I were his natural grandmother. All the same, one cannot help but admit that none of the other grandchildren possesses the flawless qualities that Boris IV does. Just think of the degree of perfection that young man has grown into! What exceptional seriousness, clarity of vision, precision, athleticism, sense of purpose, independence of thought, physical conditioning! And he chooses friends who are of the same cloth: what just one Sasha Sheremetiev wouldn't be worth! Remarkable strength of will, obvious intelligence, despite his appearance of a fierce sportsman, his impeccable manners—he was simply something out of the Junker class, a Kadet of the old school. The two lads had a curious habit of speaking to each other with the polite form of address. The boys obviously had a wonderful influence on each other. Just imagine, they had resolved never to get any mark less than an "A" in school. School is such nonsense, such rubbish, that to receive anything less than the highest mark would be beneath human dignity. Their collective, concentrated personality had to resolve the intricacies of the schoolroom quickly, exactly, and without the slightest hitch.

If there was one disquieting element in this striving for perfection, it was the so-called "Rakhmetov system" of conditioning. The two boys were absolutely mad about toughening themselves and learning self-defense. They wore the roughest sweaters, for example, on their bare skin, slept with the windows open in the winter when the temperature was twenty below zero, rubbed themselves with snow, ate only the simplest food, and one day during the previous summer had refused to eat altogether for a week, going off into the forest in the morning and not returning until dark, announcing in the most polite tone they knew, "Thank you, we're not hungry." Later on they admitted with a laugh that they had been conducting an experiment of survival in conditions of "scattered airborne landing."

What a strange quality has developed in me in my old age, thought Mary. I take delight in watching my grandchildren swallow their food. I catch myself opening my mouth at the same time that they do, like a silly goose, as though I'm descended not from the Gudiashvilis, but from some bunch like the Lamadzes . . .

Just that morning she had watched rapturously as Boris IV and his friend Alexander downed their oatmeal, not knowing that this was the last time such a magical spectacle would be played out before her delighted eyes.

Agasha, of course, also adored watching family repasts, though lately Boris IV had been causing her more and more grief. He had renounced his favorite stuffed meat pies and refused to let his friend even so much as try them. Sheer sacrilege, forgive me, Lord! Unable to control her own hands, she was constantly pushing a platter full of meat pies in the direction of the boys and also, naturally, did not suspect that she was pushing her rosy meat- and mushroom-filled temptations toward her beloved Babochka (which was her name for the fourth Boris, to distinguish him from "Boryushka" III) for the last time.

Meanwhile, however, the ideal boys were preparing to leave school and their parents' homes that day and to move to the barracks of the top secret Military Intelligence School, where they were already expected. All the preparations, of course, had been kept hidden, otherwise the household would have raised such a fuss that it would have reached even the marshal, who would have smashed their plans in a second.

"There you are, lads, one has to know how to read the newspapers," repeated Grandfather Bo, rolling up his *Pravda* and standing up from the table. "You'll see, within a month Stalin will meet with Roosevelt and Churchill, and then the final date for the opening of the second front will be decided!"

Their grandfather left, and soon the boys began to get ready. Boris kissed his grandmother and his nanny good-bye. Both of them beamed—a rare gift!

The lads walked nearly half a mile down the road toward the trolley station, then turned and doubled back toward the dacha, making for the fence on the forest side. A pole-vaulting pole was concealed behind the wall of a shed. They cast lots to see who would jump. Borka was chosen. He made a run and then flew over the fence. An effective vault, but technically far from perfect. It needs a lot of work, Boris thought. He opened the doors of the shed and pulled out two rucksacks containing recruits' gear that they had already prepared. He threw them over the fence, then climbed over himself. From the inside one could get along without a pole—from the outside as well, for that matter.

In the trolley they discussed the prospects for the opening of the second front.

"If you were Eisenhower, where would you prefer to have the landing?" Boris IV asked Alexander Sheremetiev.

"In Normandy, of course. That way the invasion forces would have to cross only the narrow strait of the English Channel, and all the English bases would be right at hand."

"Yes, but the fortifications of the Atlantic Wall are waiting for them," Boris countered. "For two years, the Germans have been preparing to repulse a landing right there, in Normandy. If I were in Eisenhower's place, I would choose an unexpected possibility and land in Denmark. The coast is practically undefended, the land is flat, the population is friendly, and it's practically a straight shot to Berlin!"

"That's interesting!" Alexander exclaimed with such heat and intensity that passengers in the streetcar turned in his direction. "Let me think about that!"

He thought the rest of the journey to the city center and was still lost in thought when they were already approaching the school, located near Mayakovsky Square. It was only at the very gates that he suddenly attacked his friend with imaginary boxing jabs, exclaiming loudly, "No, that's not right, that's not right, Boris Gradov the Fourth!"

Their school, No. 175, was unique in Moscow: the children of the upper echelons of the Party leadership and of generals studied here. The teachers were all utterly cowed and behaved timidly toward their pupils. During the breaks between classes, however, one could hear whispers: "Mikoyan played hooky again.... I just don't know what to do with Budyonny.... You know, Molotov was outstanding yesterday...." In addition to the "aristocracy," there were, of course, ordinary students, a group to which Alexander Sheremetiev himself belonged, being "not one of them."

The lads entered the courtyard, where a mob of kids was under foot. The small fry were running around after one another without regard to ancestry, enjoying their first recess. Several older pupils were walking about in the midst of the seething mass, among them a morose, round-shouldered girl in a checked overcoat. She was not talking to anyone but rather was only slapping her chubby knees with an unpretentious school satchel. She was none other than Svetka, the daughter of the Supreme Commander, as Boris and Alexander called Stalin. At a distance, not taking his eyes off Svetka, her escort, a young lieutenant from the Kremlin security detail, stood stock still.

Leaving their rucksacks in the gymnasium cloakroom, the two friends headed for the office of the director of studies of the school. Before them now lay the most difficult part of the operation: obtaining their transcripts for presentation at the secret institution. One might have expected this establishment not to give two hoots for unnecessary formalities, that they would need two young healthy lads to learn to create diversions in the enemy's rear, yet even there they had to present their transcripts with their grades in all subjects.

Boris and Alexander had spoken ahead of time with the director, an old, respected "moose" who usually moved through the school grounds as slowly and cautiously as his namesakes did through the forest. The boys had covered their tracks by saying that after receiving their diplomas, they were going to go to a top secret school for marines in Vladivostok, and that they needed to send their certificates and transcripts there right now.

"My father has all this under control," added Boris IV. That should most likely be enough, thought the lads, but if any suspicions do come up, well, then there will be nothing left to do but intimidate the old giant from the woods with main force.

Fortunately, no inhumane actions were needed: the transcripts were already prepared and were handed over with no questions asked. Either the authority of Marshal Gradov had squashed all suspicion, or the old moose trusted his round-faced valedictorians implicitly.

Happy, the two boys fairly skipped out of the school. Then their hearts sank. The previously most difficult part of the operation seemed to them the merest trifle compared with what confronted them now. They walked along Gorky Street looking at women standing in lines, coming out of stores with their meager purchases, at the old ladies sweeping the pavements, at women in police uniforms, and reflected on the fact that in a few hours they would finally leave this female world for the world of men. But first they would have to say good-bye (by telephone, of course, so as not to ruin the whole operation) to the most important women in their lives: Marshal Gradov's wife and Mrs. Sheremetiev the bookkeeper.

At the Central Telegraph Office, after waiting their turn in line, the boys slipped into adjacent phone booths.

"What's happened?" cried Veronika in an unpleasant "morning" voice as soon as she heard Boris on the line.

In an instant Boris was covered with sweat. He wanted to throw down the receiver and let matters take their own course, to do anything but carry on this unbearable conversation, but the principles he had acquired in the process of training himself told him he could not evade things, and that as a "man of direct action" he had to overcome every obstacle in his path.

"Nothing special," he said firmly. "Please, Mama, don't worry. It's just that I'm going away, not for long."

"Where are you going?" Veronika wailed even more loudly.

"Into the army," he said, closing his eyes.

The conversation was taking place practically from one side of the street to the other. As Boris stood there with his eyes closed, it even seemed to him as though they were in the same room. One could scarcely call it a conversation, though, since all his mother was doing was shrieking madly. "You good-for-nothing, have you made up your mind to kill me? What have you dreamed up, you rotten kid? You're underage, they'll send you home in disgrace! I'm going to get in touch with your father straight away! They'll catch you, you little scoundrel!" Suddenly her voice fell, and she whispered, obviously on the edge of sobbing, "Borenka, Borenka, how could you do this . . ."

He opened his eyes. "Mama, please, don't do this. . . . You seem to have forgotten that I'm not a child anymore. I've spoken with you more than once of my feelings about the present moment of history. I can't allow myself to stand to the side when my country, even all humanity, is going through this. I can't bear the thought that the war might come to an end without my participation, and as a man of direct action, I have to tell you about this directly."

"What cruelty," whispered Veronika in a voice that was scarcely audible but that then reacquired its hard edge. "Where are you going?"

"I told you, Mama, into the army."

"To your father's sector, I hope? To the Reserve Front?"

"Yes, yes," he said hastily. "I'm going to the Reserve Front."

She realized he was lying and raised her voice to a shout again: "Where are you now? Where are you calling from?"

"Mama, there's no need to look for me, don't get into a panic! Millions of fellows like me are going to the front. I don't want to be a mama's boy, and even less a 'papa's boy,' bringing shame to my father! I'll write you a letter right away explaining everything. Everything will be all right. I love you." He put the receiver down and went out of the booth into the crowd of overcoats and rucksacks gathered around the telephones. A terrible heaviness, a sensation of some insurmountable grief, took possession of the young man. He had a sudden feeling that he had already experienced this grief, the sadness of parting forever. When? He could not immediately remember.

Through the glass of several phone boxes he saw the face of Alexander

Sheremetiev. A tear seemed to be trickling down the iron champion's cheek. He was pleadingly whispering something into the receiver to his single mother. Alexander had never spoken about his father. No one knew if he had a father and if he did, where he was fighting. At times Boris felt he understood the reason for this silence. Maybe his father wasn't fighting at all? One day Sasha had asked Boris, "Is it true your father was in jail?"

Boris, a man of direct action, immediately answered, "Yes, he was in the camps. So was my mother. They were falsely accused."

The boxer bobbed his head as though he had been dealt a blow to the forehead. "What, your mother, too? Unbelievable!".

Finally, it was all over. Swinging their rucksacks over their shoulders, they walked out onto Gorky Street. In the time that they had spent being jostled in the Central Telegraph Office, the skies over Moscow had darkened. The driving snow of "direct action" struck their faces at a slant, as though falling along a straight edge.

SEVENTH INTERMISSION
THE PRESS

The New York Times:
Congressman Hamilton Fish, Republican from New York, says, "Stalin is surrounded by the same group of people who came to power with him, and their goal remains the spread of communism."

The New Republic, April 1943:
Throughout North America, in Canada, and in the U.S.A., one can hear suggestions that Russia's victory might increase the danger of worldwide revolution. . . . This idea, though, is Hitler's most important propaganda weapon. Hitler is still "saving the world from bolshevism," even though bolshevism in Russia has been dead as a doornail for some time.

The Christian Science Monitor:
The existence in Moscow of the Comintern has been a serious hindrance to more trusting relations between the USSR and other countries for some time now. . . . Now the Comintern has been disbanded. . . .

Izvestiya, November 1943:
"Guardsmen of the Red Army and Navy! Bear your banners with honor! Be an example of valor and courage, discipline and perseverance in the struggle with the foe! Long live the Soviet Guard!"

The New Republic, **November 1943, on Soviet literature in wartime:**

Nikolai Tikhonov—"Take better aim, soldier of the Red Army! Remember that by wiping out one more 'Hans,' you are saving the lives of Soviet people, you are liberating your native soil!"

Lev Slavin—"Believe nothing a Hitlerite says! Beat him without mercy and without delay, until he is finished! Hit him in the head, the side, the back, just so long as you hit him!"

Korneichuk's play *The Front* is playing to packed theaters all over the country. . . .

The talented young poet Tvardovsky has written a Kiplingesque trench ballad about a good soldier who never loses his sense of humor, no matter what the circumstances. . . .

The inexhaustible versifier Demyan Bedny has brought out a work modest in its innocence that ends with the words "Death to vampires and cannibals!" On the whole, Soviet writers are taking inspiration from Stalin's phrase "One cannot triumph over the foe until one has learned to hate him!"

The Russian Review:

Among the translators working with Soviet pilots in Elizabeth City, North Carolina, a tall, handsome lieutenant named Gregory G. Gagarin stands out. The Russian fliers treated him with contempt at first because his mother was a countess and his father a czarist cavalryman. Having discovered, however, that they could get more information about radio and radar from the translator than from any Soviet book, they changed their tune. . . .

The New York Russian émigré newspaper *Novoye Russkoye Slovo,* **1944:**

By January 1 of this year, 780 airplanes, 4,700 tanks, 170,000 trucks, 33,000 jeeps, and 25,000 other automobiles had been sent to Russia.

The Red Army has received 6,000,000 pairs of American boots; 2,250,000 tons of provisions have been shipped. . . .

William Randolph Hearst replies to *Pravda:*

Marshal Stalin calls me a gangster and a friend of Hitler. Accusations of this kind have something of the ridiculous about them, coming as they do from a man who heads the largest gangster press in the world. . . .

And who was Hitler's closest and best friend before?

Radio Berlin, February 28, 1944. Goebbels speaks:

Our enemies dragged us into this war because the form of our socialist society had begun to threaten their outmoded political system. . . .

If we lose the war, then socialism will be lost for Germany. Only when success in the war is guaranteed will we again carry out our important social plans. . . .

Uusi Suomi (Helsinki):

Russian units under the command of General Andrei Vlasov have gone over to the side of the Red Army and helped to capture Narva.

EIGHTH INTERMISSION
THE FIREFLIES' BALL

June, the month of balls: graduation ceremonies, "commencements" of all sorts where honorary degrees are conferred on illustrious guests and speakers, hats are thrown into the air, avalanches of young people rush down marble staircases with exciting expectations of wonder, happiness, and love, when fireflies light up triumphantly in tree-lined walks on clear nights, mockingbirds call and whistle, nightingales play roulades.

So it was that the graduates of the Smolny Institute for Well-brought-up Young Ladies whirled about in a park one white night, looking at the gliding fireflies, asking each other what these creatures were, what secret they contained besides deathless poetry, and not guessing the answer, or perhaps vaguely comprehending that before their eyes, in the multitude of flashes throughout the expanse of the park, over marble statues and clumps of trees, was flickering the ecstasy of all of the previous graduates of human history. Someone in devastated, partly incinerated Germany in a displaced persons camp, in the American zone of occupation, lying on the grass with his hands beneath his head will look at these tiny helicopters that have risen up to fly slowly and silently over him and wonder why they flash the way they do, what the meaning of this reaction is, what it is composed of—does it have anything to do with the process of photosynthesis?

What is the sense of these tiny flashes, this spring fairy-tale ballet, and why does it contain so much sadness? These are the thoughts of a poetess in Silver Forest. The whole house is asleep, but she is sitting on the front stoop of the terrace, holding her knees. What are these signals? A minuscule airship with a proportionally huge searchlight descends to her palm and then is extinguished, merging with the darkness. The graduation ball of the Institute of Well-brought-up Young Ladies, she thinks with a smile. Fleeting moments, funeral rites for tenderness, rebirth and extinction, June 1945 . . .

CHAPTER SIXTEEN

A Concert for the Front

☆

The American trucks arriving in an uncontrollable, almost incredible stream at every accessible Soviet port as well as across the Iranian border turned out to be useful not only for mounting guards' mortars, or as troop and ammunition transports, but also as a platform for grand pianos. Early one evening in March 1944, a Studebaker with its sides turned down was serving marvelously as a stage at the junction of the First Byelorussian and First Ukrainian fronts. On it was a grand piano, and the inspired Émile Gilleles filled a grove with the sound of Lizst's "Variations" and then accompanied the equally inspired David Oistrakh, whose "Campanella" added fire to the flickering candle of a sunset beyond the bare branches of the trees.

Nearby, however, a different sort of accompaniment was thudding away, an artillery duel across the line of the front, and echoes of machine-gun fire were constantly heard in the sky as the German Messerschmitts and the Soviet Yak-3s, La-5s, and P-39 Cobras played their dangerous games. No one paid any attention to these trifles, however. A banner reading "The Performers of the Rear for the Heroes of the Front" hung over the Studebaker, and the heroes were seated on the hillsides, which formed a natural amphitheater.

No less than six or seven thousand listeners had gathered for the concert. The barrels of tank cannons and self-propelled guns protruded from the crowd in the direction of the stage, imparting an element of antiquity to the proceedings, as though the army of Hannibal and its elephants were making a rest stop. In the front rows, on wooden benches and even on real chairs, sat the officers of units deployed in the area, among them the celebrated General Rotmistrov himself. A huge number of performers were knocking about the front these days. Quite a few of them were simply hacks who sounded like cows mooing; troupes were thrown together on the spur of the moment, artistic bohemia eagerly flocked together, supposedly to entertain the "fearless fighters" but basically to eat at the field kitchens, to stuff themselves with Spam. The "cabaret sweethearts," moreover, were always willing to go off to a dugout for a whirlwind romance. This concert, however, was a rare exception. Stars of the first magnitude were participating in it: Émile Gilleles, David Oistrakh, Lyubov Orlov, Nina Gradov, and the famous roly-poly Muscovite Garkavi, the idol of the Hermitage Garden, acting as M.C. This was why such a respectable audience had gathered in the front rows and why such excitement and joyous eagerness reigned in the back rows, or rather on the turrets of the tanks.

After the musical part of the program, Garkavi, decked out in a frock coat with a yellowing shirtfront that he had been wearing since the days of the NEP, read some sort of endless feuilleton he had written. At times he would fall into a glassy-eyed trance as he spoke of "black wings that dare not fly over the Motherland," and during these trances he would occasionally freeze in a pose of impressive majesty with his jaw thrust slightly to one side; at other times he would draw himself up to his full height and overact shamelessly, bustling about in a depiction of their despised enemies. "Bombs-billy-billy, Tuesday play the dirge, Bim-billy-billy, For Berlin and Königsberg!" he sang, raising his thighs in a cancan to a tune from the American film comedy *The Three Musketeers:* "Bombs-billy-billy, Zipping through the air, Hitler's in his bunker, Tearing out his hair, And you know where!"

"Let 'm have it!" bellowed the soldiers delightedly, laughing uncontrollably, either at the risqué picture of Hitler under a rain of bombs tearing out the hair from you-know-where or at the out-and-out lewd contortions of the famous old man.

Having finished his number, Garkavi now assumed his usual patrician manner and announced in a voice filled with noble modulations, "And now, dear friends, I am happy to have the rare opportunity to present to you our celebrated Soviet poetess Nina Borisovna Gradov!"

One of the officers stepped forward to help Nina, but she nimbly clambered up the makeshift ladder to the bed of the truck and stopped beside the grand piano. Roars of approval came from the hills and valleys bristling with cannons. From a distance Nina looked like a young girl in her Lend-Lease overcoat and boots and with her short hair. These people clearly have something else in mind when they hear "Soviet poetess," she thought sarcastically. She had been to the front with artistic troupes on several occasions and each time had felt a depressing awkwardness. Turning up all at once in a group of Soviet celebrities, she didn't know how to behave. All her life she had belonged to a small circle; now the broad masses claimed her. An aesthete inclined toward modernist and formalist experimentation, she now suddenly found herself the expression of some powerful patriotic idea wedded to the inexhaustible nostalgia of the front, and of a romantic dream as well. For some reason it was only her name that was associated with that silly tune "Clouds in Blue"—no one remembered Sashka Polker, who had composed the music. They had only to hear " 'Clouds in Blue' with Nina Gradov" and they simply went crazy. The people of "her circle" congratulated her on her huge popular success, concealing, it seemed to her, ironic smiles. So what would you like me to do at these concerts in the units? I suppose the soldiers will be expecting songs from me, not "transsense" poetry.

Nina, child, the tour organizers assured her, you have absolutely nothing to worry about. You can do anything you want, even read Pushkin aloud. People will be delighted simply to see you, especially since you're so young and attractive.

Well, if they really want to see me, then I guess they have to see me, thought Nina. They've earned the right, after all, to see what they want from time to time instead of just what this damned war shows them. She began to read from her cycle of poems entitled "Before the War." Several of them were dedicated "To O.M.," "To T.T.," "To P.Y." Verses about the blindness of guilt and love, about olive groves quivering beneath the moon and black cellars into which traveling entertainers disappeared one after another. Had she read these dedications in the House of Writers, several stool pigeons would have raced to the door to be the first to denounce her for glorifying Osip Mandelstam, Titzian Tabidze, and Paolo Yashvili, enemies of the people all of them. Up here the only ones who made their way toward the exits were those who had to stand watch or to climb into their aircraft. Those who remained greeted every line with a deafening cannonade of applause.

Encouraged, she read out several complex, enciphered quatrains from a new long poem based on erotic reminiscences of her nights with Savva and of the disappearance of her "eternal lover." Tumultuous joy again. Those on the tanks made a particular effort. With a smile she bowed, remembering how during World War I the Futurist poet Benedikt Lifschitz had read his transsense verses in the trenches to the delight of peasants from Voronezh and Pskov.

Finally, the inevitable shout of "Clouds in Blue"! was heard. "Sing 'Clouds in Blue'!"

"Comrades!" Nina pleaded. " 'Clouds in Blue' is very out of character for me! I'm not the composer, I'm no musician! And most important of all, I can't sing!"

The armed amphitheater replied with a storm of indignation. "Come on, give us 'Clouds in Blue'!" The voice of an Armenian sitting astride a cannon barrel cut through the noise: "Sing it, sister, it's your song!" She looked around and saw a thousand "loving kissers." A soldier with an accordion suddenly scrambled up onto the truck and pulled Nina in the direction of the microphone. The accordion bawled out the opening chords. Foolish tears welled up in Nina's eyes. How many of them will be killed tomorrow—for that matter, how many will die tonight? In an absurd voice, muffled by her foolish tears, she began to sing: "Clouds in blue / Recall that house by the sea / Where the seagulls flew / And that waltz in a minor key . . ." The whole amphitheater took up the tune, and she began reciting the lyrics: not a bad idea, she thought. After all, how can one sing with no voice and no ear? In this way she "sang" the song to the end, and when it was over, the soldiers yelled: "More! Encore! Sing it again, Nina!" Everyone was happy and laughing loudly, and her head was spinning. Then the face of Lyubov Orlov, the star of such films as *Cheerful Guys, Circus,* and *Volga, Volga,* appeared in her field of vision—she was supposed to bring the concert to a triumphal end, and suddenly some poetess had created this furor. That's all I need to make myself popular with Lyuba! Nina thought ironically. She begged them, "Comrades, I can't sing, I'm tone deaf! I'm already hoarse!"

The Armenian yelled from the tank, "Then don't sing, sister—just stand there!"

A rollicking laugh shook the amphitheater, after which they finally let Nina go.

She jumped down from the "stage," and someone immediately offered her a seat next to Rotmistrov himself. The general, a man with the bespectacled, sympathetic appearance of a typical Chekhov intellectual, kissed her hand and began to say something about how much he enjoyed her poetry and what great friends he and Nikita were. She was surprised: so they know even here that I'm the marshal's sister. She began to say something in reply, but just then a roar went up that would have drowned out the thunder of Mount Vesuvius. The clearing erupted with joy. The dream of the Soviet Union, Lyubov Orlov herself, had just appeared on the platform of the truck accompanied by a jazz ensemble! In the best Hollywood tradition, she doffed her top hat, twirled a walking stick, and clicked out a dance with the taps on her heels.

" 'How do you do? How do you do? I'll fly from a cannon into the blue! Into the blue!' "—it was a timeless song from the film *Circus,* loved by one and all. In order to top Nina's success, the veteran Lyubov had begun with her showstopper, and the battle was quickly won. From her place, Nina waved her hand and made a gesture of resignation: I don't pretend to be that good, it said.

Suddenly she noticed a jeep parked not far away with three young officers in it. They were clearly from rear headquarters, rather than from the trenches, if the dashing fit of their uniforms and their uninhibited posture in the imported military vehicle were anything to judge by. For some unknown reason, all three of them were watching not the stage but her, and laughingly talking to one another. What do you mean, "for some unknown reason"? Do you mean you don't know why three officers would look at a woman that way—three impudent "old hands" used to having their way with broads? It was not terribly difficult to imagine what they were saying. Take that one with the mustache, for example, who seemed the most interested: "She's not bad, boys, a good fuck." The second, with a forelock protruding from beneath his garrison cap: "Maybe you'd like to try her yourself?" The first man: "Why wouldn't I?" The third man, who had an ugly mug, spoke next: "What are you talking about, you nitwit! Who is she and who are you? She's a famous poetess, the sister of a marshal, and you're just another army lug!" "Forelock" laughed: "Chalk it up to war!" "Mustache": "Want to make a bet? I'll use her the officers' way tonight!" So they all made a bet, "Mustache," "Forelock," and "Ugly Mug" . . .

In the confusion following the end of the concert, the three young men leapt from the jeep and began to move toward her. Nina saw this from the corner of her eye but did not try to walk away, as she was answering countless questions from soldiers. She continued watching the three peripherally, though, as they approached.

The question that she heard more than any other, of course, was, "Are you married?"

"My husband is an army doctor," Nina replied as usual.

"Do you have any children?"

"My daughter, Lenochka, she's nine."

"No kidding!" exulted the soldiers. "How old are you, then?"

"Thirty-six."

Calls of disbelief were invariably heard at this point. One young infantryman even gaped in amazement. "How can that be? Why, my mama is thirty-six!"

The three officers pushed their way through the soldiers—"Come on, boys, break it up!"—and approached Nina. One of them, "Mustache," even came up so close as to be standing right up against her, so that he was looking down on the celebrated poetess from above, as it were.

"What do you say, Nina Borisovna, like to have a ride to the banquet in our 'billy goat'?"

By his sincere tone of voice, it was clear that the lad wanted to ask a more basic question. He has repulsive skin, all bumpy, thought Nina. He would do better to grow a beard than those foppish whiskers, but then that's his business.

"To the banquet?" she asked smilingly. "No one said anything to me about a banquet."

You idiot, she said to herself, you're talking to him so that he can understand. He understands that there is a possibility of an affirmative answer to his "basic question."

"How's that, then?" "Forelock" asked from the side, taking up the conversation. "The High Command is giving a banquet for prominent performers. We can ride around for a couple of hours before then, though, get a breath of air!"

"We'll show you a recently captured Luftwaffe bunker," said "Mustache." He offered Nina his hand like an officer of the old regime.

Nina did not take the proffered hand but rather walked over to the jeep, turning back to smile at the officers on the way. She noticed that "Ugly Mug" slapped himself delightedly on the backside.

Dusk was already falling, though the weaving and tumbling fighters still gleamed in the rays of the sun in the skies over the forest. Tanks, beginning to move, peeled off and sprayed springtime mud, crushed layers of firmly packed snow. Studebakers were turning on their headlights, while in the beams stirred hundreds of heads, gradually aligning themselves into march columns. In the folds of the ravine cigarettes glimmered like fireflies, and the advancing front filled the barren landscape with its own busy life—only then to move on, leaving behind countless heaps of rubbish.

"Now that's a machine!" a bewhiskered suitor pronounced, slapping the flat hood of the Willys, which had come to be known throughout the Soviet army as a "billy goat." "I remember how we dragged them over the river bottom when crossing the Dnepr. All you had to do was drag it out onto the other shore and turn the key—and the engine would start right up!"

Nina smiled. "You're not exaggerating a little, Captain?"

But all their words had a double meaning, and Nina was beginning to tire of this encoded exchange. But they couldn't leave, since they were waiting for Chubchik, who had scurried off in search of something very important, probably "fuel"—but not for the Willys.

"Nina!" someone called from the crowd. She pressed her palm to her forehead in surprise. The voice seemed to come from the past. Or maybe from the future. Or perhaps from some other dimension altogether—but not from this throng of soldiers. It wasn't a voice from her acting troupe or that of a simple acquaintance. In the twilight it was impossible to make out the face.

"Who called my name?" she shouted as if flinging a challenge and tossed back the bangs from her forehead—ready for anything, even disappointment.

For a few moments the spotlight on the tank lit up the Willys and the soldiers, and in its beam she saw Sandro Pevzner. My God, he had once been such a poignantly touching youngster, but now he was a true Charlie Chaplin in his sacklike overcoat and bent lieutenant's bars.

"It's me, don't you recognize me, Nina?" It was the same wonderful Georgian-Jewish accent! Instantly forgetting about her suitors, Nina walked around the Willys in his direction, peering out from under her hand as if into the distant past.

"First and last name!" she shouted.

"Alexander Pevzner," the comic figure muttered, as if in a sacred trance.

"Birth date! Passport number!" she shouted even louder, but unable to contain the surge of joy, threw her arms around his neck.

"Pevzner!" the officers standing behind them guffawed. "You're killing us, Pevzner!"

"Come on, let's go, Sandro," she pulled him by the overcoat collar, veered into the crowd, and slid down a slope of wet clay. Giggling like a schoolgirl back in Tiflis, she dragged him along, herself not knowing where—only to be as far as possible from those officers and their "billy goat." Even blinded by the headlights of departing trucks, she took advantage of their beams to peer into his face—also blinded, either by the headlights or by happiness. It was the bobbing face of a marionette, blissful as if in a dream.

It took only a few minutes to make their way to the gravel road, where, now calm, they walked hand in hand, like children. Now and again columns of trucks or tanks would pass, and they would scramble to the side, Nina pressing against Sandro. He told her he was "working" (evidently his tongue refused to serve him in pronouncing the word "serving") in the Propaganda Team of the First Ukrainian Front. As an artist, his job was to produce inspiring posters and caricatures of the enemy, and also to contribute to the frontline newspaper *Direct Aim!* He had heard of her tragedy and was deeply moved. "You can believe me, Nina, when I say that, although I hardly knew Savva, he was somehow a sort of measure of manliness for me, of honesty; I saw him as a true knight!"

"Why do you say 'was'?" Nina asked. "He's not necessarily dead. He could still be alive. At any rate, I'm waiting for him."

"You do the right thing," Sandro responded bitterly, "but—" He fell silent.

"Why 'but'?" She squeezed his elbow and peered into his eyes. "Tell me."

"It's just that I heard his hospital was leveled . . ." Sandro muttered.

The stamping of hundreds of feet thundered toward them in the darkness, and soon all seven stars of the Pleiades revealed to them the outlines of an infantry column. On either side of the column, next to the road, soldiers walked with rifles at the ready. From time to time they lit up the heads of the marchers with flashlights.

"Prisoners of war," Sandro said. Nina moved out of the path of the approaching column and then jumped over a trench to lean her head against the trunk of a poplar.

From time to time flashlight beams would seize sunken, unshaven cheeks from the darkness, the lifeless, almost fishlike eyes of the prisoners, random fragments of uniform, German pilots' caps, unfamiliar indications of rank. . . . From the muffled speech of the column Russian words could be made out.

"Oho, that's something worse than prisoners of war." Sandro clicked his tongue. "They're traitors."

"What do you mean—traitors?" Nina seemed to lose her breath. "And where are they taking them?"

Sandro squeezed her hand and whispered directly into her ear, "They're being taken to Kharitonovka. There's an oak grove there where they'll all be executed. They'll all be shot and their bodies will be dumped in the ravine. There's so many of them, Nina, that's what's terrible. Supposedly they all served in the German police, worked for the Germans one way or another, or served under Vlasov, but I think a lot of them were simply in German captivity. You know we don't accept any of our own men back after that; they're all considered traitors to the Motherland. . . . I must be a bad officer, probably even no officer at all; I'm just an artist, nothing more, just an artist . . . but sometimes it seems to me that it's just part of the nation being taken past us to Kharitonovka. . . ."

"You mean those cursed murderers are continuing their work even as the war goes on?" she asked in a whisper.

"And just where were they supposed to disappear to, Nina? Each unit has its own SMERSH unit—it means 'Death to spies!' . . . *Dzekhneri!*" Sandro swore in Georgian.

As the column moved past them, Nina was overwhelmed by the sudden sensation that someone she knew had caught her eye from the close ranks of the doomed traitors. It was only a flash and then was gone. She almost choked in horror: that could have been Savva! Such incredible coincidences happen sometimes. The devilish, busily woven fabric of nightmare flaps open in a moment of horror! Refusing to believe in Savva's death, Nina sometimes imagined him a prisoner of war, and Stalin's doctrine thus transformed him into a traitor. No, it couldn't have been him. The face briefly captured by the flashlight beam was quite different, not Savva's face. It wasn't his face at all, just the face of a young man who was about to be flung into the Kharitonovka ravine with a hole in the back of his head.

The column passed by and blended in with the dark knolls of the forest; suddenly everything was quiet and empty, and only the Milky Way continued to stand proudly over the despised earth. They returned to the road and all at once noticed that a crescent moon, as fine as the filament of a lightbulb, had joined the stars.

"All the same, I hope we'll be able to breathe more freely after the war," said Nina. "It can't be that nothing will change after a war like this!"

"I doubt it," muttered Sandro. "Hardly anything will change. Hitler and Stalin have driven us all into a trap with their quarrel."

In the next instant, he seemed frightened that he had spoken his secret thoughts aloud. He extended his hand and grasped Nina's wrist, as though wanting to make sure that it was in fact she and that he was in no danger.

"You know, Sandro," said Nina, "since Savva left for the front, I haven't had a single man." She walked on, her head bowed, her dangling hair hiding her face from Sandro. "I don't know what's happened to me," she went on in a muffled voice. "I haven't let anyone touch me. It made me go into a rage. Today, though, I seem to have reached the breaking point. You know, I nearly went off with those fellows in the jeep . . ."

He drew aside the hair he loved and timidly looked at her beloved face, burdened by cares at that moment but beloved nonetheless. "No, that's awful, Nina—not with those goats!"

"Do you have a place?" She raised her face so sharply that the stars of the constellation and the crescent moon rushed across her eyes.

"What?" Pevzner fearfully asked. He had been in love with her for sixteen years and had never even dreamed about such a moment.

"Is there a little room, a closet, a shed, where we could be alone?" she asked.

He drew her along by the hand, unable to say another word. They walked along the road at a brisk, businesslike pace, no longer hopping over the ditch but only changing course slightly in front of passing vehicles. Finally, after about twenty minutes of rapid walking, Nina saw a mobile frontline head-quarters encampment with large American tents, hastily erected towers and searchlights, and small trailers uncoupled from tractors. Sandro had his studio in one of these trailers. With trembling hands he removed the ware-house lock and let his beloved into the damp, cold darkness that was redolent of paint. The doors closed, and they were alone.

"Wait, wait," Nina whispered. "I want us both to take all of our clothes off, as though we were on a beach at night near Gyulripsha."

A multitude of points of light in the firmament looked down through the tiny, clay-spattered window as two naked people, first standing and then sitting on a stool, made love. There was nowhere to lie down.

"What luck that I met you," whispered Nina. "I'm so happy I didn't go with those—"

Meanwhile, the face that had flashed before Nina in the beam of the convoy's headlights was approaching its appointed destination, a ravine out-side the razed village of Kharitonovka. A mass of fires flickered in the wood before the ravine, and hundreds of shadows of human beings were moving to and fro. From the gorge came the sound of gunshots, a measured knocking that every so often increased to the feverish galloping tempo of volleys, as

though the tapping had suddenly become hysterically offended at being misunderstood and had determined at all costs, and as soon as possible, to make
its intentions known. The night shift of the executioners of SMERSH, the Red
Army counterintelligence agency, was doing its work, intensively and not
without enthusiasm.

The arriving column once again stretched out into the forest. Curiously
enough, all the men were moving with relative vigor, as if they had not yet
understood what awaited them. The light spring frost, the stars over the
pines, the fires flickering among the tree trunks—perhaps it all summoned up
something within them like the inspiration felt by Vladimir Nabokov, when
he wrote in a poem, "Russia, stars, the night of the execution / And all of the
ravine in cherry blossoms!" Then again, we are surely exaggerating—more
likely, everyone was simply tired from hatred, fear, pain, and the hope of
escaping and wanted it all to be over. These, maybe, were the feelings that
prevailed in the young face that had flashed before Nina Gradov in the truck's
headlights.

The column was marched into a hewn-out clearing, and immediately the
SMERSH agents, reeking of drink, began running down the ranks with lists,
calling out names, jerking people out of the line one after another, driving them
along with blows of their gun butts in the back and kicks in the backside. The
face that had flickered before Nina was suddenly covered with the frightened
sweat of impending death. He suddenly wanted to prolong the end, not to
be among the first groups, to breathe the night air once more and then once
again, to saturate himself down to the last cell with this strange combination
of carbon and hydrogen.·

Others wanted to fill their lungs with nicotine. The young man's neighbor,
a tall fellow of about thirty wearing the rags of a Wehrmacht officer's tunic
with a badge that read "R.A.L." still hanging on the sleeve, eagerly took a
drag on his "last cigarette," squirreled away earlier.

"So this is where the Red bastards are going to finish us off," he said in
between puffs. "So this is where . . . in the forest . . . in the open air . . . I'd
always dreamed of the Cheka cellars, though . . . Want a puff?" Having
received a negative reply, he continued to draw on the cigarette greedily,
avidly, with every drag bringing the fire closer to his fingers until it went out
right between them.

"It's all Hitler's fault, that dirty ape!" the smoker said forcefully. He sounded
like a Parisian, the offspring of a White Guard household. "If it weren't for
that dirty ape, *cette merde*, we would have had a Russian army a million
strong, and we would have finished the Red bastards ourselves . . ."

At that moment his name was called: "Chardyntsev!" They dragged him
along like a piece of baggage because his legs had suddenly failed him. "Stand

up, you son of a bitch! Stand up, you whore! We're going to hang you by the cock now, you Fascist shit!"

It turned out that the first to be called were dragged out to face not bullets but the noose. Not far from the square where the prisoners were assembled, a gallows with a long transverse beam stood in the gleam of the headlights. Studebaker trucks with their sides let down backed up to the gallows slowly. The victim was placed in the bed of the vehicle. An individual decree was read out for each victim: "In the name of the Union of Soviet Socialist Republics . . . for crimes against the Soviet people . . . to death by hanging . . . no grounds for appeal . . ." One of the SMERSH agents put the noose around the victim's neck, after which the truck—truly a multipurpose machine—moved forward and the victim plummeted downward to do his last dance, accompanied, as every connoisseur will know, by sweet erotic visions.

In the pauses between executions, a woman orderly served the killers liquor from a jug. One could either water it down to one's taste or gulp it straight from the bottle. All those who remained on the square, including the face that had flickered before Nina's eyes in the headlights of the convoy, completely lost their self-control in the face of imminent death. Some moaned in a low voice, while others vomited, falling down on their knees, pleading with the executioners, "Spare us, brothers!"

Suddenly, like a shot next to his ear, he heard his own name: "Sapunov, Dmitry!" His head whirled in a mad spiral, and, catching the toe of his boot on a stump that had not been uprooted, he stumbled and fell; his bladder and bowels gave way, covering him with urine and hideous diarrhea, but he got back onto his feet and walked toward the firing squad marching crisply across the square. He heard an authoritative voice checking off a list: ". . . Reshetov, Rovnya, Sapunov, Sverchkov . . . All right, drag those who are still on their feet over to the ravine, and the ones that are lying down, finish the fuckers on the spot! Come on, boys, move it, or we'll never finish by morning!"

Now they were pulling him along, bound together with the others, and when he fell, an oak club crashed down on his head or back and he stood up again. Still thinking they were leading him to the gallows, he said hoarsely, "Hang me, you Red bastards!" They were taking him past the gallows, though, past the trucks, into a dark clearing in the woods. It fell to his lot not even to receive the honor of a special sentence from the tribunal; instead, his was a group sentence.

How did it happen that Mitya Sapunov, who in July 1943 had joined the Dnepr partisan detachment, again found himself in a group of "traitors to the Motherland," this time to be disarmed and condemned to death? In that stifling hot month, in the Byelorussian oak forest, it seemed to him he had landed among his own people for the first time since the beginning of the war. The lads who had found him seemed to him more like cossack freemen from the era of the Civil War than a Soviet military unit forged together by army and Party-Komsomol discipline. Their forage caps perched on their heads at a rakish angle, they left their shirts and flight jackets unbuttoned, and, most remarkably, they wore German belts hung with pouches, hand grenades, and knives. Their chic lay in the fact that they carried their pistols not slung behind over the buttocks, Soviet style, but on the thigh or the belly—more convenient, they said, for pulling a gun quickly. Their manners corresponded to this idea: there was no officer protocol, the commanders were called simply "Lukich" or "Fomich," their movements were free and agile, and the general mood was that of a thieves' band: "Well, come on, you motherfuckers, give 'em the rough stuff, tear out their claws!"

They brought Mitya and Goshka back to the main base in the form of two weakly moaning sacks strapped across horses' backs. The base consisted of dugouts laid out in the ravines of an impenetrable forest. It was difficult for the scouts in the Fokker Wolfs to see any signs of civilization among the dense green treetops below, where they saw nothing but majestic nature; yet somewhere down there, turning as they tracked the bothersome flying craft, were antiaircraft machine guns.

Beneath the crowns of the oaks and elms, beneath the heavy skirts of the ancient spruce trees, all the partisan equipment and property were concentrated: stables, garages, repair shops, depots, huts with bunks for the men, a headquarters with a radio transmitter, and a *khavalka*, that is, a large mess hall, where they ate as much as their bellies could hold, beyond the military norms; sometimes, though, of course, they fell on lean times, particularly when Fritz was running search-and-destroy missions and headquarters, along with everything else, had to pack up and move on the double. They cooked at night, of course, so the smoke wouldn't give away their position, which meant that it was only by night that the boys could get hot food. But why not? It's the sort of thing a man gets used to. It was also by night that they fired up the baths, and it was there in the steam room that Mitya and Gosha went through disinfection with boiling water, and where Lazarus, or Lazik, as he was known for short, the camp barber, cut their wild heads of hair down to nothing.

Curiously, no one in the unit asked many questions about them. Just your average prisoners, what could be clearer? They'd managed to slip away from Fritz, and a good thing, too! They want to join the people's avengers, and we say welcome! At headquarters they recorded their names, dates of birth, permanent addresses, the number of the unit they were in at the time of their capture, and that was that: they hadn't needed any fantastic stories. When the lads had gotten their bearings, they were assigned to the same scouting party that had found them. They were given weapons with full confidence, including submachine guns with circular magazines, the homegrown variety. The backbone of the group, of course, was equipped with Schmeissers, though the commander, Grisha Pervoglazov, said that from now on it would be up to them if they wanted to arm themselves "good and properly."

Grisha Pervoglazov was from Rostov and, from all indications, not from one of the town's best families. At any rate he seemed to view his partisan activities as just one big round of fun. You could be lying in wait in the bushes; you might be listening to tall tales about past sexual experiences or drowsing when suddenly he—oh, what an instinct that guy has!—would call out: "Here they come! Pay attention! Anyone who starts popping off before I give the order will have me to deal with!"

A convoy appears: an armored car with a rapid-fire recoilless gun, trucks carrying materiel, officers' Horches with bodyguards. The helmets of the Fritzes have gotten red hot in the August sun, their Aryan heads are nodding off . . . they don't know that "kaput" is sitting behind the bushes in this idyllic place.

"Fire!" shouts Grisha, letting off a signal rocket to give greater force to the order. After that, everything goes like clockwork: the armored car hits a mine and takes a whipping from an antitank gun, while a dagger of gunfire strikes the officers, the helmets, the backs, and the chests of the German-Fascist bandits in the name of our Soviet Motherland! The trucks slam into one another and into the trees at the side of the road, grenades explode. Those of the guards who survive run into a ditch, where the "people's avengers" jump on them from the bushes. What fun! Well, there you have it, the convoy is destroyed, wreathed in smoke from the short battle. If there are any prisoners, we'll interrogate them on the spot. Mitya and Goshka, the two rookies from Moscow, help us out there. The lads did well in school, they know how to ask questions in German.

Then comes the best part of the operation—let's see what sort of stuff they were transporting. Sometimes some very interesting articles come our way. Once, for example, they dragged three cases of aquavit from beneath some Feldwebel. Didn't the lads get going then! They fired up a couple of trucks, put on the Fritzes' uniforms, and drove off to Ovruch to pay the local whores a little visit. Life is a carnival, brothers! No need to be sad with our ataman, Grisha Pervoglazov!

For all this casualness, the commander maintained good friendly relations and authority. It was the sort of team one dreams about in childhood—these are just the fellows I would choose, one for all and all for one, "Back to back at the mast, two of us against a thousand!"

"Sapunov, I've put your name in for the Meritorious Service Medal," Pervo-glazov said one day after the successful completion of an operation planned in Moscow that involved the simultaneous blowing up of two bridges across the Pripyat. They had a good laugh about it until, one day in December 1943, a Douglas from "the mainland" landed at a secret airfield in a blizzard and someone tossed out a sack full of medals, among them Mitya's "Meritorious Service."

By the end of 1943, it must be said, the connection to the mainland had become almost regular, and one day a baleful general with broad cheekbones arrived, bringing a whole staff of hangers-on with him. All the local "Lukiches" and "Fomiches" were demoted and assigned to newly organized companies and platoons. The whole detachment was now called "The Schors Sixth Partisan Brigade." A special dugout was built for the Secret Files Department. The bleary-eyed NKVD agents with the twisted mouths began to "sift through the cadres." Mitya and Goshka had already been summoned individually "for clarification" on a number of occasions. Over the preceding months they had completely forgotten the adventure they had concocted to start with, and they mixed up a great deal in the conversations with Major Lapshov. It turned out, for example, that even though they had run away from the bathhouse to-gether, they gave locations that were sixty miles from each other, and their stories about when it had happened differed from each other by a couple of weeks. Lapshov, strange as it may seem, did not press the issue; perhaps he had too much other business at the time. The dashing scout Grisha Pervoglazov, for example, disappeared from the brigade. Everyone wondered: where has our hero gone? Answer: he's been recalled! Recalled to where? asked the partisans, by now unaccustomed to procedure. Wherever a man is needed, that's where he is assigned, came the sarcastic reply, and then the crooked-mouthed men followed the reply with a question of their own: "Why are you interested in Pervoglazov, anyway?" Then the questions ceased. In January 1944, the front, by all indications, was approaching the partisans' zone of operations. The eastern sky was now lit up regularly by flashes of wintry light. An ever-growing thunder was heard from that direction. The order came down to relocate to the west in order to continue their work in the enemy's rear, disrupting his communications, "putting men and materiel out of action."

Then there followed two weeks of hard fighting as they advanced through areas devastated by the retreating German units. The front, however, was coming on them faster than they could advance.

"Well, Mitya, it looks like Germany has cracked," said Goshka, looking around. "What are we going to do?"

"How's that, 'What are we going to do?' " Mitya replied, pretending not to understand. "We're going to fight alongside our people."

"Our people," Goshka quipped ironically. "There's a smell in the air. Don't you understand that the whole business is going to blow up in our faces? We've got to hightail it out of this unit!"

"And just where are we going to go?" muttered Mitya, numbed by the smell.

"Hell, I don't know," Goshka whispered in reply, casting his eyes about. For this shifty glance alone he could have been handed over to SMERSH. "Maybe we could join the Ukrainians?"

There were rumors going around that in the western areas, the Ukrainians were building forces to fight on two fronts, against both the Germans and the Russians.

"What fucking use would we be to the Ukrainians?"

One marvelous evening, the "smell" was mixed with the rich, creamy aroma of Red Moscow perfume. A shapely woman appeared before the partisan outfit together with General Rudyanko and his secret agents; she was wearing a captain's tunic and turned out to be none other than Larisa the librarian. Yes, the very same one with whom Mitya Sapunov had soared away on wings of Argentinean passion, for whom the jackals from the Zarya unit had "put on a choir concert."

As soon as they saw her, Mitya and Goshka began to slip away. So what everyone had said at the time about her being a Bolshevik spy was true. All things considered, this is what had happened: the original Larisa had been raped and killed by Dovator's cossacks, and this Larisa, not a girl at all but an experienced Cheka woman, had been sent to replace her. By the time she showed up in the partisan unit she was no longer Larisa but Captain Elza Fyodorovna Vatnikov and, interestingly enough, looked quite a bit older than she had the previous summer.

At first she noticed neither Mitya nor Goshka. The agents were now calling the partisans in alphabetically, and not everyone returned to the ranks. Krutkin and Sapunov had not been called yet, and they were trying to hide from the eyes of Captain Vatnikov in the crowd of three thousand. They even began to grow beards, while at the same time thinking desperately about how to get away, what to do. They even had the idea of making a rendezvous with Captain Vatnikov in the forest, but then one day at formation, she simply came up to them and without even looking at them said with disgust, "All right, enough standing around like a Jack-in-the-box, you Vlasovite scum! Lay down your arms! Follow me!" Both of them were immediately seized under the arms and hauled off to the feared part of the ravine. Even in the woods, the secret NKVD had managed to build themselves a Lubyanka. Here they were separated and beaten individually to get the truth out of them as only the Cheka can. Then they were thrown into a pit, where another two dozen or so men under investigation were tossing about.

The next day, Mitya was dragged into a forest ranger's hut to be interrogated by Captain Elza Fyodorovna Vatnikov personally. When they were alone, the erstwhile "Larisa the librarian" drew a pistol from a holster and thrust it beneath her belt. This is my last chance, thought Mitya. I'll stun her, grab the gun, and try to get through to the Ukrainian lines. After the previous evening's thrashing, though, he didn't have the strength to lift his head, much less his arms.

Elza, looking at him point-blank, suddenly produced a tube of lipstick and smeared it on her lips thickly, like a circus clown. Then she went up to Mitya, pressed him to the log wall with her breasts and stomach, put her hand down the front of his trousers and grabbed his vital sinew fiercely. Mitya's eyes went dim, and he slid off to one side. She burst out laughing and wiped her hand on her skirt. "Stand up, you shit! Or can't you? Maybe you were counting on sympathy, you dimwit? Ha, ha. . . . I've got enough around here to fuck to my heart's content!" She opened the door and called out in a polite, Party-trained voice, "Come in, comrades!"

Two masters of strong-arm methods entered the room. Another "pertinent conversation" began. Mitya admitted that he had served in one of the Wehrmacht's Russian support units. He had been taken into it against his will. He had always hated the invaders and dreamt about escape. He and Krutkin had run away as soon as the opportunity had presented itself. "You're lying, you bastard!" shouted the agents. "Come on, tell us everything, or we'll cut your hide into belts." They obviously didn't know what else they might get out of young Sapunov, they only wanted more. Mitya, though his brains were hardly of any use to him after so many blows to the head, nevertheless managed to come up with a story that recounted only things "Larisa the librarian" could already know and was vague about everything else.

This went on for several days. To the beatings was added yet another torture, called "the incubator." Bound and gagged, he was locked in a chicken coop. The chickens, suddenly deprived of three quarters of their living space, relieved themselves on the uninvited guest and then began to peck at the exposed parts of his body in a frenzy.

One night, after an entire day of "conversations" and "the incubator," Mitya began to have delirious visions of Auntie Agasha's sweet, warm kasha descending bountifully from the heavens to the strains of Mary's Chopin. Krutkin, barely alive, crawled up to him and, laying his head on his friend's knees, racked by sobs, brought him back to reality. "Mitya, forgive me, I couldn't stand it. I confessed, I betrayed you. I said you volunteered to go over to the Germans and you dragged me with you . . ."

"Well, thanks a lot, Gosha," said Mitya with a smirk. "I wouldn't have expected anything else from you. Stay healthy and get through this—as for me, I've had all I can take."

He was sure that now they would bump him off right away, there behind the rubbish heap where they took care of everyone; after Goshka's betrayal, though, everything changed oddly. They were moved from the pit to a shed, one that even had a roof, even if it was in a bad state. And they began to give them a bit to eat: sometimes swill of the kind that might be fed to cattle, at others even military gruel—nothing like in the pit, into which a bucket of rotting potatoes was dumped once every three days. The interrogations were more businesslike, with less swearing, spitting, and hysterics, though from time to time they received a hiding as severe as anything before.

Then there appeared two quite serious types, who in all probability had flown in directly from the mainland. They wasted no time on hooliganism and didn't even smell of drink. What interested them most was the training center at Dabendorf, where the lads had spent four months before being sent to the Ukraine. "Whom did you see there, and what can you tell us about Boyarsky, Malyshkin, Blagoveshchensky, and especially Zykov? Did Andrei Andreevich himself appear before you?"

"Beg your pardon, what Andrei Andreevich is that?" Goshka interjected.

"What, do you mean to say you don't even know your leader, Vlasov, by name?" asked the serious comrades with a smile. "What kind of work did the Germans do with you, then? Did you see a certain Wilfred Karlovich, for example? Or someone named von Treskow?"

Goshka beamed. "Don't you remember, Mit, we called him *treska* [codfish]. We used to make fun of him by calling him 'the codfish.' "

"All right, enough fooling around, you traitor to the Motherland." The serious comrades scowled. Goshka immediately turned dour again, having realized he was not at all guaranteed escape from the firing squad.

Later, an even stranger series of events unfolded. In the course of an interrogation Mitya had occasion to tell his life story and naturally mentioned the fact that for eight years he had been brought up in Professor Gradov's family. They probably don't remember about the children of "enemies of the people," he hoped, not knowing that his adoptive Uncle Nikita had not been an enemy for quite some time and was now in fact a hero of the People's War, the commander of the legendary Reserve Front, a marshal of the USSR. The serious comrades exchanged silent glances when they learned of this, after which Mitya was transferred to a warm dugout with a single guard outside.

The front had already passed through their area, with the result that the partisan base was now just behind the lines of the fighting forces. One day a guest who seemed strange to Mitka came to the base. He had a large, wrinkled bald head, and he climbed into the dugout, followed by the brigade commander with a kerosene lamp. The guest wore a sheepskin coat over his uniform so that his rank was not visible, but all the same it was obvious that it was quite high. For more than an hour the guest sat in the reeking dugout asking the youth, who was in a dreadful state from exhaustion and beatings, questions about his life in the Gradov household, about which the man seemed to be surprisingly well informed.

When was your adoptive father, Kirill Borisovich, arrested? When did Veronika Yevgenievna arrive from Khabarovsk? How much do you know about Veronika Yevgenievna? Did the older Gradovs receive any letters from their children who had been arrested, and how did they react? You didn't notice . . . hmm . . . Did you have any prejudicial feelings toward your adoptive mother, Cecilia Naumovna Rosenbloom, because of her nationality? How about Nina Borisovna, what was she like? Well, I mean, what sort of life did she lead, did she come to see her parents often, did she ever quarrel with her husband, how did she get on with her daughter, what sort of things did she say? How did the life of the family change after the arrest of the eldest son, Nikita Borisovich? Did any of his old friends come around, or did they all turn their backs on him? And how did the Gradovs treat you, an adopted child from the peasantry? They didn't degrade your human dignity?

The last question seemed so preposterous to Mitya that he even spat up some phlegm, an action which he might have intended to be amazed laughter. After this, the strange guest left the dugout without saying good-bye.

A few more days of uncertainty went by. They began adding bits of preserved meat to the kasha. Mitya thought he wouldn't be "bumped off" right away: he was still useful to them for something; the strange guest would not have visited him without a reason.

Suddenly everything turned over again, capsized, and this time Mitya fell right into the wolf's jaws. All at once they pulled him out of the dugout, beat him without rhyme or reason, drove him along the road with blows of their rifle butts, beat him into the column of traitors to the Motherland, and from there began his final march to liquidation, to Kharitonovka, to the ravine. How could Mitya have known that the order had come from on high to immediately liquidate all the traitors and collaborators with the enemy held in the sector where he had the misfortune to be? The operation was being carried out first of all as an act of "just retribution" for the recent assassination of Commander Vatutin by Ukrainian partisans and second as a preventive measure, since General Hube had begun a successful counterattack with three Panzer divisions in the sector.

And now they were dragging him in the glare of the searchlights to the edge of the ravine, from which emanated a shocking smell of death. Mere shadows of people stood there, swaying back and forth, looking like targets in human form. Other shadows hastened from one shade to another, shooting them in the back of the head with pistols. The shadow targets fell, while the shadows with the guns wiped their faces, obviously spattered with blood and brains after the shots at point-blank range.

They brought up one staggering cluster of people bound together after another. When the cord was untied, the command "Spread out!" was issued, but the order led only to disorder; some nut would start putting on an act, going down on his knees: "Brothers, spare me! Brothers, have mercy!" One of them made everyone laugh. "I came just like you told me!" he yelled. "I came on my own!" As if because he came to his execution as ordered, he shouldn't be shot. Well, if you came on your own, then stand up on your own, you scum, the way you should! Come on, boys, look alive! Let's finish this amateur production, otherwise we'll never take care of them all by morning. Sometimes the shots came in a galloping rhythm like Budyonny's cavalry, as they went to work on the clustered traitors with heavy machine guns, and then the whole business became cheerier, though accuracy naturally suffered. Well, it doesn't matter, a hundred percent of them will go down into the pit anyway.

Mitya still wanted to draw himself up to his full height, still hoped to shout something into the Reds' blinding searchlights, which were so greedy for corpses, to shout out something, to bark with the hair on his neck bristling, to show the teeth of a corpse, so they would remember him. But then he was intersected by the course of universal communism, which, turned loose without any precautions, struck him in the side and proceeded on its way, cutting through an entire strata of the earth and laying bare accumulated epochs, bones, and ossified livers.

On the train back to Moscow, Nina shared a compartment with Lyubov Orlov. Nina was in high spirits, laughing, recounting funny things that had happened to her on her trips around the front, and Lyuba joined in, understanding perfectly well that Gradov had become "involved." Probably with some fighter pilot, she thought, an ace with his chest covered in medals, like Colonel Pokryshkin. However, the gaunt, round-shouldered figure in an overcoat that looked as though it had literally been through the wars, who was knocking about in the crowd surrounding the bus carrying the performers' troupe right up to the moment when it left for the railroad station, resembled anything but the hero of a wartime romance.

When the light had been turned out, Nina lay for a long time musing blissfully. Her whole body remembered Sandro's caresses, and his adoring eyes of a participant in some ritual remained in her mind. The heathen, she laughed to herself in her half-asleep state, he made himself an idol out of a ragged cat. She knew he could be handsome; once separated from his present repugnant form, nothing could prevent him from being good-looking, not even his small bald spot.

She tried to imagine their future life together, a sunset the color of old copper in the sky over immortal Tbilisi, but instead she could see only the heads of the column marching along in the darkness, the groundswell of heads, and she suddenly realized exactly whose face it was that had flickered before her eyes in the beams of the convoy's headlights. Her skin contracted all over her body, and she was shaken by a fleeting, unforgettable spasm.

Everything that trickled down from those lying over him flowed onto Dmitry Sapunov in his last hour. When that hour had passed, he began extricating himself, pushing aside the extremities of those lying heavily and unpardonably atop him. "We're short only one bullet," he muttered sense-lessly over and over again, "one bull-bull-bullet is all we need . . ." He crawled from black gloom into gray. The predawn mist covered the night's doings in thick layers. Trees—the most innocent of earth's beings—began to appear in outline. Sentries, those bullet-laden vampires, could be heard calling out to one another. In the skies above, glory roared by—the air force. He continued moving onward, pressing his elbow to his side, which had been grazed by a ricocheting bullet. Making almost no attempt to conceal himself, he hobbled along past the charred hearths of Kharitonovka. On the other side of the village, where it was bordered by fields, one could see open meadows lying in evaporating puddles. The first rays of the sun coming over the hillocks il-luminated the spots of water and made them reflect the clouds, just as they had done in the old days. Then he fell into some bushes, into leaves that had lain there since the previous year, breathed deeply of springtime mold, and, falling asleep, became the object of great interest on the part of two ravens perched nearby. The decay of the blameless and the decay of the sinful, the birds seemed to think, what is it that separates you in the heavenly places?

He woke up to the sound of whistling. It was the melody of "Clouds in Blue," which was unknown to him. A lone soldier was moving away from him, walking along the dirt road that wound through the field and toward the horizon. He was hopping cheerfully over the puddles and walking with his rucksack over his shoulder. He's unarmed, very interesting, one of the ravens suggested to Sapunov. The soldier seemed to be returning to his unit from the hospital.

Suppressing a moan, Sapunov stood up and then heavily ran after the man. He crashed onto the small back, gripped the lad's throat with his ironlike fingers that might even have been those of a corpse, and twisted the cartilage of his throat irreversibly. He dragged the body he had finished off so easily by the scruff of the neck to the place in the bushes where he himself had lain. The blue color that had come from strangulation had gone from the lad's cheeks, replaced by a rosy flush, as though he were drowsing. He reached into one of the soldier's shirt pockets and drew out a pack of crushed Nord cigarettes—there were about ten of them, more precisely eleven. There was even a lighter, fashioned out of a spent cartridge from an antitank gun.

Sapunov began smoking and did not stop until he had smoked all eleven cigarettes. A good situation, he thought—you're lying next to a military man as if he were one of your buddies, you're smoking as the internationalist air force flies by high over your head. Then he remembered that he hadn't broken the man's neck for his smokes. He reached into the soldier's other breast pocket and found his identity card. That was why he had killed him. For his ID. It was like the boy in the Russian fairy tale calling out in despair to his magic horse for help—"Go there, I know not where; bring me that, I know not what."

CHAPTER SEVENTEEN

Vertuti Militari

☆

Nine migratory geese in a graceful V formation were coming in for a landing. The slow, high Baltic sunset was reflected over the entire surface of the city's great pond. It was this surface that was the landing field for the squadron of geese. With precision the leader reduced his speed, noisily demanding that the others stay in synchronization with him: "Do as I do! Do as I do! Do as I do!" Clearly, it was not just the landing that was important to him; it had to be carried out with ideal form, in perfect synchronization. All the other geese were silent, trying to follow the beats of his wings precisely and rhythmically. They all touched down simultaneously, with a minimum amount of spray. They landed and only then broke into laughter, singing the praises of their leader. Even he now laughed without thinking, happy and proud, shaking himself all over, plunging his head into the German lake, then emerging in a spray in the rays of the setting sun. We made it! I've brought my family here without losing one of them, and in the best style!

Marshal Gradov, strolling by the pond, watched the frolicking geese with interest. They probably flew in from North Africa, he thought, from Tobruk or El Alamein, or maybe from the valley of the Nile. They had flown in a straight line, as the centuries-old tradition demanded, with no regard to antiaircraft fire or dogfights, following their navigator with precision and landing on the surface of a lake in the Danzig corridor, knowing nothing, by the way, about the so-called "corridor," yet still quite content to see that the outline of the city had not changed.

And it might well have changed, after all, and considerably, as, for example, the skyline of Königsberg had. If von dem Bode had not surrendered, the city's castle would probably not have kept its turrets. Waves of Il-2s, the "flying tanks," in concert with guards, mortars, and artillery of the three basic calibers would have turned the whole Gothic mass into "plusquamperfektum." Alas, such are the circumstances of the end game, Your Excellency "gloomy German genius."

Such were the elegiac reflections of the commander of the Reserve Front, strolling as always under the watchful eye of his bodyguards along the pond of the small Prussian city in disputed German-Polish territory in April 1945. Despite the war, the town had been scrubbed right down to the last cobblestone.

It was interesting to see the transformation of the abstract, calculated quantity of the divisions of General von dem Bode into concrete prisoners of war. It was not the first time Nikita had observed this phenomenon during the course of the war. Last summer, during the final stages of Operation Bagration, for example—at first you looked at the map, at the huge cauldron in which 60,000 of Gitter's encircled grenadiers were cooking. The cauldron looked more like an amoeba, now widening to the north, now narrowing to the south. Around the amoeba, the steel fingers of three fronts, three intangible strategic concepts bearing the names "Meretskov," "Gradov," and "Rokossovsky," were tightening their grip daily. A tactical game was being played involving the transfer of columns, the cutting of communications, the calculating of percentage losses. Gitter had only one thing in his favor—a huge swamp beneath the amoeba's belly. If he had any hope left, it was to hold out on the other side of this swamp until the arrival of some hypothetical reinforcements. "Zakharov" would arrive sooner, however, after which strategy would rapidly be transformed into blood, sweat, and tears, into the ferocious resistance of others. Thousands of soldiers fashioned Eskimo-style snowshoes for themselves out of willow branches and forced their way through the bog. Gitter ordered his grenadiers to fix bayonets and counterattack. Two days passed, and then it was all over, the amoeba was squashed, the army that two years ago had been invincible was now transformed into a panic-stricken rabble racing through the forest. The victors slurped soup from still-warm Wehrmacht mess kits that had been abandoned on the road and took boxes of Iron Crosses that had been stored away for future use but that now had been transformed into a currency of sorts among the soldiers. The strategic concept of the Bobruisk cauldron had been transformed into the somnambulist-like figure of a German general wandering all alone down a road and muttering something to himself under his breath.

Ilya Ehrenburg and the American journalist Reston were in the jeep with me then. We stopped and went toward the disoriented general. He spoke neither Russian nor English, and I'd forgotten all my school German. Ehrenburg managed to put together the phrase "Who are you?" and then roared with laughter, having received the reply "I'm a German, not a flea!" It was like something out of Zoshchenko. Of course, we had to take Ehrenburg's word for it, as there was no one to check his translation.

Later on, when they were dining in Bobruisk, that is, when the strategic concepts "Rokossovsky," "Meretskov," and "Zakharov" turned into the drinking buddies Kostya, Kirill, and Zhora, they began to discuss this notion, that is, the transformation of military, strategic, and historical ideas into the fate of one small isolated man. Then, realizing they were approaching a dangerous precipice, they cut themselves short. The mighty marshals always shied away from talking about touchy subjects.

Nikita remembered Field Marshal von Paulus emerging from the bunker, frozen to the bone, exhausted, clearly unwashed in violation of every imperial tradition. The ball of yarn was unwound, the last thread had been pulled out, and on the filthy snow of Stalingrad there remained only a little man dreaming about a hot bath and a change of underwear.

The same thing could happen to me if events were to take a different turn, reflected Nikita, just like what happened to Andrei Vlasov when he lost his army and was driven, together with his Maria Ignatievna, into one last shed. It could happen to any historical leader. Imagine Stalin driven from the Kremlin, wandering back to Georgia on foot. And what would happen in the near future to the historical concept known as "Hitler"? German generals such as von dem Bode were being turned from shaded areas on maps into prisoners of war, while I was changed from a goner in the camps torturing myself with "If I still, then I'm still . . ." into the concept "Gradov," striking fear into the hearts of the German general staff. I mustn't forget that things can work in reverse.

The surrender of von dem Bode's army took place in the Schlossburg Castle. Nikita shook hands with the captured general and even invited him to have tea in the bürgermeister's office. The German displayed no unbending Prussian grandeur; on the contrary, he was evidently grateful for the invitation and quite talkative, as if he were fairly begging for friendship.

"You smashed our forces with the help of our own strategy of deep armored wedges, concentration of fire, and massed infantry attacks. Leave us with at least that consolation, Marshal Gradov!"

Nikita nodded benevolently and left his crushed enemy with at least that consolation. He noticed the obvious pleasure with which the general sucked at a slice of lemon.

"Marshal Gradov, you won't have me shot if I ask you a personal question?" von dem Bode asked.

Nikita realized straightaway that it would be a question about the camps. The Germans know, of course, that I spent four years in prison, he thought. Interesting sort, this von dem Bode—you can already guess by his question how he will get along in the camps.

Just then came the announcement that representatives from military intelligence had arrived and that the two gentlemen, one Soviet and the other Nazi, would have to take their leave of each other. Before leaving the room, von dem Bode looked over the walls with a lucid gaze: farewell, Teutonic annals, it said. Nikita saluted him as a farewell and was pleased to see all the men of his command do the same as the German passed through one room after another.

An army must keep its dignity not only in defeat but also in the tumult of victory. What was happening now was a monstrous degradation of the army, not to mention the nation! Shame on all us Russians! Shame on our civilization! A mob of marauders with gunnysacks was running after the tanks! And this after we did such a first-class job of defending ourselves! There goes agitprop, corrupting the people again! It started with vigilance and everyone informing on each other, and today it's the squalid idea of unbridled vengeance! The soldiers' brains had been addled by four years of exploding bombs, and now this filth was crawling out of every nook and cranny, from the newspapers and radio, from the unit political officers, and every one of us, myself included, would have to answer for it. Didn't we yell, "No breathing space for the snakes!" After all, we couldn't give them any time to catch their breath. However, it was from this state of being uncontrolled, and from an inner need to remain in that state, that all this grew: Take revenge! Rage and the thirst—thirst!—for vengeance! We'll grind them into dust! Beat, rape, take trophies—in other words, pillage! The cynical "social order" was perfectly understandable. Transforming a soldier into a marauder meant making him a fearless, ferocious barbarian, but that was the price of bringing closer the goal, which was the final destruction of the disorganized enemy; and if one dug deeper, one could see something even more loathsome and sinister, something that might have come about unconsciously but arose precisely from the instinct that was characteristic of that band. For the first time after so many years of degrading reptilian life, our people seem to have accomplished the colossal moral feat of finding their own dignity. Now they would have to be turned back into swine, smeared all over with the same shit—otherwise the plan would never work! And if one wants to go even deeper, how many more circles of this hell will we have to pass through in order to—At this point, however, Nikita Gradov's train of thought was interrupted by a terse order from Marshal Nikita Gradov: "Don't plunge into metaphysics!"

One way or another, they race along in the tracks of the tanks and snatch up everything that comes to hand: sewing machines, radios, bicycles, lamps, shutters, bed linen, pillows, china tea services, watches by the pile, clothing by the armful from closets; they tear off window blinds, drag off furniture. . . . Convoys were filled to bursting with these so-called "trophies." The most terrible thing of all was that they considered any woman or little girl fair game. "They fucked our women, and now we're going to fuck theirs!" All the women who had not gotten out of East Prussia in time now walked with their legs bowed. Where had it come from, then, this passion on the part of our glorious soldiers for forcing apart the legs of old women and schoolgirls alike?

Two days earlier Nikita had not been able to restrain himself and had personally intervened in this Sodom. He happened to hear a conversation among his staff officers concerning a certain captain who had appropriated a German farm in the area and things going on there that not even Genghis Khan would have dreamed of. There was a wild commotion at headquarters: the commanding officer strapped on his sidearm, gathered together his personal "wolfhounds," and headed for the farmstead.

At the farm they found "righteous vengeance" in full swing. The captain and a dozen of his hangers-on, all of them dead drunk, covering their nudity only with pink-and-white women's undergarments, were running from room to room in the house like apes, and nothing but. The proprietor, along with his two Yugoslav farmhands, had been killed trying to prevent the rape of his three small daughters. Most of the shots had been aimed at their groins in an attempt to splatter their genitals. The girls, the eldest of whom was eleven, were crawling around upstairs in puddles of blood. Their mother had hanged herself—or had been hanged—in the pantry.

The captain, dragged to the feet of the commander, could only grin stupidly and murmur, "*Schmerz*, you say? You're lying, you bitch! *Nicht Schmerz!*"

The next day, the whole merry band was shot on the sentence of a field tribunal, that is, simply on the orders of the marshal himself. An order to the effect that any acts of banditry involving the taking of human lives would be immediately punishable by death was posted in all the units, batteries, and squadrons of the Reserve Front.

The savagery came to a stop almost immediately, which showed once again, thought Nikita with sorrow and regret, that there was no mystical fire of revenge burning in the hearts of these soldiers, only criminal permissiveness and even incitement by their superiors.

"Understanding of the just desire for vengeance burning in the breast of the Soviet soldier has been expressed at the highest level, if you know what I mean, Nikita Borisovich!" Stroilo, the chief political officer who had attained the rank of lieutenant general, fairly shouted the words at the marshal. Having learned of the execution of the marauders, he had driven off to the frontline headquarters burning with indignation no less righteous than the soldiers' desire for revenge. His large bald head with its elephantine wrinkles and its thin lips set in a permanent crooked smile seemed to have reached the limits of their ability to conceal resentment; if only Nina could see the man she had once called her "beloved proletarian hero" now!

"Aren't you taking too much on yourself, Comrade Marshal?" he yelled. "I'm afraid the headquarters of the Supreme Commander might not understand you!"

Every so often, his crude bellowing broke into the shrieks of a woman in a communal apartment.

"First of all, stop shrieking!" the marshal pronounced with his magisterial, icy calm. "Otherwise I'll have you thrown out of this office!"

Stroilo immediately subsided, reducing steam by a half turn of the wheel. "Nikita, I beg your pardon, it's my nerves. . . . It's just that I could see those lads—just because of a few Germans, they're going to be . . . after all, they made it nearly all the way to Berlin . . ."

"Those animals don't belong in the human race," said the marshal. "Here is my report to Supreme Headquarters! By permitting looting, we increase our own losses! The Germans aren't fighting for Hitler anymore, but for their own skins—they've nowhere to go, they're defending their wives and children from extermination! A mass exodus of the population to the west is under way. Have you thought about the postwar map? Go ahead, read it!"

He handed Stroilo several typewritten sheets. Without even familiarizing himself with their contents, the commissar already knew Nikita had won again. His bourgeois, pseudohumanist morality was a strange atavism in a Soviet military leader, but it was based on "our interests" and displayed a clear-eyed vision aimed at the future—and Stalin loved that. With a furrowing of his brow that reflected his mental effort he began to read the report. He hated Nikita Gradov.

The marshal sat down at the Schlossburg bürgermeister's huge, carved oak desk. He did not take his eyes off the figure of his chief political officer. The man was the embodiment of all the current vulgarity in the upper ranks. Nikita couldn't seem to rid himself of him, no matter how he tried. It was clear that Stalin himself had given the go-ahead for his appointment. Actually, he didn't do all that much harm thanks to his remarkable obtuseness. It's ridiculous, but he keeps on pretending there's some kind of trust between us; then again, all the commissars are playing up to their commanders these days as though they were friends. And all the while he's compiling a dossier on me, trying to get at me at every step. I wonder whether he has figured out that I know everything, that I have my own secret police working here? . . . But what if I'm underestimating him and I'm a long way from knowing about everything that he's up to? The marshal bristled at the thought.

A curious incident involving Stroilo had taken place in Vilnius several months before. A certain colonel of artillery had given Stroilo a resounding slap across the face on the steps of the headquarters building. The scene had been quite comical, and the orderlies standing on the steps had fairly rolled on the ground with laughter; nevertheless, the colonel had been arrested.

"You're out of your mind, Vadim," said the marshal to the colonel. "Don't you understand what might be in store for you? Why did you do that to him?"

"He knows," answered Vuinovich, standing by a window in the school and smoking calmly.

What a romantic figure, answering the question like "the hero of her novel." Nikita knew he could save Vadim and therefore permitted himself to adopt a somewhat mocking tone. He sent him with a personal letter to Tolbukhin, commander of the Fourth Ukrainian Front, with the result that Vadim was now liberating Yugoslavia, the country of his forefathers. As for the victim, the chief political officer of the front, it goes without saying that he did not know the reason for such an unexpected humiliation. Vadim had exaggerated: a Cheka agent with so much experience could not remember everyone who had been interrogated in his presence. And he did not insist that the crazed colonel be punished. Despite all his professional baseness, he was, as they say, "not a bad guy."

"I understand your conclusions, Nikita," said Stroilo, handing the report back, "but agree that you have to try to understand our soldiers! Just think what these Germans did when they were on our land, and everywhere. You yourself—remember?—were struck dumb. I can remember you gritting your teeth when we saw all that business at Maidanek. Millions of pairs of shoes from those who were gassed and burned . . ."

"Of course the Nazi beast deserves retribution," said Nikita. He had the sensation that his trachea, his bronchi, his diaphragm were beginning to quiver. "All criminals should be judged and punished, but what does the civilian population have to do with it? Most of them knew nothing at all about the death camps. Why, even our people don't know everything, not by a long shot . . ."

A slip of the tongue. A near slip of the tongue. Stroilo, as if giving him time to mull over what he had almost said, walked away to the window.

Well, there it is. A fine addition to my accumulating file, thought Nikita, walking back and forth on the path of smoothed reddish sand winding along the banks of the pond in the city of Schlossburg, now deserted by its inhabitants. There he was—marching around like a Prussian Friedrich, two fingertips inserted into his jacket opening, the turrets of the town's castle rising in the background. The background was formed by the Gothic flamboyant cathedral. From the vantage point of the flight of geese that had recently arrived from overseas, from the palace lancet window where Chief Political Officer Stroilo was standing behind barely parted blinds, the rays of the sun seemed to set the crosses and cupola on the eastern side afire in a vast Central European sunset. And, of course, from that point of view Nikita appeared as a great friend and leader to his dog Polk, already quite crazy with devotion to his master.

The marshal was in a foul mood, feeling as though the screws were tightening on him. It was the end of the war, and one might expect him to be triumphant, ready for the final exultation of victory, yet everything was giving him cause for worry and irritation: the situation in the ranks, the mood of the leaders, his personal life. The new, harmonious, and genuinely friendly relationship that had begun to form between himself and Veronika had gone sour not long after Boris IV ran away. His legal spouse now bombarded him with letters and telegrams, went into hysterics at their every meeting, during which she would remind him of everything he had done wrong, accuse him of callousness and indifference to his son. Or she would burst in, her eyes rolling, an accusing finger pointed at his face, right between the eyes: "You're a terrible human being!"

What does she want? For me to set the whole intelligence and state security apparatus into motion to look for an eighteen-year-old kid? After all, when I was his age, I left home and joined Frunze. It's clear enough that he's at the front, but where will you find him in a mass of twenty million people? I've already spoken to all of the front commanders, and they've promised to look for him, which means that the search is under way—no one could fail to take a request from Gradov seriously—but so far there have been no results. She imagines that he's less dear to me than to her, my boy, my Borka the Fourth, of whom I always think with such tenderness and pity that it becomes oppressive, and with feelings of guilt he would never forgive me for. What can you do if he wants to make this war a page in his biography? She won't listen to any of it, she goes around to all of the authorities making a fool of herself, appealing to that cousin of ours, that suspicious Lamadze, even to Stroilo. Then the bastard comes to me and announces: your wife, Nikita, is meeting with an American from the embassy.

How she changed in the time we were apart! She'll never be able to wash herself clean of the camps. It must have been there that she learned to puff herself up, to pass for a mental case. One day she had screeched at him: "You only think about her these days—that cunt!" Vika, the tender young thing from Voloshin's Crimea, from the modernist houses of Moscow! After that, all communication between the two of them had been broken off.

As for the one to whom she had referred to so unambiguously in gutter language—Taska, my faithful companion who to this day uses formal address when she speaks to me, even when we're in bed—she has turned gloomy and started to put on weight. "You couldn't care less about me, Nikita Borisovich! You've never taken me to Moscow in the plane even once!" To put the finishing touches to all of these charms, despite all their precautions, she'd become pregnant.

Stroilo watched through a chink in the shutters as the commander broke off a small twig from a neatly pruned apple tree and absentmindedly began to whip it back and forth—as though he were chasing away evil spirits—then sat down on a stone on the very edge of the pond and with the same branch lashed the innocent water. Gradovs, impudent aristocrats of fine sensibilities, why do you always feel you are the heroes of the novel, pushing us, the Stroilos, out onto the periphery? Now, it seems, another reshuffling of values is coming. He thinks I don't know who it was that insulted me with that slap in the face, and where he is now, and what kind of creeping anti-Sovietism is contained in the whole affair. Too bad the idiots had shot the young fellow in the Ukraine: he could have been useful.

It was growing dark. The shoulder blades no longer protruded from the marshal's boyish back. Polk, sitting next to him, touched a paw to his shoulder: time to go! Three massive figures in raincoats like tents approached: his personal bodyguard.

Stroilo is gathering information on me, the marshal thought. He's preparing a report, that much is clear. It's also obvious that someone in Moscow is putting him up to it, possibly Beria himself. It was not difficult to imagine the particulars: Gradov is opposed to the Party line, seeks cheap popularity with the troops, has turned the Reserve Front into his own fief, has surrounded himself with his own people and sycophants, has a harem, is making himself rich . . . a harem, maybe, that can be proved later. Making myself rich? Not very likely, but it doesn't matter: if the decision is made to devour me, they'll devour me without even spitting out the buttons. And if all that isn't enough, well . . . he's constantly expressing dubious thoughts, drawing parallels between German fascism and Soviet communism, he applies terrorist methods to distinguished military men—and then there's the Polish question . . .

"And finally, most important of all, there's the Polish question," said Lieutenant General Stroilo, completing his own drawn-out thought. "To sum up, comrades, one can draw the conclusion that Marshal Gradov is seeking personal popularity in the West and that he has Bonapartist tendencies. It's either him or me."

He moved away from the window, unaware that someone had had a pair of binoculars trained on him from a small window in the cathedral across the park the entire time.

And finally, the accursed Polish question. This damned question, the whole subject of Poland, in fact, had for Nikita become a nightmare somewhat akin to his dreams about Kronstadt in his younger days. As far back as Byelorussia, in the Katyn Forest, when he had seen the skulls with an identical bullet hole at the back of each one, he had known that in this case the Germans were not lying, that this was more dirty business of the knights of the Revolution.

Then, after the battle for Vilnius, in which Polish detachments from the Home Army, magnificently equipped, in square hats and camouflage clothing, had fought alongside Soviet forces as allies, a real regular army. . . . The first disgraceful business, a sordid betrayal! We sat down at the table of friendship with the Polish officers, and then the Chekists led them off somewhere to vanish without a trace!

"The cockroach," it seemed, had worked out his own scenario for Poland some time ago. It was no accident that one day at Supreme Headquarters he had put his good hand on the map, covering Warsaw with his palm and Krakow and Danzig with two fingers, and had uttered only one word: "Gold!"

It was not for nothing that the shameful "Polish force" had been formed of soldiers whose family names ended in "-ski."

There was more: the creation in July 1944 of the Lublin Committee of National Liberation headed by Osubko-Morawski. The main idea was to oppose the Mikolajczyk government in London with some sort of mythical Polish powers. Meanwhile, the ranks of the Communists in the Polish People's Guard numbered no more than 500 men. As for the Home Army, General Bor had no less than 380,000 bayonets under his command. Colonel Monter had no less than 40,000 soldiers reporting for duty in Warsaw alone at the beginning of the uprising. It was clear as day: it had been decided to break up the genuine resistance movement and replace it with a counterfeit Communist one. One provocation followed another in an endless chain. Radio Tadeusz Kosciuszko in Moscow exhorted the inhabitants of Warsaw to mount an uprising. "The hour of liberation is near! Poles, to arms! There's not a moment to lose!" The uprising broke out in August, and our forces came to a stop on the eastern bank of the Vistula and stood by quietly as the Hermann Göring Division entered the city, followed by special units made up almost entirely of common criminals, the brigades of Dirlewanger and von Kaminsky. We watched as gigantic mortars proceeded with the planned destruction of the city, as Goliath tanks blew up the barricades, as groups of noncombatant civilians were shot to the last man, rapes, looting . . .

For quite some time, at Nikita's orders, several young officers at the Reserve Front headquarters, intelligent lads, had been monitoring the broadcasts of the BBC and preparing a daily summary for the commander. Stroilo probably won't forget to include that fact in his report. In one way or another, Nikita learned from these summaries that the uprising was being stifled, that Churchill and Mikolajczyk were appealing to Stalin with requests for help but had received no answer. Units of the Reserve Front were stationed two hundred kilometers from the scene of the tragedy. Nikita put in a call to Supreme Headquarters. All they had to do was give the order, and the Reserve Front would force a crossing of the Vistula and come crashing down with all its might upon Bach-Zalewski. In three days they would liberate the capital of an allied power. Shtemenko had answered him with a favorite Ukrainian saying: "Don't push ahead of the boss into the fire." As it turned out, Stalin was simply making believe that there was no uprising in Warsaw. He even gave orders to stop refueling American bombers on shuttle flights to Poltava because they were parachuting shipments of arms and medicine into Warsaw.

And again: immediately after the final defeat of the insurrection, the Lublin Committee came out with a rather strange appeal: "The hour of the liberation of heroic Warsaw is near! The Germans will pay dearly for its ruins and its blood! Carry on the fight!" One was left with the impression that Stalin wanted to use German hands to sweep away everyone who was opposed to his "Polish scenario."

These victories had changed "the cockroach" considerably. He now no longer listened to his generals with particular attention as he had done in '42. A humorless grandeur, absolute and definitive infallibility, was his new pose. At times when he had been drinking, he would begin playing with people, putting the men who surrounded him into ridiculous situations, to test them. In a strange way, it seemed as though he had grown tired of power; or, more accurately, of the aesthetic, of the ethic that had grown up around his power. The ethic of Stalinist power! One would have to say the dirty ethic. For one reason or another, when he was sober, he was irritable and crude. Maybe some kind of sore was sucking away his strength? How long would he live—a hundred years, two hundred?

In February Marshal Gradov flew to the Crimea for the meeting of the Big Three as part of a team of high-ranking military experts. He was at the airfield at Saki together with the Allied "top brass" to meet Roosevelt. The president was wheeled out of the *Sacred Cow* looking pale, with dark circles beneath his eyes—not long for this world, as they say. It was rumored among the military men and journalists in Yalta that Stalin had ceased entirely to reckon with the infirm American president. He even snarled at the healthy Englishman. He presented the most outrageous demands. He insisted, for example, that the Soviet Union be given sixteen seats in the United Nations, one for each republic of the Union. His most unbridled and inflexible effrontery showed each time the "Polish question" arose. It was clear he had long considered Poland his private property. He displayed an insulting contempt for "those little émigrés," for Stanislaw Mikolajczyk; the soldiers of the Home Army he referred to as "accomplices of the occupiers." He rejected any compromise Roosevelt timidly put forth.

Well, thought Nikita, it looks now like the time for the complete Stalinist rape of Poland is coming. The committees of the London government are being broken up. The secret police are everywhere. Home Army units are being disarmed. Those that remain have had no other choice but to take up arms against both the retreating Germans and the advancing Russians.

Damn it all, how is it that I've ended up on the banks of this treacherous sea again? Once again I have a terrible choice to make, and this time I can't find the single-minded resolve I had in 1921. . . .

A Home Army division had turned up in the operational zone of the Reserve Front during the recent Soviet advance across the Danzig corridor. The scattered and severely depleted units of the division, which fielded no more than 3,000 men, were obviously making their way toward the sea in order to leave for neutral Sweden. Finding themselves in the Soviet rear, the Poles ferociously attacked their recent allies. Responding to Nikita's inquiries as to what to do, Supreme Headquarters proposed to resolve the question "in the working order of things," which meant crushing the ill-fated division and then forgetting about it. Instead, Nikita began negotiations with the Poles.

The Poles demanded free passage to the coast in the area of Elbing and Osterode. There, a long, sandy spit called Frisches Nerung extended along the five-mile-wide lagoon of Frisches Chaor, and it was from there that they proposed "to retreat," as they put it, or "to be evacuated," as the representatives from the Reserve Front insisted, to a neutral country.

More than anything in the world—even more, perhaps, than the taking of Berlin—Nikita wanted to avoid bloodshed. The "Polish question" had for some reason shaken him by its perfidy and by the brazen way in which the strong were pressuring the weak, even though one might have expected his life experiences to have hardened him to such sentimentality. Poland is Russia's disgrace, he thought. Starting with Suvorov—there was a sickening old man!—we have been tormenting this country. Then again, whom have we made suffer, them or us? Russian patriots, we still have yet to begin our noble history! A small chance has only just appeared for us, and we would be utter shits if we didn't take advantage of it. Forming the words "a small chance" in his mind, he immediately moved away from them, then and at any time in the future: it's too early, let's finish the war first. In fact, he didn't even know what he meant by the words "a small chance." Rather, he didn't want to know. Not yet.

The negotiations with the Poles had already been going on for several days. Supreme Headquarters was insisting that the division be disarmed and was silently trying to pass over the question of access to the sea. Nikita proposed to General Wigor (this, of course, was his underground code name, his real name remaining a secret) free passage to Frisches Nerung, but without their weapons. At first Wigor categorically rejected this proposal as humiliating. "When the Polish Army retreats, it is with weapons in hand!" He was trying to behave like a Polish nobleman but in fact looked like a drawing teacher. "Keep your men, General," Nikita said to him quietly as they moved away to the window to have a smoke—under the watchful eye of Stroilo, naturally. "Another two or three days, and they'll simply order me to wipe all of you out." After this they came to an agreement: the division would leave its arms with units of the Reserve Front, while the officers would be allowed to keep their sidearms. The division would be guaranteed free evacuation (in the Russian text), that is, retreat (in the Polish text) across the Baltic Sea to a neutral country. The Poles' passage to the sea was scheduled for tomorrow, that is, the day following that night whose beginning found us together with Marshal Gradov on the edge of the municipal pond of the Prussian town of Schlossburg, as deserted as a theatrical set.

The geese were swimming on the pond with a businesslike air, as though they owned the place. Some of them came closer to regard with a round eye the man who for no apparent reason was disturbing the surface of the water with a branch and to look at his animal named Polk.

"Existence equals resistance," Nikita was muttering. "There's the equation. It can turn around on you, but no one will give you a direct answer to the question: does resistance equal existence?"

Though it might seem strange, or even contrived, that same evening Boris IV, Marshal Gradov's lost son, was greatly concerned by the "Polish question." As a matter of fact, the "Polish question" had been a source of concern to him for quite some time, since he had already been stationed for a year on the territory of the country that had the misfortune to be located between Germany and Russia. At the hour of twilight, when his father was absorbed in his complicated reasonings on the edge of the pond in Schlossburg, however, Boris, or "Babochka" as his grandmother Mary called him, for the *n*th time was bringing an exceptionally sharp edge to his handling of the issue.

This was happening in the city of Tielce in the Krakow district. At eight in the evening on Market Square, where three surviving streetlights were rocking in a strong southwesterly wind and where Pan Taluba, a war invalid, veteran of some unknown army, was sitting playing "The Waltz of the Festering Street" on the accordion beneath a wall pockmarked by bullets and emblazoned with the anchor that was the symbol of the Home Army—six young men appeared on the square, which seemed to have absorbed all of the bad blood of smashed Central Europe. The group left four fast German motorcycles behind the rows of stalls as a preventive measure.

The lads were outfitted in black raincoats and forage caps bearing the insignia of the Home Army, hurriedly attached with safety pins. One of them was not difficult to recognize as our "Babochka." His young bulwark of a jaw was lightly overgrown with reddish bristles like his father's. With rapid strides the lads crossed the square and approached the town hall. All the lights were on, and there was a great feeling of animation on the front porch. People were going in and out and forming not entirely sober groups for discussion. The first congress of the multiparty City Council was in session. A detachment of soldiers trained in forest warfare was guarding the building.

The appearance of the group of six did not go unnoticed. "Hold it, boys!" shouted one of the guards. "Where are you coming from?"

"I have a message from General Bor," answered the leader of the group. "A special dispatch for Pan Wetuszinski."

The guard was just about to wave them through when he suddenly froze with his mouth open. What a strange accent! Damn it, he's not one of ours!

"Marek!" he shouted to another guard posted further up the steps. "Those guys in the raincoats. . . . Hey! Stop! . . . The son of a bitch—*cholera jasna!* Hey!"

That was the last "Hey!" of his life. The barrel of a small submachine gun beneath the coat of one of the "not one of ours" spat fire. In a flash, the six scattered through the town hall building as though they had rehearsed the whole thing more than once. Two of them took up sitting positions on the front steps and greeted the guards running up to them with daggers of fire. Two of them raced up the stairs into the meeting hall. Almost immediately grenade explosions and wild screams from the crowd were heard. The remaining pair ran efficiently around the vestibule, pouring gasoline over the velvet drapes from canisters they had been carrying beneath their raincoats, then fanning the all-engulfing flames.

The raid lasted no more than ten minutes, but in that time all the members of the Parliament sitting at the front of the hall, and all of the guards, were killed, along with a fair number of the crowd in attendance, who fell beneath the bullets and grenades.

Someone had heard the raiders talking among themselves, and now voices were raised in the town hall above the cries of horror and desperation: "Russians! The Russians did this to us! Russian bandits!"

"We're going!" Stanislav Trubchenko, the commander of the detachment, finally shouted. Everything was done according to procedure: four ran, two covered them, firing; then two others fired while four ran. Just what the doctor ordered.

Again two of the six, our "Babochka" and one other, showered the square with steel from behind a corner of the trade stalls. Pan Taluba was lying on his side wheezing, his accordion smashed. The remaining four started up the motorcycles behind the booths.

The engines roared to life. Boris jumped on behind Trubchenko. They strapped his buddy Seryozhka Krasovitsky to his seat: a Polish bullet had caught him in the arm. Tearing out from behind the stalls, they took off, shooting their Schmeissers and Walthers, tossing grenades. A chariot of fire! It wasn't very likely they would be intercepted on the road: they had demolished the telephone switchboard at the very beginning of the operation.

Now they were racing along beneath the moon like a group on a peaceful outing. The only thing missing was girls. In any case, we're going to change these hats for our own Soviet garrison caps so that our own side doesn't fire on us. You can never tell who you're going to meet on the road here in Poland: an AK Polish White unit, a Ludow unit, a regular unit of the Red Army, a stray Fritz, or even an outfit like ours—God forbid!

For the time being they roared along as though in a tranquil dream. Dots of lakes flashed by, and then treetops illuminated by the moonlight and slopes with sleeping huts and chapels. The first-class motorcycles flew up the silvery hillocks stormily, youthfully. Now and again drops of Seryozha Krasovitsky's blood stained the asphalt.

After traveling some forty miles down the highway, they turned off into the forest that served as a bandits' hideout. It was only here, beneath the hanging branches of the spruce trees, that Boris began to cool off from the heat of battle. What kind of fucking battle was that, for Christ's sake, a bandit raid on a city council? If I'd known they were preparing us for action in Poland, I'd never have joined the commandos! From the very first day in Moscow, he and Alexander Sheremetiev had been surprised: why is it they're teaching us more Polish than German? It was explained to them that numerous bands of reactionaries armed by the Germans were operating on the territory of Allied Poland; it will be your task to ensure the security of the progressive leaders of the Polish Republic and the peaceful citizenry, as well as to act in concert with the forces of resistance until the units of the Red Army arrive—this is why you need an elementary knowledge of the Polish language. So, then, repeat after me: Hands up! Lay down your weapons! Down on the ground!

If Sasha and I had known what's really going on here in Poland, how much the locals hate everything Soviet, and what we have to do here, we would never have gone to that school. It would have been better for us to sign up at the divers' school in Murmansk. And now I don't even know what has happened to my best friend, Alexander Sheremetiev, junior boxing champion of Moscow. They won't even answer my questions about what has become of him. "Have you forgotten, Gradov? No more questions until the war is over!"

At the beginning, in the spring of 1944, it had seemed to the lads that rather than having descended to the sinful earth, they had gone to parachutists' heaven. Everything was first rate! There were fifty men of varying ages in the outfit: experienced fellows in their thirties, demolition experts, mountain climbers, judo fighters, and guys just like Boris and Sasha, "coordinated guys." They seemed to be doing useful work: derailing German trains, attacking stations and airfields, blowing up supply dumps. Then everything started to go wrong, a sort of chaos began to take over. The closer liberation came, the more confused the Polish question became. One could not always tell who was in the right. Nevertheless, we carried out our missions without any "nonessential questions." Clashes with the Home Army occurred more and more frequently. They were audacious, mean fighters, though not as well prepared, of course, as the graduates of the commando school.

"As you can see, comrades, they don't have much love for us," the outfit's commissar, who also doubled as the cook, said to the men.

"Why should they love us?" Alexander asked Boris quietly. "All you have to do is remember a few moments in history . . ."

One way or another, they went on fighting and asked no nonessential questions. They no longer had the esprit de corps of earlier days. A particularly lousy—pardon me, sir!—mood was in the air, especially whenever they had to liquidate prisoners out of political or tactical considerations or haul off civilians whose identity had not been fully established.

One day, though, they landed in the worst shit imaginable. They were lying in ambush with the task of intercepting an airborne landing. Whose landing? Well, it's obvious whose—the Germans'! The last convulsions of a mortally wounded beast. The parachutists of the Himmelfahrtskommando, they're the ones we have to send back to the skies!

The results were an absurdity, absolutely ridiculous. An airplane with no identifying marks circled over the forest clearing several times in the dead of night. Then the paratroopers began to jump one after another, ten men in all. We sent up flares, and we got them all, one right after another. They turned out not to be Germans at all, but Englishmen. So they were on their way to link up with the Home Army—don't you see what a provocation it was, boys? No, Comrade Captain, we don't understand at all. How could we have attacked our allies in the anti-Hitler coalition? Shut up, you cocksuckers! These paratroopers are the victims of a provocation, a complicated provocation mounted by the reactionary forces in Poland. Understand? Don't ask any nonessential questions!

"Boris, doesn't it seem to you that this bullshit isn't exactly what we dreamed about?" Alexander Sheremetiev asked him one day, returning to the formal form of address.

*

One day toward the end of the summer of 1944, something genuinely inspiring and historic took place. They already knew a revolt was brewing in Warsaw, that young people their own age, including young Polish girls, were on the barricades, fighting off attacking SS divisions. Suddenly they were told they would be taking off that night and would be landed in Warsaw. Their overall goal was to help the heroic defenders of the city, while their specific assignment would be given to them once they arrived. "Hurrah!" yelled Sashka Sheremetiev and Borka Gradov with one voice. The other commandos were so surprised they burst out laughing, while the commanding officer and the cook exchanged glances.

"What did you mean by that 'Hurrah'?" Captain Smuglyany asked later.

"Oh, it was just for everything," Alexander replied.

"Just for everything, Comrade Captain," Boris said trustingly.

"What, are you eager to get into the thick of it?" asked Smuglyany.

"Yes, sir, Comrade Captain," Boris said even a bit more confidingly. "We're like the sail in Lermontov's poem. Wouldn't you agree, Alexander?"

" 'Wouldn't you agree, Alexander'? What the hell is all this formality between the two of you?" asked Smuglyany.

"It's just that we haven't had time to become more familiar with each other yet," Alexander explained.

Someone didn't investigate these boys the way they should have, if you ask me, thought the captain. The Special Services didn't check them out properly.

After all, it's difficult not to yell "Hurrah!" when you've just been told that tomorrow you'll be taking part in the Warsaw uprising, in one of the most important events of the Second World War, fighting alongside the freedom-loving peoples of the world! After all, it's not for the Germans that they're sending us to fight.

The next morning, two Douglases flew in from the mainland, landing at a secret airfield. Toward evening they began loading them. "Warsaw is burning," the C.O. warned. "Watch you don't get singed, boys!"

Half an hour after takeoff, they could already see in the gloom beneath them something that reminded them of the eruption of a Japanese volcano that they had seen in a newsreel before the war. There was fire everywhere, flowing in streams, flaring up and then dying down like shrubs, rolling along like balloons. Through the clumps of smoke they could dimly make out the empty holes in the sides of buildings where windows had been.

The decision was made that they would land in the Krakow district. The main objective is for everyone who survives to band together. We have three mobile radios with us. Stick close to their operators. Use your signal lamps, or your flares in case of emergency. Now move it, you cocksuckers!

Rapidly, one at a time, they began leaping out into the reddish infernal abyss. Boris made a surprisingly smooth landing, sailing right by some iron beams protruding dangerously from the gaping ruins of a building. He quickly unhitched his chute and rolled it up, then began to make his way along the wall, looking all around him. The cupolas of two parachutes appeared not far away above the burning rooftops. So the lads were landing in a tight pattern. Fortunately, there's no wind to carry them away. The heat here is hellish, though. There's a smell of decay, too, of bodies decomposing; maybe they're Poles, maybe Germans. There they are, scattered all around, bodies clustered together, along with an overturned bus, some sandbags, an armored vehicle still smoking—the remains of a barricade battle. All was strangely quiet except for the crackling of the fires. He ran to where by his calculations the two parachutists should have landed. From time to time he pressed close to walls and crawled across empty spaces. Suddenly, a terrible, prolonged, multi-faceted roar rolled through the area. Perhaps it was a house collapsing, perhaps a mortar battery emptying its barrels. Turning a corner, he witnessed a spectacle that, as the saying in the outfit went, he wouldn't have wished on Himmler. Two parachutes spread out like a tablecloth after a drunken evening were on fire. One of the men from the outfit, a soldier named Ravil Sharafutdinov, was roasting on the third floor of the building, impaled on the exposed bars of a balcony. From all appearances he was either dead or unconscious. A bit higher up, hanging upside down in a hole that had been a window, from the straps of his chute in which he was entangled, was Alexander Sheremetiev. In fact, he was suspended by only his right leg, which was wedged into something.

"Sashka, are you alive?" Boris cried upward. "Hold on, goddammit, I'm coming to pull you out!" He dashed up the stairs, leaping over the fire-engulfed landings, hearing the stairs crumble behind him.

Sheremetiev's leg, it seemed, was done for: it was crushed beneath a steel beam and the remains of a sculpted naiad.

With the aid of the parachute lines, Boris succeeded in pulling Alexander in through the window. The man was unconscious. A smile of some kind of arrogant superiority was frozen on his face. Now his leg would have to be freed as well, he couldn't just hack it off with a bayonet. After clearing away the fragments of the mermaid—breasts and nipples, a wreath of grape leaves—Boris took up the problem of the beam. Even budging the rusty three-inch-thick girder was out of the question. The only solution was to blow it in half, reducing the length and weight of the object acting as a brake lever. Running to the end of what had been an apartment—through a breach in a wall he saw an old man sprawled on the floor with the pieces of a smashed porcelain figure of an Alpine sheepherder alongside him—Boris set the explosive charge, shortened the fuse, lit it, then dashed back to cover Alexander, whispering, "Lord God, righteous and merciful, save us"—something he had heard Agasha say more than once. Then the charge went off with a roar. Everything shook, and then there was silence except for the dreadful bellowing of Alexander Sheremetiev. The remains of his right leg now quivered in the air. The beam had been hurled aside.

The roar turned to hysterical laughter. "Borka, you asshole, you've saved my life, but what the hell for? Did you see Ravilka Sharafutdinov frying? Just like a shish kebab! Ha, ha, ha . . ."

Unharmed but trembling like a pneumatic drill, Boris carried his friend downstairs, pulling him over the gaps in the staircase. Sheremetiev drifted in and out of consciousness, now and again wailing, "Don't you have a bullet for a friend? Are you trying to save on them?" after which he would laugh insanely. Finally, having reached the ground floor, Boris threw his friend over his shoulder and ran out into the middle of the street. Meanwhile, the entire wall of the house, together with the body of Sharafutdinov suspended from the balcony, slowly and majestically collapsed.

The next moment, he saw his friends running toward him, the men of his outfit, who had formed up once again. With them were several Poles, who produced a stretcher from beneath a mound of rubble and laid Sheremetiev upon it. Parachute traces were used to fashion a tourniquet around the man's crushed leg just under the groin. They gave him an injection of morphine from the first-aid kit and ran on ahead, the Poles leading the way.

The C.O. briefed them on the objective en route. To the disappointment of Boris and the other paratroopers, it was neither a raid on the headquarters of the German henchmen nor the kidnapping of Bach-Zalewski, but rather only the rescue of an important Polish Communist, General Stycharski of the Ludowa Guards, removing him from the danger zone.

The parachutists ran along behind their Polish guides, one of whom, it seemed, was a woman in overalls. From time to time they assumed a combat stance and sprayed a suspicious-looking street with fire from their automatic weapons. They took particular care to riddle a German van outfitted with antennae, after which they blew up the vehicle with hand grenades. Then they all dived down into the catacombs beneath the ruins, entered an underground cave, and unexpectedly emerged into a cellar illuminated by an electric light. On the wall, in a cozy corner, Vladimir Iliich Lenin was sitting in a picture frame, quietly reading a newspaper. Stycharski and his entourage were already there, awaiting their removal in a state of considerable agitation. At the sight of the Stalinist guard, they immediately regained their spirits. "Thank you, comrades! We knew our class brothers wouldn't forget us!"

The whole group let themselves down through a reeking manhole into the sewers. For a good hour they slogged along, up to their ankles in fecal muck. Suddenly they came out at a grille, beyond which lay the peaceful lands of the east: clumps of trees, a river flowing away into the distance, with only the glow of the city it was leaving behind reflected in it. They blew the grille away with explosives and stepped out into freedom. The rest of the night they spent making their way toward the Vistula. The rumble of the battle in Stary Miasto grew louder. Several times, from their places in the bushes, they saw German columns rolling efficiently along the roads, but they managed to avoid any skirmishes. At dawn they arrived with precision at the rendezvous point. Some motorboats were waiting for them there. Boris stood in waist-high water with a submachine gun in his hands, facing the city. At least the rapidly flowing waters of the Vistula would wash the shit from his legs.

The girl in overalls was standing next to him with an expression on her face that was at once downcast and tranquil. "What's with you?" he said to her. "Get in the boat!" She did not turn around. "Come on!" he yelled.

She turned to him. "Get in yourself!" she whispered harshly. There were tears in her eyes, and her mouth was twisted disdainfully. "Russian traitors! We believed in you, and now just look at how they're killing us! Go on! I'm going where my people are dying!" She headed for the bank of the river.

"Gradov!" the C.O. barked ferociously. Boris tossed his gun into the boat and then scrambled in after it. Several minutes later, they reached the eastern bank, where all was idyllic and a mighty army stood idle. Two drivers of horse-drawn artillery were washing down their animals' harnesses in a tiny inlet, as though they had driven their horses out to a night pasture and were quietly passing the time.

"Murderers, traitors, bandits"—that's all we ever hear from the locals, thought Boris IV as the muffled growl of the engine pushed the craft toward the outfit's secret base. Even that woman, a Communist, one of the Ludowa Guards, preferred going back to the barricades to running away. There's something not quite right about what we're doing here, something improper. Sashka was right—this wasn't the war we dreamed of. Had he survived? He hadn't heard a thing from or about him, and it was forbidden to ask questions. They sent him to the rear and threw us back into the front lines, not men but shadows, according to our instructions. Writing home is not permitted. You have no home except the outfit, no mother and father except the C.O., is that clear?

Nevertheless, he managed to send letters—folded in triangles and without envelope—home from the school. He always began them with "Dear Mama, I'm stationed in X sector of the front . . ." Alive and well, good food, proper shoes, all according to the military formula. One of my comrades will drop this off in a Moscow mailbox on his way through the city on official business. There were times when he missed his mother terribly, but not the mother who had "returned"; his mother as she was before, a young beauty, forever grabbing Bobka IV by the hair or the ear for a joke, tugging at him and squeezing him until he was almost twelve—it was she who now arose in his memory as a symbol of warmth, home, and childhood, and then, following a rupture that yawned like a black void, another appeared who was not entirely his own. He pitied the present Veronika, but as if from a distance. She did not fit into the life of the stern youth. He realized that she and his father were no longer getting on well, but his father had come back a different person too. But then, what concern are the melodramas of the old folks to people of our generation, anyway?

It was only then that he was pierced by a deep, nearly unbearable, and incomprehensible feeling that seemed to burn through to some dark foundation, when he remembered Shevchuk coming out of his mother's bedroom every morning in riding breeches, suspenders dangling down at the sides.

He often asked himself whether or not that was what he had run away from—her drunken appearance and her cynical smile?

They drove by the outfit's first checkpoint. Akuliev and Ryss emerged from a hollowed-out oak like two *shurale*—Tartar wood spirits. At the second checkpoint, Vereshchagin and Dosaev were hanging from tree branches like two pythons in camouflage clothing. Finally, the concealed clearing where the base had been set up for a couple of weeks now in a two-story "chalet" opened before them. The structure looked quite abandoned and run-down, yet inside everything was as it should have been, even the "Lenin corner" with the prescribed literature that Captain Smuglyany used to "fill up the propaganda tanks."

The commanding officer, a wiry man of about forty nicknamed "Taiga Wolf," came outside. He congratulated the six on the completion of the mission (one of the "appropriate authorities" had radioed him a message indicating that everything was "A-OK") and gave orders that Seryozha Krasovitsky be administered first aid and that the radio operators contact those same "appropriate authorities" concerning the transfer of the wounded man to the nearest divisional hospital. "And you, Gradov, Boris, report to me after dinner!" he said abruptly. Then he returned to his quarters beneath the mansard roof, where he loved to study his endless supply of maps: he had a great fondness for topographic games.

What could it mean? Perhaps he wanted to give him some bad news about Sasha Sheremetiev? Smuglyany's cooking had always been revolting, but now he couldn't get down so much as a swallow of it. He quickly drank a cup of coffee, taking it with a biscuit spread with some jam captured in a raid, then stamped up to the attic in his boots. "Reporting as ordered, Comrade Major!"

Major Grozdev (he knew his subordinates called him "Taiga Wolf," and the nickname pleased him) was sitting behind his desk as though he had been expecting Boris. "Have a seat! Nowhere to sit? Sit on the cot, then, you blockhead. First of all, allow me to congratulate you—everyone will be put in for the Order of the Red Star for today's operation, and you'll each get another star on your shoulder straps. In addition, the Polish government has conferred the decoration of 'Vertuti Militari' on all of us for the Warsaw operation."

"Which Polish government?" asked Boris without any particular joy.

Taiga Wolf smirked. "The government we recognize, in other words the only Polish government. That's not what I called you here for, though."

"Of course it wasn't for that," growled Boris. Long months of hit-and-run work behind enemy lines had taught him not to ingratiate himself before ranking officers. "Well, get to the point, Comrade Major!"

"I wanted to ask you, Boris . . . well, just as one comrade to another . . ." All of a sudden, Grozdev was mumbling in a strange tone quite uncharacteristic for him. "Why is it that when you entered the school, you didn't mention that you're one of *those* Gradovs, that you're the marshal's son?"

Boris IV only swallowed, not knowing what to say. One might say he had taken an unexpected direct hit to the head.

"Did you think we didn't know about it?" a voice behind him asked. He turned and saw Captain Smuglyany standing in the doorway, one elbow leaning against the casing. "We knew about it from the beginning, Borya. We know everything."

"Cut the crap, Kazimir," snorted Taiga Wolf, who by now had recovered his normal voice. "We didn't catch it, so drop the bullshit. Still, Boris, you've put us over a barrel, and we could really get fucked. Our unit, as you know, is the most secret of secrets. We never give out any information to anyone, and now comes this inquiry from Rokossovsky. What's to be done? I don't know myself, friend. We can't rule out the possibility that I'll have to dismiss you, even though you're a good comrade—an excellent one, in fact, a fine man! What do you have to say about all this shit?"

"If you kick me out, you'll be helping Mama to make a parasite out of me," said Boris in a somber, independent voice. Then he thought, to his own surprise, go ahead and discharge me, I've had all I can take of this crap!

"It depends on you, Boris!" Smuglyany began with a certain note of pathos. "It's all up to you whether you become a man and a Communist, or a parasite."

"Hold on a moment, Kazimir," interrupted Grozdev. "Borka, you know I love you like a younger brother, almost like a son . . ."

"I've never noticed any such thing," muttered Boris. Then he said to himself, everything has already been decided and they're just trying to make the pill easier to swallow. Taiga Wolf will realize it's a waste of time, wipe away all of this snot, and then return to his usual role: "Is that clear? You can go now!"

The commander, however, went on with his hand-wringing. What's going on? Do they really not want to see me go?

"Understand, Boris, we don't exist. You took the oath yourself, renouncing your existence for the duration of the war, right? They even put us in for medals under false names, and suddenly word gets out that Gradov's son is with us. That just can't be, since we don't exist. No one knows that we exist in nature . . ."

Someone, however, knew that they "existed in nature," though it seemed as though someone did not want them to. There was an explosion almost right next to the house, nearly on the terrace. It shook the house, and the decrepit wall of the room came apart in a zigzag. The light went out, and through the crack the dark forest came closer in an instant. Within the wood, a tongue of fire flickered rapidly from a machine gun. Grozdev, Smuglyany, and Gradov scrambled head over heels down the stairs for their weapons. Every man in the unit was already leaping from the windows and doors to take up defensive positions in a circle. They did not need any orders: the situation had been rehearsed time and time again at the academy.

The next mortar shell that came from the forest carried away the mansard and twisted the structure into ruins. The attackers sent up an illumination flare, obviously trying to determine how many men were ranged against them. While the light was still hanging in the air, the defenders sent up one of their own. The atmosphere was almost festive, like at the skating rink in Gorky Park. Figures dashing from bush to bush flickered in the green light.

What proof did anyone need? The Home Army had decided to take revenge for Tielce.

If I were in their place, I'd take revenge, too, thought Boris. If I were in their shoes, I'd wipe out every last one of these bastards!

Fire poured in from all sides. There must be a whole battalion of them out there! Looks like it's curtains for all of us—serves us right, too!

Meanwhile, from behind a stack of firewood, Captain Smuglyany was cheerfully interceding: "Where are our mortars? Bring up our mortars, you motherfuckers!"

The C.O.'s voice thundered, "Zubov's squad, stay with me. Everybody else into the trucks. Head for the gap! Formation according to Plan One!"

"I'm staying too!" Boris shouted at him.

"Didn't you hear my order, you son of a bitch?" replied the C.O., sticking the barrel of his pistol into Boris's ear. Now Taiga Wolf was displaying his repertoire.

Zubov's lads had brought up two 50mm mortars and were beginning to shell the edge of the forest methodically. Suddenly Zubov rolled to the ground, clutching at a wound in his stomach. The main body of the outfit, thirty men or so, was already headed for the forest in three Dodge trucks at full throttle. Boris was lying in the bed of one of them, back to back with Trubchenko; both of them were blindly firing bursts from their weapons and lobbing grenades. "It's a great ride!" Stasik Trubchenko, former medal-winning mountain climber and conqueror of the Pamirs, yelled joyfully. Then he twitched and seemed to shrivel away behind Boris's back. It was as though at that moment he had retreated into his own nebulous past, to the two mountain peaks that bore the names "Stalin" and "Soviet Constitution."

The whole question now was: would the three trucks manage to make it down the concealed road, going full tilt with their headlights off, or would they crash into the trees in a hail of bullets? In the aforementioned hail, however, other questions arose in the minds of the passengers. They've gotten Trubchenko, so I'll be next, right? This was a question every one of the men probably asked himself during the long minutes of flying along with roaring motors, as they rushed away as fast as possible from the ear-shattering baying of the forest.

"So, now it's . . . ha-ha . . . my turn, is it?" The words issued forth mechanically, over and over, from the lips of that same Boris Gradov whom Grandmother Mary and Agasha the nanny had loved to call "Butterfly," whom his mother, Veronika, loved tenderly, even though she had called him a "good-for-nothing" the last time they had spoken; whom Papa, Marshal Gradov, and Grandfather Professor Gradov doted upon, in whom they saw a continuer of the line; whom Auntie Nina, the famous poetess, and Uncle Kirill, now swallowed up by the labor camps . . . whose whole starry, frosty Silver Forest with its towering pines . . . "So, now it's my . . . ha-ha . . . my turn, is it?" There was no shaking off those idiotic "ha-has." "So, now it's my . . . ha-ha . . ." Seems like I'm saying it out loud. He caught a glimpse of an eye peering at him in surprise. Suddenly the sky disappeared from view, and the barking of the forest instantly stopped. One after another, the Dodges with their cargo of dead, wounded, and hysterically laughing commandos flew onto the camouflaged road.

The façade of the Saint Augustine Cathedral of Schlossburg, East Prussia, was dotted with no less than two dozen granite gargoyles, lizardlike creatures with claws, manes, and faces that frequently looked human. Some of them were functional, acting as drainpipes—the rain that had fallen before the morning was now pouring from the maws of two gangling creatures suspended above the small balcony where Siegel was sitting. Most of the figures, however, had no function other than to personify the evil spirits that had been driven from the church. The most important of these chimeras, in the opinion of Siegel, and the closest to the original state of the structure, that is, the one that had been created by Typhoeus and Ekhidna, was encamped upon the balcony itself, overshadowing the eastern part of the Baltic skies with its leonine mane, feeble-limbed goat's body, and mighty dragon's tail.

Siegel liked to stand a bottle on the curve of its tail. In fact, he liked the creature as a whole. He even detected a certain similarity of features between the creature's face and his own: the same elongated lips, the same nose with flaring nostrils, the slightly swollen eyes that were forever laughing. It was a monster with a capital M, you might even be able to mount a machine gun under its belly! It was a good thing this little balcony could get along without a lot of childish Christian prattle.

Russian soldiers were walking along below. The sound of their voices sometimes reached Siegel and his boys. The soldiers were looting the church, bustling in and out, dragging things away. What was it that was taking so long to haul away? Maybe the relics from the endless catacombs? What nonsense—he himself, Hauptsturmführer Siegel, had personally hauled the most valuable stuff from the prelate's last resting place up to this cell beneath the skies: three cases of strong, fragrant Benedictine. One good swallow will keep you going for another half an hour. All told, there should be enough to last until the end. Those Russian idiots down there are probably swilling down the lousy communion wine. Better not to even think about the *Untermenschen*. Just sit up here beneath the belly of your sister Chimera and wait for your time to come. It won't be long now. To think about these subhumans who, by an unforeseen change in the elements, had appeared in the central lands of the *Übermenschen* was unbearable. If it had been Jews who arrived, that would have been understandable; all of the Jews, though, we managed to send off to Astral. All of the Jewish *Yuga* we saw off to their proper resting place.

"Günter, did we manage to get rid of all the Jews?"

"Jawohl, Herr Hauptsturmführer."

"Very good—let me pinch your bottom, my boy." Don't shake like that, that's the way things have always been done in the brigade commanded by Oskar Dirlewanger, so underestimated by the Fatherland and by history—a pinch on the bottom as a sign of encouragement.

All three boys lay with their buttocks upward on the granite balcony that had been polished by four centuries of wind and watched the town castle through binoculars. What good fortune that I'm winding up this story with three fourteen-year-old boys! Three of the youngest boys in the *Volkssturm* and one old jackal from the brigade despised by the entire armed forces of the shattered empire, and for whom they always sent when everyone else was shitting in their pants. The ideal Himmelsfahrtskommando! Oskar and I always preferred boys, even though we were forced to conceal it, being under the imaginary command of that plebeian Schickelgruber. We even took girls and made believe there were boys beneath us.

"Hans, who do you think was first in our movement?"

"I don't understand what you mean, Herr Hauptsturmführer Siegel."

"I'm asking who came first in our great symphonic movement? If you say Adolf Hitler, you're wrong, my boy!"

"Who then if not the great führer, Herr Siegel?"

"Who I'm not telling, because I don't yet know myself, but Adi Schickelgruber was about the hundred and twenty-seventh, the lousy *Arschloch!*"

"I don't much care for what you're saying, Herr Hauptsturmführer Siegel," said Hugo, the best of the three boys, turning his clear green eyes to him. Perfect health, an ideal Aryan upbringing, an ideal slave of the plebeian forces that have seized our movement.

"It seems to me, Herr Hauptsturmführer, you ought to cut down on the Benedictine," the green-eyed boy went on. "The decisive moment is coming soon, Herr Hauptsturmführer."

He's right, this green-eyed lad. The moment is coming upon us. Brahma is moving away, Vishnu is weeping, the great Shiva is straightening his shoulders and laughing loudly.

"Law is collapsing, lawlessness reigns!" Hauptsturmführer Siegel was open to the idea of reincarnation. He would like, if need be, to come back in just this form, with these goat's legs, with a dragon's tail, with the same face as this chimera; alas, such creatures don't yet exist on the earth. With difficulty he extricated himself from his corner, downed half a bottle of the beneficial, viscous liquid, then fell with heavy groin on Hugo's muscular little backside and began to go through the motions of the universally accessible act of goodwill. The boy, who had been confused at first before turning into a steel spring, threw him off and drove him back with a few kicks from his Hitlerjugend boots to the man's limp paunch. Then he raised his pistol.

"Herr Hauptsturmführer, we have to get rid of you. You're interfering with the operation!"

"A good thought, my boy; but if I don't show you how to operate these Faust rocket launchers, who will?"

The Poles who marched through Schlossburg were a motley crowd. Their faces bore tired, indifferent expressions. They were trying not to look at the castle's main entrance, where the ranking Soviet officers were gathered, as though they wished to pass unnoticed. Anyone who happened to cast a glance at Marshal Gradov immediately looked away, as though these foresters thought nothing in particular of the fact that the commander of the Reserve Front of the Soviet Army was leading them into exile.

General Wigor drove up in a jeep with his aides. In keeping with the agreement, the officers had kept their sidearms, pistols in frayed holsters. Nikita saluted and looked at his entourage from the corner of one eye to see if anyone would follow his example. As it turned out, everyone did, even his principal adversary, Stroilo, head of the political department. Suddenly, a strange detail caught his eye: the awards on Stroilo's chest were adorned with a round medal reading "Twenty Years, Worker-Peasant Red Army." When he had only just arrived at the front headquarters, he had been wearing this medal. Nikita had stared at it quite pointedly. Then he had taken the commissar by the forearm and drawn him aside.

"Listen here, Semyon Nikiforovich, that's not quite ethical. Lots of people here know you're no army veteran. You're a veteran of another organization. Why make a laughingstock of yourself? Take it off!"

Stroilo had then turned several shades of beet red and from that time onward had never worn the decoration, so respected among Soviet military leaders. What could it mean? Why had he put it on again today?

The Poles stood up in the jeep and saluted their colleagues. The gentlemen's ceremony did not last for more than a minute. Rather an unusual fellow for one of these Soviet creeps, this Gradov, thought General Wigor, a former Warsaw architect. Can it be they're not up to anything? Looking at Gradov, it's difficult not to take him at his word . . .

This standing with palms at the visors of hats went on for perhaps another few seconds. The question of a handshake occupied several moments that were naturally awkward.

Should I get out of the jeep and go up to him with an outstretched hand? No, that would be a bit much, thought Wigor. Should I go down to them to shake their hands? wondered the marshal. No, that would be too much even for me. The Kremlin would immediately be notified that I exchanged parting words with "anti-Soviets."

In the end he made a fairwell gesture like a salute addressed to the Poles, then turned and went back inside the castle. Everyone followed him into the headquarters operations room, a large hall with three high glass doors opening onto a terrace and the lake beyond, on the other side of which the Saint Augustine Cathedral rose over the intertwining branches of the trees in the park. In the pond, Nikita noticed, yesterday's envoys from El Alamein were swimming about, looking quite at home.

Everyone was standing around a table on which a map of Germany was unfurled, with another of Pomerania lying atop it. The order for the final storming of Berlin was expected any day. There was even more work to do than usual to coordinate the various armies and divisions.

"What action will be taken with regard to Wigor?" Stroilo suddenly asked.

"What a strange question!" said Nikita with a scowl. "We part company with him. There won't be any more action."

"Surely you're joking, Nikita Borisovich?" Stroilo's voice was getting higher and acquiring a threatening, peculiar strength that was uncharacteristic of the commissar, who seemed to suffer a constant round of humiliations. "Do you mean you're going to let a whole division of anti-Soviets get away? So that they can continue their provocations from abroad?"

Nikita realized that something serious had happened in the night—he leaned on the map of Germany with both hands and gazed steadily into the eyes of the general, who was forever looking over his shoulder, whose face was hardening more and more with each passing minute.

Something serious had indeed happened in the night. Stroilo had spoken with Beria's office on the SMERSH radio three times. By morning, a group of operatives had flown in, clearly intending to deliver a blow to the marshal's immediate security. Among them was a certain Major Eryes, who, if necessary, would be assigned to carry out a particularly important task. A letter brought in a packet with Beria's personal seal contained the final instructions regarding what to do about the Poles: intern Wigor's disarmed division, and in case of resistance take appropriate action; in addition, take immediate measures aimed at creating a healthier atmosphere in the officer cadres of the Reserve Front; take stock of the specifics of continued military action, consider the possibility that new hostile action might flare up.

"You seem to have forgotten, Comrade Lieutenant General," Nikita began slowly, not taking his eyes off the chief of the political section, "that I signed an agreement with Colonel Wigor, that I gave my word of honor, that is, the word of honor of the Reserve Front, which means that—"

"So you're equating yourself with the entire Red Army now, Gradov?" howled Stroilo in a wild access of emotion that was almost theatrical, accompanied by a gesture to one of his staff officers. The latter immediately threw open the doors. The group of operatives, Major Eryes among them, burst into the hall from the corridor outside with rapid steps.

"Red alert!" shouted one of the marshal's "wolfhounds," but he rushed to the glass doors rather than at the operatives. Everyone turned and in the last moment of their lives saw three lads leap onto the terrace, their Faust rockets aimed directly at the hall. The tall one with bright green eyes . . . a burst of fire across the chest could not stop his finger. . . . Three blasts united in one mighty, disordering blow. Bodies collapsed amid clouds of smoke, while the bodiless selves of the people departed from the terrible scene, though they preserved the threads of the final thoughts of the slain.

". . . her, whom I wanted to steal . . ." was what Semyon Stroilo had time to remember.

". . . now I'm passing like a breeze in the shrubs beneath my mother's window . . ." was Nikita Gradov's last shred of consciousness.

CHAPTER EIGHTEEN

Temptation by Word

☆

A funeral procession the width of Bolshaya Pirogovskaya Street was advancing in the direction of the Novodevichy Cemetery. At the front, the sparkling boottops of a company of Guards troops rose and fell slowly. Broad bayonets glinted in the sun. After the gleam of leather and steel came the shine of brass—a Reserve Front marching band filled the length and breadth of the street with Chopin's funeral march, which could not have been more appropriate; after all, he had not betrayed the Poles.

They were carrying the Soviet Union's youngest marshal on a gun carriage. A sizable detachment of officers preceded it, bearing his decorations on cushions. There was a nervous row of mourners, in the center of whom, grieving deeply, were his wife, Veronika, and their twelve-year-old daughter, Verochka, who was holding on to her arm and whose little face was swollen. The widow was supported on the other side by Marshal Rokossovsky. In the first row were also upper-echelon military men who had found time to fly to Moscow for a day from their various fronts and armies. Intermingled with them were the relatives of the heroically fallen marshal: his mother, suffering etched on her nonetheless proud face; his father, whose aspect reminded one of the benign figures of Russian history; his sister, Nina Gradova—yes, yes, that Nina Gradova. . . . Then came the generals of Supreme Headquarters and of the General Staff, fleet admirals, celebrated flyers, leading figures of science, literature, and the arts, an entire column of celebrities, at the very end of which marched the chauffeur Lieutenant Vaskov, along with Captain Slabopetukhovsky, quartermaster of the Reserve Front, and a tear-stained young woman, Lieutenant Tasia Pyzhikov of the Medical Corps, carrying in her womb the child of the marshal whom they were all seeing off on his last journey. At the gates of the Novodevichy Cemetery, separated from the mass of Muscovites by a security cordon, one more crowd of leaders, including diplomats and the representatives of the Allied military missions, in particular Kevin Taliaferro, was waiting for the procession. The company of soldiers, the brass band, the medal bearers, the funeral horses, the carriage bearing the catafalque with its closed coffin, and the column of mourners slowly passed through the monastery gates.

During the ceremony, Taliaferro succeeded in occupying a position from which he could see Veronika. There was no doubt about the significance of the sad event—many experts, after all, had seen the future of Russia in Marshal Gradov. But this significance was lost without a trace or, at the very least, was shoved aside every time he as much as glanced at Veronika. Just think of the elegance, he thought, the nobility that shines through in her every gesture, every nod of her head, how much poetry immediately penetrates the air from every flicker of her eyes, no matter how slight. What would have become of me if I hadn't met her? Red-brick Kremlin, symbol of the world's gloom, you have become the Italy, the Padua and Verona, the Rome and Venice of my love!

Speeches were made, an artillery salute roared, the band soared to a crescendo as the lowering of the coffin began, and then commenced a Russian ritual—everyone threw a handful of dirt into the grave. Ashes to ashes, dust to dust, as they say. Walking away from the grave, the military and civilian dignitaries almost immediately began talking animatedly among themselves. Snatches of the conversation reached Kevin Taliaferro. It seemed that the Man himself, that is, Stalin, had been expected, but for some reason he had not yet shown up. Beria, however, was there, even wiping his pince-nez with a handkerchief. Malenkov, Khrushchev, and Mikoyan were present as well—the level of leadership that had shown up was quite a respectable one. In principle, what we have here before us is a serious example of "polite society," similar to the "anybody who's anybody" gatherings in New York. It was very important to be there for at least a moment, even though that moment might be only a brief flicker before the eyes of the other members of the Nomenklatura. There is no chronicle of high-society events here; only one line would appear in the newspapers: "Workers of the Party and the government attended, along with leaders of literature and art"; however, somewhere in the houses and offices of the smoky, joyless city, obviously, such things were discussed. "So-and-so was at Marshal Gradov's funeral, and so-and-so was not." This was clearly of great significance. A new class, if not an actual hereditary hierarchy, had grown up here. The development of Marxism was very curious. Now the new class had its own Anna Karenina, didn't it?

A mound rose and was covered with flowers and ribbons, a Guards company fired three salvoes into the gray, humdrum April skies, and then it was all over. The mass of people lurched toward the exit slowly, "decently." Taliaferro saw the back of Veronika's head, her golden hair pinned up beneath a small black hat, except for a few touchingly disobedient strands reminiscent of a young girl's ringlets. Princess Grace, the inaccessible dream of a Connecticut Slavicist!

Their son was not at the funeral. She never talks about him, only shrugs her shoulders—"he's somewhere at the front," and then turns away with tears in her eyes. To ask questions would be indiscreet.

What the chief of the political department, Stroilo, had been reporting to Commander Gradov, always in passing and in a friendly, "just between the boys" tone, conformed to the truth, but only in the absolutely literal sense of the word: Veronika Gradov and Kevin Taliaferro were actually "meeting." They would meet on the street, and on the street they would go their separate ways.

It usually happened by the telegraph office. Veronika, for example, would be crossing Gorky Street lost in thought. A tall military dandy in a camel's-hair coat would be coming down the steps and would raise his head. "Mrs. Gradov! What a surprise!" She, naturally, would say in surprise, "As I live and breathe! Colonel Taliaferro, I presume!" Or, to give another example: she is coming down the steps of the telegraph office just as Colonel Taliaferro is crossing the street. "Who's this, then?" he says, using a Russian phrase that he mastered quickly. "Mrs. Marshal Gradov, I presume!" She laughs out loud, a gold filling at the back of her mouth gleaming faintly. "Ha, ha, it looks like I've fallen into the hands of the bourgeois intelligence services!" They go for a stroll in full view of everyone so that there will be no gossip. They talk about the theater: the Maly and the Bolshoi are running once again, and, most important of all, MKhAT, the Moscow Art Theater! They discuss literature. Just think, Akhmatova has published something new, there's a cycle of poems by Pasternak . . . there seems to be some kind of renaissance going on in your country. You should meet my sister-in-law, she's a famous poetess. Oh, I'd be delighted! Well, good-bye, I have to run along!

Sometimes he would see her from a distance, coming out of the entrance to her building accompanied by a thuglike officer, clearly not someone from the front. In the course of his numerous trips to the forward areas, Taliaferro had learned to spot the so-called "frontline chic," by the absence of which it was easy to distinguish the "boys in the rear." The officer always had a crooked smile with a bit of the criminal about it on his lips, while a luxuriant forelock protruded from beneath the brim of his cap and fell over his brow. He would open the door of a large German car and then sit down behind the wheel himself. The chauffeur, obviously. Most likely a military chauffeur assigned to the Gradov family. That's how the Soviet elite lives: they ride around in limousines with despicable, corrupt drivers.

Sometimes Taliaferro and Veronika walked along in the crowd seemingly without noticing each other. Really, there was nothing at all surprising that they often passed one another in the Moscow crowd. What's strange about it if your office is two blocks from her house? Everyone goes about his own business, and one can pass someone several times a day without noticing the person.

One day, not noticing her, he noticed that she, not noticing him, smiled. His heart began pounding like a horse in full gallop. She was smiling not only at the fact that she was not noticing him but also at the fact that he was supposedly taking no notice of her, and in this way it became clear that in reality she did notice that he often appeared at this crowded intersection just going about his own business, not noticing her, and, not noticing him in the slightest, her smile let him know she didn't notice him either, because it would be strange to notice him too often, when a man passes by just like that since his office is right around the corner. . . .

Kevin Taliaferro, to put it bluntly, did not have a great deal of experience in love, though in Paris in the thirties his friend Rest had done a fair amount to give him the education indispensable to any modern man. The tempest of those years had passed, though, and Kevin had dried up a bit and was preparing himself for comfortable, elderly bachelorhood in the Episcopalian style. He laid the blame for his present Byronic mood on Russian literature. This is what the object of a harmless hobby can lead to, here before us is a pure incarnation of temptation by the word! The saddest thing of all is that our romance—romance, ha!, a few strolls along the street—has no future. Even in theoretical terms it's hopeless. Even in Nazi Germany before the war, if I had met a woman, we could have left together. In the Russia of the Reds it's impossible, even though we're allies. The Bolsheviks have created such a climate here that even psychologically it's not possible. In their eyes, a foreigner doesn't even belong to the human race. Even for me there's something unnatural about the very idea of getting close to a Russian woman, much less Veronika Gradov! It's practically a sort of rebellion against Stalin!

In spite of these thoughts, Kevin Taliaferro could not bring himself to stop these strolls along Gorky Street and froze in his tracks like a schoolboy at the slightest opening of the door to her building. Even the repulsive chauffeur walking her little dog—a pampered poodle in impoverished Moscow!—aroused feelings in him that he was rather too old for.

He saw her three days after the funeral. She was in a spring outfit—a short jacket with broad shoulders. I don't know what has happened to fashion in

Paris under the Germans, he thought, but on Piccadilly she could more than hold her own.

By the telegraph office—well, of course by the telegraph office. . . . In romantic novels lovers "meet by the cliff they love on the ocean shore," that is, they met by the telegraph office. . . . He went right up to her and said, "Mrs. Gradov, allow me to express my deepest condolences. For me, Marshal Gradov was always the embodiment of all the qualities of a hero!"

She shook his hand, and they went up Gorky Street together.

From time to time they caught people staring at them strangely. In that crowd, an American officer and a beautiful woman in a stylish outfit were like visitors from another planet.

By the end of the war, however, visitors of this sort had begun to appear in Moscow in ever-greater numbers: liaison missions were growing, and there was a constant movement of personnel, both military and civilian; the English had even begun selling their newspaper *The British Ally* in the kiosks, and the glossy American magazine *Amerika* circulated widely. Never at any time since the Bolshevik Revolution had there been so many lively contacts with the West. The clearly pro-Western tastes of the beauties of Moscow were beginning to contribute to this as well. Maybe things will go even further? Maybe Russia is ready to come back to us? In that case, maybe my being in love doesn't look so hopeless after all, Taliaferro thought.

All of a sudden, Veronika began to tell him about her son. At the end of 1943, seventeen-year-old Boris had run off to the front. We couldn't find him for a year and a half. Just imagine, the commander of the Reserve Front was unable to find his own son! We were almost sure he had been killed. Finally, quite recently, he was found; it turned out he had been on secret assignment in the German rear all this time. It just gave me chills all over, Kevin (yes, just like that, with no formality: Kevin; it gave her chills all over, Kevin!), when I pictured my boy on secret assignment in the enemy's rear! In short, I was feeling triumphant: he's alive, the war is coming to an end, they promised me he would be home soon—and then, suddenly, something dreadful happened. They won't tell me anything, but Boris has disappeared again. . . . Well, how do you like that? Isn't that too much for one not-so-young woman? Taliaferro, filled with emotion, sympathy, pity, delight, and some passages of strings from Mozart that were hovering in the air, suddenly burst out, "Listen, Veronika, spring is all around us now! Why don't we go to Sokolniki Park? There are so many birch trees there, it's so Russian!"

She looked at him with a wistful smile. Surely she loves Blok, she couldn't not love him. Perhaps at this moment she's thinking, almost like Blok's line, "Well, this one is in love too." A bit of English culture flashed through Taliaferro's mind: "Or ere those showes were old with which she follow'd my poor father's body!" It wasn't about that, though, that wasn't what he had in mind at all. . . . It was nothing more than the closeness of souls, ordinary human sympathy, a desire to distract the attention of the adored creature from the gloom of military matters, to return to her beauty, to nature, to the ideal Russia, if only for an hour. . . .

"All right, let's go." She smiled more cheerfully. "Are we going to take the metro?"

"No, wait a bit, I've got a car!"

He left her on Pushkin Boulevard and rushed off to the embassy garage for his Buick. Coming back, he was trembling just like the antiquated engine: maybe she hadn't waited, maybe she'd left? The lovely creature, however, was sitting on the same bench, leafing through *The British Ally*. Next to her was the ideal old Russian woman with her knitting, the true embodiment of Russian culture, Pushkin's nurse, Arina Rodionovna.

The sun was beginning to set as they headed for Sokolniki Park. It was reflected in numerous puddles on the main walk, it modestly adorned the trunks of the obviously symbolic birches. The park was empty. Kevin and Veronika slowly circumnavigated the puddles. Sometimes she extended a hand to him, and he supported her as she made a leap over the small expanse of water. You could almost become intoxicated from breathing this wonderful air, that is, the air around this beautiful woman, he thought, if she didn't smoke so much. She smokes nonstop. Interesting that she smokes Chesterfields. The smoke reminds you of a bar, of the atmosphere of a drunken throng, when sincere glances are betrayed at the counter. Of course that means those who frequent bars of that kind, not us!

She told him about the fallen marshal. Isn't it strange to hear that a strategic concept of the Second World War has the name of Nikita and has just been laid in the earth to the sound of salvoes and brass bands? When Nikita had been the young hero in 1922, he had met a dreamy young girl named Veronika at a campfire by night, and this campfire was crackling on a rock above the vast expanse of the sea in a wind she said was "purely Homeric," a wind from the Odyssey. . . . And then they had lived afterward— what the hell, fairly happily on the whole, even though he suffered from nightmares about the Civil War.

"Believe it or not, I was a first-class tennis player, ha-ha, champion of the Western Military District."

"Believe it or not, Veronika, I was a champion too, at the New Haven Country Club."

"Oh, so you're a tennis player too, that's very nice. We'll have a match this summer, unless . . ."

"What do you mean, 'unless'?"

"Well, let's just say we'll have a match. . . ."

"Tell me about your family."

"My family was his family." She told him about the Gradovs, about the evenings in Silver Forest, where it sometimes seemed as though nothing had happened to Russia . . .

"What did you say, Veronika? Why are you silent?"

After a painful interruption, she said, "It was from there they took me away."

"What do you mean, 'took you away,' Veronika, my dear?"

"Arrested."

"Pardon me, I don't understand, you mean they arrested your husband? I've heard Marshal Gradov once did four years in a military prison, but surely they couldn't have arrested you, madame?"

At every step she looked over her shoulder. At first it seemed to him that she was looking around in order to imprint the beauty of the slowly setting sun on her memory, but then he had the sensation that there was something of a nervous habit about it.

"When you talk about a military prison, I hope you don't have something like the castle of the Count of Monte Cristo in mind, Colonel. He worked in a mine and nearly kicked the bucket from hunger. As far as 'Mrs. Marshal' is concerned, she spent four years in a logging camp, in a lousy little felt manufacturing factory, in rotting barracks, and—"

In saying this, she did not look back over her shoulder but instead directly at him, as though she were asking, "Well, Kevin, has your image of the Soviet Anna Karenina crumbled now?" Her hand with its cigarette and her lips were trembling! If only I could cuddle up to those lips, just for a moment!

"Enough about it!" She flung the cigarette away and walked straight through the puddles.

He rushed forward. "I hope you'll tell me more about those days!"

"Don't get your hopes up!" she said sharply. "It's getting dark. Time we both went home!"

For several minutes they walked along rapidly in silence, spray flying in all directions. Her rubber-soled shoes and silk stockings were dirty, but the rustle of her skirt, the rustle of her skirt . . . right out of Dostoevsky, Polina and Alexei . . .

Two Russian chaps came wandering toward them. Taliaferro tried to divert his companion's thoughts from her somber recollections.

"Look at those two fellows, Veronika! Regular Turgenev characters, aren't they?"

Veronika suddenly shuddered all over and looked strangely at the two men, who were walking in different directions. They went on for another fifty yards or so, then she suddenly grabbed Taliaferro by the arm. "Kevin, I'm afraid of those Turgenev characters! Turn around!"

He turned and saw that the men had stopped and were watching the two of them walk away. Their faces were no longer visible in the twilight, but both secret police operatives and curious park officials might have followed them with their eyes that way. One had to remind oneself of the peculiar features of this country, its ever-blooming paranoia, every minute, thought Kevin.

"Don't you understand, they're everywhere," whispered Veronika. "Every time you and I meet on Gorky Street, they immediately show up around us. This evening, when I stayed behind on the boulevard, straightaway they stuck some lousy old woman with her knitting on my tail. And when we arrived here, didn't you notice the 'ambulance'? Do you think it was really an ambulance?"

By now it was quite dark. There was no one around. Any characters from classical literature were out of sight and out of mind. It was only early evening, the moon was waxing—a sure sign of forthcoming profits. It was a night in the last week of what was already called the Second World War, if, of course, one didn't count Japan, which one had to count. They didn't care about Japan now, though. Eyes were already shining among the birch trees; that was what mattered.

She took him by the hand and drew him from the walk into the trees. "Oh hell," she whispered, "let them all go to hell." She went on, "The bastards, the animals!" She was on the verge of tears. "There's no one there anymore," she continued.

Forgetting about his Parisian experiences, he put his hand on her shoulder, as though she were a trusted friend. Don't weep from loneliness, he wanted to say, you're not alone now, he wanted to go on, but he said nothing. She unbuttoned his coat. "Well, go on, kiss me!" she said. He put his mouth to her tender, though smoky, lips. She unbuttoned her own jacket and blouse, the buttons of her soft vest. He took her breast in his hand. . . . "Come on, this way! Over there, don't you see?" He saw the stump of a freshly felled tree. He sat down. "Well, where are they? Where are your buttons?"

"There aren't any, it's a zipper."

"Ha, ha, I've never seen one before."

"Allow me, I'll—"

He quickly remembered his Parisian experiences. She moaned, now throwing her head back, now resting it on his shoulder. "Bastards, scoundrels, take that, take that!" she muttered. "I hate you, I hate you . . ."

"Forget about hatred," he urged her gently. "Forget about everything, dear Veronika, I'll never give you back to anyone again . . ."

. . .

"Now there's a woman!" said Lavrenty Pavlovich Beria, apparently with some delight, after Nugzar Lamadze had told him about Marshal Gradov's wife and her artistic endeavors. Then again, with Beria you could never be sure if he was showing delight or just sinister irony.

"There's a Russian woman for you!" Beria continued, as though he were going on to deeper reflections. "Remember, Nugzar: 'She can stop a galloping horse in his tracks, walk fearlessly into a flaming hut'?"

Recalling this line from Nekrasov, which had long been a catchphrase of sorts, Beria was speaking as though it were not the "horse" and the "hut" he had in mind but other things that were more or less homonyms in Russian—"hut" and "cunt." Then he smacked his palms together, peered at Nugzar over the top of his pince-nez, and smiled as though he were imagining himself in the place of the U.S. military attaché. "On a stump, you say? Not bad!"

Lamadze, as always, was playing up to his boss, trying to figure out his train of thought, but he couldn't manage it. Beria came out from behind his desk and paced back and forth in the office, then burst out laughing in a distant corner and once again clapped his hands together. "And they say that experience from the camps can't be put to use!" Then, he strode rapidly up to Nugzar, who was sitting in an armchair, and shook him by the shoulder. "Why aren't you saying anything, Nugzarka? Why do you always prompt me to make the decisions? Don't you understand the circumstances? In a forest at night, on a stump; with an American—with a spy, what do you think! Well, say something, *sheni deda tovtkhan*, what do you suggest?"

"I think, Lavrenty Pavlovich, that we mustn't let an opportunity like this get away. In my opinion, she wants to leave with him, but there's no way we can let her go without—"

"Then do something!" said Beria and immediately turned his attention to other matters. That is, to his other crimes, as an ungrateful posterity would say.

The salvoes of the final victory salute had already thundered away, the banners of the Wehrmacht and the Waffen-SS had been tossed at the base of the Lenin Mausoleum—in other words, at the feet of Stalin—when, at the beginning of June 1945, a highly significant dinner took place in the flat of the late Marshal Gradov.

The dinner was not at all a large, formal affair, as it would be for only three people, but Veronika brought Agasha in from Silver Forest for three days to help with the arrangements for the preparation and serving.

The first of the guests was General Nugzar Lamadze. For the occasion he was decked out in a brand-new gray suit that fell flatteringly over his lithe frame. He had selected a paisley tie that went well with the suit, along with a matching handkerchief that protruded slightly from his breast pocket, so that no one would have the urge to blow his nose on it. It would not have occurred to anyone, of course, that this pleasant young man from the Caucasus was a high-ranking officer in a fearful secret organization.

The lady of the house met him wearing a dark cherry-red dress that looked as though it had just left its wearer's shoulders and did not intend to stay on her chest for long. "Veronika, my darling, I swear by the Alazan valley, you're irresistible!" Lamadze found it necessary to exclaim, and not without pleasure. "If I weren't here in an official capacity, ha-ha, you wouldn't recognize me right now, my darling Veronika. Nugzar the rake has become a respectable family man. You should take my Lamar under your wing, she's still antisocial here in the capital . . ."

The table was perfectly appointed: crystal, china, napkins in silver rings. In keeping with the Russian tradition, all the drinks were laid out on the dinner table. There was vodka—both ordinary and lemon-flavored—in heavy decanters, and bottles of wine and cognac along with zakuski that had come partly from the Supply Department of the High Command of the Commissariat for Defense and partly from Agasha's not insignificant private reserves in Silver Forest. It was precisely the Russian tradition that the principal invitee they were expecting preferred, even though he was a foreigner.

After ambling over the apartment's fine Turkmen rugs, Nugzar sat down at the table and poured himself a small tumbler of vodka. Veronika sat down beside him with her ever-present cigarette. They were just on the point of renewing one of their onerous yet exciting conversations that, it would be more correct to say, had the effect of turning Veronika's whole being upside down, when the chauffeur, Shevchuk, entered the dining room. Today his forelock was slicked down, his boots gleaming, while the buttons of his dress tunic and lieutenant's shoulder straps, protruding like small wings, vied with them. He was clearly planning to dine, even though no one had invited him.

Calmly, his mouth twisted into his unchanging hooligan's grin, he pushed back a chair, sat down, and only then asked, quite according to the rules of etiquette, "I trust you don't object, Veronika Yevgenievna?"

Lately, Leonid Shevchuk had gone nuts in a big way. The marshal's wife, whom he referred to as no less than "his lady love" behind her back, had stopped receiving him and was now traipsing around with some non-Russian officer, maybe even a Yugoslav, and Shevchuk had already filed a couple of reports about this with the competent authorities. Now another piece of shit had appeared on the horizon. That broad must be out of her mind! One day he had even had a jaunty little conversation with her: "So, Veronika, I guess you want everybody to know what kind of an alley cat I've made out of you? Maybe I should tell your Yugoslavian comrades about your 'amateur productions' in the camp?" Instead of the desired result, he received a regular hysterical fit in reply, the throwing of unbecoming objects, in particular a book not written in Russian.

That evening in his living quarters, that is, in the basement of that very building, Shevchuk downed a quarter liter of vodka, cleaned himself up, and then appeared in order to dot all the *i*'s. As for Veronika, she stood up as soon as he sat down and triumphantly walked off to the kitchen in her whore's dress as though she were going on an errand. Now that swine was staring at her in that unclean way. Well, all right, let's play this staring game, Comrade Shit, we'll see who wins.

"I'm Leonid," he said, introducing himself to the guest and defiantly reaching for the decanter.

"Well, then, get lost, Leonid!" quietly replied the guest sitting sideways at the table.

"How do you mean?" said the uncomprehending Shevchuk.

"Gather together everything that you have here, and evaporate, Shevchuk, Leonid Iliich, born 1915," said the guest in such a voice that the former low-ranking guard understood straightaway whom the camp bosses always imitated, and whose voices; this was one of those primary voices, as it were.

"How can I do that, comrade, where will I go?" He was still trying to flail his legs like a half-crushed ant, though he had already stood up from the table and had straightened his jacket.

The guest drew out a small notepad with the dreaded letters KGB on it, scribbled something, tore it out, and handed it over. "Go to Kuznetsky Most, Number Eight, tomorrow. Show this to the Pass and Permits Department. That's it. Now get out!"

When Veronika looked into the dining room from the kitchen, the bothersome chauffeur was no longer to be seen.

"Everything's been taken care of, Veronika," smiled Nugzar buoyantly. "He'll never try to blackmail you again."

She came closer and put her leg, which had almost entirely emerged from the slit in her dress, on a chair. "Listen, you devil, how do you know he was blackmailing me? What do you have here, listening devices in the walls or what?"

He smiled good-naturedly. "Well, what do you think? It was Marshal Gradov, so what do you think it would be? It was a matter of great state importance!"

"What does that mean?" She laughed with what seemed to be her former impudence, but he could see she was showing signs of fear. "So you heard everything?"

"Take it easy, take it easy," he said, pacifying the air with his palm. "We heard quite a lot, but not everything, of course. As for where we heard all this from, you'll have to excuse me. From here it was a bit worse. But that's not important, Veronika, you can rest easy. It has nothing to do with our business here. Furthermore, don't call me a devil. I may be no angel, but I'm still not a devil!"

Nugzar had appeared in the neighborhood almost immediately after the business in Sokolniki Park. He hovered around for a day or two, making no secret of the fact that his passings were no coincidence. Then he suddenly arrived with a bouquet of flowers that had obviously come not from the gardens in the suburbs of Moscow but from some special hothouse.

"What's this, cousin, are you courting me now?" asked Veronika, automatically coquettish, even though she already knew, of course, what kind of "courting" was going on.

"Ah, I only wish!" he sighed. "Unfortunately, I'm here on official business. Listen, Veronika, it looks like you're going to have to introduce me to Colonel Taliaferro."

"Whatever for?" Veronika asked sharply, as though she were not frightened at all but, on the contrary, indignant.

Nugzar smirked: he could see perfectly well that she was trembling with fear. "Official business, my dear. State interests. It has only an indirect bearing on your personal affairs."

"But it does have a bearing just the same?" she said, again in a shriek. "Whatever for?"

"This is what for," he said, suddenly raising his voice. "You're the widow of a twice-decorated Hero of the Soviet Union, a Cavalier of the Order of Suvorov, First Class, not to mention holder of half a hundred other decorations, Marshal of the Soviet Union Nikita Gradov. Don't you understand that your personal business isn't entirely your own business?"

This conversation marked the opening of the organs' campaign of psychological warfare against Veronika the beauty. The "spooks," or the "Turgenev characters" as she now called them, lay in wait for her everywhere: they followed on her heels, stood on guard by the staircase, drove by in cars, grinning at her cynically. It now seemed to her that a snout in the service of the nation was protruding from behind every birch tree in Sokolniki. One day while she and Kevin were kissing, they had suddenly been blinded by three bright lanterns. Losing his head, the diplomat was about to rush at the lights with his fists, but the lanterns had already disappeared, there was nothing but the wild laughing of the wood spirits running away among the tree trunks.

That evening a tire on the Buick turned up punctured. Taliaferro was beside himself. Veronika could not go to his place and could not bring herself to invite him to her apartment. In the huge city, there was no place for them. He could not make an official complaint. The State Department and the Pentagon would surely prefer to recall him from Moscow in order to avoid a scandal.

"We need to get married, as soon as possible!" he insisted. "We have to go to the marriage registration office, to, what's it called, your ZAGS." She was silent but offered no objection.

After one of these outbursts from the American, Nugzar struck up a most peculiar conversation with her. "You know, in spite of all his services, Nikita's reputation was not exactly beyond reproach. Those Faust charges saved him from an end of another sort, though, of course, a marshal's funeral would have been provided for in any case. What do I mean by that? Why something sinister? Come now, don't exaggerate, pretty lady! How can you prove that I'm insinuating anything? It's ridiculous! I only meant that my cousin's views were far from perfect. Forgive me for saying so, but it seemed to a lot of the comrades that Marshal Gradov was nursing some far-reaching plans. Tell me, Veronika, he didn't leave anything behind, did he? Why do you say, 'What rubbish'? I'm 'smiling like a snake'? There's something not right about the way you exaggerate, my dear. It's just that it seemed to some of the comrades that he might have left some writings behind. You aren't hiding anything, are you, Veronika?"

Now he saw that she was genuinely frightened. He laid a reassuring hand on her trembling arm. "There, there, no need to get so excited. Think about your daughter. Without a mother's care, anything at all might happen to a girl."

She began breathing heavily. He poured her a glass of wine. "Good wine always helps. No need for a theatrical production, Lyubov Yarovaya. For the time being, nothing has happened to your daughter, isn't that right? All you have to do is think about your children. As for me, I'm always thinking about my own, about Shotie and Tsisan. So you mustn't forget about Vera and Boris. What about Boris? What do you mean, what about Boris? Of course I know about Boris. We always knew about Boris. You're still not convinced that we knew? You should have thought about where to turn for information. To the point, though, about Boris. Not all the comrades are sure that he has ideal views on things. He is, of course, a hero, a brave young man. The war is over, it's true, but he's still needed. I hope he'll come back soon, if nothing happens to him. What do you mean, what might happen? Anything at all can happen to a living man. So what if the war has ended? The very same thing can happen even when one isn't at war. Philosophically speaking, of course."

Totally shaken by the conversation, Veronika stopped seeing Kevin for several days. When she heard his voice over the telephone, she put the receiver down. She tried not to go to the window so as not to see the laughably lovable figure of the aging boy striding by the telegraph office. Connecticut . . . the "c" in the middle isn't pronounced . . . a professorship at Yale . . . a hideaway in New York on Riverside Drive with windows on the 'Gudzon,' as the Russians pronounce it, though of course it's called the Hudson . . . we'll spend the night there when we go to concerts at Carnegie Hall . . . for some reason I picture it all in a clear autumn light, leaves red and dark purple. . . . In the winter we'll go to Bermuda—they say everyone there goes to Bermuda in the winter. . . . Everything is finished, why shouldn't all of this happen? They'll destroy me, she thought. As soon as he leaves, that'll be the end of me. And the end of all of those dear to me, as well. No reason why they should be left. . . .

In a panic she took Verulya to Silver Forest to be looked after by her grandmother. Mary sensed something was up. "Maybe I should take the girl to Tiflis? Bo can take a vacation."

"Oh, no, don't, I don't know myself, Mary my dear, I can't say anything, just don't take your eyes off Verulka." She jumped out from the garden gate. On the corner there were two large men smoking lazily. Were they even here, the "Turgenev characters"?

Suddenly everything changed. Nugzar surfaced again, all sweetness and smiles, making thoughtful gestures. He was afraid she had misunderstood him. Why this panic? After all, had anyone said anything against Colonel Taliaferro? Relations between our two countries have never been so good, and they'll be even better. What an enemy we brought down together! Colonel Taliaferro is a good officer, an honest, well-educated man. A Russophile at that. Let's talk everything over calmly, without hysterics, weighing everything. Of course, I work for the state, but I'm also a human being and even a relative. . . .

In these circumstances, the strange trio—Veronika, Nugzar, and Taliaferro—approached their ceremonial dinner.

Kevin also came in civilian clothes—a herringbone jacket and a knit tie.

"I beg your pardon for not having told you that there would be one more guest, Mr. Taliaferro," said Veronika with great formality. "This is the cousin of my late husband, Nugzar Lamadze. He appeared quite unexpectedly, like—" Here she burst out laughing. "—like a devil from a snuffbox!"

"Ai-yai-yai, Veronika," said Nugzar affectedly. In his stylish suit and loud tie, and with his hot-blooded Caucasian ways, he looked something like the American idea of the "Latin lover." "Ai-yai-yai, 'devil' again?"

Veronika was amazed that the all-powerful NKVD agent felt awkward in the presence of a foreigner.

"Of course I'm no angel, but still, I'm not a devil!" he said, repeating his favorite joke.

"I can see that," said Kevin.

"What?" Nugzar seemed to shudder slightly.

"That you're no angel," Kevin said with a smile.

"And you, Mr. Taliaferro?" Nugzar squinted at the American in an obvious attempt to overcome his strange self-consciousness. "You're not an angel either, are you?"

Veronika said cheerfully, "Sit down at the table, you two devils!"

At the table Kevin leaned over to his neighbor after scarcely one drink and asked, "Are you from the NKVD, Nugzar?"

The "Latin lover" was so surprised that he dropped a mushroom he had had his eye on for some time on the table. "What makes you think that, Mr. Taliaferro?"

"You can tell right away," the American explained kindly. "As soon as I saw you, I thought: well, today Madame Gradov has a visitor from the secret police."

Everyone laughed good-naturedly, but Nugzar could not stop when the others had fallen silent. He was still guffawing, louder and louder, wiping his face with his red handkerchief, and then began cackling so much again that Kevin and Veronika looked at each other with alarm.

"Oh, you slay me, Kevin!" Nugzar said at last. "I'll have to tell my colleagues, they'll get a laugh out of it too! Well then, let's drink to the American's perceptive eye!"

"Don't enlarge that to include all Americans," said Kevin. "I assure you, any of my colleagues would think you were a python handler if you introduced yourself. With me, it just comes from my studies of Russian literature."

"That's great!" exclaimed Nugzar. "Come on, let's drink to Russian literature! This nation hasn't produced a single damned thing of beauty except for literature and the secret police, as you put it. Do you find that funny? Why are you laughing? You can laugh, don't be afraid! Now that I've been unmasked, we can call a spade a spade. Tell me, Kevin, what are America's plans in the Pacific?"

All three started to laugh again, even though nothing funny had been said. It was as though the secret police were introducing some sort of laughing gas through their secret niches. This went on through the entire dinner. Agasha even looked into the dining room several times. What's going on? There was constant laughing and a ringing of glasses coming together, as though a whole host were strolling around, when in fact there was only Veronikochka and Nugzarchik (Agasha still remembered him from the dances of 1925) and one very nice citizen who was not one of ours.

Some two hours later Nugzar stood up to say good-bye. Naturally, he gave a ceremonial kiss to the Atlantic ally and made him give his word that he would come to Georgia for a wild boar hunt—that doesn't mean, Kevin, that the boar will be hunting people, but the other way around. Swinging back and forth slightly, in the proper style, he took his raincoat down from a hanger, stopped on the way to pick up the telephone receiver, into which he growled "Lamadze," and then moved toward the door. In the doorway he pinched Veronika's ear and whispered, "A fine fellow!" after which he vanished.

Silence now reigned in the apartment. Veronika put out the light in the entrance hall and took off her shoes. Then she thought, I'll go into that room in the nude! and pulled her dress over her head. When she came in, the dining room was dark as well, with only the huge portrait of Stalin on the wall of the telegraph office, illuminated by searchlights, visible through the windows. Colonel Taliaferro, after turning out the light, had also transformed himself considerably—he had removed his jacket and loosened his necktie. He was shaken by the appearance of the naked nymph. There she is, he thought, the reward for having gone through the torments of Tantalus! "Stop, stop," she whispered. "That's the way, come on. What's this, why are there only buttons here?"

They spent the entire night making love like kids of twenty, and toward morning she put a finger to her lips and wrote in pencil on a notepad: "This is our first and last night, Kevin. They're demanding that I work for them, that I spy on you. Otherwise they won't let me go."

Having read the note, he took the pencil from her, turned to another page of the pad, and wrote one word: "Agree." After a moment's thought he added an exclamation mark. Then he tore out both pages, crumpled them up, and set them on fire with his lighter. He tossed them up and down in his hands until they burned down to ashes.

The nightingales in Silver Forest were now beginning to sing exquisitely, right up until darkness. Nina, sitting on the steps of the terrace, quoted Zoshchenko: "They want their grub, that's why they're singing!" Mary Vakhtangovna glanced in her direction from afar and saw that things were not as simple as they seemed: it looked as though her daughter was in love again. Nina followed the fireflies in flight with her eyes. Sometimes they flew right up to her nose and, after hanging there for their allotted number of seconds in Diogenes-like reflection, melted back into the darkness. Their flares flickered all over the garden, rising high as the treetops, like momentary imitators of the planets. I'll tell him he should paint that sort of primitive landscape, thought Nina, an early summer night with fireflies. Let him work at it, and I'll provide the nightingales' song. It will be a primitive work, wretched human pity, a farewell to the war.

Mary and Veronika were sitting some distance away on a bench, keeping an eye on the girls flashing back and forth. Nikita's death had once again drawn them together.

"Look there, my dear," said Mary, with gentle Georgian intakes of breath. "Do you see those shrubs beneath the window of the bedroom? That day, and at that very moment, I'm sure of it, something drew me to the window. We'd only just removed the storm windows and opened everything up . . . fresh air, the smell of spring . . . and all of a sudden I had a feeling that Nikita was passing by . . . well, not so much passing as floating by quickly, on one side, through the bushes . . . I'm sure it was him saying good-bye to me . . ."

Veronika kissed her on the cheek and caressed her shoulder. "Mary, I don't want to tell anyone for the time being, but I might be leaving for America soon."

"But what about Babochka? Aren't you going to wait for him?" asked the old woman, as though she were not surprised at hearing of America.

"I have to leave as soon as possible," whispered Veronika. "It's very important. For everyone. For Borka, too. Believe me, Mary, it's not only me I'm saving."

"Whom can I believe, if not you? You're the mother of my grandchildren."

They kissed and embraced each other. Ninka, jealous, came up to them. "Can't you let me in there in the middle?" Now they were sitting, arms around one another, the three of them.

"There at the funeral," Veronika said suddenly. "The woman he loved was there. I wanted to find her, but it was impossible."

"You must find her," said Mary.

"What for?" replied Veronika with a shrug. "He loved, now he's gone. He blazed up and then went out. The whole world flickers past that way."

CHAPTER NINETEEN

The Ozone Layer

★

"Cecilia Naumovna, there's a call for you!" From the corridor came the sound of the voice of the neighbors' daughter, Marina, a well-behaved schoolgirl in the seventh grade. In the kitchen, meanwhile, the usual women, the tenants of the building, went on shouting at one another, or caterwauling, as they put it, in the kitchen, almost making a scene but not quite. The huge communal apartment on Furman Street, housing twelve families in addition to the solitary Cecilia, was continuing to live in its beehive of a routine of kitchen-toilet-corridor.

"Hey, Naumovna!" Shura Pogozhina, the acknowledged directress of the women in the flat, yelled in a hoarse voice from the kitchen. She had been at her post by her burner on the stove since morning, stirring things up and directing communal life from there. "Go bang on her door, Marinka, maybe she didn't hear!"

Cecilia Rosenbloom had moved into the apartment, her father's home, in 1939. Before that she and Kirill had lived for several happy years together in the celebrated Moscow building "Hall of Commerce," which graced Nogin, formerly Solyanka, Square. This building, which in prerevolutionary times had housed the major Moscow stock market and an agglomeration of capitalist firms, was now home to a throng of Soviet bureaucrats, ministers, and government departments. In the thirties some of its corridors, with their hotel mirrors and elevators with wire-mesh doors, belonged to the trade union housing authority. There, in the former hotel rooms, middle-level Party functionaries took up residence according to a system of vouchers. A legend of the Revolution, the celebrated "Machine-Gun Anka," had even lived there; it was rumored that her daughter Zinaida had been fathered by a foreigner. At night in 1937, the carpeted roads of commerce, even though worn thin over the preceding two decades, still muffled the tread of the "competent authorities."

One day after Kirill's arrest, Cecilia was awakened by the constant squeaking of someone's doors. She looked out into the corridor and saw several of her neighbors already gathered there. Everyone was silently watching eight-year-old Raechka Keller, who, with a smile that seemed fixed not on her mouth but on her cheek, was swinging back and forth on the heavy door to her room, in which she lived with her father, Ilyusha Keller, chairman of the Social Sciences Department at the Moscow State Pedagogical Institute. Nyusha, Raechka's mother, had failed to return home from work at the same institute several months before. The room was dark, and nothing could be seen except for the heavy curtains billowing up in the huge open window.

"What's all this, Raechka, how is it that you're swinging in the middle of the night?" said Cecilia, about to begin bustling around, still not comprehending that something dreadful had happened.

"This is how I swing," answered Raechka in a sad, endearing voice. One of the neighbors made a decision and tried to pull Raechka down from the door, but she would not give in. Still understanding nothing, Cecilia dashed into the room. "Ilyusha! Ilyusha!" There was no reply. On the windowsill she saw the print of a rubber-soled shoe. She looked down—Ilyusha, arms and legs spread out, was lying motionless on the pavement. Moisture from a water sprinkler cart left out for the night trickled beside him.

But life went on. However, the People's Commissariat for Metallurgy began to occupy the old hotel rooms in 1939. Cecilia was unceremoniously ordered to gather her belongings together: "Register at your father's address again, Rosenbloom!" Thus she had ended up in the communal flat on Furman Street, living with her modest "Papa Matvey," who had sat out the last twenty years as a bookkeeper in the district housing authority and spent all of his free time at his favorite occupation—sewing magnificent boots from the material supplied him by customers—which brought him, somehow or other, some extra income—just a little. What would you expect? In the end, Cecilia remained alone even on Furman Street, unless one counts, of course, twelve families for neighbors, because "Papa Matvey" suddenly, without making any trouble for anyone, took off for parts unknown, where maybe he would no longer have to conceal his gaze and shuffle his feet in feigned old age.

After the death of Cecelia's grandfather, the neighbors began to turn their eyes toward her room, and some of them even said straight out that she had a disproportionately large area of living space. "Fourteen square meters for one slovenly woman, it's a bit unfair, don't you think, comrades?" Naryshkin the notary public was heard to say, raising her voice, from time to time. Oddly enough, it was Auntie Shura Pogozhin who came to her defense. One evening, she showed up at Cecilia's room with a half-liter bottle. "Celia, let's have a drink to rest our souls!" Tears were trickling down the bewhiskered face of the old woman who wasn't yet old. "Eh, Matvey, Matvey," she said over and over again, sniffling. "Oh, Matvey, Matvey! Believe it or not, Celia, I never said a word about his sewing boots!" After they had embraced, they proceeded to drink the entire half liter, and from that time on, all discussion about her square meters ceased: no one in the flat was mightier than Shura.

"I'm coming, I'm coming!" Cecilia jumped out into the corridor without a skirt on, realized it with a start, rushed back, and wrapped a towel around her sizable backside, which produced an effect that was, to use one of Iosif Vissarionovich's favorite expressions, "typically not right." She ran back again and rushed about among her countless books until she had the redeeming idea of putting on an overcoat.

An atmosphere of crude guffawing already prevailed in the corridor. Next to the entrance doors the tough adolescent Sranin was tightening the spokes on his pirate's bicycle. Every time he saw Cecilia Naumovna, this young lout, who for some reason was proud of his surname, which has toilet overtones in Russian, broke into a popular anti-Semitic ditty of the time. Spicing his performance with a Yiddish accent, he crooned about a Jewish mama stuffing her Chaim with a plump chicken drumstick.

Auntie Shura often hissed at him or took a swipe at him with a broom, but he invariably finished his impressive singing.

"An artist!" Papa Sranin, an attendant from the Sandunov Baths, would say with feeling if he happened to be in the vicinity when the couplets were completed. The adolescent Sranin, having sung the song to the end, would immediately forget about "the Jewess Cecilia" and begin to think about what he could rip off that day while flying down Sretenka Street on his bicycle.

Meanwhile, the deep voice of Nadia Rumyantsev sounded from the telephone box. "Come on, Celia, a person could kick the bucket waiting for you! Rolling out into the corridor with a bare bum again?"

After their meeting at the gates of Lefortovo prison at the very beginning of the war, Cecilia and Nadia had become intimate friends, despite the elemental differences in their political and philosophical views. Nadia always came to the rescue of the disorganized Marxist. One day she came in and saw Cecilia by the stove. The silly fool, as usual she's reading the works of the "Simbirsk idiot"—Lenin—and preparing supper for herself; in fact, what she does is, she smears a frying pan with a candle and then uses it to scorch some potato peel she's managed to beg. It turned out that Cecilia had never registered with a single store and had practically no idea how to go about it; all her ration coupons were going to waste. A paradoxical situation emerged: she had been asked to leave the Institute of the International Workers' Movement even before the war as the unrepentant wife of an enemy of the people, and of course, they would not take her on staff anywhere. Practically a "free cossack," Cecilia subsisted as a lecturer for the Party's Enlightenment Society, but of course they were a lot of Marxist riffraff and didn't want to hear about accepting a loner into their coupon-rationing system. In short, it was croak on your own!

Nadia Rumyantsev herself had worked for many years as a proofreader at the Pravda publishing house, and though her pay was microscopic, she had a "V" ration card and received all the goods she needed. In general, for better or for worse, she managed to register her friend at least for a bread ration, to get her 400 grams of black bread. She took them by the throats at the District Executive Committee, bringing her demagogy with her: "A person makes the word of the Party flesh, and you wear her out with hunger?" Then she introduced the simpleton to the local "princess," Gudial Lyubomirovna Megapolis, the director of a school dining hall on Moroseika Street. "Here, Gudial Lyubomirovna, this comrade will be able to compose inspired patriotic school essays for your daughter Osanna."

Gudial Lyubomirovna sang out, "How curious!," studied Cecilia's bunch of aimless ration cards for a long time, shook it like a dead bird, then said with an unexpectedly broad, bright smile, "Come along, my dear, bring your pail along to the back door and give us your first name and patronymic. Just don't give us your surname, whatever you do!"

They now poured lentil soup into Cecilia's pail almost regularly, and sometimes even an edible viscous concoction called "soufflé." The lentil soup had to be allowed to settle, of course. After three hours or so, all the muck had settled on the bottom and the beans containing the nourishment had floated to the surface. The "soufflé" was consumed immediately, sometimes even before Cecilia got it home. The very same Nadia Rumyantsev, by the way, discovered while burrowing in the things of the late Matvey a savings account passbook with a tidy sum, a clear result of his underground work as a cobbler. She insisted that Cecilia be recognized as the legal heir.

The very same Nadia Rumyantsev, incidentally, even before dealing with all of the red tape of the ration coupons, had managed to rescue Cecilia from her temporary but nearly disastrous evacuation, where she almost departed her "existence as a protein body" at the godforsaken Ruzaevka Station. But that's another story, one that has no place in this novel.

Here we wish only to point out the luck Cecilia had in the world of "objective reality." There suddenly appeared a strong, pure friend who did so much good for her. She gave and received, we want to add, because even though "Celka" was of very little practical use herself, Nadia's good deeds were a blessing in her own lonely life. Giving always brings something in return, even though one often doesn't notice it. She did.

She had long ago given up the search for her husband and had resigned herself to the loss of her "Thunderbolt Pyotr," yet she never tried to silence her friend when the latter started going on again about her affidavits and appeals. Nadia's personal life wasn't working out at all, either. Probably better just to write the whole thing off, strike a line through it, tie up the loose ends—put it however you like. "Where are you and I going to go now, Celia?" she would ask. "Young girls go off their heads, throw themselves at the first clod that comes their way, hook themselves onto anyone, but who's going to find you and me desirable, a couple of old otters like us . . ." In saying this, of course, she had herself in mind. Cecilia didn't really understand what she was talking about. For her, sex had become a closed matter after Kirill was gone. From time to time, though, they curled up on the bed, smoked in the darkness, and remembered their husbands, their faces, clothing, voices, expressions, the romantic moments of their lives, even intimate details. So he did it then, and I— Well, what did you do? . . . I have to admit it took me by surprise . . .

These were the moments Nadia perhaps treasured the most. That was when she simply adored her "Celka." She no longer even noticed the woman's constant repulsive smell, her eternal case of vulvovaginitis.

"Then what, then what, then what?" Cecilia chattered. For some time now, she had shown a tendency to fall into a sort of stupor when speaking: she would latch onto any word and endlessly, senselessly hammer on it: "Then what, then what, then what?"

"Celka, you won't believe it, something has happened!" Nadia's voice betrayed great excitement, which was quite unusual for her. "Lvov the animal breeder has arrived! It doesn't matter what animal breeder Lvov, the important thing is that he's come from over there! What do you mean, where's 'over there'? You ninny, don't you get it? To make a long story short, come at six, he'll be here and he'll tell all. Tell what? Celka, this isn't the sort of thing you talk about over the phone. Come, and you'll find out everything. Dress more nicely than usual—put on that blue skirt I gave you. You have to put it on, and the white stockings! Understand? And wash yourself properly, understand? Heat up the water and wash yourself all over, know what I mean?"

Not having understood anything, of course, Cecilia nevertheless did as she had been told: she washed every fold and wrinkle of her body, even lightly caressing her large breasts. A puddle began to flow out from beneath the door of the abandoned bathroom that the inhabitants had long used only as a laundry. Naryshkin the notary public was caterwauling, "Don't you think it's about time to do something about people who promote unsanitary conditions?"

Wearing the blue skirt and white stockings, as well as the velvet jacket that had belonged to her father, Cecilia arrived by six o'clock at the address on Zubovsky Boulevard, where Nadia lived in a basement flat with a separate (!) entrance.

Lvov the animal breeder occupied an entire side of a table with his person: he was improbably broad, though not fat. At the sight of a new woman he stood up, filling half the hovel; he was remarkably tall yet endowed with a very small head, small feminine hands, and delicate feet, shod in fashionable (almost "Rosenbloom," thought Cecilia) boots. On the whole he was a conspicuous man of imposing appearance, an excellent representative of our engineering-technical class. Short, fair hair, Slavic eyes already slightly clouded over but still good, able to focus clearly.

"Probably not a Party member," thought Cecilia when he kissed her hand, and she was not mistaken. Lvov the animal breeder had served five years for an "ordinary" offense, had been released even before the war (the judgment had been annulled for "absence of corpus delicti"), and now worked as a civilian specialist, an "enthusiast of the far North," that is, as the assistant director of the Path of October Collective Farm near Seimchan, where they raised sable and silver foxes.

He told wondrous stories of the area from which he had come on holiday. "Vadim Kozin himself sings up our way, my girl! 'Sashka, do you remember those meetings in the park by the seashore. . . .' "

Kolyma—it's gold, girls, forests, furs, terrific wages with big raises! Know how much I brought with me on holiday? I don't know myself! Go ahead, help yourselves! He poured American chocolate bars of various sizes onto the table from a huge sack behind his chair. Where we are, guys, America is right next door! Lend-Lease goes through us, on steamers, in planes!

No doubt about it, there was an enchanting American smell coming from Nadia's tiny kitchen, where the American Spam brought by Lvov was cooking, along with potatoes and onions from the gardens of suburban Moscow. "There you have some vitamins," the guest went on. "Some people claim that vitamin deficiencies are raging in Kolyma. Don't believe it, girls! Look at my teeth, still all together, forty years old, and not a single filling! Never suffered from scurvy even in the concen—er, that is, even in difficult conditions! And why? Because Kolyma turns into an inexhaustible reservoir of vitamins! All the hills turn red with cowberries, there are heaps of nuts . . . you can gobble down enough to keep you going all winter. 'Winter lasts only twelve months, all the rest is summer!' Well, that's all just folklore! In the winter you have to drink extract of dwarf cedar, and ain't it sweet! We even mix it into the animals' feed to make their fur more downy, and on the international auction block, girls, our furs go for pounds sterling, whole pounds sterling, kilos, double hundredweights of sterling, sterling . . ."

At times his blue eyes became glassy and his hand began to dance along the table all by itself in search of the bottle with the clear liquid. Having taken a drink, animal breeder Lvov began to eat feverishly, polishing off with his vaunted teeth the salted salmon that lay in a pile on the table. And the fish, the fish! Brought this salmon myself! Go into the streams up to your knees, and you bring the stuff out by the armful! That's how it is in Kolyma!

"You don't suppose, Comrade Lvov, that you could—" Cecilia began. (In her pocket lay the letter, already written, with no address but with the beloved name written on the envelope.) "You don't suppose that you could . . ." but just then Nadia dashed in with more culinary reinforcements.

"Dear me, girls, this won't do!" laughed Lvov, pouring the spirits into the cut-glass tumblers, touching it up with cheap Three Sevens port wine. "I'm the only one drinking, and you're just eating! Intoxication ought to be mutual! Here's to friendship! To the future happiness of those present and those absent!"

Nadia was unrecognizable: she had gone red in the face and taken on a youthful appearance like a girl in the Komsomol during the First Five-Year Plan. Her cheeks were glowing like apples, as if she had come straight off a painting by Deineka.

"Look, Celka, just look what he brought me!" she cried, pulling something from her jacket. "A letter from Pyotr! He's alive and well, working on the fur farm! Oh, I just don't know what to do for you, Lvov!" And she sat down on the long knee of the guest and tousled his hair. "Go ahead, now, Celka, ask him anything, he knows everything about Kolyma!"

Celia produced the hidden letter from a velvet pocket. "I just wanted to ask you, comrade, if it wouldn't be too much of a burden, by any chance. . . . My husband, about whom they surely made a mistake, has . . . they say he has no right to correspondence, but that has nothing to do with the case, that is, formally he does have the right to correspond, although—"

"Well now, Celia, my dear!" Lvov the animal breeder stroked Nadia's back with one hand and ran the other down Cecilia's spine from the base of her skull to the coccyx. "Dear me, kids, don't whimper!" He took hold of Cecilia's letter, glanced at the name, and nodded. "All right, I'll deliver it to Kiryusha Gradov!"

"Wha-a-a-t?" Celia shrieked, jumping into the air, clutching at her heart and her breasts. "You know him?"

"Strange as it may seem, I do know him!" guffawed animal breeder Lvov.

"He and Pyotr know each other. In fact, they're inseparable friends! The thing is, though, that he just took off on a solo assignment to Susuman. I sent him there temporarily, so that the bosses wouldn't make any trouble. But he'll be fine there, Celia, don't worry. An interesting man, your Kiryusha, very positive . . ."

Trying to escape her growing dizziness, her head spinning faster and faster, Celia gulped down the rest of the burning colored liquid. A sort of stirring bravura music similar to a children's march with a steadily increasing tempo came over her. He's alive! My boy is alive!

"Animal breeder Lvov, you're an extraordinary . . . you're a messenger like something out of a fairy tale, if you're not making it all up!" said Nadia from beneath the man's arm in a languid voice. The guest had already pulled her behind the blinds, where the celibate's plump bed lay. The curtain was drawn, the bed creaked in protest. "That's how things turn out," sighed the animal breeder emotionally. Nadia giggled like a nightingale. "Celka, don't leave!" she shouted in between roulades.

It had not occurred to her to leave. Paying no attention to the rocking behind the curtain, she was pacing back and forth across the basement, a cigarette between her teeth, a cigarette at arm's length, smoke billowing from her mouth as if from a blazing blast furnace. Now and again a set of petrified toes in cracked sandals sloshed by outside the window beneath the streetlights.

So, you're alive, thought Celia. That means *I* was right, not the others, the ones in Silver Forest! That means we'll see each other again, we'll come to grips with the Erfurt Program, we'll tear Spengler's relativism to shreds together!

"Higher, higher, keep going higher!" sang out two voices in chorus behind the curtain. They could go no higher—an aeronautical triumph!

What's that? Nadka, her face all flushed as though she were her own nonexistent daughter, hopped out from behind the blinds. She was pulling on a pair of red—Cecilia had never seen anything like them before—panties. "Now you, Celka! Go on, you dimwit, it's not betrayal! This is a friend who's come to us, a great friend!"

"No, please! What are you doing, comrades? Comrades, comrades!" Celia planted her feet firmly on the floor, but the small hand of the "great friend," emerging from beneath the buttercup pattern curtain, had already seized the lap of her skirt. "Hey, little Celka, don't you understand? The war's over, and jail along with it!"

After their passion had subsided, all three went for a nighttime stroll down Kropotkin Street, up to the Palace of Soviets and back.

"Here, by the way, is where Isadora Duncan lived," Cecilia indicated to animal breeder Lvov, as was her right as a resident of Moscow. "Have you heard of this leading figure of the revolutionary aesthetic?"

"Only in connection with Sergei Esenin," said the man from Kolyma, and quite unexpectedly he quoted a passage for the ladies: "Even if you have been drunk by another / The autumnal smoke of your hair is left to me / And the autumnal fatigue of your eyes."

All three of them had wet, matted hair. For the first time in many years, an ozone layer of freshness and hope had formed around them.

"Tell me something, Lvov," asked Nadia, carrying a cigarette in the hand of an arm slightly akimbo, like a woman of the world. "You're not afraid of delivering greetings from wives of enemies of the people?"

"Yes, I'm scared," said animal breeder Lvov. "There's more to the world than just fear, though."

That very night, and given the time difference, perhaps at the very moment of this August promenade, the first atomic bomb was dropped on Hiroshima. The age of Big Science had begun.

CHAPTER TWENTY

The Path of October

★

In October 1945 a triumphant liturgy was celebrated in the Elokhov Cathedral in connection with the cessation of military operations, the destruction of the evil foe Germany, and the victory over Japan. Nikolai, the metropolitan of Moscow, led the service himself. A choir from the Bolshoi sang, and soloists and artists from the republics of the USSR performed as well.

"We bring to the Lord our God, brothers, a prayer of gratitude for the gift of victory in the great war! We proclaim the glory of our heroic army and her leader, the great Stalin!"

The choir entered magnificently: "Be glorified, be glorified, O Motherland, be glorified, O holy Fatherland!"

"Do you remember what this is from?" Kevin whispered to Veronika.

She nodded. "Yes, of course. It's Glinka's *Ivan Susanin.*"

"The opera used to be called *A Life for the Czar,*" he remembered, "and they sang different words: 'Be glorified, be glorified, our Russian czar, sovereign czar given us by the Lord . . .' "

She smiled at him across her shoulder, on which a high-quality silver fox stole was nestled.

Kevin had recently retired, gladly exchanging his Pentagon outfits for long gray and brown suits and a soft, dark blue alpaca coat. They would be leaving the USSR in a matter of days: first to Stockholm, then to London, finally to the manicured lawns of Connecticut.

I should feel deeply touched, shed a tear, thought Veronika, this is my farewell to my homeland. No, I can't, the tears won't come, I have no feeling for this country. Maybe I should pray for "the cockroach"? Sorry, you can do it without me!

The liturgy was going along beautifully, yet the clergy was feeling rather out of sorts. Only members of the diplomatic corps were present, along with a few scattered "leaders of science, literature, and art." None of the high-ranking government officials who had been expected had appeared. Once again the church was reminded that it was a thing separate from the state.

In the autumn of 1945 a blizzard came up in Kolyma, in the area of the Jelgala mines. In October a powerful wind swept over the crusted snowy spaces, sometimes rising up and swirling about the boulders like a wave against a parapet. In some of the depressions, though, the greenery was still untouched, the slopes of the volcanic hills displaying the blue and crimson of ripened berries, and the snow, falling as peacefully as in an opera, melted immediately in the warm springs. Unescorted zeks raced toward them, to store up on vitamins for the winter. They greedily drank the water from the streams weaving their way down the slopes of the depressions: the water was considered to have miraculous powers.

Sometimes even the ordinary slave laborers under escort received a portion of this blessing, if they had the luck to have humane guards. Like, for example, Vanya Nochkin, the "old shoe from Ryazan," as he sometimes called himself affectionately. Taking a group of "counterrevolutionaries" to the night shift at the fur farm, he would frequently stop at such an oasis at the hour of twilight, ostensibly to take a piss or squat down for a moment, thus giving the slave laborers a chance to get to the berry bushes. He sat and groaned, admiring the stripes of the sunset over the untamed earth, dreaming about how he would return home after his "demob" and of the lies he would tell the villagers about the war with the Japanese.

That evening, however, they tramped along the top of the depression, right through the blizzard, in the direction of the lights of the state farm. None of the "counterrevolutionaries" even so much as hinted to Vanya that it wouldn't be bad to have a rest. The whole bunch was trotting smartly and talking very little among themselves, as though they were afraid to be late to work. On the whole, they were a well-fed, able-bodied lot: they were kept well fed and warm at the fur farm.

Among the dozen men was forty-three-year-old Kirill Gradov. In his cap with earflaps, padded jacket and trousers, and sturdy rubber-soled shoes, he looked like a zek who had secured himself a cushy job of the sort that the thieves and their friends usually got, or at least one that would not kill a man. That was in fact the case at the end of his eighth year of imprisonment, but how much had gone before it, how many deaths followed by decaying and hateful resurrections!

He had landed in the Kolyma camps right at the end of Garanin's infamous reign, when the deranged major had roamed the work sites pistol in hand, when at every evening formation the thugs from the camp Education and Entertainment Division called out the names of so-called "saboteurs," who were then immediately taken out behind the barracks and shot, "right at the cash register," as they say. "Such vicious enemies of the people as you and I aren't likely to survive, Gradov," his friend from Moscow and bunkmate, Pyotr Rumyantsev, would say to him. "So don't count on living to a golden old age, sitting by the fireplace in the evenings reading Aristotle."

Suddenly, at the beginning of 1940, a new craze swept "Sevlag": conservation of the workforce. Garanin disappeared, and Gradov and Rumyantsev were temporarily spared. They lost each other in the endless reshuffling of the camp and forgot about each other, never suspecting, of course, that in a year and a half their wives, or, as the joke went in the men's camps, "our widows," would meet in the lines outside Lefortovo and become bosom friends.

Kirill wound up in the mine on the Zolotisty site, which was only a hundred kilometers or so as the crow flies from the hellhole of Zelenlag, a high-security camp for especially dangerous state criminals, where at that time his own brother, the pride of the family, Nikitushka-Kitushka, was trying to survive.

It was hard to tell what advantages the ordinary prisoners of Sevlag had over the doomed men of Zelenlag. At the Zolotisty site, Kirill rapidly turned into a "goner," and everything in his head became muddled together somehow. Not long before the war, however, another breeze, one that was not so abrasive, blew through, and instead of the morgue he ended up in the infirmary, where he began to receive the fat of some unidentified sea creature; it gave off an unbearable stench but produced clear benefits.

No sooner had Kirill been released from the infirmary than war broke out and together with a fierce hurricane swept across Kolyma like a barbed-wire broom, bringing ever more instructions to make the camp regime stricter, to be more vigilant with regard to traitors, terrorists, oppositionists, Fascist hirelings, and Trotskyites, take your pick. Swept away by the broom, Kirill came crashing down in the Serpantinka camp, the soul of which had already been frozen even in the time of Major Garanin. The traditions of "iron Chekism" were maintained in their full glory, even though the orders to shoot prisoners directly behind the barracks had not reached there yet. Once again he began wasting away, and once again chance took him away from the withering, faintly mumbling mouths of the masses. This time it was in the form of Stasis the medical corpsman, who made him an orderly.

That was the way, then, that Candidate of Marxist Sciences Kirill Gradov was tossed about during his eight-year journey through the land of practical Marxism. At one moment the roof of the sewer would burst, caving in to wash him away once and for all into the lime chloride, then he would suddenly pop back up to the surface like some worthless bubble. He went all at once from the mines into a heaven on earth, into a warm valley, as a helper in a pickling kitchen. Cabbages! Turnips! Suddenly, in the midst of the shortages of 1943, a tenderhearted lady cook gave him a whole half-liter tin of yeast. For some reason, the women in the nightmarish surroundings liked his eyes. "What eyes you have, friend! What are you standing there like a dummy for? Come on in before the digs get cold."

There was one curious detail of Kirill's fate in the camps about which he did not have an entirely clear idea himself and about which, either fortunately or unfortunately, the camp authorities had no idea at all. In '37, after two weeks of madness and abuse at the hands of the secret police, he was brought to trial before one of the so-called "troikas" and was sentenced in short order: ten years at hard labor with no right to correspondence. After that everything went as might have been expected for an ordinary zek: transit prisons, shipment, arrival in Kolyma. By this time he was perfectly well aware what the formula "no right to correspondence" meant, yet he began to have the feeling, which grew stronger the further on they went, that this formula had disappeared from his case somewhere along the way to the east.

Nadia Rumyantsev had been close to the truth when, one day by the gates outside Lefortovo, she said, "I wouldn't be surprised if things are just as fouled up in their business as they are everywhere else." Most likely the notation "no right to correspondence" had been left in one of the files on Kirill's case and not transferred to another by an oversight. It was possible that he was down on some lists as having been liquidated, while on others he was receiving a camp allowance as an ordinary member of the Kolyma slave-labor force. One day, however, he decided to tempt fate and wrote a letter to Cecilia. He received no reply, but a couple of years later, while on a wood-cutting expedition in Sudar, a parcel fell into his hands from a post office truck, producing an effect like that of a golden meteorite descending to earth from the depths of space. In the parcel, written in what they jokingly called her "pseudo-Gothic" script, was a note in which he learned his letter had reached her quite smoothly but that his previous missives had either vanished without a trace or had been rejected.

Is it worth it to risk it, he thought, getting her excited, bringing the ominous formula to light? Let her live as though I were dead, let her find herself a husband—after all, I'm not entirely alive anymore, even if I have gotten used to this nonlife and fear "the formula."

Suddenly he admitted to himself that by frequent masturbation he had crowded Cecilia to the periphery of his consciousness. The healthy young lads in the camp had resolved their sex problem in simple, if fairly inspired, fashion. It was called "meeting behind the water heaters." At night, half an hour before lights out, a group, and sometimes a whole crowd, of zeks gazing dreamily into space would stand behind the shed containing two puffing boilers. One could hear moans and occasionally roars; each man was floating along in his own imagination. For some reason or other, Kirill never had visions of his wife but rather of a slim, dark-complexioned girl who resembled his sister, if she wasn't actually her.

Some veteran zeks managed to make the acquaintance of civilians outside the camp zone and through them established reliable channels of correspondence. Kirill never made any attempt to do this. At times he admitted to himself that he didn't even want anyone out there in the "next world" to consider him alive, there where his father stood with a kindly light in his eyes in a house that even resembled him, where his mother used to drag him to the bath, laughing: "Kirill-slippery-as-an-eel! That's my Kirill-slippery-as-an-eel!" My brother must have been killed, so why should I go showing up alive? Am I supposed to debase myself *again*, show off as alive instead of him, and tell them: "Ha-ha! Kirill-slippery-as-an-eel!" is still alive; Tricky Nickie is dead, but I'm still alive—Kirill-slippery-as-an-eel! Such were the strange thoughts that sometimes raced around inside his skull, but he would catch himself and ascribe them to avitaminosis.

Sometimes it seemed to him that he wasn't alive at all. It was entirely possible that the sentence had been carried out as formulated in the court judgment but that the beatings had prevented him from taking notice. Maybe they threw me into a common pit and scattered lime over the bodies and all that is now happening to me is just a gradual posthumous fading away of consciousness, or perhaps it's quite the opposite. . . . What's opposite? What could be opposite?

Or maybe it was the other way around: his current nonexistence was only the beginning of something grandiose, a torturous transition to the fantasy of real life and the extraphysical kingdom of freedom and beauty?

But in either instance, what was the meaning of this earthly path with its triumphs and failures, its champagne and lime chloride? What could all this mean, and was not all this Marxism a simple equivocation? Can it really be that all the revolutionary ardor with which I served so arduously and faithfully was just an attempt to sidestep the question?

"What do you think, is there any sense in all this?" he once asked Stasis the medical corpsman. The muscular Lithuanian from Memel seemed by his entire appearance to deny the unreality of camp existence. Stasis made his own cross-country skis and slid across the snow's crust from one assignment to another. And when the "goners" saw this broad-shouldered, long-armed skier with ice-covered brows above the gray slits of his eyes and the apple blush on his cheeks, the bright combination of colors reminded them of bullfinches seen in childhood, and they survived another night to return the next day to this living dream.

"I don't understand," Stasis said, turning his entire body to his helper. They were sitting in a shed whose walls had long since lost all concept of the vertical and which served as a first-aid station. The wind groaned stubbornly in every corner of the shed, and the snow quickly covered the murky window. Needles were being boiled on a stove in the corner. "If you listen father and go medical school," Stasis would often repeat in broken Russian, "that mean you is doctor! Don't you understand, even in camp doctor is still doctor, and not convict!" Stasis worshiped medicine, and among the cherished books he dragged around with him from one assignment to another was a text of general surgical procedures by Professor B. N. Gradov, written in those distant days when the professor had just assumed his chair at the institute and had discovered serious shortcomings in teaching methodology.

Actually, it was that textbook that saved Kirill's life. While bandaging up frostbite cases, Stasis suddenly came upon the name Gradov and asked jokingly if Kirill were not a relative. Upon learning that Kirill was Professor Gradov's son, Stasis did everything he could to save him. Ever since then—nearly a year—and up to the time when the Kolyma winds would scatter them in different directions, they had been inseparable. Together they would make the rounds of the farthest-flung forest sites and teams, doing their best not just to go through the formalities, but actually to render medical assistance to all those "sites" and "teams."

"I mean, what sense is there in human life?" Kirill continued over the whistling and howling of the nocturnal taiga. "We joke about these so-called 'accursed questions,' Stasis, and get used to our own irony. It's some sort of Russian game, or what have you. All that is said in a patronizing tone, but never taken seriously—particularly in our family with its nineteenth-century positivism and faith in 'human genius,' in science. . . . Is all that clear to you, Stasis? If it isn't, just say so: I'll repeat it, maybe even a bit of it in German.''

"I understand it all," said the medic briefly. He was now sitting with his back to Kirill, not turning around, staring straight before him at the side of the sterilizer shining in the weak light of a lamp.

Kirill continued, "You see, the neurasthenic question seems meaningless when you have to fight for your idea, for the future, for a new society, when life is almost entirely replaced by literature about life, and you're sitting at a tea table surrounded not only by your own family, but by a whole mob of people that form the inner world of the Russian intelligentsia, people who have already asked themselves the same question so many times and seem to have answered it by the fact of their own existence in some speculative universe.

"Even in a war, in the midst of death, in the midst of constant and habitual outrages against human flesh, the question seems out of place, because passion is raging there, Homeric feelings, action is building up, a play is on. 'For the Motherland!,' there's the meaningless sense of lives extinguished in a flash, 'For freedom!' and so on, all that music.

"Music, Stasis! There's no music here, at hard labor, in the camps, behind the wheelbarrow, in the barracks, in the gruel . . . here no one has illusions, it's a decay of flesh, the death of literature, the loss of all poses of being a hero or an antihero, a simple procession into the pit . . ."

"It is here, too, there is music!" Stasis suddenly interrupted heatedly, but then, as though catching himself, immediately fell silent.

Kirill flicked the butt of his dogleg, which had burned down almost to his fingers, into the stove.

"I know what you have in mind, Medic. Faith? Christian mythology? I know you're a believer, I've seen you praying. Don't be afraid, I won't report you."

"I'm not afraid, Kirill. And it's no deception," Stasis said, now turning his face toward Kirill and sitting hunched over with his broad shoulders raised as though he were lifting sacks, his intertwined hands with their swollen veins, his long equine face drooping.

"Well, teach me to believe, then, Stasis!" Kirill pleaded with a passion that surprised even him. "I know that Marx is finished, but how am I supposed to know that God is alive when everything points to the contrary? Teach me, then, Medic!"

"Want to have a drink?" asked Stasis, indicating with a nod a concealed vial with a ground-glass top.

"No," said Kirill. "With liquor, things are easy, but only for a while. I'm serious . . . I want to learn to believe. So . . . well, tell me about yourself! Who are you?"

Evidently the wind had torn a snag from a tree and deposited it on the wire. The lamp went out. The light of the stove, weak, reddish, and flickering, could not have been better for nighttime revelations.

Stasis Ionaskis had come from Baltic stock, from a long line of Lithuanians who had settled on the sandy dunes facing the ceaselessly rolling sea between Memel and Königsberg. His father had lost a leg in the First World War and as a result had been forced to leave the farm and find other work—as it turned out, as a night watchman in a Franciscan monastery. Stasis had spent his whole childhood in the monastery. He had been an altar boy, and the monks had taught him reading and writing, along with geography, history, and biology. He had read devotional books in German and Latin, of course. Apart from that, he was a sportsman. Beg your pardon? Why yes, of course. At the age of seventeen he had joined the monastery rowing crew. So being a monk turned out to be the natural thing to do. "Yes, give me the tonsure, thanks. Unnatural, you say? Beg your pardon? No, not at all. I want to be God's servant, and I was happy. I studied medicine."

Quite so, Stasis was a monk at the same time that he was studying to be an orderly. That was in Lithuania, in Palanga. There, after the catastrophe, he fell into the hands of the Red Army. When he filled out the form, he said he was a medical orderly but not a monk. That was all. No one in Soviet Russia knows that he's a monk. Now only Kirill knows, but he has kept the faith. If they find out that he's a Franciscan, that will be the end of him, because in their eyes that's probably worse than a Trotskyite. Then again, he's very happy that they call him "Orderly Stasis" because it reminds him of "the Franciscan Order."

"You say you're happy? Is it really possible to be happy in Kolyma?" Kirill asked.

Medical Orderly Stasis was convinced that it was possible. Medical help gives a lot not only to the patient, but to the person giving the treatment. Especially if you believe in God and pray to him regularly here in the camps, you have to pray not only from time to time from a book, but every moment. He, medical orderly Stasis, had learned to live and breathe God, and that faith would always be with him, no one would be able to take it from him until the end of his earthly captivity. "That's what it is, all right, Kirill, captivity, but if you want freedom later on, then it's your will, you do it right now for the freedom of everyone—sorry for my bad Russian. Is not something you can learn, is not like sport or medicine. Life and faith are same thing—if you understand this, then you win."

"But you could still at least teach me a few prayers, Stasis," said Kirill, his eyes suddenly filling with tears as he whimpered like a child.

"Unfortunately, I don't know them in Russian," Stasis said. He did not try to persuade Kirill to stop crying; on the contrary, he looked at the other's wrinkled, severe face, the sobs growing ever stronger, with the most radiant joy imaginable. "Give them to me in Latin, I'll remember them," pleaded Kirill.

Thus began their friendship, which is not to say that Kirill immediately acquired for himself the medical orderly's treasured ability to "live and breathe God." They spent several months together as medic and assistant, then the winds of Kolyma blew them to separate camps. Sometimes their paths crossed and they joyfully rushed to each other, slapping each other on the back over and over as if each wanted to make sure his old buddy was alive; more often than not they talked about camp trivia, about how the subjects of the ferocious kingdom were staying alive, and only whispered together snatches of the Latin prayers. Sometimes months passed before they saw each other again, but that almost totally dark night in the toolshed that had been turned into a temporary infirmary, when he had poured forth childlike tears, never dimmed in Kirill's memory, not over the course of those years nor for the rest of his life.

In 1945 there was a sudden stroke of luck—he ended up beneath the safe roof of the Path of October state fur farm, which was run by a remarkable man, animal breeder Lvov. The collective was directly subordinate to the powerful Moscow organization that directed the export of furs, and therefore the local Siberian bigwigs could only gnash their teeth at it from a distance: their authority did not extend that far. Someone had calculated that fur-bearing animals multiplied better in enclosures in Kolyma than anywhere else, and Lvov had been given authority over both the development of production and the choice of his workforce.

The eccentric Lvov behaved as though he didn't understand that he was living in the heart of a giant forced-labor colony. He hunted and fished, drank, and listened to records of operettas. This did not prevent him from coming to the camps to choose workers like any good slave owner. Once he had picked them, though, he stood behind his men and never humiliated the zeks, even shaking the hands of some of them, maintaining almost friendly relations. Now he had gone on leave to the "Mainland" and had brought back living greetings to Pyotr Rumyantsev and Kirill Gradov from their wives. Naturally, the zeks repaid him with devotion, with zeal on the job. The state farm flourished. Come on, guys, let's work for those pounds sterling, said animal breeder Lvov, for hard currency! Heavier than gold!

. . .

On this day the night shift was marching from the zone in the direction of the farm through a gathering blizzard, particularly smoothly, with a firm stride, as in Blok's poem "The Twelve": "Keep up the revolutionary step / The tireless enemy never sleeps." This haste, however, was explained not only by an ardor for work but also by the fact that the arrival of Medical Orderly Stasis was expected.

As they were marching, darkness fell definitively. They couldn't see two feet in front of them, yet they could already hear the state farm's distinctive sound, a never-ending yelping of foxes. Hundreds of creatures with valuable hides were running in circles in their cages and around their feeding troughs, clarifying their relationships with one another, demanding food. They were fed better than any "wise guys" in the camps ever dreamed of being. The state knew whom to give the food to. If zeks had such luxuriant, beautiful pelts, they would have given us good food too and then later slaughtered and skinned us and cured the hides, the same way we slaughter and skin these foxes and cure their hides. The only thing I don't know is, would the people on duty here make chops out of us the way we sometimes do from the foxes? A dreadful concentration camp, that's what this is, thought Kirill in his gloomier moments. A death factory, a pagan temple of primordial sin.

He worked in the tannery, where the fresh hides underwent the first stage of processing. From there they were sent to shipping and then on to the "Mainland," to the fur center, where they were turned into elegant goods. From time to time he succeeded in taking his mind off the nature of the job and seeing the hides as mere raw material. He cleaned the bloody inner side of the hides with a scraper and even managed to think about something else, to chat with his mates. Sometimes, though, he was suddenly penetrated by what the job was all about, and he pictured himself as a dirty, debauched killer of living things, of God's creatures, so shrewd and supple, with twirling tails, sparkling fur, and a sly expression in their little eyes that took everything in in an instant. Even these creatures, though, had to kill in order to survive or, as they did here in the concentration camps, eat what was already dead; that's the way everything goes in the world of creation, a constant round of cruelty, in the final analysis, turning into a sea of human terror. Where's the way out?

They stamped their hemp, bark, or felt boots, along with their genuine galoshes, shook off their triangular hats, scarves, and mittens in the entrance hall of the collective head office, and immediately swept the snow outside with twig brooms. Vanya Nochkin stood his rifle—since it was unloaded, it couldn't do much—in a corner. "So, has the medic come today?"

"What are you on about? Come on, everyone into the recreation room for injections!"

The dozen men stamped on the wooden planks of the floor down the long corridor; all of them were friends and were hoping there was no informant among them.

On the way, Pyotr Rumyantsev, who had already had his turn, passed them, reading some fundamental work even as he walked. He jokingly poked an elbow into Kirill Gradov's ribs and whispered, "Clerics, obscurantists!"

In the half-darkened room, the bald spot of a bust of Lenin in black stone gleamed dully. Blue wedges representing "Stalin's ten crushing blows" sliced across the space of the unforgotten "Mainland." Beneath the map, the medic Stasis drew out his gear from a midwife's bag and arranged it on a small shelf: a crucifix, a tiny folding triptych of the Madonna painted by a camp artist, glasses of diluted wine, and soft American bread cut off into fine pieces for communion. Vanya Nochkin stood in a corner with his rifle: "Do your praying quickly, boys, or we might all get caught red-handed!"

Stasis turned to the twelve zeks and raised his arms. "On Easter, this holiest of holy days, brothers, to our Lord Jesus Christ we pray!"

He knelt, and the dozen men joined him; after glancing around watchfully, Vanya Nochkin followed their example.

In a low voice Stasis the orderly began to sing his own translation from the mother of languages, church Latin:

> *We believe in one God,*
> *The Father Almighty,*
> *Maker of heaven and earth,*
> *Of all that is seen and unseen.*
> *We believe in our Lord Jesus Christ,*
> *Only Son of the Father*
> *Eternally begotten of the Father*
> *God of God, Light of Light . . .*

The blizzard wailed through the corners, the ceaseless yelping of the foxes was heard.

NINTH INTERMISSION
THE PRESS

Scandinavian Telegraph Bureau:

General Vlasov was arrested in Riga by the Gestapo during a propaganda tour for talking about Russia too much. Rumor has it that he has been placed in a concentration camp.

Obnova (Belgrade):

General Vlasov, commander of the Russian Liberation Army, said his external policy was based on "sincere, steadfast friendship between the German and Russian peoples."

"Our principal enemy," he continued, "has always been and is now England, whose interests—both political and economic—are in opposition to those of Russia. After the war there will have to be a totalitarian system in Russia . . ."

Newsweek, January 1944:

It is reported that during the Teheran Conference, Winston Churchill presented Marshal Stalin with the so-called "Sword of Stalingrad" in the name of King George VI in a ceremony at the Soviet consulate. The sword was forged by 83-year-old Tom Beasley. A deeply moved Stalin kissed the sword, after which he handed it to Marshal Voroshilov. Voroshilov dropped the King's gift.

The New York Times, May 21, 1945:

General Vlasov, clearly trying to save his own skin, came to the aid of the partisans during the fighting in the streets of Prague. The partisans accepted his help, though apparently no one knows what happened to Vlasov when the Red Army arrived on May 9.

The New York Times, May 29, 1945:

As it turns out, Hitler was opposed to the idea of units of pro-German foreigners wearing German uniforms. "Any vagabond can crawl into a German uniform! . . . Let these cossacks wear their own uniforms!"

June 27, 1945:

General Vlasov is in the hands of the Soviets, reports a CBS correspondent in Moscow.

The Hitlerites used units of the Vlasov army against the partisans in Yugoslavia and against the Maquis in France.

August 2, 1946:

Moscow Radio reports that in accordance with the sentence of the military college of the Supreme Court, General Vlasov and ten of his officers have been executed by hanging.

Averill Harriman:

"Negotiating with the Russians is just like buying the same horse twice."

TENTH INTERMISSION
AN HONOR GUARD OF GEESE

At the end of our second volume, in the fall of 1945, we see Professor Gradov on the shore of Lake Bezdonka, alone, at sunset. These days, any time is the hour of sunset for me, he thought. The war is over. I'm seventy years old. The family has been destroyed. Everything that should inspire me has a false ring to it, even medicine. The sun is setting. Life could be cut short at any moment. Then again, it could happen to any *Homo sapiens*, old or young. Every day, in principle, reminds me of that tank battle in the sunflower fields, after which Nikita and I met. How right he was when he spoke of the intoxication of war, of the drunkenness that alone makes it possible to go into battle, that is, to live without concern about death. Now my intoxication has worn off completely, and these reflections of the sunset on the mirror of the water don't inspire me for a moment, not even for a fraction of a second, unless . . .

Unless the geese appear. They'll show up. Nine mighty birds, having built up their strength in the polar swamps, are on their way along an age-old route to the Nile delta. Lake Bezdonka turned out to be one of their landing fields along the way. The flying wedge comes down, the leader trying to bring in the whole team with one contact. "Do as I do! Do as I do! Do as I do!" he cries. For a moment, the squadron appears to be suspended in midair, then touches down on the water. First-class piloting!

The old professor is suddenly enraptured by his involvement with the triumph of the geese, with all of the strange fairy tale that is played out on the planet Earth. Perhaps some part of his being was once a migratory creature? Who can say by what transformation our souls pass beyond the boundaries of everyday triviality? What is to prevent us from imagining these nine as a detachment of Pavlovian Guards, drilled in the goose step to the sound of Russo-Prussian flutes and Preobrazhensky drums? What prevents us from imagining that they're pulling their boots off in order to change from the resounding goose step to the noiseless padding of cat's paws along the corridors of Engineer's Castle*? For the sake of freedom, in order to rid the Mother-land of a tyranny, in the name of liberal history—a silent jump into a dirty, bloody business. . . . And everything around writhes in sin, and everything about them gasps from love.

The old professor had the impression that someone was thinking those same thoughts together with him, sitting at the edge of the cold and dark water, someone small and infinitely loved. He turned and went down the path in the direction of home.

*Assassination of Tsar Paul I in 1801.

SELECTIVE GLOSSARY

Afinogenov, Alexander (1904–1941)   Playwright.

Alexander III (1845–1894)   Czar.

Arzamas   Literary circle in St. Petersburg in 1815–1818.

Averbakh, Leopold (1903–1939)   Critic who supported "proletarian culture."

Bakunin, Mikhail (1814–1876)   Revolutionary leader and theorist of anarchism.

Bazarov (real name: Rudnev), Vladimir (1874–1939)   Menshevik philosopher and economist, proponent of "God-building" and empiriocriticism, follower of Ernst Mach.

Bazilevich, Georgy (1889–1939)   Army commander.

Bedny, Demyan (1883–1945)   Antireligious poet.

Bekhterev, Vladimir (1857–1927)   Neuropathologist and psychologist.

Belinsky, Vissarion (1811–1848)   Radical critic, wrote famous letter to Gogol denouncing him for his conservative religious and political views.

Bely (real name: Boris Bugaev), Andrei (1880–1934)   Symbolist poet, novelist, critic.

Bernes, Mark (1911–1969)   Actor.

Blücher, Vasily (1890–1938)   Soviet marshal.

Blümkin, Ya. G.   Member of Socialist Revolutionary Party, in 1918 assassinated Wilhelm Mirbach, German ambassador to Russia, later worked for the Cheka, fate unknown.

Bock, Fedor von (1880–1945)   German field marshal, died as a result of an air strike.

Brusilov, Alexei (1853–1926)   General.

Budyonny, Semyon (1883–1973)   Soviet marshal.

Bukharin, Nikolai (1888–1938)   Bolshevik revolutionary, economist, theoretician, executed after show trial.

Bulgakov, Mikhail (1891–1940)   Russian prose writer.

Burdenko, Nikolai (1876–1946)   Neurosurgeon.

Busch, Ernst (1885–1943)   German field marshal, died in British captivity.

Cheka (abbreviation for Extraordinary Commission)   Name of political police, 1917–1922.

Chkalov, Valery (1904–1938)   Soviet test pilot.

Davies, Joseph (1876–1958)   American ambassador to Moscow, 1936–1938.

Dmitry Donskoy (1350–1389)   Grand prince of Moscow.

Dumbadze, Nina (b. 1928)   Athlete.

Dzerzhinsky, Felix (1877–1926)   Chairman of the Cheka.

Erdman, Nikolai (1902–1970)   Playwright and film scenario writer.

Esenin, Sergei (1895–1925)   Russian peasant poet.

Frunze, Mikhail (1885–1925)   Bolshevik military leader, supposedly ordered killed by Stalin during operation.

Goebbels, Joseph (1897–1945)   Nazi minister in charge of propaganda.

Gorodetsky, Sergei (1884–1967)   Poet.

Guderian, Heinz (1888–1954)   German general.

Gudiashvili, Lado (1896–1957)   Georgian painter and sculptor.

Himmler, Heinrich (1900–1945)   Head of the Gestapo and SS.

Hull, Cordell (1871–1955)   American secretary of state.

Kaganovich, Lazar (1893–1991)   Senior Soviet official in charge of collectivization of agriculture and purges.

Kalinin, Mikhail (1875–1946)   Titular head of Soviet state.

Kamensky, Vasily (1884–1961)   Poet, novelist, playwright.

KGB   Committee for State Security, Soviet secret police, formerly called NKVD, OGPU, and GPU.

Khlebnikov, Velemir (1885–1922)   Futurist poet.

Kollontai, Alexandra (1872–1952)   Politician and theorist of free love.

Koltsov (real name: Fridland), Mikhail (1898–1942)   Journalist, died in the purges.

Konev, Ivan (1897–1973)   Soviet marshal.

Kosciuszko, Tadeusz (1746–1817)   American and Polish general.

Kruchonykh, Alexei (1886–1968)   Poet.

Kuibyshev, Valerian (1888–1935)   Prominent Soviet politician.

Kulaks   Relatively well-to-do peasants, destroyed as a class during the collectivization of agriculture.

Kustodiev, Boris (1878–1927)   Artist.

Kutuzov, Mikhail (1745–1813)   Russian general who defeated Napoleon.

Lassalle, Ferdinand (1825–1864)   German socialist.

LEF   Acronym for the New Left Front of Art, an association of artists and writers in the 1920s.

Lobachevsky, Nikolai (1793–1856)   Pioneer of non-Euclidian geometry.

Lomonosov, Mikhail (1711–1765)   Inventor, physicist, poet, literary scholar.

Lunacharsky, Anatoly (1873–1933)   Marxist politician and literary critic.

Mandelstam, Osip (1891–1938)   Poet, perished in forced labor camp.

Manstein, Erich von (1887–1973)   German field marshal.

Mayakovsky, Vladimir (1893–1930)   Futurist poet, committed suicide.

Menzhinsky, Vyacheslav (1874–1934)   Senior Soviet official.

Meretskov, Kirill (1897–1968)   Soviet marshal.

Metchnikoff, Ilya (1845–1916)   Biologist.

Meyerhold, Vsevolod (1874–1942)   Actor and director, perished in the purges.

Mikolajczyk, Stanislaw (1901–1966)   Head of Polish government in exile during World War II, returned to Poland in 1945 but fled in 1947.

Mikoyan, Anastas (1895–1978)   Armenian Communist, supported Khrushchev after Stalin's death.

Molotov (means "hammer," real name: Scriabin), Vyacheslav (1890–1986)   Senior Soviet official.

NEP (New Economic Policy)   A temporary reversion to partial free trade and private ownership in the 1930s.

New orthography   A simplified system of spelling Russian, conceived before the Revolution but carried out by the Soviets.

OGPU   See KGB.

Olsufievs   An ancient, noble Russian family.

Ordzhonikidze, Grigory (1886–1937)   Georgian Communist, supposedly forced by Stalin to commit suicide.

Perekop   Town on the Perekop isthmus between the Crimea and the mainland where heavy fighting took place during the Russian Civil War.

Pétain, Henri (1856–1951)   French soldier and statesman, as premier of France concluded a separate peace with Hitler, died in prison.

Pudovkin, Vsevolod (1893–1953)   Film director.

Radek (real name: Sodelsohn), Karl (1885–1939)   Journalist and leading functionary in the Communist International, died in prison after show trial.

Rickenbacker, Edward (1890–1973)   American admiral and ambassador to Japan.

Riefenstahl, Leni (b. 1902)   German filmmaker, actress, photographer.

Rokossovsky, Konstantin (1896–1968)   Soviet marshal and minister of defense.

Rommel, Erwin (1891–1944)   German marshal, commanded Italian-German troops in North Africa, forced to commit suicide by Hitler.

Rossette-Smirnova, Alexandra   A lady-in-waiting who enjoyed the favors of Nicholas I and who interceded with Nicholas on behalf of Gogol.

Rotmistrov, Pavel (1901–1982)   Soviet marshal, joined Red Army in 1919.

Rutherford, Ernest (1871–1937)   British physicist.

Rykov, Alexei (1881–1938)   Bolshevik political leader, opposed collectivization, executed after show trial.

Saltykov (real name: Shchedrin), Mikhail (1826–1889)   Satirical writer.

Shalyapin, Fyodor (1873–1938)   Russian émigré opera singer.

Shishkin, Ivan (1832–1898)   Russian landscape artist.

Skliansky, Ephraim (1892–1925)   Party and military figure, drowned during trip to the United States.

Sobakevich   Heavyset, greedy figure in Gogol's novel *Dead Souls.*

Stakhanov Movement   Intended to increase the productivity of labor, named after Alexander Stakhanov, a coal miner who supposedly was an exceptionally enthusiastic and productive worker.

Steinhardt, Lawrence (1892–1950)   American ambassador to Moscow, 1939–1941.

"Stormy Petrel" ("Burevestnik")   Revolutionary poem by Maxim Gorky.

Surkov, Alexei (1899–1983)   Prose writer, poet, literary functionary, chief editor of Soviet *Brief Literary Encyclopedia.*

Sytin, Ivan (1851–1934)   Publisher whose business was nationalized after the Revolution.

Tabidze, Titzian (1895–1937)   Georgian poet, died in purges.

Tatlin, Vladimir (1885–1953)   Modernist artist.

Tielce   Fictitious city in Poland.

Tikhonov, Nikolai (1896–1979)   Russian poet.

Timoshenko, Semyon (1895–1970)   Soviet marshal.

Tkachov, Pyotr (1844–1885)   Russian exile publicist and revolutionary.

Tolstoy, Alexei (1883–1945)   Russian novelist, returned to Russia after emigrating.

Tomsky, Mikhail (1880–1936)   Old Bolshevik revolutionary, trade union leader, implicated during the show trials, according to one version committed suicide.

Trifonov, Yury (1925–1981)   Prose writer.

Tukhachevsky, Mikhail (1893–1937)   Soviet marshal, tried in secret and shot.

Tvardovsky, Alexander (1910–1971)   Russian poet and editor of the literary journal *Novy Mir.*

Tyorkin, Vasily   Character in long poem by Alexander Tvardovsky about World War II; symbolizes the common Russian soldier.

Tyutchev, Fyodor (1803–1873)   Russian mystical poet.

Ustryalov, Nikolai (1890–1938)   Russian emigrant, leader of Change of Landmarks movement advocating collaboration with the Soviet state, returned to Russia and perished in the purges.

Utyosov, Leonid (1895–1965)   Popular singer.

Vakhtangov, Yevgeny (1883–1922)   Actor and theater director, student of Stanislavsky.

Vasnetsov, Viktor (1848–1926)   Artist, worked a good deal in a stylized folk manner.

Veche   A type of democratic city council in Novgorod and Pskov in the Middle Ages.

Veresaev (real name: Smidovich), Vikenty (1867–1945)   Novelist and literary scholar.

Vereshchagin, Vasily (1842–1904)   Painter.

Vishnevsky, Alexander (1874–1948)   Surgeon whose methods were widely used during World War II.

Vishnevsky, Vsevolod (1900–1951)   Playwright.

Vlasov, Andrei (1900–1946)   Soviet general who after being captured by the Germans created a Russian army which fought against Stalin, executed in Moscow.

Voloshin, Maximilian (1877–1932)   Russian poet.

Voroshilov, Kliment (1881–1969)   Soviet marshal.

Vrangel (Wrangel), Pyotr (1878–1928)   White general, evacuated together with his army from the Crimea in 1920.

Vrubel, Mikhail (1856–1910)   Romantic, even mystic, painter.

Vyshinsky, Andrei (1883–1955)   Soviet political figure and chairman of the show trials of the 1930s.

Willkie, Wendell (1892–1944)   Republican candidate for U.S. president in 1940.

Yagoda, Genrikh (1891–1938)   Head of NKVD until replaced by Yezhov, shot after show trial.

Yakir, Iona (1896–1937)   Army commander who died in the purges.

Yamashita, Tomoyuki (1885–1946)   Japanese general.

Yashvili, Paolo (1895–1937)   Georgian poet, died in purges.

Yenukidze, Avel (1877–1937)   Georgian, senior government and Party official, signed the decree that became the basis for the purge trials, executed.

Yeremenko, Andrei (1892–1970)   Soviet marshal.

Yezhov, Nikolai (1895?–1939)   Head of NKVD, conducted the great purges, executed.

Zaitseva, Ludmila   Pilot.

Zetkin, Klara (1857–1933) Early feminist.

Zhukov, Georgy (1896–1974) Soviet marshal, received the surrender of the German High Command in Berlin.

Zinoviev (real name: Radosmyslsky), Grigory (1883–1936) Revolutionary and later Soviet official, executed after show trial.

ABOUT THE AUTHOR

Vassily Aksyonov is Robinson Professor of Russian Literature and Creative Writing at George Mason University. He lives in Washington, D.C., with his wife, Maya.

ABOUT THE TRANSLATORS

A former professor of Russian literature at the University of Chicago, the University of Iowa, and the University of Maryland, John Glad was also director of the Kennan Institute for Advanced Russian Studies in the Woodrow Wilson International Center for Scholars. His translation of Varlam Shalamov's *Kolyma Tales* was judged one of the five best translations of 1980 from any language at the American Book Awards.

Christopher D. Morris is a graduate of the Sorbonne, License et Lettres in Russian literature. He presently resides in Prague, where he is a contributing editor to *Traffika,* an international literary review.

ABOUT THE TYPE

This book was set in Photina, a typeface designed by
José Mendoza in 1971. It is a very elegant design
with high legibility, and its close character fit has
made it a popular choice for use in quality magazines and art gallery publications.